CW00455811

Outlawed

Guy of Gisborne
Book 2:

L. J. Hutton

ISBN: 978-1-9161020-5-7

Published by Wylfheort Books

Copyright 2018 L. J. Hutton
Previously published under the title
Prized & Honoured in 2015

ISBN 9781795833714
Copyright

Acknowledgements

As ever I have some people to thank for their help. In particular Teresa Fairhurst, whose enthusiasm for this project has been unwavering. I am eternally grateful for her patience and willingness to listen to me discussing possible plot twists, but also for her input on what it means to be a Catholic. She has made me aware of just how frightened people must have been at the threat of excommunication for something those far above them had done, and which was not their fault.

Karen Murray has again acted as a beta reader and offered criticisms. Mary Ward has been generous with her time in talking about the Anglo-Norman world even as she has wrestled with her own PhD on Anglo-Saxon literature – oh the joys of being a medievalist! And also thanks to renowned landscape historian Dr Della Hooke FSA and her husband Dr Chris Hooke for their enthusiasm and encouragement to produce this second book in the series.

I am again grateful for those members of staff who back during my time at Birmingham University gave me such a sound grounding in the lives of medieval peasants. So much is written of the lives of the 'great and the good' in medieval fiction – and never more so than about Richard the Lionheart – but the lives of the ordinary people can be just as fascinating, you just have to dig an bit harder to find them. Where I have got it right they must take their share of the credit, while any mistakes are mine alone.

And last but by no means least thanks are due to my husband for coping with me being in another century so often, and to my lovely lurchers who keep me company and (relatively) sane during the writing process.

I also have to apologise to my readers for the profusion of Williams, Walters, Henrys and Ralphs! Unfortunately these were incredibly popular names in this period, and when it comes to the real people of the time there's no getting round it other than to use their surnames. So *William* de Wendenal was succeeded as sheriff by *William* de Ferrers, and he in his turn by *William* Briwere – three Williams as sheriff in direct succession – such is the lot of a historian!

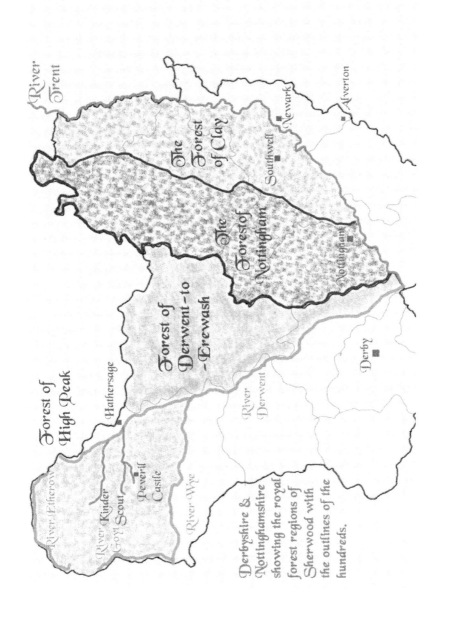

Derbyshire & Nottinghamshire showing the royal forest regions of Sherwood with the outlines of the hundreds.

River Trent

The Forest of Clay

The Forest of Nottingham

Forest of Derwent-to-Erewash

Forest of High Peak

Newark

Alverton

Southwell

Nottingham

Derby

Hathersage

Peveril Castle

River Etherow

River Kinder

Goyt Scout

River Wye

River Derwent

Nottinghamshire villages

Derbyshire villages

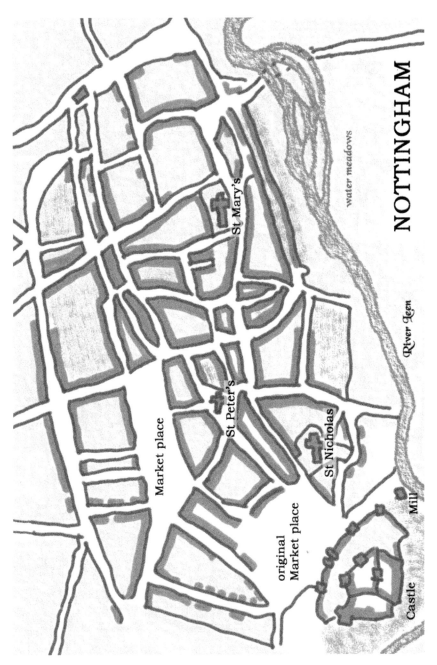

Nottingham in the 12th Century

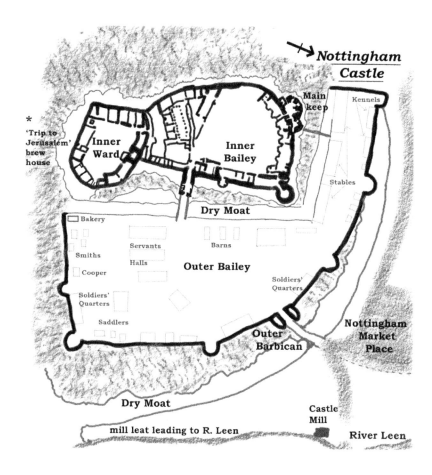

Nottingham Castle

Main keep

Kennels

*
'Trip to Jerusalem' brew house

Inner Ward

Inner Bailey

Stables

Dry Moat

Bakery

Servants Halls

Barns

Smiths

Cooper

Outer Bailey

Soldiers' Quarters

Soldiers' Quarters

Saddlers

Outer Barbican

Nottingham Market Place

Dry Moat

Castle Mill

River Leen

mill leat leading to R. Leen

Welbeck Abbey, Nottinghamshire, in the reign of Henry III.

*A*h, I dreamed once again last night, Gervase. Oh dear, did I not greet you in the way you expected? Then good morrow, dear brother! Does that please you more? Excellent! Then shall we continue with our tale? Ah, I see, you believe me not to be taking this as seriously as a last confession should be. In truth, I believe I feel much better than I did two days ago. The ague has lifted and I do not shiver so much, yet I shall continue to confess my poor life to you for both our sakes. A man never knows when that final day might come, and if mine is not now, then at least I shall have confessed all if it should come upon me unawares whilst out in the wilds somewhere.

So, dear brother, mea culpa, mea culpa, mea maxima culpa... And for all of what you call my flippant tone, I do believe most devoutly in what I am doing and why, you need have no fear of the contrary. My faith may have been moulded by my dear friend Tuck, but it is still sincere. Therefore I swear by Almighty God, and by those saints who have watched over me during my life here on earth - by Dewi Sant, Issui Sant, Cadoc the Wise, and Saint Melangell – that this is the truth, the whole truth, and with nothing altered to make me seem better at another's expense.

Now where had we got to? Ah yes, I had just finished telling you of the dreadful events of March 1190 when those poor souls perished in York Castle. What did you say? ˜Surely we have finished with Jews for now?˜ Oh Brother, now I must chastise you! That is not the response of a truly Christian man. Shame on you! Yes, well may you hang your head, for those who believed they had no choice but to take their own lives were not some devilish blasphemers against the God you believe in, but mere mortals terrified out of their minds by the cruelty of those around them. No-one Brother, no-one at all, should ever be reduced to such terror and then be upbraided for what they did as a result, especially when they harmed no other soul but themselves.

What is more, Gervase, we are not done with York and 1190 with regard to our story. For all that the man who had become Robin Hood, along with his followers and me, had brought to justice one of the ringleaders for an additional crime, there were further consequences as the year progressed which also affected us. There, are you satisfied? May I continue now? The dream? Ah yes, the dream I had last night. You are curious now, are you not?

I saw us again in my mind's eye, Brother, and I suffered a dreadful pang of longing to be back amongst those whom I came to think of as closely as brothers. There is an intense sense of brotherhood amongst those who share life-threatening experiences, Gervase, and it is hard to explain that to anyone who has not been through such a tempering fire. We became close in a way which you and your brothers will never know, and it was not unnatural or against any of your strictures, so you need not crease your brow so! If you trust a man so much that you will put your very life in his hands, then that is bound to have a deep-lasting effect on you, and so it has been with me.

So there arrayed on the hillside were Will Scarlet, Brother Tuck, Malik, Gilbert, ˜Robin Hood˜ and myself. Below us and well within range of the great wyche-elm bows we carried was King Richard. We saw him, richly dressed, tall and fair-haired in that red-blonde Norman way, and looking every bit the king. Behind him rode his mother, Queen Eleanor, and his half-brother, Geoffrey, archbishop of York; then the archbishop of Canterbury, Walter Hubert, and the truly dreadful bishop of Ely, William Longchamp; and then a stream of bishops and earls. Yet there was one amongst that illustrious crowd whom I longed to suffer more than any other and then I saw him, William de Wendenal, our bane and sheriff.

A warning was called. A warning disregarded. And then confusion. ˜Robin Hood˜ was both amongst them and with me, both with us and with the king. How could this be so, I asked in my dream? Yet I knew the answer already. ˜Robin Hood˜ was more than one man, a legend not just one person's life, and whatever happened on that day, the legend would continue.

Then I saw de Wendenal, his piggy eyes squinting up at us in the spring sunshine, and saw him point the accusing finger at the man standing on the outcrop with me. As he screamed that this was the villain, Robin Hood, we melted into the forest, but not before his fate was sealed. There was blood and anger, a dead sheriff and an indifferent king, and a legend who escaped into the forest as he would do for years to come.

I awoke then, Brother, bathed in sweat as I remembered the fear of betrayal which hung about me in those days. I will say no more of what happened on that day when King Richard rode out of Nottinghamshire for the last time until we get to it in its natural place. You will have to confine your impatience until we get to it. For now just remember that all is not quite as you might be imagining it. There was a good deal more going on there than that glimpse into my dream affords. But by the time I get there you will understand fully what was at stake, and why I woke in such a lather at the memory of it.

Chapter 1

So, Brother, we shall begin still in 1190. To save me having to stop and remind you who was who, I shall detail the members of the outlaws for you before we begin. Robin Hood was, of course, my much loved cousin, Baldwin, although by now a very different man to the lad I had played with as a child. So much so that I now have to consciously recall that he was that same Baldwin as a child, since ~Robin~ was such a very different man. Our two other cousins were with us – John, who was already starting to be known by the name he had jokingly been given, Little John, and also the youngest of us four, Allan. He had already called himself Allan of the Dales before we had reunited, but for now the name he became famous with was not in common use.

Alongside us four were the men Robin had brought back to England from the Holy Land. There was Will, a former sergeant and smith with the Templars alongside Robin, whose family name was Scathlock, but who was known as Will Scarlet on account of the tiny red burns he often wore after he had been working at his anvil. There was Malik, a former turcopole in the army of the King of Jerusalem, and the Irishman, Gilbert of the White Hand, who was a sergeant with that same army. James of Tyre had been a turcopole in the army of Balian of Ibelin, and like Malik was one of the native Christians who live in the Holy Land. And finally there was Siward of Thorpe, once a local man, who had been a squire to a knight in the service of Balian of Ibelin also, and who like Robin had gone out with one force and ended up with another. These five were professional soldiers from their hoods down to their boots, and they, as much as anyone, helped turn Robin Hood's men into the formidable fighting force of legend.

From a wholly different place came the Coshams, three brothers from out of Wales. Thomas and Piers, the oldest two, had served as archers to my own previous and formidable sheriff, William de Braose, on the Welsh Marches, and I had known Bilan, the youngest, whilst in service with de Braose. Joining them before we had even met Robin was Hugh of Barnby, another former soldier and local man, and the most ...ah, you must not draw me astray! No, Hugh's role will become apparent all in good time! Suffice it to say that Hugh was as good a soldier as the men from the East.

The same could not be said of the remainder of the gang. Walter of Fiskerton and Algar of Costock were local men who had wrongfully been imprisoned, and were now forced to live the outlaw life. Another waif swept up by the political tides crushing England was Much, the miller's son, whose family had so tragically been killed as a consequence of the riots in York. And then there was Roger of Doncaster, a thoroughgoing young rascal, but one whom I felt sorry for despite that. Brought into our midst by Allan, his great virtue was his irrepressible good humour. He was never downcast for long, and along with Allan, Bilan and Much, did a great deal to stop the older soldiers dwelling on the past. For that, Brother, I can forgive him a good deal.

And then there was Marianne – the woman of legend, who at this time was not so well known. The real Marianne had been a sister with the Knights Hospitaller out in Jerusalem, and was a far cry from the romantic waif she is sometimes portrayed as. Yes, Gervase, I know you have a problem with hearing about Marianne. She does not fit with what you wished to hear, does she? Far too fiery for you, and not enough of the meek virgin! But you must allow that having taken her vows to join what was, in effect, a conventual life, she stuck to them for a very long time, even with all the outlaws around her. Nor was she such an aberration as you may think, for later on you will meet another such as her.

Oh, has that whetted your appetite? No, you shall not draw me to reveal more right now! Mariota will appear in this tale at her allotted time, and not before. So we shall begin where we left off, in Sherwood in the year 1190.

$\mathfrak{Sherwood}$ $\mathfrak{Forest}$, $\mathfrak{June, the year of Our Lord, 1190.}$

Summer hung like a heavy, wet blanket over Sherwood. The whole of the Trent valley was sweltering in the humid heat of an early summer heat-wave, and even the birds seemed to lack the energy to sing, let alone fly.

"Is Guy really going to come?" Much asked fretfully, as he tried to find a different position to lie in on the grass in the vain hope that it would be cooler.

"He is here already," Malik said from beneath the shade of another of the great oaks.

"You've got your eyes closed!" protested Much. "How can you know that?"

"I can smell the horse," Malik answered calmly, just as Guy stepped out into the clearing leading the said horse, which looked as hot and bothered as the outlaws.

"Nicely done, Malik," Thomas said with a chuckle from beside his friend.

Guy, who had heard the exchange, told them, "I've walked her a lot of the way, that's why I'm a bit later. I hadn't the heart to make her work hard in this heat."

"What? From Nottingham?" Piers snorted incredulously.

"No, you clot-head!" John retorted, but too languid to put any malice into the rebuke. "Don't you remember? He was staying at Edwinstowe last night. He told us he'd be coming on from there when we arranged this meeting. Or did you think Tuck had got it wrong and hadn't really talked to Guy at all?"

They were north and west of Edwinstowe here – deep in the heart of the old forest, and close enough to the Derbyshire border and the safety of its highlands to be able to cross over if they needed to. Not that they would be free of the sheriff there either – given that he ruled over both shires jointly – but it was at least another set of foresters' jurisdiction, and those on foot might well give up the chase and just report it for others to deal with. It was early June and foresters like Guy were out in force, checking the royal forest for domestic animals prior to the start of Fence Month on St Edmund's day, when the forest was closed to everyone for the all-important fawning of the deer. Guy was here to play his part in that, but also for the associated agister's swanimote court at Edwinstowe. Although Guy was one of the sheriff's foresters policing the huge new expanses of royal forest – brought under forest law by the late King Henry in the 1170s – there were not enough courts set up to deal with all of the legal affairs for these new expanses of forest, and he was therefore here to sit in on the agister's court which for generations had dealt with the affairs of the original Forest of Nottingham.

"Was it bad?" Thomas asked Guy, seeing his downcast expression.

Guy grimaced. "Bloody awful! We had people coming from over in the east of the forest who are near ruined by the charges!" He shook his head in despair. "I mean, over here in the old forest, the farms have long taken into account that they won't be able to pasture their beasts in the forest for a month. And few of the farms here are that big anyway. But those poor sods in what's now the new Le Clay forest are absolutely befuddled by it all.

"And I can't say I blame them! How the hell are they supposed to know which bits are designated forest when there's hardly any real forest over there? None of their traditional boundary markers work for that! If you live within spitting distance of the Trent you're hardly going to have the kind of woodland which the deer would use for cover, are you? So even after the best part of fifteen years, the laws seem so random to them they can't work them out. And many of them have quite a large number of cattle – which is perfectly reasonable when for generations they've always had plenty of meadows and fields with good grazing. But in this heat, if what little grazing they can use for the month starts to wilt, they're going to be in real trouble."

John sighed. "They must be praying for this heat to break, and for a good thunderstorm, even more than we are!"

"What news of the chancellor, though?" asked Hugh. "Not that I'm unsympathetic to the plight of the farmers, but everyone we've encountered has been talking of the army that went north a week or so ago. Our bloody chancellor, Longchamp, is on the rampage by the sound of it! Are we facing another scouring of the north?"

By now they had been joined by all of the others, but there were noticeable absences – there was no sign of Tuck, Marianne and Robin.

"Where's Robin?" Guy asked before answering Hugh's questions. "I'd hoped he'd be here to hear this."

"Tuck and Marianne went off to collect herbs," Will Scarlet said in a tone which declared he had no interest in what they might be finding. "God knows why, but Robin went with them."

"Tuck said the oils in some of the herbs would be at their best in this heat," Allan supplied helpfully, while Hugh signalled to Guy with his eyes not to ask more, but that there was more to it than that.

Guy sighed. How typical of Robin to assume that he would not need to know what the chancellor would be up to in detail. He loved his cousin dearly, but the man Baldwin had become in the Holy Land was all too often a stranger to him nowadays, as evidenced by the ease with which he had come to call him Robin. It was almost easier to think of him as a stranger whom he needed to get to know from the start, than try and impose the memory of their childhood onto the man.

As he thought, he stripped off down to his braes, which was how all the others were undressed, yet even on his bare skin he could not feel any breeze. He flopped down onto the soft, leaf-littered ground beside Thomas and lay back with a groan of relief.

"Oh Blessed St Thomas, that's better! I've been melting in those boots!"

"Well? What's the news?" Much demanded impatiently. In the last few weeks, whenever Guy had caught up with them he had often sat down and immediately fallen asleep. It was due to the strain he was under as the only one of them living inside Nottingham Castle, but today Much wanted news before Guy dozed off. "Has Longchamp punished those who killed the Jews in York?"

Everyone understood Much's keenness to have the villains brought to justice, given that some of them had then torched his parents' mill and them with it.

Guy reluctantly pushed himself to sit upright, scraping his fingers through his thick, dark hair to try and un-stick it from his scalp. "I'm sorry, Much, it looks like that bastard de Cuckney will get off with a stiff fine. I did warn you it might be so. Word came that John Marshal has been kicked out as sheriff of Yorkshire, but God help the poor souls who live up there, because they've now got Longchamp's brother as sheriff in his place."

"That's bad?" his youngest cousin Allan asked, coming to sit a bit closer to listen properly.

Guy grimaced. "Oh aye, it's bad! If Longchamp is the deformed dwarf of the family, Osbert is the professional soldier down to the soles of his boots." He shook his head in bewilderment. "And I can't believe what I also heard at the same time – de Braose got ousted as sheriff of Herefordshire when Longchamp was making all the sheriffs pay for their offices at the end of last year! I never thought de Braose would let go of Hereford. He must be sitting in his castle at Abergavenny fair chewing at the walls! And he'll never forget the insult! Longchamp managed to get another of his brothers put in as sheriff there – Henry, I think his name is. So it sounds to me like Longchamp is using the riots more to continue feathering his family's nest than to hand out any meaningful punishments – and there's not a damned thing anyone can do about it."

"We need the king back in England!" Siward said despairingly. "By Our Lady, I was so for him going and taking back the Holy City, but not at this price!"

"Oh come on, Siward," a rich Irish voice said, and Gilbert appeared from the shade of another mighty oak, looking like some strange wight with his alabaster pale skin only broken by the faded linen of his braes, and with his flaming hair. The former crusader had been one of the first of the five who had come west with Robin to acknowledge that retaking Jerusalem might be impossible, as evidenced by his next words. "Sweet Jesu, you don't think a king like Richard will give up the chance to play the hero of Christendom, even if it's a fool's errand he's going on? We all know he's no more chance of saving Jerusalem than we have of getting cool today – or at least nothing more than some mad assault which takes it back for just a few weeks or months! But that won't stop King Richard from killing hundreds with his grand gesture! He'll not come back to these shores until he's got no other choice ...or he needs more fucking money!"

Algar of Costock and Walter of Fiskerton, the two real civilians out of all of the outlaws, were nodding in agreement with Gilbert.

"He won't come back," Walter agreed bitterly. "And Longchamp knows it and is making the most of the powers he's been given. The king just wants money, so big fines are the solution, isn't that it, Guy?"

Guy nodded. "I'm sorry, but yes, I think you're right. John Marshal will be fined some crippling amount – although I have no idea what – and Longchamp will wring as much out of the others as he thinks he can get."

"But that's asking for trouble!" Allan spluttered, amazed at the short-sightedness of Longchamp and the king. "Don't they grasp that it was the lesser nobles' indebtedness to the Jews which sparked the riot in York? That if they then bleed those same men white all over again, then they'll have no choice but to try and destroy those debts a second time or to give up their manors and trappings of nobility – which they'll never do while there's even the faintest chance of keeping them. It's a recipe for another riot! Or maybe even a full rebellion!"

"I don't fink they're finking," Allan's close friend, Red Roger, said mournfully in his broad London accent, which somehow he had never lost despite years away from the south-east. "Like bleedin' leeches, that's what they are. Get their nasty teeth into somethin' and they won't let go for anythin', even if it's goin' to choke 'em!"

"*Duw*, but that's the truth," Piers Cosham snorted in disgust. He and his older brother Thomas still had accents as broad as the day they left Wales.

It made Guy smile to hear this wonderful mixture of voices. All these men from across the kingdom and beyond, brought together by necessity and already becoming a unified force. His biggest fear, though, was that his cousin would lead them in some heroic, but ill-fated, military action against those who had burned Much's home village of Norton. Cautiously he asked,

"Robin's not talked of any plans to do something, has he?"

"Do something?" Will Scarlet repeated somewhat sarcastically. "Like what? Go hunting? Skinning a few hares?"

"Will!" Malik remonstrated softly, but to Guy's relief with remarkable effect. In his eyes Malik was becoming more of a godsend with every month that passed. Always calm and collected, the former turcopole from the Kingdom of Jerusalem was a good enough soldier to not have to prove anything to anyone, was highly respected, and so was a blessed calming influence on the more fiery of his friends.

"I meant in terms of taking action against Malebisse and Cuckney and the like," Guy said hurriedly before Will could say more. "I'd dearly hoped he would be here to hear me say this, but for Heaven's sake don't try and do anything against those men while Longchamp is in the north. With all the men his two brothers have brought with them, he's got a veritable army at his command! I'll grant you that some of them will be stupid and unused to battle, but many are the real thing – men who've fought with Osbert Longchamp in Normandy – and there are far too many of them for even the experienced amongst you to take on."

"I hear what you're saying," Hugh reassured him. "No, Guy, Robin's said nothing of trying to cut prisoners out of Longchamp's army, or anything like that."

"Good!" Guy said with considerable relief.

"Why are you so worried?" Bilan asked curiously. "They're all up in York, aren't they?"

"Not for more than a day or so longer!" Guy revealed. "Longchamp is marching on to Lincoln to deal with the troublemakers there, too!"

"Shit!" Siward breathed, as Thomas muttered,

"*Duw*! No wonder you were worried! Takes them right by the east of the shire! Or maybe through the north of it, depending on which river crossings they use."

"Too bloody close!" John agreed, now understanding why Guy had feared Robin might be tempted to act. "And with all those men it's more likely that they'll cross the Don at Doncaster where there's a bridge, rather than using a ferry further east."

Guy wiped the sweat from his brow with the back of his hand before it dripped on his already damp chest. "Now you understand! I've not heard confirmation of this, but I'd be surprised if Longchamp didn't stop at Tickhill for at least one night, or possibly Blyth. That would give him a clear day to then march to the Trent and cross it. He's got to get across it somewhere to get to Lincoln! And all of that means you could hear reports of armed men strung out through the north of Sherwood. But you mustn't let Robin try to make some sally out of the forest with you, thinking he can make a speedy retreat back into it, because he'll have a whole army on his tail! If it was just a few men, I'd have no fears you could shake them off once you got deep in here, but by sheer weight of numbers that force would be bound to catch at least some of you."

He didn't need to say who he feared that would be, for the key soldiers amongst them to be already catching one another's eyes in silent understanding. Walter and Algar were hopelessly unsuited to this kind of life. Neither had ever had to raise a hand in anger before being swept into the hands of the law by accident, not misdoing, and despite all the best efforts of the experienced soldiers, they were proving hopelessly inept at learning how to fight. Roger wasn't much better, although at least he had a healthy ability to run like a frightened hare if trouble loomed, which was more than Walter or Algar could do. And at the moment, Allan was still limping occasionally from what Guy suspected had been a torn ligament. The pronounced limp he'd had when Guy and the others had met him and Roger at Doncaster had faded, but if Allan over exerted himself the leg still gave him trouble, and Guy had dreadful visions of it giving way under him just at the crucial moment if he was running for his life.

Will spat furiously at an inoffensive beetle scuttling away from his foot. "The bastards! They're going to get away with what they did at Norton and there's not a damned thing we can do about it! Is that what you're saying?" And he glared at Guy as though he was in some way at fault too.

"It's not Guy's fault," the quietest of the former crusaders, James, remonstrated. He rarely said anything, so when he did it always seemed to carry more weight. "And he's right, Will, we can't take on a whole army! Not with just seventeen men!"

Will let out a bitter bark of a laugh. "Seventeen..." He had clearly been going to say that James was being far too charitable if he thought that every one of the outlaws would count equally in a fight, then realised that was just the point his friend from the east was trying to make him see. Malik, James, Siward, Gilbert and Will himself had all seen fighting alongside Robin in the east, and were true soldiers. Of the others, Thomas and Piers Cosham were deadly archers even if not quite so skilled at hand-to-hand fighting, and the youngest Cosham, Bilan, was getting a better archer by the day. Hugh of Barnby was another former soldier who could be counted on, but John and Allan were still catching up on refreshing the skills they had been taught as boys and would be no match for battle-hardened veterans even in an equal fight, let alone outnumbered. And of Much, Roger, Walter and Algar, the less said the better!

"No," Will sighed, his anger evaporating, "it's not Guy's fault." He looked across at Guy and made an apologetic shrug.

"It's the heat," Guy said, accepting the unspoken offering of peace. "In the castle the men are at each other's throats all the time. I've broken up three fights myself in the last week. No-one can get a decent night's sleep, and in the day the work's still got to be done. Everyone's tempers are frayed to bits."

"The dew out here in the morning is lovely!" Much teased him mischievously, and Guy playfully lobbed an old and desiccated acorn back at him, which hit with remarkable accuracy between the eyes, making everyone laugh at Much's shocked expression.

"Serves you right, you rascal!" John chuckled.

"What does?" said a voice from just out of sight, and Robin stepped into the clearing, with Tuck and Marianne behind him.

From where he was sitting, Guy could see that Tuck was watching Robin with a worried frown and wondered what the cause of that was. Marianne too seemed rather subdued, but Guy saw Hugh trying to catch his eye again and then giving a minute shake of his head. What in Heaven's name was going on there? Yet Guy had no time to wonder as Robin immediately said,

"What's this I'm hearing about the rioters in York getting off with just fines?"

He was clearly angry at this, and Guy was just bracing himself for arguing it all over again when the others began telling Robin for him. Yet before the relay of information had halted, Robin cut across John to say,

"I will not do *nothing*! Much's family, and Joseph your friend, deserve better!"

"No, Robin!" Much pleaded, to Guy's great relief. "I want justice for them, but not at the price of some of *us* getting killed! That solves nothing! And Guy's right. I do understand what he's saying. Longchamp has hundreds of men with him – we can't fight those odds."

Robin gave Guy one of those surprising angry looks. The look of one stranger to another when one has caused offence. It was not something Guy had ever seen in the boy he had known, but sometimes now he wondered just how much Robin really trusted him. Or was it a case of some days Robin remembered who he was, and others – like today – he was solely the product of the wars in the east? It was something Guy decided he should ask Tuck and Marianne about, given that they knew something of the mental sickness which seemed to afflict soldiers who had seen too much. Were there two men living inside that one body? One he could reason with, and one who would listen to no-one?

"Don't, Robin," Will's gravelly voice said into the tense silence. "We've argued with him already before *you* got *back*, and he's only telling us the truth."

Guy was rather surprised to hear a hint of criticism in Will's words. Had Robin gone off after some row within the band? That could spell trouble! Had someone questioned his leadership? Then Guy saw some of the looks going from Robin to Marianne and back. Oh no! Please not a fight over the one woman in the band! That could end up getting very nasty. Living in a castle full of far more men than women, Guy knew only too well what this heat was doing to the men's need for sex. Was that what lay at the root of this tension? Surely to God, Tuck and Hugh would have stamped on any claim to seniority over having the woman first which Robin might have made? Marianne deserved far better than to be passed around the camp – no woman, in Guy's eyes, would *ever* deserve that! But then Hugh was furtively making calming gestures towards Guy, who realised that his face must have been showing his worry, so maybe it wasn't that bad.

"We could get into the army camp at night," Robin was saying belligerently, almost defying Guy to say 'no' straight away.

"That would be easier than you think," Siward hurriedly assured Guy, knowing that for all Guy's experience in many things, he had never served in an army. "Men from one side of the force would hardly recognise men from the other. And you said that some men came with Henry Longchamp from Hereford, while the other half came from Normandy with Osbert. There can't be much common ground between the two halves." He was looking Guy straight in the eye, almost pleading Guy not to challenge Robin hard on this.

Guy sighed. "I'm sure you could get into the general encampment ...and out again! But what are you planning to achieve once you're there? Longchamp is moving fast. He won't hang around for long enough for you to do one trip in to see what you can find, then come back and plan what to do with that knowledge with the intention of going back a couple of days later. He'll be gone by then! So you have to know your objectives before you make a move."

"Is there anywhere we could find high ground to be able to spy on them for a while?" Piers asked of the group in general.

"You must be joking!" Hugh snorted. "Round there Tickhill Castle has the best view for miles, and that's up on a manmade motte! The rest of the area beyond it, and then Blyth, is as flat as Tuck's skillet! You'd have to get to the very top of the tallest tree on the edge of the forest to see any distance at all, and it still wouldn't be far enough."

"And the whole area is criss-crossed with small rivers and streams draining into the River Idle," Siward added, as the other man originally from the north of the shire. "Sorry, Robin, but you must surely see, we'd have to be lucky beyond belief to find our way back out in the dark and not suddenly find our way blocked by water."

Yet Robin was still as taut as a bowstring, and Guy felt he had to make some kind of peace offering before Robin decided to do something drastic just to prove he was in charge and not Guy. "Listen," he said calmly, "if we make a fast march through the night while it's cooler, and we can get close to Blyth, in the morning I'll ride out and see what I can find. I have every legal right to be in the forest! If Longchamp's men grab me I can *talk* my way out – of all of you, *I'm* the one who wouldn't need to fight to escape. If we can find roughly where Longchamp's army is, I'll act as your spy."

"I'll come with you!" Robin said immediately, making Guy very irritated. Damn it, did Robin think he would just ride in and make no effort on their behalf once there was no-one around to hear what he said?

"You'll have to come on foot, then," Guy warned him. "Up here the foresters' men walk! And they'll smell a rat if we pretend to be equal. Me they can check up on..."

"...But if they do that and find you had some stranger playing the part with you," Allan interrupted, "it'll put you in danger! By Our Lady, Robin! Remember Sheriff fitz John hates Guy's guts without any reason! Give him due cause and he could do anything! Do you want to be trying to break Guy out of the dungeons of Nottingham Castle?"

Guy was deeply touched by Allan's loyalty, and glad of the reminder to Robin of the risks he took on their behalf, but he feared Robin would not be the one coming to his rescue if ever there was a need. Then was even more surprised when Allan said,

"Why don't I go instead? I look more the part of the serving man. You're too tall, Robin. Who sees men from peasant farming stock growing to your height?"

"*And* you look too much the soldier," Hugh added pointedly. "The foresters aren't fighting men!"

Robin's scowl had got deeper and deeper, so that his dark brows were a single ridge above his eyes – eyes which glittered dangerously with anger at being foiled.

"Why don't I go too? I'm not as broad in the shoulder at least, even if I'm nearly your height," Siward offered. He was clearly thinking Robin believed that at least one of the crusaders should be with Guy to keep an eye on him, but in that Siward was mistaken too.

"I want to see this chancellor for myself!" snapped Robin. "To see what sort of man can destroy a kingdom in months without raising his hand to fight like a true leader!"

Guy ducked his head down under the pretext of wiping the sweat away again, so that his face wouldn't give him away, but his heart felt as if it was sinking into the ground beneath him. Was there no reasoning with Robin these days? Yet once again it was Allan who came to the rescue. The youngest of the four cousins – Guy, Robin, John and himself – was far bolder at challenging Robin than John had become of late, even though John was the oldest of all of them.

"Well if you're insisting on that, then we have to have some convincing part for you to play," Allan told Robin, but with a cheerful smile which robbed the words of any misinterpreted offence. "How many men would you have with you, Guy, if you were checking up on poachers?"

Guy sighed. "Legitimate forester's men, you mean? No more than two! There's no possible way for me to invent a reason to have mo..."

"Then Siward and I will be your men!" Allan cut across him decisively before Robin could take exception to Guy's limits. "Robin, you'll have to be our prisoner if you're coming with us. It's the only way!"

Thankful to have been given a way out, Guy seized on Allan's words. "Now that would work! We have the very Devil's own game with the sons of rich guildsmen! They think that because they have as much money as some of the lesser noble families, that they can take what they see as the same rights as those young noblemen. They just don't grasp that only the very top tiers of nobles get granted hunting rights! Certainly not the ones they see much of! ...Yes ...if we pass you off as the son of one of the Mansfield guildsmen, Longchamp is never going to go that far off his route to know any different."

"Why are you so worried about what Longchamp will think?" Gilbert asked. "Robin's not proposing going in and asking to speak to the bloody man!"

In truth Guy was not so sure of that but could not say so. He shook his head wearily. "No, I understand that. But if that army has anyone at all from around here in its midst, they'll know that a forester would have only a couple of men with him. What we can't then risk is them thinking something fishy is going on and reporting it higher. Can't you see, we don't have to walk right under Longchamp's nose to have his attention drawn to us? God damn it! If this was even a normal progress through the shires we could take more of a chance!"

"Oh!" John breathed as understanding dawned. "But they're all on the lookout for anything which might be amiss after the riots!"

"Shit! We should have remembered that too!" Will growled with a pointed look to Robin, which said that he too should have thought more.

"All of the soldiers will be on the lookout for anything suspicious," Marianne agreed, showing an interest for the first time. "They're right, Robin, you'll have to have a good covering story as to why you're with them, and the spoilt son of a rich trader suits your appearance better than a working forester."

Her words more than anyone's seemed to carry weight with Robin. "Very well," he agreed without arguing, "A poaching, guildsman's son I'll be if that's the way it has to be."

Guy managed to dredge up a smile for him. "I'll loop the ropes around your wrists so that they look good but won't be tied. For a rich man's son we'd do no more. Just enough so that he couldn't easily make a run for it the moment we got into a large village or town. Everyone else can come a goodly part of the way with us, but we'll just take the best archers right to the edge of the forest with us. That way they can keep us covered if we have to make a run for cover."

"That's us three and Malik, then," Thomas said cheerfully and Guy smiled his agreement. Only Piers was hot-headed, and with the calming influence of both Thomas and Malik, he was unlikely to start any trouble, especially as Bilan would follow the other two at every turn.

It seemed to take forever for the blessed cool of darkness to fall on the forest, time in which Guy took the chance to catch up on some much needed sleep – and sleeping meant he would not be drawn into any more arguments with Robin. As he occasionally drifted to near wakefulness he was aware of sporadic heated exchanges, but refused to be drawn in. He only opened his eyes properly when Tuck's strong hand fell on his shoulder and his familiar Welsh voice softly called his name.

"Time to go?" Guy asked as he stretched the kinks out of his muscles.

As best could be seen through the dense tree canopy, the sky still had a touch of light to it in the west, but directly overhead all was blackness. Even the stars were struggling to shine their light through the dust of air which hadn't been cleared by rain for weeks. Luckily the men knew their way through this part of Sherwood well by now, and they were heading for the Blyth road which would be safe late at night. That meant that they were approaching Blyth as the first light began to brighten in the east.

"We're close by Barnby, now," Hugh said, recognising the environs of his old home village.

"Time to get off the road, then," Guy agreed. "We'll go east of the road," then saw Robin's glare. "It's easier to avoid the villages on that side," he explained with all the patience he could muster. "If we go west we'll have to skirt Hodsock because it's right close to Blyth, but on the east side both Barnby and Torworth are distant enough not to notice us, even if someone is up this early in the fields."

James had come close to the head of the marching outlaws and now said,

"It is such a different way of fighting to what we did in the east." He shook his head as if still confused by this strange land he had been brought to. "So much farming! My family's fields were always close to the wells. We could not irrigate them if they were so distant. And of course there was always the desert as empty spaces."

"What about those groves of almonds and pistachios you told us about?" Bilan wondered. "Did no-one ever tend those?"

James nodded. "Yes, but not like you would a field like ...like this! You could predict when men would be out there. Here it is as though the farming never stops."

"In a way you're right," John agreed, as everyone gradually bunched together. "With all the taxes we need to pay, if you're not growing for your local lord to collect, you're growing in every spare space you can find to feed your family." Then he thought of something. "We'll have to go single file round the field edges or someone will see a gang of men have traipsed across the fields!"

Several groans went up at this since it would make for a very meandering passage, but now Robin was in agreement. "I know the grass is wilting in that first field, but even so it'll show if it's been trampled underfoot."

Yet they hadn't gone so very far when Guy and Robin called a halt. In the distance could be seen the first of many campfires being lit for the morning.

"Holy St Lazarus!" Robin breathed as he watched several more glows appear. "That's a whole army!"

Guy bit his lip. What had Robin thought he was talking about? Now was not the time to challenge him, though. Instead he said,

"Tuck, take Walter, Algar, Much, Roger, and Marianne back to the road and across into the forest, *now*, please! You too, John."

He was not going to issue orders to those others Robin still thought of as his men, but was grateful to hear Robin say to them,

"Will, James, Gilbert, go back to that barn down the road and keep watch from there. You'll cover our retreat if we have to come back fighting."

Thomas pointed to a small copse of ash and elm up ahead. "We'll take up positions there. If we four get up into the lower branches we'll have a good line of sight to cover you with." With no further ado, he, Piers, Bilan and Malik set off at a jog towards it.

"Time to tie you up!" Allan said with a mischievous wink at Robin and waved the rope at him.

Siward threw his sword to Gilbert and moved his two long knives further back along his belt so that they weren't visible from the front, especially with his shirt hanging over his trews. "Better take that for me! Not exactly a forester's weapon!"

"I'll come with you," Hugh said to the three former crusaders, and turned with Gilbert after giving Guy a pat of solidarity on the arm.

"Right, off we go," Guy said, swinging up into the saddle of the long-suffering mare. At least he had made sure she had had plenty of rest and had been properly rubbed down after the ride from Edwinstowe, so she would not look as if she had been worked hard. That was all to the good. He wanted anyone who met them to think they were just setting out on their day's business. Guy had reluctantly again donned his forester's hood over his shirt, and slung the distinctive horn which also went with it over his shoulder. The jerkin which he should have worn was neatly folded over the front of his saddle, though, since he believed that even the chancellor would not expect him to be sweltering in that – indeed to wear it so pointedly in this heat would be more cause for comment than not.

They reached the edge of the army camp and were quickly challenged.

"I'm going into Blyth," Guy answered levelly. "Checking on whether the head man there has got his beasts out of the forest."

The soldier looked blankly at him, then called for his sergeant, who in turn called for his knight. All the time Guy sat patiently on his horse, and Allan and Siward assumed the air of men rather bored and just doing their jobs.

"Has he been a naughty boy?" the sergeant asked Siward, nodding towards where Robin fidgeted between them. He was trying to see what was going on, but luckily his actions were misinterpreted as ones of guilt.

"Poaching!" Allan replied with a conspiratorial wink. "Don't think his father will be too pleased!"

"Not when he gets the fine, he won't," Siward added dryly.

"He's lucky," Guy said coldly from his lofty perch. "If he'd been a peasant we'd be taking him to Nottingham and his hand would come off!"

Robin flashed Guy a look of utter loathing, making Allan's heart skip in panic. God Above, now was not the time for Robin to start chipping away at Guy over his duties! With a flash of inspiration, Allan reached up and clipped Robin across the ear,

"Hear that, rich boy? You're getting off lightly!"

Robin's fierce gaze switched to Allan, but it allowed Allan to catch

16

hiseyes and signal frantically to keep acting the part. There was a momentary flicker in Robin's dark brown eyes and then recognition and understanding.

"My father will hear of that blow, *boy*!" he snapped.

"Oh don't get so above yourself," Siward said in bored tones, but exchanging a covert wink with Robin, and was also relieved to see the tension slip from Robin's posture.

Mercifully word came forward that the forester was to be allowed to ride on through the camp. Allan again was best at this pretence, openly staring at the army with all the innocence of a man who had never seen such a thing, which few of the walking foresters would have.

Right by Blyth was the camp of the important men, and as he had privately anticipated with no small amount of dread – yet had not dared to forewarn Robin of the probability – Guy was summoned to the chancellor's presence. He might have got away without an audience, but the man himself happened to come out of his luxurious tent just as Guy was passing close-by.

"Who are you to ride into my camp?" the short, swarthy Longchamp demanded in haughty Norman-French. His interpreter was about to translate for Guy when Guy replied in the same language,

"I am the forester of the sheriff of Nottingham."

He dismounted and walked forward to drop to one knee before the chancellor. It was all he could do not to stare. He had been told that Longchamp was ugly, but he had not expected this. The most powerful man in England had short, stumpy legs with huge feet and a humped back, but that would have mattered less if he had been bettered favoured in other respects. Yet his black hair grew almost to his eyebrows, while his beard and moustache were straggly and seemed to connect to his hair, given that his neck was so short as to be invisible behind its hairy covering. The impression was more of an ape than a man, not helped by the way Longchamp's belly stuck out over those stunted legs. For another man Guy would have felt overwhelming pity at having been so crippled by such a fate of birth, but one look at the cold, calculating eyes and any sympathy died and was replaced by a frisson of fear. This man was less than human on the inside too!

A trickle of cold sweat ran down Guy's spine as he saw a weeping boy being led out of the richest tent. Sweet Jesu! So the tales of Longchamp's taste for sodomy were true too! The Abbot of Rufford had once said to Guy that Longchamp was the wickedest pervert he had ever heard of, which now seemed less of a slander than an understatement. He dared not look back to Robin, Siward and Allan, but he was praying mightily that Robin would not get them all killed if he too saw that bruised boy with one hand clutching his anus protectively.

"Fitz John's man, eh?" Longchamp was saying to him.

"Yes, my lord. Fence Month begins in a couple of days."

Guy was assuming that Longchamp would know at least the main points of royal forest law, given the amount of revenue they brought in, and was not about to offer the chancellor any opportunity to take offence by daring to explain in detail. He was instantly proven right as an unctuous courtier began saying,

"Fence Month, my lord, is..." only to be cut dead by,

"Dolt! Of course I know what it is! Fool! Go away and plague someone with fewer brains than yourself – if that's possible!"

The unfortunate young man turned scarlet and fled, no doubt fearing what dreadful penance Longchamp might impose on him if he stayed.

"And what are *you* doing here?" Longchamp demanded of Guy now as he gestured him to stand up again. "Ralph fitz Stephen's man deals with this area of the forest, does he not?"

Without batting an eyelid, Guy nodded courteously and replied politely, "That he does, my lord, but I have to use the agister's court at Edwinstowe for much of where I patrol. That's where I have just been. I'm now on my way west to patrol the new forest of Derwent-to-Erewash. I intend to start in the north of the forest and work my way back down to Nottingham."

Longchamp's wicked little eyes glared at him, and Guy could almost see the wheels turning in the scheming brain, but what Guy had told him fortunately correlated with what he already knew of the workings of Sherwood. However, he was not letting Guy off that easily. "A little far north to be crossing the shire border, aren't you?" he challenged him.

"Indeed, my lord," agreed Guy, putting on the blank expression he had honed to perfection in the time he had worked under William de Braose over on the Marches. "I would have turned west much sooner had it not been for this rascal," and he flicked a thumb towards Robin. "Led us a merry chase until his horse threw him. She's no doubt heading back for her stable by now, but he's wasted my time, and now he shall have to suffer for it by walking the length of the shire with my men. That should cool his ardour for going hunting without permission again." Guy dropped his voice, pretending to exclude Robin, although all three standing behind him could hear perfectly well what he said. "A pup with delusions of grandeur will find it a humbling experience to go on foot so far, eh, my lord?"

Longchamp gave a leer which was no doubt what passed for a smile in his case. "Indeed, forester. Very well, be on your way." And with a wave of his hand that was it. Longchamp turned once more for

18

his tent and began calling for his breakfast, leaving Guy to mount up and then gesture Allan and Siward to prod Robin onwards.

The four of them now walked at the mare's slow pace through the encampment, with few taking any notice of them at all.

"See what I mean?" Siward risked saying softly. "We've got past the sentries, so now we're in the heart of the army no-one's questioning our right to be here."

It was certainly far easier than Guy had expected. Longchamp's challenge he had fully anticipated, but he had been convinced that more of the men would challenge a forester in their midst – especially one with a prisoner. Yet that also made things harder. All the four of them could do was look as hard as they could without giving the game away, whereas men speaking to them would at least have given them the chance to drop the odd question in return.

"I don't see any prisoners at all," Allan said quietly.

"Nor me," agreed Robin. "No-one who looks like they're under guard."

Guy gave the smallest shake of his head, trying to keep up the appearance of haughtiness. "No, me neither. Even from up here I can't see any clusters of men who look like they're guarding someone."

They reached the edge of the encampment, were saluted lethargically on their way by the sentries on the other side, and then began heading back for the forest, breathing sighs of relief at having got away without any trouble. Yet before they could reach the tree-line there came a whistled birdcall.

"That's Will!" Siward and Robin exclaimed in unison, Robin adding, "Something must have gone wrong!"

"Christ! I hope they haven't been taken!" Guy swore, knowing that there was no way he could talk his way back into that camp to help them, and there were far too many men for him to start a fight.

"No! Look ahead!" Allan gasped with relief.

In the shadows under the eaves of the first stand of mature trees were Will and all of the others whom they had left guarding their rear, but Will was gesturing furiously back behind them. Risking seeming too curious, Guy turned in his saddle to look. There on the very road they had come in by was another party! Nowhere near as many in number as Longchamp's army, they nonetheless were very grandly appointed. Banners flew, and even at this distance it was possible to see the vivid colours of rich garment.

"Judas' balls! Who the hell are they?" Guy gulped, squinting his eyes to try and recognise someone's pennant.

"We don't want to be caught in some squabble between these two," Allan fretted. "Robin! Make a run for it! Then we can chase you into the forest!"

Without any further prompting Robin broke into a run, his long legs eating up the ground so that he was quickly far in front of the other three. Alan and Siward took off after him, with Guy bringing up the rear holding the mare in a collected canter, so that it seemed as though she was going faster than she was to anyone watching from behind. Luckily they were all soon in the trees and hidden from view again.

"What happened?" Guy heard Robin demand of Will as they near collided in the shadows beneath the trees.

By Dewi Sant, Gervase, that was a memorable meeting! I had had heard much of Longchamp, as had everyone in England I suspect, but to meet the man in person was to feel as if you had stared Satan in the face. I jest not! Over the years I have met and had to work for some cruel and savage men, but there was a calculating malevolence about Longchamp which set him aside from the rest. Nor was I making up my description of him to paint him even blacker for you. I believe another of your literary monks, Gerald of Wales, had much to say on the matter of Longchamp's appearance too. Quite why he found so much favour with King Richard I have never understood, for even after he had been driven out of England by nobles who had taken as much as they could of his avarice and self-promoting, he was still very much the king's man in Normandy. But we have a way to go yet before we reach that point.

Was he truly a sodomite too? All I can say to that, Gervase, was that to my eye it seemed so, based on what I saw that day, and the accusations came from so many different quarters it seems unlikely that they were made up. As we shall see soon, his reputation for perversion was believed at the very highest levels, and it would not surprise me if he had enjoyed a variety of strange pleasures.

˜Did the king know?˜ you ask. For truth, I do not know. Some no doubt think he did, but my own belief is that King Richard was so intent on his own goals that he rarely saw people as anything more than tools he could use, and in that sense, Longchamp was a very effective tool for extracting money from the English. Robin never believed the king knew, but then Robin's view of our royal Lionheart was skewed for some time to come after this, and later I chose not to ask – it was safer not to by then.

˜Why is that?˜ Oh Gervase, the tales of Robin Hood and the dreadful Sir Guy of Gisborne always being at one another's throats is not without foundation. I loved him as my cousin until the day he died, but as men we saw the world in very different ways, and that led to many arguments. However, we are in the midst of wrapping up the events of 1190, which you so heartily wished to be rid of, so we must hurry on. Ah no, Gervase!

<u>You</u> chivvied me on! You cannot have your bread and eat it! Onwards we will go without digression!

Chapter 2

So there we were, Brother, wondering who in the name of St Thomas was coming to join Longchamp with such pomp and ceremony, if not with any great numbers in his retinue. The only consolation to me in those first few heartbeats was the thought that at least it was not more men to join the army. If there had been, I would have been herding the outlaws into the depths of the forest as fast as they could go, for that would have been a sign that Longchamp intended to use them to scour the shires. Mercifully that was not the case.

Sherwood Forest, June, the Year of Our Lord 1190.

"**I**t's the bishop of Durham! Hugh le Puiset!" Tuck answered for Will.

"By *Dewi Sant*, he gave us a nasty turn!" Thomas added. "We'd just seen you get in amongst those first soldiers when Will and the others came haring up to us."

Gilbert took over. "It was a sheer fluke that James looked the other way over towards the river. It was the birds coming up off the marshes, you see! A heron attracted his attention and he was following it. He spotted them first. Thank God they were a goodly way off!"

"We'd have been caught by them without a doubt if we'd stayed put," Hugh agreed. "Le Puiset must have heard that Longchamp was here. There's no other reason why such an important party would use the back roads like that. They must have been cutting across country to make sure they met him. I'd say they must have stayed last night at Retford and crossed the River Idle there – which probably accounts for them being up so early too, because Retford certainly isn't set up to receive such illustrious guests!"

Will nodded. "So we legged it as fast as we could along the hedgerows. We reckoned we'd be fine once we were on the other side of the main road. Then once we got here, Tuck said that the bishop wouldn't rough it unless he had to, so he'd stick to the best roads possible."

"Too right," Tuck sniffed. "Hugh le Puiset is one of the grand old lords of England! He'll be here protecting his own interests, of that you can be sure. My money would be on him having spoken to the king about getting at least his own lands back, if not his full office as joint ruler with Longchamp in the king's absence."

"What a bloody awful coincidence that he should turn up here just as we did," Hugh sighed.

Robin turned to Guy. "Do you believe it to be coincidence?"

Guy was surprised. "What else would it be?"

Robin sniffed suspiciously. "You don't think the bishop wants his share of the fines from York?"

Almost as one, Guy and Tuck said the very same thing,

"He's no right to them!" then blinked at one another in surprise, before Guy gestured to Tuck to carry on for both of them.

"As a bishop he has no claim on such fines for civil unrest," Tuck told Robin decisively. "Oh I know the Church has its finger in many pies these days! And that some of it is pure avarice! I'm not going to try and make any excuses in that direction. But despite how it seems sometimes, they still have their limits as to what they can set a claim to. And even if this had happened in le Puiset's diocese, he would've been hard pressed to wring some of the money out of *any* chancellor, let alone Longchamp.

"I didn't get chance to tell even you, Guy, but when I was in Nottingham I heard the gossip from the brothers I was staying with, that the archbishop of Canterbury has suspended the bishop of Coventry for buying the sheriffdoms of Warwickshire, Leicestershire and Staffordshire. So you see Robin, there are limits to how secular a bishop can become even with the Church in its current state of disarray. As it is, if anyone was in line to get a portion for the Church on the basis of the minster being desecrated, it would be the archbishop of York, not the bishop of Durham..."

"...And the king's bastard brother is the archbishop," Robin concluded, seeing reason that – however corrupt he might think the bishop to be – caught between Geoffrey Plantagenet as archbishop of York and William Longchamp as chancellor, Hugh le Puiset wouldn't stand a chance.

"I know the bishop is no saint," Tuck added soothingly, "but he's also an old man, and if what we've heard is true, he's fallen foul of Longchamp's avarice, not the other way round."

They were still standing talking several trees back into the heart of the woods, to remain out of sight, when Much's urgent call came.

"Robin! Guy! Come quick! Look!"

They swung themselves up into the lower branches of the mature trees to where Much, Roger and Bilan were keeping watch on the army and the party approaching it. As Robin edged out onto the branch where Much was, Guy stepped out onto Allan's branch with one hand holding the branch above for support. By standing up he could see more easily through the leafy canopy than Robin, even though Robin was further out on Much's branch.

The view before them needed no words. At the heart of the armed encampment there was a circle of heavily armed men surrounding a few at the centre. The ones with spears, and with crossbows ratcheted back and ready to loose, were all Longchamp's men. In the middle were a few who wore the bishop's colours, and at their front stood someone who had to be le Puiset himself, going by the richness of his clothes. He was arguing with someone too short to be seen over the heads of the armed men, and that had to be Longchamp!

What was also obvious was that the bishop was losing. Every so often the bishop would take a step backwards, as if someone had prodded or poked him. That forced his own men to step backwards, and as they did so, those with the chancellor stepped forward. The ground ceded was of no importance of itself, but symbolically it spoke volumes as to who was in control there. And beyond the circle where the talking was taking place, le Puiset's main body of men were surrounded on the edge of the encampment, and were also being threatened by cross-bowmen and men-at-arms with spears. No fighting had broken out yet, but the watching outlaws could tell that it was simply because the bishop's men knew they would be overwhelmed and dead before they could make even the slightest impression on the numbers surrounding them.

"What do we do?" Allan wondered.

Guy sighed. "There's nothing we can do. Even if we could get to le Puiset, we few would make no difference against that lot."

"You think we should defend the bishop?" John said from below them in shock. "Guy? What are you thinking of? He's no friend to us!"

Guy dropped nimbly to the forest floor and was soon joined by all of the others. "I was actually thinking that of anyone we could get to, the bishop might know what's happening with the king," he said levelly, refusing to be drawn into the rising chorus of protests. "I know he's far from being one of the poor unfortunates you all want to protect, but he might know something we could use. I'm thinking of Much's family and the folk of Norton. What if he's going back to the king? What if we could pass on the information that Longchamp has only done half the job? Has only prosecuted those who were the ring leaders at York?"

Suddenly Robin was all smiles. "Ah! Now there's a thought! Appeal to the king for justice for Norton!"

Guy wiped the sweat of another sweltering day from his brow and managed a furtive glance to Hugh and Thomas. They were back to Robin's unshakable belief in the king again. His long personal contact with the young leper king of Jerusalem, King Baldwin IV, had left him with a skewed view of kings. Guy, Hugh and Thomas exchanged covert rolled eyes of despair. King Baldwin may have been the epitome of Christian kingship, but they all felt that if ever Robin met King Richard he might find that the valiant Plantagenet would not stand up to the comparison with the near-saintly Baldwin. And whether King Baldwin would ever have actually listened to an appeal for justice for a few burned peasants, a village and a mill, was not the point – they were sure King Richard wouldn't!

Luckily it was Roger who naively challenged Robin's statement. "Wos' he goin' to do about it, though?" the scruffy lad asked in bewilderment. "'E's half way to Jerusalem by now, ain't 'e? 'E ain't goin' to turn back just for that, surely?"

"A good king cares about all of his subjects," Robin began saying, but Tuck quickly added,

"You're right, Roger. The king's already far away, but even Longchamp can't afford to take on all of the nobles who've remained if they unite against him. So this is giving the bishop an arrow to aim at Longchamp which those nobles will see quite clearly."

"Exactly," Guy said firmly, steering the conversation away from the dangerous bits. "If the other important men in London and Normandy start hearing that villages are being set on and burned with no-one being brought to account, they'll be quick to grasp that the next time it might be one of their villages. Some of *their* peasants who die!"

"And men like William de Braose might be utter bastards," Thomas added, "but by *Dewi Sant*, they object like fury to others trampling over those they think are theirs to do with as they will. No point in having the power of life and death over your peasants if some other Norman devil comes and snuffs them out like candles, and thumbs his nose at you in the process!"

"That's a real kick in the balls to men like him," agreed Piers.

Guy was nodding. "And they're who we might stir up enough to do something about Norton. It still won't be a big trial out in public with a public flogging or a hanging. I won't promise you that, Much. They'll never openly do that to a fellow Norman lord for mere English peasants! That would never do! But quietly, yes. To teach both those who did such a thing, and any who might have similar thoughts, just who is in control."

Then to throw Robin a bone and to stop him protesting, added, "And they can do it in the king's name. He doesn't have to be here in person. Because it's connected to the massacre of King Richard's protected Jews at York, we can use that to tar de Cuckney as a man who goes against the king."

"Now that's sneaky!" Will said with open admiration. "I like that!"

"But we need someone to do the work for us," Guy reminded them. "We need the bishop to be the one who takes that idea back to court. We can't!"

"Set him to do God and the king's work," Robin said with a hint of smile forming.

"Will he do it, though?" wondered Gilbert.

Guy grinned. "Out of offended dignity I think he will! Remember, the king's intent was to leave him jointly in charge with Longchamp, yet in under a year he's been removed from all meaningful power. Oh yes, if he has something to use against Longchamp, I think we can be pretty sure he will."

Siward was grinning too. "And it's all the better for him because it's nothing to do with his lands or his titles. He can blacken Longchamp's name and look virtuous because there's no clear gain to be thrown back at him."

"But how can we get to him?" Malik asked cautiously. "We can hardly march into that army."

"What's happening now?" Robin demanded. "Much and Roger, get back up into those trees and tell us where the bishop is now."

With Allan and Bilan hot on their heels, the youngest of the outlaws clambered high up into the trees and scoured the river valley.

Bilan called down, "It looks like Longchamp is marching and the bishop's just staying there!"

"Definitely!" Allan affirmed. "I can see someone who must be Longchamp on a horse up at the head of the column. His tent is still being taken down, but he's on the road and heading for the river."

"Right, we wait for Longchamp's men to get clear and then we follow the bishop," Robin declared, and for once Guy silently agreed with him.

It took well on into the afternoon before Longchamp's troops were all out of Blyth, time in which all the outlaws could do was rest to fend off the worst of the heat.

"I pity the poor sods marching in this!" Will commented at one point. "Sweating their bollocks off, I bet! This is worse in some ways than the Holy Land."

James managed to raise his head up off the bed of old bracken where he was lying. "The air is so wet here!" he said in dismay. "How can that be? So hot after so little rain and yet still so..." he groped for the right word.

"Humid," Tuck supplied helpfully. "That's the word you use when the air is like this – humid."

"Last summer was not like this," Malik observed. "Why is that, Tuck?"

"It's because we were up in the Peaks last summer," the big Welsh priest supplied. "It's always fresher up there. If you'd been down here in this maze of river channels you'd have felt it just the same."

"It's like this whenever we get a hot spell in the summer," Hugh added. "But don't worry, Malik, this won't last."

"No it won't," Siward agreed. "It's not like the summers out in Outremer we suffered, with their months of steady heat. Give it a few more days and then we'll have an almighty thunderstorm and the air will clear. I remember them when I was a lad. They'd rattle on and on through the night or day until you'd think there couldn't be any more rain up there, and then suddenly it would stop, everything would steam like it had been on fire, and then the air would get fresher."

Hugh laughed from where he too lay flat on the ground beside a snoozing Guy. "I think those are wishful memories, Siward!" He turned so that he could see Malik and James. "Sometimes it does clear the air, but other times it takes two or three goes to freshen things up. So we might get a couple of hellish days when it feels even damper and hotter than this, but it will only be days. This is England, the weather's never the same for more than a couple of weeks at a time!"

"I can see some big clouds coming up out of the south-west!" Bilan called from up above them. "That storm might even come tonight if the wind picks up!"

"That'd be handy," Guy muttered languidly from under the shade of the arm he had thrown across his eyes.

"Handy?" Marianne sniffed. "How could a thunderstorm be handy?"

"Because then I wouldn't smell myself approaching," Guy replied, deadpan. There was a brief silence, then everyone guffawed.

"Bloody hell, you're right!" Will chortled, "I stink like an old pig!"

"Me too," sighed Allan. "God, I'd love to get the sweat off my skin!"

Guy let them laugh, but had not just meant it in jest. While they were marching into the camp amongst a band of soldiers, no-one would have noticed. Longchamp's army had got so used to the sweat of themselves they wouldn't have noticed anyone except the most rank. With the army gone, though, the overwhelming aroma of ripe male had cleared, and now anyone in the village would be much more likely to pick up on so many men approaching by scent alone.

Bilan dropped nimbly onto the ground from above. "The bishop's gone into Blyth Priory!" he announced.

Robin sat up. "Into it? Actually inside? Not just set up camp outside the walls?"

Bilan shook his head. "No. He's gone in."

Tuck smacked the centre of his forehead in frustration. "*Duw!* This heat's addled my brains! Of course he would! They're Black Monks the same as at Durham! I'd be amazed if he didn't know the prior personally! The prior and many of the monks here are sent from the mother house at Rouen, you see. True Normans to a man except for the lay brothers, I wouldn't be surprised to find. Proper Normans like le Puiset himself!"

The outlaws groaned. Getting to the bishop had suddenly turned very complicated.

"What do we do now?" Walter asked.

"We pray for that rain," Guy answered, sitting up with a wince as cramp in his arm caught him unawares. By Saint Issui he needed another drink! He was beginning to feel like an old leather boot he was so dried out from sweating. No wonder he was getting cramp.

"How's that going to help us?" Algar muttered darkly. "We'll just be wet and still outside the priory."

But Marianne has caught on to Guy's thinking and was smiling brightly. "Yes we will! Soaked to the skin with any luck! And that means if some of us go to their door asking for shelter they'll have to give it us!"

Robin whipped round to look at her. "What this 'us'? You're not coming with us!"

"Who says?" Marianne bit back.

"It'll be dangerous!" Robin objected.

"No it won't," Marianne and Guy both said with the same exasperation.

Guy turned to his cousin. "She's right, Robin. If someone goes in with her acting as a man and wife, no-one will look twice at them." He threw his hands up in resignation. "All right! If *you* go in with Marianne as *your* wife, no-one will look twice at *you*. You'll just be a couple who got caught out by the weather while you were on the road."

"I'll say that my mother is very ill," Marianne decided. She looked to Siward. "You'll be my cousin who's come to fetch me." She smiled acidly at Robin. "And you'll be my husband recently returned from the wars in Normandy. No bloody good at farming, so we've lost your father's tiny farm to another tenant! So I need to butter up my father for a job for you anyway."

"Why can't we be happily married?" protested Robin.

"Because if we fake a row, I can storm off and then you can come looking for me, you addle-pate!" she snapped, more in frustration than anger. Robin could sometimes be so slow to catch on to the normalities of life, however good a soldier he might be. "You'll need a reason to be outside of the humbler guest quarters if you're spotted!"

"That's a good plan!" Will agreed. "She's right, Robin. No-one will look twice at you with a woman by your side. It's so normal. And in this heat other guests must have been snapping at each other already. You two having a row won't seem in the slightest bit odd."

"I think we should make one change, though," Siward said. "I presume you're also going in, and as what you are?" he asked Guy.

"As a forester? Yes."

"Then I think Allan and I should still be with you. You never know, one of the lay brothers might have seen us earlier in the day. Nothing's going to give us away quicker than if someone thinks, 'hey, he was with the forester earlier, and now he's saying he's never met him!' Just because we didn't see them doesn't mean they didn't see us."

"God, that's a point!" John gulped. "Well it had better be you then, Hugh, who goes with Robin and Marianne."

"No, not me," Hugh instantly refused. "It's too close to my old home. I'd be doing the same, putting you in danger if someone spots me for who I really am – and someone who once lived in my village could well be a lay brother by now, for all I know."

Tuck scratched his chin thoughtfully. "And I don't think it can be John or me – we're too memorable for our sizes. You three Coshams will never pass for Marianne's cousin the moment you open your mouths, and I'm sorry Roger, but you'll never pass for a local either. Nor Gilbert!"

They all looked from one to another, no-one wanting to say aloud that they didn't trust Algar or Walter to do it.

"I think it has to be you, Will," Robin decided.

"Me?"

"Yes. Well Malik and James are never going to pass for relatives of any English woman as blonde as Marianne, are they? But your hair is fair – what's left of it."

"You cheeky sod!" Will protested, throwing a playful punch Robin's way which was easily dodged. His hair was cropped very short but was showing signs of receding at the front, although not badly as yet.

"I think you'll make a lovely cousin!" Marianne teased, coming and linking her arm through his and making as if to ruffle the fair tufts.

"Gerroff!" Will growled, swatting her away like a fly as everyone else hooted with laughter. "Bloody hell, woman, there's limits to cousinly love!"

"Well we've got a plan. Now all we need is the rain," Allan observed.

They had to wait and wait, but just before the following dawn the heavens opened up with a vengeance. After a few enormous lightning flashes and great rolls of thunder, the storm was upon them. The only consolation for the wait was that le Puiset seemed disinclined to move on at all, making them wonder whether he was waiting for someone else to arrive, but they couldn't hope to second guess who that might be. Certainly, if there were any other guests in the priory they were showing no signs of leaving either while the rain pounded the dust to mud.

Knowing that they would have to pretend they had been on the road for at least half a day, everyone now was happy to linger and took the opportunity to scrub themselves as clean as possible in the deluge. At first it was blissful just to get the grime of the dust off them, but as the day drew on it stopped being quite such a relief. The rain was not particularly cold, but the force never let up, and soon they were squelching with every step as it ran down the inside of their clothes and into their boots. And still the thunder and lightning rattled around in the heavens above them, sometimes moving off down the Trent valley only to return later and start its circuit all over again.

"Time to go!" Guy suddenly called from where he was watching the road from up in one of the trees with Bilan. He dropped to the ground with a splat. "We can just see what looks like a small party of travellers on the road! Robin, Will and Marianne, you go now! Quickly! Get in front of them so that there's still room at the priory guesthouse!"

Robin and Will each grabbed a hand of Marianne's and together the three ran across the rain-flattened fields at an angle, just making it onto the road nicely in time before the coming party made it round the next bend to see them emerge. Feigning weariness they then trudged on just slow enough to convince the party that they had caught up with three slower travellers. Thomas and Piers scouted along behind everyone for a while, and then hurried back saying that the three had made it safely into the priory.

"What about us?" Allan asked Guy, sweeping the water from his eyebrows before it fell into his eyes again. "When do we go?"

"In just a little while," Guy answered calmly. "Let them get in and sorted first."

Allan sidled closer to him and spoke so that only they could hear. "You know what Siward said about being recognised for being with you? That applies to Robin too, doesn't it? If someone remembers he was your prisoner. You're separating yourself from him because of that, aren't you?"

Guy sighed and leaned on the mare whom he was getting ready, but it allowed him to drop his head closer to Allan's height. "Yes I am, and it does. Every bit! But these days I can't seem to say anything to him without it being taken the wrong way. And you saw how determined he was to be the one to go in."

Allan grimaced. "I know. I'm sorry, Guy. You always seem to have one or the other of us taking lumps out of you." He was referring to the dreadful pain in the neck he had been when he, John and Guy had first been reunited four years ago. As a result, Allan had been forcibly separated from John by Guy and Tuck, had spent three years in the north having to live on his own wits, and had returned substantially more grown up and wiser.

Guy smiled wearily at Allan. "You're fully forgiven. I'm just glad that now you can see why we had to do the things we did, and that nothing John or I could have done would have prevented the breakup of our little family. But I wish there was more of the old Baldwin in Robin. I used to be able to talk to him. Now it's as though he stops listening the moment he hears my voice. What's wrong with him? Or is it really just me?"

"It's not you," Allan quickly reassured him.

"But in a way it is," came Siward's voice from the other side of the mare. "Come on, I'll explain while we walk," and his gaze to the others said that he wanted to be out of earshot when he spoke further.

"So?" Guy queried once they had made it to the road, whose dips and ditches were now more like tiny streams.

"You're always ahead of him," Siward said carefully. "You were always the nearest thing he had to an older brother. And that thing you said when we were back at High Peak Castle – about John always consoling Allan, and you, him – it..." he groped for the right words. "I don't mean this in a blaming sort of way, but it almost gives you a kind of power over him. Out in Outremere he was his own man. Now he's back he's delighted beyond words to have found his family again, but suddenly he's back to being third out of four amongst you lot."

Allan snorted in disbelief. "Christ on the Cross! I'm 'the little one', and I don't go around breaking Guy's balls just because he's older than me! Well ...not now, anyway! I know I had my moments, but once I was away from John and Guy I soon realised what they'd done for me, and I've never been so glad as when I saw them that day back in Doncaster." He reached over and affectionately squeezed Guy's arm. "After what Roger and I had been through, even if you'd torn me off a strip and cuffed me, I'd still have been *so* glad to see you. It was as if the world had suddenly come right again. Nothing could ever be quite as bad if we were in it together once again." He laughed. "And you always could think quicker than the rest of us! Even when we were lads and trying to avoid old Fulk and a thrashing with that bloody belt of his!"

Guy and Allan chuckled.

"By Our Lady, I can still remember how that used to smart!" Guy recollected, and Allan grinned back, while still pulling a face at the memory of the man who had been Guy's uncle and to the outside world Allan's father – although they both knew now that Allan was his mother's bastard. Siward watched them with a sad smile. What a shame that Robin could not quite slot back into the family he had been so much a part of and loved so dearly. He had to try and get these two to understand the man who was his friend.

"At least you two were still in England, though, albeit on different sides of the country," he said to open the conversation. "That's one of the things Robin and the rest of us find hard. Things have changed so much since we left. Under King Henry everything was so stable. In our lifetimes, until we left, I'd almost say unchanging."

Guy nodded sympathetically. "I understand that. And you were all much younger then. I do understand that Robin went out while he was still little more than a boy, you know, and so his memories of home are coloured by the fact that he had no responsibilities back then. All four of us had no idea how privileged our home life was until we left the old manor at Alverton. It was a shock to me too, Siward."

Siward sighed. "Yes, but you grew up into this world as it is now. You know how it works. You see it in all of its detail as a man who's grown with the changes."

Guy nodded thoughtfully. "I see what you mean. That Robin has suddenly landed in a world he thought he knew, and which now doesn't behave the way he remembers it doing, but why does he blame me, Siward? I haven't made England the way it is now!"

"But you can out-think Robin because of that," Siward said gently. "That's one of the things which irritate him. Before he's even realised that there's a problem, you've spotted it and are halfway to finding a way around it. Will's told me how deeply Robin wanted to become a proper Templar knight, right from the moment he joined the order. It was terribly bad luck that the knight he was made squire to died, and left Robin in limbo on the road to the Holy Land and with no prospect of taking his vows. But then when we all met up and went through the hell that was the battle at Hattin, and then the siege of Jerusalem, he found something again. And he got that all-important knighthood! So now he wants to be that knight he always hoped he'd be, that leader who men would look up to. The one who is prized and honoured. And most of the time he's getting there – except when you're around!

"Without even trying, Guy, you streak past him. Even just now you did it. You had your finger right on why Marianne should go into the priory before Robin had even thought about what would look normal, and it's because he's still coming to terms with what's 'normal' for here and now. He's said to me that sometimes when you do that he feels such a fool for not knowing."

Guy turned to him in horror. "Judas' balls! He doesn't think I'm belittling him on purpose, does he? Sweet Jesu, I would never do that!"

It was a tremendous relief to Siward to see Guy's instinctive reaction. He had been pretty sure that Guy had no idea of how he made Robin feel, and he was glad to see he had been right.

In shock Guy added, "In fact, I've tried very hard to step around him, knowing that all six of you are finding it hard living here."

"But that puts you in the older brother roll again," Siward pointed out sadly. "When he realises you're trying to feed him information, or show him something, without openly doing it for the others to see, that grates too, because it only serves to show that you're still one step ahead of him all the way."

Allan sighed. "I'm beginning to see what you mean, Siward. You turned thirty a couple of weeks ago, Guy, and that really marks you out as a mature man, if nothing else did. But Robin's still got two years to go, and he's never going to catch you up with things like that. You hit all the landmarks before him, and for some reason that matters to him when he can't seem to compete with you in other ways."

Guy stopped in his tracks and threw his hands up in exasperation. "God in Heaven! I can't change that! Does it matter to you that I'm older, Allan? Does John care that I sometimes take over, even though I'm younger than him? He's never said so! What a mad kind of thought to have!"

"Aaah!" Allan said pointedly.

"What?" Guy looked at him hard. "Why that 'aaah'?"

Allan winced and braced himself. "That thing about madness."

He saw the shock wash over Guy and the sudden look of worry.

"It's not madness like the village idiot kind," Allan assured his cousin hurriedly, "but one of the things I've noticed pretty quickly while I've been with this lot in these last few weeks is that Robin doesn't sleep. I mean *really* doesn't sleep!"

Siward's huge sigh of relief told Guy that this was something both of them had independently been brewing up to telling him.

"It's something to do with battle fatigue," Siward tried to explain. "Up until you and Tuck did the whole thing for us with that Mass for the dead at High Peak, I was as bad as him. Honestly Guy, it's horrible! You get to the point where you hardly know what day it is. You're so dog-tired, and you'd give anything for the chance to sink into a deep and dreamless sleep. Yet when you lie down, sleep either doesn't come, or if it does, it's filled with the kind of nightmares which have you pissing yourself or screaming the place down.

"But it skews your view of reality too. I remember while we were still making our way across France, there was this man on the road with us, and for some reason I was convinced he was going to kill me. I couldn't even begin to explain why – not then or now. To me, I could see it in his eyes. It was complete nonsense, of course, but not to me – not at that point. Luckily he turned off the road and left the party we were travelling alongside before I did something I would now deeply regret.

"You just can't think straight. You start thinking one thing and then suddenly your mind is off somewhere else on another track altogether. And then just as you get to breaking point, you'll have a night where your head hits the pillow and you go out like a light for the full night. Just the one. The next night I was right back where I started from. It's as if it goes in cycles like the moon, waxing and waning. You have that blissful night of sleep, then some nights where you sleep for a few hours, but wake wrung out like an old rag from the bloody dreams, then it peaks when you don't sleep at all for several.

"You can reach a point where you're scared to sleep for what you'll see in your mind's eye. And that's the dangerous time, because you can even start seeing things while you're awake! It's as though your soul has to have that release, and if it doesn't come in dreams it seeps out anyway."

Guy looked Siward in the eye and said sincerely, "Thank you! That makes so much sense of something I've been thinking – that sometimes Robin looks at me as though I'm a complete stranger to him."

Siward thought and nodded. "That's possibly not far from the truth. I can only talk about what happened to me, but on one occasion I truly thought I saw a little demon looking out through a man's eyes. I've not asked Robin, but he may be getting flashes like that."

"Is this getting worse?" Allan wondered. "Because if it is, do we need to be prepared for a day when the only thing we can do for Robin is leave him at some monastery infirmarer's door to be cared for with the other lunatics?"

Siward puffed out his cheeks as he considered this. "Jesu, I hope not! No, I don't think it'll come to that." He sluiced his dripping hair back from his forehead as he tried to think things through. "I think what's really hit Robin hard, and set him back, was seeing what happened at York. It's as though it's dredged up an awful lot of bad memories."

"Are the rest of you alright?" Guy asked anxiously. "You six all went through the siege of Jerusalem. I presume that's what York reminded you of, with the slaughter that went on there?"

Siward bit his lip and winced. "Sort of. I've had a few shaky moments, I will confess – quite literally! Sometimes this battle weariness comes out in horrible tremors you can't control, and I've had a couple of attacks of them. So has Gilbert. And I think Malik and Will have had a couple of sleepless nights, but those two were coping much better right from the start, so that's all it's been for them. Will's a good man, you know. He could see Gilbert was starting to suffer a week or so back, and he got the swords out and let him batter it out of his system. Will just kept up this solid defence while Gilbert went all raging Celt on him, then never said a word when Gilbert suddenly collapsed in a heap. He just put the swords away as though nothing had happened and went and sat by Gilbert while he had a weep."

"And you?" Guy asked.

"Me? I talk to Malik. He's got such a solid, earthy view of life. I rant like a mad fool for an afternoon, and he sits there and nods and gives me the odd prompt until I've run out of words. And I'm not sure what he does for James, but it's something similar. They go off into the woods by themselves to where we can't hear what's being said and talk in their own language for what must be half the day. But you can see James feels better when he comes back. He didn't used to, mind you. The real improvement came with Tuck's service. Before that it was more as if James could manage to keep on shouldering that terrible burden he was carrying inside of him, and that after a talk with Malik he could just about get back to putting one foot in front of the other – barely. Now, though, he's lost the haunted look in his eyes most of the time. He still has days of terrible sadness, but it's not gnawing at his guts like it used to."

"I'm glad about that," Guy said with a weak smile, "although Tuck deserves all the credit for that one."

Siward didn't think so, but decided not to argue the point today. If Tuck had ministered to the former crusaders' souls on that day nearly a year ago, it had been Guy who had done the material things to make it work. "You're going to ask me why it didn't work the same for Robin now, aren't you?" he said sadly. "And the answer is, I don't know why."

"I think I can guess why," Allan said pensively. "It's all to do with the kind of people you are. Even when we were lads together, Baldwin was always the one who got so distraught about injustice. When the others of our family – Fulk, Philip and Audolph – did something horrible, something nasty and spiteful, John would be sad, Guy would be the one thinking of a way to turn it back on them, and I'd just be baffled. But Baldwin would take it to heart."

Guy gave Allan a surprised smile. "Lord, I'd forgotten that, but yes, you're right – the young Baldwin we knew always did wear his heart of his sleeve in that sense. I think I didn't see it for what it would become, because we always thought of you as the one who'd grow up struggling to fit in."

"Me? Why?" Allan was genuinely perplexed.

"Because you were always more comfortable learning to play the lute, or learning those bits of old poetry or stories. You could remember the whole tale when one of the travelling minstrels had been to the manor. All of it! And at Christmas you could remember several. But when it came to what old Fulk's master-at-arms had shown you the week before, it was like it used to wash away with the rain. It never stuck! John and I used to wonder what on earth you would ever do when we grew up. We never could see you running a manor of your own, let alone fulfilling knight's service on Fulk's behalf to one sheriff or another. And despite my mother's best efforts, yours did cosset you something shocking!"

Allan was clearly surprised that his cousin had seen him like that, but was nodding nonetheless. "Ah! Yes, I can see that looking at it that way you would think that. ...Actually, I think that has a lot to do with why I found it so hard to cope when we had to leave. But did you never worry about Baldwin?"

Guy shook his head. "Not as boys, no. I think John and I just put his idealism down to the dreams of youth. I suppose we thought he'd gradually grow out of it as he saw more of the world. Most people seem to."

But Allan didn't agree. "No, I don't think it was ever going to be as simple as just growing up for Baldwin. He wanted to be a knight and have a manor of his own – not for the having of it, like Fulk or Philip did. Not to be able to say 'this is mine! I own it all!' and gloat over that. He wanted it so that he could make it a perfect little world where nothing bad ever happened. Perhaps it was because he was separated from his own family so much. His older half-brothers really hated him, just like Audolph did you, Guy, but he was on his own facing them – not like us, all in it together.

"And don't forget, he was robbed even of his mother's share of her own inheritance by his father and brothers. The old man just swept it into his estate and redistributed it as he saw fit. At least your mother kept her portion, as did mine. Not much as money goes, but now I can see it would have paid for me to buy into somewhere small and unassuming, whereas Baldwin always knew he was getting nothing. We only realised we'd be getting nothing once we were almost grown up. He knew it right from when he was fostered out with us. It made him feel homeless.

"I know because he told me so several times back in those days. Even then he wanted some place to call his own which no-one could take from him. He used to promise me that even if I got nothing from old Fulk, because young Fulk and Philip had grabbed it all as his brothers had, there'd always be a place for me with him."

"Oh, Sweet Christ!" Guy groaned.

Siward too was looking glum at this news. "Oh shit! That puts something else into even greater perspective, then. He thought he would be coming home and would find a manor somewhere – maybe a grange from one of the Templar preceptories was what he thought when he was being down to earth about it. He said that while we were on the road – several times! Then he was going to send for you lot to come and live with us. But before we could even reach his old home we ran into all of you, and you already had control of a castle, Guy, but it wasn't how he thought it should be."

Guy was already with him on that thought. "Damnation! Of course! I was the bloody sheriff's man. So although I was already doing what he want... Oh, crap! I did it without realising it, didn't I! I got there ahead of him! I took his dream and burst it like a bladder full of wine and let it piss out on the floor."

"I'm so sorry, Guy, but yes," Siward sighed. "And what's almost worst. What at least rubs salt into the wound, is that you made it work! What should have fallen apart by Robin's lights – holding a castle only temporarily, and off one of the king's evil sheriffs, even if the rest of us can see that Ralph Murdac was as good a man as anyone can ever be in such an office – instead actually managed to give us months of respite to recover in. He genuinely can't work out in his own mind how you can work for the sheriff and yet not be corrupted by him."

Allan also sighed. "I don't think Baldwin as a child ever grasped what compromise meant, and the man he's now become as Robin still doesn't. His own innate honesty, and commitment to being as good a Christian as he can, runs so deep in him he could never, ever do what you're doing. Life is still either pure white or evil black. You're either with him or against him, and the fact that *you* still love all of us beyond any doubt, yet manage to walk that treacherous line when you're away from us, baffles him."

"And that's why he doubts you so often," Siward added. "It's not him thinking the worst of you, his cousin. He simply can't see how he himself could ever do what you do. To him it's impossible. Therefore he has to doubt whether it's possible for you."

"Then we'd better get into that priory before he gets Marianne and Will killed along with himself!" Guy said grimly, and they hurried the last few hundred feet to the large oak gate.

My dear Gervase, you sound disappointed? You ask, ˜Was that all it was? The great feud between you and Robin? Some cousin's spite over who was oldest?˜

Heavens no! Not all of it, not by a long run! But this was the start of it. If you know this, then what happened later will make more sense.

Ah me, but I must clearly give you a salve for your soul on this matter so that you do not think I malign your hero. I have known several men who were noble in the extreme during my long life, and what all of them had in common was an almost childlike belief in goodness. A kind of goodness which could manage to exist in the real world and yet never become sullied or tarnished by it. This was Robin! And if you wish me to confess further, then I shall freely admit that I never – and <u>could</u> never – rise to the heights of pure nobility and honour which he did. I never had his clarity of purpose. There, does that appease you? Good! Now let me explain that better.

You see, Siward had hit the nail on the head, right there back in those early days. Robin could never have lived under the sheriff's roof, and dissembled for him day in and day out, as I did. It was not in his nature.

He could no more have done that than grown another arm or leg. Indeed, Siward was also right in saying that Robin could barely imagine how <u>anyone</u> could do such a thing.

No, Brother! I am not saying that Robin stooped so low as to be jealous of me! I was not just offering him a compliment with one hand, then snatching it away with the other. If ever one of us was envious of the other, then it was me who wished at times to be more like him – I freely admit that. It would have been so much simpler if I could have been blind to the multitude of possibilities in certain situations, and have just accepted the outcomes as bad luck, or the ill-will of evil men, or even that I had displeased God somehow and must do better. I envied Robin his certainties too. His faith in King Richard to start with – although I also thought it no bad thing to be spared his anguish when he had to face reality on that score. But also his belief that <u>he</u> could make things better for all of the people who lived in and around Sherwood. I could see that there was the potential for a change for the better, but I also saw the mountain of obstacles which would prevent that from ever happening. I always saw the world for what it was, and if I did not have Robin's vision, then maybe I was the lesser man, but I also suffered less for being so.

His idealism was to blame, or you may to think me to blame with my worldliness, for our disagreements over whom he should help. These arguments became ever more bitter as the years went on – I suspect because he was always cut to the quick when instead of gratitude, some of those I warned him against proved false or greedy. You see, he saw all of those who fell foul of the forest laws as being innocents who were being persecuted. I, on the other hand, saw only too clearly that while many genuinely suffered through no fault of their own, there were also those who brought the force of the law down on them by their own hand. Some did it through genuine ignorance, but those were not the people we clashed over.

No, the ones we disagreed, often violently over, were those whom I could see had been trying to get away with something – often for years – and whom Robin saw as just more of the poor oppressed. Such as the cottar who had his own pigs in the forest separate to the village's, and who then did not remove them in time for a foresters' inspection, yet baulked at paying both the fine and the taxes he was due. Or the miller who had sold the grain he had taken in to mill from a monastic grange, and then tried to blame the reeve for counting wrongly when it came to paying taxes. Robin saw men like them as forced into their actions by the heavy taxes which I, in part, had to collect.

Yet he had no sympathy for men such as some of the castle guards. Men who had never wanted to be soldiers, but because they were well-built and strong, had been swept up by the sheriff or one of his sergeants and forced into service. I could see that they were doing nothing more than trying to avoid the penalty for their dereliction of duty falling on those they loved most, and so did as they were ordered. Robin saw them as too weak to make the moral stand. Some of the walking foresters in particular also came in for the most violent abuse from villagers. Yet they had no say in what they were supposed to collect, and many of those I would meet later on were sons and grandsons of walking foresters, who if they had not continued in their father's footsteps, would have been the cause of their families being turned out of the tied houses and put on the road with nowhere to go. How could a man tell his aging grandfather that he was no longer prepared to collect the forest fines, because they were so much heavier than in the old man's youth? And in so refusing, know full well that his ancient grandfather, his father and mother – also now too old to work hard – along with his young wife and children, would all be homeless? No this is no fable, Brother, I knew such a man, and well!

I, on the other hand, had much sympathy for men caught in such traps, for was I not caught in just such a way? My dear old friend Ianto was living on my charity at my manor over at Gisborne, along with Maelgwn, the blind Welshman who once had fallen foul of King Henry for being the son of one of the rebellious Welsh princes. What would become of them if I were to stand on my principles and leave the sheriff's service? No-one depended so on Robin! Nor ever had or would!

At first I used to pray that someone would come to mean so much to Robin that he would feel the weight of responsibility for them on his shoulders, as other men did. Later, as the years went on, I would pray as fervently that no-one ever should, for fear of what would befall them! And if that sounds critical and bitter, Brother, I would say again that Robin's morals were so high that we lesser mortals went in fear and trembling of where they might take him, and what they might make him do. But this is not getting our story told! Onwards, Brother!

Chapter 3

So there we were, hurrying into Blyth Priory, worrying ourselves silly over what we might find there. With me being an officer of the sheriff's there was no question of us not being allowed in to take shelter for the night, and Siward, Allan and myself were soon taking my mare to the stables for the night before intending to head for the guesthouse. I had half wondered if we might prod men's memories less if we each went in separately, but the gatekeeper made it clear that I was to be held responsible for the conduct of my men, given that the guesthouse was already full to overflowing. No doubt the fraught brother had visions of fights breaking out over who was to have a straw pallet and who would just have to make do with a hard bench! But for us it meant that we three would have to go inside together and hope for the best, or at least for the brothers being a little short-sighted or poor of memory.

Yet barely had we stabled my mare, rubbed her down and found her some feed, than we were met by Will, already coming to find us with grim news.

Blyth Priory & Sherwood Forest, June, the year of Our Lord, 1190

"What's wrong?" Siward asked, seeing Will's frown.

Will sighed. "Nothing immediately, but Longchamp's coming back within the week! That's why the bishop's lingering here. He has to meet Longchamp at Tickhill one week from yesterday. We didn't need to ask around much, the whole place was talking about it, including le Puiset's men. A couple of them are already talking about making a run for it. They reckon the bishop's had it. That he's been outmanoeuvred by Longchamp. That his claws have been cut for good. Marianne managed a casual word or two with a couple of the priests travelling with the bishop, and when she mentioned Norton and what had happened there, all they could say was that there was no point in appealing to him. Apparently he can't even help himself at the moment, much less anyone else."

"Judas' bollocks!" Guy swore, although keeping his voice down bearing in mind where they were. "How's Robin taken that news?" He was already feeling a growing dread that his cousin might be prompted to do something rash.

"Marianne dragged him off to walk under the covered arbour of the apothecary's garden by playing the slightly nagging wife, thank God!" Will reassured him. "I think everyone saw their argument as just a domestic tiff, so no-one bothered what it was about. Don't fret, Guy, she'll sit on him if necessary to stop him giving the game away, but she thought the scent of the herbs might calm him down a bit."

"God bless Marianne!" Guy said from the heart. "Well I'd best go and speak to the prior. It wouldn't be polite for me to come here and not see him, and I don't want anyone looking any more sideways at us than necessary."

By now Guy knew Roger de Pauliaco, the prior of Blyth, by sight if not to speak to, from his occasional visits to the castle to speak with Sheriff Ralph Murdac in the last two years since his appointment as prior. What de Pauliaco would make of the new sheriff, Roger fitz John, Guy dreaded to think. The prior was a florid man of around forty, full of spleen and offended dignity, and only too aware that this was considered a punishment appointment – the mother house had little time for this outpost in England, and de Pauliaco would have to work hard to rise to a better appointment! Perhaps that was why as Guy walked in, he seemed to be commiserating with an older man who had to be le Puiset? Both of them feeling that they had come down in the world from where they should rightly have sat?

Guy approached the table in the ground floor room of the prior's lodging where the two sat at the midday meal, made his obeisance, and after the most perfunctory of exchanges was waved away. Far from being quizzed by the prior, he found himself hurried out and guided by a lay brother to a seat on a bench along the side of the long main table in the guest house instead. Robin, Will and Marianne must have already eaten and left, yet there was still so little space, that Allan was at one end of the bench on the far side, and Siward at the other. He found himself squeezed in well below the salt beside a miserable man who looked as though he might be a farmer.

"If you've come to petition the prior you might as well go home now," the man said bitterly, as he passed Guy a wooden bowl into which a lay brother had ladled some hot stew. Looking at the thin stew and the coarse bread made out of mixed grains, Guy could see that the monks were hardly being generous to their ordinary guests. By any monastic standards this was poor fare.

"Not giving away much, are they?" he commented in return, hoping to draw the farmer out. It worked. With a caustic sniff the man said,

"I feed the serf who does the rough work on the farm on better than this pathetic stuff! By Our Lady, there's not even a whole turnip in this watery soup! And have you seen how badly the maslin's been ground for this bread?"

Guy bit into the bread and immediately knew it for what it was. "This bread wasn't made from maslin," he said with certainty, "it's dog bread made from mengrell!" Maslin would have been a wheat and rye mixture – making a coarse bread but usually palatable – but he could taste the peas, beans and vetch in this, which made it an altogether poorer mix. He wrinkled his nose. "And it's been poorly made! I wouldn't feed the dogs in my kennels this!"

"You're a kennel-man?" the farmer asked warily, since that could make Guy some rich-man's servant.

Guy gave him his most world-weary smile. "Used to be. Over on the Welsh borders a couple of years back. Now I've been shifted over here and spend my days traipsing around the bloody forest either sweating my bollocks off, or getting drenched, while some fancy man of the sheriff's rides along beside me and lording it over me." He had coarsened his local accent heavily too, so that he fitted the part of the lowliest of walking foresters. Down the table from him he saw Siward about to approach him and Allan putting a restraining hand on Siward's arm. *Good lad, Allan,* he thought, *for catching on so quickly.*

"What did you come here for?" he asked the man as he dunked the hard bread into the stew. He was nonchalant enough about the query so that it didn't sound as though he was fishing for information.

The farmer grunted miserably. "You know what waifs are if you're a forester's man."

Guy nodded. The 'right to waifs' was a claim lords had over what were seen to be ownerless chattels – which could be any kind of movable property from a skillet to a bull. Somehow he didn't think this was going to be about a lost pot, though.

"This lot," the farmer said with a bitter cast of his head towards the priory in general, "have claimed the right of waif over our cattle that were being grazed over towards Bilby. Not on Bilby's fields, mind, just our side of them." Bilby was the next village in line from Blyth beyond Hodsock.

"Where are you from?" Guy asked the man.

"Roolton."

That made sense. It was the next village in the same line going more or less south and a bit west from Blyth.

"But surely that's not under Blyth Priory's lordship?" he said, the map in his head meaning he was already calculating the distances.

"No it's bloody not!" the farmer snapped in disgust. "They've no right to anything of ours at all! But the prior's men came and took all our cattle while one of the village lads was watching over them. He's only a youngster! Not his fault! Nothing he could do when he was outnumbered by several big men with staffs! But our cattle are here, and now we can't plough our fields or send the calves to market this autumn to pay our rents!"

Guy felt his ire rising. So he had been right about de Pauliaco! The man wanted to make his mark here at Blyth to try and recoup his lost position within his order! And then suddenly he realised that here was a gift from God. Here was a cause he could deflect Robin towards! If they couldn't get justice for Much and the dead families of Norton, then at least Robin's desire for vengeance could be put to good use for the living of Roolton. This was a job for 'Robin Hood' and one where Robin could take the lead while Guy stayed in the background out of sight. It could hardly have been better!

For the rest of the meal he made enough of the right noises to get his fellow diner to carry on talking, during which time he got more of the details. It was easy enough then to disengage himself after the meal with the excuse that he should go and check on his riding forester's horse. If there was any confusion later if the man saw him riding out, hopefully Siward (being of the same height and colouring) would make the farmer think he had not seen clearly in the gloom of the hall – the brothers were as tight-fisted with the rush-lights as with the food!

Hurrying out to the stable area, he found the others waiting for him under a meagre lean-to, where things like the shovels and rakes for cleaning the stables were stored. Remembering what Siward and Allan had said on the way in, Guy let Robin fume until he ran out of words. If not jumping in with a solution would soothe things between them, he could be patient.

"I've failed Much!" Robin ended bitterly. "I promised him justice for his family. I promised! Now I'm proven a liar!"

"By Christ and St Thomas, Robin!" Will spluttered angrily. "Don't be such a fool! You didn't lie to him! We all thought it would be possible to get more justice for Norton than we have. All of us! It's not your fault that a twisted monster like Longchamp has got his hands on the country and is riding roughshod over the law."

"And he is twisted," Guy prompted softly, drawing the predicted tirade from Robin over Longchamp. The longer his cousin ranted the better, for then he would be calmer to hear what Guy had in mind. As Robin got to the bit about how ordinary people were being robbed blind, Guy cast the hook into the conversation.

"Oh it's not just Longchamp," he added with assumed innocence. "I was talking to a farmer in the guesthouse. He was telling me the prior here has had his lay brother out taking cattle which aren't his."

"What?" Robin spluttered, his rant cut off in mid-flow as he realised that there might be another quarry to be hunted.

Guy managed not to smile with satisfaction at the taken bait. "The farmer in question lives over at Roolton. A hamlet like most of the others round here. Our farmer says it has barely half-a-dozen families living there, and nothing much there apart from the farms except for a bit of meadow, and some woodland where they used to be able to graze their pigs until King Henry made it part of the royal forest. Not exactly a place to fight over, but since this new prior's been here they've got caught up in his scheming. Tuck was right! The prior did something bad enough for Rouen to send him here as a punishment, and now he's trying to worm his way back into favour by showing how he can turn a neat profit out of this place!"

Guy did his best not to address Robin directly, but told his story to the group as a whole, catching everyone's eye except Robin's.

"Where this gets very messy is due to the history of Worksop, which is the larger village almost next door to Roolton. Harry, the farmer, was telling me that once upon a time *all* of this area belonged to the same lord – but that's going back to the time of King Edward and beyond. Since then, though, it's been parcelled up and handed out several times over. The Norman lord who took over in the last century founded this priory, here at Blyth, and gifted it to his home abbey of Rouen – who, as Tuck told us, are Black Monks. Then when he and his son died, the first King Henry took over the estate. He kept some for himself and gave Tickhill and the rest to a noble called William de Lovetot. Now here's where it gets convoluted but relevant! De Lovetot then founded Worksop Priory and gave it to the Black *Canons* – so a whole different order of monk to Blyth – along with lands around the priory to support it. As a result, Harry tells me that he and the rest of Roolton now officially owe tithes to Worksop Priory. Unfortunately, that fat prior across the way, de Pauliaco, has decided that since Blyth was the *original* foundation for the whole of what is now the Honour of Tickhill, and more, it gives him precedence over Worksop, and the right to take cattle he designates as straying on his land."

"The sneaky bastard!" Will gasped.

Marianne was shaking her head at the audacity of such a move. "If Worksop had been in the same order as Blyth he wouldn't have been able to do anything without dragging himself even further down in the eyes of his superiors. As it is, I've seen how the Black Monks and the Black Canons are often at loggerheads anyway when there are foundations this close to each other. De Pauliaco is counting on any protest getting overwhelmed in the general tide of claims and counterclaims!"

"And the poor of Roolton are the ones paying the price," Siward added. He had quickly caught on to where Guy was going with this, and was happy to be the one casting the last piece of bait.

"Now that sounds like a job for Robin Hood," Allan added cheekily. Had any of the others said as much it would have been too much, and Robin might have spotted the way he was being manipulated, but Allan did it so mischievously and with such an open wink to Robin, it came across as too blatant for Robin to spot it for what it was.

"You could give them the money..." Guy began suggesting, but Robin was well and truly caught and in the net, and as Guy expected he was cut short.

"Not a chance!" Robin declared vigorously. "De Pauliaco needs to be taught a lesson! We're going to get the cattle!"

"How will we know which ones are Roolton's, though?" Marianne asked. "They'll have to be the right ones! I don't much fancy having to deal with a whole herd of them on the road!"

The large white cattle, which across England pulled ploughs and carts, and provided what cow's milk and ox meat the villagers had, were not the best tempered beasts to deal with in a herd, especially if there was a bull there and cows with calves. Their long, sharp horns were capable of inflicting serious injury to the unwary just from a casually tossed head, let alone when they were angry.

"There's no bull," Guy quickly assured her. "That belongs to Worksop Priory, and de Pauliaco was cunning enough not take the cows while it was at Roolton servicing them. There are three cows with calves, and four others – two yearling heifers and a couple of castrated bullocks who are a bit older – all of them from the village's plough teams. De Pauliaco's men took them with their harnesses still on! That'll help you! Put the harnesses on them and they'll be more willing to be led – the villagers need the harnesses back as well, of course."

"What are we going to do, though, once we've got them back to Roolton?" Will wondered. "What's to stop the prior sending more men out again to take them back?"

Robin smiled wolfishly, taking command with assurance now, Guy noted. "We're going to take them to Worksop Priory and ask the prior there to keep them there for safety! The villagers won't need them until after the harvest when they start ploughing to plant the winter crops. It's hardly more than five miles from here to Worksop! We can have them away and out of harm's way before anyone notices! We'll go now, tonight. With this rain the roads are all churned up. The tracks of the cattle will be all the harder to spot."

"You'll know the Roolton beasts by this cut-mark on their horns," Guy told him, keeping his voice very neutral, and scratching the mark in the dirt on the floor before scuffing it out again with his heel. "Hugh can guide you to the village."

For the first time Robin frowned. "But Siward knows the area too."

However Siward was already shaking his head. "No, Allan and I'll stay here with Guy. Remember, we're keeping us and you very separate in the minds of the monks here. Anyway, you'll need someone to bolt the gates behind you when you go."

"It'll all add to the mystery!" Allan added with another wicked grin. "You just disappear and the gates were bolted all night. Well I never! When you've gone I'll leave a cryptic sign for the prior. Just to make sure he heeds the warning he's been given! Robin Hood is watching him! It's all about sleight of hand, Robin. Make them think you're here, there and everywhere."

When everyone inside the priory's walls had settled down for the night, Guy let the others out of the main priory enclosure and kept watch, in case the sleeping lay-brother supposed to be watching the gate woke up. Allan and Siward were temporarily going with Robin and Will to help cut the right beasts out of the herd, and get them onto the road – if just Robin and Will did the sorting it would take far too long and increase the risks of being caught. Meanwhile, Marianne was going to run on ahead and alert the other outlaws that they were needed for the herding. So all Guy could do was stand in the shadow of the gate, try and keep dry and out of sight, and fret. On such a bleak summer's night there weren't even stars or a moon for him to gauge the time by. He could only hope that they would be back before the next monastic office began.

He had done the expected thing of attending the evening service of Compline, as had many other guests before going to bed. By his reckoning they then had a maximum of three turns of the priory's hour glass before a monk would start waking the brothers up for the first office of the next day, Nocturns. And once the brothers were up for Nocturns, there was very little time at this point in the year before they would be roused again for Matins, at which point sneaking someone back into the priory would become infinitely more complicated. He felt as though every nerve was on edge, and his eyes were full of water and grit as he constantly strained them for the first hint of light in the east, which would alert him to the impending danger.

Just when his nerves felt ready to snap, there was a soft tap on the gate. Easing the bar up and opening it just enough to allow a dripping Allan and Siward in, he breathed a long sigh of relief. The door-keep had begun to get restless in his sleep, no doubt used to being roused fairly soon. Together the three of them scurried across to the guest-hall, clinging to the shadows.

"All's well?" Guy dared to ask once they were within the door, but still not close to those lesser sleeping guests spread out on pallets on the floor, who did not warrant a better space for the night.

"Went like a dream!" Allan whispered back.

"Your dreams clearly aren't like mine!" Guy riposted witheringly, for which he got a sympathetic wince from his cousin.

"I suppose we'd better get some sleep, or pretend to," Siward sighed, flicking water out of his hair once more, "although we'll be lucky if no-one spots that we're drenched again."

"Not yet, though," Guy said quickly, laying a restraining hand on his arm as Siward made to head for the bench he and Allan had been allocated.

"No?"

"No! Robin Hood has a bit more work to do yet!"

Siward and Allan exchanged quizzical glances.

"What are you up to, Couz'?" Allan wanted to know.

"The bishop!" Guy replied, signalling them to follow him. "I've been praying we'd have time to do this!" He led them out of the hall to the covered walkway outside, and pulled a coiled rope out from where he had seen one of the lay brothers leave it earlier in the evening. It was not the best quality and was already old and worn, possibly there because it had already been replaced somewhere in a workshop or barn, but it would have to do.

"Allan, I'll need you to stand watch for me outside of the bishop's chamber. If anyone comes, whistle and then hide! I think there's a niche made by the angle of the wall where the stairs come up, from what I saw from the lower floor. You're small enough to fit in, I hope. If it all goes wrong, wait for any servants to go past then sneak out. Don't wait for me! I'll be going out through the window! That's where you come in, Siward. I'll drop the rope before I wake le Puiset, but I'll need you at the bottom to make sure no-one spies it. The same goes for you as for Allan. Whistle me to let me know if danger's coming, then get out! If that happens I'll leave by the stairs."

Allan pulled a face. "And what happens if we both raise the alarm? You'll be caught, Guy!"

Guy gave Allan the cunning grin he recalled from their childhood mischief. "Caught doing what? I'm one of the sheriff's men, remember? I'll have seen a man sneaking into the prior's house and up to the bishop's door, and came to protect him! If anyone asks why I'm up and about, I shall say that I woke and saw one of my men was gone. You'll have to feign a taste for the monastic mead in that case, Allan!"

Allan chuckled. "I'm sure I can manage that."

Siward shook his head, "I'm not happy about this, Guy. Don't bite my head off over this, but are you sure you're not just doing this because you've let Robin win for once?"

Now it was Guy's turn to wince. "By St Issui, Siward, I'm not that much of a wretched soul! No. I took your words to heart, and I'd been thinking all evening of a way to let Robin do something which wasn't connected to me. But I've also been thinking of Much, and I'm still of the opinion that le Puiset is still more powerful than Longchamp gives him credit for.

"Our bishop upstairs may have been deprived of his lands and power by the king's poisoned dwarf, but le Puiset is old money, old power. Longchamp is a mere upstart – a devil hidden beneath the exterior of a man of the church, as if in a twisted mummers' play. The nobles may have to tolerate him for now, but I'd bet my manor and everything I own that they're storing up his evil deeds to throw back at him one of these days. And when that day comes, I want Norton to be amongst the wrongs he has to answer for. It may take time. It may not even be le Puiset himself who throws this particular stone when Longchamp finds himself placed in the stocks, be they ever so courtly. But I'm trusting in the bishop to give this stone to the man with the strongest arm in that case, even if it is out of self-interest not Christian caring.

"So tonight I'm going to take a chance. Had you been any longer then I would've had to wait for another time and place to provide someone with this stone. I'm not intending to make a martyr of myself. Have no fear of that! But I am going to act. Now quickly! Siward, get outside! The bishop's window is the one upstairs in the prior's lodgings with the double shutters. Ready, Allan? Follow me!"

Together he and Allan hurried outside and slipped in through the door of the prior's lodging. This was a small but elegant wooden building to the side of the main monastic buildings, built on two floors. The danger for Guy and Allan was that the prior's two servants slept in the hall which formed most of the ground floor. Should they wake now it would be hard to explain their presence.

It was also pitch-black inside once Guy had closed the door. The heavy covering of clouds outside was masking the coming dawn which might otherwise have shone a few chinks through the shutters, and Guy was having to work by memory from when he had come to pay his respects to the prior. Luckily that was not the only time he had been in this hall, so he was fairly confident of his bearings. The trick was not to rush now. The worst that could happen was for a servant to have put something like a bag down in a place where they would stumble over it.

Like cats on the prowl, the two of them eased their way up the open stairs, and reached the door of the bishop's room unnoticed. At the top of the stairs there was a door on either side of the small landing, and a few more steps up to what was probably a small cubbyhole used to store valuables in. It certainly had a hefty enough lock on it!

"Don't suppose we can relieve the prior of some of that?" Allan whispered hopefully, his barely visible hand gesturing to the lock.

"Not tonight," Guy told him firmly while suppressing a grin – Allan was incorrigible, but just at the moment he was finding Allan's cheerful, roguish tendencies much easier to deal with than Robin's brittle honour. "But remember it's here," he added with a soft chuckle. "Might come in useful one day!" and he heard Allan's soft return laugh. "That room to our right is where de Pauliaco is sleeping, so that's where the danger for you is. Crouch down here on the far side of the cupboard steps to him."

Allan wriggled down into the cramped space and whispered to Guy he was ready. Guy then slid his old small knife under the latch of le Puiset's door and eased it up. Thankfully it was not pegged on the inside to lock it. The bishop must be feeling confident of his safety here. However, Guy had never intended to trust to the latch-lift on the door, locked or otherwise. He had no idea how smoothly that might or might not work, and if it dropped suddenly that might wake his target before he had even got into the room. He had his hood pulled up over his head, obscuring his face even further, and his official forester's horn was downstairs with Siward, safely out of the way. He was an anonymous man in a hood and all was set for the play he was about to act out.

Carefully easing himself through the door and closing it behind him, the first thing he did was edge his way to the window and open the shutters. Then he looped the old rope around the central timber of the window and prayed that doubled-up the rope would stand his weight. He wanted to make sure that his escape route was set up, just in case. Leaning out, he saw Siward's shade below and hissed his readiness in his turn.

Turning to the bed, the faintest glimmer of light showed him the elderly bishop flat out on his back, softly snoring. That helped. If le Puiset had been one of those who slept on his front it would have been so much harder to place a gloved hand over his mouth while waking him. Nonetheless, Guy stayed on the window side of the bed, even though it meant he had to kneel with one leg on the bed in order to reach le Puiset. It put his face even deeper into shadow as well as leaving him a quicker exit.

"Bishop Hugh, wake up!" he hissed, at the same time clamping his left hand over the man's face. His right was resting on the long hunting knife which hung at his belt. He did not want to draw it yet. There was always the chance that an old man, badly startled, might jerk hard just as an instinctive reaction, and Guy did not want to kill him – that would defeat the whole purpose of him being here. On the other hand, le Puiset was nobly born, and as such had probably been taught how to fight long before he had taken any vows.

"Wake up!" Guy hissed again and was rewarded by seeing the eyes open, the whites showing in the dim light. "Not a word! Do not struggle! I don't want to kill you! Blink your eyes if you understand me."

That was another risk. Le Puiset was Norman born and bred, and there was always the chance that he had never learned English. Far too many great nobles had only the sketchiest understanding of the native language when most of the time they spoke just to their own in Norman-French. Shit, Le Puiset wasn't blinking!

"Comprenez-vous l'Anglais?" Guy repeated. "Clignez vos yeux si vous me comprenez," and got a blink. "I shall speak in English, yes?" and got another blink. "Good! Because I want you to listen! I am about to tell you something which you can use against Longchamp." He felt the man stiffen beneath his grip and the eyes focused suddenly. So he had been right! Le Puiset was not done for yet! In return, Guy eased his grip on the bishop's mouth and jaw. He still left his hand resting there, though, just in case le Puiset got any foolish ideas about him.

"You know that Longchamp has been to York to punish those who left the Jews to their fate." He felt le Puiset slacken. "No bishop, I'm not going to deal with old news!" That got le Puiset sharp again. "What you won't know is that some of those responsible had a little more fun when they left York. Trying to evade the punishment they realised might be coming, a trio of young noblemen decided to head back to Cuckney, where one of them is the son of the manor. On their way, before they entered Nottinghamshire, they vented their miserable spleens on the village of Norton. I know there are many Nortons, bishop, but this one is just over the border of Nottinghamshire into Yorkshire, not that far from Doncaster. Do you understand me?" He got a faint nod under his hand.

"This village is on the land of the de Lacys. Young de Cuckney and his oh-so-brave friends decided that it would be fun to burn the mill with the miller and his wife still inside with their man. Many others of the village got ridden down and killed. It was sport to de Cuckney, nothing more. The villagers of Norton owed him nothing, had done nothing to him. He hadn't even been refused lodging overnight because he never even bothered asking. De Lacy will at some point want to know what happened to his mill and the money he would have got in taxes from it. There's no-one left who can tell him. Those few who've survived were far enough away to run and saw nothing in the dark. So it will get blamed onto unknown outlaws – but it wasn't any such men! De Lacy should know this!

"But worse, Longchamp was given evidence into his own hands that de Cuckney was not only responsible for trapping the Jews inside York Castle on that awful day in March. He was given proof, too, that de Cuckney fired the mill at Norton. Yet he suppressed the second evidence. He took a mere fine off de Cuckney for his part in the massacre at York. The king may be satisfied with that. I'm sure de Lacy will not! If any other money has changed hands between de Cuckney and Longchamp it was nothing more than a bribe for his silence over Norton. Money which has gone into Longchamp's pocket, not the king's!"

By now le Puiset was fully focused on Guy.

"*You* can tell de Lacy! Even if you can't get Longchamp to admit his guilt, you can pass this on to the man who has much to gain by making the accusation in public. And you can tell the king! Tell King Richard that there is proof out there that Longchamp is feathering his own nest! That money which also could have gone to fund his crusade has gone into Longchamp's coffers. I can't get close enough to the king to tell him that. You can! You can tell him that Longchamp smiles at his face and yet uses him behind his back. The proof was left with *Osbert* Longchamp in York!"

That was a bit of a guess on Guy's part. He was not sure whether Longchamp would already have burned the testimony which had been taken down by the sheriff's scribe when he had taken de Cuckney to Nottingham to face his accusers. But he needed le Puiset to believe that there was something worth acting upon.

"Have you understood what I've told you, Bishop?" He felt the nod again. "I'm going to let go of you in a moment and leave. I've taken nothing which was yours. Harmed no-one. This is about justice for the people of Norton, pure and simple. You have nothing to fear from me. I shall leave unburdened and unseen."

Guy counted to ten under his breath as he flexed the leg still on the floor to make sure he could move with speed. Then without warning he sprang back. To his dismay le Puiset made a lunge for him, bellowing,

"Who are you, knave?"

"Robin Hood!" Guy snapped. "You'll be hearing about me!" and leapt for the window and the rope.

As he did so le Puiset yelled, "Thief! Wake up! Thief!"

And in the spilt second afterwards Guy was aware running feet and the slam of the door downstairs as Allan fled, knowing that Guy would need no further warning given that he was in the room with le Puiset, and the half-awake cries of the prior's servants. Diving through the window, he slithered at speed down the doubled rope, glad he had thought to wear his heavier gloves as the smell of singed leather rose from the rope burns. He dropped to the ground and ran. There was no point in moving the rope now – le Puiset would tell everyone about it anyway. As le Puiset stumbled to the window, still yelling about thieves, Guy and Siward shot round the corner of the building into the still-black shadows.

A moment later Allan appeared beside them from the other side, and together they slunk towards the guesthouse, so that when folk began to stumble out of it, roused by the cries, they simply joined in at the back of the crowd as if they too had only just risen from their beds. Guy and Allan had long since shrugged out of their wet cloaks, which had also stayed with Siward to avoid telltale drips on the floor to show their entry point. Now Siward bundled his own cloak with theirs and shoved them behind the door of the guesthouse, out of sight. In the barely half-light the three of them therefore looked no different to the others stumbling about in just their shirts.

The chaos continued until the monks went inside to Matins, after which Guy, Siward and Allan were able to return to the hall and sleep the sleep of the righteous until everyone was roused for breakfast, by which time their cloaks were no longer quite so dripping wet. Even better, the day dawned warm and sunny but fresh. Far too warm to be bundled up in cloaks, praise be! And so Guy had the three still-damp, folded cloaks tied to the back of his saddle as he rode out with Siward walking on one side, and Allan on the other.

Indeed it was hard not to laugh as they left, for they went with the prior's blessing! As everyone had been miserably chewing on the poor bread offered for breakfast, and discussing the foolishness of old men when it had been discovered that nothing had been taken from the bishop after all, one of the lay brothers had come tearing in all of a panic. The guests could not hear exactly what he said, but most of the lay brothers left in a hurry, and there was a noticeable absence of brothers as they made to leave. Then just as Guy had mounted up, the prior bustled up to him flanked by two fawning brothers.

"Someone has stolen some of our cattle, forester!" he exclaimed with pompous indignation, as the two brothers wrung their hands and looked distraught for effect. "I want you to investigate! Immediately!"

Guy looked down coldly from his lofty perch, green eyes cold and emotionless. "Theft isn't part of my duty, prior." Then, as the prior began to sputter, added, "But since it means that beasts will be within the forest during Fence Month, I suppose I shall have to track them down. Should they be found, I shall have to take them to Nottingham, though. You may claim them back when Fence Month is over and they can be moved through the forest once more."

De Pauliaco stood making fish-out-of-water noises in his surprise at being spoken to in such a way, allowing Guy time to heel his horse forward and ride out before the prior could think of a suitable riposte.

The three of them managed to hold their composure until they were out of sight and earshot of the priory down the lane. Then Allan could restrain himself no longer and doubled up laughing. It was infectious, and Siward and Guy were soon hooting with laughter too.

"Oh blessed St Thomas," Allan hiccupped, wiping the tears of mirth from his cheeks, "did you see the expression on his face? That was priceless!"

"Bloody old goat!" Siward sniffed happily. "He and that bishop are two for a pair! But what did you write, Allan?"

"Write?" Guy asked warily. "What did you do, Allan?"

Siward grinned. "While Robin, Will and I were driving the cattle out onto the road, Allan went back with a piece of charcoal."

"Does that explain the panic this morning?" Guy asked suspiciously, although rather relishing their escapade.

Allan's smile was as cheerful as the sun above. "Bloody hope so! I wrote on the wall of the cattle shelter, above the buckets of water they must have been using in this heat,
Thou shall not steal, Prior,
And you are a liar.
Your theft will be made good
By the justice of Robin Hood."

"Holy Mother of God!" Siward gasped in delight. "That's put the cat in the dovecote!"

Guy hugged his cousin even as he laughed. "And I told le Puiset *I* was Robin Hood!"

"*You* did?" Allan and Siward hooted together, then laughed even harder.

"By Our Lady, that's going to give the locals something to talk about," Allan declared when he had sobered enough to speak. "Robin should have got to Worksop hours ago! If word gets out about that it's going to cause some confusion!"

"And why wouldn't it," Guy said with growing satisfaction. "The locals from Blyth are bound to use the market at Worksop, as will their neighbours from Hodsock, Bilby and Roolton. The ordinary folk are bound to know about Roolton losing their cattle already. Having them reappear in the fields at Worksop won't go unnoticed."

"And at the same time as Robin Hood was scaring the bishop of Durham to death too!" Siward added, already imagining the mystical attributes which would be ascribed to such a thing.

Allan gave his cheekiest grin. "My friends, I think we've made ourselves the beginnings of a people's hero!"

So there you have it, Brother, a small but notable beginning to the legend! Did Robin get the cattle to Worksop? Oh yes, indeed! He and the others had them at the fields just beside the priory's walls as dawn broke, and the

rain did as he had anticipated and covered their tracks. And wanting to make it plain where the beasts had come from, he too wrote on the priory's gate that these were the cattle stolen from Roolton by the prior of Blyth, and returned by the grace of Robin Hood. We sent Walter and Algar into Worksop for the next week's market, and Roger and Allan too. All of them came back saying how the market was buzzing like a bee hive with the tale of the cattle which had mysteriously appeared. But it was the next week when the events at Blyth caught up with everyone, and at that stage the name of Robin Hood was suddenly on everyone's lips.

Not that I had chance to revel in the moment of glory, mind you. I was already back at Nottingham and about to set out on another patrol of the Erewash-to-Derwent forest which was my designated area. Luckily, I was always conscientious, so the sheriff had no clue that I had not been there the previous fortnight, merely thinking that on that occasion I had caught no-one, if he thought at all. However, Robin revelled in his glory, and I came to realise how much he desperately needed this visible show of approval. I do not mean to imply that he had the kind of arrogant need for glory some other highborn knight have. Not at all. Rather it was as Allan had said, a need to feel that he belonged somewhere, and that what he did mattered to someone and made a difference to their lives.

For him it was not enough to know that he was appreciated by those select few he called his friends, maybe because all of them were men more than capable of looking after themselves for the most part. I believe his desire to look after those more vulnerable than his fellow soldiers was what made him so attached to Much, whom he always would regard as the lad who had lost everything. It was also a way of looking at things which gave Allan so much leeway with him when he would take no notice of John or myself – and I was to bless Allan a good deal in the years to come for that.

Did he not regard all of the outlaws as his friends? No, not necessarily. No more than any commander of men looks upon those he has the leadership and care of. Yes he was fond of them all, but close friendship was reserved for John and Allan, and the five who had travelled with him from the east. Years later, Thomas and Hugh were to tell me that they never felt he quite let them as close to him as he did, say, Will or Gilbert. And I certainly learned during this last outing with Robin, that I had to tread very carefully around him. I saw that it was all to the good that what he heard of Robin Hood being seen at Blyth was attributed to Allan and not to me, for Allan would never be mistaken for Robin personally in any light, or by voice. Therefore, in inciting the name of Robin Hood, Allan had only reflected the further praise and affection from the ordinary people onto Robin. And I saw how with me not even in the picture, Robin seemed to feel more secure as leader of our small band, and resolved to do what I could to ensure that while I might provide targets for Robin Hood, that I would stay as far in the background as I could when it came to taking action - it would make my relationship with my cousin so much simpler!

Yes, Brother, that indeed was how I saw that night upon reflection – as a chance for Robin to lead the outlaws on an act of vengeance against those in power without me being involved. Not out of cowardice on my behalf, but because I had listened to what Siward and Allan had said and realised that Robin needed to lead alone. And I let him do that – and believe in that – because I still loved him, and I wanted him to heal from whatever wound to his soul he had taken in the Holy Land. If he had made such a terrible sacrifice to his sanity in trying to save the homeland of Our Lord, then he deserved no less from me. Also, the more I thought about it the more worried I became over what Allan and Siward had said regarding Robin's inner turmoil, and I wanted more than anything <u>not</u> to be the cause of adding to that anguish.

˜So there was nothing between him and Marianne?˜ you ask. Oh Brother, you sound rather disappointed, are you yearning for a little romance by any chance? No, do not pout so, I am not mocking your mind's chastity. There is nothing wrong with wanting to hear of the happiness of others. Did not Our Lord attend a wedding and perform one of his miracles there? You are mollified. Good!

Now as to Robin and Marion, yes I did say I was worried when I spoke of them together earlier. Let me now tell you that another of the things which Siward and Allan told me of, as we rode back to join the others, was that Marianne and Tuck had recognised that Robin was suffering the most of the returned crusaders. They had gone off into the forest with him when I met the others to allow for a little privacy, in order to discuss his trials with him where he would not be embarrassed to admit to weakness. Beyond what Allan and Siward had told me before, they also said that Marianne appeared to regard Robin as a challenge to her nursing skills. If there was any deeper affection between them at this point it was very much Marianne having a weakness for Robin. To him she was a constant quandary – someone who knew from personal experience the hell on earth that the Holy Land could be, yet as a woman he could never quite bring himself to see her as a friend in the same light as the others. And there was still that vow of being a knight of the Templars which he believed himself bound by, which included chastity. Poor Robin was always finding that more of a burden than he had ever expected.

And did I manage to remain faithful to Robin and the others despite living under the sheriff's roof? Ah Gervase, and still you doubt me! Yes I did, but I too was to suffer greatly in the process of keeping the faith. If I had stepped aside from any attempt to lead for Robin's sake, I certainly did not lead a life free from sorrows of my own, and one of the great trials I suffered I shall recount to you shortly. However, first you shall have another escapade in the legend of Robin Hood. Ah, that pleases you! Good! Then I shall continue.

Chapter 4

And now we move a little further on towards the end of 1190. We heard that Longchamp actually took Hugh le Puiset prisoner when they met again, and that the bishop was confined to his manor of Howden up in Yorkshire far from the royal court, so I said nothing more of having got the message about Norton to him. There seemed little point in raising Much's hopes of justice for now, since sadly it was destined to be a long time in the coming. Indeed I have to say, I began to feel that maybe I had been overly optimistic and a little too clever for my own good on that matter – does that please you, Gervase? Yes, I thought it would. Another confession of failing on my part always cheers you.

We also heard that the dreadful chancellor then went on to try and besiege William Marshal down at Gloucester, and then took a thousand followers on what amounted to a royal progress through the country, reducing many a monastery to penury in the process. None of this touched us directly, you understand, Brother, but in amongst all of these comings and goings the justiciars still managed to visit all of the shires within the year, except for those under the control of our almost-as-bad young prince, Count John of Mortain – as he was now properly called, rather than Prince John. That certainly impacted upon me, for it meant that we in Nottinghamshire and Derbyshire had no eyre visiting us that year. In turn that meant that our gaols became stuffed to the hilts with poor unfortunates awaiting trial by the time winter started coming on.

You do not see how that matters, Brother? Well part of my role as forester involved attending the attachment courts, or woodmotes as you may have heard them being called, held every month and a half, and presenting evidence there of misdoings in the royal forest. For the poor souls dragged before these forest courts there was an added insult inflicted by no other court – they could not appeal for more time for further evidence to be found. This meant that even if the evidence against them was less than conclusive, if the verderers decided that there was a serious case to be answered for, then the man or men in question could be held in custody pending the next forest eyre. Now eyres concerning the forest could only be held every three years, but eyres for other offence were more frequent, even if not more than once in any year. So it was widely hoped by all of us involved with the evil necessity of dealing with the forest courts, that at least the general criminal events would be dealt with swiftly so that the gaols would not become overcrowded. If we foresters were immuring some poor bastards for nearly three years at a time pending trial, it was not good if those same gaols became overcrowded with regular felons!

Not only would the men within those gaols begin to suffer terribly, we could begin to run out of places to secure men! And that meant that in a place like Nottingham, where so much of the shire was under forest law that we had more than our share of poor souls caught out by those crippling laws, we had to do what few other towns or shires did and periodically use the castle dungeons. Truly, Brother, I know of nowhere else where things were so bad!

The whole of the West Country, encompassing Dorset, Somerset, Devon and Cornwall, like our two shires, had been gifted to Count John, but those shires had nothing like the areas of royal forest we did. Exmoor was probably the largest forest down there, and that was not so farmed by half as our shire. So those shires mainly just got taxed in the normal way of all shires. Only the great royal forest in Essex, and the New Forest in Hampshire, came anywhere near matching us as a single great mass of land under forest law, and neither covered so much of their shire as Sherwood did. Pity then the poor folk of our shires, and none more than those who fell foul of the verderers!

As for the verderers themselves, in any forest they were men who were initially appointed by the sheriff but then held their appointment for life, many becoming hereditary verderers. However, hereditary or not, verderers were all local men of some standing, since one of the qualifications for taking up this office was to hold land within the forest. They were also expected to be men of action, riding about their designated area of forest to their various courts – so I never got to deal with some aging fool whom I could befuddle to the advantage of their villagers. Not even those from the old forest still under the rule of the keeper from King Henry's days, Sir Ralph fitz Stephen, where such families had been in place for decades by now, and some for the best part of a century.

By royal command they had to hold a court in _each_ of our bailiwicks every forty to forty-two days, meaning usually nine a year, and we had over a dozen bailiwicks just in the old forest of Nottingham alone for the four original verderers to deal with. And worse, there were no new courts set up for the new areas of forest, so the cases heard in the existing woodmote courts doubled then trebled, and two more new verderers did not do much to ease the load. So in any given month there was bound to be a woodmote going on somewhere within the vast bounds of Sherwood, and a lengthy one at that. Gone were the days when a verderer rode in, heard a couple of cases and left for his manor shortly after noon.

Understandably this, then, was not the most popular of offices to hold, since it took a good deal of time out of every month, and there were few benefits of a physical kind, such as extra lands which could provide additional income. In my experience, I therefore found the verderers an unsympathetic lot, and all too often willing to twist their office to vent their spleen on those who had no power to stand up to them. They felt aggrieved that an already time-consuming job had become even more so, all to their detriment, and often they became disinclined to listen to even half of the evidence which could have been presented if it was going to extend the court by another day.

What you are about to hear now, Brother, is of how such men therefore corrupted what was in truth a king's court, since all of the powers of the verderers came directly from the king through the sheriffs. No doubt some sheriffs managed to keep a close eye on the verderers within their shires. In Sherwood, though, even a competent and energetic *sheriff like Ralph Murdac had had trouble overseeing the actions of his six verderers when their courts had to deal with so many cases. A weak and lazy sheriff, such as Roger fitz John under whom we languished at this point in my tale, did not even try.*

Sherwood,
Feast of the Holy Rood,
September, the Year of Our Lord 1190

Guy sat in the hall at Linby where the verderers were holding the swanimote court. As at the other villages where the courts were held, a goodly sized wooden hall had been built of somewhat greater size than the village itself warranted. Within it, a heavy table was placed at the far end, and behind this was where the verderer and one of the sheriff's clerks sat. Guy and any other foresters called upon to attend sat close by, while the villagers called upon to give their testimony congregated down the other end of the hall and came forward when summoned by the verderer's man.

On this occasion the verderer was a man by the name of Walter Ingram whom Guy heartily detested, who held lands close to Nottingham Castle – and therefore within the forest of old – and also land now encompassed by King Henry's new forest extensions. Ingram was one of two relatively new appointees to the office of verderer which had come in recognition of the greater amount of land which now had to be administered. Nonetheless, Ingram was still the second generation of verderers in his family since then, having taken over when his father became too old to do the considerable amount of riding attached to the job. Maybe Ruald Ingram had been the right sort of man for the job in the eyes of the sheriff of the time when the appointment was made, but his son certainly wasn't in Guy's. Walter wanted to move on in the world, to become an even greater lord than he was now, and that meant that he intended not only to show how tough he could be to the sheriff, but also did his best to court favour with the other nobles in both shires.

Right now he was hearing evidence concerning the killing of two red deer hinds and a young stag in the woods near Smithycote – a tiny hamlet just over the border in Derbyshire. As was normal in such cases, the men from the four villages close to the spot had been summoned to give evidence, and were now crowded nervously at the other end of the hall, and Roger – Sir Walter's man-at-arms and general aide – was calling the first of them forward.

"Smithycote! Leading man!" Roger bellowed with more aggression than necessary.

A solid-looking farmer of middle years walked swiftly up to within a few feet of the table and bowed his head to Sir Walter respectfully, keeping his gaze on the rush-covered floor until Walter spoke directly to him.

"You are the leading man of this place Smithycote?"

"Yes, sire."

"Your name?"

"Gyrth, sire."

Ingram gave a terse nod to the cowed monk at his side, who hurriedly wrote the name of Gyrth of Smithycote onto his parchment, then looked back to his master, fearful of missing the slightest instruction. That in itself had made Guy wary right from the start. A scribe could always check up on a name later and leave just a space on the page for now. Yet this scribe seemed to not quite know what he was supposed to be writing down for the record and what not. It made Guy think that there were times – possibly several per court – when Ingram did not want things to go into the official account, and that could only mean that he was bending the law to his own advantage. With Ingram living for at least part of the year so very close to the castle at Nottingham, he must surely by now have realised what a self-serving incompetent Sheriff fitz John was, and that any excessive fines which went into the sheriff's coffers would be accepted without question, regardless of how they had been acquired. So if he still did not want the sheriff to know about some things, then he must be feathering his own nest either with coin or goodwill from some other noble, and that made Guy deeply suspicious.

Gyrth was now giving a clear and concise description of how he, and two other men, had come up the remains of the deer while moving the village's swine herd to new pastures.

"You had your pigs in the forest?" snapped Ingram, interrupting Gyrth.

The leading man blinked. "Yes, sire." He clearly couldn't see why there should be a problem with that and neither could Guy.

"My lord, the people of Smithycote have paid their pannage charges on time and in full." He spoke calmly, but with enough assurance that he hoped Ingram would take the hint. Instead Ingram looked daggers at him. *Ah!* Guy thought. *So you intended to make them pay twice, did you? And no doubt that money would never have got as far as the sheriff, either!* Thank St Issui, then, that it was him who was here and not one of the other foresters who might have been willing to turn a blind eye for a small fee.

"Are you sure, forester?" Ingram demanded, fixing Guy with a belligerent stare.

"Absolutely, my lord. I collected the money myself *and* presented it at the castle where it was recorded." Guy was not about to give Ingram any chance to imply he might have pocketed the money himself, either. "They are fully paid up for the period until the Winter Haining starts in two months time. They have every right to pasture their pigs in the forest until then."

It was an overstatement on Guy's part. He knew damned well that Ingram knew that beasts were allowed in the forest until the start of the hunting season in November, but by saying it all out loud in the court, he was ensuring that the people at the far end knew he was doing what he could to stand up for them. It would be him, and not Ingram, who would have to ride alone into these villages come that time to ensure the pigs were back in the confines of the village, and it was far from unknown for a lone forester to be set upon and be given a sound beating if the people were pushed to the point of feeling they had nothing left to lose.

Ingram glowered at Guy but said nothing more to him, instead turning back to Gyrth and demanding,

"Tell me about the deer!"

Gyrth cleared his throat, and Guy suspected that any nervousness came not from guilt but from a fear of having his words twisted.

"Well, Harry, John and me were driving the pigs from the woods over in the Erewash valley a couple of miles away to the other side of the hill. There's a spot just over the hill where there's a good patch of oaks before you get to where Ripley's folks tend to pasture their pigs. We try to all get on with one another, my lord. There's a dip down to where there's usually a natural pond, so the beasts have got some water, and it was there we found them."

Ingram sniffed. "You found them? Are you sure they were dead when you saw them?"

Guy caught the implication but Gyrth didn't.

"Yes, my lord, definitely dead. There were signs that more deer had been there too, but when we got to them there were only the three of them."

"Three whole deer just lying on the ground? How very convenient!"

"No, my lord!"

"No?" Ingram was clearly irritated at being contradicted. "You mean they weren't lying on the ground? Maybe moving around a little, eh, headman?" and there was substantial sarcasm in that last.

Gyrth's face dropped into a scowl, suddenly aware of the trap this man was trying to lead him into. Guy prayed that Gyrth would not try to argue with Ingram. It would be the quickest way to ensure a heavy fine or worse, because no mere peasant farmer could hope to gainsay a man of Ingram's status. However, Gyrth was more quick-witted than that.

"Oh they were laying on the ground, all right, my lord," Gyrth ground out with as much civility as he could muster. "I meant they were far from whole! When we got to them they'd already been butchered – and I don't mean gnawed by wild animals, either. I mean butchered as if some man had taken a knife to them and cut them into joints."

Guy's pulse quickened. If villagers had taken a deer they would have taken everything they could. They would probably have left the skin, because if that was found in a village they would be convicted of poaching in a heartbeat, but anything edible would have gone. This sounded, though, as if substantial parts of the beasts had been left. "Which joints?" he demanded quickly, before Ingram could speak.

Luckily Gyrth had turned to face Guy, so Ingram didn't see the look of gratitude Gyrth gave him.

"The hind quarters had been taken, Sir Guy." Gyrth saw the understanding in Guy's eyes. So the cuts normally taken by a lord during a hunt had gone, had they?

"And the forequarters?" Guy asked quickly, still cutting Ingram out for as long as possible.

"They'd been left, Sir Guy. Along with the lights, guts and even the heart and liver. But the stag's horns had been removed."

So the intestines and various organs which most peasants would happily use as offal had been left. That too was telling. Clearly there hadn't been dogs with whoever had done the hunting, either, or they would have got the intestines cooked up with the blood there and then as their reward. That to Guy meant that this was probably a case of nobly born men out poaching, who had left their dogs behind so as not to draw attention to their covert hunting. However Ingram was either even more stupid than Guy already thought him, or he was well aware of whom had most likely done the deed and was going to cover it up.

"What difference does that make?" the pompous young lord demanded, and without giving Guy time to respond added, "Clerk? Record that three deer have been found poached within the environs of Smithycote. Who took what is not the point. The king's deer have been slain illegally."

"The fact that the hind cuts have been taken while other cuts have not should surely be recorded?" Guy prompted, although being careful not to sound too argumentative.

"Christ's wounds, man! Why?" spluttered Ingram. "Why waste valuable parchment on such a piddling detail? Clerk, don't bother with that!"

61

Guy caught Gyrth's pleading glance his way, but could only signal with his eyes to the negative. There was nothing more he could do right here and now. If he argued the toss too much with Ingram in public, he would be sure to end up being berated by Sheriff fitz John later, and fitz John would seize on any opportunity given him to tear Guy off another strip. Even worse, it might mean that the next time someone had to ride out this way, fitz John would send one of the other foresters, and that could mean Henry, Fredegis or Walkelin – all of them bad news!

Ingram had turned once more to Gyrth. "I believe you know who took these deer and won't say so!" he accused him belligerently.

That was sneaky, Guy had to concede. He wasn't accusing Gyrth himself of poaching, merely being an accomplice. That must mean that there was a much more senior figure involved somewhere along the line. Someone Ingram didn't want to upset too much by imprisoning his head tenant Gyrth, who probably answered to the lord's reeve directly, or who might even be someone of substance Gyrth could appeal to directly. That needed to be clarified, Guy thought, and instantly decided to speak to the men of Smithycote as soon as he could.

Meanwhile Ingram was in full flow. "I believe you and your conspirators are keeping information from this court. Come forward the other men who were there!"

Harry and John proved to be two young lads barely old enough to be called men, both totally overawed by the whole proceedings, and who stumbled and muttered their way through their testimonies. Yet both stuck resolutely to the assertion that they had found butchered carcasses already possibly a day dead. At this point Ingram summoned the head man from neighbouring Codnor, and although he was fractionally less belligerent with him, nonetheless kept badgering him about where the rest of the carcasses might have gone. Matthew of Codnor did his best to answer the questions, but along with those of his men who had thought they were merely coming to testify that there was a substantial herd of deer in the area, was baffled to find himself coming under ever greater suspicion of collusion.

"No, my lord!" Matthew protested as Ingram instructed his clerk to record his personal doubts. "I swear by Our Lady that no-one in Codnor knew anything about the death of the deer until Gyrth came, and then it was to ask if we'd seen anyone who'd ridden through."

"And why would a riding man be more accused of poaching than you ruffians?" snapped Ingram. "How dare you try to throw suspicion on some unsuspecting traveller!"

Unable to keep quiet, one of Matthews neighbours protested, "But someone must have used a horse to move that much venison in one go! There were no signs of a cart when Matthew went to witness the scene with Gyrth! Anyway, you'd struggle to get a cart up there with the trees so close to one another."

Ingram gave a nasty smile. "Why would you need a horse? There are enough of you strong men between the two villages. You could surely have carried a joint each?"

The village men exchanged panicked glances, but not ones of guilt, Guy was sure. They were just completely taken aback. Clearly it had never entered their heads that they might have done such a thing, but were painfully aware now of how Ingram was twisting things. Yet even Guy was at a loss when Ingram ordered his man to push the current witnesses to one side and summon the headman of Ripley.

"Ripley?" Guy couldn't help but question. "Surely if we're talking about deer in the Smithycote area the nearer villages would be Swanawick and Sumcot? They'd be the ones who could tell you if any hunters were in the area!"

Ingram glowered at him. "I would remind you, forester, that *I* run this court, and not you! *I* will decide what is relevant, and what is not!"

By now all of the hairs on the back of Guy's neck were standing. Swanawick and Sumcot were tiny vills of a similar size to Smithycote, to be sure, but there were enough men at each for someone to have been called. Why not, then? Could it be that both answered to the manor of Alfreton, and Ingram wanted Alfreton kept out of the court records? That had to be it, however odd it might seem.

As Edward, the headman of Ripley, tried to convince the intransigent verderer that his only intention in coming here had been to bear witness to the fact that a fawn had died near his own village – possibly because its mother had been one of those killed near Smithycote – Guy leaned back in the portable chair and wracked his brains for what he knew of the area. Who owned Alfreton? Ah, Hugh de Ryddynges, another power-hungry young lord! And hadn't someone told him that the de Ryddynges family had received the manor from Ralph Ingram, the verderer's grandfather? By the look of things it could well be de Ryddynges who was the culprit for the deer, but whether his star was in the ascendancy and Ingram was trying to court favour with him, or if Ingram had found a way to get a hold over Ryddynges to maybe keep him obliged to him, Guy couldn't fathom. Nor did he particularly care, but he was bothered about the fate of the poor villagers.

By now Ingram's version of events had more kinks in it than a piglet's tail, and somehow he had managed to involve the unsuspecting villagers of Pentrich in the proceedings as well. They, poor souls, seemed set for a fine for non-attendance to a court they could never have thought they needed to come to. Indeed it was only their proximity to Ripley on the other side to Codnor which linked them in any way! They didn't even share the same overlord as Codnor, as far as Guy could recall. Then he mentally kicked himself. Of course they didn't! Ingram was carefully fining villages from more than one lord! That way, one noble wouldn't find the men from a whole group of his villages on his manor's doorstep complaining. Damn, Ingram! He was good at this! Too good for it to have been the first time he had done such a thing.

Guy sighed and pushed himself upright in his seat again. All he could do for now was take note of what was done and then contact Robin and the others afterwards. There must be something they could do to help these poor folk. He was even more convinced of their need when Ingram pronounced his sentence.

"Every man of the house in Smithycote and Codnor is to be fined four pennies," he declared to a horrified intake of breath from the rest of the men there. "Maybe that will teach you to try and pull the wool over the eyes of *this* court!" For most of the men there this was no small amount of money, half a week's wages in most cases, and for many, much more. It was the maximum fine a verderer could levy without the case going on to be heard at the eyre, and it was lost on no-one that Ingram had taken all he could and yet deprived the men of maybe a fairer hearing in another court. No-one was going to protest though. It would cost them even more in bail for any of their number who were bound over to appear before the eyre. They were caught in a cleft stick and knew it.

Ingram smirked. "Furthermore," and everyone held their breath as he dangled the word for a few breaths, "the village of Pentrich will be fined a penny for each man for none-attendance, and a further penny for concealing this matter from the court." A rumble of disbelief rose from the far end of the court. This was really pushing his luck. Since Pentrich had known nothing of the deer they could hardly be blamed for not reporting the deaths to the court, but again, to argue the matter stood a good chance of only more fines, or a visit from the sheriff and his men.

"Ripley is fined three pennies for each man for the matter of the fawn." Another groan went up from the back of the hall. "And now I shall have lunch. Roger, clear the hall. I shall hear the other cases when I have eaten."

The villagers trooped out in sullen misery, but once outside Guy could already hear the anger building. Excusing himself from Ingram, who barely noticed him going, Guy hurried outside to where a couple of the women of Linby were hurrying up with platters of food.

"Where's his wine?" Guy asked them hurriedly.

"Over there," one of them gestured with her head, and turning, Guy saw the leading man of the village lifting a skin of wine from where it had been kept safely to one side. A leather beaker, ornately tooled, stood beside it and Guy had just got to it when Gyrth hurried up to him.

"Sir Guy, can you not help us? Can't you make him see his mistake?"

Guy shook his head but said, "Never mind that for a moment, just stand there and keep talking! Block me from the others' view!"

"You what?" Gyrth gulped in shock, then saw Guy pull a tiny bottle from the inside of the heavy wool jerkin he wore against the autumn chill, pull the stopper out with his teeth as he concealed the bottle in his hand, and then pour several drops into the beaker.

"Not a word about this!" Guy hissed. "Now go back to the rest of those who were in there and tell them I'll be back as soon as I've given that bastard his wine!" And Guy sloshed some of the wine from the flask into the beaker and gave it a swirl.

"What's *that*?" Gyrth whispered in horror, clearly fearing that the murder of a verderer might be laid at his door too.

Guy's smile was savage. "Just a little poppy juice to make him drowsy. The way he fills his face, the food should do the rest in the warmth of the hall. With any luck he'll be nodding off soon after the court re-sits for the afternoon. That should mean we don't have any more disasters today! I'll try to take over the proceedings once he's asleep."

"And what about us?"

"Later!" and Guy hurried into the hall on the heels of the women.

It was typical of Ingram's greed that he saw that there was some wine in the beaker and assumed that Guy had drunk some.

"Hey! You find your own wine, forester!" he snapped and snatched the beaker from Guy's hand, draining the wine in one draught, then gesturing for the beaker to be immediately refilled.

"I never touched your wine," Guy retorted. "I was just trying to make sure none got spilled. You're welcome to it. I don't drink that stuff this early in the day. I prefer to keep my head clear."

"Ha!" snorted Ingram. "If you were properly bred you'd be able to drink a man's drink." His voice already had a hint of a slur, so Guy turned without comment and, smiling to himself, made his way outside. With any luck Ingram would hold himself together to start the afternoon's proceedings, and then snore through the rest.

Going straight to Gyrth and Matthew and the cluster of men around them, Guy silenced the outpouring of complaints with a waved hand. "Yes, I know it's desperately unfair and he's in the wrong."

"But can you change the fine, Sir Guy?" Matthew pleaded.

Guy shook his head. "I'm so sorry, Matthew, but I can't." He had to wave the protests down again. "Look, that bloody clerk wrote it all down, and he's far more frightened of Ingram than he'll ever be of me. There's no way I can change the record now," although that did suddenly give Guy a germ of an idea for something which might work another time. "But tell me, who is the lord of Sumcot and Swanawick? How did they get off so lightly?"

By neatly deflecting the men's anger, Guy quickly learned that he had been right – a large part of Alfreton, plus Sumcot and Swanawick, did belong to Hugh de Ryddynges. Moreover, the word going round at the last market had been that Ingram had been at a grand feast de Ryddynges had thrown just over a week before, ostensibly to celebrate the Feast of the Birth of the Virgin Mary. That, no doubt, was where the venison had ended up – on the table before Ingram himself! No wonder Ingram was so eager to keep any mention of the Alfreton manor out of the court record!

Equally interesting was the discovery that Codnor and Smithycote answered to a different lord called Gerbod de Escalt, who himself was answerable to the sheriff of Nottingham for what taxes he collected from his manors. De Escalt's main manor was close to Bolsover Castle, so he was far enough away not to be too much of a danger to Ingram right now, but by the same token it explained why Ingram had only wanted to involve two of de Escalt's villages. He might not have thought about it while riding with his friends at the hunt, but afterwards, when he realised where the deer had been killed, he must have begun plotting. Clearly he didn't fancy arguing with Sheriff fitz John over money if the sheriff's income from the area fell because the villagers had been over-fined. Hence the fact that Ripley and Pentrich had become entangled to provide the testimony of four villages as required by law. The difference was that normally it would be the four closest to the incident so that the men could testify as to the state of the forest and deer, but this time Ingram had had to be creative.

Then Guy mentally kicked himself again. Hadn't fitz John ridden out from Nottingham a bit over a week ago? And didn't the young and petulant sheriff have a great love of venison? It wouldn't have taken him long to ride to Alfreton, that was for certain, and the more Guy thought about it the surer he was that the venison had been hunted to entertain fitz John, along with a returned promise to turn a blind eye to the hunting from that same sheriff. So de Ryddynges and Ingram had been fawning around Fitz John, had they? They might come to regret that, though, Guy thought with savage glee. He wouldn't trust fitz John further than he could spit.

Yet that did not help the poor villagers here and now.

"Listen, you have time to pay up, even if it's only a couple of weeks to Michaelmas and the next court," Guy told them, "and I'll do my best to be the one who comes and gets the fines. But in the meantime, keep your eyes open for some visitors to your villages."

"Visitors?" Matthew groaned. "Sir Guy, we can't afford hospitality to strangers now!"

"Oh you won't have to spend any money on these folk," Guy said with a wink. "I can't say any more now, but they'll be more able to help you than I can." Then a thought came to him. "What happened to the rest of the venison? The poor cuts?"

Gyrth wrinkled his nose. "We had to bury the offal. It was already starting to stink. Well it had been a warm couple of days. Even my old herding dog turned his nose up at them. They had that peculiar sheen to them they get when they're really gone off, too."

"And the forequarters and sides?"

"Hanging from a rafter in the main barn where the rats and dogs won't get to them," Gyrth sighed. "We didn't dare do else in case that bastard in there wanted them."

Guy grinned at him. "Well if Ingram doesn't mention them again I think you can probably use them. If he says anything to me later on, I'll say that the rats had got to them and they weren't fit for anything but burning. I'd suggest you cut them up as fast as possible, though. Get the meat off the bone, and do something like salt it or smoke it to help it keep. And get rid of those bones so that you can't be accused a second time of killing the bloody beasts."

For a moment Gyrth blinked at him in shock, then his face too broke into a nervous grin. "We have some charcoal burning going on in the forest. Just enough to give the travelling smith something to work with when he comes to repair the one plough share which broke at the last ploughing, you understand."

"Of course," Guy said knowingly. "I'm sure I recall you mentioning that to me and adding it to your last payments." He knew damned well that they had said no such thing, but he deeply objected to the ordinary folk having to pay to get the bits of wood they needed from the forest. Lords felling whole trees for buildings was one thing, simple gathering of fallen branches a wholly different matter.

"You could cut the venison into strips and smoke it over the fire," Matthew added enviously. "Then you'd have plenty to see you into the winter."

Guy looked at Gyrth and then at Matthew, and Gyrth took the hint. "You're paying the same fine as us. I reckon you should have half of the meat for that."

"Maybe you'll need the Smithycote men to smoke it for you, unless you too had a plough share break on you?" Guy said with false innocence, knowing that the Codnor men would also have some illicit charcoal burning going on.

"Maybe," Matthew agreed with a laugh. "Those plough shares aren't made like they used to be!"

Then Sir Payne rode in with two men accompanying him, and Guy quickly separated himself from the villagers so as not to give the game away. His fellow forester was not the evil man Sir Eric had been, nor as belligerent as Sir Henry or Walkelin or Fredegis, but Payne was scared to death of Sheriff fitz John. If Ingram complained to fitz John, and he in turn realised Payne had been at the same court, Guy knew that the young knight would come in for much questioning, at which point he would tell everything he had seen and heard. Therefore the first thing Guy said when he reached Payne was,

"Bloody peasants are already trying to wriggle out of the fines from this morning." It explained why they were speaking to him, but cut short any speculation Payne might have had on the matter. "Ingram's inside stuffing himself stupid and guzzling wine," Guy added.

"By Our Lady, at this hour?" Payne gulped. "It's a bit early to be drinking wine with a whole afternoon's court to go, isn't it?"

Guy simply shrugged and pulled a weary face, but inwardly he could have hugged Payne for making the connections without further prompting. "Personally I'd have stuck with the small beer. They make a good brew here. It's perfectly palatable, and quenches a man's thirst, but Ingram has delusions of his nobility, so he turned his nose up at it. ...Ach well, it'll be his head that thumps this evening, not mine," and Guy clapped Payne on the shoulder. "Come on, let's go and see what joys we have coming this afternoon."

This swanimote court in the tenant's year was primarily to collect grazing fees, to confirm beasts were being moved out of the forest for the winter, and to hear any presentments from the foresters. So usually it dealt with issues such as over-grazing, cutting of light woodland and clearances which had not been licensed, as well as the much rarer cases of actual poaching. So having got over the excitement of the morning, the afternoon declined into the minutia of dealing with forest life. Payne had brought two complaints of the precious undergrowth the deer needed having been illegally cleared, and had come with three more cases on Sir Henry's behalf relating to an illegal charcoal burning, a felled oak, and an unlicensed enclosure of part of a wood. As he and Guy prepared themselves for the cases to come, Guy suddenly realised something.

"You say Sir Henry asked you to bring these cases up?" he asked Payne.

"Yes," the naive forester answered and patted three pieces of parchment. "He had one of the castle's clerks write them down for me."

"He didn't mention the poaching of three deer over the shire border, did he?"

Payne frowned, puzzled. "No. But poaching up north would surely come under High Peak rather than us, wouldn't it?"

"Probably," Guy answered distractedly. That made it even odder, for Sir Henry had been the forester who had supposedly brought the morning's poaching to light. Ingram had covered the forester's absence from the court by saying that Sir Henry had already made his presentment of the facts of the issue to him beforehand, but now it looked to Guy as though Henry might not have been involved at all. That was interesting. Would the bullish Henry be any too pleased to hear that his name had been taken in vain? Possibly not. In which case, that gave Guy another angle to pursue.

For now, though, he found himself taking over the court as Ingram listened to the beginning of Payne's rambling testimony, and slowly slid down in his seat until his head rested on the table and he began snoring. Payne stopped as the first full snore echoed down the hall, unsure what to do. Ingram's clerk too looked about him in consternation.

"I'll take over," Guy sighed, pulling his chair up to beside the clerk's stool. "You take down what you think he'd want recorded, but make it sound like he did the speaking, not me."

"Can we do that?" the clerk whispered anxiously.

Guy leaned in to him and whispered back, "Do you want to be the one to try and wake him, eh?"

The way the clerk flinched as if Guy had struck him was answer enough. Patting the worried little man on the shoulder, Guy smiled encouragingly at him,

"Don't worry, he'll never know the difference. He can't read anyway, so how will he know which bits of those marks on the parchment relate to this morning and which to this afternoon?"

The clerk blinked, then brightened. He had clearly never thought of it in quite that way before. Therefore the court proceeded at an almost unheard of brisk rate, with Guy hearing the evidence and making sensible decisions on the basis of it. Payne's two cases of clearances were dealt with by minimal fines of the kind the villagers were already expecting, as were two cases brought by Guy himself of grubbed out saplings, Henry's illegal charcoal burner, and the unlicensed enclosure. The felled oak Guy threw out of court to the villagers' relief.

"That old oak got blasted by lightning last winter," Guy declared to the court in disgust. "No-one had to fell it, it came down in the spring gales all by itself. And I know for a fact that the sheriff had the timber brought to the castle." He turned to the clerk. "Make a record merely to the effect that this is an old case already dealt with at the summer swanimote and two woodmotes before that. All charges have long since been paid."

"Just that?" the clerk queried anxiously.

"Just that," Guy said firmly, but waving the leading man from Heanor away with a wry smile, since both of them knew that it had only come about because Henry had tried to wring the fine out of the village again on the sly, and had had his bluff called to take it to the court. The villagers of Heanor must have been ruing their decision this morning with Ingram's twisting of the earlier case, fearing that they too would fall for an unwarranted fine, but were now silently blessing Guy. And still Ingram snored on. The tally of livestock brought out of the forest all around the area was dealt with, with each village acknowledging how many beasts were theirs, and all the relating payments were sorted too, so that the court finished far sooner than anyone had expected.

"Good Lord," Payne breathed in awe as the hall gradually emptied. "I don't know how you do it, Guy."

Guy smiled and gratefully took a draft of the excellent small beer. "It helps to be able to read, Payne."

"Yes, I suppose it does. I noticed you taking those parchments I brought and reading them for yourself."

"It means I don't have to wait for the scribe to finish writing down the last case before he can start reading me the next one. All I had to do was wait until he could start writing again, and that gave me time to think about what to do without having to review the evidence after the clerk told me."

Payne nodded thoughtfully. "Yes, I can see how that would help." Then added, "I think that clerk of Ingram's was a bit taken aback that you could read his records, though."

Guy though so too, especially as at one point he had corrected the clerk and told him to amend the amount of a fine to the correct amount.

"But my lord always adds on something for charcoal burning," the clerk had whispered to Guy in near terror. "He says that they make money out of selling the charcoal, so he's taking that as well."

"Then in this case we'll just have to make it a very *small* burning," Guy had replied softly but with some asperity, "so that the sheriff gets the smallest of fines and Ingram gets his cut of it."

Now the clerk was packing up his parchment, quills and ink and Roger, Ingram's man, was looking at his still snoring master wondering what to do with him. Guy knew he would have to do something about that and shooed Payne off to find the horses. He then slipped Roger some coins.

"Best not mention that I had to finish off the court for him, eh?" Guy said with a conspiratorial wink. "You'll have enough on your hands when he wakes with a thick head. No point in reminding him that he made a fool of himself in front of the villagers to make matters worse." Roger shuddered, confirming to Guy that Ingram was a cruel master when the mood took him. That was the way to keep Roger happy, then. Give him a way to handle his querulous master which didn't involve him getting a beating.

"Let him think he did all the business and then went to sleep afterwards," Guy added. "Don't hesitate to show him the parchment. Even if another clerk reads it to him it'll only confirm the business went ahead without a hitch. Your master doesn't like long records anyway, so he won't think this too short. Now let's ask the good folk of Linby if they have a cart we can pour our verderer into so that you can get him home."

Under the pretext of escorting Ingram at least part of the way to his manor at Eastwood, which was the closest of his to Linby, Guy parted company with Payne, who was riding straight back to Nottingham that night with those fines and payments collected at the court. The men who had come with Payne were sufficient escort for the money for such a short journey. However, once on the road, Guy bade farewell to Roger, who had not heard his excuses to Payne, and took a different road altogether. Fording the River Leen which did not amount to much this high up in its course, he took the road into the forest, and as soon as he was out of sight of anyone, clapped his heels to his horse and rode like the devil was behind him. Before morning came he had to find Robin!

Oh yes, Gervase, I had decided that this was another case for Robin Hood to deal with. I had no doubt in my own mind that the folk of Smithycote and Codnor were completely innocent of any wrongdoing, and Ingram had been beyond heavy-handed with his fines. And it was all the worse for having happened so close to the court hearing that the people had not had time to think of what fines they might end up getting saddled with. They were about to pay out their largest fees of the year at the coming court of Michaelmas, when rents were due too. The ordinary folk never had much to spare, but as September moved towards its end and Michaelmas Day, every penny was vital. If Ralph Murdac had still been sheriff I might well have tried appealing directly to him. He would not have overthrown Ingram's decision – he would never have done what he would have seen as undermining the attachment courts and the verderers – but he would have given the villages time to pay, maybe even until the following summer's swanimote.

Yet now there was no-one I could turn to within the castle. Sheriff fitz John was such a law unto himself that our constable, Robert of Crockston, had no authority outside of the castle itself anymore. Under Murdac he had been the sheriff's valuable right-hand man, but no longer. Of the eight of us who acted as foresters for the Derwent-to-Erewash section of Sherwood, none had any more authority than I, and neither did our leader, Sir Walter. Can you therefore see that I had no legal recourse left to me? As a mere forester, albeit nobly born but only just enough to qualify as being more than a simple freeman, I was no-one in particular in the greater scheme of things. So the one and only group of people whom I could appeal to to help the folk of Smithycote and Codnor were Robin and my other friends in the forest.

So I rode, oh how I rode that night! My great problem was that I had already warned my friends to get well out of the way, far from the old Forest of Nottingham area, knowing that there would be courts at Linby,

Calverton, Mansfield and Edwinstowe within days of one another. Courts which would draw foresters like flies! I had advised them to go west. East was no good since the hereditary foresters of the old forest would be scouring their bailiwicks and keeperships, and beyond them the foresters of the new eastern part of Sherwood called Le Clay would be coming into the heart of the forest to the courts too. At this time of year more than almost any other time they were all out checking that livestock of all sorts was being brought out of the forest.

~Why was that?~ you ask.

Because, dear Brother, this was when the villagers felt the weight of the forest laws falling very heavily on them. With winter coming on they needed all the grazing they could find to keep the oxen for the plough-teams on, as well as the few pigs and sheep they might have of their own. Those who had the misfortune to have one of the great monasteries or abbeys as their masters suffered even worse than others, because your fellow brothers would have taken all the feed they could get their hands on for their great flocks of sheep. And you know how they are ever on the increase because of the money the fleeces bring. God forbid that the brothers should forego having more money to allow their tenants enough fodder for their stock to live on! And yes, Gervase, I am still bitter over the way the Church behaves on such matters, even here at what might be my last confession.

So can you see why the hard-pressed ordinary folk might risk breaking the law to sneak their animals back out into the forest? What did it matter to them whether the deer had sufficient to eat? The deer took the grazing their beasts needed, yet the villagers got no benefit from the deer being there. Indeed in some parts of this new vast Royal Forest, there were no deer to speak of when most of it was under the plough! And in years gone by they could have hunted or set traps in the forest, not for the great red deer, of course, but for hares and the lesser roe deer. Such quarry provided extra food in the cold of winter, but now the villagers were banned even from simple trapping. And that in turn meant that Michaelmas was always a contentious point in the year as the forest laws were enforced with a heavy hand.

You think that Robin Hood would have been in the thick of it? Oh in time you will hear of how he was, but remember that these are still early days. We are only a bit over a year on from all of those in his band coming together, and you should also keep in mind that none of them – not even Robin himself – had yet been outlawed. Well may you say ~oh!~ in that tone of voice, Brother. Yes, hold that thought that none were officially outlaws, for it explains why they had chosen to remove themselves from the Nottinghamshire parts of Sherwood.

Knowing that that most belligerent of knights, William de Wendenal, had the care of the other royal forest in the area, High Peak, I had advised them not to travel up to the winter hideout in northern Derbyshire just yet. With this being de Wendenal's first Winter Haining coming on he was like to be vigorous in his actions at the autumn swanimotes and woodmotes, just to prove he was the better custodian than I had been the previous year. Therefore none of us wanted him to be looking any harder than necessary at our friends up in the Peak, and so the intent was to avoid giving him even a hint that landless men were in the area for him to *hunt. So now I could only pray as I rode, that my friends would be somewhere in the cover of the Derwent valley west of where I was coming from.*

I had to hope that I would find them within a day. To delay my return by any longer was to incite fitz John's curiosity, which was the last thing I needed. One day I could cover by the excuse of returning Ingram to his manor, but Payne was not a man to think on his feet and create a cover for any longer absence for me. I had that evening and maybe the following morning, and that was all. If I could not find them I would have to return to Nottingham and try to get a message to them some other way. Yet there was not much time left if they were to help the folk of Smithycote and Codnor to find the money for the fines.

I remember that ride clearly. The light gradually dwindling, the shadows in the forest lengthening, and having to slow my pace ever more to avoid branches whipping me in the face or blinding my horse. And still no sign. None of the prearranged marks by the side of the tracks. No hint that they might be there. And then darkness truly fell and I was alone in the forest and fearing I had failed.

Chapter 5

By St Thomas, Dewi Sant and Issui Sant, I remember that night, Gervase! A thrill still runs through these old bones at the memory. Finally, in sheer desperation I decided to proclaim my presence for all to see. Stopping in a small clearing I got a fire going. I lit a far bigger blaze than I truly needed, but that was the point – to make one large enough to be visible. I had reached the ridge above the Derwent valley, the leaves were falling, making the foliage less dense for a sign to be seen through, and I was desperate. My bow was always strapped to my saddle, although I dared only carry a standard sized hunting bow, not a great Welsh bow like my friends, but it would be powerful enough for what I planned that night.

I had one way to make my presence widely seen – fire-arrows! I could not hope to do the job properly. That would have required linen soaked in something which would have burned hotly, such as pitch or turpentine. I had successfully used turpentine in the past, and for me it had the advantage of being easily accessible since it could be sneaked out from the castle's infirmary on a covert night-time visit. But I had not come prepared for such a thing when I had set out for the court at Linby, and I did not even have any linen I could use except my braes – and I am not such a hero as to ride a horse with nothing between me and the saddle but my trews! I would have to improvise.

I found some bracken which was already dead and drying nicely. With the twine I always had with me, I bound a bundle of the bracken tightly to each head of three arrows which I had cut the heads off. It was a shocking way to treat good arrows, and I mentally apologised to the fletcher in Nottingham who had made them for me, but I had little choice. I do not say this next just because I am here with you, Gervase, but then I prayed. I prayed to Dewi Sant and Issui Sant, so beloved of Tuck and myself, and to St Lazarus whom Robin would always call upon, and to Our Lady who might pity the villagers in her kindness.

˜Let these arrows be seen,˜ I prayed, ˜not for my sake, but for the sake of those I am trying to help.˜

Then I took the first of the arrows, plunged it into the fire until it caught and then set it into the bow. I had no time for finesse. No time to aim anywhere before the flames would be in danger of biting at my bow as well, but I had no need of a target either. I was shooting straight up into the air. I wanted the highest arc possible, and I pulled back the bowstring as hard as I could and let fly. The arrow shot upwards like the flame from a dragon's mouth, but before it reached the top of its flight the bracken had burned out. Swearing now, I picked the tightest bound of the remaining two arrows, set it to the fire and loosed it. This time my prayers were *answered, for it was only as it got to the top of its upwards flight and tipped over to fall that the bracken began to splutter out.*

Then all I could do was wait and pray. I had decided that I would count to one hundred ten times, then fire another arrow. I had to allow for the possibility that no-one had seen the first arrows simply because they were not looking in the right direction. Therefore my own common sense said that I should wait a reasonable amount of time so that those I sought might be in a different place. It was hard, though. By Our Lady it was hard! Have you ever had to wait like that, Brother? Waiting in what you know may well be in vain, but not daring to give up hope because so much depended on the outcome? No, I am sure you have not.

I made my count and then set the next arrow to my bow and loosed it. I had already decided that I would make two more fire-arrows if necessary, and sat staring at the skies as I counted again. By the time I had completed my second count I had realised that I would need that fourth arrow if not a fifth, and hurriedly completed my whipping to bind the bracken on. Yet no sooner had I loosed that arrow then, to my delight, a responding arrow shot up into the air from not so very much further up the Derwent, maybe three or four miles away, no more. With a glad heart I prepared another arrow, counted and then loosed again, but this time expecting no response. However, I was not so foolish as to not be aware that there were others beside my friends in the woods, and not all would be my friend. I therefore gathered my things together and removed myself to a patch of deeper cover from where I could watch the clearing still lit by my fire.

Sherwood,
September, the Year of Our Lord 1190.

Hugh burst from the woods with Thomas hot on his heels,
"It has to be Guy, I tell you," he was calling back to men unseen, and then Allan, John and Siward burst into view with Bilan. More cautiously, Robin came into the clearing, bow and arrow at the ready, along with Will, Malik, Gilbert and Piers all similarly cautious and ready to pin any attacker to the nearest tree with their arrows.

"It *is* me," Guy called and stepped out into the light of the fire.

"Told you!" Hugh said to Robin with some asperity. "Who else would proclaim their presence in the forest?"

"It could have been outlaws," Malik replied, but Thomas and John were already shaking their heads.

"Not here and now," John said firmly. "We told you ...it's the time when the forest gets cleared for the winter hunting. No-one who knows the forest is going to make themselves any more visible than necessary."

"He's right," Guy said calmly. "I hadn't thought it out myself quite that well, but I did think that as things are at the moment, you would probably be the only ones here about."

Robin still looked less than pleased, and Guy belatedly realised that once again he must have refused to listen to the local men because they weren't such experienced soldiers. At least it confirmed that he was not the only one who came in for Robin's suspicions.

"Why all the hurry, anyway?" Will demanded, spotting Robin's deepening scowl and trying to deflect an argument.

"I have some villagers who desperately need your help," Guy said, raising his voice so that even Tuck, Marianne, James, Roger, Walter and Algar – who had drifted into the clearing behind the others – could hear him. "I've been praying to the saints you'd see my sign, because I've done all I can for them and it won't be enough."

Suddenly Robin brightened, and Guy inwardly sighed – nothing like an admission of inadequacy in himself to make his cousin's day.

"Ah *Dewi Sant's* guiding hand perhaps?" Tuck added with a beaming smile.

It was easy now for Guy to smile back. "Him and St Issui and St Lazarus, and a few prayers to Our Lady for good measure. And I meant every one of them!"

"That bad, eh?" Tuck wondered. "You'd better tell us all about it, then."

With as much economy as possible, Guy brought the others up to date with what had happened at the court.

"So you see, I can't change the written record, because the moment the sheriff's scribes see it they'll know something was wrong. But that means that the folk of Smithycote and Codnor have been saddled with a crippling fine just at the worst time of the year for them to find such money. I was hoping that you'd be able to get some of the stored pennies from up in the cave to them."

He was referring to the cask of silver pennies he and the others had taken over at High Peak Castle during their temporary stay there the previous year. A hoard collected by the now-deceased constable of the castle, who had been skimming money off from taxes and fines for his own benefit. Some had already gone to help villagers elsewhere, but by Guy's calculations there would still be a substantial amount left, and more than enough to help these villagers and still leave a goodly amount.

"I know you'd be taking a risk going up to so near to High Peak at the moment..."

"...There's another way!" interrupted Robin. "We seize the fines when they're being taken to Nottingham from one of the other courts!"

Guy winced. How to tell his cousin that this was not the most viable of plans? "You'll have to very quick about it then," was all he could think of. "Because the swanimotes have a set date, they're all held pretty much on the same day. It's not like the woodmotes where there'll be several days between the one at Edwinstowe and the one at Calverton, for instance."

Allan suddenly looked up. "What about Mansfield's? When was the court for that?"

"Yesterday, the same as Linby's," Guy sighed. "All done and packed away, I'm afraid."

But Allan was still thinking. "Yes, but would they have set out with the money from Mansfield yesterday? You told us before that the Mansfield court gets almost as swamped with cases as Edwinstowe does. Don't you remember? You told us that with all the Le Clay cases having to go to Mansfield and Edwinstowe to be sorted, that was why most of the cases you're involved with were to be heard at Linby. So I'm wondering, would they have managed to get through them all in one day?"

Guy was taken a back at the thought. "Heavens, Allan, I'm not sure!" He thought some more. "Do you know, you might be right. I'm fairly sure that Walkelin, Fredegis and Henry were all going to be there, because there were cases from the north of our territory which were going to have to be heard there. That's why Henry wasn't with me to hear Ingram taking his name in vain. In fact, that was why Ingram could be *sure* Henry wouldn't be there! And knowing how those three like to lord it over the ordinary people, yes, you're right, the proceedings could well stretch out over more than one day once you add in anything my fellow foresters from Le Clay bring along as well."

Tuck was now nodding too. "And don't forget what you yourself have just told us. You got the court at Linby over and done with far quicker than Ingram would have done. Left to him you'd have been there all day, wouldn't you? So the money from Linby wouldn't normally have gone back until the coming morning at the earliest."

Walter and Algar were now grinning at Robin.

"So we could get the money when it leaves Mansfield!" Walter told him eagerly.

"Yes! That's the nearest one!" agreed Algar. "That bloody sheriff can whistle for his money for once!" Having been unjustly imprisoned at Nottingham, Algar's hatred for all sheriffs ran deep, even though it had been corrupt knights serving the former sheriff who had really been to blame.

Ever the more practical man, Will asked, "How well will it be guarded, though? If there's going to be more money in fines than there used to be, will there be more guards?"

"We can take 'em!" Algar snorted.

Will just quirked an eyebrow at Guy. He didn't need to ask just how good those guards would be. He knew Guy knew that in reality it would be the core of nine soldiers, not the full group, who would do the hard work if it came to a fight. Luckily Guy was doing some quick counting of the men he was sure had been sent north, and it was not that many.

"Actually, I think there won't be more than about half a dozen men-at-arms there. And two of them are our old friends Claron and Frani! So whoever fights them will just have to put on a show of battling it out for their sakes."

He was referring to two of the twelve men-at-arms who had been with them at High Peak, and who could be trusted to not give them away. The twelve would not be able to actively help them, being constrained just as Guy was to appear to be loyal to the sheriff, but they would do their best not to stand in the way.

What Guy was less happy about was Robin's eagerness to get into a fight with the sheriff's men. He had only ever wanted Robin to get the glory of providing the two villages with the money to pay the fine, not to be giving the Welsh archer's salute to the sheriff in the process.

"You know fitz John will go berserk when he hears you've taken his money, don't you?" Guy warned. "You'll have only a couple of days before he'll empty the castle of men-at-arms and come hunting for you. You'll have to get the money to the villagers and then make a run for it. Fitz John will throw every man he's got at the western side of the shire, and possibly over into Derbyshire if he thinks you ran that way."

Robin was looking smug. "We can outrun them! We already know more of the hidden ways through the forest than his men ever will. Places we can hide until they've gone past us and then take a different route."

John was watching Guy's worried frown deepen. "We will be careful for the villagers' sake, though," he added. "We know they can't run to the forest. We'll be careful we're not caught there." John knew all too well how Guy had had to avoid coming to see him while he was still working as a shepherd for fear of attracting the wrong kind of attention. Now he was voicing Guy's fear for him but aiming it at Robin.

Luckily, because it was John and not Guy who said it, Robin paused to think for a moment and then nodded. "Yes, I can see that we must be careful not to drag any hunt for us into a village. So we'll go for the money once it's well out of Mansfield, but before it gets near to Blidworth."

"The best spot would be before they get too close to Newstead Abbey," Siward added. "The Black Canons are unlikely to be out patrolling the forest, but they may have horses there, and if the alarm gets raised they could send a fast rider to the sheriff."

Hugh was nodding. "Yes, that's a good point. Robin, there's a slight dip as the road comes out of Mansfield. You hardly notice it on the road, but it's there. Newstead lies back from the road further up on the higher ground, but that means sound might carry. Siward's right. The best spot would be about three miles out of Mansfield before they get within hailing distance of any brothers tending the vegetable plots or fields." Then as Robin's gaze moved back to Siward, Hugh gave Guy an apologetic shrug which seemed to say 'he's going to do it anyway, so it's just a case of how.'

As Robin began discussing tactics with the soldiers, Guy strolled as nonchalantly as possible over to Tuck and Marianne.

"You're worried, aren't you," Marianne said softly as soon as he got to them.

"Yes I am. I never wanted him to all but declare war on the bloody sheriff! I just wanted some help for those poor villagers."

Marianne put a consoling hand on Guy's arm. "This doesn't help much, but I think he's desperate to lead us in something he considers to be a proper fight. He feels that in some way it will prove he's a proper leader."

"Oh Jesu!" Guy groaned, and got a sympathetic pat on the back from Tuck.

"I know, I know! *Duw*! You came with the best of intentions my friend. It's not your fault if your prayers get answered in a way you never expected."

Guy looked balefully at him. "Then I hope *Dewi Sant* looks after his followers, and St Lazarus after his disciple over there, because I think they're going to need it!" Then he noticed Roger hovering at his side. "What is it?" he asked sympathetically, expecting Roger to be asking him whether he really needed to get involved in fighting armed men. 'Red Roger' was no fighter, and Guy saw no shame in him admitting it if he was scared to death at the prospect. Yet the scruffy young thief surprised him.

"I gotta plan!" he said brightly.

"Really?" Guy was stunned.

"Yeah! We gotta be a bit more cunnin' I'm finkin'. Wos them men gonna be lookin' for when they come huntin' Robin and the ovvers afterwards? I'm finkin' it'll be soldiers and archers! That sheriff o' yours will never fink some band of outlaws, what are just farmers and the like who gone into the forest, could do it. He'll fink it's some band of mercenaries, or soldiers what ain't got no lord anymore, won't he?"

It was a very good assessment given that Roger had never as much as seen fitz John, and Guy began to wonder how badly he had underestimated the small rascal. The mischievous thief had managed to survive in some rough spots, after all. "I think that's probably all too true," Guy praised him.

"Then why don't we see if Robin will split us up?" Roger wondered. "Let that lot over there do the rough bit, then scarper to the hills. In the meantime, Tuck and me could take the money to the one village, and Marianne and Much could go to the ovver one. Who's gonna look at a woman and a young lad with a face like Much?"

He had a point. Much still had a look of wide-eyed innocence about him despite having been through so much, and he definitely looked younger than his years. "And if Tuck takes the money and I just lurk around in the background so we don't look like we're togevver, I fink we won't even get noticed. Then if the sheriff and his men come ridin' frough, we can always ask for a night in someone's barn like we was just ordinary poor travellers. We can lie low for a couple o' days in a way Robin and the soldiers can't."

Allan had come to listen and was nodding too. "We can try to convince Robin to do that. And I think it's a good plan, Roger, don't you Guy?"

"Yes! Very much so! I'm far less worried about you getting swept up by the sheriff if you can lie low."

"But," Allan held up a cautionary finger, "we'll have to make much of how we'll tell all the villagers that the money comes from Robin Hood, not us."

Tuck sighed. "Oh yes. And we must make much of their gratitude when we get back to him. He'll need that balm to his soul too."

Guy grimaced. "But in Jesu's name don't let Robin go with you! If he insists on that, then you'd be better with all of you going so that you could fight your way free of any trap. He's too easily recognisable, and having a big man like him with either pair of you will make you seem less the ordinary travellers."

"It's not arrogance," Marianne anxiously told him, "you know that, don't you? He's not doing it just to bask in the glory. It's that hole in his soul where a family ought to be."

She saw Guy's eyes go cold.

"He could have more of his bloody family if he didn't keep shoving some of us away," he said bitterly. "If what he wanted more than anything was a wife and family, I'd try and find a way to let him have Gisborne. But he'd spit in my eye if I offered it him, and worse, he won't let go of his dream to be the 'big knight'!"

Until that point Marianne hadn't really understood how deeply Robin's actions had cut Guy to the quick. "Didn't you ever dream of being the heroic knight?" she asked gently.

Guy managed to wring out a tight smile for her. "Of course I did, didn't we all, eh, Allan?" and the two cousins smiled wanly. "But I grew up, Marianne! I realised that a lot of the heroes I looked up to as a lad might have done the great deeds, but that they also stamped on a lot of people in the process. The little people who were just unfortunate enough to get in the way by accident. And these days I wouldn't want to be like that. I couldn't live with myself if I did. I'll settle for a clear conscience and a good deal less fame, thank you."

"Amen! And *Dewi Sant* bless you for that!" Tuck added warmly. "If Robin gets to the point where it moves from being healing his soul to gloating, I shall soon remind him that it was you who brought the plight of these villagers to us. Without you we would never have known in time to do something about this. Yet you'll never get to have the praise because you need to get back to the castle, and they must never know just how involved in all of this you are for your own safety. I shall offer up thanks and prayers for you, Guy, when we get chance to pause and catch our breath."

"That'll be more than enough for me," Guy thanked his friend, and meant it. "Now I must be going as soon as the first hint of dawn comes. I'll retrace my steps as far as the Erewash and then follow that down to Nottingham. That way I'll be well out of the way just in case someone sees me and recognises me."

As Guy walked away to check on his horse, Marianne turned to Tuck.

"He doesn't understand Robin's need for approval any more than Robin can grasp how he can work under the sheriff's gaze, does he?"

Allan turned to watch Guy go as he answered instead of Tuck. "No he doesn't. But I'll tell you something, Marianne, I know which of the two I'd want on my side if the worst ever happened."

Marianne turned surprised eyes to him. "You think Guy would protect you better than a seasoned fighter like Robin? I don't think so, Allan!" and she promptly turned and walked to Robin's side, where they saw her look up to him with more than a little adoration.

"Oh dear," sighed Allan, "I hadn't realised she'd fallen quite that heavily for him."

"What was that about?" Hugh asked as he came across to them.

"I sang Guy's praises and Marianne took it as a criticism of Robin," Allan said ruefully.

"But you was right, though!" Roger defended him. "I sees what you mean even if she don't. Guy might look all cold and hard, and them green eyes could give you the creeps when he gets pissed off over sommat and they go all icy, but I trust him."

Tuck looked quizzically at Roger. "And you don't trust Robin?"

The small thief wrinkled his nose. "It ain't exactly that. Most of the time I do, and I fink he's a real hero for goin' out to the Holy Land. But like Guy said, heroes can be awful single-minded! And I reckon that if Robin fought he had no choice but to choose between one of us and somefin' bigger, then we wouldn't stand a chance."

Tuck placed his big hand on Roger's skinny shoulder. "Then we must pray that day never comes, my lad!"

"We're leaving now," Hugh added, but giving them an odd look.

"Something wrong, Hugh?" Tuck asked softly as the others hurried to where Robin waited to lead them off.

The former soldier frowned. "No, not really, but it's funny that Roger should say that."

"Because you've thought it too?" and Hugh nodded.

"Oh don't worry, I'll follow Robin. We all will."

"Why? If you don't mind me asking?"

Hugh scratched the regrowth on his chin as he thought how to phrase his answer. "I'll follow him because someone has to lead, and he's as good as anyone. He's better than some of the others would be at that because he has that higher purpose in mind all the time. I wouldn't want to be part of a band of common thieves. Men who'd rob any poor soul. Robin won't let this band descend to that level. For a start the five others who came here with him all have that extra bond to him, and that gives us a stable core to our gang. So if Piers, for instance, got any daft ideas of going and robbing for the sake of it, he'd find himself very quickly alone, and because of that it wouldn't happen.

"And in truth, Tuck, I like Robin. He reminds me of an old friend I once had who isn't with us anymore, bless him. But he does worry me more than a bit when he gets that light in his eyes. I wonder whether in his head he's still just a bit on crusade even though he's back in England. He might not be fighting the Saracens anymore, but I can't help feeling that somewhere in the dark parts of his mind he's substituted the sheriffs for Saladin's captains! And when that mood comes on him he might not be open to reason."

They joined the rest and hurried off into the night, leaving Guy with his horse beside the fire. He had heard what Hugh had said to Tuck and was glad that at least some of the others were not just following Robin blindly. But the more he thought about Robin's plan the less happy he was with it. At last he could stand it no more. He would have to follow them. Of one thing he was sure, he'd had far more experience of tracking and hunting in this kind of forest than Robin had, and he was sure he could move more silently. If he kept a decent distance behind them, Robin need never know that he was there, but he very much wanted to know whether to expect to see any of them being marched into the castle on the end of some man-at-arms' rope.

Crushing his fire and walking his horse to save her strength, he hurried in the wake of the others until he was sure he had them nicely placed ahead of him. Robin would no doubt have gone faster with a smaller group, but with all of them with him he was having to keep it to a brisk walking pace. Shortly after the morning sun had climbed fully into the sky, everyone was placed up in the trees just back from the road from Mansfield to Nottingham, on the eastern side. Robin had taken them across the road so that they were in the shadows, and therefore anyone looking their way would be squinting into the sun. Guy, on the other hand, had decided to stay on the western side. It would have been hard for him to get across the road once the others had done so, and had already started looking back to the wide space below. And also something was twitching in the back of his mind. Some inner voice telling him to stay on this side, and Guy trusted that inner voice.

Luckily, they did not have long to wait. In the distance the sun soon picked up on the spears of the marching men-at-arms and the riders' mail. Knowing the men as he did, Guy could tell even from afar that the three most aggressive foresters for this area were riding with the group, and sighed. Fredegis and Walkelin had been mercenaries before earning the late king's gratitude, and been provided with their positions as foresters as a reward for good service. And Sir Henry had been known to enjoy taking part in the local tournaments, so he was definitely handy with his sword. There were certainly half a dozen of the castle's regular men-at-arms marching with them, but also another four men who must have come with the three knights who also rode with the party. One of those Guy knew to be Sir Girard, a knight currently at the castle for his forty days' service, and not someone to worry about unduly. Girard had a fearsome squint, which scared the living daylights out of many since you never quite knew where he was looking, but mostly he couldn't have hit the side of a barn with his lance if he'd tried. The other two, though, Guy couldn't be sure of, and amongst the others doing their forty day's service there were a few who were useful men to have in a fight.

"God's wounds!" he swore softly. "Why could you not have done the simple thing, Robin?"

It was surely not so very much to ask for Robin to have taken his word for once, and have simply handed out the money they had stored? After all, it had been Guy alone who had found the hoard. Robin had played no part in its discovery. So Guy felt that he had a right to have some say in how it was distributed. But it was more than pique at being so sidelined which was grating this morning. Robin had dived into this with very little thought as to what might happen if the money was more heavily guarded than Guy expected – and Guy knew who Robin would blame for that! For not knowing by some mystical means! Yet there had always been the chance that the Mansfield verderer might wish to ride and speak to Sheriff fitz John, or another knight would turn up from somewhere, and Robin hadn't given himself time to think about such possibilities.

"Christ's hooks!" Guy swore again. He was going to have to be prepared to intervene, there was no way round it. But how to do it?

Hurriedly he stripped off the finely decorated leather over-jerkin he wore. He'd chosen it for this journey because he knew it looked smart, and he preferred to never give the verderers any reason to dismiss him as being too lowly to have to listen to his opinions. Now, though, it marked him out as more than just an ordinary freeman even if it wasn't quite knightly. He tied it securely to the back of his saddle, then pulled his long-sleeved tunic off over his head and turned it inside out. The dye on the inside had faded more with his sweat than the outside had, so it looked a bit more disreputable. He wished he had thought to at least tie his lighter-weight quilted gambeson to the back of his horse, but given the still warm weather and not anticipating a fight, he'd left the extra protection behind, so he would have to hope he didn't get into any hand-to-hand fighting. The forester's hood would have to stay to give him more of a disguise by covering his face. He would just have to hope that with such a scruffy tunic no-one would think him a forester. Then for good measure he turned the hood inside out too.

His sword had remained strapped to the saddle until now. He hadn't needed it in Linby, and he had been in too much of a rush to belt it on when he had ridden to find Robin. Now he buckled the sword belt over his tunic to hold it tight. Finally he took his bow out of its oiled-cloth wrapping and strung it. Then with his quiver of arrows over his shoulder and his bow in his hand, he led the mare further back into the trees and tethered her by her reins with a knot which he could just yank free, not have to undo. He could only hope he could run back into the trees from the road, then double back to her and ride off before anyone caught him.

Giving her a last pat, Guy ran with as much stealth as he could manage back to his vantage point above the road. He was not that high up. There was nowhere in Nottinghamshire which had the kind of deep gulches and almost subterranean holloways on roads that he had known over on the borders, but it would have to do.

He looked over to where the others had been. Standing so that his eyes were shaded by an oak branch, he could see that Thomas, Piers and Bilan had moved a little closer to the road, but had picked good positions up in the trees from which to shoot. All three had their big Welsh longbows strung and ready. A flicker of movement to their side caught his eye and he was relieved to see that Allan was up there with them, also with a bow although his was a smaller hunting bow like Guy's.

Where were the others, though? He scoured the roadside and then spotted them. As expected, Robin, Will, Malik, Siward, James and Gilbert were there, and so too was Hugh. What Guy did not like was seeing John in there with them. His cousin might have huge strength, but John didn't have the aggression to be a fighter, and he certainly hadn't had much practise at fighting for real. Then Guy saw Marianne hiding in the bushes a little further back, and saw the hint of clothing with her which spoke of Roger and Much. What were they doing there? Where were Algar and Walter? And where was Tuck?

Then suddenly he saw him. Tuck was sitting by the roadside a little further on down the road, the picture of a portly monk already ruing having to walk for the day. As the party from Mansfield came into sight, he took off one of his stout shoes and began rummaging around inside it, then turned it upside down and banged on the sole. Even from his vantage point Guy could hear the laughter of the knights as they saw him, and heard derogatory comments being passed back and forth. Meanwhile Tuck put his shoe on, turned his back on them and began stomping on down the road with an affected limp.

As a piece of distraction it was masterly. The whole group was now watching Tuck, not the sides of the roads, and with any luck none of them had seen his face well enough to recognise him later on. As they drew level with Robin's men, Thomas and the other archers let fly. Four arrows landed neatly in a line on the road in front of the men-at-arms who were in the lead.

"Ambush!" someone yelled, and suddenly all of them were scrabbling for their weapons.

At the same time Robin and the other six emerged from the roadside bushes with their bows drawn too.

"Stay where you are!" Robin commanded, but the knights weren't having any of that. The six mounted men heeled their horses forward, all drawing their swords.

Now the flaw in Robin's plan was apparent. He had thought the threat of archers so close that they couldn't miss would be enough. He had not anticipated a fight. And now he and the seven with him who were exposed on the road had bows in their hands, not their swords, which would have been better at such close quarters. Guy could just about see enough of Robin's face to recognise the shock there – it had clearly never even crossed his mind that he would have to fight hard and maybe kill.

"You bloody dreaming fool!" Guy growled angrily. "Didn't bloody think it out, did you?"

Will, Malik and Hugh had reacted the quickest, firing rapidly at a knight each, then throwing their bows into the bushes and drawing their swords. Gilbert and Siward weren't far behind, although their arrows were less well aimed than the others, and skittered off the ring-mail without effect. James didn't even try to shoot his arrow, but threw the bow to one side in order to draw his sword all the faster. And the opposing men-at-arms had already run forward with their spears dropped into the attacking line, and were presenting a formidable danger given that they could out-reach any swordsman. Yet Guy had eyes only for John. His cousin stood rooted to the spot in shock as Sir Henry bore down on him bawling like an enraged bull.

An arrow, possibly from Thomas or Piers, struck Sir Henry in the shoulder, but they were shooting from a difficult angle given a slight kink in the road, and although another arrow hit one of the unknown knights too, neither penetrated enough to do real damage. Guy swept the chaos with one glance and felt his heart sink. He was the only one now who could save John. Bounding a few feet down the slope to the cover of a large coppiced hazel, he pulled back the bow until he was kissing the string, then pulled that bit harder and let the arrow fly. It struck Sir Henry just under his right arm as he raised it to cut down at John. With a howl of pain Henry's blow was stopped in mid arc as he lurched leftwards in the saddle.

Nevertheless, the sword continued its decent towards John, but it gave John enough time to regain his faculties and bring up the stout quarterstaff he held to deflect it. Luckily, with the four other archers shooting again, the different angle of Guy's arrow was not noticed in the confusion, but his friends were having to fight hard. Mercifully Claron and Frani had had the presence of mind to pretend to run on and engage with James, so the three of them were involved in an intricate dance where a lot of stabbing was going on, but nothing genuinely threatening was going to happen, and Guy gave up a prayer of thanks for that. James, he was sure, wouldn't lose his head and start forcing their covert allies into having to really defend themselves.

He looked along the fight and saw that Will and Malik had successfully knocked out two more of the men-at-arms, and with Gilbert were sending another for a long sleep too. Siward at that point grabbed a dropped spear and used the shaft to whack the final man-at-arms across the back of the head as he tried to come up behind Will.

"Blessed Virgin be thanked!" Guy breathed. At least the ordinary men weren't going to suffer any serious casualties beyond an aching head.

However the six mounted knights were proving to be a nightmare. The four archers had continued to shoot at them, but Guy could see that they had been aiming at arms and legs rather than at the body to kill. None of them would willingly kill in cold blood, and Guy again swore bitterly at Robin for putting them in this position. Yet Robin himself was battling with Walkelin, who was striking down at him at every opportunity, and only the fact that Walkelin had been on the far side of the group, and was therefore himself in the way of the other knights helping him, was saving Robin from being seriously outnumbered.

The lumbering Sir Girard tried to ride down Gilbert, but only succeeded in getting in the way of one of the unknown knights, whose resulting curses Guy could clearly hear. But then the knight was clear of Girard and turning to Gilbert again, and to Guy's horror had begun swinging a morning-star. As the three iron balls on their chains gained momentum over Gilbert's head, one of the archers in the trees must have decided they had no choice. Suddenly an altogether more lethal arrow, barbed and with a heavier head, thudded into the knight, and this time it drove in deeply. With a cry of agony the knight keeled over in the saddle and then fell to the ground.

Horrified, the other knights for the briefest of moments halted in shock, but then redoubled their efforts in their fury. Gilbert had taken up the morning-star and was whirling it above his head while screaming in his native Gaelic as he brought it down on the leg of the other anonymous knight. The spike balls embedded themselves in the man's thigh which was only partially protected by the skirt of his ringmail. As Gilbert hauled back on the morning-star, two of the balls came free with cloth and flesh attached, but the third was well and truly embedded in the chain links and began pulling the knight down towards Gilbert. Seizing the opportunity, Will dived to Gilbert's side, and as the knight slid his way, Will jumped up and grabbed his arm and hauled too. The knight went down in a tangled heap and Guy saw Will's hefty fist rise and fall twice, then the knight lie still.

Sir Henry was still trying to swat at John with his sword in his other hand, but was thankfully making a lousy job of it, and now John was holding his own, then managed to clip Henry under the chin with the end of the quarterstaff and that was that. Fredegis was now engaging Siward, but was sufficiently distracted not to see Hugh come up on the other side, cup his hand under Fredegis' boot, and shove upwards. Completely unbalanced, Fredegis lurched sideways into Siward's grasp, and he too was hauled from his saddle and knocked out. That left only Walkelin of the true fighters, and Walkelin suddenly found himself being attacked from the rear by Malik and Hugh, who had run around the others to get to him. Smacked across the head with another of the dropped spear shafts, Walkelin dropped into Hugh's grasp and was laid out on the grass to join his friends.

With the rest of the fight over, Guy realised that the wagon with the money on had disappeared. So too had Marianne, Much and Roger! In the confusion they had spirited the wagon off into the undergrowth which lay a few yards back from the side of the road. From his vantage point Guy could just about see an end corner of the wagon and it was static, so presumably the five non-combatants had grabbed the silver and were making off on foot with it, maybe even with Tuck. That relieved Guy. Tuck would be sensible and take them into hollows where it would be hard to track them later on – and Guy had the nastiest of suspicions of who would be called upon to do that! Especially as Sir Girard had taken a last look at the carnage and clapped his heels to his horse's side, heading back to Mansfield to raise the alarm.

Then to Guy's horror, he saw John come panting a little way up the hillside towards him, clearly making for a large flat stone on which to sit for a moment. But behind him Sir Henry rose to his feet. The man must have had a skull like an ox to have not been knocked out cold by John's blow, but he was upright and moving if swaying, and he had his sword in his hand and pointing at John's unprotected back. Guy could hardly believe his eyes. He looked to the others but saw that Thomas, Piers, Bilan and Allan had come down from the trees and were now too low to be able to see what was going to happen. No-one else was even looking this way!

"*Dewi Sant!*" Guy gasped in despair. Even if he called to John there was no time for John to do anything since he wasn't armed, the quarterstaff lying back beside the road.

Nocking an arrow once more into the bow as fast as any he'd ever re-aimed on a hunt, Guy brought it up, pulled back and aimed straight for Henry's chest. He'd confess his regrets to Tuck later. His cousin's life came first, and Henry was intent on killing. As Henry began bringing his left arm up, holding the sword aloft even as his face was a mask of pain from the other arrow still lodged in his right side, Guy let fly. The arrow missed its mark because in his pain Henry lurched, but it did strike him in the other shoulder, and close enough to the edges of the linked mail for it to twist and penetrate.

Henry's near otherworldly scream of agony made John spin round, and Guy saw his jaw drop as he realised what had nearly happened. As Henry crashed to the ground the others realised something had happened and all looked up too. As Will and Malik tore up the hill to John, Guy slipped back into the shadows of the coppiced hazel. He had no time now to argue the toss with Robin. If Girard raised the alarm, then Guy had to make a mad dash now for Nottingham. He could not afford to seem to be anywhere near this part of the forest. And if truth be told, he didn't think he dared speak to Robin just at this moment. If he did it might come to blows, for Guy had never been so angry with Robin as now. After all they had been through, after all that Robin had professed about wanting his family around him so much, they had come close to losing John this day, and it would be some while before Guy could speak to Robin without wanting to throttle him for that.

Yes, Gervase, I was that angry! From where I was standing, Robin had acted rashly and without thought for the consequences. He had gone running off into the night thinking only of glory, and how good it would look to hand back the villagers the very coins they had just thought were gone forever.

Was that not what Robin Hood always did? Yes, indeed it was, but later on it was to be done with a good deal more tactical thinking. I have not told you this to pull Robin Hood the hero down in your eyes, Brother. I merely want you to see that the first time he attempted to do what he would one day be so famous for, he very nearly made a tragic mess of it. The legend did not spring fully formed from out of the soil of Sherwood. Robin was a man who had to learn his fighting skills just as much as any man-at-arms, or a squire would learn to become a knight.

I have told you how he learned to use his weapons while fighting in the Holy Land, but the business of holding people up in the midst of a forest is very different to fighting other soldiers on a battlefield which your commanders have already singled out for its tactical advantages. And you have to allow that while fighting in the East, Robin had been very much the ordinary knight in training. He had not co-ordinated the defence of Jerusalem, nor had he led King Baldwin's men out on his behalf. Robin had been just one of the many brave souls out there, and he now had to learn how to lead every bit as much as practicing with his bow. It makes him no less of a hero, and I so very much want you to see the man as well.

You are mollified? Good. For as I had predicted there were consequences, and I was put into a wretched position by Robin's lack of thought, as I shall now recount.

Chapter 6

$\mathfrak{I}$ rode for Nottingham as fast as I dared take my horse, using the road first of all as the fastest route, once I was clear of the scene of the ambush. That was not cowardice on my part, Gervase. I could guess that Claron and Frani were just lying on the ground pretending to be unconscious, but I had no way of knowing if any of the other men-at-arms were also thinking the sensible thing was to lie low until these dreadful attackers left. Should even one of them have seen me, then I would have been in very real danger, for they all knew me by sight if not to talk to much – Nottingham Castle was huge, but not so very big that we would not recognise the appearance of a fellow resident. And I dared not have anyone ask where I had been. My alibi only stood up as long as everyone assumed that I had been in Derbyshire at the time of the attack, for of course I was already late in returning.

Well I rode into the castle and hurried my horse straight to the stables. Harry, the head stableman and my confident of old, took one look at the lathered mare and my face and took her off me. ˜You were riding Adiliz, if anyone asks me,˜ he said calmly, pointing to where a similarly marked bay mare was contentedly cropping at a hay net, completely relaxed. My look of relief was enough for him. He knew I would tell him what I could later on. In the meantime he took Emma, whom I had been riding, out of sight into the stables, and I knew he would work on her himself to get the telltale sweat marks off her coat and keep her out of sight until she too was rested.

For myself, I toyed with whether to try and sneak into the inner bailey across the small footbridge, which in time of peace was to the left across the rough ground at the end of the dry moat, and which ran from the stables to the picket door in the main keep. My problem would then be getting from the keep to the other side of the castle proper to where my quarters were. One route was to walk along the walls, which left me open to observation. A worse option was to go straight across the inner bailey, where I ran the risk of walking into Sheriff fitz John. Neither was good. As a result I decided to make my way amongst the servants, the soldiers, and the petitioners to the sheriff, to the servants' halls where I would be able to get some food. In desperation I could always claim that I had got near to Nottingham late last night, but knowing that the gates of the castle would be shut, had slept outside and had woken later than anticipated. It was an awful story, and I prayed to St Issui that I would not have to use it!

Did he answer my prayers? You have very little faith in the Welsh saints, Brother! Yes he did. As things turned out, I had chance to eat and then go to my shared room and change into something less travel-stained while no-one else was there, bundling my used tunic into a ball and taking it to the washerwomen before it could be commented on. I wanted that *tunic well out of sight for a day or two! Indeed, I then went to my immediate superior, Sir Walter, and reported the court's proceedings, and how verderer Ingram had had to be taken home in a cart after too much wine in the heat of the day.*

˜That man's humours are all out of sorts,˜ was Sir Walter's weary comment. ˜His are too hot and dry. He should have had something to cool him down, not inflame him further.˜ And as a general comment on Ingram's character I could not help but agree. So I was then with my fellow forester, Payne, and the sheriff's clerks, counting the money which had come in with us and ensuring it tallied with what should have been there, when Sir Girard came thundering in to the castle on a fresh horse provided by the folk of Mansfield.

Nottinghamshire,
Winter, the Year of Our Lord 1190

Guy got to the great hall just in time to hear fitz John's near apoplectic shriek of,

"They did *what*?"

"They took the money from the swanimote, my lord," repeated Sir Girard, unaware of the danger to himself.

The young sheriff had risen to his feet, handsome face now twisted in rage and becoming redder with every breath.

"And where are my *knights*?" he screamed in Girard's face. "*Where* are the men-at-arms?"

Girard gulped. "All wounded, sire! They've been taken back to Mansfield in carts. Sir Henry fitz Humphrey is dead. Our Sir Henry from here may not live, and Sir Robert fitz Ilger may never walk again. Sir Fredegis and Sir Walkelin hadn't woken when I left to bring you the news. The wise women in the village said that only when they woke would they be able to tell if there was permanent damage. I sent word to Newstead Abbey for a proper infirmarer to come and see to them and the men."

Guy now felt a little less guilty over the knight whom Thomas or Piers had shot – fitz Humphrey had been a brute of a man, notorious in the Hundred Courts for his brutal treatment of his tenants. He would not be missed, and especially not by his wife, who had been seen in church with serious bruises whilst in Nottingham visiting her family. And their own Sir Henry had been anything but a good man, and Guy was content for God to decide whether he should be called to account for his miserable life now or at a later date, believing it would make little difference to Henry's ultimate fate in the hereafter. However Sir Girard had not anticipated that his life might be in danger here and now.

"Yet you escaped unhurt!" snapped fitz John at the poor knight. "Coward! Oath-breaker! You were sent here to fulfil your father's dues to me! Yet while other men lay down their lives to protect my taxes, you come here unscathed!"

"No sire!" Girard protested. "I have the bruises to prove it! And they had archers!"

Fitz John snarled in disbelief. "Witless fool! Do you expect me to believe that a bunch of renegade peasants would know how to use such a thing? Idiot! Even if they had a wood-bow and were poaching, such a thing wouldn't bring down a *knight*! Or are you telling me you were such a bunch of incompetent ...useless ...*maidens*," he spluttered to find his words in his rage, "that you chose to travel with *my* money *without* wearing your armour?"

By now he was advancing around the table on a disbelieving Girard, stabbing at the tabletop with the knife he had been eating with, but worrying everyone into thinking he might yet use it on Girard.

"We did!" yelped Girard with rising panic. "We *all* wore our chain-mail! Men-at-arms too! And look! This is one of the bows! They dropped it at the site!"

Guy felt his heart sink. Unseen by him, Girard must have scooped up the bow James had thrown aside in the fight. But then the unexpected happened, providing him with a way to deflect things nicely.

"That's not a bow, you weasel-faced toad-spawn!" fitz John exploded. "By Christ, you should know better! And by the time I've finished with you, you will! It's a fucking makeshift quarterstaff, you snot-nosed whelp of a tinker's bitch!"

"No sire!" Girard protested, still brandishing the bow. "Look! It's got a full string! It's bound at the bottom and looped at the top!"

That halted fitz John for just the briefest moment and allowed Guy to step forwards, even as the castle's constable, Robert of Crockston, and his second-in-command, Alan of Leek, hurried to the front of the circle of aghast knights ready to defend Girard.

"My lord, it's a Welsh bow," Guy said clearly, his voice carrying in the stunned silence.

Fitz John turned to him with a sneer. "It's *what?*"

"It's a Welsh bow, my lord. I saw many of them while I worked for Sheriff de Braose. They're capable of putting an arrow right through an oak door. You can still see the one which did that at Abergavenny Castle."

Guy was never one of fitz John's preferred knights, and now he looked at him as though he had sprouted an extra head.

"This? ...This ...*thing*? You really expect me to believe that this lump of wood is a *bow*?"

Guy sighed inwardly. Being the epitome of Norman knighthood that he was, fitz John was far too used to crossbows to have ever seen any alternative use for even a hunting bow, let alone a war-bow. And that despite him having come from Chester where, Guy bitterly thought, if he had taken even the slightest bit of notice of what went on around him, he should surely have encountered at least one of the great Welsh bows. But Guy needed him to believe in the Welsh and their bows right now.

"May I demonstrate, my lord?" he asked, holding out his hand to Girard, who was only too glad to hand the dreadful thing on to Sir Guy and move away from fitz John's ire. Making rather more of a meal of stringing the bow that was really necessary, Guy then led the way out of the castle hall and out through the inner barbican to the outer bailey, where some butts had been set up in the curve of one of the buttresses. Once there, Guy called for some arrows, and while everyone waited for them – fitz John standing at the fore with folded arms and his habitual sneer on his face – Guy surreptitiously warmed the bow with a few pulls. When the arrows came he moved right back and called for everyone to get out of the way. He was going to be shooting almost the width of the bailey, albeit at its narrowest point, and immediately fitz John crowed,

"God's hooks, man! You'll never hit it from there!"

The supercilious young lord was standing rather too close to the line the arrow would take, but Guy decided it was worth the risk to give him a fright. Taking a couple of steadying breaths, Guy pulled on the big bow and felt the tug on his shoulder muscles. Thank God it was James' bow and not Will's, let alone Piers or Thomas'! Even used to the longbows as he was from his secret practising, he would have struggled to pull those. Now he felt his finger brush his cheek finding his reference point, the arrow was centred on the target, and he loosed.

This first shot was merely to get the range, but it still shot past fitz John so close that the young sheriff near leapt out of his skin. He was about to swear at Guy when the gasps of amazement alerted him to the fact that something had happened, and he turned to the target. Far from seeing the arrow wedged in the ground several feet in front of the target as he expected, going by where he looked first, it was quivering at the top of the roundel of packed straw.

Before he could say anything else, Guy was already taking aim again, forcing fitz John to skitter out of the way. This time Guy's arrow went into the top of the red, and he put three more arrows around the band of painted red cloth. At this range he could have hit the central gold without any trouble now he had got his range, but he didn't want fitz John thinking he was too good with this alien weapon.

"Christ on the Cross!" someone said.

"They've gone almost through!" the lad who hurried forward to the target called as he examined the arrows. Certainly everyone could see how close the fletchings were to the target face.

"Bloody hell, Guy, I can see how they'd go through oak!" Sir Walter muttered beside him. "They'd skewer you like a bull on its horns at that rate!"

Guy turned to fitz John. "Do you see my lord? The knights wouldn't have stood a chance. Even from a greater range than I have here, they would still have been badly wounded. The only good thing I can offer you is that if these men had wanted ours dead, they could have done it with ease from a safe distance. It seems they wanted the money more, and your men put up enough of a fight that in the end the attackers did kill, but whoever they were, they weren't originally intent on murder or we'd have a cartload of corpses to bring back from Mansfield."

Fitz John's expression was flickering between a vague relief, and the petulant anger which was still seething inside him over the loss of the taxes.

"You think renegade Welsh mercenaries did this?" Sir Walter said from the side, and Guy blessed him silently for having been the one to place that idea in fitz John's mind.

"It would explain why they wanted the money so badly," Guy said innocently. "No lord to return to. No homes. They'll need money with winter coming on to buy them places to stay."

The young sheriff turned and glared at him. "Well they're not getting away with it! You're supposed to be a good tracker, so track them! Find me these men, Gisborne!"

Everyone scurried off to prepare for the hunt, but to Guy's amusement they were kept waiting by the sheriff. When he did appear it was in full armour.

"Dare I tell him that won't stop him getting skewered?" Guy wondered to Alan of Leek who was standing beside him.

Sir Alan gave him a sardonic smile. "Perhaps best not to. Leave him some illusions, for all our sakes, Guy, and if he does get fatally stuck like a hedgehog it won't be our fault either."

Guy caught a hint of desperate hope in the last bit from Sir Alan. He and Robert of Crockston bore the brunt of the young sheriff's foul moods, and it would hardly be surprising if Sir Alan wished the bane of his life dead.

"Best hope for hoards of marauding Welsh archers deserting the army, then," Guy replied with a cheerful wink.

"Oh, if only...!" was Sir Alan's wistful reply.

With Guy and the unfortunate Sir Girard in the lead, the avenging force tramped out of Nottingham Castle with twenty men-at-arms at Guy's heels, and then ten knights led by Sheriff fitz John riding in the rear. For two whole days Guy led them along stream beds, through coppices tight with hazel and alder wands and brambles, and through waist-high clumps of bracken under oaks. He truly was following the course his friends had taken, but he was making much of the task which he could have done in a third of the time with ease. Often he cast about and then 'found' a footprint, or snagged thread of clothing, which in truth he had spotted almost instantly, and all the time the delay between his party and those they were hunting lengthened. It was a dangerous game, and one which kept Guy on his toes. If even once one of the others spotted the sign before he did, then he would be in real trouble. His claim to fame rested on him being able to follow a trail no-one else could, but so did the chances of his friends escaping. If someone else took over the lead in the hunt they might well start to close the gap.

For the first day he kept them close to Mansfield, then as the light began to fade suggested camping where they were in order to pick up the trail the next day straight away. It was a good ruse, for fitz John immediately declared that he had no intention of sleeping outdoors when the hospitality of Newstead Abbey lay not a mile or two away. And of course the abbot pressed his illustrious guest to drink well of the abbey's wines, which meant a later start to the next day than Guy would have made. From there Guy led them westwards and over into Derbyshire, but not quite to Smithycote as the foot prints did, but close enough to the manor of Hugh de Ryddynges that that became the obvious place for fitz John to declare he would spend the second night.

There was an ulterior motive for that on Guy's part. He had wanted to see if the sheriff knew the area well enough to know where he was. It took a small prompting, but then of his own accord fitz John recognised the woods of the manor belonging to his friend, foolishly declaring to the other knights that he had hunted here in the past. That really made Guy's blood boil. So fitz John had been an active member of the hunt, had he? No wonder Ingram had been so confident on twisting the law to their advantage!

Therefore the next day he took the sheriff and the others as far as the Derwent to make them work even harder, then declared that he had lost the trail but that it looked as though the miscreants had crossed into Leicestershire, and were heading for Wales. However, as a result he had the secret, savage joy of forcing fitz John to camp out on a thoroughly miserable night of squally showers and high winds. With the sheriff in a truly foul temper, they then rode back to Nottingham, and for over a week everyone walked around fitz John as if on eggshells. Yet there was nothing he could do but pay up out of his own funds. It was either that or allow himself to look an utter fool to the chancellor, and fitz John would never do that.

For Guy there was some consolation in knowing that fitz John was feeling as massively angry as he did himself, although it did mean that he had to make sure he kept well away from the sheriff for fear of losing what little self-restraint he had left. His anger at Robin's folly was taking far longer to subside than he would ever had expected, and he was still inwardly seething two months later when Tuck managed to pay him a visit to tell him that the villagers were paid, and all of them were safe. The only excuse Guy could find to give Tuck was that he was cut to the quick by Robin's thoughtlessness, and by the way his cousin was so careless of the lives of the family he professed to love so much.

"And of your sacrifice," Tuck added sympathetically. "Don't worry, Guy, I'm not about to take you to task. Even though I can see the damage done during the crusade to Robin and can make allowances for him, I can also see how you must feel. You've bent over backwards to try and help him. And this last time you came to us thinking only to help the villagers, and to give him what you must have thought was something worthwhile to do, only to have him snatch it from your hand, so to speak, and run off with it.

"John knows it was you who saved his life that day, you know. He saw you. When they all caught up with Marianne and me with our lot and the money, Robin was in a right state, and no-one said a word to me about what had happened with John. It was a good couple of days later that Will told me that they heard that knight scream, turned and saw that he must have tried to get to John. Robin had gone mad at that point, and the others were hard pressed to stop him killing all of the knights. So Will said it was only later, when the others were hustling Robin off, that he passed Sir Henry and realised that the arrow which had taken him down had come from entirely the wrong direction to be one of them. He had a word with John when he could, and John told him. Now I think Siward, Hugh, Malik and Thomas also know, but no-one's telling Robin because they're worried how he'll react."

"Worried how *he'll* react?" snorted Guy. "Robin should be worried how I'll bloody react when I see him next!"

Tuck sighed. "I thought you might feel like that. Siward said to tell you, though, that they haven't said anything to Robin because it would be another thing where you were right all along. Siward said you'd understand that. By the way, he told me what he and Allan said to you too."

"It doesn't matter a rat's left swinging bollock whether *I* was right or not!" exploded Guy furiously. "I can't be behind him every moment of every day! If he wants to lead, then he needs to bloody well *think* about what he's leading men into! The next time, I might not even be involved when he decides to ambush some other wealthy man or whoever."

"And you're scared to death that after all you've done to try and protect John and Allan, Robin will get them killed because they care too much about him to refuse to go along with his schemes," Tuck suggested gently. Guy's face confirmed he had hit the spot without words. "Bless you for caring, Guy, but you should know that Robin – not knowing that you saved John – thinks that Sir Henry tripped and fell in his already wounded state, and drove in deeper an arrow which had already hit him, and that – and that *alone* – saved John. For which he's been grievously berating himself ever since. He can see what the consequences could have been, you know, and he's been going over and over what he *should* have done. He won't make the same mistake twice."

Guy's grim returning stare, though, made Tuck realise that if Robin ever did get John killed, it would be best if these two cousins never saw one another again. He had never known Guy be so unforgiving, and he belatedly berated himself for not seeing that the separation of the family years ago had cut Guy every bit as deeply as the other three. It was just so easy to forget that when, of all of them, Guy coped the best with the trials life threw at him. Allan's earlier folly had been hard on both Guy and John, but Allan had always had an even chance of growing up and seeing where he had gone wrong; and when Allan had fallen foul of the Templars, Tuck had personally seen how far Guy would go to save one of his family.

"And to make matter worse," Guy was saying bitterly, "there's now a price on your heads! Fitz John is determined to find the culprits, so he's offered a very tempting reward."

"How much?" Tuck asked, dreading the answer, yet when Guy told him the hairs on the back of his neck prickled.

"Freedom from rent for a year for the village which hands them over." Guy's expression was bleak. "It sounds a lot, doesn't it? But what most small villages pay in rent is nothing for the sheriff to find. It's probably less than most pay in taxes these days, that's for certain. It's the emotional lure which is so cunning, though. You ask ordinary people what they think of collecting great amounts of money as a reward, and the sensible ones will just laugh and say that they'll never see it. That it would go into the coffers of their lord, more likely. They know that the chance of them ever getting to spend even one gold coin is so remote as to be not worth thinking about. But a year's rent – that's something they really know about! So be warned!"

"I'll pass it on," Tuck assured him. "Luckily our friendly villages up in the Peaks have no need of such money thanks to you, and what you should know is that Codnor and Smithycote are places which will never betray us now, either. They're too aware of what would've happened without that money, and I'll make sure they know of how the sheriff was willing to let them be ruined while he had his sport with his friend the verderer."

"Where will you go for Christmas?" Guy wondered. During the festive season there were always more hunts going on in Sherwood – legal and illegal ones by the local nobility – and that increased the risk of the band being discovered living in the forest.

Tuck winced. He knew Guy was not going to like this either. "We're splitting up for a few weeks."

"*What?* Why in Heaven's name? Surely you're safer together?"

"Yes, but Algar and Walter both want to see their families. It's been a long time now, Guy, since either of them saw anyone. Walter wants to know if his old mother is even still alive, and Algar's been worried ever since the goings on in March, because his family are at Costock right on the Leicestershire border where Sir Henry did his scouring around for the sheriff. Algar's heard rumours that his brother-in-law got a crack on the head and hasn't worked since."

Guy rolled his eyes in despair. "How on earth would he hear such a thing? Costock's the other side of the Trent to the forest!"

"A travelling merchant."

Guy felt a shiver run down his spine. "And how did Algar come to be talking to a merchant?" Before Tuck could answer he had guessed. "Robin's led them in another raid, hasn't he?"

If Tuck had though Guy was angry before he was now glad beyond belief that he had come here alone, because Guy's expression would have frozen the sea.

"Why? What excuse did he have this time? I've heard of no other villages in extreme poverty? No more rents are due yet? Why, Tuck? Why? ...To feed his *arrogance?*" The bitterness in the last word shocked Tuck.

"No! Guy, we went up into Derbyshire after we left you, but to the north-east. We went to Loxley, exactly as we planned. But we couldn't stay there forever, and we had to leave to get more supplies of food. So we were just on the other side of the River Rother when we heard another hunt going on. Hugh thinks they came on the west side of the river so that they'd be away from Bolsover Castle. We saw them take five deer – or rather the best cuts from five deer! Remembering what you'd said, Hugh told Robin we should get rid of the rest of the deer as fast as possible, and hope that winter rains and snow would wash the blood away. So we butchered what was left, bundled it up as best we could, and took it to the villages round about. We just left parcels of meat in the village at night, and buried those bones which would give the game away as to what beast they'd come from in several scattered holes."

"I'm glad to hear it." Guy's fury seemed to have eased just a touch. "But how does this lead to thieving off travellers?"

"Because we could see that there was still a good chance that someone might report the deer killed. Someone who wanted to keep in with the foresters or verderers, for instance. That would mean a similar fine for the four nearest villages to that hunt too. So Robin went in with Will and John and spoke to the headmen and left them more of the money we took. But then Robin got to wondering how often this happens, and how many more times we might have to help several villages out in one go, and he said we'd need more money in that case. Well with the Christmas markets coming up, he suggested that this would be the best time to relieve some merchants of their money."

Guy groaned. "Well you wouldn't get much *before* the markets! That was pretty pointless!"

However Tuck was shaking his head. "*Duw*, no, we didn't actually rob this merchant! We just stopped him to find out how many would be going to the York market, see? And that was when he told us about Costock."

Guy rolled his eyes in disbelief. "You mean Algar was foolish enough to ask straight out about his own bloody village? Did he not think that the merchant might report that the moment they left him?"

But Tuck was shaking his head even more vigorously. "No, Guy! The merchant told us that Sir Henry had gone like some dragon of old through the villages along the River Soar back in March. Remember? ...Back when you came north and we found Much, and Robin helped the Jews from York? ...It was when Sir Henry realised he would have to turn back for Nottingham empty-handed that his temper got really foul. Rempstone, Costock and Wysall all had men who got a beating from him. Most just suffered awful bruises, but anyone who tried to fight back got worse. We only know it was Algar's brother-in-law because he's the smith at Costock, and the merchant said he came out of his forge with his hammer in his hand just wondering what the commotion was about, and Sir Henry took it he was going to attack him. Our merchant said he got into Costock on this journey just as the men were preparing to go to the Hundred Court to complain again – that's why it was topical to him after all this time."

Guy forced himself to calm down. At least it was a reasonable answer, and not due to a wild, thoughtless moment on behalf of Robin. "So who's going where?"

Tuck too breathed a little more easily. Thank *Dewi Sant* Guy could control himself! But they really must start bearing in mind what it cost Guy to live in the castle under such a dreadful sheriff. He was only human and could take only so much. It might be better for him not to know some things for the sake of his sanity.

"Oh Thomas, Piers and Bilan are going to go with Walter to Fiskerton. Much said he'd go with Algar. I don't think he's forgotten that Algar was with him in prison in the castle. It gives them a special bond. Because of that Allan and Roger said they'd go too." He did not add that Allan seemed to need a break away from John, who had found it difficult to stop acting like Allan's surrogate father instead of his cousin. "Robin and all the others are going up to Loxley, and Marianne and I are going over to Gisborne. I would dearly like to see how Maelgwn is getting on!"

That made Guy smile at last. The blind, Welsh former-prince, whom he and Tuck had rescued from the clutches of sheriff de Braose, was someone Guy thought a lot of too. "Tell Maelgwn and Ianto I'm thinking of them. Bloody fitz John won't honour my leave to go to my manor to check on it, so I don't think I'll get there any time soon myself. Please bring me word they're all right."

"Gladly!" Tuck agreed, but also thinking that he had been remiss not to ask about Gisborne before. Guy must have been fretting about that too, and for some time. An old kennelman getting on in years and surely with not long to live, and a blind fugitive, were all that was holding Guy's simple manor together, and if either of their health failed who knew what disasters might have befallen the place without Guy knowing? And of course Guy's beloved dogs were there too. Thanks to fitz John, Guy could no longer have Fletch and Spike with him, but it didn't mean that he wasn't thinking about them. "And I'll report back on Fletch and Spike too!"

The way Guy's face lit up was confirmation enough that Tuck had guessed right.

"Make sure they have a big bone apiece for Christmas Day," Guy said with a grin. "Although I bet they're already too fat with no-one to work them!"

Tuck managed to grin back. "Oh I wouldn't be too sure of that! Young Elyas was learning fast how to set them to catch hares when I last saw him, and he was proving a quick learner with all that Maelgwn could teach him."

The reminder of the young lad who had stayed at Gisborne with his two friends brightened Guy further. "Yes, Elyas was always fond of the dogs. Thank you, Tuck. You've set my mind at rest already."

His mind would have been far less easy over that Christmas had he known of what was to come!

Was I always so angry at Robin? Ah, Gervase, that is hard to answer. And if truth be told, it came and went. The problem between us was always that I saw the broad spread and Robin went for the target like an arrow, never seeing the things going on to the side. It meant that at times

he acted when I was so bound up in trying to cope with all the side issues that I could hardly move. Times when I will confess that he was right to act decisively. But there were other times when more thought, if not necessarily caution, would have saved much grief afterwards. What you do not hear of in the stories, Brother, are the consequences to others of having a legend storm through their lives! And not all of it was good.

Chapter 7

So, dear Brother, we come to the incident which would seal Robin Hood's fate to become an outlaw. Ah yes, you have been longing for this! And I will not detain you except to remind you that, up until now, I have been very careful to not call the band of men who followed him ~outlaws~ except in the most general sense. For they were not beyond the law as yet, being merely men who had been forced to take to living rough through adverse circumstances. None of them had come to the attention of the sheriff as part of a lawless band of men as yet, and even the robbing of the taxes from Mansfield had been attributed to Welsh mercenaries you recall, and not to Robin Hood's men. Now that was to change!

Nottinghamshire,
January, the Year of Our Lord 1191

The first indication Guy had that something had gone wrong was when he was riding back into the castle, and saw Allan in the crowd making surreptitious but urgent signals to him. As fast as he could, Guy stabled the horse then made for the gates.

"Who's the lucky maid, then?" crowed Sir Henry, seeing him go.

Guy cursed under his breath that the knight had survived his injuries, but as yet was still unwell enough to have any duties, leaving him time to prowl about the inner and outer baileys spying on everyone.

"No maid, Henry. Just going to fetch my new braes. The ones I have are worn so thin my balls are freezing in this weather, even with these thick trews."

That shut him up, thank God. Nothing like something so mundane as underwear to dull curiosity. And Guy really did have new braes waiting in the town, but they might not get collected until later.

At the castle's brew-house, referred to locally as *The Trip to Jerusalem*, Guy bought a couple of pints of the heavier ale, warmed them up with a hot poker plunged into them, and then took them to just outside the door. Allan slid out of the already growing shadows of the late afternoon and gratefully cupped his hands around the rough pottery mug. He must have been waiting some time, for Guy could hear his teeth chattering with the cold.

"Aaah, God bless you, Guy!" Allan sighed gratefully after taking a good draft of the warm brew.

"Come this way," Guy told him softly, and drew him around the corner of the front of the brew-house to where it butted up to, and tunnelled back into, the cliff on which the castle sat. A slight overhang of the cliff above provided even more shelter from the wind, and if it wasn't warm it was still a good deal more pleasant for standing around in. It also meant that they were more private than if they had gone inside the brew-house, where beside the brewery itself, small rooms had been hewn out of the soft rock, and where off-duty soldiers from the castle came to get something stronger than the regular issue of small beer provided inside the castle. "Now, what's gone wrong? You look worried stiff."

Allan came and pressed close to his cousin so that he was practically whispering in Guy's ear. "By Christ and St Thomas, Guy, I hardly know where to begin. Since Christmas it's all been such a bloody mess. You know that Walter went back to Fiskerton and the Coshams went with him? Yes? ...Ah well, then I can tell you that hardly had they got there then Walter went marching into the village as if he'd not a care in the world, leaving the three brothers stuck outside. That didn't go down very well I can tell you!"

"I bet it didn't!" Guy sympathised. "Walter warming his bum by the family hearth and them stuck out in the cold! I presume that's what Walter did do?"

Allan pulled a face. "Oh yes! It turned out that Walter's mother is well and thriving, despite her advanced age – which is rather more than his brother is doing! He's got some kind of lump which is getting bigger and seems to be killing him slowly. Tuck and Marianne seem to think he won't be long for this world once they were told of it. Well the family were panicking over what would happen when the fields need ploughing again in a month or two's time, depending on the weather, of course. I managed to get Bilan on one side after the brothers got back. He was the most clear of them about Walter, because even Thomas is spitting nails for once. But Bilan told me that Walter came back out to them with some food – not much, though! Not enough! And Walter told them he wouldn't be coming back to the forest with them."

Guy's jaw dropped. "Not coming back? What was the fool thinking?"

"Oh apparently, he and his brother are very alike. So his mother decided on the spot that when the brother dies they'll tell the village priest that *he's* Walter, who crawled back to the family to die."

"Is the priest a bit blind, or daft?" Guy wondered acidly. "Surely he knows the people he lives amongst enough to know that Walter's brother has been on death's door for some time? Won't he wonder how suddenly he's hale and hearty enough to work a plough?"

Allan shrugged. "God alone knows, Guy. Maybe he's just one of those poor priests who's more villager than anything else and barely literate. I don't know. But Walter's family are sure they can pull the wool over enough eyes for the ruse to work." He grimaced. "And I think for Walter, half ...no, more than half the attraction for staying," and he rolled his eyes despairingly, "is the soon-to-be-widow."

"Aaah!" Guy sighed pointedly.

Allan nodded. "It seems that there had always been more than a little competition for her hand between Walter and his older brother. And somewhat worse, the bloody woman has decided she picked the wrong brother in the first place, and now has the chance to have Walter. Thomas was incensed that she's already been free with her favours with Walter before her poor husband's even in his grave."

"Shit! What a mess!" Guy fumed. "And he damned-well knows where the stashed silver is, and what went on at High Peak! He could betray everyone – me included!"

"I know," Allan sympathised, "and I hate to say it, but my news gets worse."

"He hasn't betrayed us already?" Guy gasped in horror.

"Lord, no! ...No, for what it's worth, Walter's so besotted with the woman I don't think he'll think of doing such a thing unless the sheriff puts such an idea into his head, and actually threatens Fiskerton specifically. Small consolation, I know, but better than it could be. ...No the next bad news actually starts with the Coshams. You see they were camped outside Fiskerton, not sure whether they should try to get up to Loxley, or wait and see if Walter came to his senses. While they were there these four men came creeping out of the night. Four archers on the run! Two of them Welsh! They told Thomas and Piers that someone had been to the villages thereabouts proclaiming a reward for information about renegade Welsh archers who'd robbed the sheriff. They were bloody terrified, as well they might be!"

"Oh shit!" Guy swore. His ruse had never been meant to endanger others. Indeed he had thought he was safe making such an inference, because the likelihood of there being Welsh archers in Nottinghamshire should have been beyond remote.

"Not your fault, Guy," Allan commiserated. "James is kicking himself too for having dropped that bow in the first place. What some of us are less happy about is that Thomas and Piers – feeling that we were responsible, and that the gang would be a man down with Walter going – invited them to join with us."

"No!" gasped Guy, appalled. Had they not learned that lesson after taking on random strangers last year?

"I'm afraid so," Allan sighed, knowing what Guy was thinking, "but you see, they thought this was different because all four men are experienced soldiers. To them this was very different to Robin sweeping up those two lads who knew no better."

Now he put a hand up onto Guy's shoulder and looked earnestly up into his cousin's face. "But I had to warn *you*! I didn't want you to come looking for us, not knowing that strangers were amongst us. Piers trusts all four implicitly, and I think Thomas trusts the two Welshmen although he's more cautious of the other two.

"It hasn't been helped by Tuck saying to many of us, if not to Robin himself, that we had to learn to stand on our own feet without coming to you at every turn. I think he feels we've leaned on you too much in the last year or so. And even Will and John think we have to be able to bring new men in at some point, although whether these four are the right ones, they're not sure of yet. Hugh, Siward and Malik are as worried as I am, especially with regard to you."

"Thank you for that," and Guy meant it. "And Robin? Marianne? What about them?"

"Marianne will follow Robin's lead, and he's welcomed them. He looks on them as recruits in much the same way that he and the others got together in the siege of Jerusalem. Men who have been brought together in adversity. As far as he's concerned, they've been forced out of whatever homes they might have, just as we were. He says they have as much right to want to fight back against the injustice of the way England's being ruled."

Guy was appalled. "Fight? What in heaven's name is Robin planning?"

"I don't know for sure, and to be honest I don't think that's the most pressing problem, because with the worst of the winter weather due in the next months, it'll be a while before anything happens. I just wanted you to know that these men are with us up at Loxley, just in case you did get a chance to head for Gisborne and came our way."

Happily Tuck had already met Guy just after Christmas and reported that everything was well at Gisborne, so Guy knew that Allan was telling him just in case Sheriff fitz John suddenly announced that Guy could visit his manor after all, and Guy then thought to take his time over the journey, knowing there was nothing to do once he reached Gisborne besides visit his friends.

"But there's something else," Allan now said, and his expression became even more worried. "I've not said too much to Robin about this – in part because of the newcomers – but I had a talk with Hugh and Siward and we agreed you need to know this."

"I'm not going to like this, am I?" Guy sighed.

Shaking his head, Allan took a deep breath to brace himself. "You know, as well, that Much, Roger and I went with Algar to Costock? …Right. Well we fared a bit better than the Coshams did. At least we got a space to bed down in the warmth of one of the barns, and on that rich soil they had a good harvest of straw and hay put up for the beasts, so we were comfortable enough."

"And Algar's family?"

"As bad as we'd heard. His poor brother-in-law has gone from a brawny village smith to the village idiot, wandering about with blank eyes, dribbling."

"God rot Henry! The bastard has always been too heavy-handed!"

"Aye, I won't argue with you on that, but…"

"But?"

"There's something wrong with Algar."

Guy felt his blood run cold. He had always had his doubts over whether Walter and Algar would withstand the trials of living rough, but Allan's tone suggested more than that. "What sort of 'wrong'?"

Allan pushed his hood back and scrubbed his hair vigorously as if to shake the words loose, then pulled the hood back up saying, "I think there's something going on in Costock. Don't ask me how this has happened, Guy, because I can't give you answers, but there seem to have been hints – I won't even call them as much as rumours – that someone is helping the villagers in the forest." He took another long draft of his ale as Guy groaned and clapped his hand to his eyes in despair. "I know. I've no idea how word has spread so fast, but it has. And I don't think it's the folk up in High Peak who've said anything."

Now Allan braced himself. This was going to be tough, because if he was to warn Guy he was going to have to betray Robin. "We did as we said after the fight by Mansfield. As soon as we could pause, Tuck and Marianne counted out what was needed to go to the villages. Marianne and Much took the money to Codnor and Smithycote, while Tuck went to Ripley and Pentrich with Roger and me lurking in the background. So what I'm telling you now is just what I've worked out." He grasped Guy's arm urgently. "You can't go and challenge Robin on this, Guy! I have no proof! I didn't actually see this happening, alright?"

Guy could feel his anger rising, but also felt deeply sorry for Allan for having been put in such a wretched position as to have to choose between two of his remaining small family. Pulling Allan to him in a hug, Guy said,

"No, for your sake I won't. However much I might want to strangle Robin when I've heard this – and I suspect I will! – I won't make trouble for you."

"Thank you! Well I got back to the meeting place with Tuck and Roger, having picked up Marianne and Much along the way. And then this is what makes me suspicious, Guy. Robin had left Hugh, Thomas, Malik and Siward at the arranged spot near Crich. What he'd told them was that he wanted some good fighters to wait for us, just in case we were running for our lives, and he'd left Malik and Thomas in particular because as the best archers they could well prove vital to our escape. He told these four on the quiet that he'd chosen them because they were the steadiest of the men.

"Well you can see how that would ring true to us at the time can't you? You yourself would have made a very similar choice, I'm thinking. Especially if you didn't want to have the whole gang lurking around and being too easy to spot. So we got back to Loxley and thought nothing more of it. Only when we came on that hunt around Barlow and Holme, and Robin said we'd need to get more money, did I start to wonder."

"Where had all that new money gone?" Guy supplied for him.

"Yes! ...By Our Lady, Guy! I knew how much there had to be coming out of Mansfield just by the weight of it! But the rub is, men like Gilbert and Piers were never taught to count large numbers as your mother taught us. And of course, when we divided up the money after Mansfield, it was Marianne and Tuck, and then John, Robin and me doing it at speed. I don't think the others really grasped the numbers at all, so it didn't seem so odd to even Siward and Hugh."

Allan's expression became deeply distressed. "But now I'm thinking about Robin, and the way he looked when we left with that money. And I'm remembering what I heard Tuck saying to you in the forest about Robin needing to be wanted, and all that stuff."

"You think he went and distributed it to some other villages, don't you," Guy sighed bitterly.

"It's the only way it makes any sense. I know he didn't give it *all* away, because some of those sacks of coin went up to the hideout to join the rest of our reserve. But thinking about it later, I've realised that Robin just took Will, Gilbert and James with Piers that time. Those of us who might have wondered about the weight never got to feel those sacks. And he did it very quickly after we got to Loxley, making the excuse that those of us who'd done more of a loop were more tired and so needed the rest. And we were, in truth. We'd done that run through the night in the forest after meeting you, so we didn't really stop for long in three whole days, and we'd had no sleep."

"Ah! But Robin and the others from the East have got used to having several nights without sleep and cope better?" It had been cleverly done, Guy thought bitterly. Move the coins while those who might question were too weary to even think straight. And Robin had clearly noticed who had sided with Guy in conversations of late, too. That was something else Guy didn't like, but that would have to wait until he could work it out in his own mind. "So where do you think Robin went?"

"I think he took a big chance," Allan replied. "I've thought about it a lot. And I've dropped the odd question in when I dared to people like Bilan and James. I found Bilan carefully colouring the feathers on some arrows and sat down to watch him. When I asked what he was doing it for, he told me very proudly that these were Robin's special arrows. 'Special arrows?' says I, 'What for?' He told me in all innocence, 'For special deliveries!' Then he looked all guilty, so I gave him a wink and said, 'ah! *Those* deliveries!' as if I knew already. It satisfied him, because I think he thought Robin had said something to me, if not the whole of what had happened. But after a bit more digging, I think I'm right in saying that they tied some coins into a bit of cloth, bound it to a special arrow, and then Robin shot that arrow into the villages."

Guy was thinking furiously. "And I bet it was done in daylight. Done when there were people about."

"I think so," Allan agreed. "It's my belief he wanted to see their faces. I don't think they went into the villages. I don't think he was that careless, Guy. But I do think Robin was close enough to see the reactions of the villagers to this gift from out of the blue. And when Roger and I had a look around the camp on the sly, he found some old dye, so I think Robin already had arrows which would be noted for their bright fletchings."

"Roger?" Guy was surprised, and that at least made Allan smile again.

"He's really taken to you. I think it's because he sees you as very stern but fair. He admires Robin, but he's also more than a bit frightened by him. Not of him as a man, particularly, but of the way he courts danger. Roger's actually said to me that if he prays for anything it's that you'll be around if something goes wrong – and Roger's not the praying sort most of the time. So he's very much with me on this one. In fact he's keeping an eye on Algar at Costock while I'm here."

"Algar's at Costock *again?*"

"Yes. But to finish my other bit first: my guess is that Robin took a big chance after we left him. I think he doubled back along our tracks towards Mansfield, but went by Skegby, Teversal and Newbound, and then crossed into Derbyshire to get to somewhere like Rowthorn or Stony Houghton. I think he moved fast and hard, because when we got back I now realise that Algar and Walter were even more exhausted than we were. In fact, I wouldn't be surprised if Robin hadn't sent them off to Loxley with someone like Bilan and James before the end, while he and the others crossed back into Nottinghamshire and made a gift to Worksop, at least. I've thought hard about this, Guy. One of those places *had* to be somewhere with a good sized market for the word to have spread as fast as it has."

Guy was nodding thoughtfully. "I can't fault your reasoning. Yes, somewhere like Worksop getting an unexpected gift would ensure that word was spread. And God rot him, Robin wanted this, didn't he? This fame!"

"I don't know about fame, but the gratitude, yes! You see at Fiskerton they'd heard of this, and Robin's face was a picture when the Coshams told him of what they'd heard when they got back at New Year. And that very evening I found him on his knees in prayer, thanking God for the chance to do such good."

"He meant it?" If anything that frightened Guy more. Robin being an arrogant fool was bad enough, but this had the touch of a man on his own crusade. And who knew what he might do if he thought the hand of God was on his shoulder?

"Yes. ...Yes he did! But that's not the truly awful bit, and I have to go back a bit again to tell you this. You see before Christmas, Algar had already asked Robin when Costock and the other villages south of the Trent could expect their share – as if it was something which could be taken for granted as happening. But Robin was shocked. He asked Algar if he'd not understood that the money which had been taken from the villages at those courts at Edwinstowe, Mansfield, Linby and Calverton weren't just the normal rents due at Michaelmas? That this was an extra burden which the villages and hamlets within the forest bore *on top of* the regular taxes and rents villages like Costock pay? Then he told Algar that because of this, those living under forest law had to be helped first."

"Oh God," groaned Guy. "Algar didn't understand, did he?"

Allan shook his head. "No, sadly I don't think he did. At heart Algar's a simple man. Taxes are taxes. He doesn't even begin to understand how they're portioned out. And he's an angry man, too. Having been wrongly imprisoned, I think he saw Robin and his quest for justice as the means of exacting his own revenge on the sheriff. He was cock-a-hoop at first after that raid, Guy! Robin was his absolute hero for taking on the sheriff's knights."

"And then, in his eyes at least, his hero turns round and spits in his eye," Guy surmised.

"Pretty much. But I still think he would have forgiven Robin refusing the money if he'd then done something like break into the town gaol at Nottingham and released the prisoners, *and* if the taking of the money had been a single event. Or if Robin had just handed out the meat to those villages after the hunt, I think Algar would have been fine with that too. He would have accepted it. But the knowledge that Robin was intent on getting more money to help others...!" He didn't need to say more on how that had been taken.

"And this is where it all started to go wrong. It was around then that Walter started asking to go to Fiskerton. He's not been happy for some time, and in truth he's older than everyone else and I think he finds the life hard. But it meant that when Algar also asked to see his home as well we all just thought that, as the two who'd never really settled to the life, it was normal."

"Hence Tuck's attitude when he came to tell me they were going for Christmas," Guy said as understanding came. Knowing the background now it made more sense of why Robin had let them go.

"And with Walter electing to stay in his home, it was less surprising when Algar asked to go back in January after the Feast of St Hilary to see if everyone was all right at Costock after the reeve had been round. But he's asked to come back to the village *again* now, and there's no good reason for why. Robin thinks he might not come back, so he just asked for two of us to go with him, and I volunteered Roger and myself, which went unquestioned since we came the last two times. I think Robin is expecting just us two to go back, but I fear that Algar has something very different in mind."

Suddenly it was clear to Guy. "Oh Christ Our Lord, save us! It's the bloody reward, isn't it?" To a man like Algar a whole year's rent being paid for his village would seem a simple choice. Possibly even a fair choice, for if other villages were being paid back their taxes, why shouldn't his gain some benefit too? "How? ...Will he stay this time, do you think, and then send someone from Costock with the information to Nottingham? Or will he go back with you and wait until Robin plans another raid, and then beat a hasty path to the sheriff's door?"

Allan's expression was pained. "Truly, I don't know. I desperately want to think that Algar won't deliberately betray us. I think he's more aggrieved than anything, but even at my worst I wasn't as innocent of the world as he is, so who am I to tell? He could do either, and the worst of it is that I can't tell you for an absolute certainty what to watch out for. All I knew was that I needed to tell you. Because if Algar walks into the castle and comes before the sheriff, I knew you had to know that he might be there of his own accord. I've been losing sleep at the thought of you risking your neck to try and rescue Algar a second time, only to find him turning round and pointing the finger at you in betrayal too."

"God preserve us from that!" Guy said from the heart, but also hugged Allan tightly again. It mattered more than he would have believed that Allan cared enough to come and warn him, for to come here was not without its risks for Allan himself. And Robin might not be as understanding of Allan's loyalty either. "Thank you! And Roger! Thank him for me too, will you? What will you do now? I think you have to warn at least some of the others, perhaps more so if Algar returns than if he stays."

"Siward, Thomas and Hugh were the first three I was going to speak to, and then maybe Tuck – but when he's on his own, not with Marianne! She's becoming ever closer to Robin."

"Then maybe Malik too. He's a thoughtful man. But not Will or Gilbert – they're too hot-headed!"

"No, they'd be likely to kill Algar! And as I said to you, I have no absolute proof of this to confront Algar with, only my suspicions."

"But they're pretty bloody convincing suspicions!" Guy responded, "And they're ones I now share. Be careful, Allan! Now let me get you a hot pie from inside before you leave."

In fact he bought three – one for Allan now to sustain him on his hurried journey back to the outskirts of Cosham, and one each for Allan and Roger for later. It was the least he could do, and he wished he could reward their kindness even more, but they and he were constrained by their circumstances. He escorted his cousin down through the town to make sure that he at least got onto the southern road in safety, then went to the house of the woman who did small needlework jobs and collected his new braes.

It was a good thing he made sure his excuse to leave the castle stood up to scrutiny. No sooner had he got back to the inner bailey than Sir Henry was there challenging him again, and this time in the company of several others including the sheriff, who had clearly been out for a ride.

"Paying your seamstress in kind, were you?" brayed the dreadful Henry. "Rather a long time to be just fetching a parcel!"

"You would cuckold Master *Brimfield*?" Guy riposted, knowing that everyone knew the massive baker and his short temper. "My God, you are brave, Sir Henry!" and earned guffaws of laughter from the group. Also, Mistress Brimfield was as big as her husband, even if she did perfect stitching, and was definitely not a woman to lust after! The laughter alerted the sheriff that something was amiss, and whatever Henry had said about provoking Guy wasn't about to happen after all.

Trying to save face, Henry demanded. "What would a man like you want with such garments? Going soft, are you, *Sir* Guy?"

Refusing to rise to the childish baiting, Guy in turn asked calmly, "And where would you get your braes from then, Henry?" knowing that the knight would notice the lack of title, even if no-one else bothered.

"Why, off Master Harby in the market!" snorted Henry superciliously. "Who would pay more for something no-one sees?"

Henry was notoriously vain about his outer garments, whereas Guy cared little for his appearance except when out on official business. However, Master Harby sold very cheap linens, all rough and unforgiving on the skin, and Guy wouldn't have touched them even at half the price. But it gave him his rejoinder.

"By Our Lady, Sir Henry, no wonder you aren't a ladies' man! Not only do you not exchange pleasantries with them, if you wear those braes your family jewels must be so chaffed as to have no feeling left in them at all!"

Those in the courtyard exploded into hoots of laughter, every one of them knowing that Henry was the most miserable misogynist, and had more than once been accused of attempted rape by those women of quality he thought to force himself on. Leaving Henry and the sheriff looking as though they were sucking lemons, Guy quit while he was ahead and hurried to his room. Fitz John desperately wanted to find some way to punish Guy for any misdemeanour he could make fit, but had yet to find one, and there was no doubt that Henry would help him if he could. Thank St Issui today wasn't that day, though. Allan's news was quite enough misery for a man to cope with in one go.

Flopping onto his simple box bed and blessing the fact that those he shared his room with were not there, Guy thought long and hard over what Allan had told him. With enemies already within the castle, he would have to be very careful should Algar appear. However, he must not make himself too scarce either, just in case Algar should accuse him when he was not there to witness it. It would not do to look as if he had run away in fear. Standing somewhere nonchalantly at the back would be best. However his logical side said that Algar would not come himself – not having been imprisoned once by a sheriff, even if it was the previous one.

For the next week or so Guy was alert to every newcomer at the castle, but with the arrival of Lent at the end of February, and then March arriving with nothing having happened, he came to hope that Allan's fears had been unfounded. Or at least that Algar had gone back to the camp with Allan and Roger, had been confronted and had an almighty row with Robin, and then had realised the error of his ways. Even a beating off Will might be seen as a preferable outcome in a way.

Then to his horror he was walking back into the inner bailey one sunny late March day only to be hailed by Alan of Leek.

"Guy! Hurry! Get ready! The sheriff is riding out immediately!"

"Why? What's happened?" Guy asked, breaking into a run to meet with the assistant constable of the castle.

"The offer of the reward worked!"

Guy felt his heart sink into his boots. "It did?"

Sir Alan nodded, although Guy noted it was with little enthusiasm. "I fear the folk of Costock may rue the day they thought it a good idea to claim this reward."

"Oh God!" The words escaped Guy's lips before he could stop them. Luckily Sir Alan was aware that Guy was no more enamoured of the sheriff than he was, and took it as an understanding of how badly things could now go wrong.

"Oh God, indeed. Whether they really know anything or not, fitz John now thinks that they must have colluded with these felons in order for them to know anything at all, so they'll be punished no matter what they say."

Guy gritted his teeth to stop himself from saying anything more foolish, nodded sympathetically to Sir Alan, and hurried off to don his gambeson and grab his sword. He hardly thought it was a matter for wearing ring-mail. Not to deal with a bunch of poorly armed peasants, for pity's sake. Yet he was sent back for the chain-mail shirt and coif, as well as the gauntlets, and that made him feel even more wretched, for nothing else said so clearly that fitz John was going to be brutal with these folk.

They rode out in a long file, with the men-at-arms marching in front of them. Quite why foresters like Guy were involved he could not fathom in his distress, until he realised that it was too early in the year for the visiting knights who came to do their service to the sheriff to be around to make up the numbers. Warfare was hardly ever waged in winter because of the difficulty of maintaining supplies to the troops, and of moving about the country when roads could become waterlogged or icy. And although there hadn't been anything which might be called a war waged on English soil since the Anarchy of King Stephen's reign, the duty of service to each shire's sheriff followed the pattern as if war was imminent. Therefore, although the castle had begun preparing for the influx of knights and their men, most would not appear until Easter, which this year was nearly three weeks away in the middle of April. And that prompted the thought that maybe fitz John was quite happy about that, because if he did overstep his authority with the villagers, there would be no outsiders to witness it.

They reached Costock as the early spring twilight fell. Fitz John rode into the centre of the simple cluster of houses which lacked even the smallest of churches, and sat there like a malevolent statue until all the men had gathered about him. As this happened the first villagers came to peer nervously out of cottage doors and barns, then gradually clustered together as far away from fitz John as possible.

The sheriff puffed himself up to his full height on his horse, cleared his throat and began to address them. "Your man... What was his name Sir Alan?"

"Robert, I believe, sheriff."

"Your man Robert came to Nottingham to tell me that you have information about the thieves who stole the taxes from Mansfield."

The villagers looked to one another with rising panic.

"He did not provide me with satisfactory answers," fitz John declared. "He will not be returning."

A shriek of grief went up from the back of the crowd. Robert's soon-to-be-widow, Guy guessed, and his heart sank that bit further. He had not known that fitz John had got his hands on one of them already.

A man who, at a guess, would be the headman of the village, took a nervous step forward. "He told you all we know, my lord. They're up in the north of the shire. At Loxley! They've been handing out money to all sorts of villages!"

"And you're a damned liar!" fitz John snapped. "Loxley? *Loxley*? There's no such place! It doesn't exist, do you understand that, you dolt? It isn't even in any of our old records."

Guy could have laughed with relief if the situation had not been so grave. Ever the overly proud one, fitz John had not thought to ask any of the older local men at the castle, who could have told him that Loxley – or what remained of Loxley after the first King William's harrowing of the north – was just over the border in South Yorkshire. Well let him think Loxley was a fable for as long as possible, since it wasn't in the Nottingham records.

Now fitz John's voice became sarcastically patronising. "We ...write ...things ...down. Yes, we do! And do you know why?" He then exploded into screaming anger. "It's so that we know when thieving *bastards* like you try to hoodwink us!" Spittle flew from his mouth, his face puce with anger – a red, frothing moon encased in chain-mail and terrifying to behold. A very Norman devil in the flesh and one who might yet kill them!

The villagers began to back away, but too late realised that they had been encircled by the men-at-arms. As they began milling in terror, fitz John sat back, icy calm once more.

"So I shall ask again. How do you know all of this?"

No-one answered.

"Very well. Kill ...oh, her there, she'll do."

Guy saw the men-at-arms falter. Clearly they hadn't expected anything this bad, and most were decent enough men that they would balk at killing a woman in cold blood. However, Sir Henry was still smarting from the indignity of being bested by a bunch of peasants, as he saw them, and he had no reservations. He didn't even bother dismounting, but drew his sword, rode at the terrified woman and slit her throat as he passed, nearly taking her head off in the process. There was a heartbeat of stunned silence, then the screaming began.

"I shall count to ten, and if no-one has told me, another of you will die," fitz John said with as much detachment as a farmer deciding which bullock to send to market.

He began counting in bored tones as the panic rose, then as he reached 'nine' a woman ran from the crowd shrieking, "It was him! Him! He came to his family telling us we could claim the reward!" And she pointed straight at Algar.

Sweet Jesu, Brother, I shall not forget that moment as long as I live. Algar looked about him like a cornered fox. I knew then in that instant that he had never anticipated that his simple plan would go so wrong. It was as my cousin Allan had said. Algar was an innocent in the ways of the world at large. It had never occurred to him that the sheriff would want to know how the villagers would know such a thing. Nor that it might not be as easy as just telling the sheriff where Robin and the others were hidden, and then returning home with the money. Algar had not intended to actually betray Robin by leading men to the hideaway. His anger did not run so deep. And to this day I still wonder whether I figured in his plan. If he thought that, as I was in the castle, I would hear of the sheriff heading for the north and would warn Robin in advance so that they would be taken. Yet at that point I dared not show my face.

You think me cowardly, Gervase? Oh, if I had been like my cousin I would have rescued Algar, would I? What nonsense! I was one man amongst over three dozen from the castle. What in Heaven's name could I have hoped to do? Especially as nigh on a dozen of those men were knights, mounted and armed as I was. Nor was I oblivious to what would happen next. Fitz John would have his blood at the expense of the village, that went without saying, but Algar would be taken for questioning back at the castle. This I knew beyond doubt. That alone posed a terrible risk for me, but if I showed my loyalties in Costock by trying to rescue Algar, I too would go back to the castle for questioning, and under torture who knew what I might reveal?

Torture? Yes, Brother. Oh, you did not think it would be used outside of war or the most treasonable crimes? Now you are being the innocent! And if you truly believed such a thing, then I am not mocking you but merely telling you the truth of the matter. Yes, I knew even then, as we sat on our horses before the terrified villagers of Costock, that the castle torturer would have work to do, and he was an evil brute of a man who had arrived in the wake of fitz John, for under Robert Murdac we had had no need of such a man.

So before you accuse me of cowardice at the prospect of torture, remember that even the bravest man can crack under such pressure. And would you have wanted me to betray Robin Hood to the sheriff? No, I thought not, for even the evil Sir Guy of Gisborne, as you have no doubt thought of me for all these years, did not sink so low.

So how did I escape? Bless me, Brother, you stop me to ask these questions, then hasten me to tell all! Bear with me, I am coming to it!

Chapter 8

Will you accept without more questions that I kept my mail coif pulled well down on my forehead, and my horse to the back of the group? Good! It was not so hard to do, for my fellow forester knights, Payne, Osmaer, Giles and Simon were also doing their best to stand back from this dire mess. Walkelin and Fredegis from amongst the Derwent-to-Erewash forest knights were as eager to be involved as Sir Henry, but so too were Sirs Mahel and Hamon from the Le Clay foresters, and we willingly ceded the right to them. It was shameful the way those big men enjoyed battering helpless villagers with the flats of their blades. We had not yet reached a point where men like that would risk actually killing a whole village, and what probably saved the people of Costock was the fact that everyone knew that three different lords had holdings there. One, had he been susceptible to fitz John's money, might have been bribed to look the other way, but out of three, one was always likely to complain to a higher authority. And that authority could well be the dreaded Longchamp – so you see, Brother, even he had his uses at times.

Therefore the miserable folk of Costock took a beating which would be remembered for generations to come, but only the headman and Algar were taken prisoner. To add to their grief, we remained in the village overnight, fitz John stripping their supplies of food far more than was necessary for one night, and I am sure that many of the women took their daughters and fled into the fields rather than risk staying with so many soldiers. Our men-at-arms would not commit murder, but they were not the most gentile of men, and taking a girl by force whilst enforcing the law was seen by many of them as one of the perquisites of their job.

I can confess to you in truth that I did some good that night, for amongst the men-at-arms were six of my old friends from High Peak, including Big Ulf and Ruald – both big, older men who were listened to. With them I went amongst the ordinary soldiers and pointed out to them that the sheriff was skating on very thin ice here as far as the law was concerned.

˜We may yet hear more of this if one of the lords of this village chooses to press charges through the Hundred Court,˜ I told them. ˜Do you want to find yourself being dragged before the sheriff of another shire when the next eyre comes around?˜

It was not much, Gervase, but it was sufficient to make them think that this time it would be better to keep their trews tied up and forego the pleasures of the flesh for once. And that shows you how much things had changed since King Richard had come to the throne. We had gone from everyone knowing exactly where they stood, and what was and was <u>not</u> permitted, to not knowing what might happen next. The old king would not have thrown over a sheriff as easily as King Richard had Ralph

Murdac, but we had already seen two changes of sheriff to the north of our shire in Yorkshire in barely a year, and Longchamp was unfathomable. Therefore if fitz John was in danger of a sudden descent from power for exceeding his authority, as I was able to hint to the men, then we did not want to be finding ourselves out of a job and without a roof over our heads along with him – and they listened to that!

I also chivvied the four more reasonable of my fellow knights into joining me in the morning to make sure that the men did not strip Costock bare. ˜You are going back to food which has already been cooked for you,˜ I told many a man, ˜you do not need to take that pig with you!˜ Or a sheep, or goat, or whole wheel of cheese, whichever someone had a rope around or tucked under their arm.

˜Why are you bothering?˜ the dim-witted Sir Jocelin asked me as he rode past, and I remember answering, ˜Because they will need to pay their taxes this year, and they cannot do that if they starve to death in the next month!˜ And yet my attempt to do good in the midst of such ill was rewarded in the oddest way, Brother, because when fitz John rode by all he saw was me ordering the men about, and knowing as little as he did and caring even less, he assumed I was for once enthusiastically following his orders.

Why would he, if he was so against me? Ah but you forget, Gervase, the first impressions I ever gave our young sheriff were of me as the dangerous killer, for I told you of how he thought I had killed my beloved dogs by his whim on the day he arrived. Yes, you recall that now. How I stood before him drenched in blood, even though it was a ruse perpetrated by Harry the stableman and myself, and then of course, I immediately led him on that never-to-be-forgotten boar hunt. So fitz John might think me a poor excuse for a knight, a poorly bred fellow whom he would rather not have sitting at his table. He might also think I was insolent to boot, but he was also just a little bit afraid of me, and that was why he hated me so much. And that was how I survived the following days too, as I shall now recount.

Nottinghamshire, Late winter, the Year of Our Lord, 1191

It was a wretched march back to the castle, and one on which Guy stayed at the back this time, grateful that there was no need for him to lead whilst following a trail on this straight road. Ahead he could see Algar being dragged along behind the sheriff, twisting and turning to look about him. The men-at-arms jeered at him for hoping that his 'outlaw' friends would come and rescue him, but Guy knew that what Algar really searched for was some sight of himself. It was the riders to the rear whom Algar was trying to see, not into the patches of woodland, and Guy was determined Algar should not get so much as a glimpse of himself, for Algar was a dangerous man now. Not dangerous in what he might do. There was no fight left in Algar now. But what he might say in panic could do terrible harm, and Guy already knew Algar could well go on the rack if he didn't tell fitz John what the young sheriff wanted to hear. He could not afford a pointing finger directly accusing him of collusion even before they got to the castle.

Once they had ridden in through the gates of the outer barbican and into the outer bailey, it was easier for Guy. He dropped quickly to the ground from his horse, and became invisible in the general chaos of the folk who served the castle and all within it. He saw Algar being dragged over the bridge across the dry moat which led to the castle proper, and knew he would end up in the dungeon beneath the great keep. With any luck he would be left to moulder until tomorrow, which would give Guy at least that night in which to think of how to play things if Algar accused him in public.

Luckily, fitz John was eager to rid himself of the bugs and muck of Costock, and to get a good meal inside him, then settled down for his normal evening in the great hall. Since Guy rarely ever stayed there beyond the meal, his absence wasn't noted as those who regularly fawned around fitz John began their nightly jostling for favour. Taking a risk, Guy walked across the inner bailey to the keep. He didn't go down to the dungeon itself, but slipped silently down the stair to it as far as he could go without revealing his presence to the couple of bored guards, who were playing dice in the chamber above the dungeon grills. From there he could hear Algar's sobs and they tore at him. It must feel to Algar as though some demon had turned back time, putting him in that dank hole again, except that this time there were none of his friends there with him.

What Guy really wanted to check on, though, was that Algar wasn't calling out his name in frantic pleas for help. Not having seen him, with any luck Algar might even think that Guy was away from the castle. After all, he knew that Guy spent many days patrolling the royal forest on the far side of the Erewash to Nottingham, so that was a distinct possibility. Whether that was the case or not, Algar was silent except for his sobs, and Guy crept away to plan his next moves.

It took another day for fitz John to get around to questioning Algar, time in which Algar had clearly not slept, and he was therefore in a semi delirious state as he came blinking into the light. As fitz John questioned him over and over, Algar's answers became more disjointed. Fitz John's ruffian of a torturer had tried to soften Algar up with what was probably considered to be a mild beating, but it had only worsened his mental state. As Guy listened from the shadows at the back of the hall, he heard Algar telling the sheriff of a band of fearful crusaders back from the East, of how they were led by a hero called Robin Hood, and how they were going to stand up for the ordinary people of Sherwood.

Yet fitz John and the other knights were openly laughing at his story by the time Algar broke down completely, and given how it had come out, Guy could see why. If they had not beaten Algar it might have been different. If they had brought him up from the dungeon first thing the following morning after their arrival, when he had not had three days and two nights without sleep, food or water, he might well have been more coherent. If they had then taken his allegations more seriously, someone might well have asked how come these men from the East had known about the movement of the money from Mansfield. But even so, Guy saw with relief that still no-one was questioning the timing of the theft. The assumption was either that the thieves had been sitting in wait for some time, or had just got lucky and been in the right place at the right time.

As Algar faded to the floor in a faint, and was dragged away to be hanged from the battlements as a dire warning to all who thought to take advantage of the sheriff, Guy thought that the proceedings were done with. Yet once the majority of the senior men had filed out, fitz John turned to Walkelin.

"How is our plan progressing?" he asked the former mercenary in Norman French. "Did you get your spies into place?" Being English born, fitz John spoke perfectly good English when he chose, so evidently he wanted no stray servant to understand his words, and that piqued Guy's curiosity!

Walkelin replied in his own heavily accented French, coming as he did from the Duchy of Brabant which had its own language, but he was still just about understandable. "Yes, my lord sheriff. The first two were brought from the gaol and freed once they were told what would happen if they did not do as they were told." He laughed nastily. "Strange how a few nights in there made them see things differently! And the warder now knows better than to let his tongue flap in whichever hovel of an inn he drinks in. He knows he will pay with his own life if he does!"

"Will the two Welshmen give us away, though?" fretted fitz John, and going by Walkelin's expression of disgust while fitz John wasn't looking at him, this must have been a much repeated demand. "What if they run for it and go to my lord of Chester?"

"As I told you before, my lord, the Welsh will do as they've been told for as long as we have their little catamites locked away!" and Walkelin laughed nastily.

"I don't know why you were so keen to involve those two," fitz John pouted, and now Fredegis appeared out of the shadows at the back of the sheriff.

"Because, my lord, it's as we told you. That bastard, Guy, may be fool in many ways, but he was right about that bow. It's Welsh. No doubt about it. Therefore whoever took the money must be Welsh or have Welshmen with them. Only they would know how to make a bow like that. They're the hook which will bring these outlaws to you. And that's what makes our plan believable. Those two renegades can truly make the claim to this gang that they've narrowly missed being blamed for the raid themselves."

"But there are Englishmen with the gang, as we told you," Walkelin added. "We heard English voices, not just that dreadful Welsh singsong. And that gibbering fool you have just ordered killed was right about one thing. We heard the name Robin. So it was probably this Robin Hood, whoever he is."

Guy froze in the shadows on his side of the hall, shrinking a little further back behind one of the great pillars and blessing his mother for insisting that he learn French in the hope that one day he might reach the court. He'd had little practise until coming back to Nottingham, but these days he had heard enough of Walkelin and Fredegis talking to one another, and together with fitz John, that he could now follow their conversation without difficulty. And what he was hearing was turning his stomach with fear. The four whom the three Coshams had found had actually been searching for them! It could only be those same four! But had they found the brothers quicker than expected, or was Fiskerton already being watched? Had Walter betrayed them too?

Never had Guy wanted fitz John's memory to fail him so much! *Ask them some more*, he prayed silently, also praying that no servant would come in to reveal his spying. *Please, Issui Sant, more information please if I'm to save your countrymen!* And his prayers were answered as fitz John demanded,

"But the two English you've sent, you're absolutely sure they won't just abscond?"

Guy thought Walkelin might just strangle fitz John going by his expression, but he managed to answer,

"We told you that too, my lord. They're from Heanor, down in the south of the forest we guard. We caught them red-handed poaching. We have their family in our clutches as well. If they fail us we shall just convict the rest of their family of the poaching in their stead – well, the sons at least. The women may not make it back to the village at all. De Wendenal must need some whores to warm his men's beds up in that frozen hole in High Peak!"

"And that's where you've taken them," fitz John said with satisfaction. "Very good. Very good! Keep me informed!" And he swept out of the hall.

"Why did you not tell him that he agreed that the women, children and catamites should be kept closer?" Fredegis moaned at his friend. "He'll only blame us if he goes to High Peak and then bloody de Wendenal knows nothing of them!"

"Phaa!" snorted Walkelin. "Did you not hear how little he remembers of what we told him anyway? No, he'll accept whatever we tell him we all agreed to, now that we're in his good books. All he cares about is that we catch these villains."

"And if he goes out and proclaims this Robin Hood an outlaw? What if that gives the game away and our men are discovered?"

"How will that give the game away, *hein*?" Walkelin demanded belligerently. "This Robin Hood is so full of himself he tells strangers his name! Half the shire is whispering his name! *Non*, my friend, if that happens it is all to the good, for it shows this 'hero' that there is a real danger for our little birds who have been taken into his nest, of them being mistaken for him and his friends!"

Fredegis sniggered evilly with Walkelin. "Well at least de Cuckney won't give us any trouble," he added confidently. "He'll keep the prisoners for us until such time as they out-live their usefulness."

"He'd better! Just at the moment young de Cuckney needs all the help he can get!" and the two of them also left the hall.

Stunned beyond words, Guy hung back long enough to ensure that he wouldn't collide with the two conspirators, then hurried into the old part of the castle where his quarters were, and went and found solace up on the deserted wall-walk. This part of the castle had the natural defence of the cliff below it, and as a result was not patrolled except in the most exceptional of circumstances. Therefore Guy could guarantee that on a cold March day, with a keen wind whistling around every nook and cranny, he could wrap himself up in his thickest cloak and know that he would remain alone up here. His other regular refuge was the stables, but there Harry would be asking him questions in an effort to help, and more than anything Guy wanted time to think this new development through alone.

Could he warn Robin? Whether he wanted to or not wasn't in doubt. No, it was how to do it that was the challenge. If these men were spies for fitz John, then he couldn't risk being seen openly in contact with the others for fear of that also being reported back to the sheriff. However, the more he thought about it, the more Guy felt sure that there were no go-betweens. No-one who was meeting with the spies to relay any messages back and forth. Fredegis and Walkelin were relying heavily on fear to keep their four men loyal. They had no idea where they'd gone to, and wouldn't until at least one of the four returned to them here, or maybe to Cuckney.

And Heanor! Guy knew where Heanor was because it was within his patrol as well. But it also reassured him in a different way, for if Walkelin and Fredegis had brought the two men from there to Nottingham, put the fear of God into them, and then released them; it was fairly natural to think of them heading off along the Trent afterwards. That might mean that as Derbyshire men, and therefore strangers to Nottinghamshire, they may well have been trying to find a way to get into the forest and got lost, stumbling on the brothers at Fiskerton by mere chance. That was a substantial relief! Algar turning traitor was bad enough, but the possibility that Walter had betrayed them too would have been a bitter blow. Now that could be considered unlikely at least. Still possible, but growing more remote all the time, thanks be to God!

It still didn't help him decide what to do, though. Dare he ride direct for the camp at Loxley? He would have to find a good excuse to ride out to the forest. Illegal hunting was definitely out of the question. That would have the bullish three knights at his heels in a trice! No, it must be something mundane. Something so boringly ordinary that they would gladly wish it on to him, and laugh behind his back at him for going. Wood gathering? It had been a cold winter and all of the people must be getting low of fuel by now, but was it enough? Was the threat of a few peasants scavenging windfall branches sufficient a reason for him to ride out? Possibly not.

But charcoal burning? Now that might work simply because of the amount of wood needed, even if it wasn't the larger pieces of timber or whole trees. Yes, he must have heard of a kiln ...no, better ...a cluster of small charcoal kilns already earthed up and cooking nicely! Something which would take some finding but with plodding persistence, not with dashing and flourishing.

And how soon? If he walked down into the town now, or at least hung around in the outer bailey for a while, then he could at least claim a chance encounter this very day. That would let him ride out tomorrow first thing, which was excellent! Time, then, to go and have a chat to Harry in the stables and talk to Tom, the man who did the real work with fitz John's hounds while Oswald, the arrogant head kennelman, sat by the fire in his tiny home by the kennels. He would take his chances regarding the four new men with Robin, and take his cousin the news of Algar.

Guy and been hunkered down, sitting on a thick fold of his cloak so as to be below the top of the battlements, and so out of the wind. Now he stood up and to his horror found himself looking straight at Algar's swinging corpse hanging from the outer wall, and it made his stomach lurch. No doubt the spot at the end of the wall above the deep dry moat had been deliberately chosen, since it too hung over the natural cliff like the wall Guy was on. From that height no-one passing by would miss seeing the corpse, but the prevailing south-westerly winds would not drive the smell into the town. That was probably Robert of Crockston desperately trying to be tactful with the burgesses of the town, who wouldn't want their wives and daughters to see such a sight either.

Yet Guy felt a growing anger inside as he looked at Algar's last, terrified expression. There had been no need at all to punish Algar this way. Had the matter gone to the Hundred Court, where it belonged, Algar would still be alive. And even if his supposed crime of collusion had been taken to the next eyre, he would have been in the gaol now and with some hope of being rescued. This was fitz John's spite, and nothing more!

Stamping down to the stables, Guy spent the afternoon helping Harry and the others groom the horses as a way of relieving his pent up feelings. Any sight of even one of the other knights might have ended in disaster given the way he was feeling. Then in the crisp frost of the first light of dawn, Guy left the castle and rode with all haste for Loxley. Not that he could do it all in one day, and he had to keep some kind of credible story going, so he stopped for the night in Chesterfield. That was suitably ambiguous with regard to his final destination, and he had stopped there before while on official business, so it aroused no comment from the innkeeper.

The following morning Guy left and followed the River Rother northwards. There were some small mines up this way which sold their coal to the smiths at Nottingham, and so it would have a ring of truth about it if he later said he had heard that there were itinerant smiths working in the area who also wanted charcoal. There had to be a glimmer of truth behind each of the tales he told, enough to not make anyone at the castle think twice about him. Once well enough away from the cluster of villages in the Chesterfield area, though, he turned off and rode as directly as he could to the border with Yorkshire, from where it was only a short ride to the Loxley valley.

Coming upon the hidden camp, Guy could hear someone shouting furiously. He didn't know whether to be glad or not that the voice was Walter's. As he led his horse down the steep and narrow track to the camp, he could see Walter standing face to face with Robin and circled by the others.

"Why didn't he do something?" Walter was yelling.

Robin, not seeing Guy off to his side, replied, "And what would you have him do? Guy doesn't have a free hand while he's in the castle, Walter, you know that! Just because Guy didn't charge the rest of the men at Costock and seize Algar there and then, doesn't mean that he won't try to help later."

It was a balm to Guy's soul to hear Robin standing up for him. At least there was some hope, then, that buried deep in Robin's heart was some remnant of the old brotherly affections there had once been between them. It also gave him the confidence to speak up straight away, knowing that he was less likely to be turned upon the moment he appeared.

"There was nothing I could do," he declared flatly, and all eyes turned to him.

"Guy!" Robin exclaimed, and there was genuine relief there. "What happened? Can you tell us? Where's Algar?"

"Hanging from the castle walls," Guy told them grimly. There was a chorus of cries of horror and disbelief. "I'm so sorry. There wasn't a thing I could do to save him."

"But what happened?" asked Tuck, bustling forwards, and Guy could see the concern in his face at the thought that Algar had died unshriven.

"I know this is a bitter pill for you all to swallow," said Guy with genuine sympathy, "but you had a traitor amongst you."

What he never expected was for all of those he knew to turn accusingly to four men standing a little apart from them.

"You bastards!" Walter howled, and was echoed by Gilbert and Will.

Yet as they made to pounce on the four, Guy's heart gave a dreadful lurch too. He knew the two Englishmen! He knew them well – or at least the older one he definitely knew well, and that man was now looking to him in despair too.

"No!" yelled Guy with all the force he could muster, as he ran to outpace the accusers. "Not them!" He skidded to a halt in front of the two Englishmen and turned to put himself between them and Will and Gilbert, whose fists were already raised. "It wasn't these two, Will! ...Gilbert! Alright? ...It's not them I'm talking about! I know this man," and he turned and put his hand on the older one's shoulder.

"You know him?" Will exclaimed in astonishment.

"Yes, I do. And I need to find out what's gone wrong before I tell you any more, but believe me, he has every bit as much of a reason to hate the sheriff as you do."

He turned to the man. "Hello Swein, how are you?" He looked to the young man beside him. "Which one of your sons is this?"

"Hello, Sir Guy," Swein answered with obvious relief and gratitude. "This is Adam, my oldest, the one whose hand you helped save."

Those words had an instant effect on the crowd around them. If the young man had been in danger of losing a hand then he must have been in serious trouble with the sheriff, and that calmed them somewhat.

"What happened to you?" Guy asked.

Swein sighed. "After I got that beating and dismissed from the castle, you mean? Adam and me and the rest of us went home to Heanor. Wasn't any reason to stay. I had no job, and I surely didn't want to stay anywhere near that mad bastard of a sheriff, that's for sure! I thought I'd done with him. I hoped that when any of the sheriff's men came riding through Heanor it might be you, so that I could thank you properly. Never occurred to me that those bastards Sir Walkelin and Sir Fredegis might turn up on my doorstep again.

"Then out of the blue a few weeks back they come with some of the castle guards. New men. Ones who never knew me for long enough to recognise me when they saw me elsewhere. They rounded us up with my wife, Maggie, and our other two kids, and dragged us off to Nottingham. But only Adam and me ended up in the gaol. We were near frantic at first, not knowing where Maggie and the little 'uns were. Then that bastard pair came again in the night. Told us that if we wanted to see our family again we had to do what they said."

"Did they give you any idea where your family was?" asked Guy gently.

Swein shook his head. "No. That was the worst of it! We'd already made our minds up that if we could, we'd not betray this man we now know is Robin, here. But how we could do that and save our three was beyond us. We just hoped and prayed we'd find the right man, and that he'd have some ideas."

Robin came forward. "They did tell me this when they joined us."

"Robin!" Will exploded. "Why didn't you tell us!"

"Because I feared exactly this reaction," Robin said calmly. "Swein said he used to work in the castle and had fallen foul of the sheriff. And, that members of his family were being kept hostage somewhere. I was planning on trying to meet Guy and ask him to see if he could find out where before telling you, so that I had confirmation that they were telling the truth before I risked telling everyone else. Now you have it."

"And I do know," Guy added, feeling just a touch smug. "Maggie and the children are being held at Cuckney, along with two people who are dear to your Welsh friends here."

"Christ on the Cross!" Will swore. "Bastard de Cuckney *again*! That little shit ought to swing from his own tower!"

However Guy was already shaking his head. "I'm not sure he's entirely to blame this time, Will. From what I overheard, Fredegis and Walkelin have something hanging over him. My guess would be that they and the sheriff kept back the evidence of what happened to Much's family, and now they're threatening de Cuckney with revealing it."

Will cocked an intrigued eye at Guy. "Oh are they, indeed! Making him do their dirty work for them where it's out of sight, and telling him they'll tell Longchamp if he doesn't do it, eh?"

Guy nodded. "That's my guess." Now he addressed the whole gathering. "Swein here was the carpenter at the castle. A bloody good carpenter too! All the time Ralph Murdac was sheriff things were fine. Then one day I rode back into the castle to find all hell breaking loose.

Heaven alone knows what fitz John was thinking that day, because what Swein, Adam, and the younger son Felix, were doing was making a stronger fence around the deer park which lies just beyond the castle."

Guy rolled his eyes in disgust. "Those bloody useless fallow deer had been escaping from the park and causing chaos in the crops. It wasn't even something which fitz John as sheriff needed to be involved in. The farmers had complained to the Hundred Court about the damage, the court had got in touch with Alan of Leek, and he as assistant constable of the castle had ordered that a better fence be made around the park. Nothing more complicated than that!

"But fitz John was in one of his tempers the day he rode out, and saw Swein and his sons and the deer park fence down. Without asking anyone, he charged up to them and started laying about him with his sword. Thank God all three of them had the presence of mind to duck down or we'd have had three corpses on our hands! As it was they were dragged into the outer bailey and fitz John declared that he would take Adam's hand off himself there and then."

Swein cleared his throat. "I've thanked Our Lady every day since then that Sir Guy rode in at that moment. He told the sheriff he had no right to take a man's hand without even having a trial. Some of my friends had already tried to tell the sheriff I was the castle carpenter, but he threatened he take their hands off too if they didn't shut up – and everyone knows what an evil temper he has!"

"I was the only knight there apart from Fredegis and Walkelin," Guy explained. "If Sir Alan or Sir Robert had been outside they would surely have stopped him too, but they weren't there and they didn't see."

Swein nodded. "Aye. Both honourable men, those two. As it was we all got a beating and a half for insolence."

For the first time Adam spoke up. "Father took the worst beating. He got whipped. It was Sir Guy who came to us in the night while we were in the castle dungeon. He got the guards to get us up out of the pit and cleaned Father's back, and put salves on it. Without him the wounds would have festered and Father would have died."

Guy shrugged modestly. "It wasn't hard to convince the guards, Adam. They could all see that but for the grace of God it could have been them that day. And you and your family were always well liked."

"Yes, but it was you who went and spoke straight away to Sir Robert," protested Swein. "It might have been a day or two before he heard, else."

"How did that help?" asked Much.

Swein grimaced. "Well as we were being held *in* the castle, and not at the town gaol, he had the say-so of what happened to us."

"And because in theory he was the one who hired you," added Guy. Then explained, "It meant that Sir Robert said that he would tell fitz John that he had dismissed you, since you'd given such offence. In reality I believe he gave you a written testimony to say that you had given satisfactory service, and were honest?"

"Aye, that he did," Swein agreed warmly. "It certainly got us out of the castle the very next day. I was near crippled, and Adam and Felix weren't much better, but we gladly walked all the way to my father's old farm at Heanor."

"Where's young Felix now?" asked Guy.

"Gone to join the monks as a lay brother at Worksop," Swein sighed. "He always was that way inclined. I blame it on Maggie giving him a monk's name! But who can blame him? I pushed him to come and join Adam with me at the castle because I thought there'd always be work for him there, but now that's all gone. And at least I've had the salve of knowing that at least one of my children is safe in these last awful days."

Robin was positively quivering with indignation. "Don't you worry, Swein! Now Guy's told us where they are, we'll have all of your family back with you before you know it!"

Then Marianne's voice said warily, "But if Swein and these others are true men, who was the traitor you meant, Guy?"

There was a sudden stunned silence.

Guy sighed heavily, "It was Algar himself."

"Algar?"

"No! I don't believe it!"

"Algar? Why would he betray us?"

The chorus of disbelief was only silenced when John asked,

"Why did you say that Guy?"

"Because it's the truth. Algar was angry that you wouldn't help his village." He had to hold his hand up to quell the rising protested again. "I know! ...I know that you told him that the people in the forest suffer more. That they had to come first. But sadly, he just didn't understand that. He was a simple man, Robin, and he didn't understand the larger picture you were trying to show him."

Guy struggled to think how to tell them more without hurting everyone. "If this helps you, I don't think for one moment he meant to betray you directly. All he thought about was getting that reward of a year's rent for his own village, so that he could help them. So he sent someone else to the sheriff to tell him to look for a man called Robin Hood in Loxley. Algar knew there was no such place anymore in terms of a functioning village, and I think he was counting on the sheriff running round in circles trying to find it.

"But that's where his simplicity let him down. He never thought fitz John would ask the scribes to check where Loxley was. So right from the start Algar's plan was doomed. Fitz John checked, realised that there was no such place in his shires, and assumed that Algar was deliberately trying to trick him – or at least that someone was. It didn't enter his thick head to ask about the neighbouring shires, just his own. So he rode into Costock with a troop of men and put the fear of the Devil into the poor souls." He turned to Walter.

"I'm so sorry, Walter, but there was nothing I could do. If even the men from High Peak had been with me I could have done nothing. There were too many others, and far too many knights. I couldn't have hoped to fight them all single-handed. And it would have been a fight! There was no other way to get Algar out once the villagers had pointed to him as the source of the information. And before you blame them, remember that they were surrounded with armed men, and one innocent woman had already had her throat slit by Sir Henry as punishment for their resistance."

"God have mercy upon her soul," intoned Tuck reverently. "Another poor soul to be added to the list in my prayers, and that list keeps growing. *Duw*, but this sheriff is the very Devil incarnate!"

Robin looked about him. "And I say he needs reminding that he's a mortal man, and not one of the Heavenly host, however far fallen!"

"Another raid on Cuckney!" Will said cheerfully. "This is getting to be a habit!"

However Guy had one more question. He turned to the two Welshmen. "I believe that you are as innocent as Swein and Adam, and I'm guessing that you've already told Robin that you, too, were under duress to find him?" They nodded. "But how did you come to be at Fiskerton? Was it just chance? Or did the two knights who imprisoned you send you that way?"

"I'm Ifor," the one spoke up. "Yes we are innocent, but you're right, we were sent to Fiskerton."

Everyone's eyes turned to Walter.

"No!" he cried, "I never said a word to anyone! Never!"

"I don't think it was you, *cyfaill*," Ifor said dryly. "We were told that someone from the village came to the castle and said there was funny stuff afoot. Something about a man who had been taken by the sheriff now coming back to take his brother's place. I reckon you stepped on someone's toes there, *ffrind*!"

Guy felt his heart sink. So it had been petty jealousy, nothing more. Maybe someone else also had their eye on the soon-to-be widow, or more likely on the land the family wouldn't be able to farm any more without another man. Whatever it was, it made little difference. "I'm so sorry, Walter, but you won't be able to go back," he said, trying to sound sympathetic. In truth he was beginning to get weary of the naivety of Algar and Walter.

"But I have to go back!" Walter protested. "There's more and more work needing doing on the farm at this time of year. They'll never manage without me!"

"Would you rather join Algar on the castle ramparts?" Guy asked him brutally.

Walter blanched, but it was reassuring to see most of the others nodding in agreement. There really was no choice.

"Don't be a bloody fool, man," Thomas told Walter brusquely. "It's not just about you! If you go back you'll endanger your mother and all the others in the house! Do you think the sheriff will give a shit about whether *they* know where Robin Hood is? They'll end up with the same crap choice Algar's village had, and like them they'll give you up, because it's lose you or lose everyone."

Walter turned to Robin and Guy. "I hate you both! You've ruined my life for me!"

Guy's gaze turned cold. "Funny that, because when I was hauling your sorry arse out of the sheriff's dungeon, you were damned near recommending me for sainthood for saving it. Or am I forgetting that you crossed the sheriff's path long before you met us?"

Walter's mouth shut with a clunk of teeth, but there was no mistaking the bitterness in his eyes.

Hugh stepped up to Walter, desperately trying to calm things. "I tell you what. When we've rescued the people at Cuckney – and make no mistake, Walter, that they come first, because their lives are in very real and immediate danger – then I'll escort you back to Fiskerton one last time. Then you can say goodbye to your family and explain that someone in the village has betrayed you already. I think you might find they're glad to see the back of you once they realise that having you home will draw the sheriff's wrath down on them. But I'm telling you, it'll be a very quick visit in the middle of the night, and we'll be gone by dawn. Does that appease you?"

Yet far from thanking Hugh, Walter looked daggers at him and then at the others. "So now you don't trust me any more? Fine friends you are!" and he made to stamp off into the woods.

However, Will and Piers were faster. The two of them intercepted him and brought him to the ground.

"Tie him up," Robin ordered, looking utterly miserable. "I'm truly sorry you've force this on us, Walter, but we have to rescue those people at Cuckney. We can't have you stamping around the shire telling everyone you meet how hard-done-by you are, or worse, bringing someone up here."

As most of them walked away from Will and Piers, who were binding Walter hand and foot with some rope Roger had brought over, Robin said to Guy,

"What on earth am I going to do with him? He can't go back to Fiskerton for the same reason."

Guy draped a brotherly arm over Robin's shoulders and hugged him. "Welcome to the shit of the real England, cousin. On days like this I wonder sometimes why I even try to make things better for people. Thank God for men like Swein, who might not be educated but understand what life's about. And I really feel for you, getting a kick in the teeth like that. Isn't it a bastard! Four strangers trust you enough to tell you they're being threatened, and trust you to help them find a way out of their mire without giving you up, yet two men whom you thought had every reason to be loyal turn out not to be. And without any cause!"

"I know!" Robin snorted bitterly. "God knows that I tried to explain things to them time and again, Guy. I thought they understood!"

Guy gave him another hug. "I fear your explanations were no competition for Walter's standing cock! That's the source of his grief! Never mind his old mother. That witch of a sister-in-law has probably been teasing him from the moment he got home. I'd bet she's let him have a few fumbles in the dark behind the cowshed, but nothing more. But if she's that lusty, I'd also bet that she's been sneaking off with one of the other village men, and it's him who's put out that just when he thought he was going to be bedding her every night, all of a sudden it looks like it's back in the barn for him again."

"I think you're dead right," Marianne said, coming up and taking Robin's other arm. "If she can think of being faithless now, when her husband is dying, you can be sure she's been faithless before then. It's not the time most women think of taking a lover for the first time!"

"But what do I do about him?" fretted Robin. "I can hardly keep him prisoner here!"

Guy felt his spirit sink. Robin was right, there was nowhere here they could keep Walter, and if they let him go free he'd be a permanent danger to them all. "I know this is a cruel thing to have to do, but I'll take him back to Nottingham with me as my prisoner. If I'm careful I can chuck him back in the hole he came out of and no-one will be any the wiser."

"Guy!" Marianne protested, but Robin nodded for all that he looked dreadfully downcast,

"It's the only option, Marianne. Walter himself has brought this on, no-one else."

Guy released Robin and let him walk on with Marianne, then caught them up again.

"There's one more thing."

Robin's head came up from looking into Marianne's eyes.

"When the two Welshmen confessed to you that they were being forced into this, did they tell you who exactly they were with?"

"Why does it matter?" Marianne wondered.

Guy turned and looked back to the two in question. "Well Walkelin and Fredegis referred to their prisoners as 'catamites'. Do they strike you as that sort?"

Robin was suddenly alert again. "No, not at all! In fact Pawl said he had been prepared to go on crusade because his wife and two children had sickened and died three years ago. They left with those men the Coshams were supposed to go with."

"Archbishop Baldwin's men?"

"That's them."

Guy rubbed his chin. "Then who is it that matters so much to them? Who is it in Cuckney castle?"

Did I put Walter back in the dungeon? How did I do it? Dear me, Gervase, you are so anxious to find fault in me! Oh, is it not that? You do not wish me to stop? Ah well, Brother, you will have to possess your soul of a little more patience, because I am not going to jump forward in my tale to tell you the outcome of that, and then go back to where I was in order to continue properly. I told you right at the start, you will have this just as it happened, and only when you have heard all will you be able to judge me.

So there we were, planning another raid on Cuckney castle. This time, because we knew exactly what its strengths and weaknesses were, and because we were not expecting anyone else to turn up uninvited, we already knew we would need fewer men. There was no need to fret that we did not have our friends, the men-at-arms from High Peak, with us to guard the roads. We few would be more than enough, for we knew exactly where we would go over the wall and when, and that there would be no aid coming from the village. The de Cuckneys were not the most popular of landlords, and if they had got themselves into trouble, their tenants would let them carry on as long as it did not rebound on them.

It was therefore not a problem when Much asked if he could stay behind with Walter. I believe he wanted to talk to his older friend to try and understand what had gone so terribly wrong, and none of us could blame him for that. Robin did take him on one side and speak very sternly to him about not letting Walter go, knowing that Much was a kind-hearted lad and would be prey to pleadings. We were then thankful that Roger said he would stay with Much. Roger was far more worldly and would soon see through Walter if he tried to manipulate Much with soft words, and anyway, Roger would be of limited use in a raid such as we were planning. We did think about asking Allan to stay as well, but he was fast becoming a competent archer and would be of use as a scout too.

Therefore we set off from Loxley leaving Walter in the care of Much and Roger, and began the walk to Cuckney. It was not so very far, and as Robin wanted to attack by night it was better that we press on that same day. Had we waited until the next morning to set out we would have barely got there by the afternoon, and therefore with a long wait until the castle men were all asleep. That would have meant a good deal of hanging about in the woods by Cuckney, which would increase the chance of us being spotted, for we were not so complacent as to think de Cuckney would set no guard at all. Indeed we suspected that he would be as nervous as a new bride, given what was hanging on his co-operation with the sheriff. Therefore, by midnight, we had surrounded the bailey at Cuckney.

Chapter 9

We had to march to Cuckney, of course, since I was the only one mounted, but you must remember that we were all young men at that time, and in the prime of our lives. Our only concern was the remote chance of meeting a party out hunting from Bolsover Castle, and that was always negligible. Moreover, Robin and the men had hunted only the day before, and we were able to eat heartily on the tender venison stew Tuck had already prepared in great quantity. More dried meat came with us to eat as we walked, so we were not marching and feeling the lack of sustenance.

Indeed the chance to eat one of Tuck's meals was a great treat for me. Since fitz John's arrival, the meals served to those of us unlucky enough to eat at his table had been repeatedly slathered in sauces. No doubt he thought this showed his quality of breeding. For me, though, it was just unappetising, and I constantly found myself picking the vegetables and bits of meat out of the overly flavoured liquid, then trying to salvage the bread from what was swimming around on the wooden platter. More than once I ended up down in the kennels stealing some of the nutty, full-flavoured dog-bread, for young Tom had begun using my bread recipe to great effect. What Ianto and I had concocted back in the days on the Welsh Marches to improve the hounds' health was now saving mine!

However, you fidget, Gervase, so I will spare you the cookery details and move on with events at Cuckney. We had asked the four newcomers to join in the raid on Cuckney with good reason - we had to make sure we were rescuing the right people! Margaret Carpenter I knew from her living with Swein close by the castle at Nottingham, but I had never had any reason to take notice of their younger children, and should she be hurt in any way, I wanted the children to see their father was one of the men rescuing them.

And then there was the puzzle over who it could be that these two Welsh archers were protecting. Robin and I had agreed that we should say nothing of our concern to the others as yet, and Marianne did not argue. For all we knew it might simply be a couple of younger brothers, just as Bilan was to Thomas and Piers – a younger man thought of affectionately did not necessarily mean something abnormal, as you churchmen would see it – and we wanted to tread careful and not offer offence if there was an utterly normal explanation. With Walter and Algar still in everyone's minds, Robin and I did not want to subject these new men to undue suspicion now that I had confirmed that two of them, at least, had every reason to want to join with Robin.

Sherwood,
March, the Year of our Lord, 1191

The men circled Cuckney castle in the blackness of the night, for once blessing the hard frost which had at least painted the ground white, allowing them to see a little by the light of the faint moon overhead. It was too close to the new moon to be shining brightly, and there was some cloud about, but once out of the trees no-one wanted to risk having lit torches in their hands. Again, Thomas and Piers had attached ropes to arrows by fine lines, and these provided a means for the same seven of only months ago to shin over the wooden walls of the simple fortification, for Guy was with them and dressed like Robin and Siward once more.

"Well he didn't learn much from the last time," Will muttered sarcastically in Guy's ear, as they dropped without challenge into the bailey.

Guy chuckled. "I suspect his greatest concern just at the moment is the bloody sheriff! Us he could eventually dismiss in his mind as just a very bad dream – fitz John he has to have regular contact with!"

"Big mistake!" Will laughed softly. "Very big mistake!"

They slunk up to the keep and spread themselves along its wall, everyone listening intently. Their best guess had been that the hostages would be in the undercroft where a year ago they had tied up Richard de Cuckney and his two accomplices. In theory that then meant that if the household was upstairs, they need never know how their hostages had escaped, but that scenario was very dependent on there being no servants on the ground floor – or at least none who were awake.

They had half considered bringing Swein in with them, but he was no fighter, and as Marianne had said, if they got everyone out, then they could decide who they took on with them later. The cellars of Cuckney Castle were no place to have a family reunion! And the last thing they wanted was for Swein to be killed as they fought their way out, leaving his family without a wage-earner.

A resonant snore right by the door made those closest to it jump.

"Shit! Have they got a man lying across the doorway?" Will hissed in Guy's ear. He was just in front of Guy on the right-hand side of the door, with Guy in line behind him, backed in his turn by James and Gilbert. Siward and Malik were behind Robin on the left-hand side. But now Siward gave a soft chuckle and whispered,

"Snoring like that I reckon it's more likely he's been banished there by the others so they can get a decent night's sleep!"

Given the resonance of the snores, audible even through the thick oak of the doorway, that seemed like a not unreasonable assumption.

"I'll pick the lock," Guy whispered, slipping forward, "but then you grab him quick, Will, before he wakes and raises the alarm!"

Guy used his fine old blade to work through the keyhole, and felt the latch click. Immediately he put his weight on the door and felt it move a little before stopping against the bulk of the man.

"Now!" he hissed, and Will shouldered the door like a bull at a gate, helped by Robin, and the two hauled the sleeping man out by the scruff of his tunic before he had realised what was going on. Robin held the man up enough for Will to deliver a mighty punch, and the man went limp.

"Bloody hell, Tom! Shut the fucking door!" a sleepy voice from the room protested, as the chill air of the morning cut through the warm miasma of sleeping men and the last of the evening's fire.

Leaving the unfortunate Tom prostrate on the frost of the motte, the seven slipped inside and shut the door silently and at speed. All held their breaths for a moment, dreading that the others within might have woken, yet all they heard was the sounds of people adjusting their positions and then sinking back into much-needed sleep. Belatedly Guy realised that it must be exhausting work dealing with a spoilt young lord like de Cuckney. No doubt they grabbed whatever rest they could for as long as possible.

Edging his way into the lead on the left past the others, Guy whispered softly in the ear of each he passed, "Follow me! Hand on the shoulder of the man in front!"

With his own hand following the wall, Guy slid each foot forward with great care. It was ridiculously slow progress and he was praying that Robin would not just shoulder past him in his impatience. But then his foot touched something and he heard a sigh at his feet.

"Servant!" he whispered back to Gilbert, who was right behind him. "Step over him!"

Bracing himself against the wall, Guy made an extended high step and was relieved to feel his foot come down onto rushes again. Having stepped fully over the man, he held out a bracing arm for Gilbert, then whispered for him to edge forward and take the lead. He himself stayed and helped each of the others over the sleeping person, and even Robin didn't pull away from his grasp. They had already agreed beforehand that if they could get inside without alerting anyone, then that would give them the advantage of surprise if they had to fight their way out, and mercifully so far Robin was sticking to that plan.

Now at the rear of the file, Guy was suddenly aware that they had reached the steps leading downwards without misadventure, and when his feet touched the earth floor of the cellar he breathed a sigh of relief. Ahead he could hear Will softly calling,

"Margaret! Margaret Carpenter! Are you here?"

"Over here!" a sleepy voice answered, then the strike of a flint heralded a glimmer of light as Siward lit a small candle.

"Sshhh!" several of the seven were hissing as the hostages blearily blinked awake, and they hurried to their sides.

Tied up in the cellars were Margaret and her two small children, and four others, all having a rope linked through those around their wrists and going through the bonds of the others, and then attached to the wall at either end at iron loops.

"Thank God it isn't a chain!" Will breathed. "No way of breaking one of those quietly!" and he looked pointedly at Guy, who nodded back in relief. Robin had refused to believe that women and children would be kept bound hand and foot, even by such a louse as de Cuckney, but Will had expressed his fear of such a thing to Guy as they had marched, relieved to find that someone else had also thought of such a danger. Now their relief was all the greater for finding the prisoners as tethered as they had feared but without the dreaded problems. Neither dared look directly at Robin for fear of their faces showing expressions of 'I told you so', but out of the corner of his eye Guy had registered Robin's surprise and horror at the sight.

"Who are you?" the smallest of the unknown four whispered anxiously, his voice identifying him as a boy whose voice was just breaking.

Robin stepped over to him and whispered back, "Friends of Pawl and Ifor. They're outside waiting for you."

"*Duw clod!*" another breathed in clear relief.

"Yes, praise God!" Guy answered with a smile as he sawed away at the rope at their end. "It was a chance remark which gave away where you were."

He wasn't going to add just yet where or how he'd heard it. And there was still the mystery of who else was with the Welshmen to be solved. Even by the faint and flickering light of the little candle, Guy was already aware that there was something not quite right about the other two prisoners. Not the kind of wrong which rang alarm bells of danger in his head, but something definitely peculiar. They jarred at Guy's senses – and not merely because some bullish knight had referred to them as catamites. He had come across the occasional effeminate man by now enough to not be taken aback by one. But these two didn't seem quite right by his measure of such men either.

However his train of thought was broken by Robin hissing, "Right! Let's get out of here!"

Unsurprisingly, James was standing with sword drawn right by Margaret and her two children. God help the man who tried to lay a finger on them, Guy thought, as he pulled the last of the rope out of the bonds and was able to slice through the cords around the Welshman's wrists now that he could turn around. James would fillet them in a heartbeat after what his own family had endured. It took all of Guy's self-control not to hurry to the head of the stairs and lead the way out, but he knew in his heart that this was something he had to allow Robin to at least make a start at doing. If it all looked like it was going to hell in a handcart, he would have to take over for the sake of those they were rescuing, but only then. He had to learn how to predict when not to seem to stamp on Robin's toes unless there was no other choice, but he was mentally praying to St Issui that Robin was remembering that they had agreed to try to go out without a fight.

Mercifully Robin was beckoning Siward forward with the candle to light the way, at the same time saying as loudly as he dared to those they were rescuing,

"If Siward holds the candle, do you think you can try to step over the servants who are sleeping on the floor?"

Margaret was already nodding, and Malik had moved to beside James and was gesturing that they would carry the two youngsters once they were up the stairs. The other four nods were less enthusiastic but still with a sign of compliance. Guy wondered about that. Clearly they wanted to be out of here, but there was a definite wariness about their acceptance of help.

Belatedly he realised that none of his own friends had bothered to try to enlighten him about where Pawl and Ifor said they had come from, or where they were going to, and that sent a frisson of fear down his spine. Just how trustworthy were these people? Robin was far too easily drawn into believing tales of woe to Guy's way of thinking, and he wished his cousin would think to question more. Guy knew he himself tended to suspect the worst more than he possibly should, but he would have felt a good deal happier just now if he had known for sure that the Welsh party's story stood up to more detailed examination.

What really made the hairs on the back of his neck stand on end, though, was hearing one of the strange two say softly to the one he knew was another Welshman,

"Some rescue! Creeping out like bloody mice! I'd like to wring the neck of that wee bastard upstairs before I go!"

Guy just about managed to stifle his gasp of surprise, and not just at the sentiment. The voice was unmistakably Scottish and a woman's! That was what it was! Those two were female! Dressed in men's clothing, and with their hair chopped short, they were carrying off the disguise well, and no doubt when they intentionally spoke to strangers they adapted their voices to sound more like boys', but Guy knew he wasn't mistaken.

"Hush!" the Welshman was whispering back to her. "Be grateful we're getting out of here at all! Save your desire for revenge for later!"

That made Guy smile. So she was a feisty lass, was she? Another such as Marianne, maybe? He leaned in closer to the two of them, who were the last of those being rescued and just waiting for Will to hand the younger two up to Siward.

"This way he gets into far more trouble," he whispered in their ears and was gratified to see them both start. "Yes, I heard you. I can tell you more when we're outside, but believe me, that the young noble you want to throttle will suffer far more if you seem to disappear."

The woman had whipped round to look him in the face and he saw her blink at his words. Then she sniffed and nodded. It wasn't much of an agreement, but Guy hoped it meant she would leave the building without wrecking their plans. Seemingly it did, because although he saw the expression of distaste on her face in one brief flicker of the candle as Siward helped her over the sleeping servant, she did nothing to draw attention to them.

At the door, Robin – or more likely Malik – had got everyone over to its latch side, allowing them to open it just a crack and let everyone stream out at speed. Will dragged the still unconscious Tom back inside, unceremoniously dumping him in a heap, to complete the appearance of the place being undisturbed. Guy was then the last one out, and even as he got his knife under the latch to ease it down, he heard rather than saw movement and someone's sleepy complaint again.

Now they were in a hurry, and everyone made a run for the main gate. Will and Malik lifted the heavy oak bar off it, and all but the two of them hurried out. Closing the gate behind the others, they then dropped the bar back into place and ran for the ropes which Thomas and Piers still guarded. Everyone else ran round the perimeter to join those two, and to man the ropes, for while the others had been inside, Bilan had scaled the walls and made sure that sufficient rope hung on the inside while allowing enough on the outside for the others to pull Will and Malik up. In a remarkably short time the two of them were on the top of the wooden palisade, and throwing the doubled-up lengths they had just climbed around a protruding spike so that they could swarm down to their friends. A tug on the ropes then resulted in all of it coming down on the outside, leaving no sign of how or where the rescuers had got in.

Once under the cover of the trees, Swein and Adam's delight at being reunited with their family was heartening to see, and Guy watched the way Robin's face lit up at seeing the family's tears of joy. That at least confirmed all he had been told that Robin wasn't doing it for the overt glory, but for his personal satisfaction, and that made it a bit easier to take for Guy. Part of him would have been deeply saddened if it had turned out that his once naive and loving cousin had become nothing more than a vain and glory-seeking shell of a man.

Off to one side, watched over by Gilbert, Siward and Will, the other escapees were being welcomed by Ifor and Pawl in a vigorous exchange of Welsh. Guy wasn't about to let it slip that he knew more or less what they were saying. It had been a few years now since he had been amongst Welsh speakers, but he was not that rusty that he could not pick out the key words. The young girl and boy were the important ones, and there was something about getting them back to a prince being said – someone who might or might not be a relative, Guy thought. And there was also something being said about the fear of not returning with the boy and girl. Words said with enough feeling to convince Guy that it had been a genuine fear for the safety of the two youngsters which had forced Pawl and Ifor to submit to the coercion of Fredegis and Walkelin.

However, he wasn't about to take any of it at its face value and in return neither, it seemed, was their rescue by the woman. Once they stopped to rest, well away from any habitation, she, rather than any of the Welsh archers, was the one who demanded,

"So why did you come for us, then, eh? Do you think *you* can get more out of their lord than the other bastards?"

But before anyone could answer, there was a shriek and Marianne leapt to her feet.

"Mariota? Is that you? Sweet Mother of God, is that you, Mariota?"

She was already stumbling over the recumbent others in her haste to get to the woman. Yet for the first time Guy heard the rescued woman lose some of her control too.

"Marianne?"

"Yes, it's me!"

"Oh Jesu! I thought you were dead!"

"*I* thought *you* were dead!"

Mariota had scrambled to her feet and the two of them met in a desperate embrace. For a moment all the rest of them heard were sobs as the two women hugged each other for all they were worth.

It was Robin who broke the moment, asking coolly,

"Marianne? Who is this?"

She turned to him and in a voice shaking with emotion answered,

"She's one of my sisters from the hospital in Jerusalem!"

That immediately explained a lot. All but Swein and his family knew by now of how Marianne had left Jerusalem, and the hospital of the Hospitallers where she had worked, to return to England as nurse to some noble ladies travelling in the party of the patriarch of Jerusalem, when he had come to plead with King Henry. Marianne had never been able to return to the Holy Land, and when she had met Robin and his five fellow crusaders, she had learned of the fall of Jerusalem to Saladin, and had feared for the fate of the sisters she had left behind.

Little wonder, then, that she was so relieved to find one of them here and in one piece. But it also relieved some of Guy's concern too. Someone who had taken her vows as a genuine sister of the Hospitaller order stood a good chance of being far more trustworthy than just a random traveller from the east. And he could also imagine that if these two youngsters had been placed in her care, that she would be as adamant about fulfilling that duty as Marianne would have been in her position.

Guy decided to take a chance and see what Mariota's reaction would be to the truth.

"We have – or rather, had – no idea of who you were," he said firmly. "We came because Pawl and Ifor were being forced to act against my friends here. They'd already told Robin that they'd been told they had to betray him or you would lose your lives. So the best way to save them from having to do that seemed to be to rescue you. It just happened that the other two men who were supposed to join our friends in hiding in the forest, and betray them along with Ifor and Pawl, were men whom I knew to be trustworthy for many years before they were forced from their home."

"And you are?" Mariota demanded of Guy.

"I'm Robin's cousin," Guy answered swiftly so that no-one gave his full name. He was not so trusting yet that he would hand them the means to betray him. "And John and Allan's," he added, pointing those two out where they were becoming visible in the growing dawn light.

Mariota sniffed. "And this is Robin?" She looked pointedly at him.

"This is Robin," Marianne agreed, and Guy thought her friend would have to be a complete fool if she didn't pick up on the emotions those three simple words were infused with. Pride, love, devotion, they were all redolent in that declaration.

"Oh aye?" Mariota replied warily as Robin came to stand in front of her. "And who might you be ...*Robin*?"

Guy had to smother a grin at that. If Robin was expecting fulsome gratitude from this woman he certainly wasn't going to get it just yet, and Guy saw him blink in surprise. No, it wouldn't do Robin any harm at all to meet someone who did not instantly fall at his feet with thanks. She wasn't biting his hand off for helping, but no doubt she'd had enough experience of false offers of help by now to be remaining on her guard for a while yet.

"He used to be a Templar in Jerusalem," Marianne tried to explain, but Mariota was quick off the mark with a comment before Marianne could elaborate.

"Oh aye?" she said with even more cynicism. "And how come he was there, then, when the other warmongering bastards left us to our fate?" She gave him a hard look. "*I don't recall any Templar knights in Jerusalem at the end!"*

Luckily Malik took a hand in the proceedings, no doubt seeing Robin stiffen at the implied insult.

"We six were amongst the many my lord of Ibelin knighted at Jerusalem," he told her calmly, and somehow, hearing his accent seemed to change something within Mariota.

"Oh? ...Oh well, that's different," she conceded. "And you were...?"

Malik gave her a small bow. "I was a turcopole in the service of King Baldwin, Sister," and he smiled.

By now Guy was fascinated by Mariota's reactions. Confronted with someone she now knew how to deal with and understood she was instantly relaxed, and even smiling back at Malik.

"You must find it very different to home being here," she said sympathetically.

Malik nodded. "For me and for James," he replied, gesturing to his fellow native of the Holy Land. "Will and Siward are English born, like Robin," he continued, "While Gilbert is from ...elsewhere." Clearly Malik hadn't quite grasped where Ireland was geographically to England yet, but the man himself was already stepping forward saying,

"From God's own country, actually," which immediately made Mariota laugh.

"Aach, there's no mistaking that!" she chuckled. "And I'd guess not so far over the water from where I'm from, at that!"

It was Gilbert's turn to grin now. "Oh, to be sure, from my uncle's farm you could see the shade of the Scottish isles across the sea on a clear day!"

"So what are you doing with a bunch of reprobates from Wales, then?" Thomas dared to ask, and coming from him it was taken as far less of a challenge than if one of the Englishmen had asked.

Strange how the Celts bonded instantly, no matter that they were from different kingdoms, Guy thought. Did they sometimes think it served the Anglo-Saxons right for taking over England that they were now repressed in their own land? That they now suffered from the Norman yoke? One day he must ask Tuck if that was just a daft idea, or closer to the truth than was comfortable to admit.

Meanwhile Pawl had reached over and ruffled the hair of the young lad. "These two, you see, *cyfaill*. Their father had brought them on pilgrimage, see? He was one of the ones who took up Archbishop Baldwin's call to take back the Holy City, and we were amongst the men who went with him. Well we didn't get that far – soon realised that it wasn't going to be easy to get there without a great lord at our head, and somehow the King of France hadn't heard of Elfael. Or at least his lords hadn't! Bloody thieving swines! We ended up having to make a run for it! Aquitaine is no place for us of the Cymry, *brawd*."

Thomas was nodding sagely. "Piers and I were caught up in that call-to-arms. We decided before we'd even left these shores we'd be on a hiding to nothing sailing for France. We grabbed our youngest brother Bilan and legged it, and hearing your story I'm bloody glad we did!"

"I wish we had," Pawl sighed. "More of our friends might still be alive if we'd done the same." He grimaced. "*Duw*, you think our mountains can be harsh in winter! You should see the ones at the southern end of France!"

"We didn't know which way to go for the best," Ifor added. "We'd gone east to get away from some of King Richard's cursed lords and their men. But then we found ourselves near Toulouse, and there seems to be trouble brewing there too. Something about a new branch of the Church creating bishoprics at Toulouse and Carcassonne, but I couldn't tell you what that's all about – we didn't hang about to ask! All we knew was that folk were saying the pope wouldn't stand for what they were doing, and that now Jerusalem had fallen he'd be even keener to root out heretics in the west."

"Lord Einion took us south again," Pawl continued the story, "and we ended up in the kingdom of Aragon. By this time we were all sick and weary, so we went to find sanctuary at one of the churches."

"That's when I met them," Mariota said. "I was at Sigena, at the convent Queen Sancha had had built for our sisters." She turned and smiled at Marianne. "I'll tell you more about that later. Many of our old friends made it to there and are safe."

"Oh thank God!" Marianne exclaimed.

Mariota smiled back. "Oh yes, God has been good to us. The queen had the building expanded once she heard of our plight, and we've been able to continue our work looking after the sick and needy. Well these three men turned up one day having been sent on to us because of the children. The prior where the rest of them were being cared for thought it improper that Suzanna was travelling with so many men, you see, and so he sent her and Anarawd to come into our care." She smiled affectionately at the two youngsters. "Anarawd is fast becoming a young man, but he's yet to put on the growth to make him look like one."

Ifor was nodding agreement at her words, now adding. "So when Lord Einion decided we should take a ship and come home, the sisters insisted that one of their number came with Suzanna so that she would be properly taken care of." He became dejected. "It was only when we landed at Bristol that he realised how things have changed here. Even in France we'd heard bad things about Longchamp and his brothers, so no-one wanted to take the chance of crossing Herefordshire now it's under Henry Longchamp! De Braose's a bastard, but at least we knew him and how he'd behave! In the winter we knew he'd be holed up at Abergavenny most likely, but who knew where this other Norman pig might be?

"We'd meant to cross the Severn at Gloucester, you see, and then get across to Ross and follow the north bank of the Wye home. But Lord Einion decided, based on word he'd had from some merchants we met at the quay at Bristol, that we'd be better going up to Worcester, and then going across to Leominster. From there, he said, we could cross the north of Herefordshire in greater safety."

Robin was looking at them sympathetically. "But I'm guessing something went wrong."

Ifor nodded glumly. "Someone betrayed us. I've no idea who. Most probably it was some merchant who'd already been primed to keep an eye out for Einion. ...Wouldn't take a miracle to work out that he'd be coming home soon, what with King Richard setting out on a wholly new crusade. Must have been pretty obvious that the one we set out on had to have failed. I hope the traitor got well paid for his efforts, because he won't live to enjoy them for long if I ever get my hands on him!"

"We were stopping near Tewkesbury," Pawl continued. "Just a quiet little inn on the edge of the town. Then all of a sudden these armed men came thundering in. Took us all by surprise, I can tell you!" And he shivered at the memory. "Several of them dragged Lord Einion out, and God alone knows if he lives or not. I swear I saw two men who served his brother, Lord Maredudd, amongst them, and that made Ifor, Hywel and me think it might be a blood feud. That Maredudd has maybe been feathering his own nest while Einion's been away, and doesn't want him back again."

Tuck sighed deeply. "There's always been bloodshed between brothers in the great houses of Wales," he said sadly, and Guy knew he was thinking of Maelgwn, whom they'd rescued years ago, but who would have died at the hands of his brothers if not King Henry's, had they known he still lived. Thankfully Maelgwn was living the peaceful life at Gisborne manor now, but both Tuck and Guy were already guessing that these two youngsters before them wouldn't live long if they fell into the wrong hands.

"But how did you manage to fall foul of two such strange knights as Fredegis and Walkelin?" Guy couldn't help but wonder. "They've not been out of the shire for months to my certain knowledge."

The Welsh archer they now knew was called Hywel grunted in disgust. "We ran north and east. Well you would, wouldn't you! The Marches had suddenly become even more dangerous than we'd ever expected! We were the only ones who escaped, and that because we'd been standing guard while the women used the privies, would you believe. Mere chance we were already outside and saw the chaos happening through the open back door. We hid behind barrels in the brewhouse and left before dawn. Mariota said we had to get Anarawd and Suzanna to their mother's folk now, but we decided we'd head for Shrewsbury first. A big abbey like that was bound to be one of the best places to hear of news from across the border."

"We got lost, though," Ifor admitted, "and before we knew it, we were into the earl of Chester's lands. That's when we got trapped. Some men-at-arms came across us where they thought we shouldn't be. The next thing we know we're being hauled before some petty lord who says he has a use for us. Something about his cousin having had trouble with Welshies over in Nottinghamshire. Before you could say "knife", we were bundled into a cart and the next thing we know we're in the town gaol in Nottingham."

"Even that didn't last more than a night," Mariota said through pursed lips of disapproval. "They sent us four up to that wee shite of a noble you've let off, and we knew nothing more of Ifor and Pawl until tonight."

"Oh he hasn't got off!" Guy declared firmly. "He's already in trouble up to his neck and sinking! His way out of it was to keep you until Ifor and Pawl betrayed Robin and the rest of us. But now you've disappeared, that evil pair of knights who dealt with you at Nottingham, and the spiteful wretch we have as a sheriff – who used to be in charge over in Chester, by the way – will be having young Richard de Cuckney's guts for garters! If we'd fought our way in and out, he could at least say he was overwhelmed, stretch the numbers and make it look like it wasn't his fault. But with not a scratch on anyone, and *all* of the servants swearing they saw nothing, he's going to be shitting himself with fright come the morning. He can't silence the servants by killing them because technically they're his father's, not his, so they can damn him with their testimony to Walkelin and Fredegis, and also at the Hundred Court if he harms them. He's caught in a cleft stick, ever serve him right!"

That seemed to mollify Mariota, although Guy could see she still wasn't wholly convinced. The greater question now, though, was what was going to happen to everyone. Under the cover of the heart of the forest, they had the time to decide what to do.

Mariota and her friends wanted to take Anarawd and Suzanna to their grandfather, Lord Rhys (Prince Rhys ap Gruffudd of Deheubarth in southern Wales), and Tuck immediately offered to escort them.

"I know the ways through the Marches like the back of my hand," he assured the party.

"I wish I could come with you," Guy confessed. "I'd love to see those lands again, but I'm going to have to get straight back to Nottingham this morning. I daren't be absent for any longer."

However, he and Tuck had a hurried conference about routes, and once done realised it had been settled that Marianne and John would travel with them. Much as Thomas, Piers and Bilan would have loved to join them, the risks were deemed too great for them. At least

Tuck, Marianne and John could claim shelter at monasteries on the way back without exciting comment as to why Welshmen were coming into England, for who would understand that the Cosham brothers were actually coming home at that point?

The Carpenter family were going to go in the opposite direction to Lincoln with an introduction to the Jews whom Robin and the others had helped. The hope was that Swein and Adam would find work helping to set right the houses in York, but if not, Lincoln was one of the more stable places to be just now. Siward and Allan would take them, along with Will, who wanted to purchase smith's tools somewhere out of the immediate vicinity, and hoped the fairs at such an important place would serve his purpose. And to be on the safe side, the Coshams and Hugh were going to keep an eye on Cuckney for one more day – just to be sure the servants didn't suffer unjustly!

Everyone would leave right now, for the sooner they split up the trail of the escapees the better. With Tuck in the lead the one group disappeared into the undergrowth south-westwards, and Siward's to the east; while Robin led the remainder of the group north-west back towards the camp, leaving Guy and the Coshams to watch them go. It was only by chance that they heard Robin's final words as he turned back to speak to Gilbert.

"Thank God for that! Some peace from the fussing of women! I thought for a dreadful moment we'd have another joining us!"

He was gone before anyone heard the reply, but Guy, Hugh and the brothers looked at one another aghast.

Hugh's face in particular creased in a frown of disproval.

"I know he's your cousin and you love him, Guy, but Robin's an ungrateful bastard sometimes!" he declared.

Guy sighed. "I won't argue with you on that one, Hugh."

"Can't he see she loves him?" Bilan asked of no-one in particular in his surprise.

At which point light dawned for Guy. "Maybe yes, maybe no."

"What's that supposed to mean?" Piers asked suspiciously.

But Guy was looking to Hugh. "Remember what we talked about? When he's Robin the crusader, the soldier, the fighter, he's as cold and calculating as the worst of men. And just now he's been in a fighting situation, yet he couldn't draw a drop of blood. Have we robbed him of one of his ways of releasing the pressure inside, I wonder?"

"Christ!" Thomas breathed. "Do you think that's made him a bit mad?"

"In an odd sort of way, maybe yes," Guy said regretfully. "By the time Marianne gets back he'll probably have no memory of having said that, and be as glad as the rest of you to know she's back safe. He's just in that other part of his head at the moment where he's all crusader and everyone is either with him or against him, and he can't always recognise who's who."

"Well he doesn't know how lucky he is to have a woman like Marianne care for him like that!" Hugh declared.

A statement which made Guy wonder whether Hugh had feelings for Marianne the more he thought about it on his lonely ride back to Nottingham. And what a tangled web that would make if it was true!

No, Gervase, I do not slander him when I say that Robin was no romantic lover. Indeed, he would always find it difficult to deal with women. I cannot say why it affected him more than any other of our band. He was no more battle-scarred than someone like Siward or James, and if he had very little to do with his own mother, he was certainly brought into my mother's wider brood along with John, so I doubt that was it.

˜Did he ever have Lady Marian as his wife?˜ you ask.

Ah, Brother, you will have to wait and see! But no, there was no ˜lady˜ of noble birth called Marian who would claim his heart in great romantic style, if that is what you are asking me. Our Marianne is the woman whose name and personality became woven into the legend, so rest assured, she will return!

But what of Walter? ˜You have not told me of what Robin did with Walter!˜ you cry. Patience, Brother! We are coming to that! Let me take a drink of this excellent beer to ease my throat and I will tell you. But let me remind you that Robin went back to that camp with just Gilbert, James and Malik, believing that he would not need the others. You would think that Much and Roger would not have had any problems keeping the wretched Walter out of trouble, and so did he.

Why do I call Walter wretched when he had betrayed Robin? Oh, Gervase, I may not have liked Walter at that moment, but I could see – as Robin probably could not – that Walter simply had not understood what Robin was trying to do, nor the subtleties of degrees of taxation any more than Algar had. He was a fool, but he had acted as much out of ignorance than anything, although I will grant you that he was a total fool where his brother's wife was concerned.

And I truly believed, as I rode away from them all on that day, that I would return to the camp as soon as possible to collect Walter, or that I would find Allan or Roger sneaking in to me at Nottingham one day to tell me they had brought him to within reach of me to save me finding another reason to be absent from the castle overnight. Indeed I was glad to be riding back alone so that I had time to scout out the dungeons at the castle, and determine who was still incarcerated in the depths. Although it may sound harsh, I wanted to stuff Walter back in there where, with luck, he would be forgotten about for several months, not the town gaol where he would have chance to chatter to his gaolers and do untold damage, and be brought out to face a judge all the sooner.

So I am the hard Sir Guy after all? Heavens! Make up your mind, Gervase! A moment ago you wanted Walter strung up from the nearest branch for being a traitor to your hero! What I was offering him was a good deal kinder than that, and with the potential for me to haul his sorry arse out of the dungeon at some later date when it would be safer for him to return to Fiskerton. A year or so down the road he would have forgotten how to get to the hideouts and camps, for Walter was no woodsman, and my friends would have been safe from any betrayal he then chose to make. I could have invented some petty tax infringement for him to have been brought in for and even found the money to pay it on his behalf – or so I was thinking at that point.

But I am talking as though that did not happen, am I? And if not, then what? Well I shall tell you right now!

Chapter 10

So, as for Walter, you must understand that the next is what I was told. Robin and the three others got back to the camp at Loxley to find Much and Roger nursing sore heads, and Walter gone. It was an understandable slip. Walter had declared he needed to use the privy pit they had dug just beyond the immediate camp, and he could hardly use that tied up like a joint for the spit. And after all, Walter had previously shown himself to be a particularly useless fighter, so although Roger said he had stood back while Much untied him, they were not expecting the violent reaction they got. Roger told the others that Walter hit Much with such force Roger feared he had been killed! One ferocious blow up under the jaw, which snapped Much's head back with great force. It is my belief that what saved Much was that he was off-balance, crouching down, so the force of the punch lifted him and his whole body went backwards in a sprawl. For believe me, Gervase, when I say that I have seen such a blow break a man's neck when the jaw and neck take the full upwards impact. Much was incredibly lucky!

As for Roger, he was stunned, he confessed, as the whole reason Much had gone to untie Walter while he stood by with one of the quarter-staffs was because they believed Walter would not harm Much, but thought less of himself. Where Walter got the strength from amazed them, for he reached out and seized the bottom of the quarter-staff before he had even gained his feet. Yanking Roger towards him, he punched him too. Not enough to knock him out fully, but sufficient to leave him dazed on the ground while Walter made his escape. Roger then admitted that as he got his wits back, he decided that he could not hope to track Walter, or do anything useful in terms of getting him back, whereas Much needed caring for. Even Robin did not argue over that choice, thank Heavens.

Yet by the time he and the others got back to the camp, it was also going to be difficult for them to follow Walter. All Roger could tell them was that their former friend had gone slipping and sliding down towards the Loxley River, and from there he could have gone in one of many directions. When I got to hear of this from Allan, when he came into Nottingham to warn me, he told me that they could only hope that Walter would have wandered round lost until he fell from hunger or exhaustion. It was a bitter thought, but they all recognised that Walter's hopeless sense of direction meant that he would be lucky to make it out of the forest in one piece, and thereby save the camp from discovery.

You are disappointed, Gervase? You thought there would be more of a grand confrontation between him and me in Nottingham? Bless me, Brother, I would have had to be inordinately unlucky to have been so accused by two of the gang in as many weeks! However I will placate you by telling you that Walter did not perish immediately. He was to reappear, *but some time later when a much bigger crisis was brewing – and that crisis was what saved me then, because no-one was listening to the ramblings of a disgruntled peasant by that time. Had he done as you so eagerly anticipated and accused me there and then in public in Nottingham, I might have been in a good deal of trouble, because some might have started wondering whether I was connected to the loss of the money from Mansfield, given that I was not far away, albeit legitimately. But I had a respite, as it turned out, and I gave thanks for that in my prayers, if not openly, for I was not so foolish as to presume that Walter might not find his way to the castle, even if it would be more by accident than design.*

However, for now we must leave Walter wandering the woods, and out of our ken for a while, and return to more pressing matters, as we are coming to a dreadful crisis. Ah, you are sitting up a little more attentively, I see! Yes, what comes next is something of much greater import – when a good man lost his life to the sheriff, and I lost someone I had come to think of as a friend. For we come to the spring of 1191 when Count John heard that Longchamp had been re-elected as a papal legate, and was also backing his nephew, Prince Arthur, as King Richard's heir, should our king die in the Holy Land. It will come as no surprise to you that our unloved Count of Mortain was incensed at being passed over for his late brother Geoffrey's son, nor that most folk believed that Longchamp was gleefully plotting to ensure that he would have a long regency in the event of King Richard's increasingly likely death in some foreign land.

Where this began to affect us in the Midland shires was in the ways that Longchamp was taking steps to make sure he had key positions already in his hands, should matters come to a fight. We had already heard that at the Michaelmas court of 1190 Longchamp had deprived Gerard de Cameville of the sheriffdom of Lincoln – something he would not have done had King Richard been at home. Cameville, you see, had a younger brother who was one of the commanders of King Richard's fleet, and Gerard himself had had his right confirmed by King Richard to remain in charge of Lincoln Castle. He was therefore holding Lincoln not only on account of having married the daughter of the hereditary constable of that castle, which would become significant soon, but more importantly by royal appointment. So you see Longchamp was definitely stretching his luck!

I was much disturbed by that news. As Norman lords went, de Cameville was a decent man. He, along with Bishop Hugh of Lincoln, had done much to ensure that the Jews in Lincoln had not suffered as those in York had done in the savage events of the previous March, and I saw him as a moderating influence in these troubled times. To hear, therefore, that he had been replaced by William de Stuteville was of little comfort. All I knew of de Stuteville was that he was one of the justiciars who had come on eyre in the past, and I also discovered that he held lands directly from Count John. So I feared that in any crisis he might be torn between Longchamp to whom he owed his office, and the youngest of the Plantagenets from whom he held his estates, and end up doing nothing to the detriment of all. This, then, was the background of the next upheaval to shake our lives.

What does this have to do with Robin, I hear you sigh? Oh far more than you know as yet, and not least because some of the conflict took place right on our doorstep! Let me tell you how that came about...

Nottinghamshire, June, the Year of Our Lord 1191

Guy looked around the hall at Edwinstowe where the swanimote was taking place on this distinctly soggy St Edmund's Day, grateful that yet again everything seemed to be peaceful. At the last two woodmotes he had attended in March and May, he had heard distant mutterings of 'Robin Hood', but mercifully nothing specific. He was still keeping half an ear open for the missing Walter, but was also glad to realise that the deer the band had undoubtedly taken, and had shared out the meat from to various villages, had not been brought to the courts' attention. That had to mean that Robin and the others were being careful and burying the bones where they would not be found.

Indeed, by courtesy of a brief visit by Allan, Guy knew that once Will had started building charcoal kilns, they had buried the bones beneath where a kiln would go, confident that the heat from the kiln would advance the breaking down of those bits they could make no use of. The antlers, of course, were valuable for making horn tips for the bows, and were swiftly put to good use. But it had been a nagging worry in the back of Guy's mind that someone would have said something by now about unlawful hunting, and he offered up a silent prayer of thanks that they had not.

Of all the courts this was the one where such an accusation ought to be made, for the swanimotes more than the woodmotes sent miscreants on to be judged at the eyres. And that was another thing niggling at Guy. When was the next eyre going to come? It was long overdue by his reckoning. The more he thought about it, the more he was sure that no-one had been since King Richard had been crowned – not for the regular eyre or the forest eyre! At this rate they would be stacking the accused like salt-cod in barrels in the town gaol before long. When he got back to Nottingham he was going to go through the scribes' scrolls and remind himself just how long it had been, hoping it was just his memory playing tricks on him.

However he had to focus on the proceedings for now. The verderer in charge of this court was Ranulph de Kirton, his manor being some four miles north-east of Edwinstowe. Because of the need to hold all the swanimotes on this day (or at the very least commencing on this day) to ensure that the forest had been cleared for the all-important fawning of the deer, each of the ancient forest courts at Edwinstowe, Linby, Mansfield and Calverton were in session – and had been since dawn was barely breaking with the current overload of cases – thereby ensuring that only one verderer sat at each.

The corrupt Walter Ingram would be fleecing the folk at the Linby court again, Guy feared, and this time without his help to stand up to him. Meanwhile Ralph of Woodborough would be dealing with the Calverton court, and Sanson de Strelley would be holding court at Mansfield. Alongside that, the two newer verderers created to deal with the expanded royal forest – Adam de Everingham and Roger de Lovetot – were sitting at makeshift swanimote courts in the bailiwick of Carburton to the north of Edwinstow, at the hall where the woodmotes were usually held, and similarly at Rufford. And none of them were men Guy would have trusted further than he could spit! To a man they seemed hell bent on getting some recompense for being saddled with the job of verderer, and since that was not to be had legitimately, they were fast becoming expert at gaining it on the sly.

Currently, de Kirton was making himself comfortable while his scribe set out his pens, ink and parchment, along with those documents brought along for the court. Like Ingram, he had taken over the role from his father when the older de Kirton had found the extensive riding required for the job too much of an exertion, and like Ingram, Ranulph was a young Norman lord who had grown up in privilege and had no idea what it was like to go without, except in those years when harvest were so bad it hit even the richest. It meant that he was singularly unsympathetic to any pleas, however justified, and Guy was bracing himself for a grim and dispiriting day.

Certainly the morning passed miserably and slowly with a clutch of fines handed down, and no-one getting away without paying something. A poor woman who had gone into the forest to retrieve an escaped chicken was fined and lost the chicken – which would no doubt end up on the de Kirton table tomorrow – while another villager was fined heavily for the two piglets he had been unable to find as he brought the rest of his pigs out of the forest, and which had been 'found' with surprising ease by two of de Kirton's men. And so it went on. Four pence here, two pence there, and all the time the pile of coins in the leather satchel on the desk by the clerk was piling up. All Guy could hope was that he was managing to maintain the mask of indifference, and that any looks of disgust would be read by de Kirton as feelings of superiority towards the peasants.

By the time the session broke for the midday meal, Guy was so thoroughly disheartened he actually joined Ranulph in taking wine with the selection of bread, cold meats and cheese provided for the court. He felt a desperate need of something to dull the ache inside, and maybe wine was better than venting his feelings later in the day. He was soon to regret it.

The shock came as the court was drawing to a close. It was hot and stuffy in the hall, and even with the main doors flung open to let in what little breeze there was, everyone was beginning to wilt as the day clouded over into sultry humidity, and black clouds appeared on the horizon. Between that and the wine, Guy was finding it hard to keep his eyes open by now, the irony not lost on him that this was exactly what he had so disparaged Ingram for. One moment they were considering the case of a charcoal burner who was protesting that he would not now be able to go to his kiln – even though it was outside of what had been the old forest, east of it in a small wood, and traditionally would not have become closed off at this time – and the next hooded men had swarmed into the hall, bows drawn threateningly.

"Stay where you are!" one of them bellowed, as the nocked arrows swept across the room. "In the name of Robin Hood, be still!"

It shook Guy, and not only into wakefulness. It was incredible how just the mention of that name took the fright away from the ordinary people. They still looked scared, but now those worried glances were aimed at the verderer's men, and the men from the castle who had come with Guy, Sir Mahel and Sir Osmaer. Would they become caught in a fight?

Guy himself felt the wine lurch acidly in his stomach. God in heaven, what was Robin thinking? To attack a court like this! He'd heard reports of the odd robbery along the Great North Road in the last couple of months. A few more than normal, to be sure, but not enough to get a useless sheriff like fitz John all fired up like some smith's forge and ready to start smiting people. But this? Fitz John would never let *this* go!

Belatedly he realised that Ranulph had turned to him, no doubt looking for support, and had seen the shock on his face. Well that was all to the good! If asked later, de Kirton would testify that Gisborne had been as shocked as everyone else, and never know that the reason was quite different to the rest of them.

In that instant, though, two of the robbers had come up to the table, one delivering a sharp punch to the scribe, which knocked him out cold – a fist which Guy recognised as Will's – and the other grabbed the satchel of coins. Beneath that hood Guy saw Malik, and the brief look of worry as their eyes met. So Robin hadn't done this without some opposition! Thank the saints for that! All Guy could hope was that those voices of restraint had made sure there was some kind of plan in place in case it all went wrong.

Then it did go wrong. Osmaer wasn't the kind of bullish man Walkelin or Fredegis were, but he drew the line at being shoved about by men he saw as common thieves. To Guy's horror, Osmaer, who unlike Guy had not been sat at the table but had been lounging against the hall wall with many of the men, yelled,

"Now!"

The men-at-arms, who had thought this would be a boring few days sitting around listening to villagers whining, suddenly found a new burst of energy and sprang into action. In a heartbeat the hall had descended into chaos, men-at-arms drawing their knives and swords, or grabbing quarter-staffs, and lunging at the intruders, while villagers got in everyone's way as they ran screaming from the hall in panic.

Guy could do nothing but join in. His heart in his boots, he drew his sword and went after the nearest intruder. To his intense relief it turned out to be Siward, who instantly winked at him and signalled with his eyes towards the side of the hall. Together they put on a show of much vigorous cutting and parrying, while at the same time doing nothing much of any harm to either. As a bench came in the way, Guy managed a theatrical trip over it and was gratified that Siward jumped over it and seemed to leap on him. As they feigned grappling with one another, Guy gasped,

"What in God's name are you doing here?"

"Robin!" Siward grunted as he heaved himself up and threw a fake punch at Guy for all to see, before Guy pulled him back down. He hardly needed to say more.

"The sheriff won't let this go!" Guy replied between loud groans. "He'll empty Nottingham of soldiers to hunt you!"

"I know! We told him that." Siward sighed, letting Guy roll to the top and seem to return the punches. "He wanted the grand gesture. To let the people know he's on their side."

"Fuck!" Guy was so taken aback it was lucky Siward had his wits about him and yanked Guy out of sight again.

"We're going to run north, then double back and cross to Loxley still north of Byth," Siward puffed. "Just so you know. In case they make you track us!"

"Knock me out!" Guy hissed.

"What?"

"Thump me! Make it look good! Give me a bruise and a half, and then run! Get out of here! All of you!"

Siward caught on and hit Guy high on the cheek, where it would show as a spectacular bruise in a day or so. It certainly made Guy's head ring, but wasn't enough to knock him out cold. He faked it, though, lying still just where he could observe things through slitted eyes. Robin was the last to leave. Well that was something. No leaving John in peril this time! And then there was the sound of a great bow's *thrum*, and an arrow embedded itself in the wall at the back of the hall with a piece of parchment stuck on it. Guy guessed that had been loosed by Bilan.

Thank God and all the saints none of those whom he thought of as the more vulnerable ones had been in the hall, which included Bilan, Much and Roger, as well as Allan and John. Aside from Will, Malik and Siward, he had managed to identify James and Gilbert, and Thomas and Piers, as the men Robin had led in. Eight of them hadn't been a bad guess at how many would have been needed, only four less than the combined knights, men-at-arms and verderer's men. Next time, though, they would need every man they had, because he would bet both on there being a next time, and that fitz John would send his men armed to the teeth to subsequent courts.

He was saved from thinking further worrying thoughts by having to play the man struggling back into consciousness, as Osmaer came to help him to his feet. When he got there and managed to convincingly look around him as if all this was new to his eyes, he didn't need to pretend his shock as fresh detail appeared. Every one of the men sported some kind of wound, but infinitely more troubling was the sight of three men-at-arms apparently dead and also one of de Kirton's men.

"Christ on the Cross!" Guy gulped, hurrying to the one fallen man. He knew him only as Godfrey. Not a good man. A bit of a brute. But now his guts had been opened up and he was staring at the roof with sightless eyes. What if this had been one of the men from High Peak? He staggered outside to heave up the wine, excusing himself to Osmaer as he returned by touching his face and saying weakly,

"Blow to the head."

"Does make you sick sometimes," Osmaer agreed, all curiosity gone now his thoughts were turned from why Guy should be so affected by one dead minion.

Together they got everyone up and sorted into those who were just knocked about, and those who needed genuine help. Luckily Guy's ability at patching men up was already well known within the castle, so no-one thought it odd that he should be calling for what he needed to apply to wounds and bandaging them, rather than being the one going to track the rogues.

There was no question of returning to Nottingham that night, not even of sending a rider to warn the sheriff. Who knew what fate they might be sending such a poor soul to if the thieves were still about? With first light Guy went out and made much of searching for tracks. The poor folk of Edwinstowe were falling over themselves to help, constantly asking him if he needed any torches or candles, no doubt desperate to prove that they'd had no idea the attack was coming.

However Guy needed no help to see the tracks heading north. The gang were doing as Siward had said, making it obvious that they were going in the opposite direction to Nottingham as fast as possible. No doubt in a few miles the tracks would get fainter and then fizzle out, but not here by the village. That was some comfort to Guy. With such a clear trail to follow there would be no question as to why he, rather than Osmaer, hadn't begun tracking. And with none of the men fit enough anymore to accompany him, even fitz John could surely not expect him to go after eight armed and dangerous men alone?

To his relief, Osmaer and Mahel, with de Kirton, agreed that Mahel would be the one to break the news to fitz John. The obnoxious knight lacked the imagination to see what a storm he would be riding into, and in his arrogance thought only of being the one to tell the sheriff as fast as possible, rather than remembering the fate of other bringers of bad news. When he tore out of the village the following morning with Guy and Osmaer's horses to use as relays for his own, Osmaer gave a sigh of relief.

"He'd have marched the wounded so hard we'd have lost Harold and Ralph as well," he said to Guy as they turned to get the men ready to march out. It was an assessment Guy himself had made, but it surprised him that Osmaer had done so too. He wouldn't have thought the knight cared that much, but maybe being the butt of fitz John's temper on several recent occasions had given him some much needed sympathy for his fellow sufferers.

Guy smiled. "Well he's welcome to the reception he's going to get off fitz John."

"Jesu, Mary and Joseph, yes! A new gang of outlaws in Sherwood *and* the court fines gone? Fitz John will burst a blood vessel!"

Guy kept to himself his silent wish that such a bursting might prove fatal, but when they got back to the castle they were mightily glad that they weren't in Mahel's place. For once the blustering knight was utterly subdued, for even cut about as he was, fitz John had erupted into a fit of violent anger, throwing everything to hand at the hapless Mahel. Even stranger was the fury fitz John then flung at Alan of Leek. Guy and Osmaer were warned even as they entered the outer bailey to tread softly, and that poor Alan was still being tongue-lashed over a day after Mahel's arrival.

Gritting their teeth, Guy and Osmaer walked to the main hall to report to fitz John, but found him in another room with the assistant constable of the castle before him.

"How could this *happen*?" the petulant Roger was screaming into Alan's face. "Why didn't you *do* something?"

As the two came abreast of Alan, Guy was shocked at the pallor of his face. How many times had this happened already?

"Yes?" shrieked fitz John at them, oblivious to how much the spoilt child he sounded. "And what have you two worthless whelps from the midden got to say for yourselves?"

Guy felt something inside unravel, and he stamped the couple of paces to fitz John and glowered down into the beetroot-red face.

"That we lost three good men and damned near our own lives! And who the *hell* do you think *you're* calling a whelp from the midden?" The last was said with such savagery and pent up fury of its own that it was as good as a slapped face for bringing fitz John down from his tantrum.

Guy didn't give him chance to get a word in, though, but stormed on,

"What in the name of all the saints do you thing Sir Alan could've done? Eh? Six bloody courts were held all on the *same* fucking day! All miles apart! He couldn't have been to every one of them if he'd been a bloody saint and the archbishops of Canterbury and York all rolled into one! Or are you so arrogant as to believe that the Lord would speak to you personally, and inform you which one of your courts would be attacked that day? Do you think yourself *that* far above us ...*my lord*? Because beware of your immortal soul if you do! And don't blame Sir Alan for not having such divine insight, either!"

Confronted with Guy's blistering and wholly justified rage, the young sheriff had gone from red to white with astonishing speed, and turned his back to cover the fact.

"They came in *armed*. Weapons drawn and ready to fight," Guy was continuing. "Our men have never known that happen at a court! *Never*! Why, then, should they have expected it this time? Why should *anyone* have expected it? All our men fought with great bravery and did the best they could, but there was little room to move in that hall, and no time or space to fall back and then launch an attack of our own."

"That's the truth, my lord," Osmaer added coldly.

"Would you like me to unbind their wounds, and have them drip more of their blood on the floor before you to prove the point?" Guy snarled.

"Get out!" shrieked fitz John. "All of you, *out!*" He no doubt hoped it would sound imposing, but the shake in his voice made Guy think that this was the first time in far too many years that someone had spoken to young Roger like that, and that he was suspiciously close to tears.

Guy made a point of slamming the door hard behind them, the men going about their business in the hall beyond all staring at him open-mouthed as he stamped past, having heard all too clearly the altercation.

Once they were back in the old part of the castle, Guy put a hand on Alan's arm to halt him, and asked more calmly,

"What in the name of Christ and all the saints was that about? Where is Sir Robert? Why are you carrying the blame?"

Alan rubbed a hand across tired eyes. "Robert's gone to talk to Eudes," he told Guy, referring to Eudes DeVille who was constable of Tickhill, and therefore Robert's counterpart there. "We had news the day you left that Longchamp's planning to besiege Lincoln Castle. Apparently he's sorted out the Mortimer uprising over on the border, and Roger Mortimer has been exiled for three years. So he's got time now to try and grab Lincoln for himself or one of his damned brothers! Robert thought we might be next. Us or Tickhill. It'd be a proper feather in his cap if he could take a castle which belongs to Count John!"

"Why?" asked Osmaer blankly. "Why us in particular?"

But Guy had already grasped what Alan was saying. "Because the one person in England who might just be able to stand up to Longchamp is the king's brother. John might be an obnoxious bastard – by nature if not by birth – but with King Richard so far away, who else could stop Longchamp from doing whatever he wants? So anything Longchamp can do to cut Count John's claws is working in his favour."

Sir Alan sighed. "And the trouble is, Longchamp already has an army at his back. He brought men together to take Wigmore Castle with the justification that he was subduing a revolt. Well if he just keeps them on the march and brings them over here, how many will question whether what they're doing to Lincoln or Nottingham is right? He's being cunning and giving them no time to stop and think!"

"Will Lincoln hold?" Guy wondered.

Now Alan managed a wan smile. "I'd actually bet more money on my lady Nicholaa holding her father's castle than Sir Gerald himself would have! Nicholaa de La Haye is a formidable woman!"

"And she's forewarned," Guy mused. "Roger Mortimer might well have been taken by surprise. The sheriffs over on the Marches have long been allowed to be something of a law unto themselves, so Longchamp's actions would be unexpected. But now Longchamp has done this, and most of England knows, too, so it won't be as easy to take a second castle."

"But Sir Robert felt we had to be prepared to go to Tickhill's aid, and them to us, just in case Longchamp comes our way," Sir Alan told them wearily. "God in heaven, it's been a long couple of days! You've made a real enemy of fitz John now you know, Guy. I started off disbelieving he could be so bloody stupid as to blame me for this disaster, but he is and this time he's not letting go. He's terrified the blame will fall on him when Longchamp finds out, so he's determined that come what may, he'll have a scapegoat ready and waiting to be sacrificed. He's worse than a cornered wild boar! He'll gore and toss us, but by proxy, sending us to Longchamp to deal with in his stead."

"I know he hates me," Guy said bleakly, "but sometimes you just have to stand up to a man like him and take the consequences, because what he'll do to you in other ways will be just as bad."

Osmaer now sighed and left, saying he would go and check on the men and then get some much needed sleep. Once he had left, Alan turned to Guy and drew him off to one of the smaller chambers.

"I think fitz John fears you," he said softly, "and men like him hate to feel fear. Be careful, Guy! You've shown him he can only push you so far. He might just think that your head fits the executioners block!"

Guy watched Alan go in his turn, but thought to himself that that fear might just be what would keep him alive. He had seen the panic in fitz John's eyes, and now belatedly realised what a fearsome figure he must have cut, for he had seen his own reflection briefly in a bucket of water. Black-eyed, leather tunic scuffed to bits and cut, and filthy from the road, he had looked more like some savage mercenary than a forester knight. And fitz John was not yet so used to dealing with men like that to be confident of what would happen if he pushed one too far. Guy might just decide to go down fighting and take fitz John with him! But by backing down, Sir Alan had made himself a much more likely target, and Guy resolved to try and watch Sir Alan's back as best he could.

The entire castle spent a tense following week, but when the change came it only made things worse. As midsummer arrived, so did word that Lincoln was besieged by a force of thirty knights, and over three hundred foot-soldiers. And to seal the panic, they were told that Longchamp had miners working to undermine part of the castle walls. Fitz John then took one look at the rock beneath Nottingham Castle, with its sink-holes and fissures, and declared that he would not be holed up in a castle which would fall around his ears.

It was a measure of how hated he had made himself that not one person bothered to point out that the miners would have little chance of succeeding with such a tactic here.

"They'd be more likely to bring every tunnel they make crashing down about them," Sir Walter chuckled softly to Guy, as they stood back and let fitz John sweep out, his personal servants scurrying in his wake with his baggage.

"What's the excuse this time?" Guy asked equally quietly.

"Says he feel the need to visit the other part of his sheriffdom," Walter replied with a sniff of disdain. "Derbyshire's never bothered him before! Still, bloody de Wendenal can have the joy of him up at High Peak for a while. Those two deserve one another!" And Guy wasn't about to argue with that.

As fitz John's party disappeared out of sight down the road, the whole castle seemed to breath a sigh of relief. For the first time in weeks, all of the knights congregated in the hall of the old keep around Sir Robert to hear what he had decided with Eudes.

"Are we going to be forced to take sides if the prince and the chancellor come to blows?" asked Sir Martin. "I can't imagine the king's brother sitting back and letting Longchamp take castle after castle!"

"Either him or the illegitimate one sitting on the archbishop's throne in York!" sniffed Sir Walter, and everyone winced at that.

Lincoln was too close to Nottinghamshire as one of Count John's personal holdings, and to York as Geoffrey Plantagenet's seat of power, for either of them to not be taking a keen interest in what happened.

Robert looked round them room with tired eyes. "Eudes and I talked on into the night and most of the next day over this. We're as sure as we can be that Count John will act. He can't afford not to! I'd be surprised if he doesn't act before Lincoln is taken, but we're both certain he'll act if it *is*." He paused and looked around at them all. "We've decided that we have to support the prince, Count John."

The room erupted in gasps and mutterings, and Robert held up his hand for quiet. "What choice do we have? The king himself gave our two shires to his brother. That makes Count John unquestionably our lord. Are any of you prepared to go against King Richard's wishes? What he asks of us we must do, or risk being accused and held responsible for being unfaithful to him, and who knows what punishment the king might hand down for that? We may have seen very little of our king in the last few years, but you all surely know of his reputation as a knight, and that he holds the knightly virtues in almost as high regard as he does his faith. Can you doubt what his response would be to disloyalty, then?"

A gloomy silence fell on the room until Mahel said what many were thinking. "But Longchamp's the devil we have to live with. We don't even know if the king will ever return from the Holy Land. Bloody Longchamp's in the next shire! If we take against him, we might not live to see the king's return!"

To Guy's amazement he could see Sir Alan nodding in agreement with Mahel. That didn't bode well! To have the constable and assistant constable taking opposite views on something as important as this could well lead to terrible trouble, and of the kind which dragged everyone in the castle in its wake. For himself, Guy could see what Robert meant. It wasn't pleasant to think that he might be taking the side of the prince he cordially loathed, but when it came to right or wrong, Robert had clearly got to the heart of it – Count John held the two shires directly of his brother as his own lands, to do with as he pleased. Therefore they had no choice but to take his side.

Guy had hoped for time to get Sir Alan on one side and try to talk some sense into him, but in little over a week they were due to go back out to the various courts again for the swanimote which closed Fence Month, and everyone was kept busy. However, Guy did find time to go and look at the clerks' records and was horrified to learn he had been right. A significant downside of the two shires being Count John's own territory was that no eyre seemed to have been held in them since their being handed over at King Richard's accession.

"God help us," Guy found himself saying aloud to the astonishment of the two monks in the scriptorium.

"Sir Guy?" one asked, perplexed. "Is there something amiss?"

Guy blinked. "Oh, not with anything any of you have done," he reassured the worried men. "It's just that I've realised how long it's been since we had an eyre. *And* how many men are still stuck in the town gaol waiting for trial! St Issui save them, the poor souls must be crammed in close and near suffocating in this heat!"

The monk gazed back at him owl-like. "Indeed, Sir Guy. We noticed that. The main eyre is overdue by a year and the forest eyre by more. That one should have come around the time of the king's coronation, but didn't. We had to get another chest to start putting the rolls in from the last swanimotes, because we'd run out of space in the other one."

"Where?" Guy asked with as much nonchalance as he could muster.

"This is the old one," the monk said, patting the top of a much-used oak lid, "and that one over in the corner is the new one."

Guy could immediately see that the new one was still coloured the warm brown of the wood, as yet not darkened by the application of much beeswax to keep the damp at bay.

"Well done. Good thinking," he praised them, but determined to come back at night and start looking through the old rolls for men who might be released on the quiet. If it got any worse, he might be asking Robin and the others to come and arrange a break-out from the gaol! Already fitz John was issuing rewards for the capture of this new outlaw, Robin Hood. How was breaking into the gaol going to do to make things any worse?

Then Guy caught sight of another piece of parchment and felt a shiver run down his spine. There it was at last, an open announcement of Robin Hood and all who followed him being made outlaw. So now it was official.

"Has this been sent out?" he asked the monks, with what he hoped was a suitably calm voice.

"Oh yes, Sir Guy! That was sent even before you got back from Edwinstowe," the younger of the two said, positively glowing with excitement now. "It's the first one of those I've had to help write out!"

"Edwin!" the older reproved him. "It's a serious matter!"

"Yes, I know," the unrepentant Edwin admitted, "but this is *Robin Hood*! He gives back to the poor. We heard that at Mansfield, brother. The whole swanimote was full of it!"

"Well he won't for much longer if the sheriff catches him," the older brother sighed, with more sorrow than disapproval, Guy thought.

Well it was to be hoped that St Lazarus would look after his supplicant, because Robin was going to need all the help he could get if fitz John decided to organise a proper hunt. Maybe this whole situation with Longchamp and Lincoln wasn't such a bad thing after all? It was certainly distracting fitz John away from outlaws, and Guy couldn't help but be grateful for that.

However, before anything could happen regarding fitz John and outlaws, Guy and the others were just about to leave the castle the following day when a rider came pounding in with further news.

"The prince!" he gasped to Sir Robert as everyone else swarmed around the two. "Count John's orders! You're to surrender the castle to him!"

"*Surrender?*" several people gasped in astonishment.

"Jesu! That makes it sounds as though he doesn't trust us to hold it for him!" Sir Henry's indignant voice rose above the babble.

"I warned you it might come to this," Sir Alan said to Sir Robert, completely ignoring the protocol of not questioning his superior in front of others of lower rank.

However, Robert just shook his head wearily and let Alan's words go. "Everyone who is here doing service should go immediately," he told the assembly. "This is not your struggle. Go back to your families and warn them that we could be seeing the start of a civil war if this turns ugly. It's very much their choice whether you then choose to come back once someone from Count John's court has come to take over. God help you all, it might even be the man himself!"

Guy saw that not everyone had picked up on how Robert had said that.

"*You* all?" he queried. "Does that mean you're leaving?"

Sir Robert gave another thin smile. "You always were quick, Guy. Yes, I'm leaving. My orders to you who are permanently here are for you to hold the castle and keep it secure. From today onwards, I think it would be best if we kept even the outer bailey closed off from the town. We don't want Longchamp sending men in disguised as peasants bringing goods into the castle, and then taking it over."

"We'll have to go out to the forest courts," Sir Walter protested. "I can't imagine our lord and master would be any too pleased to find his coffers depleted because the fines haven't come in, and the taxes not paid."

"No indeed," Sir Robert sighed. "What a time for them to pick to squabble! Very well. I shall stay until you all get back from the courts with those of the knights doing service who are willing to delay their departure. But after that I shall depart for my family's manor until I'm required."

He could hardly be blamed for wanting to do that, Guy thought, and Robert's manor was only just over the border in Staffordshire – not the farthest place to have to come back from, but conveniently out of the prince's jurisdiction. He himself was half tempted to head for Gisborne once the court was over and done with. Claim the time he was long overdue to go and check on his own holding. The more he thought about it, the more attractive the proposition became. Dare he ask Robert for his release for a week or two?

Then he heard Alan muttering to himself, "This is wrong, all wrong!" as everyone began to disperse.

"How is it wrong?" Guy asked. "What has you so adamantly against the idea of giving the prince what's already his?"

Alan started, clearly unaware that he had spoken his thoughts aloud. For a moment Guy thought he would just turn on his heels and go, but then Alan seemed to think better of it.

"Damn it, Guy, do none of you remember? When King Richard was crowned, his brother was sworn to quit the kingdom for a full three years. These shires were given to his brother for their income *only*. The agreement was that Count John had the shires, but the *castles* stayed in the hands of the crown and whoever was managing it on the king's behalf."

"Christ Almighty!" Guy was appalled. How could they have forgotten?

"Well may you call upon Him," Alan sighed. "Do you see now, Guy? Our fool of a sheriff has disappeared, and will no doubt have some half-way plausible tale worked out to save his miserable hide when the reckoning comes. He does have the care of two whole shires to think about, although we know the truth of how little he does himself in that respect. But Robert? The castle is *his* responsibility! Whatever happens to the shires, that's supposed to stay as part of the king's demesne – not his brother's – and it's Robert, as constable, who's supposed to ensure that happens."

He shook his head despairingly. "I know why you all forgot that. It's so easy when the castle sits at the heart of all the administration for the shires. This one far more so than Tickhill, or Bolsover, or Newark. All the taxes and prisoners end up here, and that's without our new duties over the extra Royal Forest lands! So it's so easy to forget that the castle's a separate entity to the lands around it, and in truth this must be the first time when it's ever mattered. I can't think of another time when a castle which acts as the seat of the sheriff was placed in such a dreadful conundrum."

"Well it wouldn't, would it?" Guy responded bitterly. "Even during the war between King Stephen and the Empress Maud, she didn't have official control of certain shires which had, to all intents and purposes, been taken out of his realm! What a mess! What are you going to do? Wait until Robert has gone, and then try to hold the castle against Count John?"

"I don't know," Alan said sadly. "I really don't know. Robert says that our un-beloved prince is the one to support. That the fact that he managed to wriggle out of the ban on coming to England within just a few months shows that his brother will be lenient towards him."

"Yes, but him coming back and living the high life at Winchester, and in the home of any baron who'd have him, isn't the same as handing him a bloody fortress, is it!" Guy spluttered.

"Two, actually."

"Two what?"

"Two castles. He's made the same demand of Tickhill."

Guy felt his world slipping into chaos again. "Judas' balls! Any word on Newark? If he wants to go up against Longchamp – who might have Lincoln – Newark's the nearest."

"Not yet. But then again, Guy, Newark belongs to the bishop of Lincoln, doesn't it!"

"Hell's teeth, of course! This heat's addling my brain! I should have thought that out for myself. Even someone as lacking in devotion as Count John might think twice about taking on Longchamp *and* the Church at the same time! He certainly can't demand the handing over of the bishop's castle as he's done with ours."

"Indeed! And Newark serves its purpose of guarding the Great North Road where it crosses the Foss Way, but it's not exactly ideal if Longchamp wanted to insist on the bishop supporting him, and using Newark to launch an attack out of. Far too much marshland around it to be able to assemble an army around it"

Guy didn't think Newark ought to be dismissed quite that readily, but he'd also thought of something else. The youngest Plantagenet was nothing if not cunning. "Count John's just been handed an excuse on a platter, hasn't he? If he'd tried this a few months ago everyone would've been on their guard. But Longchamp's made a mistake! By trying take Lincoln by force he's worried a good many of the major barons, I shouldn't wonder. So now they won't bat an eyelid at the prince wanting to have somewhere to watch his enemy from."

"Oh thank God you can see it now!" Alan's relief was heartfelt. "I'd almost started thinking I was going mad for being the only one! Yes, he's a crafty one is the prince. It's the opportunity he's been waiting for, and Robert is going to hand it to him without a backwards glance, but it doesn't make it the right thing to do. You mentioned King Stephen..."

"Jesu save us! If the king should die in the east, we're set for another such war, aren't we? Without castles at his disposal, Count John would be forced to take things more slowly. He'd have to get the support of a majority of the leading barons, get himself crowned and then challenge Longchamp, if that twisted devil didn't use his position as archbishop to block it! ...God Above! ...Longchamp as regent for Prince Geoffrey's boy, Arthur, and able to back it up with King Richard's sworn and attested will. He'd be able to call on the Church then, all right, and what would be the betting that Geoffrey Plantagenet would then throw the weight of the archbishopric of York behind him? Henry's bastard son was always more loyal to the family than Queen Eleanor's sons. ...May the saints preserve us! That's a grim thought, isn't it! I can see now why the prince is so eager to grasp this chance."

Alan was nodding sadly. "It just gets more and more twisted the more you look at it. That's why I believe we should stick to what the king's original intentions were. Hold the castle against Longchamp if necessary, but not hand it over to Count John either."

Guy grimaced but squared his shoulders. "Then I'm with you, for what that's worth."

Alan's face lit up. "It means an awful lot!" What he didn't say out loud was that he knew just how much weight Guy's word carried with the lower ranks. If the knights doing service were leaving, and some of the regular knights might too, then he would have to have the support of the men-at-arms and the ordinary men of the castle, and these were the very men who would follow Guy more than any other of the knights. If Guy made it plain that he was staying and supporting Sir Alan, then Alan could probably count on at least half of the garrison straight away.

Guy gave a terse nod. "Very well. Then we go and get the bloody swanimotes out of the way as fast as possible. I've got to go up to Mansfield this time – there's some unfinished business over what felling can be allowed now that the forest is back open again. Better I go than anyone else since I know the background. Anyway, it would look suspicious to Sir Robert if I suddenly asked to change which court I was going to to Calverton or Linby. ...Damn it! I hate the thought of going behind his back like this!"

"Me too," Alan agreed. "He's been a friend as well as a commander for many years. All I keep thinking is that I'm doing it to save his neck as well as all the rest of ours."

They parted with a shake of hands, and Guy set off for Mansfield, hoping like mad that nothing would happen in the three days he would be away.

Oh Gervase, how wrong I was to have that hope! I went off and hurried the business along as fast as I could, but Sanson de Strelley was determined to have his say on every matter, and the court dragged on for the whole of the day and into the evening. When I finally managed to leave and get back to the castle it was to find that all of my best intentions had been as undermined as Lincoln Castle's walls! Despite what he had said, Robert of Crockston had gone, and in his place was a supercilious knight brandishing his orders from the prince. Of Alan there was no sign, and when I asked after him, I was told that he had been sent back to his own manor too.

When I got the chance to ask some of my old friends from our days up at High Peak about what had happened, I was told that Alan of Leek had protested long and hard, but our new lord had come with enough men to be able to send Sir Alan off with an armed escort to make sure that he left. They had seen Sir Alan riding out with a four-man escort, his head bowed in defeat, and I myself saw those same men ride back in, for Leek might have been over the border into Staffordshire, but it was not so very far off from Nottingham, and with decent roads between the two. Now, though, I had to be on my guard for my own safety and of those whom I still felt I had a duty of care towards within the castle. I longed to be able to send a message out to Robin to tell him of what had happened, but the new man – one Ernais Malvesin by name – was keen to show his master that he had control of the castle, and I could not stir beyond the gates for days.

So there we were, Brother. It was early July and the whole world seemed to have gone mad in the space of a few short weeks. Those of us unfortunate enough to be left at the castle were now caught in the dire trap between two dreadful adversaries. On the one hand, we could be seen to be disobeying the king's chancellor; and viewed in a different light, we were disobeying the king's brother and probable heir! It did not take someone having a vision for us to predict that the tragedy would strike before it was all over.

Chapter 11

*F*or truth, Gervase, I and my friends within Nottingham Castle did not know which way to turn for the best in those dreadful days of mid-July 1191. The new cuckoo in our nest, Malvesin, had come with a party of ten knights and some thirty men-at-arms, some of whom looked suspiciously like mercenaries, and far too much the seasoned fighters for our lads to hope to overcome without serious loss of life. I therefore had a hurried meeting with Sir Walter and Sir Martin in their room, and together we decided that we must advocate a semblance of co-operation, for all our sakes. They would talk to the other knights, especially the more hot-headed ones like Henry, and try to get through to them that there was no clear right path to take. That for us lesser folk it would be better to sit tight and see what happened next. I was to do the same for the men-at-arms and men like Harry down in the stables.

You think I had the lion's share of the work? Oh no, Brother! Mine was the easy task, for all that I had far more men to talk to. Harry and the stable lads were men of common sense and no fighters. And although they wore the sheriff's badge, at this point in time the sheriff's men-at-arms were, for the most part, just the heftier lads from the local area who had had a bit of training. All they had needed to do in the past had been to break up scuffles at the various courts, keep a watch on local men hauled into gaol or the dungeons for various misdemeanours, and stop footpads and outlaws gaining entry to the castle. Not since the conflict between King Henry and the Empress Maud, some half a century ago, had there been any need for real fighting in the Midland shires. And you have to remember how vigorously the kind of young men who <u>did</u> want to fight had been encouraged to go with the king to free the Holy Land.

Remember also, that when Longchamp had wanted to find men to bring Roger Mortimer to heel, he had had to go out of his way to find them. He had to <u>recruit</u> an army. They were not there waiting for him to direct as he willed, and probably most of those he did use were men who had already served with his brother in Normandy, and had come to Hereford when Henry Longchamp had been made sheriff there. For even over there, such men were not readily found amongst the locals. De Braose would have taken his own experienced men away with him back to his lairs at Abergavenny or Brecon, and you should recall from what I told you before, that even Grosmont, Skenfrith and Llantilio on the border were hardly crammed with fighting men for most of the year.

So you see, Brother, I took one look at the scarred and battered newcomers sharpening their swords in the inner bailey, and decided that if we did have to take them on, then a head to head confrontation would not be the way to do it. And please note, dear Gervase, that these new men-at-arms did each have swords, whereas most of the men I regularly rode out *with were normally armed with spears – which are a most effective weapon when used in numbers in an army, but in the hands of one man coming up against another armed with a sword, and experienced at using it, would be at a disadvantage. However, our knowledge of the castle and time were both on our side, albeit only for a short while until Lincoln possibly fell, but we had to use them to our advantage.*

Therefore our first task was to try to find out if the king had any idea of what his brother was up to. Had the king written to Count John to act in his name? If Longchamp had fallen so far from favour, we might throw in our lot with the prince's men. We needed to get outside information, and for that someone had to get out of the castle, and oh how I wished I could get in touch with Robin!

Nottingham, July, the Year of Our Lord 1191

𝕴t was while standing on the outer wall, looking out at the town and wishing he could do something, almost *anything*, that Guy heard the commotion. Down below him and to his left, at the Outer Barbican, he could hear a woman's voice raised in anger. Sighing, he decided he'd better go and intervene. Malvesin had his own men at this vital outer gate, and because of their heavy-handed approach, already there had been altercations between them and the townsfolk bringing in essential supplies. Indeed, that had been partly the reason he'd been loitering here rather than anywhere else, because he, Walter, Martin, and the three knights permanently attached to the castle, had been taking it in turns to try and avert disaster.

As he strode along the wall walkway and then reached the top of the flight of steps, her voice became ever clearer until, to his horror, he realised he knew who this was.

"Do I *look* like I'm one of the chancellor's *men*?" Marianne's distinctive voice was saying with withering sarcasm.

Then there was a squeak, the sound of a very hard slap, and another woman's voice said sharply,

"You slap my arse, I slap your face! Simple. *Comprenez*?"

Guy knew that voice too! Mariota! And he picked up speed, taking the worn stone steps downwards as fast as he dared, but already hearing a further exchange.

"*Putana!*" the man spat, marking him as one of the foreign men in the force. Then "Aaagh...", and Guy reached the ground in time to see him keeling over onto the stone pavers clutching his groin.

"I understood that!" Mariota snarled, sounding her most Scottish. "Don't you call me a whore, you wee piece of shite!"

At which point Guy saw them, two women both bearing variants on the name of the Virgin – Marianne with her blonde hair escaping in rebellious strands and blue eyes flashing dangerously, Mariota with her dark curls writhing around her headscarf like Medusa's snakes and pale grey eyes like ice, and neither of them looking either meek or mild just at this moment. The cult of Mary had resulted in some singularly inappropriate naming, he couldn't help thinking with an inner chuckle. So many Marys, Marions, Mariannes, and Mary-Anns around, all named with hopes of divine intercession, and some of them needing it more than others! With that in mind, the next words almost came without thinking.

"Marian!" he called, hurrying to them. "What are you doing here?"

The remaining three soldiers standing turned to him, startled.

"You know zis woman?" one said incredulously.

Guy put on his most stern face as he strode forward. "She comes from my cousin's manor, where she is held in *great* respect!"

"Which one? Zis?" And he stabbed an accusing finger towards Marianne, "Or zis ...zis..." He couldn't find words to describe Mariota, whose eyes had narrowed like a cat's focused on prey at even the hint that she might be called a whore again.

"Both of them!" Guy responded, suddenly finding it hard not to laugh at the guards' discomfort. "This," and he placed a proprietorial hand on Marianne's shoulder, "is our tax collector's wife, Marian. And this," he added, beckoning Mariota forward, "is Marian of Sigena, her brother's wife. Neither of whom should be subject to abuse from the likes of you!" *And sort that one out!* Guy thought with amusement. Two women with the same name ought to muddy the waters nicely if anyone asked about them later.

The leader of the four gave Guy a filthy look, then turned and spat into the dirt, narrowly missing the back of Mariota's skirt. "You let them in, on your head be it."

Guy's amusement turned sour in an instant, and he spun back to them.

"If you four can't tell what a woman looks like after all this time, then you've been spending far too much time in solitary practices." Hoots of laughter at the sexual implication belatedly alerted him to the fact that other members of the castle's community were enjoying the spectacle of the newcomers being taken down a peg or two. Too late to stop now, though. "What do you think they have under their skirts?" he demanded, allowing the double meaning time to be caught by their audience, before adding, "A sword, maybe? Or a bundle of arrows? Or even a knife to stick you with?"

Gales of laughter rose on all sides, for with the summer heat everyone was stripped down to the minimum it was possible to wear and still be decent, and like all the other women, Marianne and Mariota were bare armed and had dispensed with petticoats. In the humid air their skirts clung to their legs showing they had nowhere to hide even a purse in some inner pocket.

Just at that point Sir Richard of Burscot came walking towards them, coming to take over the unofficial watch from Guy.

"Problems, Sir Guy?" the older man asked with a twinkle in his eye.

Guy allowed himself a weary sigh. "Dozy sods thought these two women were some of Longchamp's men."

Richard gave a snort of a laugh. "Dear me, we are in trouble if we have to depend on men like that!"

"I'm taking them to meet their relative at the stables," Guy said more quietly, twisting his story a little for his new audience – he'd hardly had a thing to do with Richard or the other two castle knights, but that didn't mean that they wouldn't think it odd they knew nothing of a family he was supposed to have in the area. "Good luck," he wished Richard, and led the women off before anything more could be asked.

"Will he cause trouble?" Marianne asked softly, clearly meaning the knight rather than the mercenaries.

Guy cast a quick glance over his shoulder and was reassured to see Sir Richard waving an admonishing finger at the soldiers, even if his words could not be heard over the general din of the bailey.

"I wouldn't think so," he answered with confidence. "I've not had much to do with him or Sir Robert or Sir Hugh, because most of the time they were doing the sheriff's business, but in the last few days I've come to realise that they're better than most of the forester knights I have to work with." They were now within the confines of the stable buildings, and he could speak more freely. "You were lucky! Whatever possessed you to come? ...Not that I'm not glad to see you," he added hurriedly, "I've been desperate to get a message to Robin, but you're taking a huge risk!"

However Marianne shook her head. "Actually we all agreed that if anyone was going to come, that it had to be Mariota and me. We heard that something was very wrong at the castle. Then the news came that it was going to be handed over to Prince John. We didn't know what that would mean in reality. We weren't even sure if you were still here, or if you'd left with the sheriff when we heard he'd gone. Robin said we had to know that, at least, but if any of our men came in, the danger was that they might get kept here to help in any fighting. Hugh, Thomas and Tuck thought it would be more likely that any women in the castle would be sent out if fighting started – fewer mouths to feed if it came to a siege, you see."

Guy had to admit that was good thinking. Marianne and Mariota had much more chance of fleeing with the townswomen if things turned ugly. With as much economy as possible, he told them of what had gone on.

"But you must tell Robin to be alert," he told them urgently, even as he kept watching for signs of anyone coming close enough to hear him. "Fitz John is absolutely seething over that theft at the court! And it's just possible that while he's not got the castle to preoccupy himself with, that he might decide to spend his time enjoying a manhunt. Remember, he'll have the twelve men-at-arms who went with de Wendenal to High Peak to use, not to mention the half-dozen lick-boots who are always at his heels from his household. They couldn't track a thing, but they're young noblemen who are hanging around him to get advancement, and that means they're as spiteful and cruel as he is – they wouldn't have lasted this long if they weren't!

"And he has his old hunting cronies, Walter Ingram, Hugh de Ryddynges and Gerbod de Escalt, with however many men they can come up with, whom he can call upon. A couple of Ingram's men *are* good foresters! They just might pick up a trail and keep it. Under other circumstances I'd be less worried, because the official business of being sheriff would limit how long fitz John could spend on such a hunt, but right at this moment he's truly off the leash."

Mariota was nodding soberly. "We'll tell them."

However Marianne was already saying, "Don't you worry, Robin's too good to get caught!" making Mariota roll her eyes to Guy.

"Your man might be clever, but that doesn't mean he shouldn't be wary," Mariota added.

"And I'm afraid there's worse," Guy sighed. "This you *must* take notice of, Marianne. Robin has been declared an outlaw." Marianne didn't look terribly impressed with this, so Guy rammed the point home. "Yes, I know you've all been living out in the greenwood for some time, and doing what Robin no doubt sees as righting a goodly few wrongs. But it's different now, Marianne. Fitz John took such offence at Robin stealing from one of his courts, he's not just made the declaration here in Nottingham, he got his scribes to write out the proclamation over and over. It's gone out to every town where there's a market. To all of the places where we hold courts. It's going to affect the villages that currently help you."

Belatedly Marianne began to look as worried as Mariota already was.

However Guy was determined that she should be convinced enough of the danger herself to pass on the warning, and all of its implications, to the others.

"Any village caught helping you will be heavily fined *at least*," he said bitterly. "Most likely some, if not all, the men from the village will be held accountable, and if fitz John is in one of his rages it's not me being foolish when I say they could be imprisoned, or even killed. ...No don't look at me like that, Marianne! I'm not saying this just to stop Robin doing what he wants to do. I mean it! This could have terrible and tragic consequences for those you all depend on for essential things like bread. You cannot now wander into villages and hope to have them help you without a second thought, no matter how much money towards their taxes you give them. There's now so much more at stake, and they may think it's better to be grindingly poor and still alive, than risk their necks being found out helping someone the sheriff is so set against."

He paused and gave up silent thanks to the saints that she was taking him seriously now. "And there's the matter of the reward."

"A reward?" Mariota gasped. "Oh Lord help us! How much?"

Guy grimaced. "So far it's only ten shillings. Fitz John assumes that Robin will soon be given up, and once he's caught Robin, he'll be able to sell off goods from whichever manor he comes from to replace his losses. So just now he's not desperate enough to part with a larger sum. But again, that could all change. Once he's back in the castle and what passes for normality has resumed, if he's not got his fines back to send to the head forester at court, he might think it worth his while to increase that reward. And that's another reason why I fear fitz John and his hangers-on might decide to hunt you while they have the time. Why pay for information when you can catch the thief yourself and have some sport at the same time?"

Mariota sighed and looked sternly at Marianne. "That's a lot of men Guy has warned us might be coming after us." Then she frowned as another thought occurred. "Do you think the prince will come here? That could mean extra men on a whole new scale."

"Yes it could!" Guy agreed with alacrity, glad that at least one of them was seeing the wider picture. "That's exactly what might happen. If *he* comes, it won't be just some royal progress through the shires with a few courtiers and some guards. It'll be with an army at his back, because who knows how many barons will throw in their lot with him? I was hoping you might be able to tell me if you'd heard anything about whether the king is backing him in this, but clearly you can't. I'm not sure which would be worse, to have the additional soldiers the king's interest would mean – but with the relief of knowing they'd be on a tight leash – or the kind of men who follow the prince and who could be wholly unrestrained. Neither seems good for us. In a matter of a week or so, the whole of southern Nottinghamshire could be awash with soldiers."

"Aye," Mariota agreed, "and you should know that we heard some rumours as we came into the town. A merchant unloading his wares had come from King's Lynn, and he said that there's a rumour that the king has sent an envoy of his own choosing. He said that he'd heard that Queen Eleanor went to the Holy Land, or at least as far as Cyprus, and took the king word of how bad things have got here, and he's acted upon her words."

Harry had come out of one of the stables and was seemingly lounging nonchalantly against its wall, chewing on a blade of hay, but Guy knew he was watching him intently.

"News," Guy called to him, and repeated what Mariota had just said.

"Bugger," Harry said gloomily. "That's all we need, the queen here as well!"

"I doubt Queen Eleanor will come in person," Guy offered in comfort, "but it would have to be someone of real consequence to sort this mess out. And men of consequence mean men-at-arms with them!" He didn't want to embroil Harry in Robin's mess, so couldn't say more, and luckily neither of the women said anything to give a further clue as to why they'd come to see Guy.

"Please tell Brother Tuck to take care," Guy concluded the conversation by saying. Harry knew about Tuck, so that was suitably innocent. "And take care yourselves getting back to him, this town isn't safe anymore!"

He escorted the two of them back to the gate and saw them safely out past Malvesin's louts, then went to join Sir Richard up on the wall – ostensibly to be companionable, but in reality to watch for signs of the two heading out from the confines of the town. It was a huge relief to see them some time later as tiny but recognisable figures heading down towards the Trent. They'd been cunning enough not to head straight north, he was relieved to see, and was then even more relieved to see someone who, by his height, could only be John getting up from where he sat beside the road and joining them. That probably meant that the two smaller men who moments later joined them as well, and were barely taller than Mariota, were Allan and Roger. That was reassuring, for those three would pass as ordinary men, not soldiers, should they be noted along the way.

Allowing himself to go and find shade now, Guy couldn't help but wonder how Robin felt about having Mariota as part of the company now. The way she had behaved had left little doubt in his mind that she was with them for the foreseeable future. But thinking about it, he realised that when she had taken her young charges to Wales, while the Welsh archers could carry on westwards with them, Mariota would likely have been told in no uncertain terms that she was unwelcome, maybe not by her companions, but certainly by those now helping them. And at that stage, where else would she have gone?

Moreover, Guy knew beyond doubt that Tuck would not have left her on her own to make her way north to whatever kin still lived beyond the northern border. No, Tuck would have insisted that Mariota come back with them, and in a way, Guy was glad. Marianne having another woman to talk to, and one with whom she was already friendly, seemed like a thoroughly good thing. It might even take Marianne out of Robin's company a bit more, and Guy was sure that if Robin had warmed to Marianne he certainly wouldn't to Mariota in the same way. So the chance of them falling out over his favours was beyond remote. And of course Mariota was another Hospitaller sister and a trained healer, so she was hardly without skills the company needed.

Feeling greatly relieved that he had been able to warn Robin, even if he was no wiser himself, Guy settled down to endure the tedium of being confined to the castle. No matter how many times he and the other knights of the forest pleaded with Malvesin to be allowed to go out and do their jobs, he was adamant that they should stay.

"We have no way of knowing if Lincoln will fall, or if Longchamp will give up on it and come looking for what he hopes will be an easier target," he told them. "I cannot let any fighting man leave."

Guy thought it was in no small measure because he feared that they would melt away into the night to their own manors given half a chance, and he was probably right. However the first news which reached them was of Longchamp himself being in the south, having no doubt left the tedious siege to his commanders, and that he had demanded that Count John of Mortain should bow to his superior authority and release the two castles.

Everyone openly laughed at that. John, the imperious prince, backing down before a mere chancellor would only happen in a fairy story! Predictably the prince's response was fast and non-conciliatory – Longchamp must lift the siege of Lincoln or Count John would 'visit him with a rod of iron'. It didn't take much imagination to work out what form that iron would take, either, when more men marched into the castle, and the residents braced themselves to be in the front line at the outbreak of a war.

Mercifully, hard on the heels of that came different news. The king had appointed Walter of Coutance, the archbishop of Rouen, as Longchamp's advisor.

"A bloody archbishop! What notice will Longchamp take of him?" Sir Osmaer groaned as the Nottingham knights congregated in the old hall.

"And a Norman one," Sir Thurstan added gloomily. "He'll be hanging onto Longchamp's tails and doing nothing."

"Oh no he won't!" declared Sir Hugh, the three castle knights now taking refuge with the foresters away from the incoming mercenaries. "Walter's a Cornishman!"

"And a cunning one," his friend Sir Robert added from by his side. "You mark my words, I met him once and there are no flies on him. Longchamp won't find it easy to pull the wool over his eyes. And if Archbishop Walter has come from the king himself, he'll have the kind of authority Longchamp won't be able to ignore."

He proved to be correct. At a meeting at Winchester at the end of July they heard that although both parties had turned up with thousands of men prepared to fight, Walter had the better of both of them, and everyone at Nottingham breathed a sigh of relief – especially when they heard that Longchamp had by some miracle summoned a third of the whole army levy of England. Two thousand knights and a sizable number of mercenaries had nearly descended on their shire on Longchamp's behalf; while the errant prince had apparently had a force of four thousand Welsh mercenaries rallied to his cause.

"God in Heaven!" even the affable Sir Giles had gasped in horror when they had learned what had turned south and away from them. "We'd have been crushed in the middle!"

Certainly, hearing those numbers, Guy was glad he had never been forced to keep his promise to Alan of Leek to hold the castle against both parties. Nottingham was a formidable fortress, but so were those opposing forces!

Then as the month ended, a new castellan arrived at Nottingham. The famous knight, Sir William Marshal, had come to take temporary command of the castle, for Count John had released it to Archbishop Walter, and Marshal was his appointee. The prince's mercenaries marched out led by Malvesin, and the entire garrison heaved a sigh of relief. It was only then that they heard news of someone closer to home and it was shocking. The ghastly William de Wendenal had somehow managed to feather his own nest in the midst of this crisis and had temporarily taken charge of Tickhill castle on behalf of the king, even though he had made no secret of the fact that he supported Count John against Longchamp. Yet Sheriff fitz John had gone fully over to Longchamp's side.

"Who'd have thought it?" Guy said to Harry, having escaped the mayhem of the main hall as everyone else tried to ingratiate themselves with William Marshal, and tell him that they'd done nothing for either side. "Bloody fitz John and de Wendenal on opposite sides!"

"They won't be able to be in the same castle as one another now," Harry observed, handing Guy some fresh blackberries the lads had gathered while exercising the horses. The fine beasts Marshal and his leading men had come with had been led on their exercises rather than ridden by mere boys, giving them chance to forage as they went. "With any luck yon' Sir William Marshal will know what kind of man our sheriff is. He'll know there'll be blood drawn before he lets de Wendenal back under his portcullis."

"I should think he found out today if he didn't already," Guy agreed, for the day had seen the welcome return of Robert of Crockston and Alan of Leek, and both had spent some hours closeted alone with Sir William. Guy wasn't sure if he was glad or not that he himself had hardly exchanged two words with the great man, or whether life would improve if, by some miracle, Marshal became their sheriff instead of fitz John. "I for one won't weep if de Wendenal never comes back, and I doubt few others will either. I wonder if he'll go back to High Peak? I hope not."

Had he been able to foresee what would happen in the coming days, though, Guy might have wished de Wendenal had kept High Peak instead of keeping Tickhill.

With the announced return of sheriff fitz John, Sir William Marshal departed in suitable fine style, his brief tenure as constable of Nottingham having restored peace and order to the place, but the sheriff's return was to prove anything but tranquil. Fitz John was due within days, but on the morning they were predicting his appearance, an altogether unexpected visitor came hurtling in through the castle gates. It was Eudes de Ville from Tickhill, pale in the face, and calling for Robert of Crockston before he'd barely got out of the saddle. He ran to meet Robert, who was hurrying out of the inner bailey to meet him, and many heard Eudes' words as they spoke on the bridge over the dry moat.

"Get a bag and come with me! We must fly, Robert!"

"God in Heaven, Eudes, why?"

"Fitz John. He's in a state of foaming wrath! I'm not joking! He was actually starting to froth at the mouth he was in such a temper. He holds us both responsible for handing over the castles to Count John."

"What?" Robert exclaimed in disbelief. Guy, who was only a few feet behind Eudes could see the shock on Robert's face. "But the damned man walked out of here! He left it to us to decide!"

"Not according to him, he didn't!" Eudes retorted. "The bastard is telling anyone who will listen that he went to visit his family over in Chester, because his mother had fallen seriously ill." Then he looked worriedly behind him before turning to Robert again. "Come on! Hurry man! We must be out of here before he comes from Tickhill! He means to arrest us and hold us for treason against the chancellor."

"Treason? Against the chancellor? That's not possible!" Robert was shaking his head in confusion, but at least looked over Eudes' shoulder to Guy. "Would you get my horse, please, Guy?" Then to Eudes, "I don't need to pack. I have clothes I can use at my manor."

"No, pack!" Eudes exclaimed in exasperation. "You'll have to come further afield than that this time! I'll give you time to run and grab some things, then I'm off – with or without you!"

Guy had taken one look at Eudes' blown horse and was running to the stables. With Harry's help he got two horses each for Eudes and

Robert, and his strongest horse for himself. They hurried the horses over to where Eudes paced the ground, and Guy thrust the first set of reins into his hands, at which point Eudes looked up, perplexed.

"Fresh horse," Guy said tersely, "and a spare," as he thrust the lead rein at him too. "You won't get far on her," and he jerked his head towards the sweating mare whom one of Harry's lads was already leading away. Then he leaned in close to Eudes. "I'll meet you both in the town by the ford." He then mounted his own horse and declared to any who cared to listen, "Sir Alan went to Derby this morning. I shall try to meet him on the way back and warn him of what's about to happen."

Turning his horse, Guy took it at a controlled trot out through the main gate, and across the open space of the old market place into the town. He was thinking frantically as to how to help both of the men who would bear the brunt of fitz John's rage. Clearly getting Robert safely away was the first priority. If anyone was called upon to witness what had been said, then it wouldn't take fitz John long to know that Robert had advocated handing the castle to the royal prince right from the start. Alan, on the other hand had been heard to openly say they should not, and only Guy knew that he had equally not intended to hand it to fitz John's chosen lord, Longchamp. That ought to afford him some temporary protection if Guy didn't manage to intercept him before he got back.

He had chosen the ford over the Trent as their meeting point as it was where the London road led out of Nottingham, and he guessed that Eudes' first instinct was to head south by road. Eudes had no reason to trust Guy, and might convince Robert to break away if he had arranged to meet elsewhere, but this way he was playing into their hands. He was pleased to see the two hurrying towards him in no time, and saw the perplexed frown on Robert's face.

"Guy? What are you doing?"

"Helping you two to get away," Guy told him laconically. "I know fitz John's sort of old! Did he come back from Chester with men?" he asked Eudes, and saw the other constable give a grim nod.

"Yes he did. Bloody mercenaries, I'm sure! Only half a dozen of them, but they scared the life out of our castle men." He turned to Robert. "You know our permanent garrison is far smaller than yours. Between the indecisive and the plain scared, I knew I wouldn't have anyone fighting on my side, and Peter hasn't come back from London yet." He was referring to his own assistant constable, Peter de Bovencourt.

"What on earth was Peter doing in London?" Robert began asking, but Guy interrupted,

"Later! Let's get you away first, and not on the London road!"

"Why not?" asked Eudes, with no small trace of fear in his voice.

"Because it's the obvious way to go," Guy replied. "Come on! Follow me!"

"Guy, where are you taking us?" Robert asked, but still wheeling his horse to follow Guy's.

However, Guy said nothing while they were in the town. He led them out on the Newark road – another good ruse as it gave the impression of either heading for the Fosse Way down to Leicester, which met the London road out of Nottingham too, or to Newark itself and the Great North Road, the more direct route down to London. Yet once out of sight of any houses, he turned off up a narrow lane normally only used for sheep and cows. Eudes paused before turning off, and Guy swung round in his saddle and told the two of them, "I'm taking you through Sherwood! I'd defy any of fitz John's men to track you by the route I'm taking you on."

"But where to?" Robert fretted, even as he followed Guy.

"The Templars," Guy called back. "I'll get you through the forest up to where you'll be able to find you own way, then I'll go and try to see what I can do for Sir Alan. If you get up to Temple Hirst, the Templars there have contacts with boats going down the coast all the time. You'll be able to get to London without having men hunting you every step of the way. And the Templars love King Richard – they won't have liked this bickering behind his back – so if they think you're being persecuted for behaving with proper responsibility towards the crown, they'll help you."

"God bless you, Guy!" Robert exclaimed with relief, and Eudes echoed him, also saying,

"I fled Tickhill as soon as they were all asleep the very evening fitz John arrived. The bastard had confined me to my own dungeon, but my oldest watchman is a loyal old chap. He undid the lock and brought me a ladder to climb out with. We got out through the sally gate – he's gone to his daughter's in Doncaster, so he shouldn't suffer for his loyalty. Luckily some of the horses were out in the fields nearby and I caught one. I shudder to think what it would've been like if this had happened in the depths of winter, with all the horses brought in. All I've thought of since then is getting to Walter of Coutance. If anyone can help us it's him. The Templars will surely know his name by now, and that he's the king's man."

"And you will get to him, but by a safer way than you'd planned," Guy reassured him. "Now hurry!" and he urged the horses into a brisk trot.

Under the dense, leafy canopy of Sherwood it was cooler once the sun came up than it would have been on any open road, and the horses were able to keep going for longer. Roughly every hour, Guy made them stop and rest them for a short while, and in this way they were able to ride on into the summer evening. When they finally stopped for the night they had cover many miles, and were somewhere between Worksop and Retford near Barnby Moor, close by where Guy and Robin had had their own close shave with Longchamp.

"Good God," Eudes breathed as he realised where they were. "I'm almost back where I started from, but I'd never have known it coming this way! Lost on my own doorstep, I'm ashamed to say."

Guy laughed. "No shame on you Sir Eudes. Don't forget I rode these forest paths for several years as part of my job. I could hardly bring men to court for chopping down oaks if I didn't know how many there were in the first place. Where the natural clearings were, and where men had dragged even the roots out. But the important thing is that fitz John is far to the south of us now, and no-one from amongst your own household has seen you back up here. What they don't know, they can't tell. Now come the morning, I shall set you on the road to Bawtry. I'd advise you to skirt east of Doncaster and head up past Hatfield to the River Aire. Temple Hirst has its own ferry, so you won't have any trouble getting across to it. You'll take the fresher horses. I'll take the other two back to Nottingham and turn them out into the fields before I get back to the castle. That way no-one will see me coming in with them, and hopefully won't make the connection that I've been with you."

When they parted, Robert and Eudes were once again profuse with their thanks, assuring Guy that they would not forget his help. He now turned south again, but was able to swop regularly between the three horses, giving them all some respite, but he also blessed the stamina of these chunky everyday horses. Fit for the lists they might not be, nor the fastest in a short dash, but if they weren't misused they would keep on going for many miles, and Guy knew how to pace a horse. It would be late at night before he could hope to reach Nottingham again, and rather than having to talk his way in through what would undoubtedly be locked main gates, Guy decided to go in with the summer dawn. If his luck really held, it might even be one of his old friends from High Peak on gate duty.

Yet after he had set the weary horses loose in the dawn to feast on the dewy grass, and began walking round the castle walls from the deer park side, he was disturbed to see crows wheeling low over the oldest part. What on earth had got them so interested? It didn't bode well. However nothing prepared him for the shock he got when he made it inside the castle.

As he got closer to the walls, he saw Skuli and Alfred were watching for him by where the kennel walls loomed over the start of the outer dry moat, and signalled him that they would drop a rope down to him. Perplexed but grateful for the help, Guy forced his tired arms to help haul him up, but at the top was surprised when the two former High Peak soldiers immediately hustled him into the stables out of sight.

"Thank God you've got back!" Harry's voice came out of the gloom, as the two shoved Guy towards him and then took up guard at the stable doors. "Big Ulf's had men watching through the night for you! Now then ...you've been here all night with me helping with delivering a foal, if anyone asks."

Walking to the loosebox at the end, Guy saw Harry was sitting on an upturned bucket as a mare known as Daisy, and her foal, dozed contentedly beside him.

"What in Jesu's name is going on?" Guy asked his friend softly, already alert to the misery in Harry's face, and the tension in Alfred and Skuli, which told of something momentous having happened.

"Brace yourself," Harry sighed, pointing to another bucket for Guy to bring over to sit on, and producing a skin of wine from behind himself.

"Wine?" Guy said in surprise. "That bad?"

"Worse. I'm sorry, Guy. Alan of Leek is dead."

"What?" Guy's exclamation came unbidden from his lips, then before the others could shush him, clamped his own hand over his mouth until he could restrain his voice more. "What happened? How?" he managed to choke out a few moments later.

"Poor Sir Alan didn't stand a chance," Harry told him, his voice full of suppressed anger. "That bastard fitz John rode in in the early afternoon of the day you left. He had Peter de Bovencourt as his prisoner. Said he'd 'caught' him on the Great North Road. Said he was a traitor! Had him dragged into the main hall by those roughs Sir Eudes told you he had with him. Poor sod was in chains. He couldn't have run if he'd wanted to."

He paused and took a ragged breath. "Two of those bloody mercenaries started helping fitz John 'question' Sir Peter in the hall. Four others went out and started asking everyone where Sir Alan was, then took up guard at the barbican. God bless him, Sir Alan never knew what hit him. One moment he was riding in through what he must have thought was his own gateway, the next, the four of them had pulled him from his horse and were dragging him into the hall to join Sir Peter. The other two roughs stood guard at the hall door and wouldn't let anyone in – and God knows our Sir Martin and Sir Walter tried, and so did Sir Robert, Sir Hugh, and Sir Richard. But fitz John's mercenaries had their swords drawn. They even cut Sir Hugh and stabbed Sir Walter in the leg! And then there were always four of them outside after that."

Harry looked across in the flickering light of the solitary lantern to Guy with baleful eyes. "I think we all thought that the two of them would end up in the dungeon. That we'd be able to pass them decent food and drink at least, and some blankets. ...Even thought that if they were down there and out of sight, that maybe fitz John would come out of his rage after a few days, and in a week or two we'd be able to get them out."

"But you couldn't?"

Harry shook his head mournfully. "The next thing we know, the mercenaries are dragging Sir Alan and Sir Peter out of the room and across to the old castle where you lot sleep. Even then I think we all thought they were headed for the dungeon there, although it's tiny and cramped compared to the main one. Everyone was stunned when they suddenly heard a man screaming from the old tower, and then saw Sir Alan and Sir Peter being swung out in chains on the gibbets used for murderers."

"Christ on the Cross!" Guy gulped. It wasn't just that Alan was dead, it was the way it had been done which shook him to the core. You simply didn't treat a nobleman like a common criminal. And to hang him from the battlements was barbaric!

"Everyone's been walking on eggshells ever since."

"I'm not surprised!" Guy could still hardly believe it. "Has fitz John gone mad, do you think? I'm serious! Has he lost his mind? Is he possessed? Do we need a priest – or several?"

Harry just shrugged. "I couldn't say. Everyone's been avoiding him like he's got the plague since then. None of the knights joined him at the evening meal. Most weren't hungry, as you can imagine, and even men like Walkelin and Fredegis just went and got some bread and cold meat from the kitchens, and went and ate it in their room. You've not been missed, Guy. That's been one blessing to come out of everyone's shock. I think most of the knights will have assumed you've come down here. They know you escape here sometimes. All of yesterday, the castle was near silent. I've never know the like! Any of the ordinary folk who have family in the town – and that's most of them – ran out of here yesterday morning as soon as the gates were opened. I certainly let my lads go. ...Wasn't going to keep them here when that mad swine's got murder in his heart!"

Guy could only sit in shock. It was beyond him to know what to do next. What *could* he do next?

"Did Sir Robert get away?" he heard Harry ask a little later, his voice seeming to come from somewhere far away.

"Sir Robert? ....Errr ...yes. Yes he did." Guy tried to pull himself together, but it was hard going. "With any luck they'll already be on a ship and heading for London."

"Saints be praised! That's the best news we've had yet!" Harry sighed with relief, then before Guy could say anything. "Yes, I know, we can't make that common knowledge, but with any luck a fast rider might be in time to have Sir William Marshal turn back here, or someone else with the authority to make fitz John pay for what he's done."

Guy nodded, but in his heart he was wondering if now that the prince wasn't involved, whether anyone would actually care?

Oh Gervase, that was a terrible few days. You throw me warnings of my soul spending time in Hell, but I tell you, sometimes I feel that I have spent time in Hell here on earth. I cannot, even now, think back on those bleak days without wanting to weep, for what made it all so desperately tragic was that, of all of them, Alan had been the one trying to do the right thing. I was told he went to his fate as the second hanged man with remarkable dignity, but that did not make me feel any better whenever my eyes were drawn to the dreadful sad shape of his body swinging high on the battlements alongside Peter de Bovencourt's.

And then a further tragedy struck. That first day I was back, I encountered the three sheriff's knights – the ones permanently attached to the castle, not the forest – seemingly sauntering across the outer bailey, but when they saw me their eyes lit up, and I knew that they had come in the hope of finding me. Taking me to walk up on the walls, they told me the part of the story my soldier friends had not known. Peter de Bovencourt had gone to London, and had sworn to the lords there that the handing over of Tickhill had been done against his advice. For once, Count John had done the right thing and had backed him up, and in writing too, but Longchamp had told him that he must return to fitz John and beg his forgiveness of his sheriff along with the others. It was Peter's misfortune that the honour of Tickhill spilled over into Nottinghamshire from Yorkshire, and was nominally under our sheriff's jurisdiction, for even Longchamp's brother Osbert as sheriff of Yorkshire might have treated him better. So Sir Peter and his squire had ridden back, and fallen in with fitz John before they had even reached Tickhill.

˜Count John himself wrote that de Bovencourt was innocent,˜ Sir Hugh told me in dismay. ˜Sealed the letter with his own seal! How can fitz John think he has the authority to hang Sir Peter and Sir Alan in chains from a gallows when someone like that has passed judgement?˜

And worse, the three told me that Peter de Bovencourt's young squire was still in the castle and grieving mightily, for Sir Peter was his uncle. We there and then decided that we must get the boy away from Nottingham, but the three were less used to deception than I, and had not been able to think of a way to do it. Someone, and I suspected it might have been Sir Walter or Sir Martin, who knew of how I had dealt with fitz John upon his first appearance, had then said that the person who might think of a plan was me.

It was then that I recalled why I had had so little to do with these three; why our paths had so rarely crossed in the past. Someone had to take the taxes to the royal court, and usually it was two out of these three, for even when the Michaelmas court came round, there were still knights at the castle finishing off their forty day's service who could see to its defence. So it was only in the winter months, when we forester knights were kept busy out of the castle watching for illegal hunting, that the three took on overseeing the castle's defences. And yet in an odd twist of fate, the forest laws now played into our hands, for the moneys from the two swanimotes had not been sent south and were overdue.

˜You must collect the coins together, along with all the documents, and set out tomorrow morning.˜ I told them. ˜You need say nothing to the sheriff, since he has asked nothing about such mundane matters in the entire time he has been here, and then if asked where you are, we can say in all innocence that you are doing your duty. But you can also then take Sir Peter's nephew with you. If he rides before you in turns, there will not even be a horse missing from the stables to indicate he left. With luck, fitz John will assume the boy has taken to his heels and run.˜

They welcomed the suggestion without question and with much relief, and yet, dear Gervase, it still all went wrong. For come the early morning when they were due to set off, the boy was found scaring off the crows from his uncle's swinging corpse, and fitz John summarily hanged him alongside Sir Peter and Sir Alan.

Yes, well may you look shocked, Brother. I can still see that awful morning playing out before my eyes even now. The three knights waiting in the shadows of the stables with their horses and the two packhorses already laden, wondering where the lad could be. Me then hurrying across the outer bailey, meaning to go and find him. And then hearing a woman scream, and then another, and looking upwards. Somehow in those days our eyes were draw involuntarily to Sir Alan any time we raised them up, so a goodly number of folk saw one of the mercenaries grab the boy, and then fitz John appear – distinguishable by his fine clothes even at a distance – and then the poor lad being swung out onto the gibbet, kicking and screaming as he went.

I confess to you now, Brother, that I did not wait to see the boy drop. I could not face it. But also I was suddenly aware that the three knights must go now, right now! They must not be seeming, in fitz John's eyes, to be reacting to the hanging of the squire. He had to believe that they were already gone when that happened, so that he would not send men after them in order to quash any report they might make. I recall running to the stables, telling them it was too late to save the boy, and then hustling them out of the main gate, but not letting them take the obvious road to the ford. I can still remember telling them that they must do as I had done with Robert of Crockston and Eudes DeVille, taking the Newark road, and in this case get to that road by going round on the north side of the town. They were so shocked they did as they were told, and I am greatly relieved to say that they succeeded in getting away.

Now please let me rest a moment and take a little wine, Brother, before I continue. These memories are still bitter to me even after all this time.

Chapter 12

hank you, Brother, for the wine. You ask me now why I did not call upon Robin Hood to save the boy if no-one else? Oh Gervase, it was more than shortage of time, and this is what makes the memory so painful for me. You see the reason why fitz John had returned in such a towering rage was not only because he had been made to look ineffective in Longchamp's eyes. He also still did not have the money stolen from the swanimote, and this new outlaw Robin Hood had not been caught – and I suspect he had indeed set men to that hunt, even if he had not ridden on it himself. In the days after those three poor souls lost their lives, fitz John had us all riding here, there and everywhere, questioning villagers as to whether they had heard anything of this Robin Hood. So can you see that Robin had in part caused fitz John to become so enraged? Have you remembered how I found fitz John berating Sir Alan over Robin's theft, even before the greater catastrophe overtook us? No do not bristle so, Gervase! Your hero had poked a wasps' nest and then left others to be stung in the swarm which followed, however unintentionally and unsuspecting of the consequences.

Yet perversely, fitz John himself had done more than anyone to ensure that no-one would speak up against Robin. The word of Sir Alan's hanging, and then of the squire's, had gone across the shire like wild fire. Royal edicts had taken longer than that! Like ever growing soap-bubbles, the word radiated out of Nottingham in every direction, and wherever we knights rode into, the word was ahead of us.

For the first time since I had come back to my home shire, I saw the sullen hatred in villagers' eyes which I had seen over on the Welsh Border whenever the sheriff's name was mentioned. No-one actually said anything, but you could see that nothing on God's green earth would persuade them to give away information which might help fitz John. And it came down to the simple fact that they no longer trusted him. That may sound odd to you when I have been telling you so much about the iniquities of living in a royal forest, but the truth was that however much people grumbled, for the most part they felt they could do little about taxes demanded from far away in London or Winchester. Until now they had not particularly blamed the sheriff himself, even if Robin had done so – it was just the way things were.

What was more, although knightly men like myself and those living and working within the castle, knew what a thoroughgoing bastard fitz John was, most of the rest of the shire had seen very little of him. His laziness regarding his office meant he personally was relatively unknown. Do you grasp that? They were still going about their business as though the tough but fair Ralph Murdac was still sheriff, for fitz John had been with us only since the end of 1189, and we were then only into the

summer of 1191 – a mere year and a half, and time in which fitz John had
left us to do the work as we had always done, while he indulged in his
pleasures either within the castle or on his friends' manors.

Now that had changed almost overnight. The people of the shires felt
that it would now make no difference whether they helped the sheriff or
not. They saw him as cruel and randomly vindictive. If he wished to visit
slaughter and mayhem down upon them, he would do so even if they had
helped him, for had not Sir Alan been innocent of letting the castle go?
Even the humblest villager knew that fitz John had left the shire at the
first hint of trouble. His thin excuses might hold with Longchamp, who
would not have known whether fitz John had left Nottingham before the
demand to surrender the castle had arrived or not, but the people knew.
And as a quick aside on that matter, Brother, I believe that Longchamp
knew full well that fitz John had run like a boy from fighting for his cause,
and was holding that back as something to be used against our sheriff as
and when he felt the need. No-one stayed by the chancellor's side for love,
so he undoubtedly had some dirty secret he could hold over each of his
followers, and why should fitz John be any different?

And so August drifted on, the three bodies still swung from the gibbet
being feasted on by the crows, Robin Hood remained uncaught, and all we
could do was pray that our two constables had had a fair hearing off the
men in power in London. If they had, then when the three Nottingham
knights arrived in their wake with the money and their news, they would
be planting seeds of concern on ground already tilled. I calculated that
even if our knights had ridden hard, it would still take them four days to
get to London, and more likely five. They then had to try and gain an
audience with someone in power, and so it would be foolish to think of
them achieving anything in under a week. Then whatever was decided, it
would take almost as long for someone to come back to us, and therefore
we should not hope to see anyone until possibly the end of the third full
week of August.

Yet when the news came, it was of a surprising and unexpected sort.
Of all people, the youngest Plantagenet had himself been furious that
someone he had vouched for should be summarily hanged by a mere
sheriff. Our royal Count of Mortain had therefore taken all of fitz John's
lands from him as a punishment – which he could do as fitz John's
overlord in many places – and had summoned him to appear in person to
answer for his actions at the Michaelmas court, which of course was now
only a little over four weeks away.

Moreover, William Longchamp had a greater problem on his hands,
and was unlikely to come to a mere follower's aid. Geoffrey Plantagenet
had been consecrated as archbishop of York, making him a full member of
the clergy at last, and he was on his way home to claim what was his. That
would mean <u>two</u> of the late King Henry's sons in England – John with the
support of many barons, and Geoffrey with many of the disgruntled clergy
behind him – and with both opposed to Longchamp, the chancellor was not
happy about that.

Many amongst us thought that Longchamp's time was now ended.
He had offended and abused so many of the major barons of the land by
now that they would seize every chance to do him down, and any who
were too closely associated with him might feel the weight of the royal

displeasure alongside him. We therefore struggled through the last week of August and the first of September, then saw fitz John off in another of his filthy tempers on his way south, and breathed what we prayed would not be too presumptuous sighs of relief at being rid of him.

Nottingham
Autumn, the Year of Our Lord 1191

Once fitz John was a day out from Nottingham, everyone began hurrying to find something to do outside of the castle. So much time penned up within the walls had been driving them all mad, and for once even the most reluctant of forest knights was itching to get out and start patrolling again, but without the flay of fitz John's temper. Yes, men had had to go out hunting for Robin Hood, but fitz John had insisted they came back time and time again to demand results, so that no-one had had time to more than ride out for a day and then ride back. And the woodmotes were also overdue, and so although the castle was without anyone in charge, a certain level of order resumed. Sir Martin and Sir Walter took over temporary command of the castle, and happily sent out those knights and men who were likely to become troublesome. Unfortunately Guy wasn't one of them.

"We need you here," Sir Walter told Guy, and sympathising with the younger man's crestfallen expression. "By Our Lady, this must be the first time in the castle's history when it's had no sheriff, no constable and no assistant constable!"

"It won't last," Sir Martin consoled Guy. "You can bet your manor on Archbishop Walter putting someone in place at the Michaelmas court, and someone who can come here straight away. Nottingham's too important for it to hang around empty while some knight comes from far away, and I can't imagine the prince being any too thrilled at having no-one minding his business interests in the shire, either!"

Yet Guy was desperate to get in touch with Robin. If there was ever a time to get men out of the town gaol, it was now. With fitz John out of the way, and very much to blame if something went wrong in his absence, Guy could think of no better time than to empty the gaol of the poor souls who had been waiting for far too long for an eyre to come around. He did get lucky in one sense, though. The castle was so abnormally empty, and the scribes so absorbed in travelling out to the woodmotes, that Guy was able to go and investigate the small hall the clerks used without anyone watching.

He still went at night, so that he could be seen to be performing whatever duties the two senior knights demanded of him by day, but no-one was there to see what hour he crawled into his bed at. And it was late, often with the sky already showing signs of growing paler by then, because of the amount of scrolls he was having to wade through. He had managed to filtch a small piece of parchment for himself, and had begun to make a list of those men who actually deserved to be there.

Hubert the tailor, for one, for beating his brother for standing up for the said Hubert's wife, and who had blinded the brother in one eye in the process. The business seemed to be doing better under the brother's care than Hubert's, Guy noted, by the fact that this time the taxes had been paid on time for the first time in years. Hubert was definitely one to keep inside!

Or Wilfred the tanner, who had thrown piss all over a neighbour in a dispute over tannery drying areas to the extent that the man had nearly drowned in it, and had then sickened and died a week later. So he was another man who could not control his temper. And the 'blind' tinker who had come in begging to the market and had stabbed a man for realising he could see full well and was cutting purses.

Yet these were relatively few of the cases awaiting trial either at the regular eyre, or the forest eyre. Guy was increasingly appalled at how many men seemed to have been incarcerated for no other reason than they couldn't pay the fines. He had thought he would only have to destroy a few scrolls to ensure the truly innocent were not hunted and brought back if Robin opened the gaol door. But the more he looked, the more he realised that if he did that the old chest would be barely a third full, instead of stuffed to the brim – and the scribes would surely know that whoever had done that had to be someone who could read, which severely limited the potential culprits to choose from.

The only way out was to do something drastic and set fire to the place, but even then he was hindered by the fact that with no scribes there, no candles were being lit, and it was certainly not cold enough yet for braziers to be brought into the room. It would never be taken as an accident but as arson, and with the inevitable investigations following which would again point to the literate. He also drew the line at setting a fire for Sir Walter and Sir Martin's sake. The last thing he wanted to do was have accusations of carelessness flung at them when they were working so hard. But what to do?

Four days after the majority of folk had left, he managed to get out into Nottingham town for a short while on market day. Sir Walter and Sir Martin could not deny him that much freedom. And so he wandered round, browsing the stalls, and praying that Robin would have sent someone into town in the hope of seeing him.

Just when he feared he would be going back unsuccessful, a hand closed on his sleeve and a voice hissed, "Guy!" Trying not to look too happy, he turned and found himself looking down into Roger's impish face.

"Tuck's at the inn up by Goose Gate," the smaller man said softly, and passed him by, as if for all the world he had just asked to excuse himself and slip between Guy and the nearest stall.

Blessing Roger's disreputable past for once, which made him so adept at remaining unnoticed, Guy hurried along Cheapside and Chandler's Lane, and then turned north up to where Goose Gate lay at the start of the Huntingdon road. A sign with a crudely painted pitcher of ale swung above the door of the inn, and Guy went and stood conspicuously by the doorway, not looking in but about him, as if searching for someone. The inn itself wasn't the kind of place he could walk into without comment, but he was sure Tuck would be watching.

"Excuse me, brother," Tuck's familiar Welsh voice said at his elbow, and Guy stood aside to let the bulky monk leave. Tuck passed in front of him, walked up the Mansfield Road until he was past the row of houses which faced onto Carter Gate, and then slipped into a field gateway. As soon as he was gone from sight, Guy followed, and with a cursory glance over his shoulder to make sure no-one was watching him, turned into the same gate.

"St Issui be praised," Guy said with relief, and hugged Tuck.

"As bad as that?" Tuck replied with a quirked eyebrow. "You'd better tell me all, then!"

Once Guy had finished, though, Tuck was frowning and clearly thinking hard. "I see what you mean. It has to be done now, doesn't it! Can't have some new sheriff coming and thinking he'll be the new broom sweeping clean, and putting even more lost souls in the gaol!"

But Guy was shaking his head. "That's not the worst of it, Tuck. It's very unlikely that the powers that be down in London would order an eyre within the first few months of a sheriff's tenure. Even men like them are going to give him chance to get his feet under the table, after all, before another one comes in and starts officiating in his own castle for the best part of a week. If he's any good, he'd be likely to shake the place up a bit anyway, given fitz John's behaviour, and that ought to mean getting the court records straight *before* the eyre comes. But all that time, men are still going to be being brought in. God knows where the gaolers are putting them already, Tuck! I don't!"

The two of them now walked back into the town and headed for High Pavement where the gaol lay. As they walked, Guy became aware that on the other side of the road, only a few paces behind them, were

Allan and Roger, and behind them in a seemingly innocent group of chatting young people were Robin arm in arm with Marianne, and Mariota playing the flirt with Siward and Hugh. Luckily, although the town was generally busy, this side, being the farthest from the market, was quiet enough for them all to converse with one another without being interrupted.

"This is the gaol," Guy told Tuck, but with Robin nearly at his back so that he heard every word. "There are men in there who've been waiting nearly four years now just for a trial. This can't go on! We could be waiting another year before the ordinary justices come round. I have no idea at all what the situation will be for the forest eyres, may Jesu help us! When the money went to King Henry it was easy – they came every third year, come hell or high water. But now it's being used to keep Count John, who knows? Maybe he'll *never* send an eyre? Maybe one day he'll come in person? He could come with the new sheriff, God save us! I don't even know if we're actually still under the king's own chief forester anymore.

"Nobody ever bothered explaining to us how this was supposed to work in reality, with the two shires being taken out of the realm's accounts in this way. So all I know is that we've got ordinary men in there rubbing shoulders with men who are truly dangerous. Murderers sharing cells with men who've committed no crime but to be too poor to be able to find bail money, and might not even be guilty of what they've been accused of."

"God curse the bloody sheriff!" Robin snarled.

"In this instance I won't argue with you," Guy sighed, "although I'd add a curse for Longchamp in with it! He created this mess! But here, Tuck, take this," and he slipped him the tatty piece of parchment. "The men whose names are on there are beyond question guilty of what they've been charge with, and most importantly, should not be set free with the others! They may well end up claiming innocent lives if you do! There're only a handful of them and most are too local to have anywhere else to go. Ask for names as you get them all out and then shove these bastards back in to any old cell."

"How can you be sure?" Marianne asked, challenging Guy before Robin could.

Guy turned and looked over Robin's shoulder into her eyes. "Jesu, Marianne! The one, I saw the near-corpse of his intended victim brought into the monks' care – his own brother! And why? For stopping that brute from near killing the woman he was married to!"

"Who? The brute or the brother?" Robin asked.

"The brute!" Guy snapped. "And no, before you ask, the brother hadn't been at the brute's wife behind his back! As soon as Hubert got locked up, his wife packed her bags and her children and went back to her family in Lincolnshire. The brother's been running the shop alone ever since, once he recovered; the apprentices have at last been seen without being black and blue, and are actually smiling; and the business is doing better because of it. In fact now, they have two more apprentices starting! Doesn't that tell you something? I'm not blackening names! There are only eight names on that list. There must be over forty men stuffed into that gaol now! For the sake of everyone, can you not trust me on this?"

"Of course we can," Siward replied, with Hugh echoing him.

"You have to do this within the next week," Guy told them. "After that I have no way of knowing when a new sheriff will arrive, or what he'll be like. He could be a reasonable man like Ralph Murdac was, or he could be even more of a brute than fitz John is. Someone, God help us, like William de Braose! And if he is, then he could come armed to the teeth with his own men, at which point he could choose to guard his own gaol. But no-one's going to tell us in advance. The first I'll know about it is when he rides in through the gates. So get these poor bastards out of there as quick as you can!"

He then turned and walked away with Tuck, leaving Robin and the others to work out how they would get inside the gaol.

"Tuck, please promise me you'll make sure those men I gave you the names of don't escape," pleaded Guy. "The wandering beggar would probably just clear off and go hunting elsewhere, as would the mercenary. But the five local men are a genuine danger to people here in the town and surroundings."

"I'll see to it," Tuck reassured Guy. "Go back to the castle and don't worry!"

That was easier said than done, though, for the days dragged on and still Guy heard nothing of the gaol being broken into. Then their own Michaelmas courts were held, and Guy was kept busy attending two courts at Linby and Mansfield over matters arising in the forest on the Derbyshire border. Yet as he rode back towards Nottingham with his scribe, and three men-at-arms acting as walking foresters, he was acutely aware that two days ago a new sheriff could have set out from London.

His anxiety was heightened when he saw someone dive off the road as they approached. He was the only one of their party who saw the man, for he was in the lead and the road curved slightly, but he knew he wasn't mistaken – it was the mercenary from the gaol! He himself had been involved in breaking up the fight at the Nottingham inn when the mercenary was arrested and had got a good look at the man, who was also distinguished by having a hook for a left hand, and this was definitely him. That could only mean one thing – Robin had emptied the gaol but taken no notice of his own warnings.

Guy found himself cursing softly under his breath. By all the saints, what would it take for Robin to trust him and take him at his word for once? And then just as he was about to tell the scribe to ride on with one of the soldiers while he took the other two to hunt the escapee, he saw another pair of figures diving off the road to get out of sight. Thomas and Piers!

"God's wounds!" he ground out in frustration, and then prayed the others hadn't heard him. The court had gone relatively well and he wasn't a man renowned for bad tempers and unwarranted anger, so one at least would be bound to ask what was wrong. But they had heard.

"Sir Guy?" Skuli's concerned voice came from behind him as the man jogged a couple of steps to come alongside him.

"A sudden stitch in my side," Guy declared rather louder, for the benefit of the others, then hissed to Skuli, who thank the Lord could be trusted, "Thomas and Piers! In the trees to our right!"

The former High Peak soldier, who knew Guy and the others of old, luckily said nothing but gave Guy a worried look.

"Shit!" Skuli muttered, then managed a nod as if Guy had said something to him, then dropped back and began a conversation with the other two men to distract them.

Then Brother Timothy, who was riding a mule behind Guy, called out, "What's that?"

Guy's heart sank into his boots as he turned in the saddle to follow the gesture. If Timothy had drawn their attention to either the fugitive or the Coshams he would have no choice but to hunt them – it was the season when the forest was closed, after all, and regardless of who they were, they shouldn't be there. With a cold sweat beginning along his spine, Guy followed Timothy's outstretched arm, praying he would see nothing.

There was movement. A bush well back from the road beneath the trees rustled, then another.

Guy did the only thing he could think of doing and drew his bow. With any luck, if it was Piers or Thomas he could conveniently miss, and if it was the mercenary he'd be solving the problem permanently. Yet even as he was fitting the arrow to the string, the bushes parted and a large red hind bounded out of the undergrowth, shot across the road mere feet ahead of them, and disappeared into the woodland on the other side. Everyone jumped in surprise, then laughed when they realised what had happened.

"By Our Lady, Brother," Guy laughed, "You nearly had me breaking our own laws and killing the king's deer!" And the others joined in the jesting.

For his own part Guy offered up silent prayers of thanks to St Cadoc, one of Tuck's Welsh saints who had an affinity with deer. Opportune didn't begin to describe the hind's appearance. It had saved him from a terrible quandary, and if the mercenary was on the loose, at least Thomas and Piers were two of the band who would be able to take care of themselves if they came face to face with him. And at least, Guy had to concede, it looked as though the mercenary was putting as much room between himself and Nottingham as he could. With any luck he would soon be out of the shire and not their problem. It didn't stop Guy from fretting over which local murderers might be on the loose, though.

Only as he dismounted and walked his horse towards the castle stables did he hear of the full events.

"The town gaol got broken into!" the newest stable lad told him excitedly, forgetting that in public he should not be quite so familiar with Guy whatever the thrill of the news.

"When?" Guy asked him, too worried to care about the lad's slip. "Last night!"

Biting his lip to stop himself cursing too vehemently again, Guy hurried into the castle to find someone who could give him more details. The first man he encountered was Sir Walter, deep in conversation with the three knights who had been to London.

"You're back!" exclaimed Guy, alerting them to his presence.

Sir Hugh of Woodham turned and smiled at him. "Yes, I was just telling Sir Walter how glad we are that you got us out without the sheriff noticing. I also bring Sir Robert's thanks along with Sir Eudes'. Both of them are grateful to you for getting them out of the shire so fast – especially with our news of Sir Alan." All present momentarily looked glum at the memory of their friend's fate.

"Has anyone listened to what you had to tell them?" Guy asked. "I mean I know that fitz John has had to go and answer to the court, but will he just get a fine? A slap on the wrist and then come back as if nothing had happened?"

Robert of Packringham's face changed to a broad grin. "Not likely! Count John is in a right temper over this one! I don't know where fitz John will go to now, but he's no longer our sheriff, thank God!"

"I'm afraid there's good news and bad news," Sir Walter added. "They were just telling me that unfortunately Ralph Murdac doesn't have the funds to buy back his sheriffdom, but he is coming back as our constable."

Guy didn't have to fake his relief at that. "By Our lady, that's wonderful news!"

"It is," agreed Walter, "but you won't be any happier than the rest of us about who's becoming sheriff."

Guy felt his heart already start to sink. "Oh Lord, who?" *Please don't let de Braose be compensated for losing Herefordshire in the past by coming here*, he prayed.

"It's bloody de Wendenal!" Richard of Burscot declared with substantial venom. "How that Godforsaken little weasel managed to get the cash together is beyond me. He hardly had two ha'pennies to rub together when he first came here! The Peak isn't that rich a place for him to have fleeced!"

And suddenly Guy knew this was the time to tell of what he knew of de Wendenal's past. "Ah, but that's what he let us think," he told the others, glad that Sir Martin had just strolled in too. "De Wendenal's to be sheriff," he told the senior knight tersely, "and I was just about to tell the others here that I reckon he got hold of the money to buy the post by theft."

All of them looked shocked, but listened as Guy outlined what had happened over the robbery when de Wendenal hadn't been with them long.

"I can go and get the trinket now," Guy told them. "It's still where I hid it, if you need the proof, but think on this – how many more times has he done something like this? He never spends a thing on himself. He might well have been accumulating a pretty little hoard even by the time he came here, especially given that, whist he's not from the wealthiest of families, he might still have inherited a manor or some bequest in recent years which we know nothing of. He's hardly the talkative type, after all!"

"But why not just buy himself a nice manor somewhere?" a baffled Sir Richard wondered. "Who on earth would *want* to be a sheriff just at the moment?"

However Guy was already shaking his head. "No, you're looking at this the wrong way. You or I wouldn't take the job for love nor money, what with the chancellor and the king's brothers set to fight it out for control of the country. But to a man like de Wendenal it will seem like a perfect time. With someone like our late King Henry he wouldn't have been able to twist the sheriffdom for his own profit. Everything was too well controlled. But I'd bet that de Wendenal has already marked out in his own mind areas where he could turn a neat profit as long as he's not too heavily scrutinised. He's the kind of man who thinks about the pennies. That's how he'll get rich. He'll skim a few pence here and a few pence there, and before you know it he'll have the pounds mounting up. I wouldn't be the least bit surprised if he'd not had his money salted away with some of the Jewish moneylenders, and because of that he's been able to get a loan from them for the rest of what he needs to get his hands on the sheriffdom."

"When's he due?" an appalled Sir Martin asked.

"The messenger rode with us," Sir Hugh told them, "so he'll get to Wendenal at Tickhill tomorrow. I think we'd better assume that the bastard will set out straightaway. He won't have to pack, because he's keeping the constable's post at Tickhill for now, so he'll be back and forth between here and there."

"So we've got only a couple of days," sighed Sir Robert.

"Hey, you three now get to work with Ralph Murdac most of the time!" Guy teased. "You're the lucky ones! It's us poor sods who'll have to deal with bloody Wendenal!"

The three castle knights tried to look sympathetic, but were unable to hide their relief. Ralph Murdac was a known quantity, his foibles and dislikes already familiar and easy enough to work around. William de Wendenal was an altogether different prospect. But as a result of that news, it was only as the evening drew to a close that Guy thought to ask more about the gaol.

"Bloody mercenaries!" fumed Sir Walter. "You know we locked one up? Well his mates must have come for him at last! The locals are all chattering about men in mail, all armed to the teeth, riding through the town in the depths of night. They pulled the bloody door off its hinges, for Christ's sake! Used their horses and iron grapples with ropes on them! And we know that because they had the bare-faced cheek to leave the rope and hooks behind once they'd done with them. The place is all smashed up because once inside, those cells' locks they couldn't break they just pulled off as well – they were mostly only iron bars, anyway, not solid oak doors."

"Jesu save us!" Guy gasped, not having to fake his shock. It was a clever idea, to be sure, and one which had no doubt been generated by the fact that he had made it clear on the slip he had handed to Tuck that such a man was inside. But this was far more of the grand gesture than he had bargained for.

"How many men escaped?" he managed to ask.

"All of them!" a bitter Sir Martin told him. "We went down into the town to see how bad it was. Every last cell has been forced open – even the ones down in the caves beneath the court."

"Caves?" Guy said weakly. "I didn't know about caves!"

Sir Hugh waved his tankard of beer with the airy dismissal of one more used to the sheriff's enforcement of the regular law than a forester like Guy. "Oh normally we don't use them. Bloody inconvenient things anyway – too much traipsing up and down stairs, and always damp. But they were discovered when the foundation stones were being put in, I'm told. My father told me that the sheriff of the day had them explored because he didn't want anyone crawling out that way. In the process they decided that they'd be useful as extra holding space if it ever became necessary. I'd forgotten that they must have been in use again, what with the way the cases awaiting the eyre have been stacking up."

And therein lay the problem, Guy thought. Hugh of Woodham was not a cruel man. He didn't wish unnecessary suffering on anyone. He simply didn't have any experience of what it must be like to be incarcerated, let alone in such a dark hole as that, and lacked the imagination to fill the gap. But Guy could readily imagine what Robin's reaction would have been! Any idea of following Guy's pleas, and only releasing those who deserved freedom, would have been blown away like a feather in a gale when he'd seen those conditions. And in principle Guy agreed with him. Even a week in a cave like that would feel like being buried alive! But there was the matter of those who would now take the lives of others, exacting what they would probably see as revenge, but to everyone else would be just further crimes and proof of their guilt.

"Have there been no sightings of some of the escaped men?" Guy dared to ask. "I'm thinking of Hubert the tailor and Wilfred the tanner in particular. Both are dangerous men, and everyone in Nottingham knows that! They might turn a blind eye to a man they saw fleeing whose only crime was taking a few hares during Fence Month, but surely they'd be screaming the place down at the sight of either of those two?"

Yet there was a general shaking of heads.

"Not yet," Robert of Burscot confessed, "but it's only been a day."

"We'd better make sure the men are out and about in the town, then," Guy thought aloud, "because it'll take more than just one sergeant to catch either of those two!"

However despite Guy's fears, the night passed without murder or mayhem in the town, but in the morning the Nottingham folk woke to a strange sight. Four of the five most dangerous local men were found trussed up at the town stocks, including the two Guy had worried most about. This time there was no report of armed men riding through the town, even though many of the locals would not have been sleeping easily. Indeed nobody seemed to have seen or heard a thing. Yet when Guy got down to the stables that night, Harry was able to shed a little more light on the matter.

"It's very strange," he said with a twinkle in his eye, clearly being careful about what he said because of the other stable men and lads being around. "On the quiet some folk are saying that a giant, a monk, a Saracen and a Templar, with a court of little folk, marched them into the market place and tied them up! Whatever next, eh? Mystical mummers playing at sheriff!"

Guy managed a laugh with the rest, but in his case it was more than a little in relief. Thank Heaven for that! So Tuck and John had taken his warning to heart after all. And it might well be that either Malik or James had come too. Which of the others was the Templar, he wouldn't like to speculate on, but it could have been either James or Siward, or even Gilbert. The Irishman seemed to be following Robin's lead at the moment, but Guy knew he could think for himself and argue for what he thought was right if need be. The only one he didn't think would have been amongst them was Robin himself. And little people? That could be Allan and Roger, and probably Much too. In the dark, with people's nerves already stretched to fraying, they might seem small compared to John's great height and Tuck's breadth of shoulder. But his big question was, had Robin approved this act, or were these members of his band acting alone? And that was something Harry couldn't hope to give him the answers to.

It took a while before I got to the bottom of the matter. For the next few weeks I was kept busy coping with the changes within the castle, for Ralph Murdac had returned a changed and bitter man. It was more than understandable. He had been expelled from a post he had filled with great conscience for no greater fault than that of being too poor to pay King Richard's bribe; and had been replaced by a man who not only had no experience, but had proven himself to be wholly unfit for the job. And now that matters had all gone to hell in a handcart, he was being expected to come back and sort things out.

Even worse, he was also being expected to nursemaid the inexperienced de Wendenal – a man who had not so long ago been one of the least of the knights who served under him, and who was now, to all intents and purposes, his superior. I do not say his outright superior, Brother, for it had been made clear – and I saw the document stating this for myself – that Murdac had the right and power in the name of both Count John and the crown to override any decision of de Wendenal's which he believed to be detrimental to the office of sheriff, or which he believed could be construed as unlawful. But it was one thing for a man like Archbishop Walter to say such a thing, and quite another in practise, since at the end of the day it was Wendenal who held the post of sheriff and not Murdac. All most of us could be grateful for was that Wendenal would spend even less time in residence at Nottingham than his predecessor had done.

But you are itching to hear of Robin Hood, not my trials within the castle. So, Gervase, I will tell you that I had contact with Roger and Allan on the times within the following weeks when I rode out to see to the clearing of the forest for the winter hunting season. If Roger has remained outside of the legend you have heard, it is because he proved so adept at remaining unnoticed. The young man whom I had feared would be the most trouble at our first meeting was in fact someone who was increasingly helpful for me, and so it was now. With the castle all of a buzz over Wendenal strutting about the place like some angry and arrogant cockerel just dying for a chance to pick a fight, Roger could pass for a local beneath anyone's need to observe, and he came several times to meet me in the town – or even on the first occasion, within the outer bailey.

On that occasion Robin had urgently wanted news of the new sheriff, so Roger had come with everyone's blessings. Therefore once I had told him all my news, he was able to answer my questions. It turned out that I had been correct in my guess over Robin's reaction to the caves. Roger said his anger had flared up like Greek Fire when they had entered the building, cleared the first cells, and then heard the cries for help from below. I knew already that five long-dead cadavers had been left behind, but Roger said that another four prisoners had been lucky to survive. The cold and damp in the caves had left them broken men in health, wracked with rheumatism and breathing problems, and sadly none were men who had in any way deserved to be there. Regrettably, the truly evil ones had proved the adage of the Devil looking after his own, and had walked out relatively unscathed.

Yet because of that it had been Hugh, who had been left guarding the door and watching for any sheriff's men, who had heard one of them – and I suspect it was the tailor – immediately declaring he would go and take back what was rightfully his. Remembering my warnings, Hugh had dealt him a blow to the head, and had dragged him outside into the shadows. Along with Tuck, he now took it upon himself to ask people who they were and where from, under the pretext of making sure that not too many people would head out all up the same road. By this means he got to pull over the ones I had been most worried about – or rather Tuck administered a smart blow to their heads with his quarterstaff to ensure their compliance. With most men only too grateful to be getting out, no-one argued.

Robin had argued, though. He flatly refused to send any man back into the gaol, no matter what his crimes, declaring it unfit to keep pigs in, let alone men. Now I learned I had much to be grateful to Hugh and Siward for, for they then cleverly suggested that Robin should therefore make sure that all the escaped men got away safely, and made a persuasive argument for some of their own number bringing up the rear on each of the roads they had sent men off along. Since Robin and several of the others were on what might be called ˜borrowed˜ horses in their guise as the mercenaries, it made sense that those mounted would take the London and Newark roads, so that they could then retreat at speed into the forest and at the same time still manage to skirt Nottingham, once their charges were clear of danger.

Therefore Robin and Marianne had ridden off on the Newark road with Gilbert; Will had taken the London road with Hugh so that Hugh, who had been the most vocal objector, was not taking part in what was to come; whilst on foot, Piers and Thomas had taken the Mansfield road, and Bilan and James had run off up the Huntingdon road. It was not how Robin had deployed them, you see, for he had ridden off believing that those not riding would be split evenly between the two northern routes. Instead, Malik and Siward, instead of riding with Will, had walked their horses and joined Tuck, John and Allan in guarding the men Tuck had laid out until they could move.

It had been Tuck's idea to make themselves look that bit more fantastical, that bit more unreal, taking his inspiration from the mummers who regularly visited with their plays. So as I had suspected, John had worn a cloak with pads under the shoulders to make himself look even larger, Malik had wrapped scarves around him to look more the Saracen, and Siward had played the Templar. The little folk I had had report of turned out to have been Allan, Roger, Much and Mariota, and they had been the scouts keeping watch while the others had tied up the criminals at the stocks. What was interesting to me was that while John predictably was unhappy about seeming to disobey Robin, the others had accepted my word that we would be doing the folk of Nottingham a great disservice by letting these few men go free. Even James, whom I had once thought so intensely loyal to Robin as to never doubt him, had seen the reasoning in what had been done. Yet more peculiar was Roger's request to me from all of those involved in the prisoners' return to not let slip to Robin what had been done.

I was able to reassure Roger, and also asked him to relay the message to Robin that none had gone back into the gaol – for the ones they had returned to prison were now occupying the dungeon in the castle as the only safe place for the time being. Roger immediately caught on to the double meaning of that message, and happily told me he would keep it simple for Robin, but pass on my thanks to the others when he could do so. And did Robin ever find out, you ask, Gervase? No he did not. There was no reason why he should. He was not present when the eyre finally came around much later, and by then other things had happened to drive that night from his mind in its details at least. He went to his grave believing that once in his life, if not more, he had emptied Nottingham's gaol of all its inmates, and was proud of that.

You are shocked? No, it was not a betrayal of his beliefs and ideals, Brother, not at all. Think of it rather that Robin had the most noble of ambitions, but sometimes more earthly considerations had to be taken into account which he could not see. And at times like that those who followed him dealt with the mundane rights and wrongs without bothering him, knowing that he would be most conscience-smitten to think that while the rest had gone free, even one of those men should have been re-incarcerated, however much they deserved it.

So as we moved towards Christmas of 1191, for the most part we were glad that the greater matters in the world had passed over us for now. All was not perfect in our small corner of the Earth, but it was better than it could have been, and we had some small measure of hope in that it had been demonstrated to us that there was a limit to what King Richard's governors would allow even a sheriff to get away with.

Chapter 13

And so we move on, Brother. You may think we have a couple of years to go before the actions of the great will impact on us once again, but I can assure you that these were far from quiet times for us, or lacking in action! For until we come to the great events of 1194 we still have William de Wendenal's shrival years to get through, and he was no easy man to deal with, I can assure you. And the gaol which Robin had broken into so easily was repaired swiftly and with greater emphasis on its security. Sadly the caves, which had formerly been seen as the last place to inter men in, had now been set up to take the more dangerous of prisoners, and I confess to you, Gervase, that I consequently had many doubts as to whether we had saved a few only to make matters worse for the many who had to come after. My conscience has been heavy on that score for many years and I am only to glad to have confessed it.

Out in the wider world we were to learn how, at that royal Michaelmas court, ours was one of eleven changes of sheriff which took place, and my fear of de Braose appearing had not been so fanciful after all, for he was one of those who got his position back in the shifting to remove Longchamp's brothers from power. Archbishop Walter was clearing out the abusers of the king's name with a vengeance, not merely fitz John! Across the border from us, Osbert Longchamp was dismissed as sheriff of Yorkshire and the king's man, Hugh Bardolf took over, who had been up to that point sheriff of Warwickshire and Leicestershire. Until the chaos of the last year or so we had seen much of Bardolf when the eyres had come around, and we were to see much more of him in the future, for he was to remain one of the chief justiciars and also sheriff of neighbouring shires for many years. Mark his name, Brother! He will become important later in this tale!

As for Longchamp himself, by early October his position had become untenable. It was declared in London that he was no longer to be chancellor, and must hand back those castles which he had wrongly seized since coming to power. It was a sharp fall down from the dizzy heights he had so recently enjoyed, and many thought it long overdue. So we all breathed a sigh of relief when we heard before October was out that he had left the country, we hoped for good. Meanwhile, for the time being the king's brother seemed to have found some sort of favour with the major barons of the land, and for once was not causing any trouble; while Walter of Coutance, the new chancellor and still archbishop of Rouen, appeared to be an altogether safer pair of hands to guide the country. So it seemed that we had settled once more into a situation which, while not ideal, was at least workable – which was very much how our situation at Nottingham appeared too.

Yet one more event of national importance was to have repercussions in my next exploit with Robin. After Longchamp's expulsion from the kingdom you may or may not know, Gervase, that he appealed to Pope Celestine for support by letter, and in the December of 1191 the pope wrote back expressing his horror at the outrages inflicted upon his holy servant – clearly he had never seen the worse side of his now former-archbishop! Incredibly, Pope Celestine called for the excommunication of the royal count and all of his advisors and accomplices. And then to pour oil onto the flames, in his retained capacity as papal legate, Longchamp not only relayed the pope's message but made it specific.

We could scarcely believe it when we heard the details. The excommunication was delayed until Quinquagesima Sunday in mid-February to allow time for repentance, but the list of those Longchamp wished removed from God's Grace was breath-taking. Aside from the prince, John, he had included the king's appointed successor to him, Walter of Coutance (and therefore a man Longchamp's equal within the Church as an archbishop); the bishops of Winchester and Coventry; the four justiciars of the realm; and Gerard of Camville, John Marshal and Stephen Ridel (Count John's personal chancellor). Such overarching arrogance should surely call down some form of divine wrath, we could not help thinking.

Mercifully, the saintly Bishop Hugh of Lincoln, who had been the man Longchamp had charge with bringing all the other bishops to heel and carrying out the excommunications, ignored the order. Then on the second of February, Candlemas Day, and with fourteen day to go until the excommunications took effect, Geoffrey Plantagenet was proclaimed archbishop at York and added poor Bishop Hugh to the list to be excommunicated for not having obeyed the pope and Longchamp's orders.

Insanity, Brother, absolute insanity! We had the pope in effect telling the king who could and could not be in charge of his own country, and bishops being cut off from God by their archbishops who were infinitely more cynical and avaricious men of the world than they were. And in the midst of this mayhem I had to deal with a trio of senior clerics who believed they were above the law now, and could hunt when and where they wished!

Nottinghamshire
Late January, the Year of Our Lord 1192

Guy reined in his horse and listened hard. He could have sworn he had heard a stag call out in alarm. Generally these woods in the

Derwent-to-Erewash part of the royal forest weren't as dense as the old forest, with less of the great swathes of managed oaks and more mixed stands of oak, ash, elm and birch; but just here there was a goodly sized wood of holme oaks which Guy knew the local deer particularly favoured to hide in. By his best guess he was somewhere on the shire boundary, not too far from the villages of Hardstoft and North Wingfield, and a goodly way from any of the major manor houses of the local nobility. So who on earth would be out hunting?

The sudden baying of hounds alerted him to where the hunters must be, a little to the north of him, and he heeled his horse into a trot. To his certain knowledge nobody had dispensation to be hunting around here, so whoever they were, they were doing it illegally. He was out here on his own, but his hood and the horn slung on its lanyard across his shoulders proclaimed his office for all to see, therefore anyone objecting to his interference in their sport would not be able to claim they had not know who had challenged them.

As he continued down the slope from Stainsby Common into the thicker part of the wood, two red deer hinds shot past him in panic with this year's fawns at their heels. Then another yearling came tearing past him with what looked suspiciously like a bite mark on her back leg. After his years working the kennels, Guy had taken to carrying a lightweight whip with him as a good means of discouraging over enthusiastic hounds from a chase, and now he unbound it from where it was strapped to the back of his saddle. It was enough to be able to deliver a stinging flick without causing the dogs any harm, because after all, if the dogs were where they shouldn't be, it wasn't their fault. Some of his fellow foresters wouldn't hesitate to maim or kill a hound, but Guy couldn't bring himself to do that, although many was the time he would have liked to do something like it to one of their owners.

Six vocal hounds came bursting out of a nearby bush and began circling him, but were quickly dissuaded of their nipping with the whip and Guy's growled commands. Recognising a pack leader when they heard it, they quickly fell in behind him, much to Guy's amusement, and followed him as he urged his horse onwards through the undergrowth. Coming out onto a track probably made by the deer themselves he was almost ridden down by half a dozen men on horseback, who were followed by a couple of panting men on foot, trying to instil some order into those hounds still with the hunters.

"Halt!" Guy bellowed at them, wearing his severest frown. "Who are you to be hunting in Sherwood without permission?"

"Qui va là?" the rider who wore an opulent fur-trimmed cloak challenged him back.

"Je suis Guy de Gisborne. L'homme de Sheriff de Wendenal." Guy riposted, making the Norman lord blink in surprise. Clearly he hadn't expected to be understood, let alone replied to in his own language, and some of the superior sneer had faded. "So I will ask again – who are you all to be hunting in the forest without the sheriff's permission or notification?" Guy added the last to make the point that, had anyone come hunting with the royal blessing, the sheriff would have been informed in advance of their arrival.

A portly man on a suitably chunky bay horse edged it forward and spoke. "Now, now, forester. No need to be hasty!"

Belatedly Guy recognised Prior Eustace from Newstead Abbey.

"My lord prior," he responded courteously, inclining his head just enough to make the expected obeisance without ceding any moral ground. "I wasn't aware that you had applied to hunt here?"

The prior's smile withered at the implied rebuke. "That would be because I saw no necessity to make such an application," he responded haughtily.

"These are still the king's lands," Guy pointed out, keeping his voice pleasant.

Another of the wealthy hunters gave an audible snort. "The Count John of Mortain's, don't you mean?"

"He's still the king's brother and a member of the royal family," Guy persisted, "and this is *royal* forest."

Yet the hunters actually laughed.

"Well he may not be in a position to tell anyone much of anything soon," the third of the fur-draped men declared disdainfully. "Count John won't be so high and mighty when he's cut off from God's Grace come Quinquagesima."

Such a reference immediately alerted Guy to the fact that these others were probably Churchmen too. "I wouldn't dismiss the prince so fast," he cautioned them. "He has a knack of surviving downfalls which would destroy other men. So who are you, my lord, to take his name in vain so readily?" The 'my lord' was something of a guess, and used to flatter the man into giving more of himself away than as any token of respect.

Instead the Prior of Newstead answered. "This is Henry Gretwold, prior of Felley, and his sub-prior Galf Furmentin, and this," he gestured to the Norman, "is my guest at Newstead, my lord Saher de Espelt. I would be wary, huntsman, of taking the youngest Plantagenet's side."

"I'm no mere huntsman, as you should have observed, my lord prior," Guy replied firmly. "I am one of the king's foresters, charged with overseeing the laws of the royal forest. Laws which you must be aware are not set at the whim of the prince but of the king himself. So whatever your argument with Count John, this is nothing to do with him."

"Oh I think you might find it harder to separate the Church from the realm than that!" the sub-prior guffawed. "Or do you wish to join the impostor chancellor in being excommunicated? You have before you three men of the cloth who could enforce such a penance upon you, you know."

'Penance' didn't come close to it! For a moment the audacity of such a threat took Guy's breath away. And not just that. Over the years Guy had been faced with all sorts of different threats to his person, but excommunication was on a whole new level, threatening his immortal soul. If he should die whilst under such an imposition his soul would spend the rest of eternity in Hell – a terrifying prospect even for the kind of man who barely stirred from his homestead, but to someone like Guy who might fall to a stray hunter's arrow at any time, it was beyond terrifying and induced a temporary mental and physical paralysis of a kind he had never known before.

What saved him was Tuck. In some deep recess of his mind he suddenly heard the strong Welsh voice saying, 'How dare they! How dare they presume to know the mind of God!' The words had been said in another time and place, but instinctively Guy knew that his friend's response would be the same right now, and somehow he had more faith in Tuck's more kindly belief than that of the self-righteous and self-serving prelates in front of him. God knew all of his sins and his good deeds and would judge him fairly when his time came, for the Almighty saw everything. And Guy was able to draw breath again.

Yet he also saw in that instant that he had made a fatal error. He had allowed the priors to see his moment of weakness, the moment when he had faltered. They had seen it and were now pressing home what they saw as their advantage.

"Oh yes, sir forester knight," sub-prior Galf was sneering, "cross us at the peril of your immortal soul!"

Prior Henry, his immediate superior at Felley Priory, was smirking as he added, "You should be careful. We have power over you not only in this life but the next!"

However it was this over-playing of their advantage which now made Guy's hackles rise. Far from being venerated Churchmen, they were now nothing more frightening than the kind of bullies he had dealt with over and over again since childhood. They were enjoying what they thought was instilling blind terror into him, and in Guy's eyes there was nothing Christian in doing that. If they had left it with the simple threat of excommunication and let his faith and imagination do the rest, he would probably have caved in, he realised. But Guy wasn't a man to stand for being bullied, whether by sheriffs or Churchmen.

He took a good look at the four closest to him, and then to the other two mounted men who, by the look of them, were seasoned soldiers escorting de Espelt. The soldiers alone he might just have tackled, but not with de Espelt as well, and the three Churchmen all seemed to be the sons of Normans and had probably been schooled in weapons as lads, just as he had, before their induction into the Church. No, six to one were odds he couldn't win.

"You leave me no choice," he said coldly, deliberately not elaborating on what he meant.

"No, we don't!" Prior Eustace crowed. "Now out of our way ...and when we're done we'll decide whether your sheriff shall hear of your insolence!"

Guy skilfully got his horse to back up out of their way and sat watching as they rode past and on down the track. The big question now was, what was he to do? He could track them and note where they brought a stag down. That would give him evidence of their illegal hunting. But would it do any good? If he took the evidence to de Wendenal he was sure that, for all that the new sheriff would bluster and fume at his authority being so openly flouted, he wouldn't actually do anything. De Wendenal was far too conscious of needing to stay close to the prevailing political wind. A man with so few high family connections, and with a limited purse to buy his favours with, would think twice or more about crossing powerful Churchmen who were allied to those who might yet bring down a royal prince and the king's own chancellor.

However Guy was also determined that these men should not get away with what was, to all intents and purposes, poaching. It would only take another of the forester knights, or one of the walking foresters, to come upon openly dumped remains of the hunt and innocent local villagers might yet be fined heavily for an offence which wasn't theirs. Angry and frustrated, all Guy could do just at the moment, though, was go and report the hunting to the sheriff. If he got there first, then any complaint that the hunters then chose to bring against him would be seen in the right light. Any delay might mean that they or a messenger from them might get to the castle first, and Guy was under no illusions that if that happened, he would be reprimanded by de Wendenal with no opportunity to state his own case.

He turned his horse for Nottingham and rode with all speed for there, but along the way he vowed he would also leave the same day and go and find Robin. If ever there was a case when Robin should help it was this, and not only because justice needed to be served. With Robin and his friends having fought to save Jerusalem, if the Churchmen did more than just threaten excommunication, the former crusaders were in a stronger position of religious grace to withstand such a horror. And Guy also wanted to talk to Tuck. Of anyone, Guy had faith in Tuck being able to tell him whether an excommunication delivered by such a trio of reprobates would carry any weight in the hereafter. He sincerely prayed not, but he would welcome Tuck's wisdom and pious insight as reassurance.

At the castle he lost no time in tracking down the sheriff and was glad to find Robert Murdac in the same hall talking to the three castle knights and Sir Martin.

"My lord sheriff, there's a serious problem," Guy declared loud enough to be heard across the hall as he strode to where de Wendenal sat. The sheriff shuffled upright from where he had been lounging on the cushioned seat and stared belligerently at Guy. However Guy gave him no chance to start one of his tirades. "We've been threatened with excommunication by the prior and sub-prior of Felley and the prior of Newstead!" he informed them all bluntly.

Anything de Wendenal might have said was smothered in the chorus of disbelief.

"Good God Almighty!" Robert Murdac exploded. "What does that pompous ass de Tuke think he's doing? How *dare* he take it upon himself to make such a pronouncement!"

"What did you do to antagonise him?" was de Wendenal's immediate response, confirming Guy's suspicions that he had been right to come here first and get his version of events in before the priors'.

"I *did* nothing," Guy told the sheriff coldly, remembering just in time not to stand so close that he would appear to be looming over the shorter man, even if he ever bothered to get to his feet. For now he needed de Wendenal to accept what he said even if he didn't like it. "I was patrolling on the shire border and saw a wounded hind go past in a panic. Then I heard the hounds. I had no idea who might be hunting so brazenly, so I went to investigate."

"They were *hunting*?" Murdac gasped in disbelief. "So openly and after the forest had been declared closed?"

"Very openly," Guy confirmed dryly. "In fact, when I asked them if they had obtained permission, that was the point when they told me that the Church now had authority over us all, and that if I disrupted their hunt any further, they would use Longchamp's instruction to excommunicate his enemies and extend it to me, and any other who dared to challenge them." He made that very pointed, staring into de Wendenal's eyes as he said 'other', and saw the sheriff swallow hard in shock.

Sir Martin came to Guy's side. "They openly admitted they were hunting and expected to be allowed to continue?"

Guy nodded. "They were very brazen about the whole thing. They were hunting with a large pack of hounds, had two men on foot with the dogs, and two men at arms with them whom I think were with Abbot Eustace's guest. A man called Saher de Espelt from Normandy. So there were six mounted men altogether."

He didn't need to say more for the other knights in the room to be shaking their heads sympathetically. No-one, with the possible exception of de Wendenal, would now have expected him to have stopped the hunt when so outnumbered. However he did add,

"The Felley prior told me he would be complaining to you, sheriff, but his intent was clearly to threaten you with the same fate if you chose to bring the hunt to the attention of the forest eyre."

De Wendenal went a strange colour and spluttered. Clearly the thought of being excommunicated was one he had never associated with being sheriff, and even such a corrupt and conniving man as him might worry over that fate. In fact it occurred to Guy that the sheriff, far more than himself, might be in need of some serious intercession and confession before he was cut off from God whilst on this Earth.

"What do you wish to do?" Guy asked him, secretly enjoying seeing the blind panic spread across de Wendenal's face, as the realisation sank in that he now had to make a decision which would affect not only the hated knight in front of him, but himself as well. "They said they would be coming to see you once they'd had their sport."

The last was cruelly taunting de Wendenal, but Guy couldn't resist twisting the mental knife he had shoved into the sheriff's dim little brain. God knew, the man deserved it!

"I must think," de Wendenal spluttered and hurried out, beckoning Ralph Murdac and Sir Martin to go with him.

Hugh of Woodham came and, with a sympathetic smile, clapped Guy on the shoulder. "Our sheriff was just telling us that he intends to make Sir Martin the assistant constable of the castle. He said he felt that with so much of the royal forest now under his administration and run from here, it was sensible that someone who knows the forest laws should have part of the running of the castle." He gave a wry snort. "Ironically we were all thinking it was probably the first sensible thing he's ever done just as you arrived with your news. So I'm guessing he'll now be shrieking at poor Sir Martin to find him a way out of this hole."

Guy sighed. "I'm not sure there is a way out of it. All I cared about was making sure everyone knew that if reports came in of butchered deer around the Hardstoft and North Wingfield area, that none of the villages got persecuted for it."

"Blessed St Thomas!" Robert of Packringham gasped from Guy's other side, "I'd not thought of it like that!"

Sir Walter, the other senior forester knight came to join the conversation. "No, but Guy's right, we can't have the villagers getting blamed for this. How much of a mess are you expecting, Guy?"

"Far too much, is the short answer! The men with the hounds were inexperienced at running their own hunt. It was the bitten deer which hadn't been brought down which alerted me in the first place. I wouldn't be surprised if some of the hounds don't escape from their control and do some savaging of their own. But they might not kill!

God help us, but they might even savage sheep if they really get the taste. And I've also serious concerns about those three priors. I'd guess de Espelt will have hunted regularly in Normandy..."

"Don't count on that!" Richard of Burscot interrupted. "You've not been to Normandy, Guy, I have. They don't have anything like the rich hunting reserves we have here. Yes, de Espelt will have hunted, but it's going to have been less often than our English lords, and it won't always have been for deer – and certainly not for the likes of our big red deer! He might be more used to fox and hare!"

Guy winced. "Then we could have a right bloody mess in the forest! I'll have to go back out. There's no way I'm leaving maimed deer to die in agony because some curse cleric thinks he's grown bigger balls just because the pope is throwing his weight around at the moment! I'll take my bow and plenty of arrows, and a three or four spears in case they decide to play at hunting boar – although I could wish the boar would win in that case! Christ help us, we don't want a wounded and enraged boar savaging anyone!"

"God have mercy upon us," intoned Sir Walter. "What possessed these Churchmen to become so bullish? It's going to be a nightmare if all the abbeys and priories in the shire suddenly decide they're above the law!"

A timorous cough came from behind them, and they turned to see one of the sheriff's clerks, a new monk who had only just arrived to replace an elderly brother whose rheumatism meant he could no longer cope with the travelling court-scribe duties.

"May I tell you something?" His face was filled with fear, no doubt already having been on the receiving end of de Wendenal's temper.

"Brother, we can use all the help we can get," Guy told him kindly. "What do you know?"

The monk cleared his throat nervously. "Well I come from Lenton Priory, but as I was leaving to come here I heard my abbot discussing something with our prior. He was disgusted that Henry Gretwold, who's the prior at Felley, had been so avaricious as to petition the new pope for further rights and allowances as soon as he was confirmed – the pope, that is!" Celestine had only been made pope that April, and had instantly gotten involved in the politics of the Holy Roman Empire before becoming embroiled in Longchamp's battles. "My lord abbot was saying that Prior Henry has clearly had some kind of word that his request has been favourably received. In what way, I'm afraid I don't know, sires, but I do know that my lord abbot used the words 'unbearable' and 'insufferable' about Prior Henry."

The knights all looked to one another in surprise.

"Well that's a revelation and no mistake," Sir Hugh said with a puffing of his cheeks in relief.

"Isn't it just," Guy agreed, smiling at the worried clerk. "Don't worry, you were right to tell us this. It's very helpful to know that not every band of monks and canons in the shire are about to start challenging the sheriff."

Sir Robert was stroking his chin thoughtfully. "That makes a lot more sense, you know. If Felley Priory has connections with the pope who's siding with Longchamp, no wonder the prior and his sub-prior think they're invulnerable – especially with the Church itself divided over who's excommunicating who. It's just our bad luck they happen to be in our shire."

"Maybe," Guy agreed grimly, "but what's the betting that de Wendenal will back down if the prior can bluster better than him?"

His words brought everyone back to the immediate problem.

"I'll make sure certain persons don't head out that way," Sir Walter declared tactfully, although all present knew he meant that he would be keeping the belligerent Sirs Fredegis, Walkelin and Henry out of Guy's hair while he cleared up the mess. "If you can do some good with this Guy, I trust you will," which was another subtle way of saying that Guy had his blessing to distribute whatever usable meat he might find to those who might need it.

It made Guy smile both outwardly and inside – Sir Walter had no idea of what Robin would make of such an order! Yet it gave him the excuse he needed to hurry out, claim a fresh horse and a spare, and leave at speed before de Wendenal could issue any contrary orders.

How on earth he was going to find Robin he didn't know. Sherwood was an awfully big place, and hardly the easiest to search. Blessing the fact that Allan and Roger had told him of where their current camps were, all Guy could do was take them in order of distance as he left Nottingham. He didn't expect to find them in the ones closest, but dared not assume so and thereby risk missing his friends. However the well-hidden camp in the patch of dense woodland on the east bank of the Leen between Arnold and Hucknall had clearly not been used for some time, and it had only ever been an overnight refuge. That close to Nottingham, except in the worst of weather when nobody was about, it was far too dangerous to remain at for longer than a day.

His next place to try wasn't so easy to decide on. There was a cunningly hidden camp south and west of Rufford not far from Inkersall, but that was taking him eastwards, and his only sensible route from there would be to go for the camp south of Worksop and then across into Derbyshire. Yet that took him too far from the hunting ground. Cursing his bad luck, Guy decided that he had little choice but to pray that they would be at the camp just on the Nottingham side of the Erewash from Hardstoft. There'd been no sign of them there when he'd been riding hard for Nottingham, though, so unless they'd arrived in the last day or so he would be out of luck there. However, if he was to make anything meaningful out of the illegal hunt, and save the deer from a painful death, he had to be thinking of butchering the carcasses now, not in several days time.

It took him little effort to find the first three slaughtered deer, and roundly cursed the churchmen for their callous cruelty and wastefulness. In each case the prime haunches had been taken, but the rest of the deer left to rot. What angered Guy even more was his discovery that the innards were still in place. That meant that the fools running the hounds had either not cared, or not been experienced enough to know, that the hounds should have had a good meal out of them. But then any huntsman worth the name would have had pack animals with him to load the other cuts onto, and would have therefore been able to carry the loaves of dog-bread, and something to slop the blood into to cook it and the bread.

The thought of the ill-used hounds brought Guy's own dogs to mind, and he suffered a dreadful pang of loss at the thought of Fletch and Spike, now up on the manor at Gisborne. He desperately missed his canine companions at times like this, not least because he could have told them to find his friends and they would have helped him track them down. He sighed and shook his head before returning to the grisly task in front of him. The guts had spoiled fastest of all the meat, even in the bitter cold of an early February day. All he could do was pile them up and pour some of the oil he'd been foresighted enough to bring with him over them, then set fire to them to destroy the evidence.

As the evil-smelling mixture burned, he cut the deer into joints and bundled them into sacks. His second horse, which he wasn't riding now, had to double as a pack animal, and was none too pleased about it. Luckily it wasn't far into North Wingfield, where he left the bloodiest of the joints. He'd not had time to get the meat off the bone, but was surprised when the villagers at first refused the offered meat. Only when he told them that the priors would be brought to justice for the hunt did they reluctantly accept some of the sides, those rib-bones being the easiest to mistake for domestic animals'.

Gritting his teeth in his frustration at how difficult even this part of his task was becoming, Guy had to turn off and go to Williamthorpe to deposit more of the meat, for he could hardly go riding across the shire with rapidly decaying joints starting to stink. Luckily the folk of Williamthorpe were less worried and more grateful, taking the lot off Guy, and immediately taking them to where they could be salted or smoked as best fitted each cut.

"Folk at Wingfield have nasty priest who keeps spying around the village," Ailred, the headman told him. "Wouldn't be at all surprised if these monks you speak of hadn't spent the night in the village too. Bit of a step from Felley and Newstead to over here. That priest seems to have the villagers under his thumb, somehow, and he's the sort who'd want to impress senior men like them. Daft sod possibly even invited them in."

Guy could have kicked himself for not having thought of that. Having ridden into them in the late morning, it should have occurred to him at the time that they couldn't have come direct from either the priory or the abbey and be hunting already.

"Is there a manor nearby?" he belatedly thought to ask. He knew that there was no-one of great consequence in the vicinity of these villages, but there was bound to be something which warranted the name, even if it was only a well-appointed farmhouse in size.

Ailred pulled a face. "A goodly chunk of the land in North Wingfield, Owlcotes and here is part of the manor at Pilsley. Old Sir Roger's our lord. Don't see much of him these days. Seems to leave most of the work to Alfred of Pilsley, his reeve. Of the bigger men, Godric, a man whose family were once thegns around here has some land at Tupton, but mostly this is still the Peverels' land, let out to their liegemen. Sir Roger's one of them."

Guy nodded sagely, hoping he was giving the impression of taking note for his business. In reality he was quietly relieved that he wouldn't be having some imperious young lord demanding to know what he was doing handing out venison to his peasants. It was something Guy knew he should have thought of earlier, but then it occurred to him that the lack of any major lord around here was also probably why the priors had chosen to come hunting here in the first place.

"Hmmm, well if you get any trouble from the reeve or anyone, refer them to me," Guy told Ailred. "In fact I'd be inclined to tell him that the priors have been hunting the area when you next see him, and that the sheriff and his foresters are aware of whom it was. That way, you've covered yourselves against any question as to why there aren't so many deer around here as there ought to be."

Leaving some very happy villagers behind him, Guy turned once more for the hunting ground. To his disgust as he followed the well-trampled trail, he found a another pair of hacked about deer further east of North Wingfield, and then a trio of hinds down by the River Doe Lee between the hamlets of Stainsby and Bramley. These last three angered him the most. They hadn't been hunted. They'd been run to exhaustion and been left to die from the bite wounds the overexcited hounds had inflicted.

"St Cadoc help me!" Guy swore furiously as he ran his hand over the soft skin so torn and bloody. "Help me find Robin and give these so-called men of God a taste of their own medicine!"

He couldn't even bury these three, the ground was too hard and he hadn't the time. All he could do was to ride into Stainsby, find the priest there, and get him to witness what Guy wrote, detailing that he had discovered the three hinds, and had purposely requested that the folk of Stainsby go and bring them into the village. He asked the headman there to preserve the skins in order to show how mauled the deer had been, for he was determined to show the skins at the next court, but again told them that if any of the meat was usable it should not be wasted.

More than ever he now wanted to find Robin. He was pretty sure that the hunters had turned for home on the same day he had met them, and had given up the hunt in time to return to a more comfortable bed for the night – possibly at Mansfield rather than their own establishments. So it was unlikely there would be more evidence he could hope to gather, and his thoughts were now on revenge.

You wonder at why I was so enraged over the death of a mere deer? What? ˜It is not as though a human being had been killed?˜

It is a good thing I still struggle to rise from this bed, Brother, or I would drag you out into the woods and teach you a lesson in humanity! No, do not tut and frown so! It is very easy for you to sit here and pronounce your judgements. You who have never had to hunt your own food, who have never had to worry if the roof over your head will be taken because of an unjust accusation by another which you cannot possibly prove to be wrong, even though you know beyond doubt it is a filthy lie. Both matters lie at the heart of this particular tale and you need to see that, Gervase.

So you think animals do not suffer, do you? Shall I take you out to the byre the next time your lay brother slaughters an old ox which has gone beyond its usefulness? Take you and stand you in front of it and make you stare into its eyes as the knife goes in. No, do not screw your nose up in such disgust! I have seen animals suffer most terribly, and the worst of those has been when a hunt has gone wrong. I have killed and killed cleanly, sometimes for food and sometimes to prevent an animal's greater suffering, such as when a horse has broken a leg, but every time I have offered up a prayer as I have done so. They are all God's creatures, Brother. He made them all, just as he made us, and for my part I would not take that life so divinely given and squander it for no other reason than to lord it over my fellow man.

Ah, that has made you stop and think. Good! What does it say in Genesis about the beasts of the field and the birds of the air? ...Yes, quote me the scripture, do – and while you do so think on those words again. Not quite so sure now, are you? Dominion does not mean a blind right to slaughter, does it? How would you feel if the lords of the Church who have dominion over <u>you</u> suddenly turned up on your doorstep, and proceeded to chase you until you could scarce draw in breath? Set dogs to harry you and bite you, not giving you a moments' rest until you fell down too *exhausted to move? Then left you broken and with your flesh hanging off in tatters for the frost and the wind to bite it again, and again, until your pitiful life finally seeped away?*

Well might your look a little sick, Gervase. There is nothing noble in such sport for any right thinking man, whatever his station. I have always loved and respected animals. I do not confuse them with people. They are not people, although some folk behave worse than they do. But most wild animals live by a certain simple order. They do not over-hunt the prey they live on, for to do so means that they in turn will starve when that prey is all gone. Only men kill like that, wantonly and wastefully, and the worst of those are men who, like you, have never had to provide for themselves. And in this instance I knew without having to be told that if this slaughter was brought before the forest eyre, those oh so holy priors would lie under oath, and push the blame onto some lesser man who would not be able to defend himself in a matter when it would come down to a simple man's word against a leading churchman.

You do not think they would have lied? Oh, Brother, you are so naive! And before you begin to chastise me over not taking the threat of excommunication more seriously, I will tell you that it comes down to the same thing – my belief that they were corrupt. Had they made such an accusation in church, devoutly and in keeping with their offices, I would have been on my knees praying for my soul in a heartbeat. Had it been a genuine threat based upon my own ill-doings I would have been even more in mortal dread. But it was done with the same careless and callous disregard as their hunting, calling upon God as if he was their servant, not they his. And at last you see it, Brother. Now do you see why I was so angry? So let us continue and I will tell you of how Robin and I taught these blasphemous clerics a lesson they would never forget.

Chapter 14

So I can now tell you that I rode with speed for the hideout located up above the Derwent almost up on Beeley Moor. This was more of a summer camp, being a little too prone to the blasts of winter winds at this time of year, given that it faced south-west, but I left a message there in case one of the company should pause there on the way back to another camp. I guessed they would be holed up at Loxley. It was where they had managed to make good permanent shelters, and would be able to light as many fires as they wanted against the winter chill without being spotted. So I rode on as fast as my horses could manage with ice on the ground and the short days, and with every mile I rode my heart hardened against those vile priors.

As I crested the ridge and looked down into the Loxley valley I was relieved beyond words to smell wood-smoke. Then I heard someone call out my name and saw Much up in a tree on lookout duty, waving excitedly to me. By the time I rode into the camp everyone had assembled to meet me, and I was glad beyond words to have found them.

Loxley and Sherwood
Late winter, the Year of Our Lord 1192

"By Our Lady, I'm so glad to have found you," Guy declared as he slid wearily out of the saddle.

"What's happened? What's wrong?" Thomas asked, cutting off Robin before he could speak.

Unable to contain his anger any longer, Guy fumed his way through the events of the last few days, often swearing volubly. Only as he ground to a halt did he realise that Robin was smiling at him with far more affection than he had seen of late.

"It's good to see the old Guy again," his cousin declared. "The one with all the passion and fire."

It took Guy aback. Was that what the matter was with Robin half the time? He thought Guy didn't give a fig about the injustices? Yet before Guy could challenge his cousin back, he caught sight of Tuck, and then realised how those closest to his monastic friend were looking at him with growing awe. Tuck was building to a towering rage.

Suddenly he exploded, face suffused with anger and shaking his fists above his head as he bellowed to the wind, *"Damnedigaeth arnyn pawb!"*

"What was that?" Guy heard Much ask Bilan timorously.

"Damnation upon them all," Bilan answered with awed respect in his voice as Tuck added,

"Dduw chyfrgolla'u at'r danau chan Annwfn! Fel anturia hwy? Fel anturia hwy!"

"Amen to that, and bloody right too!" Thomas responded, sounding as fiercely Welsh as Tuck. Then saw the questioning faces of the non-Welsh speakers and translated, "God damn them to the fires of Hell. He then asked: how dare they? And he's right, isn't he? How dare they bandy threats of God's wrath about for their petty purposes?"

Tuck now looked at all of them and they could see the fire in his eyes as he spoke. "I will not stand by and have *hyn'n waedlyd bagan Eglwyswyr* ...these bloody pagan Churchmen ...foul God's name! So help me, *Duw*, I will give them a taste of their own medicine and strike fear into their black hearts before I'm done!"

Siward and James had come with Will and Malik to stand by Guy and he heard Will saying softly, "I don't know about them, but he scares the crap out of me looking like that!"

"If that is not the fear of God about to be put into them, I do not know what is," Malik added dryly. "We could have done with a few like Tuck at Jerusalem. Salah-al-Din himself would have thought twice about facing them!"

Robin, too, was looking at Tuck with more respect than Guy had ever seen, and it occurred to him that Tuck's fury even more than his own would guarantee that Robin would act. As if hearing Guy's thoughts, Robin turned to him and asked,

"Will these clerics hunt again soon, do you think?"

Guy had been wondering the same as he had ridden to find them. "In truth, I don't know. I think much will depend on how long this Saher de Espelt stays at Newstead. He's obviously from a major Norman family and the prior will want to impress him. So if he stays much longer I'd say they'll definitely ride out again. If he's already moved on, I think the prior and sub-prior from Felley will certainly hunt again – even if the Newstead prior doesn't – if they think they've cowed the sheriff's men, but when that might be, I'm not sure. We're coming up to the start of Lent, but it's still a couple of weeks away so they've got time before it starts, and I'm not sure if they've forgotten their vows so much that they'd hunt then anyway."

"Lent? Hunt in *Lent*!" Tuck fumed, having heard Guy's words. "*Mai Celi bwra 'u i lawr*! ...May God strike them down!"

"Well that's not yet," Mariota said calmly, coming to link her arm through Tuck's and giving it a comforting pat. "Don't drive yourself into an apoplexy on their account, Tuck, they're not worth it."

"No they're not," Marianne agreed, coming to take his other arm. "In fact, I think we should tackle them in their dens. Show them they're not immune from the world coming to them if they think they can trample over the world."

Robin's face broke into a broad grin. "Oh, I like that! That's good, Marianne, that's really good!"

"Can we get into Felley Priory?" wondered John.

Will rolled his eyes in disbelief. "It's a *priory*, John, not a bloody castle! Of course we can get in!" Then he beckoned to Guy. "Come and have a look at this while you're here."

He led the way to where one of the ruined cottages had been partially repaired, and as they walked around the end of the large stone chimney, Guy saw that Will had made it into a forge. A simple roof had been put over the working area, but was mainly supported by stout timbers rather than whole walls.

With a wave of his hand to the open spaces, Will explained, "Didn't want to make it too much of a fire risk. Even being careful there's always stray sparks, and we need this place at this time of year. ...Now then, what do you think of this," and he unwrapped an oiled cloth to expose a beautifully worked sword blade. "I've just finished making the guard and handle," he added. "It's for Robin."

Guy carefully picked it up and gasped at how light it was. Carefully rolling one of his gloves around the tang as a makeshift handle, he lifted it into the on-guard position.

"By Our Lady, Will! This is the best sword I've ever held!"

By now the others had followed them round, and Robin was watching Guy like a hawk.

"You're a lucky man," Guy told his cousin enviously. "A sword like that would cost me a year's wages and then some!"

John chuckled. "Not many of those in the castle armoury then?"

Guy made a rude noise as he carefully placed the blade back on the cloth. "Armoury? You must be joking! The smiths in Nottingham knock out endless basic blades for the soldiers to use, but they're not tempered like that. They're a nightmare to keep sharp and they break if you cut at something and the angle's a bit wrong." He turned to Will. "Is this a Damascus blade?"

"It is! Learned how to make them while we were out in the Holy Land! It takes time, because you have to work the rods of steel together and then beat them out again – and the charcoal to heat it needs to be right too – but at the moment what else have I got to do when the days are so short? I'm working on some others, too. Would you like one?"

Guy felt his mouth go dry in excitement. He had heard about these blades. They were legendary. You could cut a man in half with one, they kept such a good edge.

"I'd love one! ...But not until all the others have got one! I wouldn't be able to just turn up at the castle with it, you see. Everyone would be asking me where on earth it had come from, because there's nobody in Nottingham who could've made it."

He suddenly saw Robin's face and was glad he had qualified his acceptance. There had definitely been a flash of jealousy there at the thought of Guy having what he had. "I'll have to sow the seeds now, saying I'm looking for such a blade and then leave it at least a year before I could turn up with it, you see," he added, speaking to Will but watching Robin out of the corner of his eye. "Thank you for the offer though, Will. It's much appreciated!"

The big smith accepted Guy's words with a smile. "All right, by next year. I've been trying to think of how we could thank you for what you did for us by taking us in up at High Peak when we first came here. Knowing what we know now, we'd have been in all sorts of trouble if you hadn't. And I know Tuck did the memorial mass for us, but you were the one who made it all come together. So in my eyes you've earned one of these."

Guy wrapped an arm around his shoulders and gave him a hug. "You were all more than welcome, Will, but thank you for the thought."

Only then did he see the surprise in Robin's eyes. So it hadn't occurred to Robin that Will might have had the most innocent and well-meaning of motives? Had it not entered Robin's head that the others saw himself in a very different way? Clearly not.

"Well then, cousin, what do you say you get to try this incredible new sword out on the prior of Felley?" he dared to ask.

"Felley!" Robin declared, with a grin that was now unforced. "Let's get our things together. We can decide the details as we march!"

By the time they had reached the small occasional hideaway close by Codnor four days later, they had it all worked out. Allan, Roger and Bilan would go over the outer wall while the canons were at prayer during Compline, and open the gate for the others to come in. They'd chosen that office in the hope that everyone would soon be asleep once it had finished. Certainly there would be no more tasks for any lay brothers to be doing, and they had decided to head up to the hayloft above the stables until it all went quiet.

They crept up on Felley as the early winter dusk was falling, and made their entrance without being spotted.

"They don't look like they're going without much," Gilbert observed bitterly as he kept watch as the one nearest the loft hatch. "Look at the quality of that horse at the second stall! Must've cost a small fortune!"

"That's canons for you," Tuck sniffed in disgust.

Much's voice came out of the growing gloom. "I thought they were monks?"

"Ain't no difference," Roger replied cynically. "They're all the same, an' all bad if you get on the wrong side of 'em."

Guy had to smile. He was warming more and more to Roger's healthy scepticism. But he felt he should clarify the difference before Tuck took offence. "There *is* a difference, Roger. The Black Monks who follow the rule of St Benedict, and the White Monks who follow the rule which is used at the monastery at Cîteaux, in Burgundy, are part of their communities. People can make donations of land and other things, but they all belong to the monastery as a foundation. The monks themselves don't have possessions, only the benefit of whatever income the monastery has as a whole. Granted, that can be substantial, but it's not theirs personally. Our Tuck is a Black Monk. Round here their main houses are Blyth and Lenton.

"The difference with the White Canons, like this lot here, is that each place in this monastery is provided for by a bequest or some kind of donation. The idea is that the person who makes the donation benefits from the masses said by the canons they've paid for. Storing up their benefits in Heaven, you might say! But it does mean that individually some of those canons are very well provided for!"

Tuck cleared his throat, invisible in the darkness. "Guy's right. In principle canons should be every bit as devout as the brothers of my order." He sighed heavily. "But the truth is that it doesn't work that way. Well, either way! All too often you can't tell the difference, because some of the abbeys and monasteries are filled with monks who are every bit as corrupt as these canons. Every so often some godly man comes along and tries to reform them – such as when the Cluniac reforms came along in my order a couple of hundred years ago – but sadly things always seem to degenerate again." Then he shook off his gloom. "But tonight we shall bring a little of the Anglo-Saxon reforming zeal of St Dunstan and St Oswald to these cursed priors, shall we not, brothers?"

As they were about to leave the stable Marianne and Mariota came scrambling down the stairs giggling together.

"Marianne!" Robin hissed disapprovingly, but Will recognised the signs of mischief.

"What are you two up to?" he whispered with a chuckle as they passed him.

"Worrying dirty old priors!" Mariota replied, but told him no more.

From now on they would be split into separate groups. For once, Piers and Thomas were out of the action and keeping watch with Much and Bilan, the idea being that they would bar the door to the dormitory, and then check on the infirmary and outlying buildings such as the gardener's hut. Their archery skills made them ideal for silencing trouble from a distance this time.

However, no-one was anticipating danger from outside the monastic compound, only from within if someone woke and raised the alarm before those with Robin got inside. Tuck had agreed with Guy that the six former crusaders, which included Robin, were the ones best protected against any religious threats the priors might make – because although Tuck had been most firm on the matter of excommunication, and that it wouldn't count when used for personal gain, they weren't taking any risks. The two women had been most insistent that they come with those baiting the priors in their private rooms, and John along with Guy, also wanted to see Tuck give these two ungodly bullies their comeuppance. That left Hugh, Allan and Roger to go and create mischief where the rest of the priory would see it. Allan already had something in mind, and had been checking something with Tuck, which made Guy think that another Robin Hood message would be mysteriously appearing on a wall somewhere – much to his private amusement and approval.

Gaining entry to the prior's house was ridiculously easy. Clearly the arrogant bastard had no fear of anyone taking issue with his behaviour, and in no time at all Robin, Siward and Guy in their triple incarnation as Robin Hood were lined up at the foot of the prior's bed, while Will, Gilbert, Mariota and James stood to the one side, and Malik and Tuck, along with John and Marianne stood on the other.

"Wake up, brother!" Tuck thundered, slamming his meaty fist against the prior's bedstead with a vibrating thump.

Henry Gretwold near levitated from his bed and then clutched the soft woollen blankets to him in dismay.

"Who are you? How dare you come in here like this! Don't you know who I am? I can..."

"No you can't!" roared Tuck, bringing his simple wooden crucifix out from under the folds of his heavy cloak and brandishing it into the astonished face of Gretwold. "You charlatan! Imposter! How dare you take the name of God in vain!"

"But ...but ...you're just some bloody hedge-priest!" spluttered the affronted prior. "I out-rank you!"

"Silence!" Tuck commanded in a thunderous voice which sounded as if it had come from Heaven itself in the confined space of the bedchamber. "*Alwa ar Celi a pawb 'r saint at chyfnertha 'm! Ddiarddela 'ch achos 'r bechu chan yn cymeryd Iôn s enwa i mewn 'n adfant. I mewn 'r enwa chan 'r Dadogi, 'r Ab a 'r 'n Gysegr-lân Bwci Fi sever 'ch chan dduw s Gras a 'r chwmni chan Cristion eneidiau i mewn hon byd a 'r 'n gyfnesaf. Fucheddoch i mewn arswyda chan 'n dragwyddol damnedigaeth achos Celi ewyllysia na 'n bellach drugarhau arnat!'* The Welsh words seemed to almost shake the room with their passion as he stood there brandishing the crucifix right under Gretwold's nose.

"...And if you didn't understand that, you bloody heathen, I'll repeat it in English! I call upon God and all the saints to help me! I excommunicate you for the sin of taking the Lord's name in vain. In the name of the Father, the Son and the Holy Ghost I sever you from God's Grace and the company of Christian souls in this world and the next. May you live in fear of eternal damnation, for God will no longer have mercy upon you!"

"You can't..."

"...I can! I'm a priest, fully ordained! And I call upon *Dewi Sant* to aid me in this! Him and St Cadoc, and St Melangall, and St Issui — saints you ignorant misusers of God's Grace might not know, but He does! ...*He* does!"

In the face of Tuck's righteous fury the prior had gone a pasty white, and Robin now added acidly,

"How does it feel now? To know that unless you redeem yourself, you will go to your grave with your sins hanging about you and dragging you down to Hell. That's the fate you were so happily casting upon others! Now it's your turn."

And like the big bully that he was, all of a sudden Gretwold now caved in. "I didn't mean it," he cried desperately. "We wouldn't have actually done it!"

"What, not even if you had asked Longchamp for some names to be added and then he told you to go ahead and make the excommunication?" Guy demanded, his anger rising again. "My, my, you are the brave souls! And there was me thinking you were riding along on Longchamp's shirt-tails, and making your own plays for power."

Gretwold knew he had been caught in his own trap. His eyes flickered frantically around the group, not knowing which one to look at next. And this was the point when Marianne and Mariota delivered their punch blow. Dropping the heavy cloaks they'd had wrapped tight around them, they revealed themselves to be dressed only in their underwear.

"So, prior," Mariota said as she lifted one bare leg up onto the bed, exposing a large amount of naked thigh, and then leaned forward so that he got a good look at her cleavage. "Are you having dirty thoughts now?" And she blew him a kiss. "Do like your women dark like me?"

"Or blonde like me?" Marianne asked sweetly, coming to seat herself high up by the pillow so that Gretwold's nose was practically touching her bosom.

Mariota grabbed the blankets from the unsuspecting prior's loosening grip and yanked them down. "Oh, I think he likes you best, Lady Marian," she cooed at the sight of his unmistakable arousal. Then knelt up and slapped him hard across the face.

"So now you can go to your grave with your broken vows of chastity on your conscience and no means to put it right, can't you, *prior*! You filthy old man! So much for never looking at a woman in your chaste state. And it's supposed to be chaste in body *and* in mind! If we were without these men to guard us, you'd probably have both of us and think nothing of it. How many village girls have been brought low by you and yours, eh? Well you can sweat on your lack of grace now, and realise what it felt like for all those poor souls you threatened from your place of superiority. Not so funny now, is it?"

Gretwold looked set for an apoplexy as both Marianne and Mariota got off the bed and swirled their cloaks around them, so that in an instant it was as if they had never shown themselves to him. Robin was looking furious, but the rest of the men in the room were all laughing at the prior's discomfort. Guy saw the girls scurry out and grab the bundles they'd dropped by the door which undoubtedly contained the rest of their clothes.

"I'm not absolving you!" Tuck declared. "May you rot in Hell, for the misery and worry you've caused!"

"And now that you're in no position to threaten the sheriff or his foresters, you should be more careful about where and when you hunt," Guy added. "You never know when a stray arrow might strike you down, or the lord of the forest come to exact his revenge for the suffering you caused his deer. Robin Hood is *his* servant, and a good deal more faithful to him than you are to Our Lord! You do know about the horned god of the forest, don't you, prior? And his ardour is stronger than that wilted thing of yours! He won't be so easily quenched," and onto the bed he threw a rack of antlers which had been downstairs in the prior's lodgings – except that now they were smeared with what looked like blood. As Gretwold passed out in fear, Guy reached over and daubed some more of the blood he'd found in the kitchen across the prior's face. "That should finish the job!"

Robin gave a terse laugh. "And now for the sub-prior."

He was clearly unhappy at the prospect of Marianne exposing herself again, but he needn't have worried. As they got to the door of the prior's lodgings both women were waiting and very obviously fully dressed.

"We thought that might finish him off," Marianne told Robin as she took his hand. "But it's too cold to be hanging around like that until we get to the other one."

Tuck patted her shoulder as he came past. "Nice touch, though!"

"Oh aye, there are some advantages to having nursed every kind of pilgrim," Mariota chuckled. "You get to know all their little weaknesses, and what they should and shouldn't do. The senior churchmen like him were always the worst. Always trying to stick their hands up some poor sister's skirt, or grab a feel of you as you tried to change their dressings."

"We had a fair bit of fending off to do," Marianne admitted to Robin. "It felt good to be playing one of them at their own game for once."

Luckily by now they had got to where the sub-prior slept, in a room separate from the others if not in its own building like the prior, so Robin had no time to comment.

Oddly, Galf Furmentin was a far harder nut to crack than his superior, making them wonder if he was the one who had been behind both the hunt and the idea of excommunicating the sheriff if caught. Tuck ranted with the same fury at him and made the same threats, and yet all Furmentin did was sneer at him.

"You won't get away with this!" the sub-prior sniffed disdainfully.

"And who's going to stop us?" Siward demanded. "Not your prior, that's for certain! And you can hardly go to the sheriff without admitting why we came here in the first place. Are you fool enough to stand before the sheriff and declare you hunted illegally?"

But either Furmentin was such an idiot as to not fully grasp the trap he was in, or he truly believed that whatever favours Felley had found with the current pope would override and earthly dangers. Whichever it was, he was not to be cowed or made repentant.

"Tomorrow I shall ride to Newstead, and with Prior Eustace, we will excommunicate you from the very high altar!" Furmentin declared with considerable spite. "I'll damn the lot of you for this! You ...and you ...and you! All of you! And this goddamned Robin Hood, whoever he is! You'll all feel the fires of hell for crossing me and mine!"

"*Cadoc Sant, chyfnertha 'ch gwas!*" Tuck declared in exasperation, turning away before he could resist no longer and began beating the sub-prior to a pulp.

Yet equally as affronted was John. "Yes, St Cadoc might just help us!" he declared with more ferocity than Guy had seen before. "You miserable, withered scrotum! If you won't take the warnings of someone more holy than you'll ever be ...if you wilfully spit on your faith like this ...then you'll have to face your judgement out where you committed your sins. And St Cadoc can decide when you've suffered enough!"

And with a might punch to Furmentin's jaw, John knocked the sub-prior outside, and then hefted him up and onto his shoulder, carting him out like a sack of turnips.

Most of the others gaped in astonishment at John's retreating back, but Robin was by his side, declaring, "The forest will be his punishment!"

"By Our Lady and St Thomas!" they heard Hugh gasp as they arrived outside in John's wake and found the others waiting for them. "What are you going to do with him, John?"

"We're going to take him out into the forest and let him find his own way home," declared Robin for both of them, and making Guy think that this had been planned beforehand.

"You're not going to do anything like tying him to a tree, are you?" Thomas asked, trying not to sound too anxious yet casting a worried glance Guy's way.

Guy understood why he was worried. If Robin intended to simply give the sub-prior the fright of his life, then that was one thing. But if they took him deep enough into the trees and then tied him up, he might never be found – or at least not while he still lived, and for some reason Guy felt in his heart that murder was a step too far, despite what these two had done. At the moment they had the moral upper hand if nothing else, but it was more than that. This time they had called upon God himself and the saints to take their revenge on someone who had threatened in His name. Therefore they should not take it upon themselves to exact that revenge by their own mortal hands. That would make them equally as guilty of the fault of thinking they could know God's mind, and persecuting someone on that premise.

Thankfully something of the sort had evidently occurred to Robin and John, because although they marched off into the night with great resolve, by the time the rest caught up with them, they had done nothing more than take Furmentin deep into one of the denser patches of forest surrounding the priory. James had snatched up the prior's boots and Malik a thick cloak, so the still unconscious man who was otherwise only wearing a nightshirt, was dressed enough to keep the frostbite away, and they left him propped up against a large oak on a seat of old bracken.

"He'll be crapping himself in fright in less time than he can say his paternoster," John declared with vehement disgust. "I *hate* his kind!"

It had taken this long for Guy to remember that when the four cousins had first been split up, that John and Allan had sought refuge working for the Church as shepherds. Compared to the struggles which John had gone through later, Guy had thought those earlier couple of years hadn't been so bad, but maybe he'd been wrong? Or could John no longer blame the Templars as a whole for the trouble he'd had as their tenant, given Robin's loyalty to the order, and had transferred all of his bitterness to the worldly embodiment of the Church? He found himself shaking his head in confusion, then felt some relief as he caught Hugh's eye and saw the ex-soldier shrug at him, equally at a loss.

As Robin turned with his five former-crusader comrades at his heels, Thomas called out,

"So we're leaving him here, are we?"

Malik turned and gave him a nod, although he looked far from happy.

"Just checking," Piers added, "since we weren't told about this bit of the plan, see?" Robin never replied and Piers turned to Guy to explain, "Not that I give a rat's arse about this piece of filthy, you understand. He can bloody-well rot yhere for all I care! But I don't like this thing of half of us knowing and the others not. Not so terrible yhere, but a right bastard if we'd had to fight!" In his indignation Piers had become very Welsh and his two brothers were glowering with Celtic indignation too.

Much had hurried on in Robin's wake with John and Marianne, but Hugh, Allan, Roger and Mariota were lingering by Guy and the Coshams, and belatedly they realised they couldn't see Tuck.

"Shit!" Allan swore. "We were all so much in a hurry to catch up with John and Robin we didn't notice!"

"We'll have to go back!" Mariota declared. "We can't just assume he's all right."

"Too right we will!" Allan agreed. "Christ, I don't want him getting caught after what we left in the chapel!"

They all began jogging back the way they'd come as Guy asked, "What did you do?"

Allan chuckled. "Took those other two racks of antlers from the prior's place. Got one of the very tall iron candle holders. You know, the ones with an iron circle at the top on which you spike several small candles, so as to cast light from higher up when you can't hang one so easily from the ceiling. We draped a dark cloak around the bigger set like shoulders, and set the smaller antlers on top of it, so it looks like a horned man standing behind the altar."

"I lit the candles behind it on the window sills so it was more in silhouette when you come in through the door," Hugh added.

Roger's quirky laugh came from behind. "Looked real good! Bloody scary too! And Allan wrote somethin' too, didn't yer?"

Guy looked to his cousin in what little light there was now that they'd emerged from the forest. "Not another rhyme of Robin Hood by any chance?" His cousin's laugh was confirmation. "Oh dear! And I suppose that's really going to set the fox in the hen-house when the brothers read it?" Another chuckle confirmed his fears.

They found Tuck in the chapel on his knees praying with all his might, but with the horned figure still in place and eerily lit. He was clutching in his clasped hands a breviary, and his eyes were screwed tight shut.

"*Duw*, man, get up!" Thomas hissed, grabbing one arm as Piers grabbed the other.

Between them they managed to propel Tuck out of the chapel, around the infirmary, the bake-house and brew-house, and into the shadow of one of the great barns just at the bell for Matins began to ring out. Like so many ghosts they managed to slip out through the gate as the last of the brothers had disappeared from sight to enter the chapel.

Luckily Tuck had come to his senses now, and he was running as hard as the rest of them as they pounded into the cover of the wood.

"Well that's one thing, I suppose," Guy gasped, as they all stood trying to get their breath back. "Having tramped out of the wood in such a hurry, we've all given bloody Furmentin a trail even he should be able to follow in the daylight."

Now they hurried to where Guy had left his horses tethered further back in the woods.

"I've got to go now," Guy told them. "I've taken longer than I ought to sort this out, and the others at the castle can only cover my tracks for me for so long before de Wendenal starts getting suspicious. Will you let me know what happens? I want to hear if these two try to push the hunt off onto any of the villagers in their panic. And you'll hear from the people quicker than I will."

"Don't worry," Allan told him, coming to hug him. "Roger and I will come into Nottingham as soon as we can."

Yet Guy heard faster than they did. He had hardly been back a day when there was a panic-stricken messenger from Felley Priory.

"You must do something, my lord!" the messenger pleaded with de Wendenal. "My lord prior begs you!"

"Does he?" the sheriff sniffed. "Found a use for me now, has he? Well you can tell the prior that until I have it in writing that I and my knights are exempt from his threats of excommunication, I am not lifting a finger to help him."

The monk turned pale. "But, my lord, Sub-prior Galf has disappeared, I tell you! Vanished into thin air! Spirited away by this Robin Hood! A man declared outlaw by you!"

"Not by me!" retorted de Wendenal. "By my predecessor! I know nothing of him. Did you think I would just snap my fingers and tell you where this outlaw's lair is, and send men out to get your God-damned sub-prior?"

Ralph Murdac cleared his throat and through gritted teeth told de Wendenal, "Maybe it wouldn't hurt to send one or two men to search? We really don't want the archbishop getting complaints that we'd abandoned one of his flock in the wilds, do we?" The reference to Geoffrey Plantagenet up in York gave de Wendenal cause to pause, and Ralph pressed his advantage. "Why don't we send Guy? He can track anything! And if there's no trail to follow, and the sub-prior has been taken by more unearthly forces, then that's rather more in the prior's domain than ours, is it not?"

An evil grin spread across de Wendenal's face. This was the kind of solution he liked – one where there was a chance to shift any blame onto either one of his most hated knights or to someone else entirely.

"An excellent suggestion, Sir Ralph," he chortled, completely missing how much his familiarity grated with the man who had not so long back been his superior. "Gisborne? Come here!" Resisting the temptation to bark like a dog at being summoned like that, Guy strode forward. "You will take four of the guard and go and search around Felley. You have three days to find the sub-prior, no more, starting from tomorrow."

Given that at this time of the year they would use what little light there was of one day just travelling to the priory and one coming back, it was a petty concession which gave Guy only one useful day to search in. Nor was there any point in setting out this afternoon in the darkness which had already fallen – the road heading that way was hardly a major one and there weren't that many places to stop for the night. However Guy did insist on setting out before the dawn on the following morning, choosing to take with him four of the men who had served with him at High Peak in the past.

As he reached the main gate of Felley with Leofric, Claron, Stenulf and Ketil on their shaggy workhorses behind him, he wondered what he was going to say to the imperious Prior Henry. He needn't have worried. He was ushered into the prior's lodgings expecting a tirade of abuse, and instead found the prior huddled before his fire, a wreck of a man. For a moment Guy struggled to resist the temptation to laugh, but when Gretwold looked up at him with his haunted eyes it squashed any humour Guy felt. They had wanted to frighten the prior out of his arrogance, not crush his spirit completely.

It felt like a penance imposed from Above as Guy had to stand and listen to Gretwold's faltering account of the night. Somewhere along the line, mere men had been transformed into demons accompanied by harpies, who had tempted and tortured the prior, and who had vanished into the night. It was the rest of the canons who told him of the appearance of the horned god in the chapel, of how they had fled in terror, only returning in the morning, by which time the forest spirit had departed taking the sub-prior with him, and leaving nothing but his horns fallen on the altar.

"I'll do what I can to find him," Guy reassured the assembled community, although noticing that the less well-fed and clothed lay members weren't looking any too anxious to have Furmentin return.

There was just about enough light for him to go out and make a cursory inspection of the area around the priory, and was able to say with confidence that aside from the actual road there were only two sets of tracks leading off into the forest.

"Did none of you check the forest round about here?" he asked, as he and the men enjoyed the hospitality of the canons, tucking into beautifully fattened trout in the refectory.

"What? Go into the forest?" a rather portly canon in his forties exclaimed in dismay. "Oh no! We wouldn't venture into such a wild place!"

A lay brother with heavily callused hands rolled his eyes in disgust at the canon's fear. "We went to the edge of the forest, Sir Guy, but from what we've heard of this Robin Hood, his gang is heavily armed, and we were far from well enough prepared to be able to fight back. With not a single weapon between us, we'd have been at such a gang's mercy."

"A sensible choice," Guy agreed. "However tomorrow we'll go and see what we can find."

However, after he had led his men in a rather circuitous search before coming to the place where he knew Furmentin had been left, he was shocked to realise not a trace of the man remained. He could see no obvious sign of which way he'd gone from the oak tree, and got down off his horse to make a more detailed inspection of the ground. As he inspected the old leaves, now breaking down in the winter wet and frosts, what he did find and had not seen in the night was signs of boar – a very big boar and one who had been here quite recently.

He was just standing upright to call a warning to the men, when a snort and a crash behind him told him it was too late, the boar had arrived. Flattening himself against the trunk of the tree he yelled to the men,

"Fly! Boar! Get out of here!"

But the boar was faster. It thundered out of the dead bracken, scattering fronds in all directions, and charged at the horses. Ketil's horse promptly threw him and bolted, leaving him to be gored by the boar and his life was only saved by the fact that it turned and then spotted Guy. With a squeal which would have done a dragon proud, the boar spun round and charged at him. Guy had no blade large enough to defend himself with, and the only thing he could do was wait until the boar was close enough to him to be committed to its path, and then dive to the side.

As he threw himself to the side of the oak and slid in the muddy soil, Guy's hand brushed against something and instinctively closed around what felt like metal. It wasn't a blade, though, and he feared what would become of him when the boar turned back to him. Braced as he was for the attack, it took him a moment to realise that the boar was crashing on into the distance and not coming back. While the other's hurried to bind the dreadful gashes in Ketil's lower leg and thigh, Guy flicked the dirt off what was in his hand and found himself looking at a heavy silver crucifix. A crucifix he had last seen around the neck of the sub-prior.

Sending the others off to take Ketil to the priory infirmarer, Guy now began inspecting the area very carefully, and came to a grisly conclusion. Furmentin couldn't be found because he had been killed and eaten by the boar. In patches he found what was probably dried blood, although the light was less than ideal for being sure. Indeed the reason why the boar had passed on killing and trying to eat him and his men, was probably because it was still gorged on the sub-prior. He continued the search until dark, but then had to return to the priory with his grim news. The crucifix and the soles of Furmentin's boots he took with him. The gnawed skull, stripped of all its flesh, he'd tactfully shoved down a badger's hole – he didn't think it would do the brothers any good to see that. As it was they were seriously worried by what Guy had found, even the more resilient lay brothers, for they were the ones who had to work the fields beyond the security of the priory walls.

For their sake, Guy stayed to organise a hunt for the boar after sending an explanatory message back to Nottingham. Yet try as he might, he could not find the boar again. He could track its path to a small stream, but then after that it was as if it too had vanished into thin air.

No, Brother, you are wrong, by that time I was most definitely doing my best to find the beast, not ignoring signs I could have tracked. Whatever had happened to the sub-prior, I genuinely did not want the beast going into one of the isolated hamlets around those parts and causing death and destruction. A big old male boar like that was incredibly powerful, and it would take a skilled hunter to bring it down. The villagers had had too little practice at such hunts to have been able to bring it down effectively, and having tasted human flesh, the beast could not be allowed to live to try it again.

In truth, I increasingly saw it as divine vengeance. Both prior and sub-prior had crossed a line of propriety with their threats, and I believed then and now that Tuck's heartfelt prayers to St Cadoc had been answered with a true Welsh saint's understanding of divine retribution. It was even appropriate that the prior, who had been swayed by his more corrupt subordinate, at least was spared his life, although his wits were permanently damaged. The next I heard of Henry Gretwold, he had been demoted to sub-prior and another had taken over as head of Felley Priory.

Moreover, when I got chance to speak to Allan and Roger, they too said that Robin had heard of a boar terrorising the priory, and had gone to see if he could find it. Even with all of the gang on the hunt they never found hide nor hair of it again, and Tuck too saw that as a sign from God.

St Cadoc had an affinity with the deer of the forest, he reminded the others, and took exception to such wanton cruelty – especially when coupled with blasphemy!

You may well sniff at such things and deride them as Celtic superstition, Brother, but you were not there when Tuck was calling for God's aid. You did not hear the power and the passion in his pleas. Nor do you understand the purity of his faith and of his intent while he was doing so. If ever there was a man to reach the ear of the saints it was him, for he never asked for a thing which would benefit himself, only others. Can you say the same? For all your life spent in holy orders, Gervase, I fear you would struggle to rise to Tuck's heights in such a case, where the name of God was being shamed by the very men who ought to have preserved and lauded it. In your shoes I would think twice about declaring again that God does not care for animals or their suffering, he may decide to teach you a lesson as he did the sub-prior!

Chapter 15

$\mathfrak{N}$ ow, though, I must return you to the matter of my friends, and in particular my cousin. I was at a loss as to understand why John of all people had been so angry on that night. What the Felley men, with de Tuke from Newstead, had done went against what all of us held dear in terms of our faith. Yet John's anger had seemed far more personal, more intense, but I could not fathom why.

When I had first left him and Allan in the care of the Southwell monks, he would have been with a very different order to the White Canons of Felley. Southwell was a minster church and under the authority of the Archbishop of York, not some abbot who could do as he wished without fear of inspection. And there were only such monks and priests at Southwell from amongst the Black Monks as were needed to cater for the spiritual requirements of holding services there. Theirs was an open church, not a monastic one wholly closed off from the world. Moreover, as I told you before, John and Allan were swiftly moved off to one of the minster's farms – they were not living with the lay brothers. So where had John's fury come from?

It was a matter I spoke to Allan about at the earliest opportunity, and was disturbed by what he told me. Apparently Robin had been having long private conversations with John, conversations Allan had been excluded from. He told me that if he got up from whoever he was with and casually strolled over to join them, there was an obvious change in the conversation as soon as he got near. The odd snatched word which he did hear was no help in discovering what was being talked about, but it was definitely Robin doing the talking and John mostly listening.

˜I am sure he is working on John to get him to see everything from his point of view,˜ Allan told me, and clearly feeling as much concern as I did. ˜I have seen the two of them praying together as well. Not with all of us, as when Tuck leads us in our prayers when we hear the distant ringing of church bells on a Sunday.˜

This was late at night and almost furtively, I was told. Allan said that the first time he discovered them was purely by chance. He had been unwell all day, and had woken with an urgent need to visit the privy pit again. Only when he had relieved his griping gut did it dawn on him that he should have stumbled over John in his haste to get out of the hut they shared with Roger and Much. Loitering with his blanket wrapped close about him, for no other reason than making sure that he could actually leave the privy safely, he had then heard the voices in prayer. At that point he had felt too ill to be curious, but once the malaise had passed, he realised that while it was not a nightly event, it was certainly more than once a week. Allan, Roger and Much had by now all realised that *something was going on, but even Roger's inventive curiosity had failed to discover anything remotely useful.*

My own suggestion was that they talk to Siward and Malik. Of all the former crusaders, these two were the most down-to-earth and the most sensible. Yet it was Will who sought the younger men out, and with the same concerns. For despite his complete loyalty to Robin, Will was a man with little time for those who became so saintly they were no earthly use. And Will was a worldly man who could also see that sometimes Robin's high ideals were as dangerous to those who were fighting alongside him as those they opposed!

Nottinghamshire & Yorkshire
Spring, the Year of Our Lord 1192

Standing outside the *Trip to Jerusalem* brewhouse with mugs of ale in their hands, along with many others enjoying the first truly warm and sunny day of the spring, Will had joined Allan and Roger in coming to seek out Guy. To any observer they were strangers who had struck up a casual conversation as they leaned against the sandstone cliff which the brewhouse was built into, and which had warmed up nicely in the sun. In reality they were by the cliff so that no-one could come up behind them and accidentally overhear what was being said.

"Won't you be missed by Robin?" Guy asked Will, careful to keep any tones of concern from his voice which might be picked up on by the noisy group of soldiers just in front of them.

Will shook his head and smiled. "Naaa! Told him I was coming with these two to go to the market. I've made some good tools over the winter, but what I haven't got is properly seasoned wood to make the handles out of. There's a tinker who comes here quite often, Roger tells me, who has such things. It's going to be useful, because if necessary I'll only buy what I desperately need, and then say he hadn't got what I wanted and be able to come back another time. He never thought to question it."

"*Dewi Sant* be blessed!" Guy breathed in relief. "Well I'm certainly glad to see you, Will! So what can you tell me about my cousins?"

The burly smith took an appreciative swallow of his ale before speaking. "Damned good brewhouse, you lot have got here! ...Hmmm, John. ...Well I think the problem started with that ambush which went wrong outside of Mansfield. Robin had a right old panic about nearly losing John, you know! I know you were spitting nails about how carelessly Robin went in on that one, Guy, but he's not so stupid as not to have seen where he went wrong. You see, he hadn't appreciated how out of training John was.

"Daft, I know. The rest of us could see it, but somehow Robin's view of John was coloured by the bigger cousin who'd always been able to best him at every turn when we were all lads. So it was a huge shock to Robin to find that John desperately needed training to come up to our standards.

"He set me to do that. Well I didn't take long to realise that John's adequate with a sword, but that he'd be cut to bits by any decent swordsman in no time. On the other hand, with his height and build he's a demon with a quarterstaff! And I think it fits John's nature better, too. He's too kind-hearted to be comfortable with seeing his opponent bleeding in front of him from cuts and stabs he's made. The quarterstaff's more of a paralysing weapon than a killing one."

He saw Guy's dubious expression and smiled while making a dismissive gesture. "I know! Smack someone hard enough on the head with one of those things and you'll still kill them. But it's not so bloody. Not so obvious. And for some reason that matters to how John sees it. So I've been putting John through his paces. God bless Tuck, because he's joined in as John's sparring partner, so I've been able to stand back and coach them both without getting pummelled to bits in the process.

"But what makes the difference between Tuck and John, is that Tuck is happy enough just learning a new skill. As a man he's content in his own skin. John, on the other hand, was also very aware that at Mansfield he came close to letting Robin down – or that's how he sees it! He's been getting a right old fit of the guilts, I can tell you. He was kicking himself hugely for not having been more alert. Felt he could have drawn us all – but Robin in particular – into danger if we'd had to carry him wounded from the fight. So he's made some kind of vow to be more of Robin's right-hand man in the future. To look out for Robin as much as Robin looks out for him, if you follow me."

"By Our Lady and St Thomas!" Guy groaned, muffling his response in his ale mug and taking several long swigs to stop himself from swearing further. When he could trust himself to speak without drawing attention to themselves, he turned to Will again. "So was that business with the sub-prior some kind of cockeyed way of showing Robin that he's got the balls for a fight now?"

The other three chuckled at Guy's despairing incredulity.

"Not quite that," Will reassured him, "although I won't say there wasn't a hint of that there. No, it was more that, with this new sense that he should be watching Robin's back, John was incensed that the old goat would threaten to excommunicate someone who had fought so hard for Christ."

Guy leaned back against the hard stone and wished he could scream in his frustration. "St Issui give me patience! ...Did John not grasp that the sub-prior would have known nothing of all of your times in the East? *Could* have known nothing?"

Allan gave him a weary smile. "If he'd stopped to think about it ever, maybe he might. But even now I don't think that's something that's crossed John's mind."

"That could be dangerous if it happens again," Guy warned them.

"You aint' kiddin'," Roger agreed morosely. "These days he's lookin' sideways even at us if one of us disagrees with Robin over sommat."

"Not that we mean the company is splitting," Allan hastily assured Guy. "But there's been a bit of dissension about what Marianne and Mariota did."

"Oh dear," Guy sighed. "I did wonder about that."

Will chuckled and rolled his eyes. "Honestly! Robin can be a right St Paul at times! Too bloody sour and prim for a chap of his age! Most of us thought it was funny. The dirty old sod being exposed for what he was. And why shouldn't the girls have had their bit of sport? Like Mariota said, they're neither of them wilting violets straight out of the nunnery. They've both had to fend off men for years when they were out in Jerusalem, and long before they ever met us. They knew exactly what they were doing and how far to take it – and it wasn't that far! Those shifts were made of good linen, not your flimsy stuff, and in a camp as small as ours we've all seen a glimpse of them that undressed before. Couldn't help but! So none of us were shocked. Good on them, I said, and so did several others."

"Aye, but Robin got himself into a right state," Allan added. "He really went to town on Mariota when we got back to Loxley, saying if she wanted to lower herself like that, then she had no right to drag Marianne down with her."

Guy sucked air through his teeth and winced. "Ouch!"

However Allan forestalled any question. "Yes, but not quite how you might imagine! You see it turned out it was actually Marianne's idea."

"Bloody hell!"

"Quite! And Marianne got really angry at Robin taking that tone with Mariota. She tried to explain at first, and then when it became clear that he wasn't listening to her, she got really mad. What a shouting match!"

"I ain't never seen a couple go at it like that!" Roger declared, clearly still somewhat in awe over what he had witnessed. "Marianne went and stood in front o' Robin and began yellin' in his face. Then he tried to push her to one side to carry on his yellin' at Mariota. Then

Mariota starts screamin' at him for pushin' Marianne around like she was some piece o' baggage, and Marianne slaps him for bein' so high an' might wiv' her. Bleedin' awesome it was!"

Guy became aware that Allan and Will were smothering giggles at the memory, though. "And...?" he asked them.

"And," Allan answered with a grin, "then the silly bugger took it into his head to order them to go into the cottage they share and 'rethink' what they'd done. God help us, he doesn't understand women, does he?"

"Never has," Will added sagely. "Always been a right tit where that's concerned. ...Well they went, but it was more them storming off together than going because he sent them."

Then suddenly he became serious. "But now it's become a real problem, Guy. If Robin had calmed down and got off his high horse, things would have been different. Several of us tried to tell him to just let it go now he'd had his say, but he wouldn't. Then he came out with some crap about not being able to trust the two girls. Thank God he didn't say it to their faces! But most of us told him what complete bollocks he was talking."

"*Most* of you?" Guy had caught the inference.

Allan nodded. "Even Much, who looks up to Robin so much he hardly ever questions a thing, said that was taking things too far. But then John spoke up and said that Robin, as leader, had to have the final say in matters. If he hadn't said that, I think we might have worked Robin round. Got him to realise he'd been a fool. As it was, we then went off and did a little," he gave a quick glance around, "...erm, 'aquisition' in south Yorkshire, if you get my meaning?"

Guy did. So it had been them who had liberated a quantity of coin from a party of wealthy churchmen just west of Doncaster, had it? He'd had his suspicions it might be. Not that they dared discuss *that* more fully here – that would really be taking too much of a chance.

His nod prompted Allan. "When we went and did that, I think we all thought that Robin was leaving the girls behind as a token punishment. Not a good thing to do, but if it settled the matter once and for all maybe it was worth it. But after that we hit on the very problem you thought of, Guy. A lot of this money was in *gold* coin, and like you said, it's become obvious that we're going to need someone who can change it for us into silver we can use to hand out to the ordinary folk. And your mother came into the conversation once again. Well it was equally obvious that the ideal people to go and speak to her were Marianne and Mariota. Who else would be able to just walk into a nunnery? But would Robin have it? Oh no!

"And this time the two took real offence. Pretty understandably, Mariota said there was no way they were staying if all they were going to do was stay in the camp and act as skivvies for us men. So the row blew up all over again. Robin saying what else was Mariota going to do if he couldn't trust her to come on raids? And then Marianne screaming at him for doubting their loyalty. But the worst of it is, Guy, we've lost them."

"Lost them?" Guy gasped. "What do you mean, lost them?"

"They left in the night," Will said sadly. "I can't blame them. They've known one another for years, and in some pretty horrendous places too. They know they can rely on one another. The way things have been going, they couldn't really have said the same about us! They must have thought that with none of us actively stopping Robin, how long would it be before we threw them out anyway? And the worst of it is, we didn't even notice they were gone until the next day! We just thought they were staying out of everyone's way while there were some pretty heated conversations going on between the rest of us."

"You stood up to Robin?" Guy asked.

"Aye," Will sniffed, "but I'll never be his right-hand man again, I reckon. That's John now. The only one amongst us who didn't challenge Robin at some point. It was only at the very end of the day when Tuck went to get the two of them, so that we could all say we were sorry, that we found they'd gone. That really shook Robin. Really deeply! I don't think he ever thought Marianne would just walk away from him without so much as a goodbye."

"Pfff! 'E deserved it!" Roger declared.

"He did," Allan agreed, "but it still came as an almighty shock."

And then full understanding came to Guy. "Oh Lord, it's that same thing about him needing to see the faces of those he helps, isn't it! That need to have approval. To see that he's appreciated. By Our Lady, that kind of outright rejection must have cut him to the quick!"

The other three were all nodding.

"He's in bits now," Allan continued. "Rather late in the day, but he's blaming himself and doing a far tougher job on himself than we ever could. And what's worse, when we tried to track them come the next morning, we lost their trail. They truly intended us not to find them, and certainly not easily. It took three days, but we finally managed to find what we thought was possibly their trail until we got to the Great North Road. But beyond that we'd got no chance. A big party of pilgrims had just gone north, heading for York we supposed, but they'd obliterated any tracks we might have followed either way for miles."

Now he gripped Guy's elbow furtively but with some urgency. "We need to know they're alright! Some of us have talked it over, and we reckon they might have gone to Kirklees and your mother, despite what happened. Because of what we said about Aunt Alice, I think they see her as the kind of prioress they could cope with, but we can hardly turn up on the doorstep of Kirklees and ask to see her. Not a bunch of scruffy renegades like us! They'd probably bolt the gate in fear and never listen to a word we said. But Mariota and Marianne could have doubled back on us, and Kirklees isn't such an impossibly long journey from Loxley for two women alone."

"I thought you said they'd gone to the Great North Road?" Guy protested.

"No, I said we followed *a* trail to the Great North Road," Allan clarified. "None of us is wholly sure it was the right one! And they could have turned back at several points at the places where we struggled to find any signs. Anyway, if they've gone that way and got that far, there's very little more we can do. All we're trying to do is make sure they're not in trouble closer to us."

"Will *you* go to Kirklees, Guy?" Will almost pleaded. "We've tried all the places we can get to, like the villages, and they're not there. But there've been some other robberies up on the northern border of the shire in the last week or so, and they've been brutal in comparison to what we do. We're all worried sick Marianne and Mariota might have fallen prey to these new ruffians!"

"I've heard of these," Guy admitted. "Probably only four men, but extremely violent. Probably mercenaries from Brabant, was the message we got from the sheriff of Yorkshire, and it sounds about right. It's anyone's guess as to why they're here. For all anyone around here knows, they might have been paid by somebody with the king to escort someone to see the archbishop, and then they've been dismissed and left to make their own way back. They killed for a second time only the day before yesterday right on the border near Doncaster."

"Oh crap!" Will groaned.

"I don't need to explain why Robin himself won't ask you to do this, do I?" Allan asked Guy.

He didn't. Guy was painfully aware that having to make the comedown and ask his irritating older cousin for help would have rubbed salt into Robin's spiritual wounds in the worst possible way.

"Oh Hell," he muttered, swallowing the last of his ale. "I suppose I'd better go and dig out Ralph Murdac and ask if I can go to Kirklees. Try to find some reason which might just make sense. No point in asking de Wendenal! That would be a straight 'no', no matter what the circumstances."

"As it's over the border, could you say you'd heard here in the town that these new troublemakers had hurt someone who'd been taken to Kirklees for care?" Allan wondered. "Maybe someone who'd said they'd been followed by them from here in Nottinghamshire?"

Guy paused. "Ooh, that's a good one! I like that! Thanks, Allan, I'll use that."

"We'll meet you on the Mansfield Road once you're well clear of the town," Will declared. "Thank you, Guy!"

Luckily the new trouble was sufficiently on everyone's mind that Murdac was only too willing to let Guy go. As it was, it was past the end of the closed season in the forest, and there was a week or so to spare before the round of woodmotes began again, so there was little for Guy to do officially. Certainly nothing beyond the normal checks for unlicensed felling or grazing, which pretty much anyone could do.

Therefore Guy found himself out on the road within the day, and relatively unconstrained by duties. He found not only Will, Allan and Roger at the roadside, but Malik and James too.

"I do not understand Robin," James told Guy with a fretful shaking of his head. "I would never have spoken to my wife in such a way. Never! I may have been the man of the household, but that did not give me the right to abuse her – in words or in body. Is this something which happens here in this country?"

"Not if the man has any sense," Guy assured him. "I gather Will's told you much the same? Well believe it! A man may head the household, but if he has a good wife he's a fool if he doesn't take her into consideration. And I know Robin and Marianne weren't married, but for Heaven's sake, they were as close as any betrothed! If he had any sense at all, he wouldn't have made such ridiculous accusations.

"Sometimes I wonder about my cousin, James, really I do! This isn't any behaviour he learned as a boy, I can assure you. Granted, old fitz Warin was a brute, but even he knew how far he could go with his wife. And he treated my mother – who, more than her sister, ran the household – with a good deal of respect. I can't ever remember an occasion where he openly questioned her loyalty to his family, and in practical terms that's what you all are, Robin's surrogate family."

James and Malik seemed to take this as considerable reassurance, and together the six of them travelled on foot as fast as they could up to, and across the shire border into Yorkshire.

Kirklees stood in the Calder River valley on the north bank, sheltered by the escarpment behind it and the similar rise in the land to the south-west across the river. Having only been established in the middle of the century, it was a relatively new nunnery, but it was well-endowed for its size, and the inhabitants clearly lived a reasonable life going by the well-tended fields close by. That at least reassured Guy that his mother had chosen well – and he was as sure as he could be that Kirklees had been her choice, since there were other nunneries she could have chosen which were still within Nottinghamshire.

What his reception would be was something he was increasingly worried about, however. His mother had made no attempt to contact him, as far as he knew, and given the disappointment his older half brother, Audolph, had turned out to be, it would be understandable if she had decided that she didn't want to know what became of either of them as they grew older.

"I can't make any promises, you know," he told the others, as he prepared to mount up and ride the last few yards out of the riverside woodland to the nunnery gates. "For all I know she might have died at some point in the last fifteen years. I've not heard a thing, and it's not been helped by the amount of times I've had to move around."

"Oh don't be daft, Guy!" Allan chided him. "Aunt Alice always adored you. She'll be glad to see you whatever's happened in the meantime."

However Guy was far from feeling confident as he rode to the gate and then dismounted to ring the bell. A small hatch in the gate was opened some moments later, and a coarse female face glared out of it at him.

"What do you want?"

Guy managed to brace himself and put on what he thought of as his 'official' face. "My name is Sir Guy of Gisborne," he replied civilly. "I would like to request a ...conversation ...with whoever is in charge here. The prioress, maybe?"

The disembodied face glowered back and demanded bluntly, "Why?"

Oddly, it was her plain rudeness which quashed Guy's nerves. Had she been more gentile, more devout in her manner in rejecting him, he might have found it harder to insist. Now, though, he glared back at her and said with all the authority he could summon, "I am enquiring about two women who may be in great danger. They have been missing for some time and I wish to speak to the prioress concerning their safety."

"They ain't here!" the gatekeeper snapped and shut the hatch in Guy's face.

"Bollocks!" Guy swore softly, and turned to shrug in question towards the wood's edge where he knew the others were watching. What to do now? Then it occurred to him that had he really been here on the sheriff's business, he wouldn't have been so easily put off. So he turned and gave the bell a longer and more vigorous ring.

"Go away!" the voice of the harridan came from over the wall.

"No!" Guy yelled back. "I demand to see the prioress!"

"Go *away!*" the voice screeched, this time sounding even more irate.

"By St Thomas, woman, I am not here to rape, pillage or plunder!" Guy snapped. "I'm trying to find out about two women who might be in great danger. Women who, if they aren't here with you now, might well be in the near future! Now will you let me speak to the prioress?"

"No!" the voice came over the wall again.

"Judas' balls!" Guy growled softly, then drew his dagger and used the heavy pommel to hammer on the gate as being less painful than using his fist.

Moments later another voice was heard demanding, "What is all this noise? Sister? What's going on?"

"Madam?" Guy called. "My name is Sir Guy of Gisborne – a knight of the sheriff's. I'm alone and here to speak to whomever is in charge here. It concerns two women who have been lost in the forest. I'm not here to threaten any of you in any way. I just want to speak to you – and not yelling over this bloo... this *wall*!"

There was a pause and then the hatch opened to reveal a much more pleasant face.

"You are seeking two women?"

"Well at least news of them," Guy replied, manfully crushing his growing annoyance. "And if they've not come here or been brought here wounded, then at least to give you a description in the hope that you might let us know if they are found in the coming days."

"You are not trying to take them to an unwanted marriage or the like?"

Guy shook his head. "No, nothing like that. It's more that there's a group of four men – mercenaries, we think – who've already robbed and murdered on two occasions in the last week up on the Yorkshire-Nottinghamshire border. These are very dangerous men! Their first victims were a merchant and his journeyman travelling with three guards of their own. Now they're all dead! I'm a forester, not a guard, but when I heard these women were missing while out amongst the villages, I became very concerned. The sheriff will need to know if he's to search for two more bodies."

The sister had put her hand to her mouth in dismay at what Guy was saying, and now stepped back and gestured to someone unseen.

"Open the gate."

"But sister...!"

"Open the gate, Sister Hilda."

"But Sister Constance, what will the prioress...?"

"I'll take full responsibility, sister, now open the gate."

Guy heard muttering under the other sister's breath, but there was the sound of a bar being lifted and bolts being drawn back. The heavy oak gate creaked open to reveal a courtyard area, and Guy stepped into the nunnery grounds.

"May I bring my horse in? I don't want to leave her outside and have her stolen."

The more amenable sister smiled and gestured for him to lead the mare in, while the gatekeeper stood glowering to one side. Heaven alone knew where they'd found that one, Guy thought. She looked more man than woman, and going by her attitude, a calling to a life of submission to an order of prayer seemed unlikely. A moment of mischief made him turn to her and smile while saying, "Thank you, sister," but all she did was scowl even harder at him.

The other sister was a tall and graceful woman of middle years who responded more favourably to his smile.

"Please excuse Sister Hilda," she said as she turned and began leading Guy across towards the main buildings. "She had a wretched life out in the world before she came here. It's not you. She hates all men."

"I've had worse in my line of duty."

"I'm sure you have! ...Our prioress is over this way. I'm sure she'll be willing to listen."

Guy's heart was beating like a drum as they entered one of the buildings, and then came to a closed door which Sister Constance knocked on. This was the moment of truth. Would he see his mother in this room or a total stranger? His mouth was dry and he swallowed hard, forcing his tongue to unstick from the roof of his mouth. Ridiculous to be so nervous at his age, but he was.

Beyond the door a muffled voice called, "Come," and Sister Constance lifted the latch and led the way in.

What Guy saw was a simple but comfortable room. No luxuries, but a cushion on the seat which was before a well-polished old oak desk, for the benefit of those visiting the prioress. For an instant Guy couldn't see anyone, then Sister Constance stepped aside and he saw the back of a woman, dressed like the other sisters in black, getting up from her knees at a small altar at the side of the room, and having to place her hand on it to help herself up.

"Aagh," she hissed softly, then smiled. "Age doesn't come alone, I'm afraid. My joints are reminding me of my mortality!"

But Guy barely heard her words. There was no way he could mistake her, she was still the same. Her face was more lined now, but the eyes were still as bright and lively, and the smile was all her own.

"Are you well, young man, you've gone very pale," she asked solicitously. "Sister Constance, do fetch this guest some wine."

"No ...no, it's all right," Guy managed to croak, "I'm well." He coughed and managed to say the words, "Hello, Mother. Do you not recognise me?"

"I'm not an abbess, my dear," his mother began to say, " 'Sister' will do." Then caught his expression. "Did you not mean...?"

"It's me ...Guy. Your son."

For a second Guy thought he might have been too blunt. She went very pale, then with a cry of joy, ran and threw her arms around him. He hugged her back, both too emotional to be able to say anything for now. When they did separate, Guy saw tears of joy streaming down her face.

"Oh thank you, Lord! My prayers have been answered!"

"Your prayers?" Belatedly Guy realised that Sister Constance had tactfully left them alone for now.

His mother sniffed and rummaged for a cloth to blow her nose on. "Yes, my prayers. I've prayed so often that I might see you again just one more time before I die."

"You're not ill are you?" Guy gasped, feeling a momentary surge of panic.

"Oh no, dear, but I'm not as young as I was! I'm becoming increasingly aware of the fact that I don't have as much time left here on earth as I would like. So much to do, you see." Then she held him out at arms' length. "You've grown into a fine looking man, Guy, the very image of *my* father! Who'd have thought it? Giles was dark like you – or rather you're like him – and that's what I saw in you as a boy, but your father never had those cheekbones, or those colour eyes! No, you're very much your grandfather instead. Well, well!" And she smiled broadly. "Come, tell me what you've been doing."

It took rather longer than expected for Guy to satisfy his mother's curiosity. From her he hid nothing of his time on the Welsh border, of helping rescue Maelgwn with Tuck, and his subverting of de Braose's cruel authority. Then there was his meeting with the Coshams, and of course his reunion with all three of his cousins. That in particular delighted his mother.

"Oh praise be to Our Lady!" she exclaimed in delight. "All well, and all in contact with one another. That pleases me more than I can say. I always worried about those three. Baldwin was such a dreamer, poor John was never encouraged to be his own man, and may her soul rest in peace, but my sister was a terrible mother to Allan. Spoiling him rotten one moment, then wailing over him the next. It wasn't healthy."

Yet Allan was the easiest to talk about. Guy happily told her of how Allan had struggled at first, but now seemed to have found his feet, and how he had taken on board her teaching from when they were all young, and had found someone in Roger who needed caring for. John he found himself saying less about, because the man he'd become of late was someone whom Guy couldn't quite fathom. Instead he moved on to Baldwin as fast as he could, telling her about his return from the East as Robin, and of the mental anguish he still suffered.

"And that brings me to why I came here," Guy finally managed to say. Recounting the story of how Marianne, and then Mariota, came to be with the company in the forest, he then explained Robin's hopeless mishandling of the situation.

"Oh dear," his mother sighed when he'd finished. "Yes, I can see that this is an awful mess. And you thought they might have come here because they knew I'm your mother? Well I'm so sorry to have to tell you this, but they've not come. Not to here. We've had a few visitors claiming sanctuary here for a night over the last few weeks, but definitely not two young women alone."

She took in Guy's expression of sudden worry. "You really are very worried about them, aren't you?"

"Very," Guy admitted, and made the point again about the new threat from the mercenaries. "Quite aside from what it would do to the men if they find their behaviour has brought the two into harm's way, I can't bear the thought of Marianne and Mariota being raped or worse – although in some ways rape by such men might very well be the worst they could experience. Death might be welcome after such a thing."

"You must come and eat with us," his mother insisted, but now Guy had to admit,

"I'm not quite as alone as I said to your gatekeeper. There are five others out in the wood waiting for me – although one of them is Allan!"

"*Allan*? Then go and fetch them in!" she commanded, forgetting her religious status and swiping him on the arm in a light reproof he remembered only too well.

To Guy's amazement, not only the five he had left emerged from the woods at his calling, but Tuck, Much and Bilan too. Allan found himself being mightily hugged too, and Tuck was welcomed with much enthusiasm.

"Will you say mass with us, Brother?" Sister Constance, who turned out to be Guy's mother's second-in-command, asked. "Sister Marian clearly approves, and we've not had a priest here regularly for some time. Our old priest died and his house has been empty over the winter. We're waiting on the archbishop's pleasure to assign us another."

Guy and the others were looking for who Sister Marian was when his mother spoke. "I'm Sister Marian, Guy. Alice isn't really a suitably conventual name, and it's normal to take another name when you enter orders."

"Sister Marian." Guy couldn't help but grin.

"Is there a problem with that?"

"No, Mother, it's just that now we not only have a Marianne and a Mariota, but a Marian as well. All these names from the same root, and all sisters of one order or another – it could get a bit confusing!"

Luckily his mother still had her sense of humour and once she laughed, the other sisters saw the amusing side of it too. Yet now that they saw the nuns altogether it was very clear that Marianne and Mariota weren't amongst them, even under assumed names.

"What will you do now?" one of the sisters asked.

"I honestly don't know," Will admitted. "Go back into the forest and carry on searching, I suppose. It's all we can do."

"I'm Sister Adelaide," a foreign sounding sister spoke up. "Like the two you're searching for, I was once a sister of the Hospitallers, although I chose to become one of the order here rather than be herded down to Devon. I think you're underestimating them."

Will groaned. "I wish it were that simple, sister. But just at the moment Sherwood is a very dangerous place to be. I know they know how to defend themselves, but it's going to take a bit more than that to keep them safe."

But Sister Adelaide was shaking her head. "No, that's not what I meant. Out in the great hospital in Jerusalem we got to know what men are like. How they think. What I meant was that I think your two missing sisters deliberately wanted to give this Robin a fright. I didn't know either of them personally, although maybe by sight. But I do know that we all knew enough of the world to know when a man's being a fool, even if his heart is in the right place."

"Thanks for the vote of confidence," Will growled into a mouthful of bread and rolling his eyes to the other men.

However Guy was beginning to grasp what the sister was saying. "Ahh! So you think they wouldn't have gone far. Just far enough to give Robin a fright, because they know he thinks the world of Marianne even if he's not behaving like it at the moment?"

"Exactly!" Sister Adelaide agreed. "I'd stake my next month's rations that they've gone somewhere they know they'll be safe. Somewhere they can hide away and then come out of when they think this Robin's learned his lesson."

"So one of the other camps, maybe?" Tuck wondered.

"I'd say so," Adelaide confirmed.

And then light dawned for Guy. "Derbyshire! They'll have gone to Derbyshire! From the main camp to the one by Hathersage would be an easy journey even at this time of the year. And Marianne knows the villagers there even if Mariota doesn't."

"Aaagh!" Will groaned. "And then they could walk in daylight up to the other camp up the valley! Might even have got a lift on a cart part of the way."

"And you didn't check those camps?" Guy asked in frustration.

Will shook his head. "We thought they were leaving us. *Really* leaving us! I mean, once you get up by Kinder there's nowhere to go except up onto the moors, and that's a rough journey for anyone. We didn't think for an instant they'd go that way because we were thinking of the onward journey."

Bilan piped up, "But if there's no onward journey intended...!"

Will banged his head twice on the table to the sisters' amusement, although only Guy to his right and Bilan to his left heard the muffled, "Bleedin' Hell!" in exasperation.

"I'll ride with all speed that way tomorrow," Guy declared. "You lot head back for the main camp on foot and try and stop Robin from doing anything even more..." He desperately wanted not to say 'blindingly stupid' but words failed him.

Luckily the others understood and were all nodding before he needed to finish the sentence.

"You can stay the night here," his mother insisted. "We don't have guest rooms for you all, but there's a good warm hayloft you can use, and we can provide you with a goodly breakfast to see you on your way."

Some of the sisters looked more than a little worried at the prospect of having so many men within the confines of their walls at night, but Tuck was quick to assure them that they had nothing to fear. He led the sisters in prayer that night, and then Guy and Allan spent the remainder of the evening in the prioress' room talking with her.

In the morning they all departed, but with the promise that what gold coin they had would be gladly exchanged by the sisters. Apparently they had a good deal of coin at the moment as the rents from the farms came in for the half year, but it wouldn't be paid out by them to the Church until Michaelmas, so storing a smaller quantity of higher value coins suited the sisters as well. Gratified that they had at least succeeded in one area, Will and Tuck led the others off into the forest, while Guy mounted his rested horse and began a brisk ride due south. This would bring him to the shoulder of the moors, and thence to the River Derwent, which he intended to follow straight down to Hathersage.

What he found there would then determine what he would do next. He had no qualms about asking for the two women in the village. His reputation with the folk there was still good from his time at High Peak Castle, and he knew he would get truthful answers, not evasion, and he was hoping the sister at Kirklees had guessed right.

He knew that Will and Tuck would have followed the River Calder and then the Holm to get to the moors, and then to Loxley, but didn't want to go that way himself, even though it would be easy to get to Hathersage from there. Partly it was so that they covered two of the main routes down to Hathersage, but also because he didn't want to have to spend a night at the camp with Robin just at the moment. That Guy might yet succeed where he hadn't would not make things any better, Guy knew, and he wanted Robin contrite for when Marianne reappeared, not pent up and ready to snarl again. Because of that he was praying that he would learn that the two had been up to Kinder, and returned back through the village by the time he got there. He could then just track them and make sure that they got safely to close by the camp, then head back to Nottingham.

He therefore thought his prayers had been answered when he saw Skuli's daughter herding some geese near their cottage, and heard that Marianne and Mariota had passed through only the day before heading back to Loxley. Happily letting his horse wander at her own speed, he was therefore unprepared for what happened next.

The scream was his first alarm. He was crossing Bamford Moor and was not far from the old cairns when he heard it. Then there were two screams. Mariota and Marianne!

Kicking the horse into a canter – the fastest he dared risk on such ground – he made straight for where he thought the cries had come from. As he crested the top of the hill and saw the group of cairns rising around him he also saw his two friends. The mercenaries had found them!

By Our Lady, that gave me such a fright, Gervase! I had thought them safe and on their way home, and then out of the blue our greatest fear for them went and appeared. I could scarce believe such bad luck – theirs or mine, for I could hardly stand by and do nothing. Yet there were four well-armed and expert fighters arrayed against just me and two women. The odds seemed heavily weighted towards us losing.

With all that in mind, the moment I saw them I hauled my horse around to get the nearest cairn between me and them. No do not tut, Brother. It was not cowardice on my part. I had every intention of fighting, but I wanted to even those odds, and I had belatedly remembered that I had my bow with me. It might only be a wood-bow for hunting, and not the great long wyche-elm bows which all those with Robin were now becoming proficient with, but it was bigger than most of the similar bows in the castle. I had wanted to get used to pulling a heavier bow so that if I ever got the chance to use a longbow I would have the strength. Therefore Thomas had made me a bow of a sturdier construction so that while it would not attract attention for its style, it would still punch an arrow far harder than it ought to.

Oh every bow is different, Gervase! If your bowyer knows his craft he should tailor the bow to the one who will use it, and Thomas and Piers Cosham were very experienced. Therefore my bow was far superior to the general store at the castle, and I made sure it stayed with me in my room when not in use. Now I was blessing the brothers and calling upon the Welsh saints to aid my aim. For my intention was to try and take two of the men out of the fight before I even got to close quarters with them, yet as I crested the small rise of the cairn, bow strung, arrows at the ready and the first one nocked, I was shocked by what I saw.

No, do not shake your head in that way! What I saw was not what you are thinking. A little wine to wet my throat, and I will tell you all.

Chapter 16

So there I was, sitting on my horse for all to see on the knoll, all prepared to shoot fast and then ride down, sword in hand and fight it out, only to be stunned by what I saw. Far from being the feeble victims, Marianne and Mariota had gone on the attack. For a moment I failed to grasp what their tactic was. Marianne was running for all she was worth for the next cairn, and it took me a breath to realise that she too had a bow in her hands. Behind her Mariota was working on preventing the two nearest of the men getting to Marianne, by dodging and ducking in their path. As the bigger of the two women she stood the better chance of not being crushed into helplessness when caught, whereas Marianne had the speed, and both were working to their strengths. Meanwhile the two men further back were completely focused on getting to the lead two and helping them – they never even looked my way.

As I calculated my aim, pulled the bowstring back until the nearest flight was nearly brushing my nose, and gave an extra pull for good luck, Mariota went down. Yet even then she did the unexpected. Her fall was more of a controlled collapse than falling hard on her back which might have winded her. As the ruffian crowed with delight and spread-eagled himself upon her, she allowed him to think her defeated, so that as he released one of his arms to grope at the ties on his trews, she took advantage of the fact that he had partially hoisted up her skirt already. Her hand went to her thigh and came up with a small but deadly knife from a garter belt, and before the man even blinked, she had driven it deep into his neck. With her knowledge she hit the vein first time, and I saw the gush of blood spurt out even from where I was.

In the instant I changed my aim from him to the man who had passed Mariota and was nearly on Marianne. My arrow took him in the small of the back, and he threw his arms wide and sank to his knees. With any luck I had hit him in the kidney and given him a belly wound to boot, but I was too busy nocking the next arrow to look hard. Marianne, meanwhile had only faltered for a heartbeat and then loosed her own arrow into the nearest of the remaining two. At that range even with a light bow she would have done some damage, and like mine, Marianne's bow had been made for her by the Coshams. What was more, she had been practising and her technique would have put many a man-at-arms to shame. Her arrow took the man through the throat and dropped him instantly. My second arrow took the remaining man similarly as he turned to look in shock at where the unexpected attack had come from, and in that instant what I had feared would be a defeat turned into victory.

Instead of riding pell-mell down the uneven slope and risking my mare's legs in unseen holes, I was now able to ride down at a steady walk. Mariota had already rolled the dead man off her and was wiping her hands on the grass to get the blood off, and Marianne sauntered down to join us from her higher ground.

I recall her greeting me in her usual no-nonsense northern way.

˜Fancy you being here,˜ she said. ˜Right useful to have an extra pair of hands.˜

No, Brother, there was no gushing thanks from either of them, but then I was no Robin either, needing to hear my praises sung. And you must remember that these two women had seen men brought into that great hospital in Jerusalem missing limbs and worse. A little blood was never going to turn their stomachs, or have them fainting like some highborn ladies I have encountered.

I also knew that it would be fatal to act as if I was their saviour. They had been doubted and slighted by Robin, if by none of the others outwardly. Therefore if I was not to be left with four dead bodies and talking to empty air as they stalked off again, I had to be tactful. I also wanted to begin the healing process if I could, so I said,

˜And to think that Robin was worried that you might need a man's help,˜ and followed it with a smile. ˜Nothing left for me to do but the mopping up!˜

I tell you, Gervase, that I was secretly holding my breath, though. I had hardly had much practice at dealing with women over the recent years, particularly offended ones, and I was far from sure my approach would work. Yet work it did! Both immediately smiled back, which seemed to be a good start.

˜Did Robin send you?˜ were Marianne's next words, and I was sure I heard a trace of longing for the answer to be a yes.

Now I was caught in a pretty trap. If I said 'yes', it was not exactly the truth, and might rebound on me badly if they thanked Robin for doing that as soon as they saw him – for I knew in my heart that Robin would be instantly affronted at even the thought that he should ask for my help. On the other hand, if I said 'no', he had not asked me, then it would sound as though he was uncaring as to their fate, and might make a reconciliation all the harder. I therefore answered hesitantly, telling them of how Robin and the others had been scouring the forest, frantic for their safety, and that I had been brought in because of the visit to Kirklees. I then tacked a small lie on to the end, telling them that of course Robin would not ask me in person, guessing that they knew him well enough to understand that, but that he had sent Allan to do the asking. I knew Allan, of all of those who had come to me, was quick-thinking enough to guess why I might have twisted the truth like that and react appropriately if questioned, and as cousin to both of us he was a plausible messenger.

I can tell you with the benefit of looking back all these years that that day was a turning point in my relationship with both women. Firstly my ploy worked. Neither were silly girls who wanted to be constantly fussed over, but it made a big difference to them to know just how much the men of the group felt badly for possibly having driven them into harm's way. They now had proof that they were valued by the whole company, even by such different souls as young Much, despite his hero-worshipping of Robin; quiet James, who hardly said a word to anyone except Malik and Tuck; and gruff Will, who might not know quite what the right words were when speaking to women, but whose heart was true and loyal.

And then there was how the two of them and I got on. I had been deeply saddened by the coolness which had developed between Marianne and myself since she had become so enamoured of Robin. Was I in love with her, you ask? No, I do not think my feelings ever ran to the kind of love you are thinking of, Brother, but there was some affinity between us. Marianne was the sister I would dearly have loved to have had. She reminded me of the women I had grown up around at Alverton – our cook, the reeve's wife, and indeed my own mother – all of them very capable and intelligent, and strong-spirited enough to cope in many a crisis.

And you must allow, Gervase, that I was singularly starved of that kind of female company. The castle at the heart of any shire is mostly a man's world, and as long as I lived there I only came into daily contact with such women as came into the castle to do basic tasks, such as the laundry, and I was not having lengthy conversations with them. Also, remember it had been I who first met Marianne, and then introduced her to Robin and the others, and right from the start we had shared our feelings of loss at being separated from friends and family. So now I was very glad to be talking normally again with her as we walked back towards Loxley.

As for Mariota, I had had no chance to really get to know her at all since she had been with the company. So it was an unexpected pleasure to find someone who shared my dry sense of humour, and there was a sparkling wit twinkling in her eyes at times when she spoke of events in the camp. The fact that Robin had actually managed to rile this woman so badly said more than I liked of how tactless and insensitive he had been. Had my cousin been within striking distance at that point, I might well have dragged him off into the forest for a private conversation, and shown him what I could be like when I really wanted to play the older brother! Instead, I revelled in having two very amiable companions for the walk back to Loxley, for I insisted on Marianne and Mariota taking turns to ride my horse.

And what of those we killed? Ah, we shall come to that now, Brother!

Loxley & Nottinghamshire
Spring, the Year of Our Lord 1192

They did not have to go all the way to the camp to run into several of the others. Much and James had gone on to find Robin and tell him of what had happened, but Will had come looking for Guy accompanied by the three Coshams, Allan, Roger and Malik, all of whom made no attempt to disguise their relief at the two women being found safe and unharmed. It also allowed the two to meet Allan without Robin's presence, so that they were able to thank him, and allowed Guy to have a quiet word with him long before any potential complications set in. Things could hardly have worked out better for once.

There was much swearing at the encounter with the four mercenaries, but happily the Coshams were as pleased as dogs with two tails to learn that their coaching at archery had paid off so well, and Mariota got serious praise for her knife-work from the non-archers present. Standing back a little and watching the conversations, Guy realised that this had unexpectedly cemented the two women's place in the company as active members. Whatever Robin's reaction to the news, he would now be at risk of everyone else turning against him if he continued to disregard their abilities, and that was a comforting thought. The last thing Guy wanted was for either of them to feel that they had no choice but to return to a dreaded cloistered life for want of anywhere else to go. He knew how that would feel, for at times the castle felt more like his prison than any home.

It wasn't long before the rest turned up, and Guy retreated to the back of the group while Robin and Marianne met. Thankfully, Robin had had such a fright, his first reaction was to sweep Marianne into his arms and hug her tightly until she protested she was struggling to breathe. And if he was less overjoyed to see Mariota, it was made up for by the others, who lavished all of their relief onto her since they were clearly not going to get a turn at hugging Marianne.

At the camp, Tuck had begun a celebratory feast, and they were greeted by the mouth-watering scent of cooking. Four hares were cooking in a pot in oak-leaf wine, along with a goodly portion of dried mushrooms which Tuck had had stored away; and an enormous pike was being baked stuffed with herbs, provided by John's increasing skill as a fisherman. Only he and Tuck had the patience for that kind of hunting! And to complete the celebration, Tuck brought out more of his own wine – light refreshing birch sap for the white, and a rich elderberry and damson so dark it was almost black. If any proof were needed that Marianne and Mariota were valued and wanted, the way everyone joined in the celebrations with gusto was it.

Moreover, that night Robin did not get to sideline Guy as much as he might have wanted. Will and Malik made a point of asking what he was going to do now, and would not let the conversation be diverted.

"I think you need to take those four bodies back to the sheriff," Will declared firmly. "They know you're a good shot at the castle, and with three of them having arrow wounds it's plausible that you brought them all down by yourself."

"Leave them to rot where they are!" Robin declared savagely. "They don't deserve a burial for what they've done!"

"It's not about burials, you twit!" Will retorted, robbing his words of some of their bite by lobbing a crusty chunk of bread playfully at Robin, and catching him on the forehead with it. "It's like Guy just said, technically they're over the border here in Yorkshire. So if someone comes on them, they'll report the deaths to the sheriff up in York. You don't want the bloody sheriff of Yorkshire coming and scouring the area for murderers, do you?"

"That's true," Gilbert agreed. "Guy's sheriff sent him to look for them, so he can legitimately drag four bodies back and no-one will care much. Leave them a couple of weeks and it won't be anything like so obvious that they're mercenaries, and that could be our undoing, even though we've not had an actual hand in their deaths. Well not us men, anyway!" And he raised his cup of wine in a toast to Marianne and Mariota with a comrade-like wink.

"And if someone thinks four shepherds have been murdered...?" Allan dropped in sneakily, but making Robin frown in thought, for even he could see that someone might want that answered for.

Siward nodded. "They have to be accounted for in Nottinghamshire where we can control what's said about their deaths."

Now Allan grinned mischievously. "Why don't I take Marianne and Mariota to Kirklees to meet Aunt Alice? And you Robin, and John! She'd love to see you two again! That way, if asked she can say that there really were two sisters who came to stay who'd been attacked on the road."

"Oooh, that's cunning!" Will approved.

"And it accounts for my journey times, too," Guy said with some relief. "De Wendenal doesn't have to know which sequence the events happened in. I doubt he'll bother to look at the bodies himself anyway. So I can say the men attacked Marianne and Mariota and were killed, then I escorted them to Kirklees and came back for the bodies."

"Why don't I come with you?" Hugh suggested. "We'll borrow a cart from Hathersage, and Will and I can play two of the local men you've commandeered to help lug the bodies back."

"Good idea!" Will exclaimed before Robin could speak.

"I'll come too," Siward added. "It might be no bad thing for three of us to get a look at the inside of the castle. You never know when that might come in useful! And this is one of the rare times when we can legitimately walk in without anyone asking too many questions. If Will plays the cart owner, Hugh and I can play men from the village who needed to come down to the Nottingham market anyway. A quiet word with one of the lads from High Peak to get some names, and we can give our testimony as real men from Hathersage. It can all go on record as a perfectly legal hunt."

"And de Wendenal gets the praise for sorting out four dangers to travellers," Guy added, making the distinction that the sheriff would get the credit and not himself. "He'll be crowing over that for weeks! And because he loathes me, he'll not say a word of who it was who brought them in. My name will never get mentioned when the eyre comes around – whenever that will be!"

It deflected Robin nicely. "What? You mean the justices *still* haven't been?"

"Not a sign," Guy sighed. "It has to be something to do with our shires being taken out of the normal run of things to support Count John, but quite how I don't know. The fact that we're not submitting our monies directly to the chancellor anymore, I can understand. But why the courts haven't been mystifies me. All I can think is that it's more profitable to keep levying bail money for those in prison than the small fines they'd have to pay if it came to court, and those payments are going to the damned prince too. That and the fact that everyone's too busy trying to stop him and Longchamp dragging us into some awful civil war to worry about the small details.

"With half the sheriffs of England having changed yet again last year, it must be getting hard to work out who should be going on eyre and where to. Not to mention those sheriffs who aren't settled enough in their shires to be able to risk leaving them just yet. Any shire which was under one of Longchamp's brothers must be in quite a mess administratively speaking. There's no way those two could have been keeping a proper track of all of the shires they each held, and the under-sheriffs probably went in the purge too. So some sheriffs must be struggling to get their shires back to a kind of normality."

"Rough on those in the prisons, though," Gilbert sympathised.

However Hugh waved a cautioning finger. "Yes, but don't forget, pretty much none of the other shires will have been so overwhelmed with men brought in for offences against the forest. Nottinghamshire must be unique for the amount of land under forest law, isn't it Guy?"

"You're absolutely right. At least in the other shires most of those in the town gaols, or castle dungeons, will be murderers and thieves of the worst sort, not just some poor lad caught red-handed poaching a hare. Nottinghamshire must be the worst shire to live in at the moment."

That seemed to give Robin a strange sense of satisfaction, as though it made him feel that he was in the right place to be launching his personal crusade for justice, and therefore he made no argument about the three who would accompany Guy.

Guy himself made a point of thanking Allan again on the quiet for offering the diversion. Also, if anyone could straighten Robin and John out it was his mother. It was strange how the relationship between the four cousins had shifted again. Where Guy and Allan had been the least close as boys, they were now becoming very much in sympathy with one another as men, and John and Guy were drifting apart from the closeness they had once shared. Quite what he would have done without Allan this time, Guy wasn't sure, for Allan seemed to have a knack of directing Robin without being so wholly under his spell as John was now.

What surprised him further was the appearance of Roger in his party. The young former cutpurse expressed a disinclination to return to the nuns' company so soon, and instead offered to act as Will's lad. So Hugh and Siward hurried off to Hathersage to borrow a horse and cart, and Will, Roger and Guy made all haste back to the site of the fight. Luckily it was such an isolated spot that no-one had been back in the short time the bodies had been left, and so a day later the five of them set out for Nottingham with their grisly cargo covered by old sacking, to keep the flies at bay as best they could.

Guy's return worked like a charm. De Wendenal puffed himself up, and immediately sent for a scribe to write to the other sheriffs in the adjoining shires to gloat over his success at dealing with the problem, quite disregarding the fact that he'd had no hand in the affair at all since he hadn't even sent Guy. Ralph Murdac was full of praise for Guy, though, and immediately ordered that Guy should take his witnesses to the scribes and have the whole account recorded.

"I know just the one I want for this job," Guy confided to the others as he led them through the castle to the scribes' room. "He's been intimidated a few times into writing false accounts for various verderers. He also knows that I can read what he's writing, so he won't try anything like putting down false accounts to ingratiate himself with the sheriff."

"Is everyone in this place twisted and corrupt?" Will asked softly. "You can't even trust a bloody monk to write things down right?"

Guy chuckled. "It's not that bad, and to be fair, Will, the scribes are in an unenviable position. What they write will get read out for all to hear at courts in the normal way of things. So if a sheriff or verderer has told them to write something down and they don't, then even if he can't read it for himself, it doesn't mean that their words won't come back to haunt them.

"The only advantage they have is that if they cross a man like de Wendenal, they get sent back to the monastery they came from not turned out on the streets. Even a sheriff like him won't risk punishing a man the Church sees itself as owning, and some of these bishops and abbots are very protective of their status, as you've seen all too clearly! They can be quite a law unto themselves in the cut-off space of an abbey. But that also means that a scribe would do well not to go back with the sheriff's complaints following him, because his abbot or prior could make him suffer for making the abbey or monastery look bad.

"And they have a tough time living here too. They're neither fish nor fowl. Not one of the common press of servants and craftsmen who do the everyday work. Not part of the fighting men, and definitely not part of the sheriff's own world and his senior men. If they came originally from noble families they wouldn't be serving here as a mere scribe, so they get looked down on by just about everyone."

They found Brother Oswine miserably sorting through a pile of scrolls.

"I have to find the charter for one of the sheriff's manors," he told Guy glumly. "It's not here and I don't think it ever was. The sheriff says that there's a manor up in the north of the shire by Barnby, but no-one else knows a thing about it."

"Oh that one!" Hugh said without thinking. "That belonged to the fitz Ranulph family!"

"Good grief, that's going back a way," Guy exclaimed. "Robert fitz Ranulph and then his son William were sheriffs when I was a boy. God knows what's happened to them these days."

"I think the manor got taken over by a distant relative the best part of twenty years ago," Hugh told Brother Oswine, "but it was the family's, not a manor of the sheriff's. That's why you can't find anything."

Oswine's face puckered into a frown. "How do you know about Barnby if you live at Hathersage?"

Belatedly Hugh realised just how much he had given away. "Oh I was born near Barnby," he covered, "But I went away to fight and then settled in Hathersage. A local lass caught my eye," he added with a knowing wink which made Oswine blush, and mercifully he left the matter there.

"Just refer de Wendenal on to me if he gives you any trouble over this," Guy told Oswine comfortingly. "Now, I have a job for you, so get your portable writing desk and come with us. I need you to take down these men's testimony."

It was a pleasant spring day, and so Guy took them all up to the roof of the old tower under the pretext of not being disturbed. In reality it gave Will, Hugh and Siward a glorious view over a fair part of the outer bailey, the inner ward of the oldest part of the castle, and a chance to look at the walls of the other half of the castle proper. As each came in turn to sit by Brother Oswine and Guy in their shelter out of the wind and recount their version of events – all carefully rehearsed beforehand – the others were left to gaze undisturbed.

"I wouldn't want to be besieging this place," Will observed softly. "You'd be taking it piecemeal."

Siward nodded thoughtfully. "And that natural cliff on this side would complicate matters no end. There wouldn't be any point in bringing up a trebuchet to this side. Even if you knocked holes in the walls it wouldn't do you any good. The only bit worth battering would be the main barbican, and like you say, after that you'd then have to start on the inner gate over that dry moat."

"Why do you want to know how to get into the castle like that?" Oswine's worried voice suddenly said behind them.

"Don't worry," Guy reassured him, "they're just old soldiers. Habits die hard."

Oswine looked dubiously at the three men before him and then at Roger, who had been the last one whose account he'd been writing, and suddenly he must have realised how tough they looked.

"No need to look so pale, brother," Siward added kindly, then pulled his shirt up to expose a wicked scar on his side. "See that? Done by a Saracen sword close by Damascus! And this," he showed the other side where a puckered circle lay just below his ribs, "that was a lucky escape from a Saracen arrow. An inch further in and instead of giving me a nasty scar it would have given me a gut wound I'd have died of. That was at Jerusalem."

In an instant they transformed in Oswine's eyes from frightening ruffians to heroes. Clearly anyone who had fought to save the Holy City was a different matter.

"That was why I asked these men in particular to come and bear witness to the nature of these mercenaries," Guy added, deciding to build on the advantage. "They know what a mercenary looks like, and their word is good."

Totally convinced, Oswine was now smiling and came to stand with them looking out over the castle. "Some days I wish I could fly," he said wistfully. "I'd take to the skies and fly so far away from here I'd never have to come back."

"Is it that bad here for you?" Hugh asked sympathetically.

"I never wanted to be in the Church," Oswine answered. "My father's a merchant, and my mother died when I was too young to remember her. He didn't want the bother of a baby when he already had two strapping sons and a daughter, so I got given to the Church with a good donation and forgotten about."

"Is that why you were glad to come out to act as a scribe for the sheriff?" Guy wondered.

Oswine nodded but his face became sad. "I thought it would be wonderful to get beyond the gates of the priory, but I never imagined the suffering I'd see." Then he bit his lip and looked fearfully at Guy, suddenly aware of what he'd let slip.

"Don't worry, Brother," Roger said cheerfully. "He won't tell on you. G... Sir Guy ain't like the rest of 'em."

Oswine turned to Guy and frowned. "No. No you're not, are you? You were the one who stopped Sir Walter Ingram from over-fining that village for poaching." Then he frowned even further, looking from Guy to Roger and clearly wondering how someone so clearly from the south would know Guy so well. These really were the strangest of men!

"He works on the same manor as us," Siward said before the damning question could be asked. "Roger's heard me talking about Sir Guy because he and I grew up in the same area."

That at least was convincing given that Siward was obviously local to the shire at least and of an age with Guy. Certainly it satisfied Oswine for now, and he left them to happily go and tell the senior scribe that de Wendenal couldn't claim his manor in the north.

Meanwhile, Guy took the others by the most circuitous route he could manage back out of the castle, largely by taking them on a walk of the walls where they wouldn't be likely to encounter any of the knights. Sgt Ingulf and Big Ulf had walked into them as they had come in, and hurriedly passed on names when asked, but now it was clear that Ingulf had informed the others who had served with Guy at High Peak, for the rest of the twelve were out and about the castle. Ruald, Claron and Stenulf were loitering on the wall, and cheerfully greeted the three former soldiers, and were introduced to Roger. Then Ricard and Alfred seemingly accidentally walked into them just by the main keep, and Frani and Osmund met them as they were walking over the drawbridge to the outer bailey. Leofric, Ketil and Skuli finally caught up with them as they left through the barbican and were about to head for *The Trip*, Will wanting to sample the fine ale again before heading north.

"Some days I wish we'd made a run for it and come with you lot," Ketil confided to Will as they clunked mugs together in a toast to everyone's continued good health. "If it wasn't for Guy being here I don't think half of us would have stayed."

This was news to Guy, but somehow didn't seem so unexpected to the others.

"Robin's not the easiest leader to be with, though," Hugh offered as consolation. "He has very high ideals, but putting them into action sometimes isn't quite as straightforward as he'd like to make out."

"It beats watching one of you swing from the battlements," Skuli snorted, with a shake of his head at the memory of Alan of Leek's fate. It was going to be long time before anyone forgot that, but Guy hadn't quite realised how deeply it had affected the ordinary men. That the knights who had to work so closely with the sheriff should be fearing for their lives was understandable, but now he realised that the regular garrison must have been thinking that if a man as senior as Alan could come to grief, then they stood no chance if the sheriff took a dislike to them.

Leofric's next words confirmed his suspicions. "I know bloody fitz John's gone, and may his soul rot in Hell when his time comes, but de Wendenal's not that much better. Sir Ralph hasn't got the control over him he had when he was sheriff, and de Wendenal can be like a mad dog some days. You never know who the bastard is going to bite next!"

The three left soon after, but as Guy strolled with the others to reclaim the cart, Will said thoughtfully, "I reckon this sheriff needs taking down a peg or two."

Siward looked at him in surprise. "Strange you should say that, I was just thinking the same! What we've heard here makes me wonder if we're trying to dam the flood of taxes and bad deeds against the ordinary folk the wrong way. We're trying to plug the gaps after they've happened, when maybe we should be going for the source?"

Guy felt a shiver run down his spine. "Woah! Hold hard a moment! I understand your thinking, but would all of you please remember something before you go suggesting such things to Robin? ...You will never get to a point where there's *no* sheriff, alright? It just won't happen. The king wants his money, and the way he gets money from the shires is through the sheriffs. It's that simple. So if you get rid of de Wendenal, then someone else *will* come in his place. The best you can ever hope for is that the replacement will be someone like Ralph Murdac used to be – fair, and strong enough to know when he's being asked for the impossible, and not be fool enough to try and make it happen even so."

"You say used to be?" Hugh queried. "Has he changed so much?"

Guy's fallen expression alone said enough. "He's a different man. So embittered by the way the king treated him. He served King Henry faithfully for all those years, and then when he was in his prime and had the shire turning like a well-kept mill-wheel, he got cast off like an old boot. And for why? Because of King Richard's desire for money to fund the crusade. It might be a good cause, but the money he got in those single sales of the sheriffdoms in a way squandered a resource he could have used better. The money itself went in little more than a click of the royal fingers, but then the wrong men were in place to get him more. He'd have been better to have been more cautious and settled for less in the short term to get more in the end.

"And the very fact that Murdac was cast off and yet nothing's been achieved rankles, too. I think he'd have been far less bitter if the king had sailed into the East and taken back Jerusalem within the year. At least then his conscience could have reasoned that his own suffering saved that of hundreds if not thousands of others, not to mention the matter of souls and salvation! But from where he's sitting it all looks like the act of a foolish king too full of his own quest for glory."

He looked around them to make sure no-one was close, even though they were now walking the horse and its cart out of the town by the deer park.

"What worries me, to be frank, is that Murdac now sees Count John as the man to back. I think Sir Ralph would be quite happy to see King Richard die in the Holy Land and Count John take the throne. In his eyes, John might be an irritating and petulant royal pain in the arse, but he knows England. He knows how the systems here work. He knows what he can get and what he can't. And unfortunately John is crafty enough to dangle promises which at least *look* as though he might keep them. Promises of offices and rewards which would, if he were king, be in his power to grant.

"I'm not being an old worry-guts when I say that, since the chaos of last year, when we got so entangled in the grabs for power, I don't like the thought of becoming involved in another political storm. But that could happen if Count John thinks that his brother is too far away to halt any act on his part to claim the throne for himself. Last time, Count John and Longchamp were fairly closely matched, and John was a blessing in disguise, but I don't think that Murdac can see just how dangerous he really is now that the counter balance of Longchamp is gone. And if young Prince John makes the call to arms with all the weight of his Plantagenet heritage behind him, I'm seriously worried that Murdac will answer! Especially if for some reason there's no sheriff here."

"What about de Wendenal?" Will wondered. "I thought you said he was useless? How will he make any difference?"

Guy grimaced. "He's useless at his *job*, Will, but when it comes to being crafty and looking after his own interests it's a different matter. De Wendenal will think very carefully before backing anyone against the king! And about the only good thing about him being sheriff is that he has the final say-so on whether any of the men under his command fight."

"What about men who are in the castle doing military service?" Hugh asked. "Surely they wouldn't be so easy to command against the king?"

For the first time Guy smiled. "No, Hugh, you're right about that, God be praised! Once we're at this time of the year when we have knights and men from all over the shire rotating in and out of the castle it's a different prospect altogether. Some might side with Murdac for old times' sake, but far more will have a healthy caution over taking part in any action against the rightful king. They've got too much to lose! They're not the ones with family estates across in Normandy or Aquitaine, or wherever, which they can run to. If the king loses his temper with them and grants their manors away to someone else, they're done for. I tell you I've been breathing a whole lot easier since the first lot arrived!

"But that's something else you need to make sure Robin understands. We now have a full compliment of men in the castle and rising. Whatever you come up with to rattle de Wendenal's cage with, it can't be a show of brute force. Not right now, anyway. In the winter, maybe, but I'd guess Robin won't wait that long."

Roger had been walking along with a far-off gaze in his eyes, and Guy thought he'd been taking little note of the conversation, but now he suddenly said, "What about that scribe we was just talkin' to?"

"What about him?" Guy asked as the others too looked confused at the sudden shift.

Roger's thin face was screwed up in concentration as he thought his idea through. "Well you sez to us that the scribes has to read stuff out in court. Read out what they writ."

"Yes," Guy agreed cautiously.

"So, can't we get Brother Oswald to put stuff into those scrolls on the sly, like? Stuff what would make the sheriff look a fool? He sounds like the sort who'd get more upset over that than someone givin' him a chance to fight."

The four others all stopped in their tracks and stared at Roger in amazement.

"Bloody Hell, he's right!" Hugh declared. "The worst you could do to de Wendenal is make him look an idiot."

"We'd have to be ready to rescue Oswald," Siward cautioned.

"Yes, you would," Guy quickly agreed, "but it's also a brilliant idea, not least because if it's words going into the accounts going with the payments of taxes, then de Wendenal won't have heard them read out back here in Nottingham. It'll happen when he takes the money south for his royal lord and master. Just because we're not sending money directly to the King's Exchequer doesn't mean it isn't being accounted for, or that de Wendenal isn't answerable for what he collects."

"But what's he going to write?" Will wondered.

Now Guy grinned broadly. "Why the truth, of course! ...That the full amount of fines were taken from these villages, but that Robin Hood took it back despite the sheriff's men, and then raised the full tax from those villages, but it was taken back by Robin Hood's men too!"

Will was already chuckling softly and Siward was beginning to smile. However Hugh wasn't wholly convinced.

"Wait a moment, though, Guy. You were furious with Robin for taking the money from Mansfield, saying that it brought nothing but trouble for the villagers. What's changed?"

It sobered Guy a little. "Point taken, Hugh, but that time you took so much all in one go. It was the kind of grand action guaranteed to inflame the sheriff, and God knows fitzJohn took little inflaming! His kind of revenge would be petty and wholly unpredictable. I could never hope to predict which way he'd lash out. He was the sort of highborn fool who'd slaughter a whole village and then rant when there was no-one to tax later. And you have to remember that poor Sir Robert, as constable, had no more control over the vicious young swine than I did.

"It's very different with de Wendenal and Ralph Murdac. Murdac's got the remnants of the authority he had as sheriff. He knows the job inside and out, and there have been many times already when de Wendenal's had to lean on him for that. So Murdac's our brake on the sheriff if his cart starts to run away. He'll make sure that there's a limit on what punishment de Wendenal hands out. He might well steer him towards hunting you lot down, but it's coming up summer, the undergrowth in Sherwood is thickening up nicely..."

"...And we can lead the sheriff a merry dance!" Will chortled.

Ah, Gervase, you think we had scant thought for the poor scribe. Not so, Brother, not so! In that moment I had already had the idea that if we need to extract Brother Oswald in a hurry, then this was one person I most definitely could send to Gisborne manor. In comparison to the confines of the cloister, my little manor would seem like blissful freedom for Oswald, and I knew that his skills in writing would come in very handy for Maelgwn now that Tuck was permanently away. So you see, I was not disregarding your fellow brother at all. And I believed that he would seize the chance to do some good before escaping from a vocation he had never expressed any desire for. Clearly you have taken to the monastic life, Gervase, but it must be torture for those who have it imposed upon them from early childhood, and then grow into men wholly unsuited to such a life.

You understand now? Good! So let us move on to that summer of 1192 when Robin led the sheriff in a merry dance through Sherwood!

Chapter 17

I do not know what was said to Robin by Will, Hugh and Siward, but somewhere along the line Robin was convinced of our plan. Yet because of my location within the castle, I would be the one to direct Brother Oswald in providing the means by which de Wendenal would be made to look a fool, and you must by now realise that Robin would never have been content to sit back and merely do the raiding for Oswald and I to record. He needed to see that axe fall on de Wendenal's neck, even if it was only in the form of a quill and ink! Therefore I knew it would not be long before Robin would do something to provoke our truculent sheriff.

It was no surprise, then, when he made a strike against the woodmote at Calverton when it next met only a few weeks later. Indeed I was more surprised that he had waited that long, and suspected that it was only the lack of a target which had held him back. I was not present, but arrived back from the Linby court to find de Wendenal in a fine temper. Of all of the four forest courts, Calverton was the one closest to Nottingham, and therefore was never thought to be under threat. In this I therefore thought Robin had been most cunning, for not only had he shown that he would dare to strike right under the sheriff's nose, but also, because it raised the serious question of how effective de Wendenal could be if such a thing could happen on what was virtually his own doorstep.

As I had foreseen, Ralph Murdac was managing to hang onto de Wendenal at least enough to prevent him from going out and putting half a dozen villages to the torch in his fury. He even went so far as to call the sheriff foolish for thinking that the villagers of Epperstone, Woodborough, or even Thurgaton further off, would have the remotest clue of where such outlaws might be.

˜For truth, Sir William!˜ I recall him saying in exasperation. ˜Such a man might come out of the forest, commit his crime and be on his way before the local folk even knew he was there. Or do you believe that they would defy you so when your own verderer lives within the village?˜

And for that he had a point which even de Wendenal could not argue with, for Ralph of Woodborough was an energetic scourer of the forest within a day's ride of his manor, even if he was hardly the sheriff's man, given that his grandfather had been appointed a verderer by the Keeper of the Forest in King Henry's day. No-one within three or four miles of his home could fail to know who he was, or that he had a comprehensive understanding of the forest thereabouts and would miss even the smallest oak, or spot even an extra couple of furrows on one of a village's strip fields which had not had rent paid on them. So much so that there had been occasions when he had come to harsh words with his fellow verderer, my old arch-enemy Walter Ingram, whose court at Linby was close enough for there to be disputes over whose court a case should be heard in.

I confess to you now, Brother, that there were times when I played them off against one another, and in the process managed to ensure that a case became lost to both. There, does that appease you since you have had few admissions of my sins of late? I thought it might!

But to return to our actions of that summer, the taking of money from the woodmote at Calverton caused ripples through the castle at Nottingham, and de Wendenal declared that he would not be made a fool of by some local rogue. We would take those knights and men with us for their forty-day service and scour the forest, he declared. And then he made the statement which chilled my blood. He would not, he said, give Count John reason to call him incompetent. He would show his royal master that he was the man to be looking after the shires which provided for the royal princely household – and by master I sadly realised he was not meaning the king.

For that, at least, I was quietly glad of Robin's grand gesture, for without it I would have continued working under the mistaken belief that de Wendenal was the king's man. I knew that he had loyalties to the royal prince when he had held Tickhill, but had foolishly assumed that from seeing the fate of Eudes de Ville, that taking sides was not a good idea, and that he had learned by seeing others' fall from grace that a sheriff was deemed to be the king's and no-one else's. Clearly he was not someone who learned such lessons!

That was the point where I believe I came to realise that de Wendenal in his dim, thoughtless way, would be as much of a danger to us all as the petulant fitz John, and I decided to do what I could to help Robin get him moved on. Oh I knew someone else would come in his place, but I prayed that that someone would be cast more in Murdac's role, and would be someone we could all work with better.

Sherwood
Summer, the Year of Our Lord 1192

For all of Ralph Murdac's restraint, Wendenal was still not a man to let the raiding of a forest court go without some effort to catch the miscreants. And so a scouring of Sherwood was called for. Something the sheriff organised with relish. However because this had taken part very much within the bounds of the original royal forest and at a forest court, this time both de Wendenal and Murdac were insistent on the Keeper joining in in person with his men.

Guy had never seen much of Ralph fitz Stephen, the official hereditary keeper of the old forest, primarily because his own duties kept him involved with the newer swathes of the expanded Sherwood. However while Ralph Murdac had been sheriff there had been cordial visits between the castle at Nottingham and the Keeper's substantial, if not quite so grand, castle of Laxton. All had changed when fitz John had come as sheriff, and fitz Stephen had maintained a tactful distance for the whole time of his tenure. During that time, the Keeper had still directed his own riding and walking foresters, and had collected the fines due from the courts which sat to deal with matters arising within the old forest, but had carefully made sure that verderers' courts for the two new bracketing forests of Le Clay and Derwent-to-Erewash were heard on different days to his own. In other words, fitz Stephen had all but washed his hands of the problems of dealing with the greater forest.

That was something Guy found hard to forgive him for, because if nothing else, the knowledge that all of the woodmote and swanimote records had passed through Laxton before going to the sheriff might just have restrained the verderers. Of anyone, fitz Stephen ought to have known if someone was being over-fined for a minor matter, or have suspected if a village was being fined twice over for something already dealt with in a court a year or two back. The original four verderers – Ralph of Woodborough, Sanson de Strelley, Walter Ingram and Ranulph de Kirkton – had all been much more under fitz Stephen's lordship in the past, and Guy was certain that while Ingram was someone who had always needed restraining, that de Kirkton at least had probably been fair and even-handed until he had seen the degree to which Sheriff fitz John had been getting away with little short of murder.

Yet as fitz Stephen rode in through the outer gateway of Nottingham Castle, Guy could understand Ralph Murdac's gasp of surprise. Fitz Stephen had gone from a man of middle years but active, to an old man. He was now portly and rode a staid horse fit for long plodding journeys, but certainly not for any sort of speedy chase. And as fitz Stephen dismounted there was an audible groan of relief at getting out of the saddle and the massaging of the small of his back. The Keeper of Nottingham Forest was going to be of no use to them at all!

"How old is he?" Guy heard someone behind him ask, and an equally unseen voice which he thought was Sir Walter's answering,

"About fifty-two I think, but by Jesu he could be ten or fifteen older by his looks! God's hooks! What's happened to the man?"

Guy felt a tap on his shoulder and turned to see Sir Martin at his side. "Guy, do you still have some of that liniment you gave me for my rheumatism in the winter?"

"Yes, most definitely!"

"Then would you go and offer to rub some into his back for the Keeper?"

Guy was quick to catch on. "You want me to find out what's happened?"

Sir Martin and Sir Walter were now by him and nodding, and even Murdac turned and added his agreement.

"You know enough to be able to tell me if he's just lost the will to do his job or if it's something worse," he said softly. "This isn't the man I knew! But I need to know fast if he's going to lose even more of his grip on his office. I've thought it odd since I've been back that we hardly seem to have any communication with Laxton these days, but I never expected this. I just thought Ralph was trying to keep his dealings out of the way of an incompetent sheriff, not failing himself."

Shouldering his way through the press of men in the outer bailey, Guy got to the side of the Keeper and proffered an arm to lean on.

"You seem to be in some pain, sire," he said solicitously. "I have a warming balm which might help. Would you like me to bring some for your servant to rub in?"

The Keeper raised pain-filled eyes to Guy's. "Dear Lord, no! That ham-fisted oaf would only cripple me further!"

Guy managed to keep his face politely blank. "Would you like me to do it, then? I have some experience in helping with wounds and injuries."

Fitz Stephen looked at him assessingly. "If you can do it without rendering me incapable of walking as the last fool who touched me did, then yes."

That sounded serious. No mere twinges of aging joints, then.

"Have you received an injury then, sire?"

Fitz Stephen nodded as he hobbled along beside Guy. "Just before King Henry died I was riding through Sherwood. A bloody boar came straight out of the undergrowth at my horse. Nothing I could do about it. She bolted, I got swipe off by a low branch and fell on my back onto a rock."

"Christ and all his saints!" Guy gasped. "You're lucky you can walk at all!"

"That I know," fitz Stephen said witheringly, but without malice having realised that Guy had recognised the damage done without further explanation.

Guy took him up to one of the rooms which were reserved for special guests. The large bed was soft and comfortable to lie on, and with Guy's help, fitz Stephen stripped to his braes and lay face down on it. Leaving the Keeper with blankets draped over his back to warm the skin, Guy raced down to the stable where he kept his stash of ointments and healing salves, and then ran back. At some point as he crossed the inner bailey he heard de Wendenal's voice calling his name, and Murdac firmly telling him that Guy was on his business.

As he rubbed his hands to warm them, and then began gently easing the honey based liniment into the Keeper's back, he also began feeling for the damage. At the top of the spine all felt normal, but as he got further down he reached a point where he dared only use the lightest of touches near to the spine itself. If fitz Stephen hadn't actually broken his back he had come perilously close to it. Indeed Guy wondered whether a clean break might not have done less damage. With that there might have been the possibility of it healing if it hadn't killed him outright. What he was feeling now were chipped and partly crushed bones, and all he dared to do was ease the tension in the surrounding muscles. The only consolation was hearing fitz Stephen falling into a relaxed sleep and giving small involuntary grunts of relief as painfully contracted muscles were unknotted.

Leaving his patient well-wrapped up and to sleep off the strain of even such a moderate day's journey, Guy went down to find Murdac and discovered him with de Wendenal in the main hall, still working out who would ride with who.

"Sir Ralph won't be able to ride with us," he told them regretfully.

"Why? What's the matter with the daft old sod?" de Wendenal snapped irritably. "I'm counting on him doing his bit with his own men!"

Murdac visibly winced at de Wendenal's disrespect. "What did you discover, Guy?"

As Guy detailed the extent of Ralph fitz Stephen's injury, however, even de Wendenal had to admit that he couldn't expect a man in that much distress to spend several days in the saddle.

"I think it would be best if he stays here and waits for us to get back," Guy concluded. "I can ask Harry to come up from the stables and continue with the massaging while I'm out with you – I trust him to do no harm far more than that servant of Sir Ralph's. That should at least ensure that Sir Ralph can ride back in less pain than he arrived with. And I think he's well aware of what you're intending to do and will lend his authority to any actions you take. It's just not possible for him to do it himself."

"Thank you," Murdac said quickly, before de Wendenal could add some snide remark. "I had wondered what had gone wrong."

"Bloody man should have given up the Keepership if he can't do the job!" de Wendenal snorted in assumed pious outrage, although Guy and everyone else present knew that he was simply thinking of how much more power he could draw to himself.

"And would you have him divorce his wife too?" shot back Murdac. "You forget at your peril, Sheriff, that it's Lady Maud de Caux whose family have the hereditary keepership of the Forest of Nottingham, and it's only Sir Ralph's by virtue of his marriage to her. A position conferred on him by King Henry, you should recall, as part of that same marriage settlement. If anyone is going to appoint someone in his stead it would be her or the king or, should the situation become truly desperate, the king's head forester. The likes of you or the chancellor have no say in this at all! It's one office which is not available to the highest bidder!"

The sheer bitterness of Ralph Murdac's tone as he said the last told Guy just how deeply the loss of his sheriffdom had cut the former sheriff. De Wendenal had never been one of Ralph's favoured knights when he had served under him, but Guy wondered just how much he truly hated the man now. That was another thing he must bear in mind. Murdac might not have the power he once had, but what was the betting that he still had the ear of those old friends who still did? That might make him another route by which de Wendenal's name might be blackened. It would have to be subtly done, with no hint of Murdac having been directed by a third hand, but Guy felt certain that if he found the right arrows, he had found in his old sheriff a very useful bow to shoot them through.

"Well whatever's the matter with him, fitz Stephen will have to moulder here!" de Wendenal was declaring brutally, bringing Guy back to the present. "We have work to do! We shall set out at first light tomorrow morning. Make sure everyone knows what they are doing! I want no loitering and stalling by idle men-at-arms under the pretext of not knowing what's happening!"

As de Wendenal turned and stomped back to his private chamber the entire company sighed with relief.

"Judas' balls!" Hugh of Woodham growled from beside Guy. "Is there any situation he can't cause offence over?"

"Excepting that I wouldn't wish it on my friends over on the borders, I could say it's a shame he didn't get Herefordshire in the latest shuffling of sheriffs," Guy sighed. "A few cross-border raids by the Welsh might sort out whether it's all bluster with him."

Murdac sniffed. "I know what you mean. Unfortunately he's such a cursed ruffian, he'd probably cope."

"Oh he's probably had his share of rough and bloody fights," Guy said dryly, "but I meant the kind of skirmish where you have to outwit a clever enemy and lead your own men while you're doing it. God knows I loathe de Braose, but against de Wendenal I'd put my money on him chewing him up and spitting him out every time. De Wendenal is fine when he can bully and bluster, and batter the odd poor sod with his fists, but the more I see of him, the less I think he's a proper fighter."

To his surprise he saw a genuine smile break out on Murdac's face. "By Our Lady, Guy! You're right! I knew there was something not right with all this excess of ill humours. I fought in Normandy as a young man, you know, and it's a long time ago, but until now it never occurred to me that I might still be able to give that brute a run for his money."

Guy and Sir Hugh grinned back, although Guy was quick to add, "Well before you get too taken with the idea, hadn't we better do something with this mess?" He pointed to the list of men the scribe had left, detailing who was going where and with whom.

"Mess?" Sir Hugh queried. "It's not that bad, surely?"

Yet Guy quirked an eyebrow and said to Murdac. "Wendenal going into the heart of the old forest with just men-at-arms? Isn't that asking for trouble?" He paused to let them see what he was meaning. "You, Sir Ralph, are fine taking us forester knights who normally patrol Derwent-to-Erewash, and heading straight up towards Mansfield. And although the Le Clay knights now won't have fitz Stephen leading them in a scouring of the eastern side of the forest, I'm sure they'll be alright with Sir Martin leading them. Only Mahel of those knights is a hothead likely to cause trouble in one of the villages. But not all of Sir Ralph's foresters are familiar with that dense forest immediately north of Calverton. In fact, I am right in saying that only two of them are, aren't I?"

Murdac suddenly saw it. "Oh, Holy Mother of God! He'll get lost, won't he?"

"I'd say there's a grave danger of that," Guy sighed, "and there'll be no point in him losing his temper with the men-at-arms who are with him. They won't know any more than him! And we all know what he'll be like if he comes back having had to be rescued just from getting lost! That would truly cap what he sees as outlaws taking the piss out of his authority."

Sir Martin and Sir Walter had joined them, and now all shuddered at the thought.

"You'd better go with him, Guy," Murdac hurriedly decided. "Someone had better be there to keep him from falling in a boar wallow or getting stuck up a tree. Yes, I know he was a forester himself, but the bloody man isn't a natural out in the wilds like you are. If you ride with me, Hugh, then he can't say I'm a man down. I'm sure Robert and Richard can supervise those men left to guard the castle at such a time!" The last was said with a twinkle in his eye, knowing that the remaining two castle knights, Robert of Packringham and Richard of Burscot, could practically supervise those knights and men here on service with one arm tied behind their backs once the disruption de Wendenal brought to the place was gone.

For Guy it was a huge relief. He hadn't wanted to end up with the Le Clay knights, because that would most likely take him through or at least close by Fiskerton, and who knew if Walter was back there by now? But he also wanted to steer clear of his normal places just in case one of the villages he had been more reasonable with forgot, and appealed to him for help if Henry, or Walkelin, or Fredegis started trampling crops or worse. With their blood up on a hunt it would be a miracle if no-one got hurt somewhere out in one of the forest villages, but Guy knew he had no means to avoid that happening this time.

Yet Guy also had the beginnings of a plan to truly humiliate de Wendenal. It all hinged on whether Robin and the others were close enough to take part, but with a bit of cunning plotting to ensure that the twelve men-at-arms who were his friends marched with him, Guy thought it might be possible.

Come the morning he was feeling quietly confident as the massed men streamed out of Nottingham Castle. Calverton was six miles north and a touch east of Nottingham – a comfortable morning's march for the men – and with plenty of time for them to pause for food at noon before spending the whole afternoon hunting. Once they had spilt up, Sir Ralph and his part would overnight at Linby, and the Le Clay party at Southwell, but de Wendenal had already expressed his intention of returning to Calverton that night. That might mean that Robin would hear of it and come searching. Never had Guy wanted his cousin to be spoiling for a fight so much!

There was a heart-stopping moment when de Wendenal started to protest at Guy's inclusion in his party. Luckily Ralph Murdac drew the belligerent sheriff to one side and after many hissed words, during which Guy would not have been surprised to see Murdac thump the sheriff, their despised leader saw sense and the hunt began.

"I want to cover the ground around this place!" de Wendenal roared to his men. "Spread out and search as you go! Gisborne! Find me a bloody trail!"

However the ground immediately around Calverton had been so trampled by the passage of the massed men that even someone as dim as de Wendenal could see that there was no hope of that. All they could do was march off a little more north and east than the Le Clay knights' party had done, and then swing into the north avoiding Oxton Bogs. The inappropriately named Darcliff Hill – little more than a slight rise in the ground – was as far eastwards as they went, and the men tramped on northwards. The men-at-arms were spread out so that even in amongst the plentiful oaks and the undergrowth beneath, they could see the man at either side of them, and Guy was watching as many of those he was not sure of like a hawk, just in case they found some clue as to who had stolen the money. He wanted this fight to come on his ground and in his time.

Therefore he allowed de Wendenal to bawl and shout at the poor folk of Fansfield, and threaten them with all kinds of fates if they did not report any sighting of this outlaw band, and then to repeat the process at Blidworth as they began the loop round to come back to Calverton. None of it achieved a thing, but it was giving de Wendenal a chance to vent his fury, and Guy wanted him weary when the time came. Footsore and dispirited, the men tramped back into Calverton, and while de Wendenal forced himself on the hospitality of Ralph of

Woodborough, just a mile away, Guy made sure the men were cared for. In the process he managed to have quiet words with all twelve of his old friends from among the men-at-arms.

"Stay together!" he warned them. "Stay where you can seem to be fighting Robin and our friends, but then fall to the ground without anyone questioning you afterwards. I want this to be an utter shambles!"

And then when all of the weary men had gratefully curled up in their blankets for the night, he took his horse and the two belonging to fitz Stephen's riding foresters and headed north as fast as he could. Having been constrained to the pace of the walking men all day, the horse were not that tired, and by sharing his weight between them, Guy hoped not to draw any suspicion over weary horses the next morning, but he very much wanted to get up to the outlaws' hideaway which was not far from Inkersall. Mercifully he knew it was only five or six miles away, and so accomplishable in the night when someone knew the forest as well as he did.

On the outskirts of the camp he heard an owl hoot and then as he got closer the sudden calling from above of,

"It's all right! It's Guy!" in James' voice.

"What brings you here?" John asked out of the gloom, as James could be heard rousing Robin.

"Trouble and a plan!" Guy told him, now looking forward to the rest of the day.

As he outlined his plan he could see Robin bristling in the light of the fire which had been poked back into life. That was until he said,

"But you must tie me up with the sheriff! In fact it would be wonderful if two or three of you were seen to pile onto me right at the start. Make me seem as though you think I'm a real threat! I'll happily fake being knocked out while you deal with him. But when he comes round he has to see me tied up like a hog for the slaughter."

"Don't you worry, we'll make it look good!" Hugh reassured Guy. "He'll think you fought tooth and nail to protect him by the time we're done!"

Guy was relieved that Hugh had grasped the necessity, and was sure that some of the others had too, yet he was gratified to hear Gilbert's broad Irish accent ask,

"Where do you want us to ambush you?" And then seeing Robin's inflamed glare add, "Because we don't want to leave it too long and have the bastard sheriff turn back so he can get to a proper bed for the night, do we?"

Now Guy looked Robin straight in the eye as he said, "I don't want to lead them here. No chance! That's asking for trouble! If the brutish boar wants to come back for a second helping and revenge, it has to be to somewhere well away from your camp. So can you spend tonight laying a trail I can follow, from somewhere near by that rise by

Blidworth, and take it westwards? You know, that trickle of a stream which runs down past Inkersall, but makes a puddle of a pool a couple of miles south-west of there? I'm thinking of you catching us just the other side of there."

"Oh, that's nice!" Thomas approved quickly. "Some nice boggy ground to leave some footprints in just to egg him on, perfect!"

"Exactly!" Guy agreed. "Don't make the rest of the trail too clear. He needs to think we genuinely found you, rather than being lured there, but a last clue that the quarry is in sight and I think he'll play right into your hands. I've told the lads from High Peak to lag, so the others will be the first in line when the sheriff flays them onwards. That way you can come out fighting in earnest! I managed to shift the castle men around so that none of the ones likely to fight you in earnest are any loss to anyone."

He saw Tuck looking at him sideways. "No, Tuck, I'm not playing God with men's lives. All of those men are ones who've been creeping round de Wendenal trying to advance themselves. If he doesn't get them killed in this fight it won't be too long before he does in another. They have no thought for those they might trample on as long as they rise to the top of the heap. So I need to focus on those who I know I can save, and who will help us save others. It's as simple as that. We can't do this and have no casualties at all! I'm just trying to limit the damage."

Tuck nodded sagely. "A little harm to do much good. Well let's hope that we bring this sheriff down a notch or two in the process."

Did we succeed? Ah Brother, you will hear soon enough! But I meant what I said. I was not trying to play God with men's lives, but if we were to cut de Wendenal's claws it could not be done without some spilling of blood. I had chance in a brief few words with Tuck, Will and Gilbert to say that I was not asking for those soldiers at the front to be deliberately cut down. Simply that the Sherwood men need not hold back and risk getting wounded themselves for fear of taking down a friend, and they understood that.

As for me, I was desperate to see de Wendenal's ego pricked. He had had his own way for far too long, firstly at High Peak, where I had heard only too well of how he had tried to trample our miner friends underfoot, and then at Tickhill, where by all accounts he had been unbearable. Yet as constable of Tickhill, while he had the means to make the household's lives horrendous with his cruelty and pigheadedness, at least he had had no means to affect the lives of villagers and farmers in the wider shire. As sheriff he was in an altogether different position, and I wanted him brought down to ground from his fanciful imaginings of how powerful he had become, before he brought tragedy upon some poor innocents.

What could he have done? Oh, Brother, you should never underestimate the power of a sheriff in his own shire. He was the one who could decide whether a man should be brought to trial, and if he could not sit in judgement on them within his own shire, he could nonetheless choose to put someone in harm's way or remove them from it. Who would gainsay a sheriff if he had records falsified to say that a village had not paid its taxes? Or that the fees to pasture animals in the forest had not been paid? Or that they had been harbouring a wanted criminal? And this was the kind of thing I was worried about with de Wendenal. Fitz John had been personally dangerous with his uncontrolled temper, but if he was the sword cut, de Wendenal was the bludgeoning hammer – able to kill and cripple despite its dull edge.

Chapter 18

So, Gervase, to return to the tale in hand – I returned to the hall at Calverton where all the men were bedded down, and managed to slip in unnoticed. Despite the nights being light, and the men being far from unused to walking, no-one was in a hurry to rise. De Wendenal had had them all kitted out in their gambesons, and although it had not been a hot summer as yet, it was still too warm for marching across the shire with several pounds of packed wool on. Everyone had drunk thirstily as soon as we had returned to the village, and it was a measure of how much they had sweated out during the march that none of them were getting up in the night to find a privy or simply a convenient tree to piss against. Therefore I was able to get a couple of hours' sleep before we got roused by the village cockerels announcing it as time to rise.

Even better, it was far later by the time de Wendenal appeared with his host, Ralph of Woodborough. Both had the air of men who had drunk heavily the night before, and I guessed that they had misguidedly slacked their thirst with some of the best of Sir Ralph's cellars, and were now suffering for it. Happily we then only had the two riding foresters and the two walking foresters, who were fitz Stephen's forest men for the Keeping known as High Forest, to contend with, and they were only joining us for the first time that morning as we headed north. These four met us as we once again tramped northwards between Farnsfield and Blidworth, and came into their territory, for the three Keeper's foresters who saw to the area close to Nottingham Castle (officially known as Leen to Dover-beck) had gone with Ralph Murdac's party, but even so they would not impinge on another forester's territory.

De Wendenal was most waspish about such niceties, but I was only too grateful for him having something else to worry at like a bone. It kept him nicely distracted from me! Yet I now had to be most careful. I could not cause offence by saying outright, or even implying, that these four foresters had missed the signs of a band of outlaws on their own patch. And so I made a point of asking them when the last time had been that they had been in this particular part of the forest. I do not blaspheme, Brother, when I say I was praying that they would not say within the last week.

These men had a huge area to cover, for their territory ran right up to Edwinstowe in the north, and from the river which ran through Ollerton and Rufford in the east, right over to the shire boundary with Derbyshire beyond Mansfield. Therefore they had something like twelve miles of dense forest in width at its widest in the southern half of the Keepership, and nigh on eight miles as the crow flew from north to south. It does not sound much, does it? Eight miles one way, and eight expanding to twelve the other. Little more than half a day's ride if you took either in a straight line.

But neither was in a straight line even where the roads ran through it, and the rest was a tangle of dense woods, sometimes of the famous Sherwood oaks, but even in the lighter patches it was still filled with stands of sliver birches and elms and ashes, with a mass of undergrowth beneath. I do not know how you are at calculating, Gervase, but Tuck and I once whiled away a winter's night working it out, and we came to the conclusion that those four men had something like a hundred square miles to deal with when you took it as a block of land, not in lines. Now do you see how Robin Hood was able to lead those who hunted him such a merry dance in the heart of the forest?

Even in winter, you could be thirty or forty paces away from men and never see them. The trunks of the great trees obscured any long vistas, and in the summer, with the bracken and small bushes burgeoning beneath the heavy green boughs, the line of sight was even more limited. And so I was praying that those foresters had not been in <u>this</u> patch of forest of late – these three or four miles north of Blidworth and little over a mile in width – when they had so much more to patrol. Had they been, then I would have had to proceed with a great deal more care, for I could not seem to stumble upon signs which they too ought to have recognized, and yet by the same token, I could not start examining one area most intently without there being some reason why I would do so.

However my prayers to St Cadoc must have been heard, for the four announced that they had been variously over by Rufford, west of Clipstone, and beyond Mansfield in the case of the two riding foresters. My approach was clear and I could begin the dance!

Sherwood
Summer, the Year of Our Lord 1192

"My lord!" Guy called out, gesturing to attract the sheriff's attention. When de Wendenal finally turned to look his way, Guy stood in his stirrups and reached up to pull a snagged piece of cloth from a branch above him. "Someone kept watch up here!" he added, just in case the man was too thick to see the significance. "See? He caught his trews or shirt as he jumped down!" Then before the sheriff could make a mess of such a carefully planted sign, Guy bawled, "Everyone stand still for a moment! We have a trail to follow! Wait until I've come to you before moving on!"

Now came the risky part. Would de Wendenal let him do his job? Would the bullish sheriff stand back and let the acknowledged tracker do what he was good at? Or would he flay the men blindly onwards? Realising that he must let de Wendenal have his head, if no-one else, Guy vaulted down from his horse and hurried to the patch of ground in front of the sheriff's horse. Casting about him he was relieved to see that whoever had laid the outlaws' trail had not been so obvious as to do it on the track which the sheriff was riding down.

"No, they weren't on this side of the track," Guy said affably to the sheriff. "Would you continue to search for further signs, my lord?" It was said with a forced smile, but it placated the sheriff's ego into thinking he had not been actually told he could ride on.

To make it clearer, Guy also called to the men beyond the sheriff and told them that they too could walk on as long as they were alert. He then hurried back to the side of the track where the tree was and began searching. It didn't take long for him to find an expertly placed foot on the bank of a small streamlet.

"This way!" he called across to the sheriff, and then called for the four foresters to come and track with him. It was a cunning ploy, for now Guy went on foot, asking Ketil to lead his horse for him, and if Guy – a knight – was walking, then the riding foresters could hardly refuse to do the same.

"Keep behind us, no more than ten abreast," was Guy's next instruction, and was gladdened by the sight of the twelve men from High Peak muddling about so that they got behind the ten others men-at-arms, who in turn were behind the sheriff and Verderer Ralph. Not that they could go ten abreast. The trail went off into the undergrowth, and soon it was all they could do to have the five trackers questing side by side.

When Hubert, one of the riding foresters missed a fairly obvious sign, Guy realised that this sort of work was not either of the riding men's forte. Felled trees and deer's carcasses they could deal with, but not this kind of work, and he gestured the two walking foresters to close on him as the trail narrowed, forcing the two riding foresters to drop back.

With a triumphant, "Ah-ha!" he managed to pounce on a bent and trampled bracken frond before the forester John stamped on it. Then was surprised to see that the same John was looking at him in shock that he had so quickly spotted the sign. Judas' balls, this was going to be harder than he had thought, and for wholly different reasons! If the four foresters were going to be so bloody useless, then he was going to be much more conspicuous as the one who led de Wendenal to the ambush. Please God that Robin would make it seem authentic! The last thing they needed right now was a fit of cousinly pique, and Robin only going at the attack half-heartedly just because it had been Guy's idea. That would drop Guy right in the mire!

Luckily the trail petered out briefly, and Guy had to call everyone to him and explain the basics of what they should look for, and then spread them out again to comb the forest at a snail's pace. It was Big Ulf who spotted an artistically broken branch at the same time as one of the other men-at-arms triumphantly found a snagged thread on a ragged piece of oak bark. By now the sheriff was fairly champing at the bit, for they had been proceeding at a crawl for nearly a mile, and so when they finally dipped down to the stream where Guy had arranged for the ambush to take place, de Wendenal was wound tighter than a crossbow.

Guy made sure he had turned aside to look at some fictional clue which mercifully Claron played up to, so that even as hopeless a tracker as Walter, the other riding forester, could triumphantly find the footprints in the bank.

"Here, my lord sheriff! Here!" he squawked, and nearly got trampled as de Wendenal and Verderer Ralph spurred their mounts forwards.

Seeing their sheriff surging forwards, the men whom Guy had guessed would be clamouring for a fight broke into a run to follow him. Better still, the four foresters ignored Guy and the other men-at-arms and promptly sprinted after the others, Hubert and Walter frantically swinging themselves up into the saddles of their horses having snatched the reins back from the soldiers.

Big Ulf gave Guy a wink. "Better keep up, I suppose if we're to play our part," and together the thirteen of them hurried in the wake of the rest who were rapidly disappearing into the darkness of a dense patch of oaks.

They were halted by an arrow whistling past Guy's nose to embed itself into a tree beside him. Instantly he recognised Malik's fletching and looked up, wondering why the experienced soldier was not up ahead as he heard fighting breaking out. Instead he saw Marianne and Mariota slithering down out of the tree.

"Quick! You twelve back to that slight bend and then make noises like you're fighting like mad!" Marianne ordered, and the twelve immediately caught on.

"I've got blood!" Mariota added, brandishing a small bladder. "It's been the very Devil stopping it from drying and going too dark in this weather. We had to pen a small wild boar piglet and then kill it late this morning to make sure we had some. Now you two, come here!" and summoning Alfred and Ricard, she proceeded to artistically splatter them.

With the sounds of fighting still going on ahead, the two Hospitaller Sisters soon had all the twelve looking as though they had fought tooth and nail against vicious attackers. They had even used a small knife to give some of them surface cuts, and rubbed dyes into patches of skin to make them go convincing bruise-coloured purples and greens. The twelve soldiers were not complaining. A few small nicks from a clean knife wielded by an expert were infinitely preferable to getting a real wound, because the danger was always that the other soldiers might force them into a situation where they had no choice but to fight in earnest if they appeared to be too disengaged. Now they looked as though another group of outlaws had come up from the rear and attacked them, giving them a convincing reason not to have joined in the fight up ahead.

"You'll need to thump one another as well," Mariota warned them, as Marianne turned her attention to Guy. "Use those spears to clout a few shins so you hobble convincingly on the way back. We can't have you forgetting and stopping limping when the others are struggling to stay upright!"

For Guy they had a different technique, streaking the blood to look more like missed sword strokes with a bloody blade, for he would surely have drawn a more experienced fighter to him. Quickly turned into a bedraggled state, Guy then got Ruald and Ingulf to land a few carefully chosen blows on him, and then hurried forward. He was glad that both women had been quick to say that the plan was that Guy would join in up ahead. That meant that Robin had to have taken to heart the need for him to know just what had happened for his own protection – if questioned at the castle he could not afford to be surprised.

As Marianne and Mariota disappeared into the undergrowth out of harm's way, Guy trotted to the bend in the track and peered carefully around the trunk of a conveniently massive oak. As he had predicted, the other twelve men-at-arms had put up a spirited fight. Two were out cold close to where he stood, and he guessed that Tuck and John had come up behind them and laid them out right at the start of the ambush. Three more had been pinned to trees by arrows which had to have come from the great Welsh bows, and Guy had to admire Thomas, Piers and Malik's aim, for all three men were pinned by their gambesons only, there was no blood. Now they were being guarded by Much, Roger and Bilan with their slightly lighter bows, and Guy was glad to see that the three youngsters had hoods pulled well forwards, shading their faces and concealing how young they were.

"*Arhosa ble ach!*" he heard Bilan snarl. "Stay where you are!"

That was cunning! Not only did it reinforce the misconception that they might be deserters from amongst the Welsh archers sent on crusade, it sounded far more threatening coming in another language. The soldiers certainly believed it. They glared furiously back, but made no attempt to tear their padded jackets free.

He looked to the rest of the fight. Will was fighting a brute of a man whom Guy would not be sorry to see the last of. Sometime over the winter, Will had made himself a war-hammer and was wielding it with amazing dexterity in his left-hand even as he used his sword with his right, creating a whirlwind of attacks which it was proving impossible for the man to get past, even though he was one of the few who had a sword as well as his spear. Guy had heard in the castle gossip that the man had fought in Normandy in the past, and he certainly had a professional technique, but he was no match for Will. Luring the soldier into lunging at him, Will finished the fight with a swipe of the hammer which nearly staved the man's skull in. He wouldn't be getting up again, but Guy knew that there had been little chance of them getting away without a single fatality, and if it had to be anyone then this was the least awful outcome.

He turned and looked again, as Will stopped and leaned on the hammer to get his breath back. James had disarmed another man and had taken him out of the fight by the simple means of a well-placed fist once the man was on the ground. Tuck and John stood over two more unmoving figures, and Malik had just clipped another with the pommel of his sword under his jaw, and Guy saw him fold up gracefully at Malik's feet, otherwise unhurt.

Meanwhile, Thomas was already binding the hands and feet of the two walking foresters, who were also unconscious, and off to one side Guy could see the protruding and unmoving boots of one of the riding foresters. Clearly the two Welshmen had recognised that they weren't the close-quarters fighters the others were, but were making themselves useful in other ways, and Guy was relieved to see Piers – whom he had suddenly realised was missing from the scene – stand up hoisting the other riding forester's limp form onto his shoulder, already trussed like a chicken for the spit. Praise the saints, Piers had kept his head, then! Maybe he was finally learning some restraint after all?

Guy allowed himself a sigh of relief. This was good, it was all good! The remaining two men-at-arms had lost their fights with Allan and Hugh, and although they were cut about, as were James and Malik's opponents, none were badly wounded. So with only one fatality out of twenty-four men-at-arms, Guy felt sure that it would not seem such an affront that someone like Murdac would feel the need to lead a second hunt for the outlaws.

However, that left Robin battling it out with de Wendenal, and Gilbert fighting Sir Ralph. The flame-haired Irishman had his blood up, and was screaming in his native tongue,

"*Dia curse tú, tú bastaird!*" which Guy was pretty sure meant, 'God curse you, you bastard!'

To give Ralph credit, he was giving Gilbert a run for his money, and he would surely testify that these were no mere farmers on the run whom they had encountered. Yet with a final,

"*Tóg sin, tú muc Béarla!*" (Take that, you English pig!) Gilbert feinted one way, and then brought the pommel of the sword back straight into Sir Ralph's face with such force that the verderer was lifted off his feet and was hammered back into an oak, guaranteeing that he would not rise again for several hours.

That only left Robin and the sheriff, and to Guy's horror he realised that Robin was toying with de Wendenal. The sheriff was no mean fighter, and he fought unconstrained by any ideas of knightly codes of honour. Wherever de Wendenal had learned his fighting, some of it had been very dirty indeed! But he had not had Robin's experience either, and that had allowed Guy's cousin to get the measure of him early on and be confident of the game he was playing.

Guy heard Robin taunting, "Oh come now, sheriff! Is that your best stab?" as the sheriff's blade went wide, and hacked uselessly at a sapling instead of Robin's arm. And all the while they were dancing further and further away down the track and away from the others. That could not happen! Guy felt panic rising. What in God's name was Robin playing at? Why was he trying to get de Wendenal alone? Yes, it was a good thing that Robin was drawing him away from the end of the track where their twelve allies now lurked, but there was something in Robin's tone, and that weird glint in his eye which chilled Guy to the marrow. Christ be merciful! He surely wasn't planning on killing the sheriff, was he?

Feigning an exhausted stagger, Guy ran as convincingly as possible into the wider clearing as the track expanded for a short way, which he appreciated had been the ideal place for the ambush, but which now meant that he was still exposed to the glare of the three men still pinned to the trees. He had to make this look good.

"You bastards!" he snarled and managed a feigned stumble over the legs of Will's dead opponent, then didn't know whether to be glad or sad that as he momentarily distracted the three lads, the three soldiers tried at last to make a break for it. It meant that Will, Tuck, John, Malik and James, all piled in again to make sure that the three did not get chance to escape, but also masked Guy's onward progress.

He was aware that as he tore past, no longer needing to fake any limping, that Hugh, Siward and Gilbert now came after him having also been freed of the need to put on a show for fear of what might be reported back.

"Robin!" he heard Siward call in dismay, as all four of them rounded the next kink in the track and found that it narrowed, but also that Robin was still dancing lightly in and poking de Wendenal with the tip of the beautiful sword Will had made for him. In contrast, the sheriff was clearly tiring, but was as enraged as any wild boar Guy had ever hunted – and just as dangerous! One miscalculation by Robin and de Wendenal would fillet him with his butcher's cleaver of a sword. But worse, close to Guy could see that strange mad light in Robin's eyes. Unless he did something and fast, one of the two would be dying beneath these oaks and a catastrophe would ensue.

Launching himself at de Wendenal's back, Guy catapulted the two of them beyond Robin's reach and into the undergrowth, and they went down into the fronds of bracken in a tangle of limbs. By some divine intervention, as he went down beneath Guy, the back of de Wendenal's head came into sharp contact with a large protruding root of one of the oaks, and to Guy's intense relief, he felt the sheriff go limp. Before he could draw breath, Siward was with him, and then saying what Guy was thinking,

"Oh Blessed Virgin, thank God for that!"

He helped Guy to his feet and together they turned back to the track to see Robin struggling wildly in the grip of Will and Gilbert, who were all but screaming at him to calm down and get a grip on himself.

"Stop it!" Will bawled into his face. "Enough!" and then as Malik came up to help, thrust Robin towards his friend, and with his meaty fist Will laid Robin out too.

They all paused, panting, and gazed at one another in shock.

"That wasn't what we planned," Siward said softly in Guy's ear as they gasped side by side.

"I didn't think so," Guy replied, clapping a hand of solidarity on the crusader's shoulder. "By Our Lady, that was too close for comfort, though! I thought it was going too well." He waded out of the bracken and went and put his hand on Will's shoulder too. "I know you had no choice back there, but this ...this was just..."

Will nodded. "You don't have to say it. He was completely somewhere else. In some other world in his head. I don't think he even knew me. Not properly. He knew I was an ally, but as his friend Will? No, I don't think so."

Hugh came running up to join them. "We have to move and fast! Those men are only going to stay unconscious for so long – we did our best not to hit them too hard in case we did real damage." Then he saw Robin on the ground. "What...?"

"Never mind!" Gilbert snapped. "He's not hurt, the fucking idiot!"

"We'll explain later," Will added wearily. "Let's get the sheriff back to the others and all you lot trussed up. We'll come back for him when we're done."

In the end James went back and sat with Robin just in case he woke up sooner than expected, but Will confessed he had hit him hard, and Robin remained out cold. The men-at-arms were trussed up with the aid of various belts and straps, and some old bits of rope which had been collected by the gang for just such an occasion. They were then laid out in two lines – each roped together by two longer lengths – somewhat apart from one another, so that the twelve who had been in on the whole thing would have some advanced warning of the others waking.

Marianne and Mariota reappeared with three of the horses, although the riding foresters' beasts had clearly been on their home ground enough to decide to head back to the safety of their respective stables, and Sir Ralph and the sheriff were hoisted aboard their own horses by Tuck and John. However, not before they had been stripped down to their underwear. This was supposed to be an exercise in humiliation, and Guy intended to stick to that part of the plan.

The men-at-arms had also been relieved of their gambesons. It was too good an opportunity for the gang to get their hands on some useful protection, and they were sure that in the sticky warmth of the summer forest, the men would be glad to be free of them. And the men would not be so keen to be standing on their dignity that they would worry about going into Mansfield, as the nearest town, in just their braes – unlike de Wendenal and Sir Ralph! All they would be wanting was a decent meal and an alehouse to drown the pain of their bruises in, while complaining vigorously at the sheriff's insanity at charging ahead as he had done.

Guy, too, could not care less about who saw his underwear if it did what he prayed with the sheriff. He would be prepared to put up with a lot more than that for the pleasure of humiliating such a man. For now he hoisted himself across his saddle, and then went limp to allow Will to tie his hands to one stirrup and his feet to the one on the other side, echoing the way the sheriff and the verderer were tied up. This way they looked like three pale deer being brought home from the hunt!

For now the majority of the gang melted away into the forest, leaving Much to lead Guy's horse – for they needed his help, but Guy wanted the most naive of the horse-leaders well away from the sheriff should he wake – and Roger and Bilan the other two, while Thomas, Piers, Hugh and Malik harried the hobbled and strung together men-at-arms into starting the slow march back to civilisation, albeit not the way they had come. With great care they took them by a route through the forest so that they avoided all roads until they came right by Mansfield town itself.

Guy had originally hoped to go back to Nottingham, but he now realised that the others had been right to say that it was too far if anyone was badly injured, and that it would be dangerous taking a man like the sheriff tied up all that way. Mansfield, as the next largest place in this part of the shire, would have to do, but at least it had plenty of men of some standing to witness the sheriff's humiliation; men who would not be easily intimidated into not repeating what they had seen. At that point it was already coming into the early evening, and many of the inhabitants of the town were taking their ease in the lowering summer sun whilst chatting to their neighbours and friends, for it was the kind of evening to incite folk to make the most of it. And for what Guy wanted it could not have been better.

"Send us in first!" he hissed to Hugh, who had dropped back to walk by the horses, and Hugh immediately grinned.

"Come sheriff!" he declared loudly. "No time to be hanging around at the back! You shall get home first. Never let it be said that Robin Hood is not generous to his guests!"

De Wendenal opened a malevolent eye to glare at him, which Guy saw through his lashes as he kept his eyes as closed as possible to avoid being thought to be conscious.

"You'll pay for this, you bastard son of a poxed whore!" the sheriff growled, trying to spit at Hugh but lacking the saliva. "I'll have your head on the battlements of Nottingham by the end of the month!"

"You can try," Hugh laughed from beneath one of the hoods which were now part of the whole Robin Hood disguise. "The Hooded Man will be harder to catch than you think."

Yes, Brother, that was the first time anyone actually attached the name of The Hooded Man to Robin Hood, and I can see by your smile that that pleases you. But you are not so happy that it should have been Hugh who got the name? Ah, but you see, we had long agreed that if necessary there should be three men who could pose as ˜Robin˜ to repeat that night when my cousin, Siward and I had put the fear of God into young de Cuckney. It had worked so well then, and it meant that should one of the three become incapacitated by a wound for a while, ˜Robin Hood˜ could still put in an appearance should it be necessary. Therefore the guise of the hood had been an obvious one to keep. Yet with me being away from the others for so much of the time, Hugh was the obvious choice to become the third ˜Robin˜, for if not quite as tall as Robin and myself, he was only an inch or so shorter than Siward, and his hair was as dark. He also spoke with a local accent which was something which added to the confusion, since we three original actors did too. Ah it was a good trick we had conjured up on that night, as was proved by the way it lasted!

But I have left you in mid-crisis, Gervase! Hugh slapped the arse of the sheriff's horse and let it trot off down the street between the houses, to be swiftly followed by Sir Ralph's and then mine. The poor men-at-arms who were suffering for following the sheriff so eagerly, then followed us in at a more sedate pace, with our twelve friends bringing up the rear. The whole thing worked like a charm for the ordinary men, for the battered men at the front brought those townsfolk running to their rescue who were of a sympathetic turn of mind, while the rest fell about laughing at the sight of the sheriff. I had a prime view of this since my horse had ambled up to just behind his and Sir Ralph's, and I feigned being still knocked about rather than yelling to be set free as the sheriff did so that I could savour the moment.

Very well, I will confess to you a most un-Christian enjoyment of that. Is that better? Mea culpa, mea culpa, mea maxima culpa – I truly relished every breath of being strapped across my horse for the pleasure it gave me watching such a beast being brought low. A better man than I might have felt just a twinge of remorse as I watched de Wendenal writhe and swear and demand to be got down, I did not. In my eyes he deserved exactly what he got that evening, for it took quite some while before anyone believed that he really was the sheriff.

Indeed it took the appearance of Ralph Murdac and the other party out of Nottingham from the road coming up from the south with the intention of spending the night there, and their shock and horror, before it was truly believed by the worthies of Mansfield that it was their sheriff hog-tied in his braes before them. Until then they had been treating him like some lowly riding soldier, made to wait his turn along with the others. And who could blame them? All they had ever seen of him was in the mangy furs he wore in all but the hottest weather, and now I realised why, for they bulked him up something amazingly. Beneath all the trappings of his finery, William de Wendenal had lost the muscles of his shoulders he had had when he first came to Nottingham to the paunch spreading around his middle, for clearly he had enjoyed the table as sheriff with little restraint!

With much cursing and blaspheming, de Wendenal was hauled down off his horse and escorted into one of the guildsmen's house. With it being high summer, no-one had had so much as a cape to drape around his shoulders to cover his state of undress, and he had to endure the short walk still listening to the badly stifled guffaws of laughter; for if the folk of Mansfield now dared not laugh out loud, it was still a sight to bring mirth unbidden to the lips, and choking it off was no easy matter. I, too, was helped down off my horse with considerably more sympathy than the sheriff had received, and being left alone with the ordinary folk while Ralph Murdac and the forest knights scurried around the sheriff and verderers, I was able to feebly joke that at least it had been a good deal cooler returning than riding out. My failure to make a fuss over being seen so undressed must have endeared me to the townsfolk, for thereafter I was always made most welcome in Mansfield.

Yet now I come to the truly sad part of the tale, Brother, for Ralph of Woodborough's collision with that oak had done serious damage. No, Brother, I will not censor Gilbert for what he did. It was an accident, a genuine accident. The bruise to his jaw certainly came up a princely purple, but I had had far worse and not been so harmed. The following morning I professed myself well enough to accompany the local wise woman in to see Sir Ralph, and then the brother from Newstead Abbey who was sent for in a hurry. We all agreed that it was the oak – the bark of which was still embedded in the back of Sir Ralph's skull – that had done the damage, not the clip to his jaw. And so we waited another day, while Murdac took our seething bundle of fury back to his castle at Nottingham, and then another day, and still Sir Ralph did not wake.

Finally we managed to get a litter strung between two horses, and along with the brother and six of my friendly men-at-arms, we carried the verderer to Newstead and its infirmary. Poor Sir Ralph lingered for another two weeks, slowly fading away and withering up like an old ear of wheat for want of water, for despite the brothers' best care, they could not get enough water into him to keep him alive in what turned out to be one of those rare blasts of hot English summer. When the message came to Nottingham that he had passed away, I found myself in the strangest of circumstances, for I had another job for Robin Hood of a kind I had not anticipated.

Chapter 19

So you are all agog, Brother. What was the job? ...No? Oh, you wish to know what happened to Robin first. Very well then, I shall fill in that gap for you. When Roger and Allan crept into Nottingham and found me, they told me of what had happened.

I had not needed to be told that the reason why none of the former crusaders had come with us to take the sheriff back was because they all felt they would be needed to calm Robin down when he came to his senses, and they were right! It took all of them insisting that he had gone into what Gilbert called ˜the red mist˜ before he would believe that he had lost control so badly. Even so, I believe that only Marianne adding her voice to the others finally tipped the balance to him fully believing them.

Tuck told me that when he came to, Robin was still teetering on the verge of falling back into that miasma of rage, and it had taken some persuading for him to take a draught of the poppy juice which Tuck had carried with him in a small flask, thinking he would have it there for anyone who was wounded. As the poppy took hold, Robin calmed down, and finally he was able to see reason. Truly, Gervase, if he had not agreed to let Tuck and Marianne medicate him at that point, I believe that my cousin would have either have been killed or would have killed someone he cared for so dearly that it would have made him a broken man forever. However, for the concluding of this tale you should know that Mariota and Will waited for Hugh and the others to rejoin them, to let them know where everyone had gone, while the rest retreated northwards and a touch west towards Derbyshire, Will willingly separating himself from Robin's wrath as the one who had administered the felling punch.

Yet Tuck did not want to make the journey to get Robin over to the Loxley camp, even though they could have marched fast and on into the night with the summer light, and done the trip in two or three days. He knew where he wanted to be, and it was where there was a monastery's medicinal garden which could be raided. Therefore they pressed on to just north of Cuckney, and to the Derbyshire border by Welbeck Abbey. I am told that Robin began to falter on that journey, and that our dear, loyal John carried him the last miles across his shoulders, and would not let any other help him.

There, does that make you happy, Brother? Good! Well they got to the border which just there is formed by a trickle of water known as the Millwood Brook, but once upon a time it must have been a fearsome torrent, for long, long ago it carved out a small gorge and created a series of caves. And it was here, in this secluded spot between the two tiny hamlets of Whitwell and Elmton, where my friends took refuge while Tuck went to work on Robin.

The first thing, he insisted, was that Robin should get some sleep. Not just the light naps breaking up the night which had been going on for far too long, but a deep and healing sleep. I am told that Robin protested long and hard, and that what finally convinced him to submit was the combined insistence of Tuck, Marianne and Mariota that he would almost certainly go mad if he did not, and John's equally firm determination that if they had to move in a hurry, that he would and could carry Robin even to the ends of the Earth. And so Tuck's treatment began with more of the poppy being administered.

Robin, I was told, slept for three days straight through while his friends kept guard, which of itself spoke volumes of his state of exhaustion. At the end of those days he woke with a blinding headache but with his fury finally gone, and at last he was open to reason. To my cousin's credit he now saw how badly things could have gone wrong, and how he could have endangered all of the others by departing from what had been arranged. However, I have to say, Brother, that I do not believe he was ever relieved that he had <u>not</u> killed de Wendenal. Never in his life would Robin understand what I told him, which was that there would not be – could not be – a time when there was no sheriff for the two shires. No king, whether it was the late King Henry, King Richard, or any other to come, would allow the revenue from a whole shire to slide out of his grasp, and therefore there would always be someone to do the king's dirty work for him. It was just that some did the job with a fairer mind and a less brutal hand.

What Robin did agree to was to take the herbs which Tuck and Marianne would mix up for him over the coming weeks. I believe that he was shocked when Malik and James led the others in saying that they could not continue to follow him if he would not do this thing, and that they feared that if he did not get regular sleep, that he would reach a stage where he would not know reality from the nightmares, and would get them all killed in the process. Allan told me that only John did not say anything on this matter, but that even he sat staring at Robin with a look of anguish and fear on his face which our cousin could not ignore, and that too helped convince Robin that his friends were genuinely worried for him, not turning into his enemies.

They also convinced him that having baited the sheriff so resoundingly, that they must wait and see what ensued before they raided any more courts, or robbed any more rich merchants risking passage through the forest.

˜God be merciful and not let the hammer of the sheriff's wrath fall on any of the ordinary folk for our temerity˜ Tuck told me he had said, and Allan and Roger in particular had held sternly to the need to speak to me and find out what might happen, rather than blunder on making any retribution fall heavily where it should not. And so they set up a permanent camp at the Crags, raided Welbeck's gardens for Tuck's herbs, and waited to hear from me while Robin rested and made a good show of returning to sanity.

So shall I continue, Gervase? Good, because we have not finished with this tale just yet.

Sherwood
Summer, the Year of Our Lord 1192

Back at the castle Guy had made a point of seeking out Brother Oswald, and had set to with him to record the whole sorry mess. Man after man was brought to the scribes' room to bear witness to the fact that they had been assaulted by a formidable force of experienced soldiers, each swearing with his hand upon the Bible that he was telling the truth before the castle priest. So by the time it dawned on de Wendenal that he should put something to the official record, he was too late to twist things to cover his ineptitude. Moreover, Guy had been very careful in his choice of words as he had dictated them to Oswald. Time and again he chose a phrase or sentence which, to the unassuming men coming to add their marks to the parchment beside where the clerk had written their names, sounded like the truth. Yet when read out in other circumstances, they could also sound very much as though the sheriff had bumbled the whole thing from start to finish.

For instance, 'Sir William took no foresters with him but the four of the Keeper's for that keepership,' would sound reckless when read in the safety of London or Winchester. No-one but one of their own would understand that having Sir Walkelin or Sir Mahel with him would not have helped de Wendenal one jot in tracking the thieves. But taking only men-at-arms, who could only be expected to follow orders, sounded as though de Wendenal had tried to fight some kind of pitched battle in amongst the trees, in a place which any soldier worth his pay would have avoided like the plague. By the time Guy had finished with him, de Wendenal's account to be sent with the rest of the sheriff's records was going to condemn him at every turn. And to crown it all, the sheriff had taken men traipsing through the forest right at the end of Fence Month, just when the deer were supposed to be left in peace for the all-important fawning; for St Cyril's Day – when the forest became open to all and sundry once more – had still been a week away on that fateful day. A legal nicety maybe, but one which Guy felt sure the king's head forester would be quick to grasp and not let go.

Yet there was one unexpected victim whom Guy could never have anticipated. When the news came of Ralph of Woodborough's death, the sheriff wanted to waste no time in getting a new verderer appointed. The next round of woodmotes was less than a couple of weeks away, and with the courts already over-stretched, having one less verderer to sit in one was little short of disastrous. Ralph fitz Stephen had agreed grudgingly to come from Laxton once more to Calverton to give the new verderer guidance, as long as Guy was there to ease his pain, but the question was who that man should be? Messages to and from Laxton Castle resulted in it being confirmed that the late Sir Ralph had had a cousin who might be prevailed upon to take up the role, but to do that he would have to have the verderer's house, since he lived in Leicestershire and could hardly fulfil his role from there.

"No doubt he'll grab the offer with both hands," Ralph Murdac sighed as he broke the news to the forest knights.

"You don't sound overly pleased," Sir Walter ventured, and Murdac shook his head.

"I've met Griffin Presbiter, and he's another such as de Wendenal – all brute force and ignorance! And with a massive chip on his shoulder because he comes from the cadet branch of the family, and therefore is no-one in particular. I know we're in dire need of another verderer, but I could wish most devoutly that this wasn't the man fitz Stephen has come up with."

"You think he'll be trouble?" Guy asked, and was worried at the speed with which Murdac nodded. "Because he'll want to be proving he's as good as his cousin was?"

Murdac sighed heavily. "At first, yes. I think he'll be heavy-handed to prove that he's the man for the job. That he'll milk the forest for every fine imaginable, and think that filling the king's coffers is the way to rise further. But once he knows he's secure in his job, I have a dreadful feeling that he'll continue as he started, because it's also in his nature to be such a man."

"Well he's not exactly starting out the right way, and he's not here yet!" Sir Martin hurried up to them saying. "We've just heard, he's said yes, and he wants his cousin's widow and her children out of the manor house by the time he arrives."

Everyone looked shocked.

"Does he have a wife and so many children of his own?" Sir Walter wondered aloud.

Sir Martin shook his head. "Apparently it's just him and his old mother, and a couple of household servants. No word of any wife."

"How old is he?" Guy asked Murdac. "Surely a man of his age would be married if he had a place of his own? Or is he like me – too far away from his actual house to have a family?"

That earned him a strange look from Murdac, as if this was the first time he had seen what Guy's life was like. Murdac could ride over to his manor and visit his wife and the rest of his family, but clearly

Guy's distance from his humble manor had not been thought of in those terms before.

"No Guy, he's not like you. Sadly there have been two wives, and both died within a couple of years of their marriage. Of what, I don't know, but he does seem to have been unusually unlucky in that respect."

"Or unusually brutal," Sir Martin added softly, hurriedly clarifying by saying, "Not that I'm accusing him of outright murder! But if he's too free with his fists, a woman with-child could end up not surviving the birth for reasons other than the normal perils of the childbed."

Murdac inhaled sharply. "Blessed Virgin have mercy!"

"I think we might be calling on her to watch over Sir Ralph's family," Guy said bitterly, "But where will they go? Where can they go? Do they have other family who might take them in?"

"Find out!" Murdac declared. "No, better than that, you go and see them, Guy. I know I can trust you to be sensible about this. We can't let them stay. Not with the sheriff in his current mood. The bastard would be as likely to throw them all in the town gaol – or worse, into the dungeon here, if he feared them coming under the scrutiny of another sheriff at the gaol when the eyre comes. He'll keep this brute of a man on his side, I have no doubt about that. But if we have to evict this poor woman, then I want it done by someone with some tact and conscience. For pity's sake, Guy, go and sort this mess out!"

It was a grim task, but Guy knew what Murdac was hinting at – this was a forest matter, and of the other forest knights there were many who would simply turn this unfortunate soul out on the road and never think twice. And he was quietly glad to have a reason to be away from the castle for a few nights. He had done as much as he could with Brother Oswine, and now he had to find out if his plan would succeed. Would de Wendenal ask for all the statements to be read back to him? Guy thought not, but if he did, then de Wendenal might just have the wit to scrap some of them. A clever man might ask for a section to be cut out of the parchment, so that it would look as though two smaller pieces had been used. There was nothing odd about the records being on different sizes and different shapes of parchment – after all, sheep did not come in one size just to provide skin to write on!

Also, Guy wanted to leave Oswine alone with the sheriff. He was pretty certain that Oswine was sharp enough to have picked up on the ambiguity of some of Guy's phrases. If he then told the sheriff, then that would mean that he was of no use to Guy for further distractions and deceit. This time Guy had not actually done anything wrong, and he knew he could avoid trouble by simply playing the innocent, so it was the ideal time to test Oswine's resolve.

Therefore he rode out and turned his mare northwards once more, glad to be out of the oppressive atmosphere of the castle, for he had been struggling to keep his feelings hidden these last few days. There was more than just the widow to worry about, and he was hoping that he might just be able to ride on and see if he could find the others, for he had grim news. The entire band had now been officially outlawed! As of the second day they had been back at Nottingham, de Wendenal had issued the proclamation and had it sent out to the whole two shires – anyone found aiding and abetting this bunch of marauding Welsh fugitives would be bringing the full weight of the law down upon them. And as for their leader, this elusive Robin Hood, the reward on his head had gone up to ten shillings.

That was a huge temptation, Guy knew. In a world where the rent on a simple cottage was two or three shillings a year, that would set a family up nicely. And for a more well-off man, such as a guildsman, that would buy a new tunic and cloak befitting his station made of good quality wool. Even a craftsman could set his son or other apprentice up with a whole new set of tools for that sum, which meant that now the reward for Robin would tempt men from all classes. Suddenly the rules by which Guy's friends had to live by had changed, and he desperately wanted to let them know that.

He was so absorbed in his thoughts that he was completely taken by surprised by Allan and Roger dropping out of the boughs of one of the great oaks, right into his path. But much as he was relieved at hear that Robin was allowing Tuck to try to heal his inner pain, his lack of enthusiasm was soon picked up on by the perceptive pair, and once he had told his news, they too were worried.

"We're going to have to be very careful with which villages we approach, aren't we?" Allan said glumly. "It's really going to have to be just the ones we know beyond doubt that we can trust."

"I'm afraid so," Guy sympathised. "In fact, I was thinking that for the next outing of Robin Hood's gang, you might want to be thinking of aiming for milled grain and the like, rather than money. For once taking actually what you need to survive."

Roger was nodding thoughtfully. "I fink you're right, Guy. We needs stuff to tide us over. That bleedin' sheriff will soon over-step the mark and do sommat horrible. Then folks'll start rememberin' who's on their side, and it won't matter what reward the sheriff puts up, 'cos they won't believe for a moment that he'll actually give it to 'em. But we has to give 'em time to get over the shock of how much it is now."

Guy smiled for the first time since meeting the two. "Very perceptive, Roger! That's exactly it! And if you two can see it, then hopefully others like Siward and Hugh will too, and between you you can convince Robin. God knows, there are enough corrupt millers about who skim ground-up flour off their customers for their own purposes, and whom you could relieve of several sacks without causing any but them grief. Do you think you can steer Robin's need for action that way?"

Allan was already smiling reassuringly. "Don't worry, Guy, I'm sure we can. In fact, I think everyone else will jump on the idea with enthusiasm just for the fact that it gives us a way of keeping Robin active and feeling he's doing something without risking life and limb for once."

Guy didn't like that 'for once' one little bit. How many other times had Robin led the rest of them into danger? He resolved to try and ask someone slightly less caught between two cousins than Allan in the near future, but felt it would be grossly unfair to expect Allan to keep divulging all of Robin's secrets every time they met. He wanted Allan to keep coming to see him, but that meant not putting him under the same kind of pressure to be loyal as Robin did – and Guy was sure there had been more of that than Allan had let on, even if it did not yank his feelings around as much as it did John's.

Yet they were now coming into the fields around Woodborough, and ahead Guy could see the trim little manor which belonged to the verderer. It was bigger than his Gisborne manor, but then that wouldn't be hard – Guy's house just about qualified as the smallest kind of manor house, and was barely larger than the average farm house. This one had a modest undercroft made of stone, above which was a neat dwelling which Guy guessed would have a hall running a little over a half of its length at the one end, and a couple of private chambers at the other, divided from the hall by a corridor made of simple wooden screens. To the side of the house was a small building from which smoke rose up out of a substantial chimney, proclaiming this to be the kitchen. No-one in their right mind would put a kitchen beneath the living space for fear of fire, and so it was only in the old longhouse style of manor like Guy's where the kitchen was part of the manor house itself. Yet this was a goodly sized kitchen for the size of such a manor, making Guy think that Sir Ralph, or whichever forebear of his had done the building, had enjoyed entertaining his fellow worthies of this part of the shire.

"Shall we wait for you?" Allan asked.

Guy smiled. "You can come with me, if you can bear to. This isn't the happiest of visits. But because of that it would be nice to have someone to talk to later on."

"We'll be your men, then," Allan said with relish. "It'll probably lend some credence to anyone watching that you've come to chuck them out, anyway. One man to do the job seems not quite right. If this new monster asks around he won't want to hear you've been kind to this family."

"You have a point," Guy sighed. "Very well, come on."

He dismounted at the gateway to the small open space around the house and handed Allan the reins. Before he could climb the stone steps to the main door, an enormous woman came bustling out of the kitchen with a wooden mallet in her hands.

"Who are you to disturb my lady's grief?" she demanded belligerently.

"I'm Sir Guy of Gisborne, come on the sheriff's business, and with more bad news, I'm afraid," Guy told her with such sadness in his voice that it seemed to take the wind out of her sails.

"It's happening, then?" she demanded. "She's being turfed out?"

"I'm so sorry, but yes. And this time it's not the sheriff's decision. It's the cousin of her husband's who's coming to take over as verderer, Griffin Presbiter."

The woman spat into the dirt and made a sign to ward off evil, crossing herself as a last precaution. "That evil little rat's turd? By Our Lady, I hope his balls shrivel to walnuts and rot in the wrinkles!"

All three men blanched at the thought and at the venom in the cook's voice.

"You know him?" Guy ventured.

The cook glared. "Wish I bloody didn't! He comes here scrounging a meal for him and that old crone of a mother of his every Christmas. Puts a blight on the festival for everyone else! Why on earth Sir Ralph never turned him away I do not know." Then she realised just who she was talking to and her face darkened again. "Are you trying to trip me up? Spying on us for him, are you?"

"Not at all," Guy hurriedly assured her. "Sadly the sheriff needs a new verderer in place as soon as possible, because the courts are due. Presbiter could have stayed at the castle for this first one. It's not like there isn't room! Our constable, Sir Ralph Murdac thought it harsh that your lady should be thrown out so fast after the news of her husband's death, and he was the one who sent me. He wanted it done with the least cruelty. Do you know if she has anywhere to go to? I can provide an escort to ensure she gets there safely."

Instead the cook sniffed resignedly. "You'd best come in and see for yourself."

She led the way up the steps and into the hall. The place lay cold and unused, fresh rushes scattered on the floor ready for when needed and logs in the fire basket, but no sign of life. However, beyond in the private chambers, there came the sound of children, and Guy immediately looked worriedly back at Allan and Roger, because they sounded like very young children.

"Milady, there's a knight from the sheriff," the cook announced, her bulk blocking the doorway and all beyond it to Guy's view.

"He'd best come in then," a frail voice answered, and the cook shuffled sideways to allow Guy through.

What he saw made his heart sink into his boots. The poor woman was heavily pregnant, and there were two little girls of about three and five playing with rag toys on a mat in front of a small fire.

"Madam, I am so sorry for this intrusion," Guy said gently, trying his best to seem non-threatening as he came forwards and went down on one knee, so that he could look her in the face without looming over where she sat. "No, please don't try to get up!"

Already the tears were welling up in her eyes as she said, "Do we have to go?"

"I'm sorry, but yes." Then he saw her wince as the baby must have given her a kick. "How long do you have to go before your baby is due?"

"Six weeks, if all goes well."

There was another snort from the cook behind Guy. "Except it hasn't been, has it, milady? You've not been well all the way through this pregnancy!"

"Martha!" the lady remonstrated, casting urgent glances towards the children, who had stopped their play and were now watching the adults with wide-eyed worry.

Luckily Allan and Roger stepped in.

"Would you like to see some juggling?" Allan asked. "Why don't you come into the hall with me and my friend Roger, and we'll show you some tricks. Would you like that?"

He scooped up the younger, and Roger came and took the older girl by the hand, pulling such a ridiculous face that she giggled and went with him, her fear temporarily forgotten. For a moment the two women looked almost panic-stricken, but then when they heard the voices in the hall beyond and realised that this was not an excuse to spirit the children away, they relaxed a fraction.

Guy took the lady's hand. "What's your name? I only know of you as Sir Ralph's wife, not even your family name. He was always Ralph of Woodborough, or Ralph the Verderer, to me."

"I'm Annora, daughter of William fitz Waland. My father still lives up in Steeton village, not far from York." She looked down, and Guy saw the tears starting to fall. "Although whether he'll want me back is another matter. I'm the youngest of three daughters. Once upon a time our family were thegns under King Edward, but now there's nothing much left but a farm and the title. Ralph wanted a wife with some pretensions of nobility and who could bear him sons. His first wife died during her first pregnancy, you see. She brought him a good dowry, so he could afford to take me with my poor pittance, but he wanted a girl from a family who produced children. My older two sisters both have several children already, you see."

"Passed on like a bloody milch cow!" Guy heard Martha grumble softly. "She deserved better!"

"Have you been with your mistress long?" Guy asked standing and turning to her.

"Long enough to know that a sweet soul like her was mismatched to a man like the master!" Martha retorted, clearly expecting Guy to pick a fight with her over her interference.

"So do you want to serve this new master, or would you be prepared to come with your mistress when we take her?" Guy asked civilly instead.

Martha's shocked silence gave him time to turn back to Annora. "Look, it's obvious that you won't be able to travel far, but we can try and get you somewhere safe just for now. Saints be praised that it's summertime and warm! I've no idea what I'd do with you if it was winter!" He turned to Martha. "Can you pack what she and the children will be able to take with them? Don't worry about the weight, we'll use the horse."

Turning on his heels he strode into the hall. "Allan, Roger, can you run as fast as you can and bring Marianne and Mariota to the camp east of here? I think we're going to need their expertise!"

The two instantly grasped why and set off immediately.

"I'm sending for two women who used to be sisters with the Hospitallers in Jerusalem," he told the two women. "They worked tending to women pilgrims, and what they don't know about helping a woman through a birth isn't worth knowing. Now can we start getting ready to move? We won't go tonight, but tomorrow morning I'm afraid we must. I'm taking you to a secret place of safety, but if we're to go at a pace you can manage, milady, then it has to be then."

Yet once he had managed to calm Annora and get Martha set to packing, he went outside and found Roger seated on the bottom step.

"Allan took your horse. I hope you don't mind. But he said he was worried and we should get Marianne and Mariota here as fast as possible. He's taken your forester's lanyard and hood too, just in case someone sees him and starts wondering why he's on such a horse."

Guy sank down beside him, enjoying the warmth of the sun-baked stones and the sense of relief. "No, I'm not cross. I'm bloody glad he thought of it! He can push the horse as hard as he likes, because he'll have to walk her back anyway if he's got the others with him. Please God he'll get to them tonight or early tomorrow."

"You takin' 'em to the camp by Thurgaton?"

"Where else can I take them? That bit of high ground is dry and the woods are thick. And if the worst comes to the worst and the camp is discovered, then at least it was only a place you used occasionally. There must be others you could use. It's not like Loxley."

"I don't like the look of her." Guy turned to Roger in surprise, but then realised what he meant as the smaller man went on, "I ain't no expert on kids and fings, but she looks proper poorly to me. And I reckon it ain't just the news her old man's dead, either."

"Martha, the cook, said she's had a bad confinement."

Roger looked at him sideways. "I don't fink you gets your nose broke by havin' kids."

Guy gulped, then realised that what marred an otherwise pretty face was the slight twist to the nose and its slightly lumpy bone. "Christ on the Cross! So Griffin isn't the only self-made bastard in the family!" He clasped Roger's shoulder in solidarity. "Then thank God you and Allan thought to get our friends as fast as you did! I could probably help with a straightforward birth – heaven knows I've done my share with animals – but if she's been on the end of a beating or two then we really need a woman who knows what to do."

From above Martha's voice said, "You're a funny sort of knight." The big woman stood staring down at them from the top step with a puzzled expression. "Most care nothing for the women around them."

Guy twisted round so that he could speak more easily. "I was born on a small manor, my father a knight tied in service to the man who owned it, who was also my uncle. My own father died when I was still a lad, but it was my mother who ran the manor house and did all that the lady of the house ought to have done. Her sister never managed to get to grips with it all. And because my mother wasn't his wife, and he depended on her to keep things running for him, my uncle treated her more respectfully than he might have. So I grew up in a world where the men were away a lot and the women were the strong ones. I suppose it makes a difference."

"Local lad, are you?" Martha asked boldly.

Now Guy had no trouble smiling. "The other side of the Trent, by the River Smite close by the Leicester border. God knows who's got the manor now. My uncle died and we all had to take service where we could. One of King Henry's sales of a manor to the highest bidder, you see. So I know what it's like to suddenly lose your home and know you can't ever go back."

Realising that Guy was not so very highly born seemed to win Martha over, and she came bustling past them saying, "Well since you're helping us, I'd better feed you, then, hadn't I?"

In the morning, Guy shouldered a heavy pack and Roger another and they left the manor behind them. Guy had the smallest child sitting on top of his pack, and Roger held the other's hand, while Martha carried what little she had of her own and had an arm around Annora. As they turned onto the unpaved street running through the village, people came to the doors of their humble houses to watch, and Guy could see the pity in their eyes.

"Where you takin' her?" a burly farmhand called out.

"Somewhere safer than she'll be here," Guy called back, doing his best to sound calm.

There were some ugly murmurings going on by the time they were halfway down the street, and for an awful moment Guy thought he might get mobbed by the locals. Yet it was the way Martha time and again shook her head when a man started to come forwards which seemed to save them. Whatever the locals thought, they clearly trusted Martha to do right by her mistress.

Then to Guy's dismay, Annora had to stop and sit for a moment at a stile just beyond the village. This was going to be a very slow walk, and more than ever he was glad he wasn't going to have to take her far – if they even made it there! Annora was not faking her need to rest, and they had only come a matter of a couple of hundred yards. What surprised him more was hearing the steady clip-clop of hooves and to then see one of the men from the village leading the horse with a simple peasant's two-wheeled cart behind it. And with it came four sturdy looking women.

"Her can't walk," a grey-haired matron declared, as if daring Guy to argue.

"Come on, into the cart with you," another older woman said firmly, and with another, helped Annora to her feet.

Guy couldn't argue.

"Now, where you takin' her?" the man demanded.

"First off, to Epperstone," Guy told him, desperately wondering how he was going to get Annora to the camp at this rate.

"He's got someone coming to meet us," Martha intervened. "Two Hospitaller sisters, he said."

That roused everyone's interest, and Guy felt forced to attempt an explanation. "I may know nothing about childbirth, but even I can see she's going to need someone who can help beyond what the local midwife can do. These two women have served in a proper hospital in Jerusalem. If anyone can help her, it's them."

"But why would they help?" the older woman demanded. Clearly she was the spokeswoman for them all and a force to be reckoned with.

For a moment Guy panicked, but before he could think of anything to say, Roger piped up with,

"Because they're with Robin Hood," and Guy felt his heart sink into his boots, for now the cat was truly out of the bag.

Yes, Brother, for an awful instant I thought we would be dragged back to the village and handed over to the sheriff for being the ones who had brought this sorry mess down upon the village. However what will please you is that I was totally unprepared for the expressions of delight which I then saw. The name of Robin Hood worked like a charm, and you must

not chastise me for doubting, because up until then I had never seen it for myself. You must have a little charity and allow that, bound as I was to the sheriff's castle for so much of the time, and with such a pair of sheriffs as I had served under recently, that I had not seen how the word had spread.

Now, seeing the way the villagers went from suspicious of me and in no small measure hostile, to wanting to do all they could to help me, was both thrilling and disturbing.

˜Have you ever seen him?˜ I asked as calmly as I could, and was stunned to see the nodding heads.

˜Up there on the ridge˜ the man told me, barely able to restrain his awe and excitement, and pointing to the small rise between the village and the villages of Arnold and Carlton. Compared to the ridges I had seen in my time on the Welsh border it was barely a hillock, but to the locals who had lived all their lives in the flat Trent valley it was proper high ground. ˜After the raid on the hall in Calverton we all saw him. Him and that giant who goes with him, although Robin Hood is no small man. He had his great bow with him, and we saw him aim into the village, and then a purse with all we had paid out came with that arrow. God bless him, we all said, and meant it.˜ And I sighed for it meant my fears of Robin taking risks to be <u>seen</u> to be the villagers' saviour were confirmed.

For a monk and a man of God you take inordinate pleasure in hearing of a man outside the law, Brother. Yes, Robin had done his characteristic display of generosity again, but I was more surprised to hear that a great cheer had gone up from the villagers. It was my first personal experience of just how loved he already was by the ordinary people, and for the first time I felt I might get this poor family to safety.

And I have to give Roger credit for having read the villagers better than me, for he then revealed that we were taking Lady Annora to one of Robin's camps and the need for secrecy. I think I near fainted on the spot at that, but far from my expected reaction of every man and his dog wanting to come and see this fabled place, suddenly two of the women said that in that case they would stay behind, and the other two and the man said that they would come with us as far as Epperstone. I then had to confess that we would not be going as far as Thurgarton, and that we would be able to return the cart to them in a matter of an hour or so. I had no need to swear them to secrecy either. They understood without being told that if they did not know where this place was, then they could not reveal it under torture.

Truly, Brother, I was humbled by their courage. I, more than many men, knew what their fate would be if the sheriff ever found out the extent of their support for this outlaw he had set such a price on. And to my surprise I realised that while Robin continued to hand these people their rents and fines back, that reward money would not look so tempting. In that respect, my act of kindness came back to me in the comfort of peace of mind.

And did Robin help the Lady Annora? Well not him personally, but Marianne and Mariota came with an escort of Will, Hugh, Siward and the Coshams, and a goodly supply of medicines created from herbs plundered from Welbeck's plentiful gardens. I had to leave them to it, for there was only so long I could be away from the castle for, and Will had a quiet word and said that as Robin was calming down just at the moment, it might be politic if I did not appear just at the moment. I could not take offense, Gervase, because I could see how hard he was taking his own rejection by Robin, and in truth I felt for Will. He had been through as near as this earth could produce to the fires of Hell, through war and death and darkness, and surely that should have been enough to bind a friend to him? Not to be thought faithless and untrustworthy. It cut Will to the core, and although Robin apologised later, I know that their friendship never fully recovered to how it had been when we were all at High Peak together.

However, you should know another codicil to this story, for it established Marianne and Mariota as valid members of the outlaw gang. Not only was Robin much gratified to hear of how they had saved Annora's life when they returned – for I was told that she would undoubtedly have died had they not been at her side when she gave birth – but he could now see that not everyone they helped could be aided by men alone. The two of them had come to a decision that Annora would be better giving birth sooner than her allotted time, and did something of which I am ignorant to have her produce her child while at the camp. Then with the men's help they took her north to her family in a borrowed cart. But to the villagers of Woodborough and Epperstone another link in the legend had been forged – that Robin Hood had a lady and that her name was Marion!

No, Brother, do not frown so. You do not understand the simple faith the people have in Our Lord's mother. When the high and most glorious saints could seem far above them and remote, a simple carpenter's wife was someone they thought of as one of their own, someone who would understand their humble problems. And clearly Marianne's name must have cropped up in conversations between the men when they had gone for food and to borrow the cart for Annora's journey, and so the link was made in folks' minds of a lady here on earth doing the divine Lady's work, who also shared her name. It was not blasphemy. No-one worshipped our two ministering sisters. They simply saw them as one of the earthly mysteries rather than the heavenly ones. And you have to allow that when Robin Hood is spoken of even now, the name of Marion is not far behind! So that is how it began, that there were fabled women with your hero too, therefore be satisfied and let me continue with our story.

Chapter 20

And now I shall come forward several months Brother, for Robin recovered well over the summer and autumn of 1192. I am sorry to relate that Lady Annora's fate was not a kind one, for she was soon married off again, and what became of her and her three little girls I do not know. No, Brother, I did not hear of the fate of everyone whom Robin Hood helped, and neither did he to his discomfort – like you, my cousin did so love a happy ending!

I heard of raids on a couple of mills, and they were strangely discounted because those same millers had been foolish enough to cover their skimming off of sacks of flour onto petty thefts before, and so they had cried wolf once too often and were dismissed. Therefore there was nothing new in their respect to inflame our volatile sheriff, and we managed to get through the next few months in relative peace. I say relative peace, for de Wendenal moaned on and on every night about what had happened to him, until every last person was so sick of hearing about it that had anyone such as the chief royal forester, or one of the chancellor's men, come to question them about it, they now would have dismissed it as something of nothing – and oh how I relished that, I can tell you! To have de Wendenal ridiculed a second time was something more than I could have dreamed of, although it turned out that I had done rather too good a job in the first place, and he was dealt with at Court without any need for anyone else to come to Nottingham to investigate the matter.

Therefore, my ploy to discredit de Wendenal bore fruit at the Michaelmas court. He set off with the rents and fines for his master, Count John, who was going to be at that court, and arrived back with us in late October with his tail between his legs and portentous news.

Nottinghamshire
October/November, the Year of Our Lord 1192

"King Richard has made peace with the Saracens! The bloody king is coming home!" de Wendenal announced as he thundered through the great hall at Nottingham. "God's hooks! Could he not have done the decent thing and died out there?"

"Welcome back, my lord sheriff," Ralph Murdac said dryly, as the rest of the company did their best to stifle groans that de Wendenal had not taken his own advice and expired in London. It had been blissfully peaceful during the month he had been gone. Time in which the castle had gone back to running like a well-kept mill – forest courts had been held on time, rents had been collected, and Guy had prayed nightly that his ambiguous records had done the trick and de Wendenal would be gone for good.

"Do you know what happened?" the sheriff demanded instead, ignoring Murdac's welcome. "That thrice-be-damned head forester of the king's, fitz Peter, had the God-Almighty nerve to accuse me of incompetence! Me, incompetent! And all because of that cursed fiasco with that by-Our-Lady-cursed Robin Hood!" De Wendenal glared at the assembled knights and other unfortunates who happened to be there when he rode in. "So we are going to find this Robin Hood and I am going to deliver his head to fitz Peter on the brightest, shiniest silver platter I can lay my hands on! Is ...that ...clear?" he roared, every vein in his neck standing out, and some on his forehead throbbing too.

Guy wanted to scream. So a bawling out by the most senior forester in the land had done nothing to bring de Wendenal down at all. Another man might have been severely chastened. Another man might not have mentioned it even if it had happened, and Guy would have had to work out just how bad that encounter had been. But not de Wendenal, he was just too dim-witted to know when he was beaten. There were a couple of dogs whom Guy had seen in the bear-baiting at the fair like that. Great brutes who lacked a glimmer of the intelligence of Guy's much-missed hunting dogs, and who only lived to inflict pain on others. And that was what de Wendenal was – a human version of those dogs who were only good for coarse fighting, and whom none would miss when they were gone.

As it was, several folk could not contain their groans of dismay at the thought of another expedition led by de Wendenal – not because they feared its outcome so much as it would now provide fuel for yet more dreary evenings listening to him pound on about it while in his cups. And that was something Guy had definitely picked up on. The resounding humiliation had clearly cut de Wendenal deeper than it had seemed at the time, for the sheriff was drinking more and more heavily of an evening, to the extent that it was now rare to see him appear before midday, and then like a bear with a sore head – which he undoubtedly had!

Therefore his absence had been a blessed relief to almost everyone, and to a man they were all doing their best to hide their dismay as de Wendenal bawled to the room in general,

"I want him found! I want you useless bunch of whore-sons to turn every stone and blade of grass for this whelp of a tinker's bitch. I want to know where he haunts, where his hideout is. The poxy bastard must be holing up somewhere, and I want to know where that is!"

"But he might already have left the shire," Sir Fredegis objected, clearly not fancying the prospect of what he saw as a wild goose chase. "You said there were Welsh with him. That sort don't like the English, so why would they stay?"

That Fredegis himself also did not much like the English was well known, and neither did his fellow knight from the Lowlands, Sir Walkelin, who was murmuring his agreement even before Fredegis had finished speaking. The two of them normally enjoyed favour from this sheriff, given that they were as brutal as he was, but it was a measure of de Wendenal's anger that their habit of speaking their minds now brought his wrath down upon them.

"Fools! Imbeciles!" he ranted, grabbing a lighted taper and hurling it at them and missing wildly, but causing several people to begin a frantic stamping on the rushes it landed on, to make sure they did not all go up in flames. Yet oblivious to all of that, de Wendenal was ranting, "Back to Wales? Back to sheep-shagging, arse-end-of-the-known-world, Wales? Why would they go back *there* when they can plunder one of the richest shires in England, eh? Eh? Tell me that!"

The two were already backing off, horribly aware that their leader and protector was not going to be reasoned with this time, and Guy knew it wasn't the time to point out to the sheriff that while Wales might not have the wealth in terms of grain and sheep that Nottinghamshire did, the chance to live a life free of the heavy taxation of England – let alone the added burden of living within a shire which was three-quarters under forest law – might be a heavy incentive for anyone to leave.

Ever since King Henry had levied the Saladin Tithe five years ago, wheat prices had been steadily rising, and if the peasant farmers were getting more for their wheat at market, it was also crippling them to buy the seeds they needed to sow again for the next year. And few could afford to keep back much even to feed their own families. Guy knew that more and more was being sold abroad to those who could afford the higher price for good English wheat, and that the peasants he saw were planting ever more crops of the mixed seeds for their own use – barley and rye prices having risen by substantially less.

No, de Wendenal was wrong about that, there was plenty of incentive for men to leave England for Wales or elsewhere, and even bombastic fools like Fredegis and Walkelin knew it. So he silently rejoiced that de Wendenal had just robbed himself of two of his staunchest allies within the castle. Maybe another hunt for Robin Hood would be done with little enthusiasm, even by the most belligerent of the forest knights?

For now everyone fled the main hall, glad to be leaving de Wendenal on his own with his wine, which he was already calling for.

"Rather worrying, de Wendenal's response to the king coming home, don't you think?" Sir Martin said softly to Guy, as he joined Martin and Sir Walter on the way across the inner ward of the oldest part of the castle.

"I wondered if I was the only one who noticed that," Guy admitted. "Yes, it sounds very much as though he's worried that the king might discover he's been a bit too much in Count John's favour, doesn't it?"

"Please God we don't end up caught like we were when Alan died," Walter said fervently. "One of us dying like that was one too many. By St Thomas, who'd have thought doing your duty could end up being so dangerous!"

"And it sounds like the king might even be home for Christmas," Guy added.

Sir Martin was aghast. "So soon? I mean, not that I won't be glad to have a king back here again, but for those who've backed Count John..." he didn't need to say more.

Guy shrugged. "Well if a messenger has already arrived, and he set out just ahead of the king, even allowing for King Richard to linger for a week or two in Cyprus, or for bad weather on the sea crossings, it's perfectly possible." He didn't want to add that he knew rather more of the time it took to come home from the Holy Land than anyone here knew about.

Sir Walter puffed his cheeks out and looked to them with dismay, "Lord! No wonder de Wendenal is suddenly all keen to make it seem as though he's the best sheriff we've had in a while. He must be remembering Sir Ralph's fate as sheriff at the hands of King Richard and wondering if it'll be his turn next!"

Guy left them to their commiserating and took himself off to his shared room, and then finding Sir Osmaer already there, and young Piers there grumbling to him whilst perched on Guy's box-bed, retreated to the stables. He needed to think and think fast. Where could he direct de Wendenal towards if necessary? Would he even be able to do that? There were only so many times that he could be seen to be the one taking the lead in the hunt for Robin Hood, and then failing spectacularly, before someone started wondering how he seemed to know so much.

In the end he retreated to the castle walls and up onto the battlements of the oldest keep of the castle. He still had the clasp hidden up there which de Wendenal had stolen whilst still just one of the forest knights, and just now he wanted to make sure that it was still safe. With Ralph Murdac back at the castle for the foreseeable future, it meant that there was someone who would remember what had happened if it became necessary to blacken the sheriff's name. But how that would help just at the moment Guy couldn't decide, and so he would keep it safe and plot behind the sheriff's back.

And could he risk warning Robin? How far would he have to ride to reach them? It was only a week until the tenth of the month and the last swanimote courts of the year, when all animals had to be clear of the forest right through until St Felix and St George's Day. Would Robin show up at one of those? This time it could be bloody dangerous if he did – especially if de Wendenal thought to lay a trap at one of them! Moreover, he couldn't begin to predict which one of the four courts Robin might attack, or whether he was likely to be attending it at the time. Please God he wouldn't have to fake fighting his friends again so soon!

Then with the evening meal came a pronouncement from de Wendenal.

"I want you all out scouring the forest!" he declared, his anger directed at his foresters for want of anyone else. "Make sure that not one chicken or pig is in there by the time the Feast of St Martin comes round!" referring to the Feast of St Martin of Tours, which fell on the eleventh of November, and which was the date when the forest was officially now out of bounds to all but the foresters and those licensed to hunt. "And while you are at it, you shambolic, incompetent excuses for foresters can find me this thrice-be-damned outlaw!"

Guy saw instantly that the sheriff had alienated every one of the knights. There were hardly any left now of those who had come to do their service at the castle over the summer, which was a small blessing, but the two who were there were looking to the three castle knights in poorly disguised surprise. It simply wasn't done to berate men of quality like that in public, although it would have sat better if de Wendenal had been of a significantly higher station himself. But the man was of no better origin than many of the same men he was haranguing, and already men like Sir Mahel were visibly bristling – Mahel and Sir Humphrey having every reason to be outraged given that they both came from very good families, even if they were the third and fourth sons, and therefore likely to get nothing in the way of bequests.

The three knights who would remain at Nottingham were also getting sympathetic glances from the forest knights. If they themselves were on the end of de Wendenal's temper, at least they were going to escape soon. Sirs Hugh, Robert and Richard would be stuck here at the castle with no-one to deflect the sheriff's temper except Ralph Murdac, especially at times like these when the household assembled to eat. Guy caught Richard of Burscot's eye and rolled his own despairingly, then saw Richard return a minute cringe of acknowledgement of their shared suffering.

Not since fitz John's day had the castle emptied so swiftly when the morning arrived, and Guy along with all the others escaped with relief. Of the eight knights who rode for the Derwent-to-Erewash part of Sherwood, the more war-loving Henry, Fredegis and Walkelin had already claimed the ride to the north of the forest along with Sir Humphrey, for once on their side even if he didn't like them much. Guy let them go, knowing that they might well take refuge at Bolsover Castle for at least one of the nights, and also that for Henry, the wounding he had taken from Robin Hood would ensure that he would scour that section of forest with truculent zeal. That was something Guy had no desire to witness.

He also let Osmaer and Thorsten claim the narrow middle section. He could understand why they would want to – they both needed to improve their lot in life, and the dense forest up where Guy had witnessed the debacle around Codnor and Smithycote had every appearance of being a good place to hide out in. That the outlaws only had two temporary camps up there, was information he was keeping firmly to himself. And so he rode out with the timid Sir Payne, and headed west and a little south. They would cover the southern tip where the two shires came down to the confluence of the Trent and the Derwent, which was mostly farmland caught up in the forest laws, and with little in the way of the kind of cover needed for a whole gang to be living unseen.

"Do you think they'll catch him?" Payne asked Guy wistfully.

His tone made Guy look at him in surprise. Was Payne a secret admirer of Robin Hood? Carefully choosing his words, Guy replied, "Well if venom and ire were all it took, I think you could guarantee that those four heading north wouldn't come back empty-handed."

"Oh." That sounded distinctly despondent!

"Not that they stand a cat in hell's chance of catching them in reality."

"Oh!" Definitely happier! Then hurriedly asking to cover his slip, "Why do you think that, then, Guy?"

Guy allowed himself a chuckle. "Well for a start off those four couldn't track a bullock through a snowdrift!"

"Oh! ...Get your point. I see..."

"And when we were tracking them in the heart of the forest it was taking me all my time to find signs. These aren't some peasants blundering around in the woods, Payne, they're clever soldiers and they know what they're doing. They knew enough to split us up in that last ambush! And if they still have most of the same men with them, they'll have at least a dozen of them. What are our four going to do out-numbered like that, even if they all happen to be together at the time?"

Payne definitely brightened at that thought, and Guy had to smother a smile, then thought to risk another comment, just to make sure where Payne's sympathies lay.

"He impressive, this Robin Hood, isn't he? The way he's taking the sheriff on. I'm sure I saw a crusader's badge amongst them, you know."

"Really?" Payne's eyes lit up like candles. "By Our Lady! A crusader, to boot!"

Guy couldn't resist mischievously adding, "And if that's so, he might find more favour with King Richard, if he ever comes here, than de Wendenal will."

Payne gave a wistful sigh. "Now that would be something I'd like to see. And if we could have Ralph Murdac back as sheriff, too, that would just be wonderful."

"Not much chance of that, I'm afraid," Guy sighed in sympathy as they came to the place where they would part company. They had just reached Trowell, and Payne was turning slightly north for Ilkeston to go up as far as Denby and then loop back round to return to Nottingham through Mapperley. It was his usual route and one which contained very little dense woodland at all, so that his job was relatively easy in making sure that the farm beasts were all contained within fields.

For once Guy was taking the very southern part of the shires which Sir Humphrey usually patrolled – his taking of this without argument earning him gratitude from Sir Walter, having been faced with Sir Humphrey's strident demand to be allowed to try his luck at besting outlaws elsewhere. It would ensure he was well away from anywhere the outlaws might be, and although Guy knew he was taking the coward's way out of this situation, he also knew that at some point Robin had to face the prospect of one of the sheriff's hunts without forewarning or collusion from someone on the inside.

On the other hand he was not looking forward to a night spent at the home of Roger de Buron. Horston Castle sat where the land rose up from a brook which drained into the Derwent a mile or so away, with the small hamlet of Coxbench cowering on the other side of the brook and the other de Buron holding of Horsley only half a mile away. And these were far from being Sir Roger's only holdings, as he was quick to let any guests know, for he was quite the grand Norman lord even if his family had been in England since the Conquest. Sir Humphrey welcomed these forays to grand homes which were close to his own, but Guy dreaded such close proximity with men of this kind for fear he would let slip his true feelings on how they treated their vassals. Yet there was nothing for it, Sir Roger would be expecting a visit this close to the swanimote, and so Guy would have to go.

As he approached the castle Guy was mentally bracing himself for the night to come, and noticed the way the local peasants ducked their heads and steadfastly refused to meet his eye. That said much for the way Sir Roger treated his underlings, but he was horrified to see a sturdy young man herding a small group of pigs turn white when he saw Guy.

"They'll be out of the forest on time, I swear, my lord," the man gabbled in total panic.

Guy reined-in his horse and looked down at the man. "You don't need to panic," he said in his most reasonable voice. "You've three more days until the swanimote. Surely you don't come from so far away that that's an impossible distance to cover in the time?"

The man gulped and shook his head, "Little Eaton, sire, just over a mile away."

Guy shrugged, "Then you've nothing to fear from me."

Yet the man still looked worried to death.

"Is there something else?" Guy asked, now genuinely curious.

"Little Eaton ain't in Sir Roger's demesne, but these woods is."

"Ah!" That explained a lot. "So how come you're here?"

"Mildred," the man said, gesturing to a huge sow who was clearly getting on in years. "I don't know why, but she surely loves the acorns from Sir Roger's woods, and her breaks down her pen to get to them. If her didn't give such grand piglets her'd have been on the butcher's block long since, but her gives twelve piglets every time, and they all lives to be good-sized pigs."

Guy laughed, which seemed to disconcert the man even more, forcing Guy to explain further. "Listen, I'm not the regular forester knight who comes this way. I know what sows are like! They're a bloody law unto themselves! So I don't give a tinker's cuss if she's here now, just as long as she's not still in the forest after St Martin's Day. Do you understand? And as for Sir Roger, I'm not much of his sort of knight, so I don't see any point in mentioning to him that I've seen you. He ought to be more reasonable. There's no marker or fence that a beast would recognise or honour between his bit of forest and the rest of it. Who owns the nearest bit, anyway?"

"My lord de Ferrers."

"The earl of Derby? Ah, no ...he's not earl even though his father died, is he? With the king being away he's got the estates but not the title as yet. ...But even so, de Ferrers is one of the great lords of

England." Guy laughed out loud. "Good grief, even Sir Roger ought to be thinking twice about antagonizing such a man – especially over a few pilfered acorns! Don't worry about your pigs. Go on, I've never seen you."

The man nearly fell over himself bowing and thanking Guy, but at least it made Guy feel a bit better about the coming visit. Yet when he got to the castle it was clear that more than just Sir Roger's household were there. Horses were tethered all around the castle, with men seeing to it that they were fed and watered.

"Who are you?" a rather well-armed soldier demanded as Guy rode up.

"Sir Guy of Gisborne, come on the sheriff's behalf to see to matters of the forest."

The soldier immediately relaxed somewhat. "Oh, well you've come at a rotten time. I doubt there'll be room for you at the castle. The lord's here."

"William de Ferrers?"

"Aye."

Guy tried not to look too askance. Talk about predicting what was to come! The very man he had been talking about with the peasant was here in person. Oh well, no point in hanging about, he should go and announce his presence before someone did it for him.

In the crammed hall, he managed to work his way through the lord's retinue up to where the two most important men sat at the top table.

"Who are you?" the man whom he assumed to be Sir Roger demanded before he even got to the board groaning with food.

Mentally sighing at the attitude of imperious lords, Guy repeated his credentials and was then surprised to find that the William de Ferrers was now scrutinizing him.

"Gisborne? That's not around here, is it?" de Ferrers demanded, fixing him with an intense stare.

"No, my lord, it's over in Lancashire – part of my lord of Chester's lands," Guy replied as politely as he could, at the same time noticing that de Ferrers was probably not much older than he was, whereas Sir Roger was a portly man of middle years.

"Good God, what are you doing serving the sheriff of Nottingham, then?"

"Doing what the king wanted me to do – King Henry, that is, not King Richard," Guy riposted, then hurriedly thought to soften his words by adding, "There was a delicate matter concerning Prince John a few years ago, in which I was able to be of some help. I was knighted by my lord Chester and was given a manor on his lands, but the king needed more men to patrol the extra lands which Sherwood now covers, so I was sent here as part of my lord Chester's due service to the king."

Yet he was totally unprepared for the way de Ferrers suddenly broke into a grin. "Oh! You're *that* knight are you? Ah well, that explains a lot!"

Guy was totally baffled. How on earth had a lord whose lands were here in Derbyshire, and whose castle was at Tutbury just over the border into Staffordshire, come to hear about him?

Seeing Guy's expression de Ferrers laughed again. "My new wife is Ranulph's sister," he said easily, "but also, my mother was the daughter of William de Braose – the sheriff I believe you were serving at the time?"

Guy gave a silent "Oh!" That explained a lot! De Braose had been far from pleased to have a knight he thought of as his to do with as he wished – even if Guy was really in service to the king – being cut out from under his nose. No doubt the entire extended family of de Braoses had been regaled with that tale, and probably several times over too!

"And how is my lord sheriff?" Guy asked with as much grace as he could summon.

De Ferrers cocked his head on one side. "Have you not heard? Sir William senior, my grandfather, died last year. It's his son, my uncle, who is now sheriff."

Guy blinked in surprise. "No, I hadn't heard. Did the older Sir William get to be sheriff again when Longchamp got kicked out?"

De Ferrers shook his head. "Sadly he was too ill by then, although I know he would have loved to have tried. In some ways it's probably a good thing that my uncle has had a fresh start as sheriff – it could have been very messy if Grandfather had been trying to issue orders too. He was still a force to be reckoned with!"

"I wouldn't doubt that for a moment!" Guy replied with feeling, then thought he should change the subject before he gave himself away as to how much he had loathed the old man. "And is my lord of Chester well? I haven't seen him since the day he knighted me and sent me off to come here."

William de Ferrers gave him a sly but still amused look. "Oh he's very well. Indeed he was much taken at the way you took his young liegeman and your former sheriff, fitz John, out hunting boar."

Guy felt his knees nearly buckle at that. Christ on the Cross! So Ranulph of Chester, the man who could whisk Gisborne manor away from him in a heartbeat had heard about his run-ins with fitz John, had he? That was bloody unnerving!

"Don't worry," de Ferrers was saying with an airy wave, "Ranulph was laughing himself sick at the thought, the last I heard. I probably shouldn't say this, but there's not much love lost between the two of them. I think he's almightily relieved that fitz John's family stumped up the money to buy him the sheriffdom. He's certainly not rushed to offer fitz John a place back at Chester after his fall from grace over here, so I think you can breathe again, Sir Guy." Indeed Guy was suddenly aware that he had been holding his breath, and gratefully gasped as de Ferrers added, "But therefore I'm not surprised that you're proving to be a useful forest knight for the sheriff. I have a license from the king's forester, fitz Peter, to be able to hunt as soon as St Martin's Day comes. Would you be able to lead us?"

What could Guy say? He was a mere forest knight, and de Ferrers damned near outranked the sheriff as a lord, and was far more influential as a person than de Wendenal would ever be.

"I'd need a message to be sent to the sheriff," Guy cautiously answered. "Not about you hunting, my lord, since you have the needed permission, but to explain my absence. He'd be expecting me back the day after the swanimote, you see."

De Ferrers waved a be-ringed hand in dismissal. "De Wendenal owes me his service for his lands. I'll send a man to tell him. Now do sit yourself down Guy, and enjoy some of this excellent trout!"

So it was as simple as that, Guy thought – de Wendenal was outranked on all fronts, but it was worth knowing just how much he must be indebted to Sir William here. And with Ranulph of Chester and William de Ferrers being brothers-in-law, if de Ferrers told Ranulph of how well his liegeman had done, then that was praise Guy would gladly accept – anything which cemented his position with his overlord for Gisborne manor was not to be sneezed at.

Therefore Guy resolved to find William de Ferrers a first class hunt, and as he worked his way round the forest over the next two days, thought long and hard about where he would take this fine lord. Mercifully the swanimote passed without incident at Linby, and no sooner had it finished then Guy was riding hard to make sure he reached Horston Castle again that night. Much would depend on what de Ferrers wanted to hunt. If he fancied his chances at wild boar, then Guy thought he might take him northwards to the rougher forest above the Derwent. It was less well-hunted up there, and Guy knew there were more boars to be found in those woods than in the patrolled forests eastwards. On the other hand, he could take the lord north-east towards Clipstone, which would have the advantage of giving them somewhere appropriately grand to stay in the form of the royal hunting lodge, and still have a good chance of a successful deer hunt.

The northern route was definitely Guy's preferred route, because it took him clear of any of the outlaws' hideouts. He could plan as much as he liked, but if the hunt went the wrong way, then there was little he could do about it – and he now knew that de Ferrers had come well-prepared with a pack of hounds, which would not be under Guy's command. North of Crich was a temporary camp, and Guy was pretty sure that Robin and the others would not be lingering there just at the moment.

On the other hand, Clipstone was rather close to a major hideout which lay between Clipstone village and Inkersall, albeit deep in a cluster of veteran oaks. It was a little too densely wooded to be knowingly leading a hunt through, and Guy would do his best to either stay south and west of the spot, or go north and west into the dense forest between the rivers Maun and Meden. Yet if de Ferrers wanted stags, then that would have to be the place to go, for there wasn't time for Guy to lead the hunting party into the truly empty parts of Sherwood further north.

To his dismay, de Ferrers laughed good-humouredly at the offer of a boar-hunt, but declared that while it might have pleased his blood-thirsty grandfather, de Braose, it held little attraction for him. He wanted the thrill of hearing his expensive hounds baying after deer, and seeing them truly running, not watching them being gored by a vicious pig. For that Guy had to respect the man, as he loathed seeing dogs of any sort hurt, and he was filled with a deep longing for his own hounds when he saw de Ferrers' pack. In fact he was so engrossed in making much of the dogs that he failed to realise that de Ferrers had come outside and was standing watching him until he said,

"So you're a dog man, Sir Guy!"

As Guy looked up, startled, de Ferrers waded his way through the milling hounds towards him, cheerfully fending off their affections and wagging tails. "Always a good sign when my dogs like a man."

Guy had no trouble smiling back. "Yes, my lord, they're usually a good judge of character, aren't they?" A huge white greyhound with black ears and a black saddle-mark promptly put his feet up on Guy's shoulders and slurped up his cheek with a rough tongue.

"Down, Favour!" de Ferrers commanded, and the dog dropped down, but stood there wagging his tail un-cowed. "My prize dog," de Ferrers said proudly, "and Grace, my best bitch is this one here."

"Beautiful dogs!" Guy enthused, beginning to heartily wish that he could serve this more amenable lord. "I can see why you wouldn't even consider a boar hunt – I certainly wouldn't with hounds like these! I was always wary of using dogs for that, even with my old deerhounds I had back on the Marches."

"You had deerhounds? Tell me about them!" And so began an amiable ride across the shire boundary into Nottinghamshire which was in danger of lulling Guy into a false sense of security.

Guy led them as far as Mansfield on that first day, drawing de Ferrers' attention to the best coverts as they followed part of the Erewash's valley to cross the shire boundary at the hamlet of Selston. At that point it was clear that a first day's hunt ought to be possible coming back to this area after an over-night at Mansfield, and as Guy had asked for word to be sent to the town of the imminent arrival of an illustrious guest, he was sure that it would not cause too much consternation amongst the town's folk to have them stay a second night. In the prime woodland just north of Codnor, Guy was able to lead de Ferrers to an elderly stag, who would probably not have survived another winter, but who had an impressive rack of antlers for the lord to have as a trophy, and two hinds who would be no great loss to the herd in terms of breeding.

With de Ferrers now a very happy man, and his kennelman wholly on Guy's side after the way he had helped to reward the hounds with a good feed after the hunt, Guy spent a relaxed night in Mansfield courtesy of one of its leading guildsmen. He even felt able to join in with the merriment of de Ferrers' household, and it had been such a long time since he had felt so comfortable in a large group. So he had few qualms about the next day's hunt, and was happily sleeping the sleep of the just when he was rudely awoken by a hand over his mouth.

"Shhh!" a voice hissed in ear.

Guy opened his eyes a slit, and then wasn't sure whether to be pleased to see that it was Roger, or worried sick that he should have come to him in such dangerous circumstances.

"Can you come outside?" the small ex-thief whispered urgently.

Guy nodded and silently eased himself off the bench, and together they crept out of the guildsman's hall, carefully negotiating the other sleeping forms by the glimmering light of what fire remained in the grate. Outside he found Siward, Hugh and Allan lurking around the corner of the street from the hall where he had been sleeping.

"What's wrong?" he asked the moment they met.

They all looked faintly guilty.

"Robin wants to know what you're doing with a lord and hunting in Sherwood," Hugh said apologetically.

"That's why we came," Siward added. "With everyone else's help Tuck managed to convince him that he shouldn't come himself. I think we could all see that he'd come in here like the wrath of God before he'd even bothered to find out what's going on."

Guy felt a rising anger. "What I'm doing? What I'm fucking *doing*? St Thomas stay my hand! I'm doing my God-damned job, that's what I'm *doing*!" He couldn't believe how fast his cousin's mistrust had cut him to the quick, and it must have shown in his face by the light of the wan moon overhead, because Allan quickly came and put his hand on Guy's arm.

"I'm so sorry, Guy, we tried to tell him that that's probably what it was."

"Probably?" Guy was so angry now that he snatched his hand away from Allan, oblivious of how that shocked his youngest cousin. "Fucking 'probably'? Christ on the Cross, I could walk away and never look back! Does nobody comprehend what it is to be a forester? Do you?" he hissed with savage fury, wanting so much to shout and just about hanging on to his presence of mind not to.

Without giving any of them chance to reply, he stabbed a finger towards the large house where de Ferrers slept. "That man in there is the brother-in-law of the lord who grants me Gisborne! My bloody hall! The place which houses a Welsh fugitive wished onto me by Tuck, and a dear old friend who committed no crime but to get on the wrong side of a bastard Norman lord! What would you have me do, eh? Tell him to stick his hunt up his arse, and have him report back that Guy of Gisborne is an ill-mannered cur who should be demoted to a mere castle knight, devoid of any holding?" Guy slapped the wooden post of the nearby stables furiously. "And would my pompous cousin step in and provide those two, and young Elias, with a home elsewhere? Would Robin climb down from his fucking high-horse to commit to service with a lord for the sake of others? Don't bloody-well hold your breath on that one!"

Having run out of breath himself Guy turned away, panting, and leaned forward to grasp his knees with his hands.

"Jesu!" he heard Hugh's soft sigh. "Lord, Guy, that's harsh."

"I'm harsh am I?" Guy flung back over his shoulder without looking. "Well my life is fucking harsh! You try being equable dancing around bastard de Wendenal, the king's laws, and a cousin who wants to be some kind of twisted cross-breed between Saint Lazarus and Sir William Marshall!"

He jumped as he felt someone pull him upright and into a hug and a voice in his ear said. "No, you twerp! He meant the choices you have to make are harsh."

Belatedly he realised it was Siward, and then that the other man who was hugging him from the other side was Hugh. For the first time in a long time Guy felt the tears coming to his eyes, and despite his best efforts a sob escaped from his lips.

"This is exactly why we wouldn't let Robin come," he heard Allan saying softly from somewhere just behind him.

"Do you know what's the worst?" he said when he could managed to get the words out. "I *like* William de Ferrers! Yes he's very much the high-born lord, but he's got a sense of humour, and he's a fair and honest man. These last two days have been the best I've spent in a very long time. I've had good company. I've had a chance to show what I'm really good at, without it being tracking some poor unfortunate who's got on the wrong side of the sheriff's ire. And I've had some truly gorgeous dogs to handle. ...And I've actually had the chance to handle those hounds at the hunt because Sir William isn't a jealous man, but gets as much pleasure out of watching what I do as if he were doing it himself. So just at the moment I like him a good deal more than I do Baldwin - or Robin as this twisted version of him wants to be known now! And it would serve my bloody cousin right if I asked de Ferrers if he could find me another position where I could be his huntsman, and to hell with the sheriff and the forest!"

"Please don't!" Roger said in clear panic. "Don't leave us!"

Guy turned to the smaller man and managed a weak smile. "No, I won't. And not just because I'd lose Gisborne manor if I did. However angry I am at Robin, there's all the rest of you, and I have no wish to see a single one of you swinging from the battlements at Nottingham the way I had to see Alan of Leek's corpse doing until it got cut down." And he heard the sharp intake of breaths as his words sunk in. It was too easy for them to forget that those in the castle were not all Guy's enemies, and what it cost him when things all went wrong.

Yes, Gervase, those four in particular were always more sensitive to what my ongoing deception cost me. And did I lead de Ferrers on another day's hunting? Yes I did. But I had meant what I said to my friends on that night. We four were once more comfortable with one another when we parted, but I was to hear later on that when they got back to the camp they were not slow to let Robin know how disgusted they were with him for making me feel so ill-used. I also understand that when they repeated my words concerning Alan of Leek's fate, that Will and Malik were joined by the Coshams and the two women in expressing their revulsion at the thought of having to watch a friend's corpse hang and rot, and what that had to have been like.

It is a bitter pill, Brother, to feel so used by someone you hold dear. This is why I said to you at the very start of my confession that although I always loved my cousin, there were times when I disliked him intensely! And so I got up the next morning, and excused my slightly less than enthusiastic appearance by saying I was unused to so much wine, and had been woken in the night by a nightmare which I was cunning enough to say had come about from being back in Mansfield for the first time since I had been here as a prisoner of outlaws. Yes, Brother, I confess that I lied, and was not proud of it. I did not like deceiving de Ferrers, or being forced into untruths just because of my cousin's prickly notions of honour!

Yet we did hunt the next day, and the pleasure of being in such good company and with the robust company of the dogs, did much to restore my good humour before midday had arrived. And at that point I resolved to take as much pleasure as I could from such a day. Therefore I led our party to the high land north and west of Mansfield Woodhouse and just across into Derbyshire, and there Lord William brought down another stag and three hinds, and pronounced himself well happy with his hunt and content to leave any others to later hunters. It was something which endear him further to me, for many a hunter I had known before and since, seeing themselves as being lucky on such a hunt, would have demanded that we hunt on, thereby forcing me to step back into my role as preserver of the king's game, and causing me to call a halt to any over-hunting regardless of whether I incurred their wrath. That de Ferrers was conscious of the limits set him by fitz Peter, and stuck to them without prompting was a blessed relief for me. Maybe it was easy for a man who usually got whatever he wanted to be that way, but de Ferrers was utterly lacking the prickles and ego which made Robin such a constant burr under my saddle at that time.

As for Robin himself, I also learned later that he had threatened to come and cause mayhem to my hunt in a fit of pique over me pulling cousinly rank, as he saw it. To my surprise it turned out that of all people it was Tuck who put a stop to that, declaring that unless Robin wanted to wake up the next time and discover that he had missed not only Christmas but the turn of the year, he would do no such thing. Normally Tuck tried to stay outside of any arguments, preferring the role of arbiter, but maybe the timely reminder of the fact that it had been him who had got me involved in the rescue of the same Maelgwn who was now at Gisborne, provoked him to act.

So I was left to hunt undisturbed, although not unnoticed, for as the hunting party returned to Mansfield I was aware of being watched, and when I scoured the trees I saw Robin's face looking down at me from high in an elm. Coldly ignoring him, I rode on, not even bothering to signal that I had seen him. When I then rode past him a month later on the outskirts of Nottingham, where he was lurking disguised by a heavy hood in the winter gloom, I believe it finally sunk in how much he had hurt me, because the next attempt at a meeting was conducted by Tuck. Of course I could never treat Tuck so coldly, and after much discussion I reluctantly agreed to continue listening on their behalf in the castle, but I made it clear to Tuck that I was doing it for the rest of them, and that if Robin was caught that was his bad luck.

Chapter 21

Oh, so you think I was in the wrong, do you, Gervase? Well do not be so quick to condemn me at this late hour. I have since learned that my hard words woke Robin up. You see he had been rather carried away by Much, Walter and Algar's descriptions of me rescuing them from the dungeons of Nottingham Castle, and somehow in his head he had developed the notion that he would always be alright, because even if he got caught, I would rescue him and whisk him away from the castle before he truly felt the weight of the sheriff's law and got the lash, or lost a hand, or even felt the drop from the hangman's noose.

Talk about double standards! I was too much the older cousin when I stood in his way of getting his own way, but he still thought that the big cousin who had hauled him out of scrape after scrape as children would still be doing the same for the man. And I confess that I was angered by that when I learned of it. Yes, Brother, I confess to the sin of too much anger at times, and of not being forgiving enough. Yet I must plead my case, and say that even as a man who had just turned thirty the previous April, Robin still needed to grow up in some ways. No stripling youth anymore, he could still be infuriatingly naive and far too blind to the consequences of his actions. Yes, I was undoubtedly too fast to see the wrong in him, but the faults were not wholly mine.

However, we need to move on, for greater events than those in just Sherwood were about to catch up with us. And just in case you think that I recounted that episode with de Ferrers simply to make you feel sorry for me and the way Robin Hood treated me, I will tell you that de Ferrers will appear again soon. At that point I was grateful beyond belief that I had got on his good side, for my life would then depend on him looking kindly upon me. Yet we must get there first, and so we shall pick up the story just after the turn of the year into 1193.

Nottingham
Late January onwards, the Year of Our Lord 1193

The news came to Nottinghamshire in a flurry of messages, but they all said the same thing – the king had been taken prisoner on his way home from the Holy Land by Henry IV, the less than spiritual Holy Roman Emperor. Rather worse, it transpired that the message had first gone to King Philip of France, who was King Richard's sworn enemy by this stage.

"Bloody de Wendenal's going round like a dog with two tails!" Richard of Burscot complained to Guy as they left the castle chapel together on the Sunday after the news had come. The forester knights had already gone on ahead and it was just Guy left with the three castle knights.

"He certainly seems to think he's had some kind of reprieve," Sir Robert agreed. "The damned man's insufferable at the moment."

"I've heard him say that Count John will go and swear fealty to King Philip if he in turn acknowledges John as king in his brother's place," Sir Hugh added morosely. "By Our Lady, what a mess!"

Robert looked at Hugh in horror, "You think Count John would go that far?"

"He probably wouldn't give it a second thought," Guy told him dryly. "Those two have always fought like cat and dog – King Richard and John, that is. No love lost there!"

"God preserve us!" Sir Richard groaned. "Just when we thought we could get through a year without the threat of civil war coming up to bite us, here we go again!"

"It's definitely wearing thin, this constant state of living on a knife edge," Guy agreed, "but what choice do the likes of us have?"

"Sod all!" Sir Hugh snorted in disgust. "But I tell you all, we'd better start treading very lightly for the next few months. May St Thomas help us, but if we rub de Wendenal up the wrong way and Count John does become king, then we could find him looking for ways to take his petty revenge on us once he knows he's secure here, so be careful!"

It was a warning Guy took to heart. De Wendenal did not need any more reasons to dislike him, and he did his best to stay as far from the sheriff's presence as possible. In early February he gratefully escaped, and volunteered to do the longest ride up to the border of Derbyshire to deal with cases to be brought before the first woodmote of the year. Most of them, he knew, would be petty complaints brought against hard-pressed villagers who had gone out gathering wood for their fires during the long chill of winter. The unfortunates who lived in the cluster of villages around Bolsover Castle he could do little to protect, they were too close to the castle and the eye of its constable, Richard Vernon. And Vernon, Guy knew, was doing his best to look good in order for his temporary appointment to be made permanent. But the villages north of there and up into the Peak, where so many miners needed wood for various uses, were unpopular with the other knights for their begrudged respect and sullen responses, and so he was glad to be able to do what he could for them.

It would also give him a chance to sneak over the border into Yorkshire and visit the camp at Loxley. Over the Christmas period he had heard nothing from the outlaws, and if he was still quietly seething over the way Robin was behaving, he still wanted to know that the others were alright. The fact that Tuck had only come the once – and very briefly - to see him particularly gave him guilty moments, fearing that one of those who had come on that night with de Ferrers had repeated his words all too accurately, and that Tuck had taken offence at Guy's referring to him wishing Maelgwn onto him. So he rode north and quietly prayed that he would still be welcome at the camp.

He had declined the offer to travel with those who would base themselves at Bolsover and ride out from there, preferring to stop at Mansfield and then ride on that bit further north to stop at the little village of Beighton, right on the northern edge of the forest and shire. From there he would work his way westwards via small places like Coal Aston and Holmesfield and then up to Hathersage. Every time he got to Hathersage he felt as though he could breathe more easily, could let the mantle of forester slip into the background and become himself once more, even if it was only for a short time.

He would probably have to make a courtesy call to the new constable of the Peak – or rather the man who was doing the job on his behalf – but just at the moment that was not such a chore. The man who had taken over from William de Wendenal at that castle in early 1192, when the dust of the changes of sheriff had settled, was a mature man, Sir Richard of Lea, and like de Wendenal, Sir Richard's allegiances ultimately led to William de Ferrers. Just at the moment, with so much political turbulence going on around him, Guy was thinking that keeping in with a man who shared his ties was no bad thing, and Sir Richard did not make it hard.

"Guy! Come in! What an evil day to be out in, come closer to the fire!" were the heartening words which greeted him when he strode into the familiar keep at High Peak. He was rewarded with a smile from a woman who had been here back in his brief tenure, and was glad to see that after the grim times of de Wendenal's tenure, the people were once again looking happy.

"Sir Richard," Guy responded thankfully, and taking the proffered hand of welcome, "I won't say no to getting warm again. By St Thomas, that wind's biting! Straight out of the north!"

"Have you heard the news?" Sir Richard asked, as Guy gratefully accepted a tankard of dark beer into which Sir Richard had just plunged a poker to warm it.

"That rather depends," Guy said warily. "That the king's been taken prisoner, yes, but anything beyond that, no."

Sir Richard waved him to a chair beside the blazing fire and settled himself opposite. "God help us, but that fool Count John has gone to France – and we can all guess what for!"

"So he's gone? The sheriff thought he would."

Sir Richard rolled his eyes despairingly. "There are few men to whom I would risk saying this, but what does the fool think he's doing?"

"Plunging us into civil war if he's not careful," Guy replied dryly.

"Then may St Thomas intercede for us that that doesn't happen," Sir Richard said, and meant it. "But there's more! I heard from a messenger heading north that there's a rumour which could yet prove true that Count John and King Philip are planning an invasion. And there's been a Great Council called for the end of the month to decide how to raise the ransom for the king – that's what the messenger was riding out with, the call for the great barons to attend."

Guy sat there aghast, too appalled to say anything at first. All he could think of was: how are the ordinary people going to find more? His face must have given him away, because Sir Richard was giving a bitter chuckle.

"I'm glad I was the one to tell you, because your face is picture! I know what you're thinking, because it was the first thing which came to my mind too. Where in the name of all the saints are we going to get the money from? It's all very well for the great lords to decide it, but those of us closer to the ordinary folk know how hard it is just to find the rents and various payments we have to get off them."

Guy took a long swig of his ale. "Dear God, the price of wheat is already way up from when King Henry called for the Jerusalem Tithe and the Saladin Tithe. This last year or two it's been up to a shilling and sixpence a quarter at the very least – that has to be half as much again, or more, of what it was when we had to collect the Jerusalem Tithe! No-one's income's gone up by those sorts of proportions!"

Sir Richard shook his head wearily. "And the miners are no better off. I tell you Guy, I fear what I may be asked to do in the name of reclaiming a king who's spent barely a few months in his kingdom since he was crowned four years ago."

On an impulse Guy decided to test Sir Richard. It was just a feeling he had about the man, and not enough to tell him that the folk in this long valley would be seen right by their friends come what may, but enough to drop a question.

314

"It's no wonder they adore this Robin Hood," he said, keeping his tone world-weary.

"No wonder at all!" Sir Richard replied without hesitation. "He must seem sent from the Lord himself to some poor souls! I can't find it in me to try to stop their chatter about him, because what can the likes of you or I offer them instead? If it gives them some hope, then with the lives they lead at the moment, it seems cruel to me to crush it. I doubt he'll last long. A sheriff like de Wendenal is brutal enough to make it impossible for the villagers not to tell him where the outlaws are."

The sympathy in his voice emboldened Guy. "I'm not so sure. The reward won't work."

"By Christ, why not? It's a small fortune to many of them!"

Guy gave a bitter laugh. "And that's why they don't believe for a moment that they'd ever get to see it. Don't you see? They think that the moment they open their mouths, and their lord gets a whiff of the fact that a reward was likely to be paid to this village or that one, that he'd be there like a shot, claiming it himself. The ones who know me well enough to speak openly just laugh at the thought that they'd ever see as much as a penny."

Sir Richard looked at him in open astonishment. "Good Lord! ...Do you know, I've never thought of it like that? But now you say it, it makes perfect sense. They've been stripped of everything which has a value, so why would they believe they would get the reward?"

The older man seemed genuinely dismayed at what had been forced upon the ordinary people, and Guy thought that maybe under the right circumstances he would be a willing ally. Not yet. Sadly it would take this next round of wringing money which wasn't there out of the people before Sir Richard would be ready to be subverted, but he was definitely on Guy's mental list now. It was also useful that Sir Richard's own manor was deep in the thick woodland above the Derwent, and conveniently further north than Horston Castle and Sir Roger de Buron to be sure that their paths would not cross often. If one of the outlaws was wounded then that might be the point when Sir Richard would help, for it would be an act of Christian charity rather than subversion.

In the meantime, Guy collected those pleas which would be dealt with by the sheriff, rather than by Sir Richard himself at the High Peak forest court at Tideswell, and in the morning went on his way. In theory he was now due to ride back to Hathersage and visit the nearby villages of Bamford and Hurst, then make his way south again. However he barely showed his face at those two, setting his horse to the short ride over Hallam Moors to the Loxley valley. He had to skirt Stanage Edge with its rugged cliff-face, but still made the camp before the winter light gave out on him.

For once he rode in, worried that he might have to make a fast exit, and that all by itself made him feel faintly sick. If he was no longer welcome here life would be bleak indeed. Yet the moment he edged into the warm light of the large cooking fire which was going in the middle of the encampment, he heard Thomas' voice call out in clear relief,

"Guy! *Duw* man, you're here at last!"

Then Tuck bustled forward and took the horse's bridle. "Get down and come and eat! Much, where are you? Ah, there you are! Take this beast and feed her, will you?"

Guy allowed himself to be hustled forward and plied with a bowl filled with one of Tuck's delicious stews, a stew which contained more meat than Guy normally saw in a week at the castle. As he gratefully ate, he looked about him. Not a sign of Robin or John, nor of Marianne, Gilbert, James or Mariota. No Allan or Roger either.

"They went into Sheffield market today," Siward explained before Guy had chance to ask. "They won't be back for a while yet."

"Am I safe being here?" Guy asked bluntly. All of them looked shocked that he would ask such a thing. "I'm the traitor, remember?" Guy found himself saying before he could stop himself. It was frightening how quickly the hurt at Robin's mistrust had surged back up.

"Don't be bleedin' stupid," Will's gruff voice came from behind him as the bulky smith came and plonked himself down beside Guy and proffered a tankard of their home-brewed ale to him. "Now don't go upsetting the apple cart on us. We've already had strong words with Robin over that. He knows he was beyond wrong about it, so can you please not bite his head off the moment he walks into camp?"

"I'll do my best," Guy said with a sigh, then felt the need to make it clear that he had never been angry with the rest of them. "I came to warn you – I have news! Sadly not of the good kind, though," and he proceeded to tell them of the planned Great Council. "I can't see the outcome being good for the ordinary folk," he concluded.

"But the king will be back!" a voice said from the darkness and Robin strode into the camp with those who had been with him.

"The king will be back *eventually*," Guy corrected his cousin as blandly as he could manage. "But everyone agrees that Emperor Henry will demand a high price. England's perceived as being wealthy! Therefore the ransom will be high, I can assure you of that. So it's going to take a while to get that money together, and King Richard won't be home before it gets to the emperor, you can bet your boots on that."

Yet the light had come on in Robin's eyes and Guy knew that already he was looking forward to meeting the great crusader, even if it was from a distance.

"I came because we need to set up some means of me getting in touch with you," he said firmly. "News could come at any time which you might need to hear, and I can't guarantee that I'll be able to ride out to find you. De Wendenal is champing at the bit to prove himself. He could decide to purge the forest at any time and throw every man who comes to give service at it this summer. That could mean a huge number of men hunting you, but I have to have some way of letting you know they're coming."

"We'd been thinking that," Thomas said quickly, "well some of us had, anyway. Sherwood's too big for us to keep relying on chance meetings. We've been worried we've missed you!"

"That we have," Tuck said warmly. "It's been decided that we have to get better at what we're doing and come to you more often."

Guy wondered who had done most of that deciding, but was pleasantly surprised to look towards Robin and see his cousin's expression was open and smiling. No sign of the masked eyes and distrust which had been present so much in the last year or so. Maybe Tuck's sleep remedy was helping more than anticipated? He almost looked like the old Baldwin – almost.

"We'll be coming in in pairs once a week from now on," Robin said with something verging on enthusiasm. "There are enough of us to be doing that. Marianne or Mariota with one of us will work, because we'll look like an ordinary couple coming in to the market. That, we've learned, is a good disguise."

Guy bit his lip and refrained from saying that he had been the one to first say that when they'd been trying to get into the priory at Blyth. As long as Robin had learned the lesson that was all that mattered. A bit of credit would have been nice, though.

"I'm one of the few who won't be coming," Gilbert was saying with a sheepish grin, pointing to his flame-red hair which was so bright as to be memorable anywhere.

"And you only have to open your gob and you give yourself away," Will snorted. "The word would be all over Nottingham that the Irish were invading if you went!"

"That's why I won't be going either," Piers said with a sigh. "I'd love to taste that beer that Will keeps on about from your castle brew-house, but Thomas and me are too Welsh."

Robin was laughing with the others at his downcast expression. "And that's as good a reason as any to keep you out of the town! Too much of that beer and we'd all be in trouble!" Then he turned to gesture to Malik. "And he won't be coming either. James will just about pass as a local if whoever he's with does the talking, but Malik's too dark even in winter. That still leaves lots of us, though."

"It certainly does," Siward agreed and gave Guy a grin, as did Hugh.

Those two seemed to have struck up a close friendship, Guy thought, and was glad. If the gang did break up he would like to think they would stay in the area with Allan and Roger – friends in the area he could still meet with sometimes. But now he had to ask an awkward question.

"What will you do if the call comes to raise a large ransom?" he asked Robin directly, but made sure he then looked to the others. "Will you try to take some of it back to help the people? Or will you let it be gathered in because it's going to free the king?"

He knew it would be a real conflict of interests for Robin, forcing him to choose between the king he admired and his own personal crusade to help the people of these shires. His question took Robin by surprise, and Guy was glad that at least he paused to think before answering. Had he instantly replied that the king must be released at all costs, Guy didn't quite know what he would have done.

And at that point he had to recognise that in his own mind, he would quite happily sacrifice the king if it would save the misery of the ordinary people whom he knew. A king who had cared so little for the people he ruled wasn't much of a king at all in Guy's eyes. And as for what King Richard might have laid up in store for himself in Heaven for trying to take back Jerusalem from the Saracens, well that might benefit him personally, but Guy had spent too long with Tuck not to think that such Grace would be vastly diluted by the time it got distributed to every last man, woman and child in England as their allotted due from their king. They wouldn't be feeling much benefit in the hereafter at all, so why make their lives worse now?

To his astonishment, Tuck was suddenly voicing those same thoughts, concluding with, "It was a worthy dream – going to take back the Holy City – but not one to crucify your people with!"

Robin was now wearing a frown of consternation. "Yes, I can see that we must help the people. How bad can it get Guy?"

With a sigh and a shrug, Guy had to admit, "I can't say for sure, but I think we'll be lucky to get away with having a second tithe levied this year. Heaven preserve us, but it might be worse, depending on the Emperor's greed."

Malik shook his head in despair. "A tenth of everything to the Church, the rents and fines to their lord, and then you think another tenth for this ransom? What will they live on?"

"Even at its worst, with the crusade rolling over it, it was never this bad at home," James said sadly. "Not for the ordinary people. Why is it like this here? Is it like this in Normandy too?"

Hugh, the one of all of them who had spent a fair amount of time in the great swathe of lands across the water which were still the primary holding of the king, answered, "Not at all, James. Over there each baron is far more his own man. That's why it was such a choice prize to become the king of England for William of Normandy when King Edward died. Edward's kingdom had been organised for centuries. The difference is that the old English kings never abused the system like this. They let the Hundred Courts give the freemen a voice, and although I suspect we've always been the most taxed people of any country, it was done fairly."

Siward was nodding. "By St Thomas, even the Danes knew better than to get too greedy! They had the wit to know that you don't kill the sheep that has a fleece of gold as well as shearing it every year – and given the price the best Lindsay wools from the east of our shire and into Lincolnshire get, they might very well be bloody gold!"

"But all that money's in the hands of the big monasteries, or great landowners like the Templars," John added bitterly. "And while I dare say that they'll be as unhappy about this ransom payment, it won't have them starving like the villagers will."

Robin suddenly looked up, smiling, "I know what we'll do! We'll anticipate this tax. If the great and good of this land can still afford to eat, then we should be taxing them heavily now. Let's tax every rich merchant and lord who passes through Sherwood, so that when the time comes the whore-son sheriff can collect his money off the people, and then we'll go round after him and give as much back as we can manage."

There was an enthusiastic response to his idea from most people, but Guy had to add a note of caution. "If you give back this time, it will have to be to all of the villages, you know. This time you can't leave out those on the other side of the Trent, because the Bishop of Lincoln will be scouring everyone in Newark and for miles around for every penny, and so will the lords of the other villages not in the forest. I know you won't be able to give money out to all the villages across the Derwent in the rest of Derbyshire, but then the sheriff won't be as bothered with them as those on his own doorstep."

Will instantly agreed. "Remember the trouble with Algar and Walter! Let's make sure we don't give the villagers east of the Trent cause to hate us! We may need their help one day."

"Wise words, Will," said Tuck, and several of the others were no nodding too.

Guy expected Robin to argue, but he was already saying, "Very well, we include all of Nottinghamshire. It will mean less for each village, but we can do our best to share it equally. But that means we have to start as soon as we can!"

"York at Easter would be a good place to start," Gilbert said thoughtfully. "All those rich men coming to the great Minster and the archbishop to save their souls. It would do them good to give to the poor at such a time!" And everyone laughed.

"But we're still going to have to be very lucky to get enough in time," Marianne warned them when the laughter had subsided. "We can only be in one place at a time. What a pity there aren't any great places of pilgrimage in this shire we could visit on the way."

"She has a point," Mariota added for emphasis. "By the time you've got up to York and then come back, you'll have used up several days just on that alone. And from what Guy's said, the ransom could appear at any time."

Tuck's face suddenly broke into a beatific smile, making Robin ask, "What? What have you thought of?"

The Welsh monk's grin got broader. "Well you can't be in more than one place at a time, but 'Robin Hood' can! Siward's been your double before, let him be it again! If you take Little John, Gilbert, Malik, James and me, and Much and Marianne, that's six of us to tackle any guards a merchant might have, while Much and Marianne spirit stuff away. Then let Siward take Will, Hugh, Allan and Roger, Mariota and the Coshams. That way, both lots will have good archers. But even better, the numbers will be the same, and both lots will have a woman with them, should anyone ask!"

"By Our Lady, Tuck, that's brilliant!" Will enthused, as Marianne declared,

"What a wonderful plan!"

Guy immediately looked to Robin, wondering whether there would be a flash of temper at being so manoeuvred. After all, it would mean someone else taking the instant credit, even if it came back to rest on him later. But Tuck was being even craftier, and before Robin even had time to think, added,

"We'd be cracking the big nut of York and the archbishop, of course, but Repton's likely to attract more than a few visitors at that time, as will Beverley Minster, Southwell and the big abbey at Selby. If we relieve the merchants at Selby on the way up to York, then by going over to Beverley afterwards we won't be going in the direction anyone would expect – they'll think we'll go the fastest way back into Sherwood. But if Repton and Southwell get visited by Robin Hood too, then that's going to confuse the living daylights out of anyone trying to track just one party."

Guy had to hand it to Tuck, it was a masterly piece of directing and one which his cousin swallowed without wincing because it was clear that he would still have the major part. Without batting an eyelid, Robin was instantly discussing the ways and means of carrying the plan through, rather than arguing with anyone. It meant that Guy was able to sidle back out of the immediate light of the fire and watch, but was surprised to be joined by Will.

"Tuck, Siward, Hugh and Malik, and me, came up with half of that plan some time ago," the big smith said softly. "We thought it would be best if we had some kind of plan as to how to divide the group up if needs be. John, Much and Marianne would never be separated from Robin, and we had a feeling that he'd also kick up an almighty fuss if such a thing was suggested. So Tuck and Malik agreed that they would go with Robin to try to keep things calm, whatever the situation turned out to be."

Will now scuffed a boot at a piece of root before saying even more softly, "And we wanted a plan where we could save as many as possible if Robin decided to do something really fucking stupid! James doesn't say much, but if pressed he's a good fighter, you know, and Gilbert you've seen in action. Working with Tuck and Malik they're probably the best placed to fight their way out of a bad situation."

Guy was more than surprised. "You'd separate Robin from the others? ...I don't mean out of cowardice, or anything! I'm just a bit surprised after all you six went through to get back from the Holy Land together, that's all."

Will shrugged. "We're loyal but not stupid. And we can all see that as time goes on it's Robin who's the one who's been worst affected by the experience. Sometimes he just doesn't seem to think straight. Do you know what I mean? He gets these ideas and he goes after them like a bloody bull, seeing nothing in the way, not even a sodding great brick wall straight ahead or a cliff right at his feet!"

Sighing, Guy agreed. "Oh yes! I've foreseen that situation coming several times! I'm just glad that you all have."

For that he got a sympathetic smile from Will. "Thought you might have! Once we'd decided that, we roped your Allan in. He's a bright lad when it comes to the ideas. He thought we should start giving Robin Hood a company. Names to go with him as his helpers, you see. So Tuck's going to make sure that the names of Little John and Lady Marion get heard, along with Brother Tuck. And while Siward or Hugh plays 'Robin Hood' with our lot, the names of Allan of the Dales and Will Scarlet will get dropped as well, along with our Lady Marion. If we're going to be an infamous band of outlaws, Allan thought we should have names we could attach deeds to. He said half a dozen was enough for people to remember, but he also said that those names shouldn't be attached to anyone who'd be in trouble just for what they were either – so not the Coshams, because they'd be in enough trouble just for being lord-less Welsh in England. Gilbert would be in the same boat just for being Irish; and Malik and James could be in a very bad place if they got caught too, because who would understand that although they're from the East, they aren't Saracens? So Allan said we should stick to names which could be local, and as a result, much harder to pin on any one person."

"God bless Allan!" Guy said from the heart. "That's the kind of planning I'd have been proud to come up with. And he's absolutely right – it's been the Welsh accents which everyone's noticed so far, you know. I think it's a great idea to start giving your hunters some other people to fret over."

So there you have it, Brother, the start of the famous names which would be eternally linked with Robin Hood! That Lent and Easter-tide the wealthy merchants travelling through Nottinghamshire and Yorkshire got well and truly fleeced of their wealth. At every turn the sheriff got word of this troublesome outlaw lifting purses on the Great North Road, or brazening his way into inns where merchants were staying and removing their purses. And the raid at Repton was particularly effective thanks to Allan's inventiveness, for a voice from the crypt echoed up proclaiming that Robin Hood was doing Christ's work in protecting the weak and the poor.

Oh do not pull such a face, Gervase! If it had been Robin himself making that echo in the crypt you would be all agog, so do not pout so because his young cousin did it on his behalf. Not fitting for a house of God, you say? For truth, many of those gathered in that holy place on that most holy of festivals, were thinking more of the money they would make out of those devout enough to want to come to one of the great places of worship, than their eternal souls. Do not doubt that, Brother. Your own aspirations may be spiritually high, but those who were relieved of their wealth worshipped money almost as fervently!

So as Lent progressed I heard first of a train of merchants being robbed of all of their portable property on the northern border of the shire, and then after a week or so, of the astonishingly bold robberies at York. Yet Robin was too far away for his deeds to be the ones we heard most of at first. It was Siward's band whom we heard most of, and if they did not make quite the same grand gestures, they were to my mind far more effective. They must have been travelling fast and light. Because one day they were at Repton, then another up by Mansfield, then Blyth, then down to cheekily raid some merchants on the Great North Road just as they were about to ask for shelter at Rufford Abbey, and then to catch the ones whom they had missed the night before as they came close by Laxton Castle. That really rankled with the sheriff! But before we could ride out to apprehend the rascals they were gone and next heard of relieving nobles and merchants of purses at Southwell. And they finished on a triumphant note by fleecing the bishop of Lincoln as he came to Newark Castle just before Easter.

Moreover, the names Will had mentioned to me were already being muttered in the marketplaces. Allan o'Dales, Will Scarlet and Lady Marion were the ones I heard of first and had to cover my smiles over, but Allan and the others must have been creative in their calls, because I heard of Little John and Brother Tuck long before the word came of the antics over in Yorkshire where the real John and Tuck were. But of all names it was Robin Hood's which everyone was now mentioning. This sudden clustering of events where his name was being broadcast took the name from being one which was whispered in dark corners to one which could be openly heard on the streets.

For myself, the only thing which dampened my amusement at the panic these raids caused was realising that it was the gang without Robin who had had the most effect, who were the ones whose exploits had most tickled the public fancy. I hoped that by the time Robin and his half of the gang got back, the individual events would have become blurred in the gossip, and he would not notice. But it was also clear as I heard those snippets of news coming in, that Siward's half had acted with a good deal more humour and good grace than had hitherto been part of the raids. In one merchant's family who came to the sheriff to report their losses at Repton, the father was stamping fury in the hall, but the wife and two daughters had clearly been far from frightened, even seeming to see it as a rather romantic escapade. ˜Robin˜ had bent and kissed the lady's hand, and Allan had flirted outrageously with the girls, telling them that with such beautiful eyes they had no need of jewels. And these were far from the only report where aside from the loss of money and jewels, little had been hurt but pride.

All of which seemed to be saying to me that while Robin had all of the passion, those with cooler heads were the ones who were doing a better job of getting people on their side. And that was only emphasised when we heard of the fury and indignation which rattled around York for weeks after Robin's visit. No such anger lingered where the others had been, and I was very glad that, albeit by chance or divine intervention, they had been the ones to stay closer to home – to those places where they had their hideouts. We all needed the people of Nottinghamshire to be on our side, and I gave thanks to whichever saint had been watching over my friends and had ensured that things had gone so well, for come the next winter the outlaws would be needing more than purloined jewels and gold, even if my mother was now acting as our banker.

And should you wonder further about signs and portents, just as that Great Council was taking place in the south, there was also a great rumbling and shaking of the earth felt across England. Yes, an earthquake! And it was felt far and wide, and seen as a very bad sign of what was to come. Some even wondered if we were seeing the start of the end of all days, and that the Day of Judgement would soon be at hand.

Did I? No, I cannot recall thinking that, but I did think it a terribly bad sign of what was to come, and I was very glad when I did get to see my friends again to discover just how much money they had been able to amass, for I believed we would need it all and soon. There was so much that Robin had decided that they must pay a visit to the Jews in Lincoln and ask them to exchange the jewels for coin. They would be sure to remember Robin kindly after what had happened back in 1191, and our needy peasant farmers could hardly present their lord with an exquisite ring as payment for rent or ransom without getting into serious trouble.

Yet before the axe could fall on our necks in the form of the ransom demands, we had rather more pressing matters to deal with right on our doorstep, and once again Count John was right in the thick of it!

Chapter 22

So what was this crisis? Well right in the middle of Lent we heard that Count John and King Philip were assembling a fleet at Wissant in Flanders, with the intention of launching an invasion. Ah yes, you have heard of this. But did you know that disaster was only averted by the prompt action of the king's mother? Old though she was by then, Queen Eleanor rallied the justices, and with them called out the fyrd. You do not know the old word? Ah, well the fyrd was the Saxon name for the army obliged to rally to the defences of towns, which was created back in the far-gone days when the Danes were our enemies and greatest threat. Not being a military man, you would not know this, Gervase, but for every length of town wall there was a most careful calculation of how many men it would take to defend it; and those calculations still governed my life because they lay behind the terms of military service for most of those knights and their men-at-arms who came to the castle every summer. Such service to a castle was one thing, but it had been a long time since the full summons to arms even for the townsmen had been used, but Queen Eleanor used it now.

We learned that the rebellious Count had many mercenaries in his pay, and I saw for myself how that worried Walkelin and Fredegis. After all, they were just such mercenaries from the old king's hiring, and I could see that they did not fancy having to fight a younger generation of fighters from Brabant and elsewhere, the shoe suddenly being on the other foot for them. I was also concerned on another front, for it was said by so many that it must have been true, that Count John had recruited Welsh mercenaries, and that made me worried in case Thomas or Piers got taken captive. Allan's words of them suffering simply because of where they had been born seemed horribly likely to come true.

I was therefore most relieved when Easter had passed and I had a visit from Allan and Roger informing me that everyone had finally arrived back at camp and without injury. Yet my relief did not last long, for within the week we had had word that Count John had taken those same mercenaries to Windsor and Wallingford castles, which he already controlled, and was preparing to defend them. That was bad enough, but apparently on Easter Monday, the justices and their force then besieged the count and his men at Windsor with over five hundred foot soldiers plus various mounted men, and with siege engines. Then to crown it all, William Marshal had ridden in to join them with another five hundred men. Clearly these men meant to quash the prince's ambitions once and for all, but those of us at Nottingham pitied the poor souls in Windsor Castle who had not chosen any side, but were trapped there. It is one thing to say a thousand men, the number trips off the tongue with ease, but it is something else to see *such a force of men and know that you might soon be on the receiving end of their weapons, and for that they had our sympathy.*

I tell you, Brother, about the only good thing I could see in all of this was that the Scottish king stayed true to his vows to King Richard, and despite Count John's best efforts, the Scots refused to be drawn into the fight. I know it pleased Mariota that her fellow countrymen stayed true, and the rest of us were heartily glad that we would not have to be watching the north as well as the south. Yet it seemed like barely had the news arrived of Windsor then we did have to look to the north, although only as far as the border between Nottinghamshire and Yorkshire, and that was way too close for comfort!

Nottingham
Spring, the Year of Our Lord 1193

"Hugh Bardolf has raised his men from Yorkshire," gasped Ailred, an agister for the far north of the old forest, as he hurried in to where the scribes were gathering accounts for the forest courts.

"God help us, what for?" Sir Walter asked, looking up with a worried frown. "He's supposed to have been one of the king's most loyal servants for years – that's why he got the sheriffdom. What need does he have of an army?"

"Doncaster," was Ailred's terse answer.

"Doncaster? What have the poor folk of Doncaster done to him?" Guy couldn't help himself from asking. It was not his place to question messengers, but at least de Wendenal was still sleeping off the last night's bellyful of wine and not likely to rise for at least another hour.

Ailred winced. "It's not just Sheriff Bardolf. The archbishop is there too, and my lord de Stuteville. A farmer who spoke to some of the foot-soldiers said that it was because they wanted a fortification close to Tickhill – just in case Count John decided to come up here to his castle, you see?"

Guy looked to Sir Walter in horror, both of them thinking that the other castle the prince might want to claim was this one they were in. "I'll go and tell Sir Ralph right away," he said, and seeing Walter's worried nod, dashed out and took the stairs down two at a time.

Finding Ralph Murdac in a small anteroom off the main hall, Guy had no compunction in disrupting his meeting with one of the millers from Nottingham who was discussing delivery of more flour for the castle kitchens.

"Trouble, sire," Guy said as Murdac looked up in surprise at him coming in without waiting for his knock to be answered.

"We'll have those thirty sacks by Thursday or there'll be trouble," Murdac said with a warning wag of his finger at the miller, and then curtly dismissed him with a sharp wave of his hand. As soon as the door had closed, Murdac quirked an eyebrow at Guy who immediately told him,

"The sheriff of Yorkshire and the archbishop have summoned a force and are fortifying Doncaster. We just heard from Ailred, the agister for Rumewood keepership. He said it's because they're worried about John deciding to hold on to Tickhill."

"Christ on the Cross!" Murdac sank back into the leather chair, shocked and horrified.

"We didn't say more in front of Ailred," Guy continued, "but both Sir Walter and I immediately saw where that might go. May God help us, but we've been down this road once before, haven't we! The shires are the prince's, but the castles are the king's. Does Count John never learn?"

Murdac snorted bitterly. "Well given the way his brother's behaved since he became king, he must have thought he was in with more than an even chance of becoming king himself soon. King Henry always had more sense than to be drawn into that unwinnable war in the East. And the old king knew his duty too. He was a hard task-master, but he worked as hard himself. He was a man you could respect, but all Richard thinks of is money for his next fight, and all John thinks about is power; yet of the two John is the one who has the better grasp of what it's realistic to ask."

Guy felt his guts churn. St Issui and St Cadoc watch over me, he silently prayed, Murdac will go with the prince if he has to make the choice, and then we may all end up dead! "Should we wake the sheriff and tell him?" he managed to say without his voice shaking badly. Then wondered what the point was of that. De Wendenal was certainly on the younger Plantagenet's side, and if Murdac wasn't going to restrain him in this matter, then they were damned before the first arrow was loosed.

"No, don't bother him. He wouldn't be alert enough to take it in anyway. Do we know how many men?" Murdac asked, but Guy had to shake his head.

"Ailred only spoke to someone who'd spoken to the foot-soldiers going to Doncaster. He didn't go there himself."

"Then we need someone to ride up there and find out. Get one of the others to go with you and get me some information I can work with. Go! Bring me some numbers, Guy!"

Hurrying out, Guy wondered who on earth he could ask. Ideally he would have ridden alone, but Sir Ralph must have been aware that a knight on his own could all too easily get thrown from his horse or have some other accident, and wanted no delays. He might even have been thinking of the dreaded Robin Hood for all Guy knew! So there would be two of them. Then a bright idea came to him, rather than taking one of the forest knights he would ask one of the three castle knights to come with him. The three were closer friends with him these days, if not quite so much in his confidence as Harry and the soldiers. With any luck, should they run into Robin or any of the others he could presume on that friendship to ask any one of them not to say anything. He would have to say something in such a scenario, and he resolved to say that one of the outlaws was his cousin – it was enough of the truth and yet didn't say that his cousins were in the Robin Hood thing up to their necks. Just please don't let it be Robin himself I see, Guy prayed, because he feared he was the one who wouldn't be tactful regarding Guy's position.

There was little point in setting out that afternoon, but Richard of Burscot was down at the stable waiting for him in the hazy light of the following chilly spring dawn. The first of the primroses in the hedgerows bobbed their golden heads in the breeze as they clattered out of the town and onto the open road, reminding them that warmer days would come even if it was cold now.

"By Our Lady," muttered Sir Richard as he pulled his cloak a little tighter around him, "it's early in the season to be thinking of sieges. I pity the men who have to keep any castle surrounded when the nights are still so cold." He looked up at the leaden clouds piling up from the east. "We could yet have snow, you know."

Guy followed his gaze and nodded. "They look awfully heavy, don't they? It might not stay for long, but as you say, rough on men camping out in it."

"Are the men we're looking for surrounding Doncaster or in it?"

"Hopefully defending it," Guy said after wiping his nose which was running fiercely in the sharp air. "Judas' balls, I've only just got rid of my cold, I hope it's not coming back again!" The entire castle had coughed and sneezed its way through Easter, and Guy had got off lightly, but he had every intention of finding somewhere warm to stop for the night under the pretext of feeling groggy, and with luck that would be Edwinstowe. There was an old lightning-blasted oak near the inn there which he and the outlaws had designated as a message point. A bit of red wool snagged up at rider's height would mean a message in the secure crack beneath, and Guy already had one written out and tucked in his shirt. A trip to the privy in the night would be the means of putting it there, he hoped, because he was desperate to warn his friends to stay clear of both Doncaster and Tickhill.

They had passed Bilsthorpe when Guy became aware of movement off to his left. Under the guise of a sneeze, he managed to duck his head sideways and look behind Sir Richard, then wave a warning to stay way to Gilbert and Piers, whom he identified by Gilbert's red hair and Piers' massive bow. Thereafter he saw Gilbert disappear in the direction of the camp which was deeper in the woods, and Piers kept pace, but out of sight.

It didn't take long once at Edwinstowe, though, for Hugh and Will to come stamping into the inn, bemoaning the cost of wheat and how much it was going to cost to replace a hammer-head. They played the part of local travellers to a nicety, joining in the locals' conversation and barely giving Guy a second glance, but as night fell they paid up their farthing to sleep in the stable loft, indicating that they would be there for Guy's benefit.

Never had it seemed to take so long for a man to get to sleep, but Guy had to admit that although the castle was crowded, and Sir Richard shared a room with Sir Robert and Sir Hugh, the general noise of coughing and snoring from all sorts of men bedding down on the benches was something the knight was not used to. Finally convinced that Richard was deeply asleep, Guy managed to ease himself softly to his feet and slide to the side door out into the yard. Mercifully Will and Hugh were already standing waiting for him at the stable door, and he gratefully slid into the warmth given off by the horses.

"What's up?" Will asked softly.

"Another bloody army on our doorstep!" Guy told them, then explained.

"Jesu!" Hugh breathed when he finished. "Will they attack Tickhill, do you think?"

Guy shrugged. "I truly don't know. I think much depends on Count John. At least Hugh Bardolf is a reasonable man from all that I've heard. And he's very much King Richard's man, so with any luck he has enough authority to halt any war-like feelings of Geoffrey Plantagenet's."

Will gave a chuckle. "He's about as suited to be archbishop as I am!"

"But a good deal more dangerous," Guy countered. "You never know which way the cursed man's going to jump! At the moment he's all Richard's, but I wouldn't trust him further than I can spit not to change sides if he thinks it would be to his advantage. But what worries me more is that it's our unloved sheriff, de Wendenal, who's technically still constable at Tickhill, and he's very much Count John's man. Honestly, I don't know what he might do. If we had a constable who was very much for the king, I'd say he'd stay at Nottingham and protect his interests as sheriff. He won't risk someone handing that castle to the king behind his back. But these days Murdac's so embittered he's for the prince too, and that may well mean that de Wendenal will feel he can safely leave him to mind Nottingham while he goes and fortifies Tickhill. So you must be careful! There could be armed men, and in some numbers, moving between any one of those places."

"Thanks for the warning," Hugh said warmly. "But what about you? Dare you stay on at Nottingham?"

"I don't have a choice," Guy sighed. "I have to go through the motions of staying loyal. As for now, the knight riding with me is Richard of Burscot. He's a good man, but I don't want to test his friendship to the extent of him knowing I have cousins who are outlaws, let alone Robin Hood! We're riding to Doncaster tomorrow. If you can loiter around here and watch for us coming back, I'll try to work what I know into a conversation with Richard, which you might be able to overhear. Otherwise we'll no doubt stop here on the way back. Can you sneak in to meet me here again without being customers at the inn? It might look a bit suspicious if you come back that quickly."

Will clapped him on the shoulder. "Don't you worry! Even Much could get into here after the training we've given him! We'll be about the place and waiting."

That reassured Guy immensely, especially when they got to Doncaster the next night. Camp fires were all around the town, and just going by them it looked to be a formidable force.

"Do we go to the leaders and ask?" Sir Richard wondered. "What do we say?"

However Guy at least felt confident on that score. "We have every reason to ask what's going on! Remember, Richard, our own castle is linked to Tickhill in many ways, so we have no reason to feign our concern."

They were taken into the presence of Hugh Bardolf, and with suitable deference to the Sheriff of Yorkshire's status, Guy requested information on what was going on, concluding with,

"We are all aware that Nottingham is not a castle to be easily besieged, my lord, but with our sheriff still the constable of Tickhill in name – even if the practical side is deputised – he is understandably concerned."

Hugh Bardolf snorted. "I bet he is! Well you may tell your sheriff that as long as he makes no war-like moves, he has nothing to fear from us. However knowing what the youngest of King Henry's sons is like, we felt it incumbent on ourselves to make an appropriate showing of force on the king's behalf. Do you understand?"

Guy nodded. "I do, my lord. You could not afford to let Count John think that the north was his for the taking, and using two such formidable castles as Tickhill and Nottingham to do it with. We get enough trade passing through to know that the main roads to the north on this side of the country are dominated by such castles."

Bardolf gave him a smile. "Good. You're shrewd enough to see the position. You might remind your sheriff that both Sir William de Stuteville and myself are enfeoffed to Count John as he is. Therefore we cannot make any move of aggression directly towards him without breaking our oaths. However, should he do something which could be seen as acting openly against the king, that would another matter. Do you see?"

"The king is the higher authority," Guy ventured, and saw that he'd got it right. "So you cannot attack the prince because he is your lord unless he attacks the king, who is his lord in turn." Then couldn't help himself from adding. "What a bloody mess!"

Now Bardolf laughed out loud. "That it is, young man, that it is! And our war-like archbishop is positively itching to get his armour on and have a fight. The bloody man's remembering his days fighting alongside his father, no doubt, but it's far from ideal to be having him trying to wrest castles from his half-brother just at the moment."

"Well I hope you succeed in getting him to keep the peace," Guy said from the heart, and was relieved to hear the same feeling in Bardolf's,

"So do I!"

As Guy and Sir Richard prepared to ride back the next day, they got a better chance to see the force encamped at Doncaster. There were more than twenty knights milling around the main leaders, but Guy was relieved to see that it was unlikely that there were more than a hundred foot-soldiers.

"How many do you reckon?" he said softly to Sir Richard, as they rode out.

"About a hundred and thirty ...a hundred and forty? Allowing for the ones we can't see, but by the number of tents, no more. But what's going on over there?"

Guy looked in the direction of Richard's nod and saw the piles of long timbers with activity all around them. "I'd guess a palisade. The town's not got much in the way of defences these days, so I suspect that Bardolf and Stuteville want to make sure they have something to retreat behind if necessary. Not that I think Count John will come up here when he's got William Marshal camped at his gate at Windsor. But they no doubt want to be safe rather than sorry."

At Edwinstowe, Guy once again managed to slip out to meet Will and pass on the warnings.

"I hate bloody sieges," Will sighed. "Give me a good fast battle any day!" Guy could understand that. They had all suffered too much at Jerusalem, and Will was clearly thinking of there too when he added, "Think we'll try and get Robin clear of here. Time to go and take some of that money up to your mother, eh? And then take the silver on up to Loxley."

"Excellent idea!" Guy enthused, glad that Will was already thinking that if Robin was on more of an even keel at the moment it was best to try and keep him that way, not rake over the old ashes again and get them burning in his soul once more.

He was less reassured by de Wendenal's reception of the news.

"Ha! They don't dare act openly against Count John!" he chortled, swinging his wine goblet in his enthusiasm and dousing Ralph Murdac with a goodly portion of it in the process.

"I don't think that's quite it," Murdac countered waspishly, as he wiped the red wine off his face and looked grimly at his shirt, which was now liberally splattered too.

"Don't you?" de Wendenal sneered. "They're too scared of what he might do when he becomes king, that's what I think!"

Murdac gave him a filthy look, which de Wendenal was too drunk to notice, but once the sheriff was snoring, sprawled across the table with his head resting on his platter with the remains of his dinner, he said openly to the others,

"We're walking a tight line here. This news of the king's mother acting against her youngest son is troubling. And Richard's not dead yet, however much Count John might wish it. He's more than capable of issuing orders still. And his bloody half-brother is sitting on our border – is he likely to be too scared to attack? I don't think so! God help us if Geoffrey comes to us with sword and fire, because he's outside the regular constraints now he's archbishop!"

Guy thought it significant that Murdac would refer to the king as merely 'Richard', but gave his brother his title of 'Count' – another hint of which way Murdac's sympathies lay, even if he was too astute to risk openly acting. But he agreed with Murdac's assessment – Geoffrey Plantagenet was the one to watch at the moment, the one who could plunge the whole area into chaos.

Yet the weeks dragged on with no sign of the prince coming north, or of those fortifying Doncaster leaving it. Bardolf had to be keeping the king's half-brother on a tight leash for now at least. And then at the end of April the blow came. The ransom demand had been received, and it was truly shocking.

"Seventy thousand marks?" half of those in the hall to hear the news gasped in unison when it was announced.

"Does England even *have* seventy thousand?" someone wondered, just as Murdac cried out in appalled tones at what his clerk had just read to him,

"Christ have mercy on us!" Hurriedly adding, "The emperor has actually set the ransom at one hundred thousand marks, but is willing to set the king free on receipt of seventy thousand. Blessed St Thomas, that has to be double what goes into the Exchequer in any single year! That's like asking us to raise a year's taxes over again and with twice as much on top! We'll never do it. The people don't have that much." His clerk read on very quietly to him, then he looked up at his frozen audience. "It says here that this time the Church will have to pay too. Well that's something, at least!"

"Thank God for that!" Sir Hugh breathed to Guy, who dared to ask,

"How much have they got to pay?"

The clerk's tremulous answer was relayed to the room by Murdac. "The clergy have to pay quarter of all their income apparently, and the churches have to give up all their gold and silver. And the abbeys of those orders who do not have gold and silver are to give up their wool-clip for the year."

"We'll have trouble there, no doubt about it," Sir Richard declared. "They've not been used to being bled white like we have. And I presume we are going to be bled white, Sir Ralph?"

The constable had already gone very pale. "A quarter of every man's income, it says here, but for knights it will also be twenty shillings for every knight's-fee."

Guy felt himself go cold. For knight who barely qualified as such, like himself, with a tiny manor, that was a lot to find on top of the quarter of his income – it was a fifth of the yearly knight's-fee for someone a good deal further up the scale of nobility than he was, the kind of man who was one step below becoming a baron and far above himself. How would he come by such money? With shock he realised that this time he too might have to ask for help from Robin. If he wasn't rich, he was also not poor under normal circumstances, but these demands might just impoverish him permanently.

"We have to start collecting the ransom immediately," Murdac sighed, and a collective groan went up.

Miserable beyond belief, everyone began a slow shuffle out of the hall, and Guy found himself beside Giles, his amiable but rather dense former room-mate.

"What's that in English pounds, Guy?" Giles asked him, his face creased in anguish as he desperately tried to calculate how much he would have to pay.

"A hundred thousand marks? Probably about sixty-six thousand pounds."

"Oh God!"

"Oh God, indeed, but spare a thought for the soldiers here, they're lucky if they get tuppence a day for the days they give service. They're even worse off than us."

He didn't dare say what he was thinking, which was of how the cottagers who could find paying a penny for a sheep or sixpence for a pig hard to find, would then find more.

"Pray that the coming winter is a mild one, Giles, or we may have people starving to death after we've collected this lot. They'll have nothing left to buy seed to sow. Even we'll be tightening our belts, I fear."

It certainly made Guy's daily life an utter misery, for aside from his regular duties he now had to help with the collection of the ransom. No-one with even a vestige of authority was exempt from this onerous task because of the short time they had to accomplish it in. In just five months the money needed to be all in for it to go to the Michaelmas court, and so he found himself going out accompanied by two soldiers at all times, for everyone expected trouble. Luckily he usually managed to ensure that it was two from the twelve he regarded as his friends, but he made sure he had words with the other soldiers too.

"For God's sake tell the people that everyone is being taxed!" he urged them. "Tell them the Church is to lose all its gold and silver. Tell them that the knight who rides with you not only has to pay the same tax of a quarter the value of all income and property as they do, but the fee on top as well."

"Why?" one of the soldiers demanded belligerently. "Why bother?"

Guy glared at him. "Because they're used to it being them alone who bears the burden of taxes, you fool! And if they see that even those they see as high above them and untouched by the misery they normally suffer getting hit too, they at least might not stone you when you come grabbing what little they have left!"

He saw his words start to make a dent in their truculence. "Remember, even in the smallest places there might be a dozen men and lads. There'll only be two of you and a knight. What will you do if they choose to resist? They won't have swords and spears, no. But a few young lads off to the side with slings and several sharp pebbles could still do you a lot of harm. If one hit you in the eye it might even kill you! Do you want that?" Now he really had their attention. "So this time, make an effort to explain that we're all suffering."

He wasn't sure how long his words would last with those who marched out with the likes of Walkelin or Henry, but at least he'd tried. Time and again, for himself he found that if it made no-one any happier, at least nobody tried to brain him with a shovel or impale him with a pitchfork when he took the ransom amount. And more and more he was desperately hoping that Robin had amassed a small fortune, because they were going to need it if the folk of Nottinghamshire and Derbyshire weren't to starve.

He said as much when he travelled up to High Peak again at the start of May to see Sir Richard. A local lord had felled four great oaks to build a new hall, and was arguing that they had come from the western bank of the Derwent, and therefore out of the forest. But Sir Richard was sure they had come from close by Hathersage.

"The man must think I'm blind," Sir Richard snorted in disgust as he welcomed Guy. "I can't find even one stump where he says, much less four! Yes, his hall is outside of the forest, but I need someone to swear that those oaks came from right where our two forests meet, and a knight, not just one of my walking foresters."

"It's my pleasure to come," Guy assured him. "By Our Lady, I'm glad for some respite in collecting this damned ransom."

"Aye, it's bad," Sir Richard sighed. "My miners have paid up ...grudgingly, but they've paid. I was dreading what I might have to do to extract it if they didn't."

At that Guy had to bite his lip. It was almost certainly that the miners had learned from his time at the castle, and when they had hit a rich seam, had hidden the extra away against such a time as this. He saw one of the serving women looking anxiously at him, and managed a covert wink at her, at which she smiled and hurried out. Yes, he'd been right. They'd been just a touch worried he might say to the genial Sir Richard that he should look at some of the supposedly worked out mine caves and see what was hidden there. That Guy had kept their secret would ensure that not only he, but Robin and the others as well, kept their goodwill. And of anywhere the people of this valley would be counting on Robin Hood to help later on, but it could prove fatal if that faith was crushed, because they could betray Guy with ease.

"I fear for the farmers in the Trent valley," Guy said, turning the conversation to places further afield. "They have such good soil they're used to planting wheat and buying in animal feed. I don't think they have reserves of oats and the vetches to plant mixed crops for themselves as those on poorer land do. I never thought I'd see the day, but for once the ones who farm poor soil and have maslin or mixtil coming up from the winter sowing, or even a pure crop of rye, will be better off later on, I'm thinking. No-one will want to seize a crop that's mixed grains. And I've done what I can to encourage those I've seen, to plant at least one field with mengrell this spring. Again, oats with a good mix of peas and beans in it won't be good enough to sell, but it will keep those folk alive. The only trouble is that I don't get to go over to the east side of the shire much anymore, and the folk over on these higher lands don't need me to tell them to grow more of the unsellable mixed crops to save their lives."

"You think it will come to that?" Sir Richard asked worriedly. "I've not been away from here apart from visits to my own manor, so I've not seen as much as you have."

Guy's expression was grim. "In some cases I reckon they've practically had to pick the wheat seeds up off the floor to scrap the means together to pay this levy. It's the bit the great lords never seem to see. Peasants don't have that much coin about the place! So when the demand comes for a quarter on their income and portable property, what do they think these people have? It's going to be pretty much all portable property until the wheat harvest gets sold, and even then we'll have to take the wheat instead of coin. I tell you, I don't know how rents will get paid at Michaelmas. I reckon most lords will have to wait a good six months this time before most folk will be able to pay."

"Thank the Lord that mining isn't so seasonal," Sir Richard said with some relief. "At least the folk here will have a new lot of ore to sell and buy food with."

Yet Guy shook his head. "No, I think you're missing the point. What will they buy? If all the grain goes to markets across the sea to raise money, what's going to be left? Not much, and what there is will likely treble in price because of the shortage. And I fear the wheat will go straight out of England, because after we've bled everyone of their last coins, who will have any to buy wheat with? Certainly not soon enough to satisfy the ransom time limits!"

"Blessed St Thomas!"

"Yes, I hope he looks after his people, because they're going to need it!"

Then realised that Sir Richard was looking at the castle anxiously too.

"Is there something else?"

The older knight gave a grimace. "What do I do if they come to besiege me here, Guy? That's my other worry. I'm going to send what I have to the sheriff with you, if that's alright with you, because I've got to admit I'm worried I might get holed up here."

Guy blinked. "Why would you think that? It's been over a month since the lords fortified Doncaster, and they haven't moved on Tickhill yet."

"Oh dear, you haven't heard?"

"Heard? No, not if you mean there's been a change. Mind you, I've been in and out of the castle so fast I've barely had time to change my clothes and get a meal and night's sleep. What's happened?"

Sir Richard puffed out his cheeks, then answered, "Quite a lot! Did you not hear that King Richard had heard of his brother making trouble, and offered him a truce?"

"Lord, no!"

"Well he has! The king has told him that he must give up Windsor and Wallingford, and this castle here. I've been on my knees giving thanks in the chapel that the count never made it this far north, because I don't know what I'd have done with him claiming this place as his own."

"Jesu!" Guy gasped in horror. "I'd not heard he'd laid claim to High Peak as well as Tickhill and Nottingham."

"Well he did. But in that whole truce between the brothers, it now means that Hugh Bardolf and William de Stuteville have declared that they cannot in conscience take arms against the Count now, and they've left Doncaster. But not the archbishop. Oh, no, not the archbishop! He wants a fight! So now he's gone to Tickhill thinking to join Hugh le Puiset – another bloody war-mongering Churchman. And the bloody archbishop is also calling the other two cowards! To give le Puiset credit, he's abiding by the truce and leaving, although I heard he's not happy about that, because he thought he wasn't far off taking it. That has to be why Archbishop Geoffrey has gone there – he thinks he'll just pick up where the bishop of Durham left off, and he'll have a castle in his hands."

Guy was so shocked he couldn't think of anything to say for a moment. This was turning into a regular squabble between the remaining three sons of King Henry, and with half of England caught up in the fray.

"So what's bothering me," Sir Richard was continuing, "is what if he takes Tickhill and then thinks he can come here? Or if Tickhill resists more than he expects, and he comes here under the guise of making sure High Peak stays loyal to the king. I mean, he can lie through his teeth and say he's holding either for the king, can't he? Who's to say he won't hand them over when King Richard gets home? Geoffrey's not the one who's been collecting castles like they were feast day sweetmeats, and he was famously loyal to the old king. He'll get away with it. But what do *I* do if he comes here?"

Guy was thinking furiously. "Do you know, I'd open the gates and let him in. You can't possibly fend him off with just twelve men, and if King Richard is even half the fighter he's supposed to be, he'll know that. And you are way outranked by the archbishop. De Wendenal, as the king's sheriff, has a certain authority, but you're just a constable charged with the care of the castle in the absence of any greater lord. In your shoes, I'd be going out the back door as he comes in the front! Take advantage of the fact that anyone bringing the horses to the stables will still have to ride around the valley and come up the long way."

"But where would I go?" Sir Richard asked him. "Especially if they come in the evening!"

Guy's conscience tweaked at him. He had to tell Richard about the cave beneath the castle now. "Get a horse, hide in the valley on the far side of the castle, and then when they're all inside, come back round to the front as if you were going to ride up the valley yourself. The entrance to the cave beneath this castle looks narrow, but there's room in there for you and your horse. The villagers know about it, but few others do, and you've been fair to them – I can't see them betraying you."

Sir Richard looked at Guy in amazement. "A cave beneath the castle? By Our Lady, is there? I thought it just some old rock-fall."

Guy grinned. "Get beyond that and you'll soon find differently. It doesn't have the ores our miners want, you see, so it isn't worked like some of the places you see round here, but it's a cave all right. And if it saves your life..."

Sir Richard nodded mutely, only too glad to see some way out of his predicament.

"I hope it doesn't come to that," Guy added, "but if it does, I can't imagine that they'll come hunting for you at your own manor. If you'll forgive me for saying it, it's the castle which is important, not you."

Now Sir Richard laughed. "This must be the first time I've been so glad to not be higher up the ladder. There's much to be said for being one of the humbler knights!"

"That there is!" Guy agreed, and poured them both some more ale.

When he left, he made for Nottingham with all speed, not wanting to take any chances with the money he had laden onto a pack-horse. Once there the sheriff and Murdac both expressed approval for Sir Richard's thinking in making sure the money got out before the archbishop got too war-like, but Guy was gladdened to hear Murdac add,

"Although I hear that even the archbishop has had to go back to York and his minster. The news that all his plate is to be sent to help release his half-brother hasn't gone down well! The last we heard, he and his men were seen riding north, no doubt so that bloody Geoffrey can salt some of it away before it all gets sent south!"

Yet some good came of it at last when Guy caught up with Robin again. The jewels they had taken across to Lincoln had been received with delight by the Jewish families they had helped before. Having had all they possessed in York taken only two years ago, they had been horrified to hear that the king intended them to bear one of the heaviest taxes on his behalf, as the Jews of England had to raise five thousand marks of the ransom all by themselves.

"They near snapped our hands off for those jewels," Will told Guy with a laugh. "Much easier to hide, you see? I know some folk see them as grasping, but the poor souls round here have been hit hard these last few years, and who's going to help the likes of them?"

"No," Tuck agreed woefully. "It won't be like in the villages, where everyone will do their best to help each other. There they need every person to be able to work and do their share of ploughing and harvesting, so they'll pull together. But few understand what the Jews have to do to earn a living when they're barred from so many trades."

"I am glad we were able to help them again," James agreed. "It was not like this back home."

Will draped a consoling arm around the younger man's shoulders. "No, it wasn't like this in the Holy Land." He gave an apologetic glance Guy's way. "There were some idiots amongst the Templers and other knights, but not this turning on one another amongst the ordinary folk like us."

As Robin seemed to bristle at the implied slight to England, it was Marianne who saved the day by adding, "I saw one of the young women we met from York. She's still in Lincoln with her family. She said the women don't like going to market on their own any more. They wait until a couple of the men can go with them. Isn't that horrible! To be too scared to even go and get food."

Deflected, Robin sighed and said, "People see the local knights going to the Jews to borrow money to pay their share of the ransom, so they think there must be even more money hidden away. It's a short step then to thinking that if the Jews have money to spare, then why aren't they paying up and saving the ordinary people from going hungry. They can't begin to grasp promissory notes. They wouldn't be able to satisfy their lord with a note saying they would pay up in instalments, so it never enters their heads that the Jews' wealth is all in pieces of paper tying others to giving what money they had back to them." He gave Marianne a hug. "But we've helped them by taking what coin they had and leaving them with the jewels. If they have to flee, at least they have something to start a new life with."

Guy was glad that Robin had found something positive in the situation, but he was more worried by James. The young turcopole had never seemed to quite settle in England, and now he was looking positively miserable. When it was possible to draw Malik onto one side without causing comment, Guy asked him,

"Do you think James wants to leave?"

For a moment Malik looked startled, but when he answered it wasn't to tell Guy he was foolish to think such a thing.

"You noticed? ...Then you are more observant than Robin!" The older of the two natives of the Holy Land sighed and drew Guy even further off. "I have not said anything to Robin. I do not want him to start trying to talk James round. That would be unfair to James – to make him so much the centre of Robin's attention."

It was carefully said, but Guy thought it was as much because Malik didn't quite know how to put into English that Robin would badger James witless. He could easily see that happening, though. Faced with one of his trusted few leaving, Robin would do all in his power to make him stay.

"Don't worry," Guy reassured Malik, "I won't say a word. But do you think he'll try to leave?"

Malik shrugged. "Maybe. I think what has stopped him so far is that he does not know where to go to." He dropped his voice confidentially. "But while we were with the Jews the one family said they were packing to go to some more of their family in Spain. They said that if things get bad there, then it is only a short journey to the North African coast, and from there they could go east more easily." He shook his head sadly. "There are always ships working that coast if you have the means to pay them, so they are right. But they said they would welcome someone who could act as a guard. I suspect that James intends to go with them. He has said nothing to me yet, but I am sure he will go."

"He was very taken with that young widow," Guy recalled.

Malik managed a watery smile. "Oh yes! And that is another matter which may sway him, because she is one of those leaving."

"And being James, he would not be upset by her bringing her children up in her own faith if they should wed."

Now Malik was surprised. "You have James ...oh what are the words?"

"Weighed up?"

"Yes, weighed-up!" Malik looked to Robin. "You spend so little time with us, and yet you see what Robin does not."

There was a lot of sadness in those last words, and Guy wondered if Malik himself was half thinking of leaving too. He didn't want to ask, though. Losing James would be a bitter blow to Robin, but Malik would be a loss he himself would feel, for he felt sure that Malik worked well with the steadier heads amongst the gang to curb Robin's wilder plans.

"If you get a chance, will you tell James that I understand why he would want to go?" he said instead. "I would hate for him to think that all of us are so uncaring of the sorrow he feels, or that we haven't seen how he missed having a young family about him."

"You are a good man, Guy," Malik said with feeling, and with that Guy had to be content.

You do not understand why I have mentioned James leaving? Ah but it is all part of that great suffering which made Robin Hood into the legend he became. You see James and Malik provided a wider perspective on what went on in our small corner of England. They had grown up in a distant land, but one which was very like England in the way that it was governed. There were lords there whose families had connections with England and France and the Holy Roman Empire, and who raised their taxes in much the same way. But they did not have the kind of officials we had in England. For that matter, Brother, neither does Normandy! Indeed I shall break from telling you this in strict order for once to tell you that

the balance of that ransom was ultimately paid from Normandy, and for the simple reason that it took so much longer to get money out of those lords. His mother and her loyal nobles managed to quell any resistance in Aquitaine, but Normandy only paid up when the king himself went there in force once he had been released!

So to Malik and James it was a huge shock to see how put upon the ordinary folk of England were. It made our lovely land feel more alien than ever the lush greenery and rains did. And to James, already feeling the pain of losing his family, to see families with young children being used so cruelly was more than he was able to bear. Did you think to hear such a thing, Gervase? That one who had fought his way through the hell on Earth that was the Holy Land in those years, would find England even more unbearable? No, I did not think you would. Yet that was very much the case – it became insupportable for James, and you will soon hear of him leaving, but also of others from his homeland arriving in our shire.

Ah, that tempts and teases, does it? Well then I shall press on! But before I do, I would urge you to remember our fears about Geoffrey Plantagenet, because they were to come back to haunt us within only a few months, and with disastrous consequences. That triangle between King Henry's two remaining legitimate sons and the illegitimate one had not finished with us yet!

Chapter 23

So we have reached the height of the summer of 1193, and by the end of June the means of handing over the ransom had been worked out, although we in the shires had little knowledge of that. When two-thirds of the ransom had been raised, the king would be released as long as hostages were provided in his place. And here we come to an old adversary again, because for reasons I think only the king understood, the person he nominated to take those hostages to the emperor was the dreadful Longchamp. It says much for his evil reputation that Queen Eleanor, even in her desperation to get her beloved Richard home again, refused to hand over her grandson to Longchamp's care. This boy was not the only hostage who was refused to be handed over to Longchamp, so it was not merely the queen's dislike of him personally.

I have never understood why the king kept such a man close to him. It did nothing to enhance the king's reputation, that was for certain, and came close to halting his plans to be released. I am not sure who eventually took the hostages. It may have been the queen herself, because she certainly travelled to meet the king. But I tell you this fact now to emphasise just how little thought King Richard gave to others. He was not such a devil as his younger brother was to become, but equally he was not the good man my cousin Robin thought him to be either. I now see that the only way anyone ever got King Richard's attention was by rebelling against him. Otherwise the fate of others never entered his head in his single-minded pursuit of his own goals. Maybe he was as great as you think him for his holy quest, but he was also bitterly cruel in his disinterest.

As for Archbishop Geoffrey, he was now kept busy with his own canons at York, who refused to pay towards the ransom and barricaded themselves in. There was also some quarrel between them over who would become their dean – an argument I know little about and cared even less about at the time. All I was bothered about was that Geoffrey travelled to see King Richard, because he wished to appeal to Rome and the king forbade him to – or so Tuck was to tell me was the case once he had spoken to fellow priests.

For me, though, there was much relief that my friend Sir Richard was not to be plagued by the archbishop and his men. He did not have to use the cave beneath the castle, but when I confessed that I had told him of it, Robin was less than pleased, and I knew that I had somehow slipped in his estimation again by seemingly being over-friendly with the enemy. Luckily he was later to meet Sir Richard and liked him, so I was forgiven, but this constant misjudging of my actions was exceedingly wearing to me, Brother, and I confess to some very un-Christian thoughts at the times when he did it.

For the time being, however, we were in the midst of the whole ransom affair, and it was to come to impact on us personally in a most unexpected way as the summer moved on. For some things were about to change in the outlaw's gang, starting with James' departure.

Sherwood
July onwards, the Year of Our Lord 1193

"Did you know?" was the demand from Robin, as Guy rode up to them for a prearranged meeting at the camp they had right on the shire border with Derbyshire.

"Know what?" Guy shot back, having no trouble in looking confused since he hadn't a clue what Robin was talking about.

"James has left us," Gilbert said sadly. "Just up and left with not a word to anyone except Malik." He gave his fellow former-crusader a baleful glance.

"I gave him my word not to warn you," Malik said calmly, although Guy got the hint that he was already getting rather tired of having to justify himself.

"And that makes it alright?"

Guy was rather shocked that the challenge came from John. When had his cousin become so blind to another's suffering? And that made Guy throw back,

"And what would you have had Malik do? Be faithless and break his word? It wasn't his decision. Anyone could see that James was getting more and more miserable in England."

That had all of them turning to him in surprise.

"You thought that?" Piers said, quite amazed. "But you hardly ever saw him."

"Then maybe that's why it stuck out like a sore thumb to me," Guy replied with an apologetic shrug. "I didn't say anything because I assumed you all saw it too – you all being with him so much more of the time."

"Hugh says he saw it, and I did too," Mariota spoke up, "but I don't think either of us thought that he would leave. We didn't think he had anywhere to go to."

"I should have taken more care of him," said Tuck sadly. "I have failed one of my flock."

Will gave a grumbling noise in his throat. "For pity's sake, Tuck, give it a rest! He wasn't only your responsibility! We should all be looking out for one another, and just because James was so quiet doesn't mean we shouldn't have been a bit more watchful."

Guy cast his eye around the assembled group and saw that Allan and Roger weren't looking as bothered as some of the others. That didn't surprise him. He would have been more shocked if they had not noticed James' misery. He also thought Siward was carefully avoiding Robin's glance, so that probably meant he, too, had been aware all was not well with James. But to Robin the leaving was obviously a cutting shock, and Guy remembered back to when they had all come to High Peak, and how Robin had confessed that James had become a substitute for Allan in his affections during those years away in the East.

Dismounting, Guy walked over to Robin and wrapped his arms around his cousin in what he was hoping would taken as a familiar, cousinly gesture, not the embrace of a traitor.

"Don't take it so personally," he urged. "The times when I saw James most unhappy wasn't when he was with you in the camps. It was when he saw what life was like for the ordinary people. It was England he couldn't come to terms with, not being with you." He held Robin back at arms' length now, and saw to his relief that his words were having an effect. "Come on ...you've said yourself that sometimes it feels like you've come home to a strange country. Well how much worse do you think it would be if this really was a strange country, and there was nothing at all which was familiar for you to hang onto?"

Robin took a deep, ragged breath, then looked over Guy's shoulder to Malik. "Is it that strange to you? Is it that bad?"

Malik gave a very eastern shrug. "Sometimes. The way your people are so tied up with laws and rules is far worse than at home. I think that is what James found very hard to accept." His eyes met Guy's and there was gratitude there for helping get this out in the open without an argument raging around it, and Guy knew there must have been arguments – Robin would not have accepted this quietly!

"Do you want to go back?" Robin was asking him, appalled.

Again, Malik shrugged. "Not particularly, but then I can guess what our home must be like now. It cannot be as it was when James and I were boys, that is certain. If we return to our homes we will have Saracen lords, and it may not be so good being a Christian there anymore."

"But you didn't have a family there, either," Guy piled in, trying to help, hurriedly clarifying with, "At least I don't mean you never had a father or mother or other family. I meant as a married man." He turned to Robin again. "Can you see that what James probably missed most was being able to go and see a wife and children? Maybe not every day, but he knew they were there. And then suddenly they weren't, and neither were his brothers. So during the first couple of years he was with you and mourning them, all of you as his friends helped fill that gap. But at heart I think James is a family man, and it's all the worse for him, because of all of you, he had that once and so he knows exactly what it is that he was missing so badly." He gave Robin the small shake he used to give back when they were children, and he needed to make the idealistic younger boy see sense. "He wasn't rejecting you! He just needed something you couldn't give him anymore."

Belatedly Guy recalled that he wasn't supposed to know where James had gone and thought to say. "How did he go? Did he join up with some merchants heading south? Please don't tell me he went to the Templers and volunteered to go back!"

Robin scowled. "He went with some of the Jews from Lincoln who are going eastwards."

"Well that's not so bad, surely?" Guy released Robin as he threw up his hands in a questioning gesture. "What's so terrible about that? He's gone with people he knows. He's not alone. He's not going to fight – or at least not unless he absolutely has to, because I know nowhere is totally safe these days. You don't have to worry about him so much in a company." But Robin's scowl darkened even more, annoying Guy. "What is the matter Baldw... Robin?"

Guy's tone and the slip into his old name brought the full focus of Robin's glare onto Guy now.

"He broke his word to me! He promised to stay and fight!"

Now Guy didn't have to feign anger, and he riposted acidly, "So this is all about your wounded pride, is it? Not poor James' misery at all? You miserable little shit! James didn't do what you wanted. Oh-fucking-dear!"

"Don't you take..."

"I damned well will! By Our Lady, when did you turn into such a pompous little prick? Get off your high horse and think about James as the man he is – not some wretched servant bound and tied to you! How long ago was it that he promised to stay and fight, eh? No, I can guess! It was probably back when you were all leaving High Peak, or sometime around then?" Guy spun on his heels and strode back several paces, and then turned and marched back to Robin when the urge to slap him had momentarily passed.

"You ask too much of these men! You aren't some crusader commander with a force to do with as you will! These are people who follow you because they care about what you are fighting for. But that doesn't give you the right to ride roughshod over their feelings and needs! Bloody grow up!

"James left because he no longer felt he could do what you asked of him, and he had every right to do that. He promised to try, and he's given you more than two years of trying to prove it. If that's not good enough for you, then I suggest you go and closet yourself in some monastery somewhere, far from the world! Because in the real world people change, and people's needs change, and if you can't love them as they are, then you have no business demanding promises from them which they may not be able to keep!

"Fucking hell, Robin, he hasn't betrayed you as Algar did! He hasn't tried to force you to do something like Walter did. He's just quietly got up and gone and taken your secrets with him! Over the sea, and there, who's going to give a tinker's cuss who Robin Hood is, or what he's doing? Even if he falls foul of some great lord and gets questioned – which I pray to St Issui he doesn't – he can't betray you because you don't mean anything where he's gone! So get a grip on yourself!"

Robin was now furious too. "Always the big cousin, aren't you! Piss off, Guy, I'm a grown man now! And don't you ever speak to me like that in front of my men again!"

"Well I wouldn't bloody have to if you'd stop behaving like some spoilt half-grown lordling!" Guy spat back. "Oh don't think I don't see it! I may only meet up with you once a month or so, but even just riding in now, I can see that you've been badgering Malik over this. No, don't shake your head, I can see it! So I'm telling you that if you don't stop this, one by one these men who are so loyal to you at the moment will start drifting away.

"I don't give a shit if you don't want to see me again for telling you the truth! Once I ride out of here you can't spend the next two weeks giving me earache over it. But that means I'm the one person who can speak up and tell you that you're behaving like some petty warlord. Stop looking to get all the glory, and start giving the others some credit for what they do to make your barmy ideas happen, and then give them some bloody choices! You don't have to hang onto them like they're children or moonstruck fools, who'll fall down a well without you controlling their every move! In fact most of them could lead this gang as well as you've been doing this last year! So stop throwing your twisted piety about oaths in their faces too, or you might find you're in a gang of one, and they go off without you!"

And with that Guy didn't wait to hear if Robin replied, but marched over to his horse and pulled the reins out of the thorn bush which he had flung them into to tether her. Yet as he turned back to be able to mount up, he saw Robin had stormed off into the forest, and the others were all just standing there open-mouthed. It made him pause, and so he saw that John was the first to move, making as if to follow Robin, then was surprised to see Tuck and Allan catch John's arms.

"No, John, leave him!" he heard Allan say gently, as Tuck added, "Sometimes the truth hurts, but it has to be said."

John turned to look at Guy, who had put his foot back down on the ground from the stirrup and was standing watching.

"You didn't have to be so hard, Guy," John remonstrated. "That was unnecessarily harsh."

"No, it wasn't," Will said bluntly. "I'm actually glad Guy did that."

John was aghast. "Why?"

Will tutted. "Bloody hell, John, are you so blind too? Haven't you seen how Robin's been to Malik these last few days? That wasn't fair. It wasn't called for. And I don't care how much he's haunted by Hattin and Jerusalem, he's overstepped a mark this time. We've all been pussy-footing around him because of how fragile he's been sometimes, but I'm thinking that maybe he's taken our kindness the wrong way!"

"You aren't thinking of leaving, are you?" a shock John asked.

"I won't say it hasn't crossed my mind," Will replied honestly. "I'm getting pretty sick of his attitude, to be frank, but actually leaving ...not yet."

"I'm glad you said it too, Guy," Mariota's voice said, and Guy turned to see that she was holding onto a sobbing Marianne, who had probably tried to follow Robin too. "And not just for James and Malik's sakes. If Robin wants to recruit new men; or we come across someone who ought to be with us; we can't have him tearing into them and demanding they take Templers vows or the like, and berating them when they don't show some weird kind of monastic subservience. They'll just go! And you made a good point when you said that even if – God forbid – James comes to harm, he can't betray us. Because the next time it might be someone who's been with us a shorter time, and who only goes a couple of shires away, and would give us up to save them or their family."

Her words seemed to finally hit home with both John and Marianne, who stopped crying and looked up at her friend in shock.

"Oh my God, I hadn't thought of it like that!" she gasped.

Hugh cleared his throat, and when everyone had turned his way, then said, "Well that's the advantage of having someone like Guy, isn't it? Someone who has a different view on things. Who spots stuff we don't see because we're too caught up in what's in front of us." He walked over to John and put his hands on his shoulders. "And you mustn't be so hard on Guy. To say what he did, it had to come from a member of his family. Someone close enough to shout back. Allan couldn't do it. Robin wouldn't have taken it from his younger cousin."

He shook his head, "And you've been so close to Robin you wouldn't do it. You're a good man, John, but you're too soft with him. So Guy was the only one left who could – and don't fool yourself that what he said wasn't necessary. It was! I've been holding my breath these last couple of days in case we lost Malik, because I know Will wouldn't have let him go alone. And then we'd not only have lost two good friends. We'd have lost two of our best soldiers as well. How do you feel about going into a fight without them?"

There was another cough from the other side. "We'd half talked about trying to get back to Wales," Thomas said apologetically. He wrapped a brotherly arm around Bilan. "Found it very upsetting, all this blame throwing, did our Bilan. And me and Piers weren't too happy either, see? Never got further than a bit of talk, mind, but don't think Malik and Will were the only ones."

Tuck went and wrapped both of them in one of his big hugs. "*Gwisga t adawch 'm 'ma ag hyn 'n waedlyd Saesneg baganiaid!*" (Don't you leave me here with these bloody English pagans!) And the three Coshams laughed, breaking the tension, although Guy alone knew what Tuck had said.

"For God's sake, let's go and eat! I'm bloody starving!" Will declared, and everyone trooped back to the campfire, where Tuck had something aromatic brewing in a large cauldron.

It took until nightfall for Robin to come back, and it was clear that he was far from pleased that Guy was still there, but he must also have heard how the others were all chatting freely to him. Guy was half hoping for some kind of apology to the others, but evidently that was not going to happen while he was still there. He knew he wouldn't get one himself. Instead Robin went and sat himself down beside Marianne, and seemed reassured when she immediately looped her arm through his and smiled up at him.

"We were just talking about handing out the money we have," Gilbert told him. "Guy's been telling us that we might be best waiting until after Michaelmas."

"If we give it to them now, there's the danger that some lords – having been hard pressed for money themselves – will start searching peasant homes for anything they can take in lieu of rent," Siward added.

"We've decided that we'll hand out small amounts of flour or grain for now," Tuck said firmly. "Stuff they can use straight away, not have to store. That way we know they'll get the benefit from it."

"They didn't get all of the ransom in this sweep, either," Guy warned. "I was telling the others that there's a real danger that there'll be another collection. Some of the churches have been very resistant to handing over the silver, and after the threats of excommunication last year, no-one's too keen on battering down the monastery doors."

"You can't blame them for that," Tuck sighed. "Some pompous priest putting the fear of God into them is bound to have an effect, although I'd like to get my hands on men like that. Fair gets under my skin, it does, mere men twisting the fate of someone's soul just for worldly reward!" And everyone laughed, because Tuck was struggling not to break into Welsh in his disgust.

"Are you suggesting we target churches?" Robin asked cagily.

Guy looked to the others, not daring to say the plan that was coming had been his idea. Please let one of the others speak up and tell Robin.

Mercifully Siward winked at him as he said. "Hmm, not exactly the churches. Let's face it, the poor priests in many village churches are no better off than those they're serving. No, we were thinking more of the bishops and some of the bigger monasteries. We thought it might be worth paying a few visits to some of those big tithe barns."

Marianne looked up into Robin's face, saying, "They've made such a fuss about their gold and silver, you see, that maybe no-one's looked hard at how much grain they have? Gilbert said they might be playing with loaded dice, so to speak. Making everyone look at the one hand with all the gold and silver, so they don't look too hard at the other one, which is the barns stuffed with grain."

"Nobody asked them specifically for their grain, you see?" the Irishman expanded. "A fourth of income, that's what those fat bastards were asked for. But who do you think was allowed right into the monastery precincts to see what they'd got? Damned few if any, I'd bet! And some of those monasteries got visits real early on in the gathering! Apparently nicely before the harvest was got in! Maybe a wee word was had in certain ears that prayers would be said if the visit was got over and done with nice and early, you see? So that by the time the harvest came rolling in, they could shut the doors on their barns and sit back all smug."

"The sheriff isn't quite that daft to trust in promises in the hereafter," Guy felt able to add now, "but he was fair champing at the bit to go and scoop up what he could, when the word came that the churchmen would have to pay. He made sure they went straight to the top of his list to visit! The first ones he paid a visit to."

"So we need to get in and grab what we can for the people before someone realises that there's been a wee hiccup!" Gilbert said with a mischievous grin.

"Newstead, Rufford and Blyth are all rich enough to cope with losing their harvest," Guy said grinning back, "but Lenton has never felt the hand of Robin Hood!"

"Right by the castle!" Gilbert responded, keeping the momentum going. "Think of it! Snatching it right from under the sheriff's nose!"

Guy following with, "He's at Newark just at the moment, and the Prior's away too! No-one's guarding the henhouse against foxes!"

"We're thinking, two night's time!" declared Will. "Start tomorrow, use the temporary camp by the Leen tomorrow night, then get into positions so that we can start loading a cart with grain as soon as it's dark and the monks are in their beds."

"Best time to do it," Tuck agreed. "Between Compline and Matins is when most will sleep the heaviest, because they'll be tired from the day. Once you get to the hours between Matins and Lauds they'll be more easily woken by any strange noises."

"For now we can take a cart west on tracks that are well used," Will said firmly. "No need to worry about us being followed on those. Then we'll offload what we've got and hide it. Guy knows a covert not far from the Erewash where there's an old stone building."

"The roof's off these days," Guy explained, "and it's derelict, but I think once upon a time it was a small chapel. There's a stout old door which is jammed shut, but if you pull a cart up to it, you should be able to drop stuff over the wall. There was a hunt there only a couple of weeks ago which I led to get rid of a wild boar who was terrorising the local villagers, and nearly had the local lord off his horse! We took a cart that way to drag the beast's carcass back, because he was a huge old boar, so there are already tracks and the grass is crushed by the passing of the hunt."

"Let's do it!" Roger enthused, and there was little Robin could do but go along with them.

Guy left them to follow him on foot, and made a fast return to the castle so that he could go out again in a couple of days without anyone wondering why he was departing so fast. With every one of the knights still going in and out to try and keep some semblance of the woodmotes and forest laws going, Guy had few worries about getting out, especially as just at the moment Ralph Murdac had had to go to his own manor to sort out what he owed for the ransom. That the sheriff had then chosen to go and talk to the Bishop of Lincoln and leave the castle unsupervised was all the better in Guy's eyes, because the blame would not fall on Murdac.

Therefore he wandered down to the stables to Harry and warned him that he would be taking one of the horses from out in the fields, and got him to send one of the lads out with a saddle and bridle, and leave them under a big old oak which had a useful cleft in it. Then as the late summer dusk fell in shades of golds and reds, Guy made vague comments about going to meet a friend in one of the inns in town, and walked out of the castle. Since most of the rest of the household were still at the dinner table, no-one noticed him go, or that he was carrying his saddlebags with him. He would need their contents for the coming woodmote which he would be riding on to, so with luck, folk would just think he had made an early start – which in Guy's case was not unusual anyway.

He toyed with the idea of walking the one and a half miles to Lenton. It was hardly an arduous walk. But then thought perhaps it would be better to have his horse caught and saddled before any fuss started. The last thing he wanted was someone to come running to the castle, and commenting that they had seen Sir Guy out in the dead of night trying to catch a horse, for the fields were flat and open roundabout the castle. It was a glorious night for it, clear and bright even though the moon was not full yet. They would have little trouble finding their way around this night, and with any luck, even in the great tithe barn some light would come in through the doors.

Tuck was waiting for him at the roadside, and gestured him off into a stand of small sliver birches, where Guy tether his horse and then followed Tuck onwards on foot.

"I wanted to be the one to come and meet you," his old friend said warmly. "I said I was the best one to be seen loitering by a priory, but in truth I wanted a quiet word."

Guy felt his heart sink. Was Tuck going to take him to task for berating Robin in public?

So he was surprised when Tuck said, "I'm glad you said what you did to Robin. I was trying to find a way to tell him that his reaction to James leaving was all wrong. I wish I could go to confession, because I feel most guilty over the way I seem to have given your cousin the idea that he's the only important one amongst us all. I've been trying to help him, but God forgive me if I've made him think his way is always right."

Guy stopped and grasped Tuck's arm. "No! Don't you go blaming yourself! As a boy he was always prone to having high-flying ideas, and then getting all upset when they got burst for being the soap-bubbles they were. I can't imagine that anything you said would have led him to get himself worked into a froth over James leaving. I think it's got far more to do with that weird state of mind he had which put James into Allan's place – the youngest cousin who was someone he could play the older and wiser one to!

"And it's not been helped by coming home and finding Allan all grown up and not wanting to act as Robin thinks he should. When Allan was a boy he hung on Baldwin's every word. But just as Baldwin's grown up into Robin, Allan's his own different sort of man too, and not one to follow in the way John does. So I'm guessing that because James was quiet, and didn't argue, it was all too easy for Robin to think it was alright to expect him to follow no matter what."

"And James making a decision for himself was unexpected? Yes I can see that that would have come as a nasty blow. Thank you, Guy, I've been feeling awful over that, and not least because you got drawn into being the bad one again."

Guy snorted. "Sadly I'm getting used to that! But I meant what I said – I don't have to live with him! So if anyone has to straighten his tunic for him every so often, then at least I don't have to suffer the results for days afterwards."

"May *Dewi Sant* bless you," Tuck said with feeling. "There are times when I wish it was you leading these men."

Now Guy laughed. "No you don't. I'm too good at seeing everyone else's point of view! By the time I'd weighed up everyone's needs and reasons, nothing would ever happen!"

Tuck laughed with him, but added, "I'm not so sure of that, but after the few weeks we've had, I find your modesty a lot easier to deal with than Robin's constant taking of offence where none exists."

Any further comments were halted by Will melting out of the shadows and saying, "The others are just up ahead," but whispering in Guy's ear, "but I agree with what Tuck just said too!"

It made Guy feel somewhat better to know that he had taken some of the pressure off the others, and at least they all seemed in a cheerful mood as they followed his lead around to the fields at the back of the priory. Away from the imposing gate house, it was relatively easy to shin over the wall at the back and get into the greater compound of the priory. Over to one side was a massive tithe barn, easily accessed from the main gate by carts bringing grain and other goods inwards, and now they were able to slide the bar off the double gates and allow the cart in which Marianne and Much led, followed by a second led by Mariota and Roger.

"We borrowed them off the villagers at Smithycote," Thomas told Guy as he passed him the first of many sacks of flour. "Funny how they've not forgotten who helped them," and he winked conspiratorially. "Your hiding place is ideal for distributing the flour to the Derbyshire villages on the way."

"Wonderful!" Guy agreed, feeling some more of the weight coming off him. Whether Robin stayed as leader or not, at least the others were seeing the benefits of him consorting with the local nobility on hunts and the like.

It didn't take long to get the first cart loaded, and in the process removing most of the already milled flour from the barn. There was enough piled high on the cart to keep several villages going for weeks, and by the time they had done the same for the second cart with the un-milled grain, Guy was sure that this night they had saved many families from starvation over the coming months. Used wisely it would help eek out their precious supplies for a good while.

Finding a stack of sacks of barley as well, Guy said, "Bring as many as you can carry of those too! We can tie them across my horse! That's beer for a few good brews too!" Beer brewing and bread making went hand in hand pretty much everywhere, as the yeast from the beer was needed for the bread. Without new brews of beer going on, Guy knew that eventually it would get hard to make anything other than flat bread on a griddle, which wasn't as satisfying as leavened bread, and the villagers would be needing all the sustenance they could get soon.

Barring the gates behind the carts, Guy went with Allan as he chalked on the front door of the abbey,

As gluttony it is a sin,
And all your harvest is gathered in,
We have taken it to do more good,

To be given back by Robin Hood.

"Like it?" Allan chuckled as they scurried away.

"I haven't had this much fun in ages," Guy admitted, unable to hid his broad grin. "Can you suggest to Robin to go for Felley Priory and Newstead Abbey as soon as possible?"

Allan laughed, "I'll do my best."

The immense haul had put Robin in a good mood, for the carts they had brought were the big ones normally used to bring bulky loads like hay and straw in from the fields with. On the slight inclines, the men had to push to help the horses out, as the villagers only had stocky work-horses more like ponies, and the load was far heavier than they normally pulled. But by the end of the night, the haul had been hidden away in the ruined chapel, and Much with the three Coshams were on their way to take the un-laden carts back, although with a suitable thank-you gift for the villagers of Smithycote.

"Makes a pleasant change to do this without having to practically stick an arrow up someone's nose," Gilbert said cheerfully, as they all walked northwards with Guy.

The way Robin whipped round and stared at him in surprise made Guy think that his cousin hadn't considered that even the soldiers were glad not to be fighting all the time. But he was even more shocked when John said with clear relief,

"Yes, so much better if we can do it without having to threaten people until they're scared for their lives."

That more than anything seemed to tweak Robin's conscience, and so Guy unexpectedly found himself with Robin for company at the head of the column, as they wended their way along a narrow track through the forest.

"I thought you were just taking your frustrations out on me," Robin began guardedly. "After you left us the other night, Tuck told me I was being most un-Christian towards you."

"Did he?" Guy was genuinely surprised, and the way Robin watched him so carefully for it made Guy wonder whether Robin just wanted to make sure that Guy and Tuck hadn't set him up for this conversation.

"He thinks a lot of you, you know," Robin continued. "Sometimes I think more than he does of me. He said you make terrible sacrifices. That your duty, as you see it, is every bit as binding to you as my vows to Balian of Ibelin are to me. He says that I am wrong to doubt you. And that I should be wary of committing the sin of too much pride over my taking of my vows as a knight at Jerusalem. He says that while it puts me in a state of Grace for defending the Holy City, that it would count for less than it might if I carry on being blind to others' needs. Was I really so blind to James' misery? Was it so obvious to you?"

Guy was quite taken aback, both over Tuck's faith in him and that he should think that Robin was in such danger of wiping out the spiritual good he had done in the East. And just how much of the truth should he tell? He could bluff his way out of this, but then it would negate Tuck's hard work, and so he mentally braced himself and said,

"I'm afraid it was – terribly obvious that James was homesick, I mean. Every time I met up with you all, he was asking me about why things were so bad here. Mind you, I think Malik is right and that he'll have a nasty shock if he goes home too, because I suspect he thought things would return to what he thinks of as normal, and Malik's right, that's never going to be the case."

Robin shook his head in dismay. "Why did I not see it?"

"Maybe because you put him in the place where Allan used to be in your mind? But he was never Allan, and even Allan's grown up." He took a deep breath and then said, "You have to listen when these people tell you they're worried about doing something, you know. They're all adults, and while sometimes you'll be able to reassure them, you're still going to have to give them reasons. Just saying it's all going to be fine just because you're leading them only makes them feel worse."

Robin's eyes went wide in shock. "I don't do that ...do I?"

"Well not in those words exactly when I've been with you, but in the way you act, yes! Look at them tonight. They're so much happier because they've had chance to talk it out, and they knew from the start what was likely to happen." Then felt sorry for Robin as he saw how crestfallen he was. "I'm not saying that there won't be times when someone has to take the lead. Or be the one to make the casting vote. Of course there will. That's why any group needs someone who's at least nominally the leader. But they were starting to feel that you were taking their loyalty for granted, and that's bad."

"Oh dear." Robin looked over his shoulder at the others again and then back at Guy. "Why do you make it seem so easy?"

Guy rolled his eyes in exasperation. "It's not about making it easy or hard, Robin. It's about seeing the people around you for what they really are. For instance, if I was in your place I would never, ever ask John to kill for me, because I know it would tear him up inside. That doesn't mean he won't have to kill at some point, and he's not so foolish as to not know that. But if you need to dispatch someone, then for pity's sake send Will or Malik or Gilbert, not John. And for God's sake don't use it as a means to test his loyalty to you!

"In fact never test anyone's loyalty like that! Nothing will make them hate you faster than that! And you need to realise that they are with you for as many different reasons as you have people, and not all of those reasons are going to coincide with your grand plan. But if you want to do this thing you are setting up – this being the rescuer of the common folk – then you need people with you, and you have to accept them as they are. You can teach them to hold swords and shoot arrows, but don't keep taking the moral high ground over them."

"You're an irritating bastard when you're right, you know," Robin said, making Guy's gut do a little flip, but then felt his cousin reach out and squeeze his arm in the darkness of the clump of oaks they were walking under. "Any more advice for tonight?"

Guy managed a laugh. "Well apart from the fact that Felly and Newstead are up the road and close together with barns stuffed with grain, no. But then I'm sure you'd thought of that already."

"I think I've managed that by myself," Robin answered dryly, but at least without animosity. "It's their turn tomorrow night!"

"Can I come too?"

"Do you want to?"

"Bloody hell, Robin, it's only knowing I can twist these crippling taxes back on the rich bastards that keeps me going when the sheriff has one of his tantrums. Of course I want to come!"

"Really?"

"Yes! So can I come?"

An arm came out through the gloom and hugged him tight. "Of course you can, cousin!"

And so we went and relieved Felley Priory and Newstead Abbey of their grain and flour in one grand night of mischief, and oh how I relished it, Gervase! Those barns were not as packed as Lenton's had been, but they were still far fuller than they should have been, given what had happened over the last month or so. We stashed sacks up oaks, in ruined cottages, and anywhere else we could find which would keep them temporarily dry and safe. It was with much regret that I then had to go on and deal with the woodmote at Mansfield, but I heard only days afterwards that Blyth Priory had been hit. That I was glad about, for the monks there seemed to have learned nothing from their last visit by Robin Hood, and had been trying to claim taxes they had no right to, even in those straightened times. Then Rufford got a night-time visit, and after that Southwell.

By this time the word was round the two shires like wildfire, and the people were all but cheering on Robin out in the streets. It was the monks' own faults. If they had not squealed so loud about how much had been taken, the vast majority of the people would never have guessed how much they had squirreled away, or that it was the food which they so very desperately needed. Then de Wendenal came flying back to the castle in a fine temper, swearing blood and vengeance at this pestilent outlaw, only to have Robin in brazen cheek lift the contents of the bishop's tithe barn at Newark the day after he had left. The sheriff was nearly apoplectic!

Yet the final straw was a return trip by Robin Hood to Lenton, in which the six ruffians whom Abbot Alexander had hired to guard the barn got knocked out and hog-tied, and a large quantity of what was left was removed. Oh you do not need to purse your lips so, Gervase, the brothers were in no danger of starving. They would have been as fat as butter if they alone had eaten the contents of that great barn. Most of it was destined to go to market and fill their coffers, not their bellies, and I knew this from hearing firsthand how meagre the meals were for the ordinary monks from those of them who came to act as scribes at the castle. No, you need not fear that the brothers suffered.

But the sheriff did! Suddenly he had the heads of the respective orders complaining vigorously to the justices and to him personally. To my secret joy, de Wendenal was fast becoming seen as unfit to hold the office of sheriff, and this was then confirmed in a special message which came from Walter of Coutances – whom you will recall had been sent by the king to sort out the mess in England – that de Wendenal was no longer to be sheriff. According to the Norman archbishop's letter, Ralph Murdac was to assume the responsibilities of sheriff once more, based on the fact that even if he was not in favour with the king or rich, that he had served King Henry loyally for many years, and was seen as trustworthy. When the king returned, we were told, the matter would be properly settled, but for now de Wendenal was to step down.

Moreover he was to be deprived of his position at Tickhill. This was a major disaster for him, for there he had had no sheriff in the same castle watching over him as he would now. I wondered whether there had been doubts in some minds as to how much attention he was paying this key castle, because the man chosen to take over was King Henry's former sheriff of Oxford, Robert Delamere – another man very like our own Ralph Murdac. It almost seemed as though in our corner of the kingdom there was a return to those days of King Henry, with Delamere and Murdac taking over the two most powerful castles, and bringing some order to the world again.

Oh how I revelled in that news, Brother, not least because I knew that Robin could afford to take a rest from his activities, and so it would seem that Robin Hood had backed away at the return of Murdac as sheriff. And I was delighted to find Robin himself come to meet me in the town along with Allan and Roger in late October, when we were all having a much needed rest from tearing about the shires for months on end. We were on cordial terms for once, and I was genuinely glad about that, and even more so when I found that he had come asking if I had heard anything which would indicate that James had been apprehended before he got onto his ship. For there was a worrying rumour which the villagers had passed on to Robin, and it was that there was a reward posted for the capture of several young men who had abandoned their lord upon returning from the Holy Land. I was able to reassure Robin that this was nothing to do with James, but that we had heard the same news only that morning. Someone else was in trouble and needing the help of Robin Hood!

Chapter 24

We were most mystified by this word of men from the East. Both Robin and I were concerned that somewhere along the line someone had seen Malik and James and labelled them as Saracens, and therefore thought that calling them deserters from a crusader would make folk more willing to hand them over. I did not credit de Wendenal with the brains to do such a thing, but Ralph Murdac was no fool, and if word of our shire had got as far as men like Sir William Marshal enough to make him dismiss de Wendenal, then he might also have acted. Yet within a couple of weeks I was able to tell the others that this was nothing to do with them.

Whoever these men were, they had absconded the moment their feet had touched English soil, and the news of the reward had come up from the south-east because one of them had connections with the north. And then more came out – they were with two who had been laymen with the Templars, and suddenly all began to make more sense, for who would have cared about mere serving men in the normal way of things? But the Templars losing men they saw as their own was a very different thing, and the reward had been issued from the Temple in London, centre of the order in England. Things had somehow become blurred and blown out of proportion when the regular authorities had heard of it and heard the name of one of those missing – a Robert Hode!

Oh what a misfortune for the poor man to have a name so close to someone who by now was known about beyond our own two shires! Robin Hood had not quite achieved the notoriety he would eventually have, but people in and around the court had heard his name, and that had sealed this man's fate. Blurring the two names, some fool had decided that these renegades must undoubtedly be heading back to Sherwood, although what they thought ˜Robin Hood˜ would have been doing coming <u>back</u> to England baffled us all. It must surely have been a very short trip given what we had done only a few weeks before! Maybe some fool thought the mysterious Robin Hood was consorting with King Philip as Count John was doing – who knew?

However, when I heard about the muddling of names, I was positively itching to let Robin know, and it was agonising having to wait until I saw one of them again. You see we had found very swiftly that weekly meetings were just not practical. For a start, as the year drew round towards its end and the daylight got less and less, just coming down from the hideout at Loxley and then getting back took up a week. And that meant that barely had one lot got back with my news then the others would be setting out, or might even end up crossing, with the result of conflicting messages both to and from me. Moreover, even I did not normally have that much to pass on that a weekly report was necessary.

So it was sheer misfortune that the news came only a day after I had last seen Robin and Tuck.

As for how I was managing those covert meetings – I had begun to take walks into the town on a Sunday, varying my times between mornings, afternoons and evenings. It was the one day when we would not be sent out on the sheriff's business, and on those occasions when I would be away for more than a week, I generally knew about in advance. And by making it a set day of the week, we had agreed that if for some reason I did not appear, then those of them meeting me could leave, for I was unlikely to be in danger, but it avoided anyone else loitering for several days and risking being arrested for being a vagrant.

Sometimes I went for a walk by the river, sometimes I went to one of the churches in the town to hear mass, and on others I went to one of the better alehouses or joined in the archery practice at the butts which had been set up outside of the town. No, Brother, there was no compulsion for the townsmen to practice, but after the recent incidents many of them thought it would be no bad thing to have some means of defending themselves, and by practicing openly they could at least give lip-service to the idea that they might come to help defend the castle – an idea which I might have let slip to some of those whom I got on with, you may wish to hear. Yes, even in Nottingham I was not quite the obedient servant of the sheriffs they might have thought I was!

But to these returning men... There was no doubt in my mind that they would need our help if they came up to the Midlands. Of course they might have fled towards Wales and never come our way, but some small voice within me said that they were coming to Sherwood. You may call it a lucky guess, but when that inner voice prompted me it often had the most unforeseen results, and I have long thought of it as one of Tuck's Welsh saints whispering in my ear where only I could hear. And so I waited with barely contained impatience for my next covert meeting, and meanwhile tried to keep an eye out for anyone who might seem out of place, or listen for the odd dropped word which might give me more clues.

Nottingham
December, the Year of Our Lord 1193

"Going out again, Guy?" Sir Henry brayed across the smaller hall, where some of the forest knights had gathered on what was turning into a very chilly night, the great hall being as cold as charity this night. "Your piety will be the end of you kneeling at mass in this weather!"

Sir Walter was just passing the open door as Guy was leaving.

"Is there something wrong, Guy," he asked as Guy flipped a finger at Henry and shut the door before the thrown lump of hard bread could hit him. "I don't normally agree with Henry, but it is a shocking night to be going out in."

Guy drew Sir Walter away from the door. "There's nothing wrong, and I haven't been smitten by guilt or anything, either." He pulled a face, then leaned in conspiratorially. "I just fancy a pint in an alehouse without Henry or Humphrey bawling down my ear! If I say I'm going to the *Trip*, or any other alehouse for that matter, they'll want to come with me. And not only will that defeat the object of going out, it'll make me the most hated man in Nottingham for inflicting them on the ordinary folk who just want to take their ease on the day of rest."

Sir Walter was already chuckling. "You're a sly one, Guy, but I know what you mean. Thank God Martin and I can use our rank to avoid having to be with them too often. Go on then, enjoy your pint! I'll tell Martin and Sir Ralph, just in case one of the malicious swine tries to cause trouble for you over it. May God forgive me for saying this, but it would be just typical of Henry to start implying that you're too pious to be able to do your job and ought to be replaced."

Guy thanked him and they parted amicably, allowing Guy to don a heavy felted cloak and head out into the driving rain. This time he was making for a church – St Mary's up on High Pavement. St Nicholas' church was close by the castle, and St Peter's was not much further, but for now Guy wanted to have time to check if he was being followed, and so he had picked the most distant of the three and the one with easiest access for getting out of town in a hurry for the others, just in case. In time his Sunday walks would lose their novelty, he knew, but for now Sir Walter was right, Henry and a few of the others were spiteful enough to want to cause mischief if they thought they were being left out of something.

Easing the big oak church door open, Guy slipped inside and stood to the side of the door allowing his eyes adjust to the even deeper gloom inside. The last publicly witnessed service of the day had been said, and there were no candles lit except for a single one up at the altar. By its flickering light he gradually made out four figures kneeling in prayer in front of it, and he softly padded forward, recognising the backs of Malik, Siward, Gilbert and Robin and not wanting to disturb them. However before he had got to them, Siward and Malik were already rising to their feet and coming to greet him.

"What a filthy night!" Siward said softly as Guy draped his dripping cloak over one of the iron candle stands. "We spotted the priest running for his home before we got here. I don't think he'll be back to trouble us! We'll probably wait here and see if the worst of this blows over during the night. No point in getting drenched if we don't have to."

Robin's hand fell on Guy's shoulder. "Cousin! Any news? Anything interesting happening?"

"More than you would believe!" Guy said with feeling. "I've heard more on those men the reward is out for, and it isn't good." By the time he had explained the confusion over the names, Robin was pacing up and down before the altar, gnawing at a fingernail and wearing an expression of furious concentration.

Malik was the first to speak, though. "So not Saracens, at all?"

Guy shook his head. "No. Nothing at all to do with them. I wish I could tell you where they're heading for, because they must be up here or nearly so by now, but in all the confusion all I got was 'the North', and that's an awfully big place to have to search!"

Gilbert looked startled at Guy's words. "God have mercy on them! Of course, it's been weeks now since that reward was issued. Even if they've been ducking and diving like foxes with hounds on their heels, they must still be close to here by now."

"And it's unlikely they've been caught," Siward added thoughtfully, "because if it had been far away, there's been time for word to get here. And if they were taken in one of the closer shires – Leicestershire, for instance – then that's close enough for word to have reached the sheriff, even if not to get back to London or Winchester yet."

Robin came to a halt in front of them. "But that's good news then. It means they must still be out there somewhere! Have you any idea where they might be, Guy?"

His cousin shrugged. "Could be anywhere, if you're asking me if we've had any sightings ...because we haven't. On the other hand, I've had a lot longer to think about this than you have, and if we're now talking about Englishmen – and with at least one or more of them having lived up this way – then I think they'd be daft to come anywhere close to a castle, wouldn't they? They'll know about Leicester, and Nottingham, and to a lesser extent Derby, and will stay well away. On the other hand, I wouldn't expect them to want to go as far east as Peterborough, because that would give them a real problem heading north through the Fens. So my money would be on them taking a course between Peterborough and Leicester, but staying well clear of both of them. After that, well, they could be canny and go up the east side of our shire and just avoid Newark. But the problem with doing that is that they're going to be going through some countryside which will be ankle-deep in water at this time of the year."

Siward was nodding already. "I see what you mean, Guy. If they've got enough local knowledge to avoid the big towns and the sheriffs, they'll also know that."

"Exactly! So my best guess is that they'll come into Nottinghamshire and try and cross the Trent somewhere between here and Newark, before the river gets too many side channels and marshes."

Robin was nodding his agreement. "I suppose it all depends on where they're heading for, of course. If it's Lancashire or further north on the west coast, then they might go west of Derby, but the Peaks aren't territory for the unwary or unprepared to travel through – especially at this time of the year! We've already seen snow up on the top of Kinder, although it hasn't come down to the camp yet." He turned to Malik and Gilbert. "Can you two go and fetch the others? We'll meet up at the temporary camp by Epperstone a week today. In the meantime Siward and I will start looking. It has to be us. We're the ones who know the area best." He turned and gave Guy a faint smile. "Don't suppose there's much chance of you being able to come and help us?"

Guy pulled a face. "Not remotely! It's all way out of my allotted territory for inspecting. Normally I'm glad to be in the wilder country of the Derwent to Erewash side of the forest, well away from seeing farms being made to suffer for the king's arbitrary boundaries, so I can't ask to change. Anyway, it would be so out of character that it would draw all the wrong sort of attention."

"That's a shame, it was fun having you along," Robin said, and seemed to mean it, giving Guy hope that maybe they really had moved into having more of their old relationship. Perhaps Tuck's sleeping draughts and that massive row had between them cleared the air? As a result he hugged Robin tight when they parted and whispered in his ear, "Never doubt that I love you, cousin! I would lay down my life to save yours," and was rewarded by Robin whispering back,

"I know, and I would for you."

It made for much consolation as Guy splashed his way back to the castle, and if he got in cold and wet, inside he was glowing inwardly in a way he'd not done for a long time. And that was the last he expected to hear of anything for at least a week or two. They had made a tentative arrangement to meet again, but it was already the beginning of December and by two weeks' time the days would be exceedingly short, and the places where they could meet busier than normal. Inns would be building to the Christmas festivities and lacking quiet corners, and the churches would be receiving more visits from the pious, especially now that Advent had arrived. So Guy expected to go to St Peter's for the last Sunday mass before Christmas itself, and maybe meet with someone, but not to worry if he didn't.

That all changed three days later when Sirs Mahel and Hamon came back to the castle like cats who'd had the cream, dragging behind them seven miserable wretches.

"We have him!" Mahel crowed before he had even dismounted, gesturing to a man in tattered clothing, barely able to stand. "We have Robin Hood!"

It was pure luck that Guy had been in the stables at the time, and even so he only came out in time to hear the words 'Robin Hood'. His heart sinking into his boots, Guy shoved forward through the crush of people, then saw the men and began a slow clapping. The crowd looked at him in astonishment, and as the babble died away to nothing, Guy declared,

"Sir Mahel, what a marvel you are! Robin Hood, eh? And which one of these men is capable of pulling a Welsh bow, pray tell?"

Mahel just looked blank, but Hamon gave the line Guy wanted, "What about Welsh bows?"

"Why, have you forgotten already?" Guy declared with withering sarcasm. "The Welsh bows which were used to ambush Sir Henry over by Mansfield. If you wish, I can go and get the captured bow and give you another demonstration. Then you can see which one of these half-starved men is capable of pulling such a bow! And before you reply to that, think on this – Robin Hood was using those same Welsh bows to terrify the guards of Prior Alexander at Lenton not seven weeks ago. Do you recall what they said?"

Mahel's face had gone a dark red between his embarrassment and his anger, but it was de Wendenal's voice which answered, and belatedly Guy recalled that Murdac was away at Derby. Having got his sheriffdom back, Murdac was trying to repair the ravages of de Wendenal's tenure, starting with the substantial neglect of the second shire of the sheriffdom.

"Always so quick with the ripostes, aren't you Sir Guy," the former sheriff sneered. "Don't be so quick to deride Sir Mahel for doing what you couldn't. It's winter, you dolt! Of course they look half starved! Take a look at half the people in the shire, they all look the same!"

Guy almost literally had to bite his tongue to stop himself from saying that the shire folk were starving because of the king's ransom, not because it was winter, and that Robin Hood hadn't had to give everything he owned to pay up to the sheriff's soldiers. Giving de Wendenal and Mahel filthy looks, Guy turned on his heels, his parting shot being,

"Well the best of luck convincing the eyre of that ...my lord," the latter delivered with such contempt he later thought he was lucky de Wendenal hadn't called him back for such insubordination in public. As he stormed off to his own rooms, Guy was frantically thinking. Could he pull off the prisoners' escape before Murdac got back? The last time anyone had escaped from Nottingham Castle's dungeon had been when Murdac had been sheriff, when Guy had rescued those now with Robin, and Guy had no wish for him to become known as the man who couldn't hold prisoners even in his own keep. God forbid, but that might just mean the return of de Wendenal to office, and Guy dreaded that. But could he just leave men to rot knowing that they were innocent? He had no doubt about that, he couldn't. Nor could he rely on Murdac to set them free, even though he would see they couldn't possibly be Robin Hood's men, for Murdac would honour the Templars demand for capture.

He made sure he was absent from the hall when the men were questioned in front of de Wendenal. He knew he would never be able to keep his feelings from showing under such circumstances, and the last thing he wanted was for the collected knights to think that the reason he had taken such a shot at Mahel was because of sympathy for the men. Much better to have his absence attributed to wounded pride at being dismissed by de Wendenal in public. Of course, those who did the menial work around the castle knew and liked Guy well enough to not think that. But he had deliberately kept his distance from the knights, and was mostly indifferent to what they thought of him, expecting that at some point this kind of confrontation would occur, and quite consciously wanting them to come to the wrong kinds of conclusions.

It worked rather better than Guy had expected, several giving him pitying glances the following morning when he encountered them about the place. However he was prepared to suffer that if it meant that he was seen as no threat to the security of the prisoners. That night, when Osmaer was snoring enough for a whole pen-full of pigs, Guy slipped unnoticed out of their shared room and crept down to the dungeons. After the time when he had released Walter, Algar, Hugh and Much, Guy had long since worked out the best route to and from the dungeons, depending on time of day and who was in residence. So it was almost second nature to him to flit through the castle like a ghost, unseen and uncared about.

It said everything for the foolish extent to which de Wendenal had accepted Mahel's story that before Guy got to the deepest chamber he heard the guards. Creeping down the stone spiral staircase, he peeped round until he saw them. Six men! God in Heaven, who did de Wendenal think was coming to rescue them if he already had Robin Hood?

Guy went back several steps and leaned his head against the cold of the stones as he tried to think. De Wendenal was stupid, that was the greatest problem. A man with even a degree of intelligence would have decided on one of two things. Either, he had Robin Hood, in which case there was no need for a guard, the dungeon being sufficient once someone was down in one of the two pits.

Or he didn't believe he had Robin Hood – in which case he ought to have been loudly putting it about that he did in the hope of catching the real one, but would be keeping the guards hidden and further back so that he could catch the outlaw in the act of releasing the prisoners. No, de Wendenal was just blundering on, as usual, hoping to get the credit for catching the outlaw instead of Murdac, and the worst of it was that Murdac was not due back for at least another week, maybe two. Time in which de Wendenal could do God alone knew what.

Could he get Robin in here? Could he affect an escape aided by the real Robin Hood? Even for Guy that was a tall order, and he thought he was able to out-think most of the castle on a good day. In desperation he went to the scribes' room, hoping that de Wendenal had put something to parchment already. He was hoping for pretty much anything, just something which would give him a clue as to how the deposed sheriff was going to react. By the light of a solitary candle, Guy began rummaging, and was almost immediately rewarded by finding three slim pieces of parchment with a message to each of the Templar Masters at Faxfleet, Temple Hirst and Temple Newsam – the nearest Templar preceptories – informing them that their errant laymen had been caught.

Could he be one of those to taking the messages? If he went for Temple Newsam, which was close by the prosperous little town of Leeds, he wouldn't have to travel with the other two messengers. And with Leeds being primarily the land of the king, there were no great landowners who other volunteers might want to take the chance to impress with tales of catching Robin Hood. It would also be a pig of a ride in this weather, and Guy guessed there would be few takers. He had no intention of delivering the message, but it would give him a chance to ride in the direction of Loxley and maybe meet those who were coming to Nottingham for their next meeting on their way, for he mostly knew which way they would come.

He went to the hall in the morning but to his silent fury, de Wendenal would not take the bait of offering him the ride in the wet. Instead he sent possibly the three dimmest knights in the castle – Sirs Payne, Joscelin and Giles – all incapable of doing other than exactly what they were told, and Guy dared not push too hard for fear of rousing de Wendenal's cunning. The messages were going without him, and with them his chance to alert Robin.

Yet as he fumed with frustration, fate lent him a hand. That night he went down to eat with everyone else, thinking that he had to show his face, only to find that since it was a Friday it was a fish pie as the main dish. Maybe because Guy had only walked into the hall as the pie nearest to him was being cut, and therefore his nose had not become numbed by the miasma of unwashed men and rushes damp from the passage of many boots, but he reeled back from it. That fish was off!

Not just a bit old. It was absolutely rotten if he was any judge. The cook must have been literally scraping the bottom of the barrel of salt cod for this one, no doubt because de Wendenal had interfered and countered Murdac's order to get rid of anything which was too old to be any good – another attempt to relieve the castle's suffering after de Wendenal's rule.

Guy looked at the portion of pie as it slopped onto the bread trencher of the man at the end of the table. It had a nasty sheen to it, and Guy immediately decided that he would rather eat dog-bread than that. Luckily de Wendenal had already made heavy inroads into the wine, and was past noticing what Guy was doing. So he grabbed three of the apples which were piled up on a plate further along the table and left. Apart from any Christmas feasts, in the winter no-one used the great hall for eating because of the amount of wood it took to stoke the great fire enough to make it even vaguely habitable, and so the ordinary soldiers were spared the company of the knights and ate in the servant's hall out in the outer bailey. Hurrying across to it, Guy was horrified to see that some of the pie had made its way out here too, and frantically gestured to Big Ulf not to eat it. He nudged Ingulf, who was the leader of the twelve from High Peak, and the big man hammered on the table for silence. Immediately Guy shouted,

"Don't eat the fish pie! It's bad! The fish is rotten."

Several men spat out mouthfuls, but others looked in horror at the remains of what they had already devoured, too hungry to have looked at what they were eating, and eating too fast to have been aware of how it tasted. 'That's what comes of bolting your food,' Guy heard his mother's voice from the past echoing in his mind. Never had her words been so appropriate!

"Pass the word," Guy said wearily, "and be prepared for the latrines to be in demand. I'd be making sure there are plenty of buckets available."

Sure enough, by the time Guy had wandered over to the kennels and found some bread and eaten in with the apples, there were already sounds of people being very unwell. He made his way up to his room, but before he opened the door, the sounds from within said that Osmaer was suffering badly, and so Guy left him alone with his bucket and went for a walk on the walls. At least the air was fresh up there.

As the night drew on, though, it occurred to Guy that for once there might be no guards down in the dungeon. In no time at all he had made it to the main keep and down the stairs, and was gratified to see the evidence of a game of dice hastily abandoned and no-one in sight. Making sure no-one could see him from through the iron grills over the pits, Guy coarsened his accent to become thoroughly local, and called down softly,

"You men what got brought in, how come you got caught?"

There came the sound of coughing and stirring, then another very local accented voice called back,

"Who are you? Why do you care?"

Guy sighed. What would it take to win these men's trust quickly enough to give him time to at least find out what he was dealing with here? He couldn't trust what de Wendenal had had written down – that was likely to be a pack of lies, as much to do with what the former sheriff wanted to be said than the truth.

"You got hauled in for being Robin Hood," he called down. "Well maybe the real Robin Hood might help you. But I have to know who you are first. He won't set criminals free to hurt the locals."

"We're not bloody thieves or murderers!" an indignant second voice snapped back.

"Good, I'm glad to hear it. So if you're not those, then what or who are you? Someone said you're Templars' men? Where have you come from?"

An older voice answered wearily, "Aye, three of us have come back from Acre. As for being the Templars', I suppose that depends on whether you think they have a right to our lives after having left us to rot in that city through the siege. If the king hadn't come to raise it, would they have ever thought to come back and try to get us out? I don't think so, and neither do my friends."

Guy could understand their bitterness. Word of the long siege at Acre had filtered back, and Robin and the other five who had been in the Holy Land had been glad they had not been there, telling the rest of just how dreadful it would have been. They had his sympathy.

"How did you get back here?" he asked gently. "I don't imagine you had money to buy your passage back."

The same man gave a bitter bark of a laugh. "No, we'd have rotted there if we hadn't been swept up by those with King Richard. At first we thought him our saviour. We hoped we'd be shipped home at some point. But then we got pulled back into the fighting. Just because we were one step short of having starved to death didn't stop those with the king making use of us. By the time the king had made his truce with Saladin, we were just praying that we could get on one of the ships without being thrown off to make room for some lord's looted treasure. There were five of us. Two died on the voyages. We were crammed into the holds of the galleys like bloody slaves. The old man who's with us was a slave of the Corsairs we encountered in Crete whose ships the king hired. We got separated from the great and the good by the time we got to Corfu and he managed to stick with us. The group we were with chivvied us like cattle all the way home."

"So is that four of you? What of the others? There were seven of you brought in. Who are the others? Which one of you is Robert Hode?"

"That'd be me," a very broad northern accent said. "I'm a carpenter from up by Holy Island, what some call Lindisfarne. I did some work for the Templars at their preceptory at Temple Cowton, up just off the Great North Road close by Northallerton. Right pleased the Master was. Said it were some of the best carpentry he'd seen in a long time. So he arranged for us to go by boat down the coast to London to do some work in the big Temple in London. Seemed a good deal. The wage we got offered was as much as we could earn in a year at home. So me and my 'prentice lad, Edwyn, went. Wish we never had now!"

"What went wrong?"

"Bloody Templars thought we'd be even more use to them over in France or somewhere! Every time we tried to collect our wages and go, there were always some new excuse. We hung on to get the money, see? Couldn't go back home with nothing to show for months of work."

A younger, stronger voice now chimed in bitterly. "Eventually we realised that the bastards weren't going to pay us at all! They kept on about deductions for our keep and other shit like that! As if we'd had more than a few pennies-worth off them! We certainly weren't over-fed, I can tell you!"

"What did you do?" Guy was now fascinated to know how these two had got here.

"They thought we were beneath notice," the younger man told him. "Stupid fuckers forgot that we did the work on the doors and locks on their bloody strong-room! Never thought that what we put together we could take apart."

Instantly Guy was laughing because he could guess what had happened. "Let me guess, you took the locks apart and took what was owed you?"

"Too bloody right we did," Robert Hode answered.

"That explains a lot!" Guy chortled, dropping the accent now that he was surer of them.

"Does it?"

"Oh yes! You see it must have been only a week or two earlier that Robin Hood emptied the tithe barns of the local abbeys and monasteries up here. The Churchmen are screaming fit to raise the dead! So you then relieving the Templars of some cash and having a name similar ...well no wonder they thought you were him!"

"Shit!" another voice said from the gloom, with an accent so Irish it made Gilbert's pale by comparison. "We're going to fucking swing for this!"

"Good grief, how did you end up with this lot?" Guy asked him.

"Oh I'm just the miserable Irish bastard who knows everything there is to know about horses," he replied bitterly. "These two hadn't been gone a day before some evil little scrot' started pointing the finger my way. The fact that I wouldn't know one end of a lock from another meant nothing. I just heard the words 'lashes' and 'loosen his tongue' and I took to my heels like the hounds of hell were after me!"

"He caught us up and then we all started running!" Robert said with audible anger. "We knew there'd be no reasoning with them if they caught us. But we got to by Windsor and met these four from off the ship. By then we'd heard about the siege there, and there were still too many soldiers lurking around for our liking. None of us wanted to get scooped up by the likes of them. So we joined together and made a run for it."

The Irish voice came again. "I cannot fucking believe we got caught by a pair of thick-as-pig-shit knights and a bunch of local bully-boys!"

"How did it happen?" Guy prompted.

"Fucking Newark!" the Irishman declared, and Guy heard him spit. "I hope the bastard place sinks into the mud and on down to Hell!"

"We took a wrong turn," the younger man Guy now knew was Edwyn explained. "We were trying to get across the Trent but somehow we got into a bog. Some men out catching eels pulled us into their boats but whacked us over the head as they did it. We woke up tied up like so many ham-hocks waiting to be smoked! We reckon they stuck to our money, because it wasn't on us after that. Then those two bloody knights came in, and the rest you know."

"By Our Lady, you've been unlucky!" Guy sympathised. He sat back on his heels and looked around him. Dare he break the men out right now? He wouldn't get them out and across the outer bailey without being spotted tonight, not with so many going to and fro to the latrines. Then he had an idea.

"Are all of you fit enough to do some climbing?" he asked. "It's downwards, not up, and you'd have some rope to help you." He was thinking of the trouble he'd had getting the frail Joseph out the previous time. If they couldn't clamber he would have to try and hide them somewhere in the castle and sneak them out a couple at a time. Luckily there was an instant chorus of yeses, and even an older and frailer voice said,

"I'll try, and you lads must go whatever."

Guy immediately pulled back the bolts on the grating and hauled the heavy iron up and over. It was a weight even for a fit man like Guy, and it took all his strength to not let it fall with a crash. Grabbing the nearest ladder he lowered it down and was relieved by the speed with which the first man appeared.

"Wait over there and watch for anyone coming!" Guy urged him, gesturing to the doorway to the stairs.

The three who must have been in the East came up first, and then the old man, who had Robert right behind him ready to catch him if he fell, and finally the Irishman and Edwyn. The younger man helped Guy lower the grating back and shoot the bolts home again.

"Right, you all need to stay right behind me," Guy said sternly. "Half the castle is puking its guts up after some bad fish pie, so although hardly anyone is in a fit state to do any running or fighting, there are folk about later than normal. I'm going to take you right up to the walls, and then it's going to be a cold and miserable walk along them, because you're going to have to stay crouched down so that you aren't seen above the parapet. No-one's going to be up there on guard tonight, but I don't want anyone looking up and wondering why eight men are traipsing about up there in the dead of night."

"How late is it?" the Irishman asked.

"Time most of us are normally in our beds," Guy said dryly. "So that pie's been a mixed blessing – no guards, but a lot of people not sleeping!"

"Jesus, that bad?"

Guy nodded. "Very bad!" However he didn't give them time to ask more but set off. He just kept going up the stairs, blessing the fact that there weren't many living quarters in the keep itself. Potentially the sheriff could sleep there, but the place was a cold alternative to the building King Henry had had built in anticipation of his son John coming to live there, and Guy had never know a sheriff sleep there.

Two floors up, he led them off to the left and then paused for them to rest briefly in a tiny side chamber before attempting the walls. A sleety drizzle had started up, which was no bad thing, and Guy set off with them, encouraging them to bend at the waist so that at least they could rest their hands on their legs to ease their backs. Thankfully the wall was wide, and going single-file and keeping as close to the parapet as they could, they were invisible to all except if someone came up to their height, which no-one did. At the junction with the oldest part of the castle, Guy led them on the odd dog-leg which got them to the old walls, then shooed them into one of the turret rooms.

"Stay here, I'm going for the rope!" he told them, and disappeared off into the gloom. With no need to be covert, he walked briskly through the castle, clamping his hand over his nose and mouth against the awful stench. This was turning out to be the most awful case of food poisoning, and when he got out into the inner bailey and saw people on their knees in the open, he began to worry that some might not survive the night. It was far too bitter to be out in for long even when well, let alone as sick as these folk were. And there were too many of them for him to be able to help, even if he had not been on a mission. The only thing to be said was that those who were still anything like conscious were too wrapped in their own misery to even glance his way, let alone call for help.

He went back into the keep and took the narrow footbridge which ran from a picket door straight to the stables over the inner dry moat. There was no sign of the grooms tonight, and Guy guessed that if they weren't sick themselves they would be trying to help their friends. He seized two good sized coils of rope, slung them over his shoulder, and hurried back the way he had come, never once seeing anyone who might question him later.

At the top of the oldest castle keep once more, he summoned the men from the turret.

"Those of you who don't think you can manage to go down the rope by yourselves will get lowered down by the others," he told them, "although I hope most of you will be all right."

"I can't do that," the older man immediately said, "but I'll take my chances. Don't you dare give up the chance for you to leave because of me!"

Guy looked at him hard. He was a very ordinary man, nothing remarkable about him at all.

"Do you know, I think I might be able to walk you out of here," he said thoughtfully. "One's a very different matter to seven. Right, let's get the rest of you down."

He made them wrap some of their ragged clothing around their hands against the rope burns, and tied a rope around the first man.

"This is in case you slip," he said. "Hopefully we won't have to take your weight all the way down, but it's there as a brake if you need it." He got the man to take a loop of the other rope around his middle below the tied one, and then gave him simple instructions about walking down the walls and then the short stretch of cliff below it.

"You haven't got to go all the way down," he explained to them. "We're right above the *Trip to Jerusalem* brew-house, and you should come down on its roof. Wait until at least three of you are on the roof before you slid down to the edge. Stay on the ridge tiles until then – you can sit astride them. Then two of you can lower someone, but importantly, once you have someone on the ground, they can tell the rest of you where to lower yourselves and help catch you so you don't make too much noise, or risk someone spraining an ankle. Beside the brew-house there are some over-hangs of cliff. Wait there for me and I'll come with this man and lead you to somewhere you can hide out."

The three former laymen of the Templars managed the slither down without disaster, and Guy realised that although they hadn't an ounce of spare fat on them, they were wiry but strong – no doubt a result of the hard labour they had done. And with them not being heavy men, they managed the ropes without resorting to the safety one.

"You next," Guy told Robert. The carpenter was the one he was most concerned about. He had to be in his late forties at least, and although his arms were strong, he was also carrying the most weight. As Robert disappeared over the edge of the wall, Edwyn came to the rope with Guy without being asked, taking a good grip on the rope behind Guy and taking it round his back before grasping in with his other hand. It was a good job he did. Twice Robert lost his footing and slipped, leaving Guy and Edwyn to take his weight, although the second time the Irishman was already on the rope with them.

"What's your name?" Guy asked the Irishman.

"Colm."

"Right then, Colm, you next." And Guy saw Edwyn look at him and nod, understanding passing between them that the youngest man would also be the best to go down last. Yet Colm proved to be more able than Robert, and got down without incident. It wasn't that hard a climb down, Guy knew. An absolute swine to get up, but not that hard to go down, because there was some kind of angle to it and it had hand-holds or places where you could dig your toes in in the soft rock. Edwyn went down with the natural ability of a spider, and Guy wondered whether he'd been the kind of lad who had climbed every tree in the neighbourhood, and whatever bits of cliff there might be up in Durham, because he was the most sure-footed of the lot.

Guy turned to the oldest man. "Now then ...what's your name?"

"I'm Walter."

"Right, Walter, let's get you out of this place. Stay close behind me unless I tell you otherwise, all right?"

Together they walked at an easy pace through the inner ward, through the inner bailey, and out through the first gatehouse into the outer bailey. This was where Guy was most worried they would be stopped. Here fewer people had partaken of the fish pie, but as they passed the wooden buildings housing the servants' halls, they could hear the sounds of scrubbing going on, and the sloshing of water. Steam hung in a haze about the doors, and Guy guessed that those who were not afflicted were doing their best to clean up before it became even more disgusting.

They reached the outer barbican without incident and now Guy was genuinely shocked, because the castle gates stood open. He cursed himself for not having checked this – it would have saved all the scrambling – but it was so normal for the gates to be shut tight once night came that he had never dreamed they wouldn't be. Outside, two of those who should have been at least watching the shut gates were slumped semi-conscious in a dreadful state. Guy knew he should do something for them, but first he had to get Walter out, and they hurried past and over the bridge across the outer dry moat, and then on to skirt the castle around to the north and come down to below the cliff and *The Trip*.

The others were lurking in the shadows as they got to them, and Guy led them off into the deserted town. It had to be near midnight by now, and not a soul stirred. When he had got them to St Mary's, Guy took them in and showed them where to hide.

"I'll be back for you as soon as I can," he told them. "But if I'm held up, the moment it's light, walk east until the houses end, then turn left and go north on that road. When you see three old oaks clustered together, there's a track off to your right. Take it! It becomes little more than a pathway, and a lot of people get put off using it because it goes right into the heart of the forest, but that's a good thing for you! No-one can chase you on horseback there, and there are lots of places to get off it and into the undergrowth where you can't be found. If I don't catch up with you, keep on on that track. You'll probably meet some people coming the other way. They'll have a huge Welsh monk with them, and another man even bigger than him. They're my friends and they'll help you."

"God bless you!" said Walter, clasping Guy's hand and pumping it.

Now that he could see Walter in the light of the candle they had lit, there was something familiar about him which Guy could not place. He was sure they had never met before, but something was niggling at his brain.

"Where are you from Walter?"

"Oh a farm up Skipton way. Nowhere you'd know. I'll be all right, don't you worry. I have a brother up there to go to."

Ah, Gervase, that was to be a significant meeting! But before I finish with this tale, I must tell you that I went back to the castle and wondered what on earth I could do to start sorting the dreadful mess out. And it was dreadful in every sense. I went in to the servants' halls and managed to get those who were not sick to come and help me drag those poor souls who had collapsed outside at least indoors. I had them laid out in the great hall as the one place which as yet had not been fouled, and then we went in search of those within the castle who had heaved themselves dry or simply become unconscious.

I am sorry to say that when dawn came we had lost over a dozen souls – people who would never wake again. Some had choked to death, while others had succumbed to the cold outdoors in their weakened state, and three were a dreadful colour and seemed to have taken even more harm than most from the poison of the pie. Barely a quarter of those within the castle were still on their feet, a terrible situation for one of the greatest castles in England to be in. Of course I had closed the gate once we had retrieved those two outside, and in one way I was relieved to discover that they were amongst the dead, and undoubtedly had been already when I had passed them with Walter.

I left Harry and Ingulf getting the wise women brewing up what herbal medicines we had which might help and went into the town to summon assistnace. The first thing was to assure the townsfolk that dreadful though things were, this was no contagion but simply bad husbandry. Relieved that they would not catch something fatal, the townsfolk rallied, and I was able to go and find the priests to come and do what was necessary for those who had died. In the processes I was able to check on my escapees, and was relieved to find that they had left the church and with no sign of them ever having been there.

The place was still in turmoil three days later when Ralph Murdac returned in answer to my message to return immediately. Of the knights I was the only one left standing, apart from Sir Robert and Sir Hugh, and even they had taken a mouthful of the pie and swallowed it before realising how bad it was, and still felt shaky. For the rest of those who had been taken ill, it was over a week before many were able to rise from their beds, and my only consolation was that de Wendenal took the longest of anyone to recover. When Murdac and I got to the bottom of the situation it transpired that the head cook had utterly refused to cook the salt-cod, and had marched off into the town, leaving only his helpers to make what they could of the mess. Even Murdac had not the heart to chastise them further, for all of them were terrified beyond words of what their punishment might be for laying the garrison so low. However, de Wendenal received the brunt of Murdac's anger, and rightly so.

Therefore it was a week before anyone remembered the prisoner who was supposed to be Robin Hood and in the dungeon, and that only when a party from Temple Hirst returned with Giles to claim their prize. They were irate at having had a wasted journey, but their anger was soon deflected towards de Wendenal, and I was now sure that he would never be in a position to return as sheriff. Sadly he knew it, and was unbearable to be around after that, to the extent that Murdac suggested forcibly that he should take himself off to Derby for a while and try doing some of the work he had neglected for so long.

Meanwhile, I was covered with glory for having held things together. Murdac was even understanding about the prisoners escaping, realising that they could have gone at any time during the night given that the gates stood open. And there was no chastising of the gate-keeps when they were dead. We all believed they had had enough punishment while they lived, for to die from the cold having been so violently purged was something the thought of which gave us all the shudders.

But what of my escapees? Ah, I will come to them now.

Chapter 25

*N*ews of what had happened at the castle must have spread like a
summer grass fire through the shire, because barely had Murdac
returned than I found Roger loitering in the outer bailey. With so many
townspeople still going in and out, he was not conspicuous, and we were
able to converse. I told him hurriedly of the men I had sent into Sherwood
and he made off at speed. I gather that Allan had been waiting not far
away, and so while Roger ran to alert most of the gang to start searching,
Allan went and fetched Robin and Siward from their prearranged meeting
place.

The next I knew of it, I was being informed by Murdac that my
reward was to be able to go and spend Christmas at my own manor, and I
accepted with heartfelt thanks. It had been far too long since I had been
able to make the journey to my humble home, and so I rode with all speed
northwards, intending to briefly stop at Loxley and then ride on. Ianto,
Maelgwn and Elias had been preying on my mind a great deal, and
although Tuck kindly went and checked on them from time to time for me,
I still felt that they were ultimately my responsibility.

So it was a great surprise to me to ride into Loxley and have
Marianne come flying at me and throw her arms around my neck,
hugging me until I could barely draw breath and thanking me. When I
finally got free I had a huge shock – the old man, Walter, was her father.
There, Brother, you see? That was why I said I later felt it was more than
mere instinct to do what I did and help them. He had been taken captive
by the Corsairs, which was why she had heard nothing of him for all those
years, and on getting free his first thought had been to try and get back to
find her. Not realising that she had become a Hospitaller sister, he had not
thought to even look in the Holy Land, but had assumed that she would
have travelled back with some other pilgrim family, and would find her in
Yorkshire if anywhere.

Yet now there was a problem. Marianne had long since taken a trip to
Skipton and found no trace of her Uncle Roger or his family. Whether
they had died or just left she did not know, their farm always being a little
isolated and having been taken on by a family from far away to whom the
name Roger Shepherd meant nothing. Walter, though, was not in a fit
state to continue living rough with Marianne at Loxley or anywhere else.
He needed a proper house, however so humble, and I had to say that I did
not think he could go to Gisborne as he would be unable to help much with
anything. Too old to do the heavy work, he did not have Maelgwn's talent
for organising, and with Ianto already there as someone who could no
longer do much to contribute, I did not feel we could hope to support
another. As I said to my friends, if King Richard had not skinned us to the
bone it would be a different thing. In good years there was plenty at

Gisborne now that it was being run well, but this year even the best of manors was struggling to get through the winter.

It was then that I had the idea of asking Sir Richard at the Lea if he could find a place for Walter at his own manor. I asked Tuck to come with me up to Gisborne and then to accompany me to High Peak on the way back. I had high hopes that if I played up the fact that Walter had gone as a pilgrim and ended up a slave, that Sir Richard's kind heart would be moved, especially if I had a monk with me to plead as well. The Lea was an ideal place, for with it being within Sherwood, Marianne would be able to go and see him frequently without taking too many chances. Initially we decided that Marianne would be married to a charcoal burner who also did a little fletching as well. That would help explain her itinerant lifestyle to Sir Richard, and why Walter could not live with her, for he was bound to ask that if nothing else. Later he was to know the truth, and good man that he was, continued to harbour Walter at his manor.

However, when Tuck and I appeared at High Peak we spun the story that it had been Tuck who had found him, and that we had left him in the care of the nuns at Kirklees. That had the advantage of making him somewhere where he could not stay, since the sisters would help the sick and injured, but would hardly keep a man about the place. Tuck then said that he had traced the daughter and we wove Marianne into the tale. Being the kind man that he was, Sir Richard willingly agreed to find Walter a place at The Lea, and I got the impression that he had always had trouble finding men for his household when the surrounding farms on his manor needed every man they had. Moreover The Lea was a far bigger manor than mine, even if it was far from being grand, and with Sir Richard residing at High Peak and having no need to entertain his neighbours, food was not as tight as at Gisborne. And so we obtained a written instruction from Sir Richard to his housekeeper – which she of course would not be able to read, but would recognise Sir Richard's seal – and Tuck agreed to take Walter to The Lea as soon as he was fit to walk that far. But you see, Gervase, that is where the connection between Marianne and Sir Richard of Lea occurred. He was not her father, but he did employ her real father as a household man, and in time Marianne became very precious to him as the daughter he had never had.

Does that satisfy you? Good, for we must now come on to portentous times before I pause once more. My Christmas visit to Gisborne was a delight, but it gradually became clear to me that I would now never settle in such a small place myself. By the end of the week, although I was so very glad to see my friends there again, I could all but feel the walls closing in on me. What on earth I should do if I ever found a woman I wished to marry was quite a sobering thought, because there was no way I could bring her to Gisborne and then abandon her for months on end with just an old man, and a blind man and his boy for company. I said as much to Tuck on our journey down to High Peak, but I could never have believed how close I was to come in the next few months to losing everything, including Gisborne manor.

Yet we started 1194 in calm enough fashion except for a couple of small changes. The three who had been Templars' men decided they would continue north and try to find service with some nobleman on the Scottish border or even in King William's kingdom itself. They had no desire to stay in Nottinghamshire even with Robin, declaring that they had seen enough fighting for one lifetime once they heard of how often we seemed to have trouble courtesy of Count John. They therefore decided they would hire themselves out as workmen, not soldiers, since they had a wide range of skills to draw upon. Robert Hode also chose to continue on north to his home, and when Tuck and I got back to the camp, it was to find that Robin, Hugh, Malik and the Coshams had gone to escort all four north and ensure that they at least got beyond York safely.

However to my surprise, Colm the Irishman had decided to stay. In one of those strange coincidences of life, it turned out that he and Gilbert came from the same general area of the far north of Ireland called Ulster, although they did not know one another, nor did they even know each other's families. But their respective clans seemed to have some common affiliation to the same grand chief, which was enough for them to regard one another as kinsmen. Gilbert, it transpired was from the leading O'Neill family, while Colm was a Magennis from the Mourne mountains – names which meant little to the rest of us, but which bonded them with remarkable speed. He was not the seasoned fighter Gilbert was, but he was far from being helpless, and this brush with the unfairness of the law had given him an appetite to learn how to defend himself. In the meantime, though, they were having great fun trying to teach Roger Irish, which was hilarious for everyone since Roger had about as much aptitude for languages as a log of wood, but huge enthusiasm.

More surprising was the discovery of Edwyn Carpenter of Durham still at the camp. He had started talking to Will, and by the time Robert had been ready to leave Edwyn had decided he was staying. He told me that he felt there was little to go back for. The business that Robert had left behind had to support Robert's wife and children, and although Robin had given them money to make up for what had been taken from Robert when he had been captured, it would still mean lean times for the family without having another man to feed. And Ewyn, too, had had enough of false promises and being at any lord's mercy. He was not a fighter, but he had a craftsman's ingenuity, and if nothing else, the experience he had of dealing with door locks and other such devices made him an ideal recruit.

So we went into the new year with the outlaw band up to sixteen members, and if neither of the new recruits was as skilled as James, neither were they the liabilities that Algar and our Walter had been. And Walter of Fiskerton was to reappear again shortly just when we thought he was gone forever!

Nottingham
The start of the Year of Our Lord 1194

The new year began with a series of startling pieces of news. First came word from out of Normandy that although King Richard had ordered some castles there to be handed over to his brother in the truce of the previous year, the Norman lords loathed the youngest Plantagenet so deeply that they had utterly refused to do so.

"That's telling!" Murdac declared to those who were sat with him at dinner that night. "It certainly gives us some hope that they, at least, won't take any claims of kingship on his part seriously enough to fight for him. And I suspect it weakens Count John's position with regards to France, too, because what King Philip really wants is Normandy back under his control, and if John can't guarantee him that, then he's not such a useful ally any more. Certainly not one worth going to war for, I'd have thought."

Then hard on its heels came word that the Count and King Philip had tried to bribe the emperor to keep King Richard locked up, but had been foiled when letters had been intercepted.

"What was he thinking?" Sir Martin said in conversation with Murdac, Guy and Sir Walter. "To send a message intended for the likes of us, and openly saying we should get ready for war to back his claim to the throne, is insanity!"

Walter sighed heavily. "I think we've had another narrow escape. Can you imagine trying to resist the forces of the king? I for one wouldn't want to come up against Sir William Marshal."

Ralph Murdac was shaking his head. "But I would have had little choice but to do as the Count said. He is my liege-lord after all. You're right though, Walter, at times like these it's hard to know who your enemy is. And you too are right, Martin, because in the rest of that message it became clear that the only reason we're not fending off King Philip yet is because he wanted to see more of Normandy rising up to support Count John. Lucky for us, then, that the letters got taken by the archbishop of Canterbury, who's put a stop to this nonsense. And to crown it all, the archbishop and the bishops of Lincoln, London, Rochester, Winchester, Worcester, Hereford and Exeter – and more abbots and high clergy than you could shake a hat at! – all got together at Westminster, and have excommunicated Count John and all those who supported him, for being disturbers of the king's peace and of the realm."

"*Dewi Sant!*" Guy gulped, "Not that threat again! That could have been us too!" Then saw the worried expressions on the others' faces, and wondered whether just being in a castle under Count John's lordship brought them into that group. "Would we know if we've been included?"

Nobody knew. It was hardly the kind of thing which was a daily occurrence, and most people would assume that they would personally have to do something so extraordinarily evil to be removed from God's Grace as to be hardly worth thinking about if you lived a normal life. This concept of being cut off and condemned remotely, and for nothing more than being in the wrong place and at the wrong time was terrifying, for what could lesser men do to redeem themselves? And the thought of dying in battle took on a whole new level of fear under those circumstances, when no matter how good a life you might have led, you would be condemned to Hell for eternity without reprieve. Guy had a feeling that the local priests might be in heavy demand over the next couple of days as men hurried to make confessions and get what absolution they could while there was still time. No-one wanted to die unshriven!

"Is there any news of when the king is likely to return?" Martin asked hopefully. "Maybe a king who cared enough to go on crusade will be less careless of his peoples' souls than his brother, do you think? Do we have a date for his release even?"

Murdac shrugged. "Not yet, but Queen Eleanor has gone over there and so has Walter of Coutance, so it can't be too far off. I suppose we must just pray that since Longchamp is out there and fawning around the king, that he doesn't come back and pick up where he left off, because I can't imagine Richard will settle to ruling as his father did. Please God, Walter of Coutance stays as chancellor, and doesn't get sent back to his Norman cathedral!"

That gave everyone pause for thought, and even more so when they heard that after a Great Council on the tenth of February, Hubert Walter – the archbishop of Canterbury – had decided that steps must be taken to seize Count John's castles.

"What do they think we're going to do?" Murdac asked of nobody in particular as he listened to the scribe reading out the message. "Start our own bloody war up here?" He turned to Guy. "I want you to ride to Tickhill with a message for Robert Delamere. Find out if he knows any more than I do! Not that I expect him to. The poor man's barely had time to get to grips with his new appointment, much less start causing trouble – and he never was a warmonger like de Wendenal. I liked and trusted him back in the days when we went out on eyre together. He must already be ruing the day he ever accepted the post at Tickhill."

Guy was glad to go, not least because he very much wanted to talk to Tuck again. The Welsh monk always had strong views on political

Churchmen, seeing them as men first and possessed of an unseemly arrogance. And his response was everything Guy could have hoped for, and set his mind to rest.

"*Duw!*" Tuck growled in exasperation. "What's the matter with these men? No Guy, I don't think any of you are in peril. Count John, yes! That young man should be far more worried than he is by the sounds of things. Excommunication is no laughing matter, but equally it's not something to be handed out like a week in the stocks either! I have far more faith in God and the saints to be able to distinguish between the good and the bad than these men seem to, and it's beyond arrogant of them to think that they should know His mind. But I would be careful of something your sheriff doesn't seem to have thought of, and it's that with you and all of the rest of Count John's followers being in theory down on the same level as the heathens and the Saracens now, you may find that the archbishop sees you as a valid target."

Guy groaned. "Then you'd better pray for us, Tuck, because we haven't forgotten how eager Geoffrey Plantagenet was to swop his mitre for a helm over Tickhill the last time. In fact I'm sure it was partly de Wendenal's reticence to defend Tickhill which has led to him being replaced. His failure as a sheriff was just the excuse those in power were waiting for."

"Why did they need an excuse?" Much asked innocently, although Guy could see that several of the others were also struggling with the political shenanigans.

"It's complicated, Much," he sighed. "Last year the worry was the same as now: that in giving castles to Count John, the king had effectively given him fortresses he could hold against all comers, including the king himself. King Richard's noble desire to do right by his youngest brother had the potential to be the very thing which robbed him of his kingdom, and still has, do you see?

"Now originally de Wendenal had been seen as a safe pair of hands to put Nottingham and Tickhill in, even though he was not only in shires which were and are given over to the count for his income, but also – because having William de Ferrers as his liege-lord for his own lands, and who is himself very much tied to the count in the same way – de Wendenal has a several stranded personal alliance to Count John. You might think that that made de Wendenal one of the worst men to put in a position of power. But there are other lords who manage to juggle the mixed loyalties without too much trouble.

"Hugh le Puiset, for instance. He was happy to reinforce Doncaster in case the count made any aggressive moves, but his ties to the count meant that he was constrained from making the first move against him. It's all about loyalty and being faithful. Everyone, from the lowest peasant to the highest lord, is considered to hold fealty to the king above all else except God, even if most are too humble to know it, or care! Then they owe fealty to the man next down from the king in the line of authority and land-holding – which in this case means the count. So while Count John was just rattling his sword and saying he wanted to take power, there was a limit to what anyone could do against him without being called faithless and honourless to their sworn lord. But the moment he fortified Windsor he'd gone beyond talking and done something against his own liege-lord – the king – and that's why the lords then besieged the castle.

"So if you want to take his vows literally, de Wendenal was in the right by not defending Tickhill on behalf of a man who wanted to usurp the king. But on the other hand it shows a distinct disregard for the loyalty he ought to have shown the count. Ideally he should have fortified Tickhill better and just held it until help came, which would have sorted things out one way or the other. And it means he's disliked by both sides now! He didn't do the right thing in the eyes of the count's men, but he didn't do any better by the king either."

"Blessed St Thomas! What a complicated way of doing things!" Edwyn declared.

"Oh it's that all right!" Guy laughed bitterly. "We may end up quite literally being damned if we do and damned if we don't!"

"No!" Tuck said emphatically. "Not damned! Not you lesser men. Hold to your consciences, do no more evil than you have no other choice but to do, and do your penance afterwards, and God will judge what's in your heart, not these lordly bishops!"

"Thank you, Tuck! That's a very comforting thought!"

Yet as Guy got to Nottingham he had another shock – the entire town was filled with soldiers! Clearly someone was intending to lay siege to the castle, and although at this stage it wasn't clear who that might be, Guy felt it his bound duty to get back in. He skirted the town, trying to look as inconspicuous as possible, and realised that the greatest crush of men were actually on the town side. That made sense given that the great gates and the only way in lay there. Round on the opposite side, the cliff gave the castle protection from any assault unless men wanted to climb on ropes, and that brought its own problem of not wearing armour. Nobody would make that climb even in a simple ring-mail birnie, because with the weight of the gambeson beneath as well, few men would have the strength to haul themselves up. Yet no-one would make that climb unprotected when the defenders had all the time in the world to throw things at them or loose arrows at them.

Guy, on the other hand, was one of their own. He rode round to where the stables were, and staying well back, waited until someone appeared on the battlements. Keeping a big old oak between himself and the soldiers, Guy frantically signalled by waving his foresters hood, and was rewarded by seeing the man stop and peer hard towards him. Gesturing climbing a rope and seeing the message was understood, he then unsaddled his horse, and made sure she was loosed into a field, then crept back as close to the wall as he dared.

Within minutes he saw the familiar faces of Big Ulf, Ketil and Ruald peering back over the wall, and then a rope snaking down towards him. He grabbed the end as soon as it was within reach, and tying the end around himself – just in case they had to haul him up like a sack of turnips – began to climb. The cliff was no problem, although it was disheartening to find that something he would once have gone up with the ease of a squirrel, now had him puffing and panting after the first yard. Once at the foot of the wall proper, though, he had to rely on the others. He saw them put a loop of the rope around one of the great stone parapet blocks, and so had no worries about leaning his full weight on the rope, but it was taking too long for him to climb.

Suddenly there was a shout from behind. He had been spotted!

"Hold tight!" Leofric's voice called down, and suddenly Guy was being hoisted up at speed.

He slithered over the stone edge with little grace, and landed in a panting heap on the walkway at the feet of those he had spotted, plus Ricard and Frani, all of whom were still holding the rope. No wonder he had gone up so fast with six of them hauling him.

"You're a daft sod coming back," Ingulf said genially.

"Well someone has to watch out for you lot," Guy quipped back, and was rewarded by their laughter.

His greeting from Murdac was less joyful when he found the sheriff further along the walls, looking at the surrounding army pitching its tents and settling in.

"What news from Tickhill?" Murdac asked.

But Guy could only shake his head. "Not good, my lord. Sir Robert knows no more than you. He could only say to tell you not to worry about them, because Tickhill has enough stores to last a long time. He's going to shut the gates and wait. He'll sit tight and let those above him argue it out." Then Guy gestured to the soldiers, "But I don't think he was anticipating this! I didn't see any heading his way, but given that they seem to be coming up from the south, that means nothing, I suppose. Some might go on from here to Tickhill."

However Murdac didn't think so. "No, I'm afraid all those are for us, Guy. We're the one with the man-power, and even if the power of being the sheriff's seat is less tangible, it still makes us the greater prize. We're the main target. They'll only bother with Tickhill once this place has fallen, or if they start thinking that Sir Robert has the means to come to our aid. Or if the count should send men to there before coming to help us, or something like that – not that I think for a moment he will. I fear Delamere will have Hugh le Puiset to deal with again, though. The bishop of Durham seems determined to regain favour with the king after his spat with Longchamp, come what may."

Guy felt deeply sorry for Murdac. He was caught in the most unenviable position. "At least I didn't hear or see any sign of the archbishop joining in," he added, trying to sound reassuring.

"Well you wouldn't, would you?" snapped Sir Mahel who was standing a few feet further along the wall. "Hubert Walter might have sent these bloody men, but I don't think he's going to be doing his own dirty work! Really! Sometimes you can be so dense about those above you."

"I wasn't talking about the chancellor, Archbishop Walter," Guy said coolly, "or the archbishop of Canterbury! We're not even in his archdiocese. But we are in York's, and do you think the archbishop of York will just sit on his hands when he has the excuse to fight men who have been excommunicated, and sitting in a castle virtually on his shire border, and certainly within his archdiocese?"

Murdac turned to Guy in horror. "Judas' balls! The bastard! I'd forgotten the bastard son."

Guy sniffed. "I have a funny feeling he would have reminded you himself sooner rather than later, my lord."

Even Mahel had gone pale at the thought. When you had no idea whether you had been excommunicated or not, finding yourself on the opposite side to an archbishop was about as bad as it could get.

And things just got worse and worse. From the top of the walls those within Nottingham could only watch as more and more men and equipment arrived, and set themselves up around the castle. They had now been cut off from the outside world for some two weeks, and everyone was wondering what had happened about the king. Had the ransom been accepted at last? Was he on his way home? Or would the emperor prevaricate and wait to see what King Philip and Count John could offer him to keep King Richard captive?

"What do you think those barrels are, Guy?" Sir Simon asked him as the two of them and Giles and Osmaer watched the particularly careful unloading of many barrels from off a line of wagons.

"I have no idea, but they're being awfully careful with them, and that worries me," Guy sighed.

"It's Greek Fire," Fredegis' voice said from off to the side as he wandered up to join them, the threat of the siege making him less keen to be so distant with the other knights. "May God have mercy on our souls if they start using that!"

"What does it do?" Simon asked with a wobble in his voice. If an old soldier like Fredegis was dreading this, then it had to be truly awful.

The former mercenary gave an involuntary wince. "It burns! And you can't quench it! If you throw water on it, it just floats on the water and keeps on burning. The only thing you can do is let it burn itself out. But the worst is if you get it on you. You can't wash it off, but then you won't get the chance! It burns hotter than embers! I have only seen it used once, and then men died screaming in agony and were nothing but charred lumps when we could get to them." He shivered. "I do not wish to face Greek Fire again."

"How will they use it?" Guy asked in dread.

Fredegis shrugged. "Just load a barrel onto one of the trebuchets and send it over – that's what normally happens. If we're unlucky it will hit something hot and start burning straight away. If not, then they'll use fire arrows I expect."

Outside of the castle the first trebuchet had arrived with a mangonel to keep it company. Alone they were not a threat as yet, and there had been no sign of wagons arriving with the great stones which would be loaded onto them, and would then be hurled at the castle walls. Yet the fact that any siege-engines had arrived at all said that this time there would be no hanging back. This time the lords would not be content to sit at a distance just sealing the castle off, they clearly intended to take it.

The castle had ample stores for now, and a good deep well which would keep the water flowing, but with it being only early March, the stream of knights coming to do service at the castle had not fully begun, and so the defenders consisted of the regular garrison with only half a dozen extra knights. It was hardly an ideal place to be in with such an army camped at the door. And what an army it was! What it lacked in numbers it certainly made up for in importance.

"Jesu bless us and save us!" Guy heard the normally indifferent Sir Henry say one morning, as they realised a new banner had appeared beside an equally grand tent. "Is that the Earl of Huntingdon's arms?"

Already Guy had felt his heart sink as he watched the other banners being hoisted, now that there were enough lords for it to be necessary for their men to know who was where. He recognised not only the banner of William de Ferrers – who was no doubt hoping that a display of loyalty would ensure that the king made him earl of Derby in his father's stead – but also his very own lord, Ranulph de Blundeville, Earl of Chester. For Guy, being on the opposite side to the man whom he held Gisborne from was disastrous, and he had no illusions that the earl might have forgotten who Guy was, and that he was his the moment he saw him. Please God that the earl would be understanding that Guy had little choice but to be here – sneaking out would be seen as him being untrustworthy and faithless, and that too could cost him his manor.

It had already been much discussed amongst everyone within the castle as to how many of the local lords, who held land of these great families, had come along to help in the siege. There was no doubt that these three great lords all had territory close enough to Nottingham to be able to call upon those knights who owed them service and get them here with speed. One of the visiting knights, Fouchier de Grendon was already positively sick at the thought that he might have to face his own father. For Serlo de Grendon held land in Derbyshire from the de Ferrers family, and would have been forced to answer the call to arms.

And all their lives were made more unpleasant by the presence of a rather grand knight by the name of Roger de Montbegon, who had come to get the service he owed the king for his three manors in Nottinghamshire out of the way. Normally he would not have come himself, and Guy had been keeping well out of his way and his complaints, and so had not heard the details of why he was here just now – it was bad enough that he was without listening to his often-aired grievances. Everyone in the castle had something to lose in this situation, and just because Montbegon was grander than most did not mean that that those more lowly, like Guy, would feel their losses any less keenly.

The man he did feel sorry for was Henry Russell. He had the misfortune to be the man who had come from court with the letters for de Ferrers and the earl of Chester, but had then been sent onwards by them to Murdac, with the demand to give up the castle. Yet with the sheriff not being sure which side anyone was on, he had not only sent one of the villagers out with the refusal, but had also hung onto Russell, telling those outside that should they wish to negotiate further, he had no intention of sending one of his own men out to be then held captive. They would have their own man back when and if that time came. And so now Russell was trying to stay well out of everyone's way, and had been sent to sleep in the same chamber as Guy and Osmaer, although Osmaer had promptly decamped for another room, saying he would not sleep alongside the enemy. Guy just felt sorry for the man, and did his best to make his stay bearable.

March dragged its way onwards, and the siege held although nothing much of any excitement happened. More siege-engines arrived and there had to be half-a-dozen of each type spread out round the castle walls now. All they were waiting for were the stones to hurl. Fredegis and Walkelin, as the two who had had some experience of being on the other side of a siege, said that they would not start the bombardment until they had enough to keep going.

"No point in making dents in our walls and then giving us time to mend them before the next load of stone arrives," Walkelin explained. "Once they start they'll keep going all day, every day, until something crumbles."

The lesser folk, who would normally have been busy within the outer bailey keeping the castle running, had been allowed out before the siege had really bitten. They could do little in the way of fighting and would only be extra mouths to feed if things got bad. But now Guy was glad they had gone for another reason – if those stones cleared the outer wall they would fall on the wooden halls and buildings of the outer bailey, crushing anyone who was within. Harry had emptied the stables of all but a couple of horses, sending them out with the young lads who normally helped out from the town. At the time they had only been thinking of fire arrows hitting the thatch of the barns, but knowing of the Greek Fire now, Harry was doubly glad.

"The horses don't deserve to burn," he said morosely to Guy as they shared a beer in the quiet of the stable with Henry Russell, since the poor chap was welcome nowhere else. "I just hope that if they get taken as prizes that they're well treated."

Few other ordinary men remained, but the baker and his lads had been forced to stay as essential to the welfare of the garrison, and so had the smiths and their men, for more than ever they were now vital to the defence of the castle. There had been no exchanges of arrows as yet, but when the time came Murdac was determined that while there were men left who could pull a bow, the defence would not fail for want of arrows. Most were the short bolts for the crossbows the regular soldiers used, but Guy had been practising with the big Welsh bow they had taken and which only he knew had been James'. The former crusader might be gone, but Guy was glad he had his bow. It had the advantage of a much greater range, and if pressed he could loose arrows at almost twice the speed the crossbows could shoot, even though Guy was hardly as practised as the outlaws.

And thinking of Robin, Guy made sure he went to the walls several times a day in the hope of seeing him or one of the others. Several times he saw Will and Hugh in the first week, but as the siege dragged on Robin himself came more and more frequently along with John, both clearly wanting to make sure that their cousin was surviving. No doubt Allan was there too, but the smaller man was harder to pick out in the general press around the castle, even on the cliff side. On a couple of occasions they were able to shout a few words to one another, but to be heard over the all-pervading racket they had to shout so loud that they almost immediately attracted someone's attention. Instead they had to make do with large gestures.

But it was by this means that Guy heard first of anyone of their impending doom. Robin himself came as close to the castle as he dared and then began gesturing furiously south-eastwards, then mimed someone putting something on their head. Then John appeared and made as to put something onto Robin's head, and then knelt before him, and suddenly Guy knew what they were saying – the king would be here soon. Yet how could he warn any of the others? It wasn't as simple as saying,

"I've been talking to my cousin over the castle wall."

And then they all saw a dark line on the horizon which gradually grew.

"Christ help us! More men!" Harry declared. "How many do you reckon there are, Guy?"

"I have no idea." And that was true, because although they could see the men, Nottinghamshire was not so flat that they were advancing across an open plain. The road dipped and rose, and went in and out of trees, at which points men disappeared. Then something caught Guy's eye and he pointed to where more men seemed to be appearing. "Looks like it's too many to get across the bridge here at any speed, though. Someone's either sent them to another crossing, or that's a separate group arriving."

"Looks like a royal banner up there by Earl Ranulph's," Henry Russell observed.

"Aye, but which one?" asked Guy, and heard Murdac behind him say as he came to join them,

"That's the big question, isn't it? Is it Count John come to aid us? Is it the bloody archbishop? I know he's not fully royal, but King Henry recognising him as his own gives him a right to use colours very like the king and his brother. If the damned wind would get up and move the bloody thing a bit, we might be able to see! As it is, it could even be that twisted dwarf, Longchamp, come to plague us in the king's name – and I'm not giving this castle up to him come what may!"

It was a desperate conundrum, and not helped when they saw that the new host had come to join the besiegers.

Then someone pointed and called out, "Look! The archbishop's cross! Down there!"

Sure enough, in amongst the fighting men and the tents was a beautiful gold cross gleaming in the spring light. It had not been carried before anyone on the march, as far as anyone in the castle could see, but its presence confirmed who was now here.

"That settles it, then," Murdac sighed. "Bloody Geoffrey Plantagenet couldn't resist the chance for a fight. Let's hope we get through this without him excommunicating us all over again!"

It was as though the world had come to Nottingham in all its finery, for by now the number of those coming to attack the castle had far outstripped the town's capacity to house them all, and tents with banners were springing up in the fields beyond it.

"I have a dreadful fear I will not be leaving here alive," Giles confided to Guy as they watched the men pitching tents even closer to the castle walls. "They look very determined to have this place."

Guy knew what he meant because it was his worry too. He had already made sure that he had a length of rope hidden away, but which part of the wall he might go down was quite another thing. However he tried his best to cheer the younger man up. "Hopefully it won't come to that. Murdac's not a fool. Hopefully he'll start treating with them."

However all they got was a huge man in armour coming forward and bellowing at them,

"S'ouvrir les vanne, au nom de le roi! Vous devoir se rendre!"

Harry jabbed Guy with an elbow. "What did he say?"

Guy leaned in and said softly, "'Open the gates, in the name of the king. You must surrender.' Sounded as though he expected to be obeyed, too."

However others were not impressed.

"Shoot him!" Murdac commanded. "I'm not giving up to some uppity Norman baron!"

Several of the soldiers brought their crossbows to aim and shot, hitting several of the men around the knight but not quite hitting him. It seemed to enrage the man for he stormed off yelling furiously in French.

"Do you think he was someone important?" Payne asked of no-one in particular.

"Not likely to be the king," Sir Martin sniffed. "Sir Ralph said that King Henry always spoke English, and Count John does, so the king must do. So no, it's pretty unlikely that it's the king."

Yet even before they had retreated from the wall, things began to happen.

"Christ! They're launching an attack!" someone yelled in warning, and there was a mad scramble to get to armour and weapons.

By the time Guy got back to the inner gatehouse there was a strong smell of smoke.

"Shit, they're burning the gates!" came another called warning, and Guy could see the smoke rising from the barbican.

After a worryingly short space of time, there came some mighty thumps, and what was left of the outer gates cracked open to allow men to stream in, and the big knight who had called the warning was in the lead. Nottingham castle had been breached!

Ah me, that was a day I shall not forget in a hurry, and we are not done with it yet. However you have no doubt guessed that the big knight who challenged us was none other than the king. It was typical of the man that he never thought that he might not be understood. He was the king, therefore we must understand him – such arrogance, Gervase! He may have fought for Christ in the Holy Land, but he was never one to think of what others might need or know.

And in defence of my sheriff, Murdac had never even met the man! Remember, Brother, that before any Great Council could be called at the

start of his reign, King Richard had dismissed the likes of Murdac and Delamere, and was holding out his hand to the highest bidders for the posts of sheriffs of the shires. The sheriffs of King Henry's reign were also, of their personal stations, not men of such high standing as to be the ones at the front when he was crowned, either, even if they had gone. And then after that, he was gone, first to Normandy and then to the Holy Land. So how would Murdac have known him as one man to another? Nor had the young prince Richard ever spent much time here in England, spending more time in his mother's province of Aquitaine, or in Normandy fighting his brothers. In this if no other, Prince John had the better of his older brother, for he had grown up here and could speak English as well as any of us, albeit with a distinct French accent.

If you will allow a moment's digression longer, I will also say that my experience in that breaking of the siege did something for me – it gave me new insight into what my cousin and his friends had gone through at Jerusalem. Our siege would not be anything like as bad as that, not as long or with such dire consequences for such a huge number of people, and for that we would all give thanks when the time came. But for me it opened my eyes as to why the siege gave them all such nightmares, and I knew I would not look at that episode in their lives in the same way ever again. There is an incredible strain in just waiting, Brother. In doing nothing, because you can do <u>nothing</u>! You ask why we did not do anything before the seige began in earnest? But what could we do? There were too few of us to fight our way clear of the surrounding soldiers even if we had thought it right to abandon the castle. No Brother, a seige is slow, exceedingly slow until whoever is on the outside chooses to launch an attack, and we had no way of predicting when that would happen until we saw it begin.

However, we must press on! King Richard had fired the main gate and gained access to the castle, and was coming to fight for it!

Chapter 26

e prayed then. To St Thomas and to any other saint whom we might think would look on us with favour. For the gates opened and easily double our numbers streamed in just while we stood too stunned to instantly respond. They were screaming murder and we instantly knew that these men would not give quarter. Later we also had our suspicions confirmed that these were the men who had come with the king. The local knights who had been camped around us with the three earls – for in thanks for his part in the siege, de Ferrers had his right to the family title of Earl of Derby confirmed – were not so keen to be slaughtering their neighbours. They knew only too well that there but for the Grace of God went them. A different castle, a different month of the year, and they too might well have been doing nothing more than their sworn duty to end up on the wrong side in these family quarrels. For that was what this ultimately was. It was the fight between one son and another over who should inherit, but few such family spats are the cause of so many innocent men losing their lives, praise be!

That Friday the twenty-fifth of March was an awful day, Brother. I went out armed and ready to fight, although with little heart for the task, if I am to be truthful. I had no appetite for this political war-making. This was no defence of our land against marauding foes. Not even of the kind I had fought against on the Welsh border. Some may think that there was more nobility in fighting other knights, the culmination of the training they had undertaken since boyhood and finally putting it into practise. I did not.

Those Welsh war-bands we had fought against had been fighting for something I was not entirely without sympathy for – the right to live without feeling the constant heel of Norman over-lordship on their necks. Therefore they fought with passion and fury, and all of us who stood against them knew we must kill or be killed; it was as simple as that. But this? This was the kind of fight where a man might do the right thing for the right reasons and still be wrong. And worse, might find himself facing a member of his own family who had likewise been swept up in these rich men's games. No, I had no relish for what I was about to do.

And what seemed even worse to us was that we could see a second archbishop's cross in amongst the banners of knights, and this one was much more prominently displayed. With both archbishops amongst those attacking us, we did not know what to do for the best. Was Geoffrey with Richard or John? Had Hubert Walter, the archbishop of Canterbury, come as the king's right-hand man in the literal sense of being by his side in battle, or simply to take the castle so that no-one else could make a bid for the throne? Or even Walter Coutance? Would he have his own cross *carried before him, even though it was not for an English archbishopric? Was that the chancellor? We did not know.*

I went out into the inner bailey and joined with the other knights from the castle, and together with our men-at-arms we sallied out to meet with the attackers. They came on in close ranks at first, kite-shaped shields interlocked and bearing down on us in sheer weight of numbers. However in the confined space between storehouses and other buildings that superiority did not last for long, and as they had to break ranks it became a more evenly matched, grim fight. In one way it was a good thing, because it never allowed the attackers' superiority of numbers to overwhelm us. At best we were only ever six abreast and facing the same number. Any closer and there was no room to swing a sword without the risk of beheading one of your own!

In the castle at this time we had thirty-six ordinary men-at-arms, of whom my friends numbered twelve of them, but in addition we had twenty-four sergeants – and those, dear Brother, are the ones who were mounted in a normal conflict – plus the same number of crossbow-men. Then there were us sixteen knights who normally saw to the forest, our three regular knights of the castle – Hugh, Robert and Richard – and the six knights who must have been ruing the moment they had answered the summons to come to do their service. And to lead us we had Sir Ralph Murdac, our visitor, Roger de Montbegon, and William de Wendenal who was so drunk in his fear that he could barely move in a straight line. I was glad that the sheriff nonetheless thrust de Wendenal into the fray. It would have been a cruel fate if he had taken no risks while others died.

And they did die. Step by step we were beaten back until our attackers had the taken the outer bailey, and until at dusk all we could do was shut the gates of the inner gatehouse and lick our wounds. At which point we took stock of our losses, and they were not good. We had lost a third of our men-at-arms, amongst them my friends Ricard, Alfred, Ruald and Claron, all of whom had been seen to fall. Osmund was missing and we feared he must have been taken prisoner.

More than that, we had lost seven of our sergeants and three of the crossbow-men. Of the knights, we had lost two of the visiting knights, and Payne and Sewel were missing along with two more visiting sergeants. We also had many men wounded by crossbow bolts, for the enemy archers had been more successful than the swordsmen in that respect, and I spent much of the night helping to patch our men up. As night fell we realised that our enemies had also retreated back to outside the main gates, and so I led a sally out to reclaim the bodies of our friends. We had no desire to leave them to be trampled and hacked at the next day. Then Sir Ralph led another sally out who deliberately set fire to what remained of the gates, and to several of the buildings which stood in the way of our being able to see what was coming through the gates.

Yet that did us no good, for come the morning we realised that all we had done was make it easier for the attackers to bring the siege-engines closer to the castle itself. But worse, whoever was leading this attack did something truly terrible in my eyes. As I have told you, I did not at this stage know that this was the king. All I knew was that whoever this man was, I now hated him with a passion, for he had rough gallows built where we could see them, and had those prisoners they had taken the previous day strung up – some from amongst our force, but others known to be supporters of Count John within the town. Even now after all these years I still get a lump in my throat at the memory of seeing young Payne swinging there. He had spent his whole life being afraid of someone or other, and just at the point where some of us had worked on him enough that he had stopped quaking in his shoes on a daily basis, that had to happen to him.

Yes, Brother, I am still angry about it. He had done nothing! He was a lowly knight just doing his duty. And as a soldier, King Richard should have understood that. I fully understand that in such a situation prisoners were bound to be taken, but why simple men like Payne could not have been ransomed I have never been able to grasp, particularly as King Richard had an unquenchable thirst for money. It certainly meant that come the morning our resolve stiffened considerably! If we were to swing anyway, we might as well go down fighting!

Nottingham Castle
March, the Year of Our Lord 1194

"Vous devoir se rendre! Se rendre aux roi!" was the cry which presaged the next round of fighting – 'You must yield! You must yield to the king.'

Murdac turned to Guy. "Can you use that damned great bow? Right, then get up to a vantage point and start killing some of their leaders for me! You're the only one with the range to do that. And if you can get rid of some of those bloody crossbow-men too, do it!"

With relish Guy bounded up the stairs of the small tower which stood to the side of the castle's inner gate. Harry was at his back carrying those arrows Guy couldn't manage, and at the top of the tower Guy looked out at the renewed battle and swore savagely. He strung the bow, flexed it a couple of times to warm it and then picked up the first arrow.

His first target was a crossbow-man who was coming forward under the cover of two shields, and was heading for Murdac. Pulling the string back until he was kissing it, he sighted down the arrow, pulled back a touch more so that the flight brushed his chin, and loosed. The arrow hammered into the archer, going straight through him and hitting the man beside him too. They went down in a tangle, shocked cries going up all around them, but Guy had moved on and was already taking aim at his next target. Another archer went down in a welter of blood, and another and another. Then when he could see no more of the lethal bolts aimed straight at his friends, Guy went for the knights, taking only a fraction longer to take aim in order to find the more vulnerable parts where an arrow might go in through a gap in the ring-mail.

Once he had Earl Ranulph in his sights and almost loosed, but then thought better of it. As lords went, Ranulph had been more than fair to him. If he died, who knew which member of the family might take over? And they might be a lot less willing to leave even a small manor in the hands of a knight doing service elsewhere.

Feeling his arm begin to tire, Guy paused and flexed his shoulders, then became aware of Harry staring at him slack-jawed. His friend had just shown a whole new side to him – an avenging killer like no nobleman with that great bow, yet far removed from the ordinary men too, menacing and dreadful in his black leather jerkin, and nothing like the kind man Harry thought he knew. Yet Guy had no idea of how terrifying he had seemed as he struck with lethal speed.

"What's wrong?"

"Sweet Jesu, Guy! Do you know what you've just done? How many arrows you've just loosed?"

Guy blinked and looked down to where only a handful remained. Then looked out over the parapet and realised how little time must have elapsed, given that the defenders were still clustered around the gatehouse, and the attackers had not pressed forward that much. He had been utterly absorbed, at one with the bow and letting his fury provide him with the energy to pull and pull again.

"They were trying to get you," Harry said, awe still in his voice, "but we're too high here."

Guy shook his head. "More like the angle was wrong."

"Well whatever it was, I could hear the bolts rattling off the stones below us! I thought we were done for. How many did you hit?"

Guy gave a lupine grin. "Most of those I aimed at! Didn't get all of them quite where I wanted, mind. But at least those crossbow-men will think twice about coming forward again." He flexed his arms as the soreness really hit him. "Good job I kept practising, eh?"

"You must be as good as Robin Hood," Harry said in wonder.

"Not a chance. I don't get to practise daily like he does," Guy said, then realised just how much he had let slip. Harry knew that Guy had been able to help his family, but belatedly it occurred to Guy that he had never made the connection explicit between him and Robin before – or at least not since Robin Hood had become so famous that the name really meant much to Harry. Yet he would just have to trust Harry now. He had not betrayed him before, so it was to be hoped he wouldn't do it now.

"How many arrows left?" he asked Harry. "Are there any downstairs?" But Harry shook his head. "Right, better save these last few in case of an emergency," Guy decided. "Can you go and take this bow back to the old keep? That's where the weapons taken from outlaws and the like are stored. Put it and the arrows in there. If the castle falls then that's where it ought to be, and hopefully no-one will ask about it. I'm guessing they'll be thinking it was one of our archers up here."

He flipped the string off and handed the bow to Harry, then loosened his sword in its scabbard and took the stairs at a run to go and join in with the others. Finding Murdac at the rear of the gatehouse, momentarily leaning on his sword and gasping for breath, Guy reported,

"Out of arrows. The bow's back where it was."

Murdac gave him a funny look. "I'm not going to ask where you learned to shoot like that, Guy." Guy stared back blankly, genuinely not sure what Murdac meant. The sheriff pointed a finger upwards. "It was like death fell from the sky for a while. Mother of God! You hit damned near every one!"

"Did I? I was so busy finding the next target I didn't have time to stop and look."

Murdac's expression became even more unreadable. "Yes. Well it was the speed which was the other thing. By St Thomas, I've never seen the like!"

"Oh I'm not that fast," Guy said without thinking. "There are many Welsh bowmen who could knock spots off me for speed and accuracy. I've seen them do it."

He was thinking of Thomas and Piers, but was brought back to the present by Murdac saying,

"Then I shall remember to give extra thanks the next time at church for the fact that we never had Count John's Welsh mercenaries at our gates!"

At this point Guy became aware that men were streaming past him back into the castle.

"Siege-engines!" someone called, and almost immediately there was a strange sound overhead and then a thump.

"Everyone take cover!" Murdac roared. "Get inside! No-one stays out in the bailey!"

He didn't have to say it twice. Another large lump of rock announced its imminent arrival with an unearthly whistle, and then exploded on contact with the flagstones of the inner bailey, and showering the place with razor-sharp shards. Guy saw one man clap his hand to his face and then blood start to well through his fingers, and somewhere off to the side someone screamed in pain. The siege had begun in earnest.

For the rest of the day Guy was kept busy tending to the wounded. There were others who could keep watch on the parapets, and now that they were sealed in, there was little else anyone could do. Their remaining crossbow-men kept a watch for likely targets, but with the siege-engines doing most of the work now, few target presented themselves. Only one of the machines was actually inside the outer bailey. Most were on what level ground there was to the north and north-east, where they could be moved into position away from the houses.

It meant that when night fell, the old castle where Guy slept had not been damaged in any way, although the stables had been badly damaged, and so too had the fine hall which King Henry had had built. Dog-tired, and yet unable to sleep, Guy finally went up onto the southernmost corner of the building and stared morosely out over the little River Leen. Across the water meadows he could see the Trent meandering away by the moonlight, and wondered whether he would live to see another day. It was Sunday tomorrow, as good a day as any to die on.

He was so lost in his own thoughts and prayers that it took a moment to register that someone was calling his name urgently, and it wasn't from within the castle.

"Guy! Guy!"

He looked down and saw Robin and the others grouped at the bottom of the cliff. Then Thomas pulled back on his bow and Guy saw an arrow arc up towards him. A rope was attached and he swiftly tied it off.

"Come down!" Robin hissed frantically.

"I can't," Guy called back sadly. "There are wounded men here. I'm the only one with the knowledge of how to treat some of the worse wounds. Murdac let the scribes run back to Lenton when he saw how things were going, and the women went back into the town. I've got two men with belly wounds and a sergeant whose arm I've had to take off. I'm the last person who should be doing such things, but at least I knew to put a poultice of honey and a turpentine bandage on the stump. If I leave they'll definitely die, if I stay they might just live."

"Do you know it's the king you're fighting?" Robin called back in disbelief. "What do you think he's going to do to you when he gets into that castle?"

Guy stared back at him in shock. "The king? *Really*? Oh God preserve us!"

"Who did you think it was?" Will's voice came out of the darkness full of exasperation.

"Geoffrey – the archbishop – and the earls of course, but it all changed when the archbishop came."

"Did you not see the king's banner?" John called.

"No. Not with all the others around and the houses in between."

Now Robin was calling to him again. "Do you know that Tickhill has surrendered? The bishop of Durham should be here by tomorrow bringing the prisoners from there to the king. For pity's sake, Guy, you have to convince the sheriff to yield! There's nothing but death and damnation if you continue to hold out!"

Guy sighed. "Look, there's some local men caught in here. One of them is Harry the stableman who's helped me in the past. If I bring them up here, will you take them to safety?"

"Do you have to ask?" Robin's voice came back.

Running as quietly as he could down the stairs, Guy went and found the three smiths who had been trapped in the castle and the baker, none of whom could do much now that they were separated from the tools of their trade, and in the baker's case, his ovens. With Harry he led them up to the tower and then explained that they were getting out and that friends were beneath who would help them. Luckily all the men were strong of arm, and John and Tuck had come up to the top of the cliff to help any who needed to pause before making the second part of the scramble down.

As the last smith made it down to the ground, and John and Tuck joined him, Guy undid the rope and dropped it back down to them.

"Good luck, cousin, we'll be watching for you," Robin called back up. "If you get taken prisoner then we'll be coming to get you, never fear!"

"Then make sure you're quick about it," Guy said, wishing that his voice did not sound so scared. "They were awfully quick to hang yesterday's prisoners this morning!"

"Don't you worry!" Thomas' reply came. "There's four of us now who could cut the rope with an arrow if needs be. We'll be in that crowd and cutting you down before they know what's happened."

It made Guy feel a little better knowing that his friends would be there for him, but once he had seen them melt safely off into the darkness he felt obligated to go and wake Murdac. As it happened the sheriff was having no more luck in sleeping than Guy, and he called 'come in' as soon as Guy knocked.

"I've just been called to by people on the outside," Guy said softly, closing the door and coming to sit beside the sheriff, who was perched on the edge of his bed, a small candle lit and a leather cup of wine in his hands. Not that he was as drunk as de Wendenal undoubtedly was. Ralph Murdac looked as sober as Guy.

"It's not good news, I'm afraid, my lord." Guy said sadly. "They say Tickhill has surrendered."

"Oh." Murdac's one word held a world of misery in it.

"And I'm afraid there's worse. It really is the king out there."

Now Murdac snorted. "And how would peasants know that? Unless you're telling me you've had a conversation with one of the knights out there?"

Guy cringed inside. "No, not a knight." How could he convince the sheriff to accept the truth? "But they were quite sure it's the king."

"I didn't have you down as one to give up," Murdac sighed.

"I'm not giving up!" Guy objected. "But don't you think it would be an idea to send someone out tomorrow?"

"And who am I going to risk? You saw what they did to poor Payne and Sewel! Or are you volunteering to go yourself?"

"I'll willingly go rather than send one of our own to the gallows," Guy told him truthfully. "But I was actually thinking that this is just the reason why you held onto Henry Russell. It is, isn't it?"

Murdac's head came up and he was suddenly less gloomy. "By God, I'd forgotten about Russell!"

"And then there's young Fouchier de Grendon. His father and brother are outside. Of any of us he has someone there to intercede on his behalf. They're both senior to him in their family, and they're on the winning side, so surely they should be able to speak up for him? Send those two, my lord. Between Russell and the de Grendon family we should be able to get some sense of what's going on out there."

Murdac sighed. "You talk a lot of sense, Guy, and for the sake of everyone else I shall send them, but I think I'm doomed come what may. I've been on the wrong side with this king from the moment his pompous, proud arse hit the throne. He won't spare me now no matter what I do."

Guy felt sick at the thought that Murdac might end up getting hanged. If he could get to Robin he might just be able to save Murdac at the last moment, and he reconciled himself to leaving the castle later that day if the chance came.

Their first sight however, was that of the bishop of Durham coming in from the north in much pomp and ceremony, and even from the walls they could see the prisoners who had come from Tickhill. Guy desperately wanted to say who they were to the others, but Murdac was saying nothing, and Guy felt he couldn't undermine the sheriff now. However the sight of them seemed to make up Murdac's mind that Guy had maybe spoken to someone who did know what was going on.

"Someone find Russell and de Grendon," he ordered, and when they were brought to him in the keep, he instructed them,

"I want you to act as our messengers. Go out under truce and find out who is out there. I don't believe for a moment that the king is home already. This is probably just Geoffrey Plantagenet mischief making. But you two are the only ones I can send who have an earthly chance of surviving."

Neither of them looked happy, but the prospect of getting out of the castle also held its own appeal. Dressed in their ordinary clothes and without armour, the two of them were taken down to the gate and then let out. Guy was up in his spot again with the Welsh bow and the last few arrows. If either of these two were brought to the gallows, he would do his level best to make the shot Thomas spoke of and cut the rope before they choked. It was the least he could do for them given that it was his idea.

Both men were white as sheets, and walked out with their hands up to show they had no hidden weapons. Halfway across the outer bailey, men swarmed out to meet them, and they disappeared from view. A tense hour passed, and then another, but then to Guy's intense relief they were seen coming back, and the gate was opened to let them back in.

Everyone congregated around them all asking questions until Murdac roared for silence.

"It is the king!" Henry Russell said emphatically. "Beyond any shadow of a doubt it's him! He towers over everyone, and even with his teeth half gone from his sickness in the Holy Land, and the way he's lost weight, it's still unmistakeably him. No-one else can fix you with his eye like that!"

"You're sure it's not his half-brother?" Murdac asked dubiously.

But Russell was immediately shaking his head vigorously. "No, not even Archbishop Geoffrey can match him. It's the king!"

"My father says it is, too," Fulchier declared with no small hint of desperation in his voice. "Our lord, Earl William, has been quite clear on that matter, and you can't think that someone of his status would be fooled by anyone else?"

Yet somehow Murdac could not, or would not believe them. "Anyone who wishes to go may leave," he said, although Guy knew that this only applied to the knights. The ordinary men were condemned to stay, come what may.

As the argument raged on, Ingulf came to Guy's side and hissed in his ear, "Go! Please, for our sakes! Make sure that our families don't get turned out because we were here! You're the only ones we can trust – you and Robin."

Guy felt dreadful but nodded his reluctant agreement. Then de Wendenal spoke up,

"Well you can stay here if you want, Murdac, but I'm leaving. I'm surrendering. This bloody place isn't worth dying for. Who's with me?"

Unsurprisingly Fredegis and Walkelin were there like arrows from the bow, and Henry not far behind. So too were the remaining two visiting knights and Roger de Montbegon. After that there was a pause and then Murdac turned to the rest of the knights and said,

"You too Simon, and you Joscelin. Both of you are too wounded to fight on. Osmaer, Simon, Thorsten and Guy – you'll go too. None of you are well enough placed to withstand getting caught up in this. Throw yourself on the mercy of that man out there and pray it's enough. Guy, I'm sending the wounded out in your care."

And that was it. Shortly after noon the small party trooped across the singed and trampled ground of the outer bailey to their besiegers. De Wendenal practically ran, and no sooner had they been marched unceremoniously into the royal presence, then he was declaiming Murdac loudly.

"He's the one who said we should fight, Your Grace! He wouldn't believe us when we said it was you!" And on and on he went, shifting every ounce of blame away from himself until the king roared in his Norman French,

"Be silent! You faithless wretch! Whatever your sheriff has done, you own him more loyalty than that!"

De Wendenal subsided, whimpering, although Guy wasn't sure if he had understood every word said to him. And now the king's gaze travelled over the rest of the knights kneeling before him. Everyone kept their heads bowed until the king said,

"And have any more of you anything to say for yourselves?"

Hoping his French was suitably good, Guy cleared his throat.

"Oui?" the king sniffed derisively.

"For myself, nothing, your grace," Guy said politely as his brain scrambled for the right words in the language he hardly ever used now, "But we have several wounded brought out with us. I would plead for clemency for them from Your Grace."

"Would you now?" The king sounded surprised.

Guy gulped and hoped what he was about to say would not overstep the mark. "None are great men, Your Grace, they were simply soldiers following the orders of their lord. None would know you from any other great lord. They are overawed by all such men."

"That is a remarkably noble sentiment coming from such a ragged man. Who are you?"

"Sir Guy of Gisborne, Your Grace."

Another discreetly coughed from somewhere just behind the king, and then Guy heard Earl Ranulph saying softly, "He's a knight of mine, my lord. It's complicated but he's here by the direct wish of your late father."

Guy saw the king turn in surprise. "Is he indeed?"

"Yes, sire. And he has done no small service for your family in the past." Guy was aware that Ranulph was leaning in closer to the king, and was no doubt giving an abridged version of how Guy had hauled Prince John out of the wilds over in Wales.

The king gave a terse bark of a laugh. "The Welsh, eh? Well, Gisborne, it seems you have your uses."

"And if you wish to hunt as you expressed a desire to," Guy heard de Ferrers speak up, "then the man you want tracking the deer is the one kneeling before you. He provided me with excellent sport not six months ago right here in Sherwood."

The king gave another sniff. "Very well, he is released into your custody, Chester, and I shall hold you and Derby responsible if he causes any trouble."

And with that Guy was dismissed and ushered away into Ranulph's entourage. Despite his desire to know more of what was going on, he found himself watched every moment of the rest of the day. In fairness, most of the earl of Chester's own men were more than sympathetic to his plight. They needed little imagination to see how easily they might have been caught in such a cleft stick.

When the evening stew was brought round, someone found Guy a bowl and he was not stinted of his share of the food. Yet the greatest surprise was to see Roger coming towards him when someone came to collect the large pot the men had taken their portions from. The former thief just about managed to contain his relief at seeing Guy, and under the excuse of visiting the latrines, Guy managed to brush past him and say, "I'm fine. I'm in no danger," before his accompanying guard caught up with them. Roger disappeared after that, and Guy presumed he had returned to let Robin know that he lived and was in no immediate danger.

The night seemed to drag on forever, and many times Guy thought about trying to make a run for it. But every time he thought he might, he also thought that if he did, it would make things so much worse for the others. If he could not be trusted to stay put when men such as the earl of Chester and the earl of Derby spoke up for him, then the other lesser men would never have a chance of getting on the king's better side. Not that Guy was sure that there was a better side, but at least they could maybe steer clear of the wrong side.

As Monday finally crept in, the archbishop of Canterbury took matters in hand, and went to speak with Murdac and the remaining garrison, and to Guy's intense relief the rest of those left within the castle marched out and that was the end of the siege. They had been cut off from the outside world for over a month, but the real fighting was over and done with in three short days.

Our siege may have been short, but its aftermath was as bloody as any other. I was compelled to take the king hunting in Sherwood on the next day, of which more in a moment. But I must tell you that I was appalled

when this so-called great king hanged all of the sergeants from our castle to make an example of them. The rest of us had to pay fines as we had feared we would, but I never did understand what the king thought hanging common men achieved. They had had no say in whether they fought or not, and were hardly likely to incite a rebellion on their own behalf. I am told that overall we got off lightly, for if the king had had to storm the castle, then he would have thought himself within his rights to put all to the sword – such was the knightly code he and other such great men lived by, Gervase. But to me it seemed unnecessarily cruel.

Ralph Murdac was taken into the king's custody and had to throw himself on the king's mercy. I am told that he and other men who were deemed to be too close to Count John were lucky to get off with their lives, and two noblemen were actually hanged. Yet for my part the one whom I wished the full weight of the king's anger to fall upon was William de Wendenal, but never had the saying that the Devil looks after his own seemed so apposite, for the dreadful man suffered no more than the rest of us, although he would never again hold an office such as sheriff or constable of any castle.

Chapter 27

Over that first night I prayed that my friends would be spared too, for I had little faith in this legendary king of ours. As a young man I might once have been blinded by his awesome reputation, but I had seen too much of the world and what rich men did without thought for the ordinary people by now. Having stood as close to King Richard as I am to you now, Gervase, I can tell you that he was indeed an imposing sight: exceedingly tall but broad in the shoulder to match, and with those piercing blue eyes which often go with the red-blonde hair which signifies ancestry with the Danes. Yes, Brother, the Danes, for do not forget that the very reason Normandy bears that name is because it was the domain of the Norse men, allowed to settle on the coast by a French king some two or three centuries back. And King Richard would have fitted well into those times. I could easily imagine him as some bear-skinned berserker, as at home looting the monastery out on Lindisfarne as wading ashore at Acre in the face of the Saracens, or besieging the castle of some rebellious lord in Poitou!

But close to, and past the point where the legend blinded you to the man before you, I found myself leading out on a hunt an imperious man who used his piety as an excuse to do just as he wished without thought for others, and with dreadful breath! Truly, Brother, those rotten teeth from his illness in the Holy Land meant that he could have felled a bear just by breathing on it! While he kept his mouth shut it was bearable, but his smile was now gruesome in sight and smell, and men did not keep a distance solely out of respect.

So now we come to the one and only time our so-called illustrious king ever came to Sherwood, and I for one am glad it was only the once. With his household men dancing attendance on him, King Richard rode out, and I led him up to Clipstone. As king he had every right to be hunting in the royal park there, but I had also had urgent words with both Ranulph de Blundeville and William de Ferrers. I had no wish to repeat my error with fitz John and go seeking red deer and boar if the king was not used to them! And I was most glad I asked them to subtly find out.

At first both earls looked at me slightly askance, but as I explained that I was worried because the king had spent so little time in England – and was undoubtedly more used to hunting in the East or in Normandy – they suddenly realised what I was doing my best to say, without calling the king hopeless where others might overhear. Knowing that they had spoken up for me, they had as much to lose this time if I fell flat on my face, and Earl Ranulph knew that he would not be chortling this time if it was the king who ended up having to be rescued by a mere huntsman forest knight. And when both came back looking slightly shaken, I knew I had been right to ask.

~By Our Lady, you were right to worry, Guy!~ Earl Ranulph said to me, and even now I can remember his horrified expression as we stood in his tent that night. ~Earl William made some comment about the spotted deer which have recently been introduced at the royal park at Clipstone, and we both expected him to make some withering comment about them not being worth the hunt.~

De Ferrers sat beside him, and I could see that he too had been shocked as he told me that the king had been full of how many of those fallow deer he would be able to bring down, adding,

~And no wonder he expects to bring down many when they are there and waiting for him and without the sense to run hard!~ And then he added something which cheered me immensely.

~We are both in your debt, Guy. It would have gone very badly for us if the king had been displeased by his hunting, for – may St Thomas help us – he wishes to be back at Nottingham tomorrow for a Great Council the day after!~

It turned out that while his half-brother the archbishop of York, and also the earl of Huntingdon, would be accompanying the king, the archbishop of Canterbury and my two earls would be doing their best to move heaven and earth to get the great hall ready to hold a council in. And both men were experienced enough hunters to know that we could not ride the fifteen miles to Clipstone, take the time to track and then hunt the wild red deer, and still ride the same fifteen miles back. As it was, I would be up before dawn and riding like the wind for Clipstone to ensure that even the fallow deer were still where we prayed they would be.

Some other poor soul would be guiding the king to Clipstone, and I was most grateful that it would not be me, for I had no desire to spend any longer than necessary in the king's company. I had all the patronage I could have asked for in the gratitude of the two earls I had helped out. And I knew this would not be forgotten by them, and that Gisborne was therefore secure for now, even if I had trouble paying the forfeit due for being in the castle during the siege.

Already by then I would not have trusted the king to remember what he had promised a lesser mortal like myself – and that is putting the most charitable view of him forward, for I know you will suck you teeth in horror if I say he would not think twice about lying to the likes of me. Yes, I knew you would, Gervase! But King Richard saw the entire world in black and white, good or bad. He was so like his ardent admirer, Robin, in that! There was never any middle ground for him. People were either with him or against him; they were either nobles not so far beneath him as to be companions, or peasants so far below him as to be little more than cattle to be moved around and disposed of as required. And while he would have honoured any promise made to the likes of the earls to the death, he would have regarded those below him as likely to be utterly faithless, and that therefore there would be no reason not to change what he had agreed if he thought it necessary. He would not have seen it as lying, do you see, Brother? I was never Prince John's man, but I could see very well why after a while, men thought he would be the easier one of the two brothers to deal with, and I understood why men like de Ferrers saw the younger Plantagenet as a man worth cultivating. He could not have been any worse than his brother, as we saw it back in 1194, although in the long run John as king would become an even greater nightmare

However, with King Richard still in our shire, I shall tell you of the hunt.

Sherwood
March, the Year of Our Lord 1194

Guy took the horse at the fastest pace he dared out of Nottingham, but had not got far under the eaves of the forest before several figures melted out of the shadows.

"Guy! You're safe!" There was no mistaking the relief in Robin's voice.

Guy reined in the horse and vaulted off. "Yes, but I won't be for long if I don't get to Clipstone fast! The bloody king wants to hunt today!"

Several of the others groaned even as they clapped Guy on the back and murmured their own relief at him having survived. Yet Robin was immediately taken away by the prospect of the king coming into his demesne.

"The king is coming to Sherwood? At last!"

Guy wasn't quite sure what to think about that. Did Robin think that King Richard would welcome a known outlaw with open arms?

"Don't be quite so joyful," he warned his cousin. "This isn't King Baldwin of Jerusalem we're talking about here, you know. King Richard is a very different kind of man, haughty and proud! He won't take any challenge or criticism."

"Surely he wants to know what England has been like without him here?" declared Robin in disbelief.

"I wouldn't count on it," Guy replied dryly. "And I suspect that he's heard as much as he wants to know from Walter of Coutance. His nominated chief justiciar he might just listen to. Someone he'll see as a mere hedge knight he won't!"

"But it's the truth! We can swear to it as men who have fought for Jerusalem as he has!"

Guy felt a cold trickle of sweat run down his back in fear. "Christ on the Cross, Robin! No, you must never claim any comparison between what you did and his ventures! He won't stand for it."

"Why?" His cousin seemed genuinely incapable of grasping that the king would never wish to be compared to someone as lowly as Robin. How to explain?

"Robin, you have to understand, he's been made to believe he is better than everyone around him from the moment he could walk and say his first words. This man truly does not believe himself to be like any other unless it's another king. And I'm not sure he even thinks of King Philip as being on quite the same scale! If I were you I would steer well clear of him."

"No! I must see him!"

Guy sighed. "Well you won't have any trouble with that. He towers over almost everyone else, even on horseback. Seeing isn't the problem, talking is! Truly you don't want to be doing that!"

"But can you introduce us to him?" Robin insisted.

It was a very tall order. "I can't make any promises," Guy said quickly. "And if I do you must drop to your knees the moment he spots you! I can't be responsible for what he will do otherwise."

"Very well, we'll do that. But will you?"

Inside Guy was still feeling the dread. What in God's name did Robin think would happen? Yet clearly he wasn't going to take no for an answer, and if anything it would be even worse if Robin chose to approach the king with anyone to present or intercede for him. No, he would have to try, and hope for the best.

Guy sighed. "Very well, but listen to me Robin, because I'm not saying this to be awkward or to push you to one side. His moods are very changeable, and if he becomes irate at anything, I won't dare – no-one would, not even one of the great earls! You don't mess around with the king when he's like that!

"You have to understand, that he's not best pleased to have to come back from captivity and immediately besiege a castle in his own realm. The fact that he could have made it a lot clearer to us who he was, hasn't entered his head. We'd been so sealed up in the castle for weeks there was no way we could have known he was even in England, let alone at our gates.

"And if he'd thought for one moment how things looked from our side, he could have done a lot more to make it clear to us that he was the king. One man standing outside and bawling at us in Norman French, which most of the garrison don't understand anyway, was never going to do the job. And that's the way he thinks, so for pity's sake don't try to make any claims or present any causes to him, because if he takes offence this is one time I'll be able to do nothing at all to help you. He could call his guards and have you swinging from the nearest tree and me alongside you!

"So if he has a good hunt and seems placated, then I will do my best for you, because I know what it means to you to meet him. But please don't be angry with me if I don't. I'll only be trying to save your skins."

Will spoke up out of the gloom. "Why don't we come up to Clipstone with you? We can patrol the perimeter of the park and make sure that no deer try to escape. And then we'd be on hand but out of sight. Would that help?"

Guy could not hide his relief. "Lord, yes, Will! We've had one fright already when we thought he would want to hunt red deer. But that doesn't mean that if he starts a wholesale slaughter of the fallow deer herd that they won't panic and run. I'm going to have to ride ahead now. I daren't delay because I'm taking word to those at Clipstone hunting lodge that they need to prepare for the king today. I never thought I'd be glad for Tickhill surrendering so early on, but at least it means that the servants there must know the king is in the shire. They won't know, though, that he'll be at their door later today! So I must ride on."

"We'll linger on the edges of the hunt," Siward's calm voice reassured Guy, and with that he had to be content, although he prayed that Robin would not be foolhardy and try to accost the king as he rode through the forest – that would be fatal, and could well cost Robin his life and the lives of all of those with him.

In the meantime he rode into the courtyard of the hunting lodge and informed the servants of the impending arrival, impressing on them that the king was not likely to be forgiving of even the smallest slip. Then having grabbed a hurried breakfast of bread and little else, he got a fresh horse and went to inspect the deer. The fallow deer were so used to being fed over the winter that they were not at all bothered by Guy riding near to them, and for a moment he wondered whether they would provide enough sport for this war-like king. Yet there was little else he could do.

He did go so far as to ride out a way from the park boundary looking for signs of red deer. In one spot near a stream he did see evidence that a small herd had come down to drink, but by the look of the prints they were youngsters, because none were of the size and depth he would have expected for a decent sized stag or hind. Maybe that would be all to the good, though, if he had to drive them the king's way. Yearlings who had never even heard a hunt would be all the easier to catch than a wily old beast who knew how to evade – or worse, who would go on the attack straight at the king. And the youngsters would still be bigger than the fallow deer.

He had not been back at the lodge long when the sounds of a large group of people chattering announced the arrival of the royal party. As had happened with fitz John's party all that time ago, Guy realised that these courtiers were never going to be quiet enough to do a proper hunt with, and thanked St Cadoc that he had been divinely prompted to ask what sort of hunt the king was expecting. What he had not anticipated was being drawn off to one side by the earl of Huntingdon, while the king drank a leather cup of mulled wine against the chill of the March day before starting the hunt.

"Can you really offer the king a hunt today?" the earl asked anxiously. "Derby and Chester say you can..." and he looked worriedly at the chattering starlings in their gaudy colours, swirling and darting around the king and never shutting up.

In that instant Guy realised that the earl was used to what he himself thought of as a hunt.

"I asked the two earls you mentioned to make discreet inquires as to what sort of hunt the king expects," Guy answered softly. "Praise God, he is expecting an easy slaughter of fallow deer – and those we have a plenty, contained within the park awaiting the royal pleasure."

"Fallow deer?" the earl looked perplexed.

"The daft spotted things you'll see shortly," Guy said, not bothering to hide his disgust. "The blessed things have to be fed through the winter because they are from the Norman territories south of Rome and on Sicily originally, although the ones we have here have been bred in England."

The earl looked at him aghast. "Really? And the king wants to hunt *them*?"

Guy grinned at him. "If you will forgive me the familiarity, my lord, I am guessing that you are used to our native deer? The sort you would have hunted as a young man in Scotland?"

Huntingdon gave him an assessing glance. "So you know who my brother is?"

"Oh yes, my lord, he's King William of Scotland."

The earl puffed out his cheeks, then seemed to decide that Guy was even more trustworthy than he had been led to believe. "Then you should know that even now my brother is riding south with all speed to meet with this king. He wishes to make sure that King Richard knows that he declined Count John's invitation to join in trying to overthrow him. He is hoping that because of that he may be granted something he will ask of the king."

Now Guy understood. "And you want to make sure that the king is in a good mood after having to besiege one of his own castles? Yes, I can understand that the last thing you want is for him to be in a temper having been thwarted even in his pastimes."

Huntingdon breathed a sigh of relief. "I see why my friends put their trust in you. You are a sharp man to grasp that."

Guy chuckled. "I also have a great desire not to have my neck stretched! And I fear that if I fail in this, your illustrious brother will not be the only one to suffer!"

David of Huntingdon laughed with him but then became grave. "My brother and I have both felt the wrath of this Devil's brood, and it's only in recent years that I have been able to return as earl of

Huntingdon. I have lands in Scotland to be sure, but my shire here is a wealthy part of my inheritance I would not willingly give up again."

"Then I shall do my best to ensure that we both come out of this day with what we had this morning," Guy reassured him, but was then summoned to the hunt.

As he had feared, those riding in the king's wake were hardly conducive to a proper hunt, but what they did for Guy with their racket was make the fallow deer more skittish than they had been when he had seen them earlier. To give the king his due, he was a good shot, but his illness and time in captivity had eroded much of his strength as an archer, which was another reason for Guy to be glad that they were hunting the softer, more domesticated fallows. Cutting the courtiers out like poorer members of a hound pack, and steering the king's horse with his own, Guy managed to get him close enough to the deer so that, even with a light bow, the king could strike hard and make a kill.

Three hinds and then a young buck went down to the king, and the courtiers had enough sense of self-preservation to back off on hearing the king's howls of glee at each kill. In the end they retired to the lodge and the king was left hunting with just his half-brother and David of Huntingdon alongside Guy. The archbishop was a fair shot with a hunting bow, but not as good as the king, but managed to bring down two hinds.

Rembering his own first encounter with Geoffrey – then just a haughty bishop who nonetheless expected to come out on top in every situation – Guy wondered whether he, like the earl, was desperate to stay on Richard's good side and was being very careful not to outdo him. Someone had said in the camp that Richard was peeved that Geoffrey had started an argument with Hubert Walter over him carrying his cross of office of Canterbury in Geoffrey's ecclesiastical province. Clearly the king was not going to have Church spats interfering with his own plans to sort the wheat from the chaff amongst his own nobles, and Geoffrey was treading very carefully around him. Guy thought that if a man like Geoffrey Plantagenet was going on cat's paws around the king, then that was no small comment on what Richard could be like if enraged.

The earl brought down one small hind and left the rest to the king, although in his case Guy was sure he could have done far more had he wanted. Yet it was finally Guy who had to say tactfully to the king,

"Your Grace, if you wish to return to Nottingham for the night there is little time to hunt further."

Mercifully the king's blood-lust had been satiated, and his desire to meet out some kingly justice to those who had so defied him over-rode any pique at cutting the hunt short.

"I shall get the household to bring the jointed beasts to Nottingham for you, my lord king, so that you may feast upon them," Guy said subserviently, and was rewarded with the king's black-toothed grin.

Earl David was visibly breathing a sigh of relief from behind the king, the archbishop already having given up and begun riding away to where the king's bodyguards sat on their horses at a discreet distance. At that Guy thought that maybe he would live to see another day until he saw Robin lurking in the undergrowth not far away. Steeling himself to have to grovel to this man whom he was disliking more with every day, Guy managed to wring out in his most courtly French,

"Your Grace, may I crave your indulgence to present someone to you?"

The king turned towards him, but at least the frown was one of puzzlement, not anger.

Guy swallowed hard and ploughed on, "He's a former crusader, Your Grace. Wounded before your arrival and shipped back home." He was trying desperately to tactfully avoid saying that Robin and the others had only been knighted at Jerusalem. Somehow he had the feeling that despite their heroic efforts, the king would not see them as proper knights, and refuse to grant them even the briefest of audiences.

Mercifully the king inclined a regal head and beckoned, assuming that wherever this person was he would see the gesture. Guy urgently gestured Robin forward with a jerk of his head, and as Robin and some of the others came forward, frantically gestured them to kneel.

"This is Sir Baldwin de Hodenet, my cousin," Guy said with great deference, although Robin looked at him somewhat askance at the use of his old name.

" 'Odonet?" the king said with puzzlement, and mispronouncing it in French. "I do not know this place,"

"It is close by Shrewsbury on the Welsh Marches," Guy supplied, praying that Robin played his part and didn't start arguing.

King Richard sniffed his disdain the moment the word 'Welsh' left Guy's mouth, but he demanded of Robin,

"And where did you fight?"

"We were at Hattin, Your Grace," Robin replied, sufficiently servile to not arouse comment.

"Ah! Where the True Cross was lost! Not a great day, was it?"

Robin turn pale at having the day when he had seen so many of his friends slaughtered so dismissed, but hurriedly added,

"And at Jerusalem, my lord king. That's where we received our worst wounds."

The king quirked an eyebrow. "Then you seem to have much to make up for, young man. Get your equipment and meet me at Nottingham! You will march with me when I leave!"

Then the king seemed to become aware of the others. His experienced eye travelled over Will, Gilbert, Siward and Hugh and marked them as soldiers, then stopped at Malik.

"Who is this?" he asked Guy.

"He was a turcopole serving Balian of Ibelin, my lord king, released from his duties on account of his wounds. He was sent here by Lord Balian because he is kin to him, and the lord feared he would be the butt of retaliations if he stayed."

"You too will come with me!" the king declared imperiously, including the other four in the wave of his hand. "And the others?" His wave then travelled over Much, Allan, John and Roger, and Guy was beyond glad that the Coshams and Tuck had stayed out of sight, because he was able to say softly in French,

"Just peasants overawed by your presence, my lord king. They will be part of the party bringing the deer in to skin and butcher." Heaven alone knew what he would have said if there had been even a whiff of Welsh in the air!

"Hmmph." The king instantly lost interest in them and heeled his horse forward, leaving Guy to gesture Robin to get out of the way and fast. He was glad to see Siward and Gilbert grab his cousin's arms and all but drag him off into the woods, as Robin stared after the king in a stupor.

"Was that really your cousin?" Earl David asked softly as they followed in the king's wake.

"Oh yes," Guy sighed, then was glad that they were talking in English which the king did not even understand, and was able to say, "He's utterly in awe of the king. Thinks him a great hero for what he did in the Holy Land."

"And you don't?" Earl David sounded a touch shocked.

"Oh for what the king did out there, yes, he is undoubtedly very much the hero. It's rather that my cousin got properly knighted at Jerusalem, as did the others, and I fear that if the king grasps that, then he won't think him a knight at all, even though Baldwin is the son of a knight."

The earl's eyes opened wide. "Ooh, one of *those* knights! Oh dear, I see your predicament. As you say, a delicate situation, and one I think you handled about as tactfully as could be done."

"Thank you, my lord."

"But you might want to tell your cousin that his majesty is not returning to the Holy Land but to Normandy. He has expressed his intention to return to what he sees as his main territories, and to deal with those lords whom he feels did not respond fast enough with the ransom, or who have caused trouble in his absence. It will be bitter work taking back castle after castle."

Guy cringed. This was not the sort of fighting Robin would have expected, he knew, and the earl had been subtly returning the favour of the good hunt by giving the information to him. Gratefully he said,

"Thank you, my lord. I shall pass that on. I appreciate what you have left unsaid, too."

"Somehow I thought you would!" and Earl David gave a tight smile. "We walk a dangerous path in this king's wake."

It made Guy feel he could share another confidence with him. "My cousin was amongst those who attended King Baldwin of Jerusalem in his final months. From what he tells me of him, the Leper King was as saintly as he was kingly, but it has given my cousin a rather ...unique ...impression of what a king would be like."

Earl David's expression was now of total surprise. "He was close to the Leper King?"

"He led his litter when he had to travel, and was one of those who kept the king company when required. He even saw his body after he had died before it was embalmed. Apparently it took the king's fancy that they should share the same name and be the same age, and asked my cousin often about what his home was like in England."

The earl shook his head in amazement. "That's close indeed! Well I never met that king, but you should warn your cousin not to expect the same from our king. These days he's a bitter man who feels that all those he once thought of as friends abandoned him out in the East, and now that he's come back to this trouble with Count John's men, he's even more so. If your cousin is seeking another king to serve closely, this isn't the one to try with."

Guy nodded. "I'd thought as much, but I don't think he'll fully believe me if I tell him – although I shall do my best. Will you return to Scotland with your brother, my lord?"

"I'm not sure. Much depends on how well his requests are received. I may have to linger to plead our case."

"Then I wish you the very best of luck with that, my lord, for I fear you will need it."

The king and his bodyguard had already disappeared from view to where another relay of horses was waiting, and it was then that Guy saw the stag. He was an old male, made thin by the winter, but with an impressive rack of antlers.

"My lord," Guy said softly, and took his bow from where it was strapped across his saddle. As he nodded towards the stag, Guy strung the bow and handed it to Earl David with one of his own heavy arrows.

The earl's face broke into a wide grin, and taking the bow from Guy, pulled back on it and sent the arrow whistling into the stag. He brought it down with the one clean shot, earning Guy's approval. It was the shot of an experienced huntsman, not the lucky ones the king had made at close range.

"Go and join the king," Guy told him. "I'll do the deed with it and bring the rack to your camp late at night."

He knew he had just made a friend of this earl too. The Scottish Norman was more pleased with that one worthy kill than all the pandering to the king's ego, and Guy had high hopes that he too would not forget what Guy had done. Not a bad day's work after all!

When the earl had vanished from sight, Guy slumped forward in his saddle and breathed easily for what felt like the first time in too many days. As he lifted his eyes he was surprised to see the outlaws swarming towards him.

"Did you hear him?" Robin demanded, eyes shining. "He summoned me to fight with him!"

Guy was horrified. Had Robin not seen King Richard's disdain? "Are you going?" he couldn't help himself from asking.

Robin stared back at him as if he had lost his mind. "Of course, I'm going! He's the king! How could I not?" Then as he turned to the others as if expecting to see them looking as eager as he was, saw their downcast expressions. "What?"

There, you see, Gervase? That is how I know that Robin Hood was not the earl of Huntingdon! I liked the earl right from the start, and we will meet him again before my story is through. But for now we shall leave him ingratiating himself as best he could with a king who was determined not to be pleased. I did not envy him his position in the slightest. He had poor choices to make, that I understood, for he could either leave his earldom and return north to his brother's court – but take the risk that the earldom would be taken from him by the king – or stay and represent his family at the English court, in the hope of at least being able to warn them if the king should turn his attention and armies northwards. And unlike my cousin, I could like the earls of Derby and Chester for what they were, knowing that they were imperious lords, but also that by their lights they did the best they could – unlike many others!

I gutted, skinned and otherwise dealt with the earl's kill while others did the same for the king's, and the venison was loaded onto a cart which I would accompany back to Nottingham. With several great men coming to Nottingham for the coming council, there would be a need for the extra meat, and the castle's stores were definitely depleted just now. You will no doubt take little pleasure in hearing that the earl was most pleased to find the rack of antlers in his tent after he retired from the royal presence, and sent a brief message to me thanking me.

However that was not what kept me awake most of that night, despite being so tired that I could have normally slept on a grave and not worried.

Yes, Brother, it was Robin. You did not think to hear of him abandoning the people? No, neither did I until that point. I had thought it would be his life's work to protect the weak and innocent of our shires against the worst of the forest laws. I could not believe that he would simply pack his bags and walk away.

Mercifully, the next day everyone was so taken up with the council that it was a simple matter for me to slip away. You see I was not under guard as others who had been in the castle were, on account of me taking the king hunting, and so while my fellow knights were kept cooped up, I was able to slink out of the camp and head into the forest. And it was not because I had no interest in what the council would decide. I knew full well that Ralph Murdac would now never return to the castle in any capacity, and that meant there would be a new sheriff. But more than anything my mind was occupied with Robin, and whether he would stay or go.

Chapter 28

I met the others not far out of Nottingham, for they had followed me, and from the moment I saw them I knew that there had been high words between them. Robin had a set to his jaw which said that he was going, come what may, but others amongst the gang looked shocked and not a little frightened. As for Marianne, she was red-eyed and pale, and I knew she was stunned at the ease with which Robin had decided to leave without even speaking to her. Yes, well may you look surprised, Gervase. People think of them as very much a couple, but the way he had made his own decisions made it clear to her that he never had thought of her in the way she thought of him.

As soon as I had dismounted I told Robin,

˜He is not going back to Jerusalem. He is for Normandy and retaking castles lost to him there.˜

I thought it would shock him, and emphasised it by telling him that I had heard this from those closest to the king. Yet to my horror this news seemed to have little impact on Robin.

˜But I will be a proper knight in the service of the king!˜ he declared, as excited as the small boy I had once known had been on his birthday – and back then, every year he had hoped for some special gift, and then been so disappointed when only we boys and my mother ever remembered. And in that instant I realised what he thought he was going to get, and the resulting battle of words between us was as bitter as any we ever had.

Sherwood
Spring, the Year of Our Lord 1194

"**G**od's wounds!" Guy fumed. "Is that what this is all about, Robin? Are you still harping on about the damned knighthood?"

"It matters!" Robin spat back.

"Does it? What in Heaven's name do you think you are going to get?"

"If I am a knight to the king then I should get a manor. A place where we can all live in peace when we return. Something *you* can't give us *all*, can you, Guy?"

To have that thrown in his face was too much for Guy. After the strain of the last weeks his nerves were worn to shreds, and this was the final strand to unravel.

"You fucking fool!" he threw back. "A manor? Ha! Really? You honestly think that the king is going to give some ragged half-knight a manor? Oh and you clearly think it's going to be some grand place since you sneer at my Gisborne!"

"Half-knight? How dare you!"

"Oh I dare! I dare because that's how the king sees you and all of those like you! You're nothing special to him, Robin. He saw humble knights like you die like flies in the Holy Land and thought nothing of it. The likes of you come ten a penny to him! And what do you propose to pay him with for that manor you think he'll grant you? Because I tell you straight, you *will* have to pay! You'll have to pay just as our cousins Fulk and Philip were asked to pay for the fitz Waryn manor. They couldn't, so how are you so different, eh? What are you going to do to come up with the money? Use a great chunk of what you stole from the rich so that you can now become one of them?"

Robin's hand flashed out to slap Guy, but was caught in Guy's own vice-like grip.

"No you don't, Couz'! I'll take a good deal of shit being thrown at me by you, but *never* try that again!" Robin managed to wrest his hand free, but before he could rage at that, Guy was storming on, "You need to fucking grow up, Baldwin! If you want to be the legendary hero of epic poems, the man who gets sung about by minstrels in *chanson de gest*, you have to wake up and see the world how it is! Look at you! You're like a child staring at the sweetmeats at saint's day fair and never thinking there might be a price to pay! All you can think about is yourself, and how you can become this mighty knight you dreamed of being as a boy.

"Well listen to me, and listen hard! The king has come back for two things and two things only! First and foremost is *more* money! He'll give *nothing* for free! He's not interested in rewarding anyone with anything unless they can pay and then pay again. And be warned! – No, don't give me that look, seriously, take warning! – *Never* tell him that you are Robin Hood!"

"Why not?" Robin finally managed to get in to snap back. "He's the king. He should know what his sheriffs have been doing to his people behind his back! Someone had to stand up for those who couldn't!"

"Judas' balls!" Guy howled, throwing up his hands in disbelief. "What's the *matter* with you? Those sheriffs weren't doing *anything* behind his back! They were doing whatever they had to do to fulfil his orders! *His* orders, Baldwin! If he finds out that you are Robin Hood, and then someone tells him – which they will – that Robin Hood stole from the sheriff's courts, and from the Church when the ransom was being collected, he won't stop to ask what you stole or *why*! He'll string you up from the nearest tree, and being the king, not a soul will lift a hand to stop him! Why do you think I introduced you to him as Baldwin and not Robin, eh? It was to try and save your stupid neck!"

Robin had gone pale, but Guy wasn't done yet. "And talking of not looking to your people – take a hard look at yourself! You and your precious king are two for a pair for that! You've gone and given the people of these two shires more hope than they've had in years. They actually believe, because of you, that they might get through the next couple of years without starving to death or worse. And now you're going to turn your back on them and walk away, and for what? This lunatic need of yours to do better than me?

"Well I'm telling you, I don't give a rat's left swinging bollock if you get a manor ten times the size of Gisborne! Go ahead and have it! And then when you do, maybe you'll start to realise just what you're going to have to do to hold onto it! How you, too, will have to grovel and watch your every word around men you despise, but have to bite your lip and take what they hand out, or else risk losing that fine manor. So don't you dare sneer at me and what I have! I know the price I pay for that alone, and I don't want much more! You can out-do me as much as you want, because it's nothing I'd ever want. But what you're doing to the people, and these friends of yours here and now, is something I won't stand by and watch you do without saying a word."

The two of them stood almost nose to nose, breathing heavily, both furious, both convinced they were right, but it was Robin who broke the gaze first.

"Phaa! I knew you would never understand! You know nothing of kings! I don't know you anymore, Guy. Once upon a time you, too, were as hungry as the rest of us to become a proper knight and serve the king. And if you can't see what he's offering me, I don't have the time to try to explain. I *will* go with him!"

In the silence which followed, Hugh's calm voice came clearly, "Then you'll do it without me. I'm sorry, Robin, but I'm not going back into that man-killer that's Normandy. I've been through that once before, I have no desire to go there again."

Much's young voice piped up, "But it surely won't be as bad again this time, Hugh? Not like you were telling us on the way here. Like Robin says, the king will be there!"

Hugh shook his head. "No, Much ...it'll be worse! When I was there he was *Prince* Richard, and he was fighting his *father's* barons. Now *he's* the king, and he's going to punish those who weren't fast enough to come to his aid, or sided with his brother. And it *will be* a punishment! If you think what went on at our castle here was bad, it'll be as nothing to what you'll see in Normandy!

"But there the ordinary people will hate you as well, because *you'll* be the paid soldiers trampling their fields and their crops. And your fellow soldiers will steal from them, because while the mighty lords close to the king will eat well, scant thought will be given to just how much a man needs to eat to lug arms and armour around all day, and those men will be bloody hungry. So when the supplies run out they'll scavenge and to hell with whoever gets in their way. I know, I've seen it!"

Much's innocent face turned to his hero. "But you won't let them do that, will you Robin?"

Robin had been momentarily distracted by Marianne, and had not listened to all Hugh had said, but now smiled benevolently at Much and declared,

"Of course I won't! If others don't tell the king if his men suffer, then I shall."

Guy and Hugh exchanged shocked glances. It didn't surprise Guy that Much would be going. Ever since he had first known the lad his head had been full of tall tales, and Robin had done nothing but fed those ideas. And if Hugh's words carried no weight, then there was little either of them could do.

As Robin stood straight and cast his eye over the others, demanding, "Who else is with me?" Hugh wandered over to Guy.

"I'm sorry, I can't go through that again, not even to save Much," he said sorrowfully.

Guy turned slightly so that he could grip Hugh's arm without Robin seeing. "You have nothing to apologise to me for," he said softly and with great sympathy. "I'm just glad you're staying – and not just because it means it will be one less of you who'll get wounded or worse. It's probably selfish of me, but I think of you all as my friends, and I don't want to be left here alone. Half our friends in the garrison are gone as it is. I need to be able to come and talk freely with *someone*, or I'll go mad!"

Hugh gave a watery smile at that, but gripped Guy's arm back, both of them glad to have a friend.

Yet when they looked back at the group the separation was something which surprised Guy. He'd expected that the former crusaders would all be with Robin, but Malik and Will were still standing back. Gilbert had gone to Robin, leaving Colm hissing urgent words in Irish at him to try and make him change his mind, but rather more serious to Guy's mind was that Siward had gone to Robin. However in the midst of the heated exchanges which were going on, Siward caught Guy's eye and winked. It was such an unexpected gesture that Guy was taken aback. Clearly this was not quite what it seemed, and then he saw Siward mouth silent, "in camp," and knew they would be talking alone at some point.

Robin, though, was calling to Malik and Will, who now was the one shouting back.

"Are you really going to leave me to go without you?" Robin was saying, genuinely perplexed, whereas Will was clearly becoming exasperated.

"Christ's hooks, Robin, can't you hear what Hugh and Guy are trying to tell you? If you thought Jerusalem was bad, this is going to be worse! Then we were in the right, protecting the women and children of the city. Now we'll just be mercenaries for hire, slaughtering as we go. No, I won't become that! And Guy's right, what about the people here? What about helping them?"

"I can help them, and all the people of England, by getting close to the king and telling him how things really are," Robin declared, equally frustrated that Will wasn't seeing his point of view. "I can do more, not less, where I'm going!"

But Will shook his head and turned away.

"Malik, are you not coming?" Robin now turned to the next of his old friends.

Yet the former turcopole shook his head. "This is not my fight, Robin. Why would I go and bring war to people I do not know? These folk in Normandy are no threat to us here, and I have left one home already, I do not wish to leave the one I have here."

"But you could have a better one!" Robin insisted. "Fight valiantly for the king and he'll give you one! One no-one can take away from you."

Malik shook his head sadly. "And where will he get this wondrous place from? Look around you! This is not like my homeland, where men could be given land out of the great empty spaces no-one else wanted. If I have a manor like Guy has, then who am I making homeless? And why would the king give a man like me the home of one of his loyal subjects?"

Robin stubbornly riposted, "Well there are plenty who backed Count John! They'll be losing their lands!"

"But that is now," Malik replied reasonably. "He will do this thing before he leaves, and there are men he must reward right now. They are the ones who will get those lands, not new men like you and me. We will be at the very end of the list of men who might get lands, and I do not think we would get them even if the king is the man you think he is. I am sorry, Robin, I will not go."

He turned and went and joined Will, who was standing beside Tuck and Mariota. The Scottish woman was glaring at Robin so hard that if looks could have killed he would have dropped on the spot. And there was no need to ask why. Her friend Marianne was distraught, absolutely devastated by Robin's decision to leave. But her worst glare came as they all heard Robin say to Marianne,

"But you could come with me! Other women follow the army and tend to the wounded."

Marianne wrenched herself away from him and curled her lip in disgust, and through her sobs declared. "A camp follower? You want me to be a *camp follower*?"

"No! One of the healers!"

"Oh, and what do you think would happen to me if something happens to you? Or probably long before then? I don't want to be passed around the camp from man to man! And don't tell me you'll stop it, because you won't be able to! I'd be in one part of the camp and you in another. How would you know if I'd been raped by ten or twenty men until you came to find me? No, Robin, I love you more than life itself, but I won't do this!"

And she fled towards Mariota and was enveloped in her hugs and Tuck's too.

That John remained standing loyally by Robin was no surprise to any of them. Guy would have been more shocked if he hadn't. But he was surprised to see the Coshams standing closer to Robin, if not actually with him.

"But you're all coming," Robin declared with satisfaction on seeing them.

"No, we're coming as far as Nottingham," Thomas said carefully. "If it looks like Guy is wrong, and there's a hope that we can fight for this king and then go home to Wales with honour, not as fugitives, then we'll come."

"You'll be able to fight as my men!" Robin announced, as though there was no doubt about that, but Thomas was already looking troubled at his certainty.

With Colm and Edwyn standing with those who would stay, there remained only Allan and Roger who hadn't declared what they would do, and the moment Guy's eyes travelled to Allan he held up his hands, and with his usual light touch laughed,

"Oh no, Couz'! I'm no soldier! You know that! Me, in an army, taking orders? You know that will never happen. No, I wish you well, but we'll not go. Not Roger and me, we'll be staying. We'd rather spend a lifetime in the forest than go where you're off to."

Somehow Robin took that news better than the others, but he still turned his back on them and said to the seven who were with him,

"We must go to the camp now. We are expected, and I won't keep the king waiting."

As they tramped out of the clearing, the others clustered together.

"Is he really in such danger?" Allan now asked Guy outright.

Guy sighed. "I fear he is. Honestly, Allan, this king is nothing like King Baldwin of Jerusalem. Nothing at all! He's imperious and headstrong, and he certainly doesn't like to be corrected, much less gainsaid. If Robin tries to speak up he'll feel the full weight of the king's wrath, and I fear it's going to come as an almighty shock to him."

"What was all that with Siward?" Hugh asked Will and Malik, and the big smith grimaced,

"He's going with him, not to fight with him, but to be there to help him leave when he comes to his senses. Siward's worried that left to himself, Robin and that warped sense of honour of his will mean that he'll stay even when he's lost all faith in what he's doing. And Siward knows that that will kill him. He'll just give up and let someone slaughter him in battle, because he won't fight on but he won't leave."

"*Duw!* That's a truly Christian thing Siward's doing," Tuck sighed, "but I wouldn't want to think that he would get himself killed in the process."

Now Will grinned. "Oh don't worry, Tuck, Siward's not a martyr! He said that if Robin hasn't seen sense by the time they're about to leave England, then Robin's on his own. Siward's only going because he doesn't think it's going to take that long for King Richard to shit his nest, so to speak. While you were in the camp, Guy, we had a chat to one or two of the soldiers, making out that me and Hugh were men come to join them, you see. They say that after they leave here, the king will go to Winchester, and may well sail from Portsmouth. So that means that they'll be close by to the New Forest, and that'll be somewhere they can hide out in until everyone's gone, and then they'll come north again – or at least Siward will."

Everyone breathed a little easier at that, but Guy had another thought. "Allan, if Bilan and Much are still with the army after they leave here, will you and Roger follow them? You two will have as much chance as anyone of getting those two lads out, because I don't think they'll be with the main army. Neither of them is useful enough, unless Bilan gets taken for an archer with his brothers."

"You think they'll get split up?" Mariota asked anxiously.

Will sniffed. "I think it's almost certain! That's another reason why I wouldn't go. If we'd all be staying together that might have made a difference. But I know – and if he'd get his head from up his arse for a moment and think, so does Robin – that armies don't work like that. All the archers will be together, so that's the Coshams off in one group. Then the ordinary men-at-arms will be somewhere else, and that'll be John. Much is likely to be sent to be with the cooks and other rough workers, and that means that Robin, Gilbert and Siward will be in another part of the camp. And I think we'll all be asking you to lead us in some prayers for John, Tuck, because he's going to have a terrible time all on his own. I'm just hoping that Siward's right, and that it'll be John being taken from him that will wake Robin up."

Tuck nodded sagely, "I think we're all praying for that, Will, but we will say prayers rather harder tonight, I'm thinking."

As they all took deep breaths and tried to feel a little calmer about what had just happened, Guy tentatively asked,

"I know Robin isn't gone yet, but ...do you think 'Robin *Hood*' can carry on? I meant what I said earlier on, the local people have come to rely on him. I'm even more worried about them than I am about Robin, if I'm honest, because he's making his own choices, but they've had no say in this. I don't believe for one moment Robin's rubbish about getting close to the king. He might. He might be deceiving himself into thinking that's another excuse to follow the dream he's had since he could barely walk. But I don't, and I'm willing to carry on bringing you what information I can get if you are willing to carry on without him."

Hugh's face split into a grin. "Lord, I was hoping you would say that! No-one's ever seen 'Robin Hood' without the hood. They're not to know that it's a different man beneath it!" He saw Marianne's dismay and added gently, "Even if he comes back, Marianne, it could take weeks. What do we do if a situation comes up where Robin Hood would normally act? And I've also been thinking, that if our Robin is foolish enough to open his moth and start making out that *he's* this people's hero, then one way to save him from himself is to make sure everyone knows that Robin Hood is still here in Sherwood. That way, Robin's just some daft young knight with dreamy ideas of being a hero, not a danger to the king."

Guy's laugh was one of relief. "By *Dewi Sant*, Hugh, that's a brilliant bit of deduction! Oh yes, I like that idea! I have to get back to the king's camp now, but all of you have a think about where Robin Hood might show himself to the leaving army. Somewhere with some trees he can disappear into. And for yourselves, some trees you can get up into and hide amongst in case someone orders men-at-arms to come chasing after you."

Marianne's voice, hoarse from her sobbing, said, "If you don't mind, I won't come on that one. I don't think I can watch him riding away and never looking back."

"I don't think anyone expected you to," Hugh said gently, and wrapped his arms around her, and suddenly Guy saw why Mariota was smiling. Hugh loved Marianne far more than Robin did! And he would stay, no matter what. Yes, Hugh was a far more fitting person for Marianne than ever Robin would be, and hopefully this break from Robin's attention would give Marianne a chance to see Hugh's qualities, and what a good man he was.

Therefore Guy rode back into the camp feeling a lot better than when he had left, and just to cover his absence with a believable story, he hunted and brought down a sizable wild boar, taking it into the army camp saying that it had been terrorising a local village. He had to walk his horse back with the boar tied onto it, but at least he had worked some of his anger towards Robin out on the hunt too, and was quite calm when he took the beast up to where the food for the nobles was being prepared in what remained of the castle's kitchens.

That night he joined the rest of the throng in the great hall, although its windows had suffered from the impacts from the siege-engines, and there were a couple of holes in the roof which made the fires gutter and smoke terribly as they were drawn both by the chimneys and the holes. The great lords at the table at the top end of the hall were the ones offered the choice cuts of the boar, and Guy saw the king raise his eyebrows at the choice of a second meat besides venison.

"Who has hunted this?" he demanded loudly, forcing Guy to stand and acknowledge what he had done.

"The forest still needed to be patrolled, my lord king," he said subserviently, having had to walk up to the top table in order to be heard. "The beast was digging up fields and making wallows in the newly planted wheat, quite apart from causing havoc with the lambs."

That was always a problem with boar. They were as carnivorous as any wolf or fox when it came to small and easy to catch creatures like lambs, and no ewe would be able to fend one off a lamb too young to be able to run yet. Every year around this time there were sporadic problems with boar which had come too close to villages, and as the king turned to de Ferrers and asked him if this was true, Guy saw the earl nod and say yes, even if the racket of the hall had risen again now that they saw that no-one was about to feel the king's wrath.

The king stared down his imperious, long Norman nose at Guy. "Clearly you are an excellent huntsman," he declared. "I have a mind to reward you for the enjoyable day's hunting I had yesterday. I do not think you will make much of a soldier, though. The forest is where you belong. Huntingdon, you have forests in your lands in Scotland, do you not?" The name came out as 'Untingdon with his French accent. "Give this man a manor on your lands! Your brother will not say no when we meet," and the king laughed uproariously.

Guy heard the next aside to de Ferrers, on the king's other side to Earl David. "You see, Derby, I can even give away land in another king's realm when he is subject to me! And this hedge-knight will never know the difference, or even see his manor if he goes on hunting boar just to impress. I wonder if he even brought it down himself? Do such men know how to hunt properly?"

Guy saw de Ferrers wring out a smile, and then cough when the king turned back to the hall. The way the king had leaned in to him must have given him a full blast of the royal rotten teeth, but more than that, Guy knew that the king was not being subtle in his implications that he could take whatever he wanted, even from the highest men there. Meanwhile, David of Huntingdon had risen from the table, bowed towards the king, and then gestured Guy to come to one side.

"You know that was meant as an insult," the earl said to him with a sour smile.

However Guy grinned back at him and said, "It's a good job I didn't take it as such, then, isn't it. I would be deeply grateful to have a manor, however humble, in the realm of another king who is less capricious. I'm also very aware that for all of the king's proclamations, he'll be gone in a few days, at which point he will never know whether you gave me that manor or not. You can easily invent some suitably Scottish sounding name of a place which doesn't even exist, tell the king you have given it to me, and then ride away knowing that the moment he turns his back on Nottingham he'll have forgotten my existence, let alone that he asked you to do this. So I know that should you grant me such a manor, that it is very much your bequest and not the king's whatever he may say." It was a subtle piece of flattery, and one which Guy hoped would appeal to an earl who had himself been on the rough end of the Plantagenet's fickle natures.

For a moment Earl David stared and blinked, then turned away to guffaw merrily. "By Christ, Sir Guy, you do give me the most excellent sport!" he declared when he had composed himself enough to reveal his face once more to those in the hall. "And you're a smart man to be thinking like that! Very well, I shall ask my brother to find you a small manor somewhere within my lands. I have not had chance to go north for a while, so I cannot say where it will be, but I do know that between the crusades and other fights we have many small manors only being kept going by their reeves for want of a knight. Having you as lord of one at a distance would make little difference. I suspect ideally Galloway would suit you, as it is close to the border, but it may end up by being in Angus, which is much further north."

Guy nodded. "I understand, my lord, and I still gratefully accept wherever it is. All I would say is that you appreciate that I will not be able to come and fulfil any terms of service which involve me personally coming to fight for you or your brother."

Earl David smiled back. "I think I can make that plain to my brother, but assure him that if he's ever in need of a good forester than he has one to hand. I do understand that you have little choice but to be here."

"No, my lord, I was set in this post by the king's father in person. That makes it rather hard for me to leave."

"Were you indeed?"

"You may wish to have a quiet word with the earl of Chester on that matter, sire, but only when the king isn't around since it concerned his brother."

The earl's curiosity was clearly piqued, but Guy had to resume his place much further down the hall. Only when he sat down did he realise that right at the very far end, almost so far below the salt as to be out of the door and with the ordinary soldiers, sat Robin, and that his cousin was glowering at him furiously. Of Siward and Gilbert there was no sign, and Guy did not like the look of that.

He took the longest way round back to his place on the benches so that he passed Robin, and having exchanged a few words on the way with men like Sir Richard of Burscot, it looked normal for him to stop and speak.

"Where are Siward and Gilbert?" he asked softly. "Please tell me they aren't with the ordinary men. And where's John?"

Yet Robin turned angry eyes to him, and instead of answering, delivered a question of his own.

"And what were you doing with the king, eh? Making sure you get in first to be the one who is given the prize and be honoured?"

Guy glowered down at him. "Actually I was making sure that he sees me as nothing more useful than a forester! And for your information, he thinks I'm so close to becoming a peasant that he thinks I didn't hunt that boar on my own! There was no courting favour there."

"So why was the earl laughing, then?" Clearly Robin was determined to see everything in the wrong light, setting Guy's teeth on edge. Things were dangerous enough already without his cousin getting a fit of pique.

"If you must know he was simply asking if I could lead his brother, the king of Scotland in the same kind of hunt I took this king on. He laughed because I risked implying that his brother would be up to hunting red deer. There, are you satisfied?"

Robin simply looked away, refusing to respond in any way.

"Oh have it your way," Guy sighed, too tired to carry on arguing, and feeling too out of sorts to continue at the feast, took himself outside to where the air felt a good deal sweeter, even though it was still filled with the smells of cooking fires and too many men crammed into a confined area.

As soon as he left the castle proper, he went to look around the camp. He found Much and Bilan easily enough amongst the cooks, working with the most lowly of the army's company. As yet Much was not ready to give up and leave, but Bilan softly whispered that the younger lad had already been in tears over where they were. He still had faith that Robin would coming looking for him and haul him out.

"But if he doesn't come by nightfall or first thing in the morning it will be a different thing," Bilan confessed after Guy had chased a bullish cook away, telling him that these boys had come from his manor without his permission and would speak to them. "Thomas and

Piers are with the archers. They shoved me this way fast so that Much wouldn't be alone."

"Good! As soon as you want to leave, Allan and Roger are nearby to help you."

Bilan nodded. "It'll definitely before we march from here, I can tell you that! Much won't cope with more than a couple of days of this."

"Good! I'll go and find your brothers and tell them that you're all right for now."

Guy gave a lordly curt nod to Bilan for the benefit of anyone watching, and strode away as if he owned the place, the epitome of a haughty lesser lord. Thomas and Piers were harder to find, but he managed it, and once they were reassured that Bilan and Much would make a run for it, admitted that they would not be lingering as soon as an opportunity came.

"We thought we might be segregated," Thomas admitted. "The good thing is that we've had chance to talk to another couple of Welsh lads, and they're saying that they're thinking of running too. They've been hauled back from Normandy with the archbishop of Coutance, and say that now that they're this side of the Channel they have no intention of going back. They've confirmed what we feared – that once we get over there there'll be no coming back except with some great lord. There'll be no end to the time of our service, nor an honourable return. More like a shallow grave in some French field! We're not going out for that, not even for Robin!"

Relieved that others would be staying, Guy went in search of John, but to his discomfort could not find his cousin before the camp settled for the night and he would be drawing unwanted attention to himself by continuing.

The Great Council continued and the fate of the sheriffs was decided. The king placated his half-brother by granting the archbishop the sheriffdom of Yorkshire, compensating the loyal Hugh Bardolf with Northumberland instead. That did not bode well, Guy thought, and there was a moment's panic when William de Braose's name came up, but luckily the younger de Braose was one of only seven sheriffs who kept his original shire. For that Guy was glad to have half the country between them, for he feared that he would be as brutish a sheriff as his father had been. However the news for Nottinghamshire and Derbyshire was not good. The king's loyal man William Briwere would be transferring to them from the similarly joined Oxfordshire and Berkshire, and his reputation was not good. In the mean time William de Ferrers would hold the shire until Briwere had been out on eyre, and the king made it clear that the dreaded Briwere would be visiting his new appointment as a judge before he took over. That was a crafty move Guy did not like at all. It meant that Briwere would be legitimately able to come down hard on all in the shires who were even thought to be against the king, and then come in to take his post and see that the sentences were duly meted out in a way he would not have been able to do if he took up his post straight away and had had to by-pass his own shire.

Seven weeks' grace was all they had. Seven weeks for Guy to try and get Robin back, or if not, to set things up so that Robin Hood would continue come what may. Because with William Briwere as sheriff Guy had no doubt that the ordinary folk would need a saviour more than ever.

Oh, Gervase, that was a terrible time. Was Robin proven right? Did the king listen to him? Ah, I will come to that shortly. But what I will tell you is that it is true that this was the only time King Richard ever even came to Nottinghamshire, much less to Sherwood. There are some twisted tales which tell of the great king taking the great outlaw as his knight and going to fight in the Holy Land together. That is arrant nonsense! Both of their times on crusade happened separately and long before they met – it was simply not possible for their paths to coincide any other way. And yes, it was me and not Robin who took the king through Sherwood. But however much he might have been a great hunter of men, unlike his father he was not a great hunter of beasts. Old King Henry would have known the difference between a noble red stag and a half-tame fallow one, and would have poured scorn on his son for not knowing how they varied in temperament and size. Oh, the old king surely hunted fallow deer, for it was on his instruction that the blessed things had been sent to deer parks in our shire in the first place; but he would have also made it clear which he wished to hunt too!

You think it was disloyal of us to plot to replace Robin even before he had left? No, Brother, loyalty had nothing to do with it. And before you cast blame our way, remember that Robin had shown precious little loyalty towards the people who loved him. I would have had more patience for his naivety towards the king if he had been asking me to get him into the castle so that he could petition him on their behalf, and then intended to return. I would have been far less angry at that.

It would have had no effect, of course, and might well have led him to end up in chains in the castle dungeon, but maybe a day or so in there until I could have got him out would have sorted his mind out a little. A blunt and brutal riposte by the king straight away would have saved everyone a lot of heartache, and would have achieved much without Robin suffering for long. I would be having scant sympathy for him when he woke up to the king's true nature now, though, because of his lack of empathy with the others.

So what of my cousins and those others who had followed him to King Richard at Nottingham? I will conclude this episode before we must stop for the night, for I would not leave you in quite such suspense!

Chapter 29

$\mathcal{S}$o we come to the Easter of 1194, for in the midst of the siege and telling you of it all, I have forgotten to tell you that the three terrible days of our siege took place in the last week of Lent, and Holy Week loomed. The king lingered at Nottingham until the end of that week when I had taken him hunting on the Tuesday. Yes, Brother, I recall the exact days of the week – one does not simply forget the day of meeting a man like King Richard! So we endured three days of his royal anger, in which I constantly saw Robin trying to get close to the king, and being fended off by those around the great man, as others far more important took his attention. I did not know whether to be glad or sad when it was announced that the king would be departing on the Saturday in order to spend Palm Sunday at the minster church of Southwell.

Much work had been done in those three days to make our castle secure again. You should know that the outer bailey walls had for much of their length only ever been in stout timbers supported by some stonework in places. The stone walls were reserved for the inner bailey, and so the outer bailey was more easily repaired than other parts of the castle, some of which took months to get back to their former states. But for our purposes it meant that Much and Bilan were trapped within the outer bailey at the kitchens, and therefore would find it hard to escape just yet. Their best hope was as the mass of men travelling in the king's wake moved to the area around the minster, they would then be in an ordinary camp and much more accessible.

And I for one could not wait to get them out! Much had become wan and haunted even in those few days, for Robin had been so single-mindedly pursuing the king that he had not thought to look for the lad, assuming that he would be well. Yet Much was not well at all. He had had no experience of what life could be like under petty tyrants such as the cooks, and he was constantly on the end of both tongue-lashings and clouts for not knowing what he was doing, or being too slow. I blessed Bilan in those days, because he kept his head, remained inconspicuous, and kept Much from doing something foolish in his extremis.

Consequently, when it was announced that they would all pack up camp, move on to Southwell, and then from there move on to Melton Mowbray on the Monday, with the intention of the king spending Easter at the great royal castle at Northampton, I was relieved. And not only for the two youngest! Gilbert was at the end of his tether, and twice in the halls I had to pull him to one side before he began a fight with someone who had insulted him and his heritage. Only by telling him that, if Robin's knights started leaving before we had even left Nottingham, he would jeopardise the chances of the boys who had also arrived with Robin, did I manage to keep him under some kind of control.

And for myself there was the additional complication, if you wish to think of it as such, of trying to sort out how I would care for that manor in Scotland. While we had a moment's grace before the dreaded William Briwere arrived, I had done some serious talking with the remaining eight men I knew from our High Peak days. Frani, Stenulf and Osmund were all now getting older, and we contrived that with the exodus they would simply slip away and go back to their villages up in the Peaks. They no longer looked the tempting fodder for those who would come rounding up young men to serve the sheriff, and were not such competent soldiers as to stand out in a crowd. And you must bear in mind that we suspected that the kindly Sir Richard of The Lea would be replaced, but that the new incumbent would have no idea of who had been in the villages prior to his arrival. Therefore our three friends were unlikely to be spotted as new arrivals back in the area.

But the others also no longer wished to serve in the castle, and we finally came to the arrangement that I would send the remaining four men-at-arms with Sergeant Ingulf in charge of them to hold my new manor. None of them were frightened of hard work, and I knew that they would take part in tending the manor, not just sit back and lord it over my tenants. But I also guessed that I would need someone to take my part up there and stop my tenants from fleecing their absent English lord, and it might well need a little physical persuasion until they got the idea that I was not about to make their lives a misery. With Ketil and Skuli having Norse heritage, they at least might be looked on more favourably, I hoped, and act as intermediaries if necessary. Therefore I sought out Earl David, and arranged that Ingulf and Big Ulf would travel with him until such point as he met with his brother and arranged the manor. They would then travel back north with King William's retinue.

Then more august visitors arrived in the form of Queen Eleanor and the dreadful Longchamp, when there was a deal of shuffling and moving men around, and we had an opportunity for some to leave. So, Leofric, Ketil and Skuli slunk out of the camp with the older three, and headed for Hathersage in order to collect what they would all need. In time it was hoped that they would be able to send for their families and friends, but for now they would simply be telling them where they had gone. These three would then meet Ingulf and Big Ulf on the Great North Road as they came back north again, and would travel with them to my new manor. It suited us all. Five strong men who were reliable were enough to hold a small place for me, and got them out of the castle as well, and it showed the earl that I would be treating my responsibilities seriously. I half thought of asking Marianne's father if he would like to go too, but then I thought that if this was to make a permanent rift between Marianne and Robin, then she might well be very glad to have her father nearby still.

No, do not yawn, Brother! I will continue, and I have not been boring you with unnecessary domestic details. If you have been alert you will realise that now I would be going back into Nottingham Castle with no allies amongst the soldiers any more. Ah, that has woken you up a little! Yes, I would be alone, but my anxiety to do that was in part based upon Robin's actions, for you see, I was definitely worried for what might happen in the future.

If Robin could walk away from Marianne and his friends from the Holy Land so easily, the thought scared me of what he might do if he returned and then thought to attack the sheriff again. Would he care that some of our friends were in the way? That if he did not set his ambushes up with more thought than he had shown to date, he might well put our friends in a terrible place where they <u>had</u> to fight him? And if they did, would that strange mind of his flip over to where he no longer recognised them as friends at all and killed one or more of them? I could not take that risk anymore, I decided. It would be awful for me, but not half as awful as having to fetch even one of their bodies back to the castle with an arrow through it from Robin's bow.

So, we come to that Saturday when the king rode out in splendour, once more content that all he surveyed was his, and the time had come for some of our gang to leave him.

Nottinghamshire. Spring, the Year of our Lord 1194

"Thank Christ for that!" Gilbert exclaimed softly, as the main party disappeared from view.

Guy had managed to draw him to one side, and just at this moment Gilbert was within the stables and Guy on the outside watching. Thankfully the king of Scotland had arrived the previous night, and with his additional retinue it was difficult to see who was supposed to be with whom, making Gilbert's absence from amongst the knights harder to spot. To all intents and purposes it looked as though Guy was just chatting to one of the grooms, and as Guy was quite purposely wearing his forester's uniform, the few who had looked his way with the intent of rounding up stragglers had looked away again. One of the advantages of having de Ferrers as sheriff, albeit temporarily, was that he had been able to impress upon the king the need to keep the forester knights to milk this valuable resource.

"That's it, they've cleared the town," Guy told Gilbert with relief, then called a little louder, "It's all right, you can come down now."

Bilan dropped nimbly down from the hayloft above the main stable, and then helped Much down.

"Thank you, Guy," the youngest outlaw sniffed tearfully, coming to hug his saviour. "I couldn't have stood another day!"

Guy hugged him back tightly, but Gilbert saw the anger in his eyes and mouthed,

"I know. He never came!"

That Robin had not once come to look for Much had cut the lad to the quick, and for that if nothing else, Guy was angry.

"I know Siward went with Robin," he said to try and cover his rising ire, "but have any of you seen John?" They already knew that he had seen Thomas and Piers and told them he would spirit Bilan and Much away, and now the two archers were only waiting until they got to a particular grove of oaks before they too melted away out of the army. However none of the three there had seen hide nor hair of the big man.

"If he's with the men-at-arms it'll be all the harder to cut him out," warned Gilbert, giving Guy a sympathetic look. "You might be better hoping that Siward can find him. I spoke with Siward late last night when I warned him that I was leaving. He knows what you were doing with the lads and said he'd do his best for John."

Guy gave a thin smile. "I know, and for that I'm grateful. I just hope Siward doesn't put himself in danger in the process."

However Gilbert was encouraging. "I don't think Siward's that keen to swing from a rope, and of all of us who came with Robin, he's the one who's the local lad, don't forget, so he'll know where he can leave around here."

With a sigh Guy nodded, but then began ushering the three to a spot high up in the outer bailey's wall where there was still a ragged gap. With the aid of some of the rope from the stables, Guy managed to lower Gilbert with Bilan's aid, then the two youngsters scrambled down to join the Irish knight.

"Go!" Guy hissed, having already talked the best escape route out with Gilbert beforehand. He was even happier when he saw Tuck melting out of the shadows from an alley on the northern side of the town, and taking Much by the arm, leaving Gilbert to concentrate on covering their rear. Then Tuck handed Bilan something long and thin, and Guy saw him pause and bend it, at which point a longbow appeared in his hands and Guy felt sure they would escape. The worst thing he could do now was stay looking, thereby making someone wonder why he was looking in a totally different direction to the king's party. Big Ulf and Ingulf were long gone with the king of Scotland's party, and the rest of their friends were already well on their way up to the Peak. Everyone who could be saved right now had been, and that was the way he wanted it to stay.

As de Ferrers was travelling as far as Northampton with the king for the Easter court, the castle was now in the hands of Sirs Hugh, Robert and Richard, and there was a collective sigh of relief from the entire population of Nottingham, within and without the castle walls. It was therefore not hard for Guy to request that maybe a couple of days' rest would benefit everyone, and that the first step might well be for several men to go out searching for horses. Those that had been at the castle were now with the king, yet without them the knights would have a hard time visiting the more distant parts of the forest. Harry had high hopes that his stable-lads might have taken those he sent away to avoid the rocks of the siege-engines deep into Sherwood, and would soon return, but they had to assume that more would be needed. It said much for how exhausted everyone was that no-one bothered to ask Guy where he was going to search, and he managed to slip away into Sherwood at dawn the next day.

Beneath the boughs of the trees just showing the first bright sprig of green leaves, he met the outlaws. If anything they were in better spirits than he was.

"Good news!" Tuck declared. "Thomas and Piers got out last night! And they have friends with them – all Welsh archers!" Guy looked around for them, but Tuck shook his head. "They've taken Much and are going back to the camp by Inkersall to wait for us there. We didn't want to drop the new lads straight into a fight – didn't seem fair."

"And there are plenty of other places in the heart of the forest we could use if that camp gets compromised," Hugh said with a smile. "Better than taking them straight to Loxley. Marianne and Mariota are at the Inkersall camp too. They came this far, but although Mariota really wanted to join in the fun, she wouldn't leave Marianne alone when she's so upset. They've got Colm and Ed with them."

"That was kind of her, and good thinking not to put the new men to the test so soon," said Guy, thinking that Hugh was showing a good deal more sense over bringing new men into the group than Robin had. Then he blinked and looked at the others again. Granted there were only Will, Gilbert, Hugh, Malik and Tuck there, but they seemed to be dressed very much alike except for Tuck – and even Tuck seemed to be sporting a new monk's habit which was more green than black.

Hugh's grin got even wider. "Both women were as much angry as upset. They offered to stitch us all forester's gear! We've never dared ask them to do something like that in the past, but this time they volunteered! Luckily there were only going to be four of us this time round, but what do you think?" and he held out his arms so that Guy could see the doublets. They were the simplest of shapes, more like lengths of cloth with the head hole cut in them and the side seams stitched up than neat garments. However they were definitely effective. "Mariota says they'll make a better job of them when we get back," Hugh added, "but we wanted them for the show even in this basic state."

"Where did the cloth come from?" Guy asked in amazement.

Tuck's deep chuckle was part answer, with the rest coming from Will,

"A couple of bolts of cloth we 'acquired' from a rich merchant. Sheer good fortune that they happen to be this nice dark leaf-green. But Roger had a quick look at it before he and Allan ran off, and he thinks he can remember enough from his apprenticeship to that dyer to be able to colour us some more if we get him some un-dyed cloth. We'll be able to have our own hoods of office, just like the foresters!"

"And all the better for our disguises!" Hugh said cheerfully. "And talking of disguises, we've been having a think about this appearance of 'Robin Hood' to throw the scent off Robin. It would've been nice to do it in Sherwood, but I don't think the king is going to oblige. When Gilbert told us that the king is going straight from Southwell to Melton Mowbray, it seems to me that he'll cross the Trent at Newark. If he does that, then he can go straight down the Fosse Way until he's about six miles outside of Leicester, then just turn off to Melton. He'll have a good road and a clear route that way. I don't see him coming all the way back to Nottingham to cross the river, because there are no roads over this way as good as that old Roman road."

"Do you agree?" Malik asked Guy. "You are the only other one who knows that side of the river. We cannot help Hugh on this matter."

However Guy was already nodding thoughtfully. "Yes, I think you're right, Hugh. With that many men to move, the old Roman road makes a lot of sense. It runs straight and true in the right direction, and it's that much higher than the roads on this side of the Trent. I'd bet that especially around Lowdham, the road he's just taken will be churned to mud by now with that many men and horses tramping over it – it lies too low to drain well, and we've not had any hot weather to dry it out yet. Yes, I think we can assume that the king will go that way."

Looking relieved, Hugh then said, "In which case, I think we make our appearance by Owthorpe."

"Oh yes!" Guy approved. "The Owthorpe Wolds!" He saw the others looking blank and hurriedly explained, "They're not hills as you think of them, Tuck, but the ground definitely rises away from the Trent there, enough for the land not to be so flat as to be able to see for miles, that's for sure. And there are some nice dense woods around Blackberry Hill, as I remember. There's just enough of a nice rise off to the side of the road to mean that anyone chasing after us will have an uphill run. Yes, I don't think we could do better, Hugh, not without following the king into Leicestershire, and we want the name of Robin Hood to be remembered here, not there. So what are we going to do?"

Now Will took over. "Well we thought we'd let the king himself go past. Given what Gilbert's told us of how arrogant he is, I doubt he would take much notice anyway – more likely just send some soldiers after us. And he's the one who'll be heavily guarded. We can't get into a fight with so few of us and so many of them. It's got to be showing of defiance more than any act, wouldn't you agree?"

Guy's immediate nod of agreement led Will to continue, "We think it's got to be Hugh who acts as Robin Hood even though you're with us now. There are men in that group who might know your voice even if your face is hooded. 'Robin Hood' is going to tell the king to go and not come back, that he's taken all he's going to get from the poor of Sherwood. Or that's what we'd come up with. If you can do better we're all ears, because this is more Allan's strength and he's not here."

Together the six of them carefully looped around Nottingham as they talked, and crossed the river at the bridge when it was busy. If nothing else, at the moment there wasn't a soldier left in Nottingham except for a handful of wounded men left to help the castle knights, and that made life a little easier since they knew they would have to be exceptionally unlucky to be stopped by one of the knights, and the ordinary folk were too harried and weary to notice anything much at present. By nightfall they had found a suitable spot in the woods above Owthorpe, and with it only being five miles from Nottingham, it meant that Guy could go back to the castle for the night, thus allaying any suspicions he might have caused by staying out over night.

In the early dawn he left the castle again, having made sure he had been noted there the previous evening. It was the kind of spring morning where there was a bit of a frosty haze to the air early on, but promised to clear to a bright day. He had brought with him one of the large loaves of dog bread from the kitchen's first bake, although at the moment it was keeping the ordinary folk going rather than any dogs, since the kennels were empty. The best wheat had all been used up with their illustrious visitors, and even before they had left, those lower down the social scale like the soldiers had been on mixed-grain bread. Gnawing on the bread and some rather withered but sweet apples, the six of them sat on a fallen log just under the shadow of the trees.

They had picked a good spot where an easily climbable oak was close by a huge old elm. The elm had few branches near to the ground, but once up in the oak they had strung a rope across to the elm, and would be able to get much higher in that. The oak had the width, but the elm was half as high again, certainly higher than most men would think of looking up into, and even Tuck was confident of making the climb.

So they waited, and shortly after noon the first of the royal party came into view over the brow of the small rise in the road just past Cropwell Bishop.

"Here we go, lads!" Will declared cheerfully. "Time for Robin Hood to wave the king off!"

They pulled their green hoods up over their heads and took up their places behind the trunks of the great oaks' at the wood's edge. An advance guard went past and then in a flurry of bright banners and rich cloth, the two kings rode past their spot. Behind them came the two archbishops, then Longchamp – who seemed to have weaselled his way back into the king's good books – and Queen Eleanor.

"Let her go," Guy called softly to the others. "She can't speak English so your words would be lost on her anyway."

They had decided that it was not worth Guy trying to coach Hugh in Norman French. If he mispronounced something in the heat of the moment it could become incomprehensible, or worse, he could just be laughed at for his poor French and the impact would be gone.

"Robin Hood's an English hero, let him speak English," Will had declared, and the others had agreed.

So the elderly queen passed by, oblivious to the men watching, and was followed by seven bishops and six earls. Behind them came the noble prisoners being taken south to await the king's pleasure on what their punishment would be. It saddened Guy to see Ralph Murdac with them, but he couldn't help but smile to see William de Wendenal there too, and it seemed fitting to give him sight of the man who had so plagued him.

"Now!" Guy hissed as de Wendenal, who was on their side of the road, looked up and about him.

Bounding out and up onto a small rock, Hugh struck a pose with a wyche-elm bow strung and held out for all to see in one hand. In the other he held arrows, but with the sun now behind him they were not so easily seen.

"Leave and go back to your Norman lands!" he called out. "This is not your land, these are not your people! They have given all they have. There is no more! Try and bleed them again and you will answer to me, Robin Hood!"

The others made sure they were spread out on either side of him, Tuck closest to the wood, and then Malik. They had decided that Malik should have a fast run back to the wood in case he needed to provide covering arrows for the others to flee. Guy stood a little back behind Hugh to be less visible, and then Will and Gilbert were on his other side but also a few paces back. All brandished Welsh-style longbows, and now, just in case no-one was watching, Guy loosed an arrow straight up into the air, a fluttering tail of red silk cut from a tattered banner streaming behind it to make sure it was noticed. He made sure it would come down on open land, though. The last thing they wanted was an accidental killing sparking a fight.

It certainly worked! Suddenly there was chaos down on the road as some slowed their horses to look, and others near rode into them. The small number of men-at-arms strung out along the line of illustrious horsemen milled about, wondering whether they should attack this strange group, and waiting for a command.

"The king!" someone – possibly the earl of Chester – called out, and suddenly the men-at arms were hurrying forward to protect the rear of the main royal party. Yet when the unexpected men showed no sign of chasing after the king, Guy and Hugh had more of the attention of the rest of the party.

"Go back to your Norman lands!" Hugh insisted loudly. "Go bleed them white if you can! I am Robin Hood and you will not rob my people anymore! Sherwood is mine! Be warned if you come hunting me, *you* will be the hunted! You have levied taxes you have no right to. Now I, Robin Hood, will tax all those who dare pass beneath the eaves of Sherwood!"

There was already some restive movement down below, and Guy called softly, "Get ready to run," as Will now called out,

"And I, Will Scarlet will forge such arrowheads as you have not seen before! They will pierce your rotten hearts!"

"And I, Brother Tuck, call down the wrath of God on you wicked men of the Church! For you forget your vows and who you serve in your avarice! *God* will judge you and find you wanting!"

As some swords came free of scabbards, Robin and Siward were seen riding forward amongst the knights of lower rank – all on shaggy work horses, not destriers – and Guy was relieved to see some of the other lesser knights speaking to them, probably trying to coordinate an attack up the hill. But since he could not be on the hill and on the road at the same time, at least Robin was now safe from suspicion, or so Guy thought.

Yet in a moment of total insanity, Robin could not resist taunting de Wendenal.

"So this is the man you could not catch, sheriff?" he called out loudly for many on either side to hear him.

"*Dewi Sant*, what's he doing?" Tuck gasped softly. "Shut up you fool!"

They saw Siward pluck at Robin's sleeve, but he was too far back to be able to catch him properly as Robin's horse moved closer to the former sheriff. The worst of it was that he was still not that close, though, and so he had to stand in his stirrups and shout to get the next words heard,

"Were you ever even safe in your own castle, sheriff? Did you never wonder how ...Robin Hood knew your every move?" He had stumbled over the giving of the name, and the six watching had gasped in horror as he nearly said 'I'.

Malik had already disappeared, and now Guy melted into the shadows with Tuck, feeling his guts turning to water as he realised that Robin had as good as given him away. Mercifully Siward had now caught up with Robin and was hissing something vehemently in his ear. It made Robin pause as he turned a puzzled face towards him, but it gave De Wendenal that brief time to think. He looked upwards to Hugh, and the six watchers saw something change in his face.

"I know you!" he screamed. "Traitor! You're one of mine! ...You're..."

"Kill him!" Will snarled to Malik as he plunged into the wood with Hugh on his heels, and Malik, who had already had the bow tensioned, pulled back and let the arrow fly even as de Wendenal began,

"You're G...!"

The yard-long barbed arrow took him through the neck. The superb shot of a master bowman – and no-one would know that it had come from Malik's bow and not 'Robin Hood's'.

As some cried out in shock, others roared furiously, but those closest to de Wendenal were too busy wiping the massive spray of blood from his arteries out of their eyes to be able to react, and they got in the way of those trying to give chase. It gave the six time to swing up into the oak, and then on into the elm, and to pull the rope after them.

High in the branches they watched as finally horsemen spurred up the hill to the copse. Guy could feel himself still shaking at how close he had come to being unmasked as the traitor in the camp. For that he dared not even look towards Robin and Siward for fear of his emotions getting the better of him – it was all he could do to control the fear-induced griping in his gut. He had to trust to the others to keep watch, and he was grateful to feel Tuck's strong grip on his arm as the big monk eased himself around the elm's trunk to reach him.

He heard a man not far below calling,

"They've vanished!"

And someone else calling, "Come back! We must protect the king at all costs!"

Then another closer saying as the other voice faded away,

"Oh well, he's saved the king the trial of one less traitor. I can't imagine he'll worry too much about that when his brother's escaped to France. He's the worst of them."

"And what was that all about, anyway?" another said distantly.

"Aach, de Wendenal had become a drunk!" the previous voice replied. "He was probably seeing double for months!"

A blessed silence followed in which Guy did his best to even his breathing. After what seemed an eternity Will's voice came from just above him saying,

"That's it, the last of them have passed. For Christ's sake let's get out of this bloody tree!"

They worked their way down to the lowest branches and then let themselves down with the rope. It was still a bit of a drop given that they had to use the rope doubled, but as the last man down, Gilbert managed to pull the rope with him as he made the final leap. Immediately Tuck pulled Guy into a bear-hug.

"*Duw*! I don't know what came into his head! Idiot!"

Guy felt Will come and put his arm around his shoulders from the rear.

"Stupid, stupid bastard!" the burly smith growled. "Jesu, Guy, you didn't deserve that!"

Gilbert spat furiously. "Fucking idiot! What was that? Wounded pride or something? What did he think we were going to do once he'd left? Did you hear him? Bloody near tried to tell them who he was! God in Heaven!"

"I do not think he thought at all," Malik's calm voice said, but there was a definite underlying thread of anger there too. "If you ever get to ask him, Gilbert, I have no doubt that he will be shocked that you think he purposely tried to betray Guy."

"Well if he does come back, he can be Robin Hood again," Hugh declared, "but there'll be no doing something just because he says so anymore! He can be our leader, but we'll all be having a say in what we do in future."

As Guy lifted his head from Tuck's shoulder to look at them, Hugh looked him squarely in the eye and said firmly, "You're too valuable to us, Guy, to have you risked like that again. From now on we'll make sure that it's anyone *but* Robin who comes to meet you. We five will make sure that he knows only that which everyone else knows. There'll be no calling on your feelings for him as your cousin now, no confidences directly from you to him. He'll only get information through another. That way he won't have enough knowledge of what you've been doing to betray you, and I don't know about the rest of you, but I say we keep quiet about that new Scottish manor of Guy's?"

"Definitely!" Will declared without having to even think about it.

"I agree!" said Gilbert emphatically. "God alone knows how the rest of us would have fared without you, Guy, and I'm not blaspheming there, Tuck! It would truly have taken an act of God to get the two lads and me out of that fucking castle by ourselves; and that's before we even get to the men-at-arms we owe so much to whom Guy has saved!"

He turned to Malik. "I don't know how much of this you've picked up in your time here, my friend, but the likes of Colm and me aren't welcome in England because we're Irish, but Scotland is another country like our own. We could go there and not be persecuted. And the same goes for Welshmen like Tuck and the Coshams.

"By getting that manor, Guy has given us somewhere to run to if things get too bad. Somewhere were the lords are a bit thinner on the ground than round here! Somewhere where we might be as poor as church mice, but at least with a place where we could build a simple house and not die in the wilds. I'm not going to spit in his face for that kindness just because Robin might take offence! So I say we protect the man who's thought about us, and been there to help us, first."

Malik nodded and smiled at Guy. "Do not worry, I agree with the others, you take too many risks already. If Robin returns he will not get the chance to do this to you again – not from my mouth anyway."

Suddenly Guy felt totally drained as the relief hit him. "Thank you," he said weakly. "Thank you all! It means a lot to me. And thank you for offering to be intermediaries between Robin and me – I don't think I could stand seeing him face to face now, or at least not for a long time." Then another thought came to him. "Did any of you see John?"

The way horror spread across their faces told them that they hadn't.

"Fuck!" Will exploded and punched at a low branch of the oak in anger.

"Poor John," Malik said sadly. "He will be feeling very left alone."

Gilbert shook his head, "No it's worse than that, Malik. I hate to say this, but we may have seen the last of Little John. Once in that army he's not the sort to have the guile to get out. Poor bastard!"

Tuck had his hands clasped in prayer, his lips mouthing silently something in Welsh, but as he felt their eyes on him, he said aloud, "God forgive him, your servant Robin, for he knows not what he's done. Bring him to his senses for all our sakes, and for those of your oppressed people in this country." Then he smiled faintly at Guy. "For what it's worth, I truly believe that he has no idea of what he nearly did."

He waved Will and Gilbert to silence at their outraged spluttering, "No, that does not excuse him! I know that! But I have come to know that young man as well as any of you. Remember, I have heard his confessions! And I wholeheartedly believe that it never crossed his mind that he so very nearly destroyed Guy. It makes him a fool. It makes him selfish – for I do agree that he was full of wounded pride that his place was so easily taken! But it does not make him evil. He did not do this with wicked intent, of that I am sure."

However Guy was shaking his head. "Believe that if you will, Tuck, but from where I'm standing just at the moment, it looked as though he was furious that I may have replaced him." He turned his baleful gaze to Hugh. "I don't think he even thought it might be you, you know. We're of a similar height and build, and from that distance when he first saw you he probably had no doubt that it was me, because the other one who's been 'Robin Hood' alongside him is Siward, and he was right there beside him. You've never shown any inclination to lead, but I've been the one to challenge him time and again. I think he couldn't bear to see me take his place – and that's despite it being him who was the one to leave. He's betrayed me, and quite deliberately."

He turned to Will and Malik. "Thank you! I mean that from the bottom of my heart! To you Will for guessing what de Wendenal was about to call out, and to you Malik for that amazing shot! I may not have been in the line of an arrow or a sword cut, but you saved my life as surely as if I had."

Will grinned and clapped him on the arm. "My pleasure! And you're definitely having that sword now! It's all made, I just need to put it together. If you have it now, then you can say it was given to you by one of the fancy lords. And with a whole new lot of soldiers coming in, few are going to know that you didn't have it before."

Guy's smile was weak but genuine. "And I accept with thanks."

Together they made their way out of the wood and began their walk back towards Nottingham, looping around the back of the woods and avoiding the village of Cotgrave. It was as they got to the Polset Brook that three figures suddenly rose up from out of a clump of bulrushes.

"Nice distraction there!" Allan's cheerful voice declared. "Look who we managed to haul out of the ranks!" and there was John.

Guy couldn't say a word, but ran to embrace his cousin.

However Tuck's *"Dewi Sant!"* said it for all of them.

Allan's cheer faded as Guy reached out and dragged him into a three-way hug. "Guy? Guy, what's wrong?" and still Guy could not speak.

With a heavy heart Hugh explained to the three just what had happened. John just hugged Guy tighter, and even the normally chatty Allan could only say, "Oh Guy! I'm so sorry!" as he now hugged Guy back hard.

It took Roger to shake his head and say philosophically, "'E's lost 'is 'ead. Robin's gone barmy. It's the only explanation. 'E never came to see John, you know. We was watchin' and he never even came lookin'. We saw you, Guy, but we was on the other side of the camp, and we didn't dare move in case we lost sight of John."

Allan cuffed his eyes and added, "Thomas signalled us, as he promised, to let us know that he and Piers had got away, and that Bilan and Much had too. We guessed that John would be the one having trouble getting out, so we chose to stick by him."

John pulled Allan into another embrace. "And I'm glad you did! I never wanted you to pay me back for all the care I took of you when you were young, but if I had, the debt was repaid today. I owe you two my life."

Roger pulled a face and rolled his eyes in mock desperation. "Oh give over! If it hadn't been us, it would've been some of the others."

"Yes it would have!" Guy said firmly. "You were *never* forgotten, John!"

"Do you think will Siward bring Robin back?" Allan asked generally.

But Guy shrugged and said, "I don't know and I don't care! I hope that Siward returns with all my heart, but Robin's a stranger to me now. He made a choice back there, and now he'll have to live with it. The rest of you I'll continue to help, and if that means him too, then so be it. But if he calls on me for any favours to him alone, he'll be denied them. If he chooses to see me as his enemy, then he's made his bed and will have to lie on it. At least I know where I stand now, and it's too late for him to change his mind."

And with that Guy turned and continued to walk towards Nottingham, not seeing the worried shaking of heads of Allan, Hugh, Malik and Tuck. John, however, nodded thoughtfully and then hurried to catch up with Guy, falling into step with him, and if nothing was said, there was a brief exchanged smile which said that things were now right between them once more.

"Oh shite, there's going to be trouble over this," Gilbert said sadly, and Roger agreed.

Yes, Brother, I was deeply hurt by that betrayal. My soul was cut to the very quick that my cousin was so full of his own importance that he would do such a thing. I have not over emphasised this episode. Had de Wendenal got one word more out of his mouth, then I would have been condemned for all to hear. With so many present it would not have been possible to silence all those who knew Guy of Gisborne was the traitor. I would have had to go on the run and hope that I could get Ianto, Maelgwn and Elias out of Gisborne manor before retribution came their way.

And with such a public declaration, the king of Scotland would have withdrawn the offer of the manor up there too. Yet I would have had no way of telling my friends that they were walking all that way for nothing – let alone Ingulf and big Ulf who were right in the midst of that army! They too may well have been hanged for my sins. So you see, Brother, there was so much danger to so many from that one act of spite by Robin.

Yet the king passed on and never looked back, and for that we were grateful. I am told that the Easter court at Northampton was a very grand affair, but all of us at Nottingham were thankful to have missed it. He then travelled on down to Winchester and had himself crowned again to emphasise to all and sundry that he most definitely was our king. Ingulf and Big Ulf were down there as King William had to be part of the coronation ceremony, and when we saw them next they said that the ordinary people down there were ecstatic at seeing the heroic king returned safely from the crusades. I suppose he made a very grand spectacle, and from a distance he was certainly the epitome of a great king in appearance. What none knew until after he had departed was that he was demanding more taxes of England. Had those ordinary folk known of that as he paraded through the streets, there might have been a few rotten eggs thrown instead of cheers!

Our king was proposing to levy a land-tax which went back to the time of our great need to defend against the Danes – the hideage or carucage, or as most now knew of it, the Danegeld. This was a crippling tax of two shillings on every hide of land as had been laid out in King William's Domesday Book, and would be due from all land, even the Church's. It had last been levied back early in the old king's reign, but at that stage the people had not been subject to the two extraordinary tithes, nor the purge of the ransom collection, and those of us who saw things at a local level knew beyond doubt that it would not be collectible. It was simple – we could not collect what was not there! And worse, this was for the defence of Normandy. What did we care for Normandy, and why should we pay when we had already paid so much? The lords and people of that province had not come up with the ransom money required, and we all felt that they should now pay for their own defences.

However the illustrious King Richard would never again set foot in England, although he would reign for another five years. From Winchester he went to Portsmouth, and after some false starts due to the weather, left England for good in mid May. I was not sorry to see him go.

As for ourselves, we returned to the forest. That night I could not face the thought of returning to the castle. I was too wrung out to even think of facing the likes of Walkelin or Sir Henry, and had I had to do so, I would not have wanted to be responsible for the consequences. Instead, at the camp I sought out Marianne and told her of what had happened, and we wept for the man we had lost together. Yes, Gervase, I am not ashamed to say that I mourned the man I had once loved so dearly. Baldwin or Robin – whichever you wished to call him – might still have been walking this earth, but the man he was now was someone I was no longer capable of caring for in the way I once had. And so the old person, the one I had wanted so desperately to be reunited with when we had left Alverston all those years ago, might as well have died that day.

I know Marianne's deep devotion died that day too, especially when she heard from the others of how Robin had never come to seek them out at the castle. How he had not once thought to check if they were as well as he assumed they would be. Oh she still loved him! Her feelings did not die so fast for her love had been true, but her devotion – that bit which would have made her follow him even to the very gates of Hell – had been blasted like an oak in a thunder storm. Many times in the next few days I was to hear that she would ask Tuck why God had taken the man she loved and changed him out of all recognition, and Tuck for once was unable to supply her with an answer.

As for myself, the next morning I had to resign myself to either leaving the castle for good or going back, and because of what rested on me, I went. However, in the process I did find three of Harry's stable-lads with several horses, and was able to guide them through the forest back to the castle. Therefore I arrived back to much gratitude and few questions, and that suited me.

We were lucky enough to get the Earl of Derby back with us before the end of April, and so he was there when the eyre came round. However, since the town gaol had been damaged in the course of the siege, and I had had time to flit up to the scribes' room and remove certain scrolls, there was little William Briwere could do when he came through the shire in late May. I was glad I had done what I did with the records, though, for my first glance at our new sheriff told me we had not changed for the better. Our new sheriff was more cunning than de Wendenal had ever been, and I did not like the way his eye roved over us as if measuring us up for when he returned.

Yet I am ahead of myself here Brother. I must rest for the night before we get to Briwere's tenure as sheriff. And there is more to tell of Robin, which I know will please you!

Chapter 30

*I*n that night at the camp I met the new men who had been bought in. And once I did, I understood why Thomas and Piers had so willingly brought them. The first was an older man, grey-haired but burly and still fit.

~This is Aneirin ap Gwillam,~ Thomas told us with great pride. ~He is a master bowyer – a man whose name we had already heard of years ago as a great bow maker!~

Coming from Thomas, that was praise indeed, and even more so when Thomas told us that if we thought the bows he made were good, we should wait and see what Aneirin could do. And Aneirin was more than willing to stay and become our very own bowyer. He was canny enough to know that going back to Wales was not an option, or at least not as himself. And if he did not go back to practise his trade, then how would he live? And with him came a scrawny man of a similar build to our own Roger – and Roger was very much our own now, Gervase. He was always to be in Allan's shadow, but he was just as valuable, and now more than ever, for it turned out that this scruffy Welshman was called Rhys ap Morgan, and he was the master fletcher to Aneirin's bowyer.

Will took one look at the pair of them and immediately suggested that Roger learn from Rhys, for if Rhys could do such a job, then strength was less of a factor than dextrous fingers – and we all knew how light-fingered Roger could be! He also told Aneirin that Edwyn – who had already become called more familiarly ~Ed~ – was a carpenter, and the older man's face lit up and declared he had found the ideal apprentice. And so without any leader making the decisions on their behalf, our outlaw gang decided that these four would never take part in any raids unless Roger or Ed's skills were particularly needed. They would take up permanent residence at the Loxley camp and become our armourers, with Will joining them as often as he could. The basics of arrowhead making he could teach them quite quickly, given their talents, but he would be the one to make special heads for special tasks, and over the winters he would create swords when he could.

I was much comforted by this, for it was done in the right spirit. No-one was forcing these men to take vows they had no desire for, nor determinedly setting out to make them into fighters when they had no appetite for the job. And yes, Brother, if you wish to take that as a criticism of my cousin, it was. I was not so naive as to not think that at some point someone would have to become more forcefully the one to take the lead, but for now it was a blessed relief to have breathing space from Robin's intensity of purpose and design. Nor do I think I was the only one who was feeling that way on that particular night.

It was all the more apparent when we found that there were two more men who had escaped with the Coshams. Martin was a young man from Walesby, whose father was the head man of that village. He had been unjustly accused of poaching, and I knew his name from the scrolls I had seen. His family had somehow scrapped together the money to keep him out of the town gaol, but he had then been virtually thrust into the hands of the king's army by the resident forester at Kirton. This was more than a little illegal if anyone had wanted to be picky about it, but given that Laxton Castle and its keeper, fitz Stephen, were almost next door to the villages, the forester had known he could get away with almost anything short of murder with Ralph fitz Stephen in his current state. I immediately confirmed to the others that there was no way that Martin could go home, but that if we reimbursed his family the fine and kept their son safe, then Walesby would be another village which would be firmly on our side.

Then to our shock the other young man who had come with them announced that he was the smith's son from Walesby, taken up by the army to serve them. Will all but fell on his knees in thankful prayer at that, and I am not in jest, Brother! Will was not endless in prayer as Robin was, but when something so fortunate happened he was as fast to give thanks where he felt it was due. And so Simon, the smith's son, would make another member of the outlaws who would become the backbone of the band. He too knew that he could not hope to return home when the dreadful forester, Hubert, would be coming through the village on a regular basis, and I made a mental note to watch out for this man. Hubert might be fitz Stephen's man, not ours, but if I could somehow bring him down a peg or two I would, for Simon told me how he had conducted a campaign of persecution against his father because he assumed the charcoal at the forge had been obtained illegally from within the forest even though it had been bought legitimately.

Now I must rest for the night, Brother. I will continue in the morning, for despite your glum expression Robin Hood is not done with yet. Ah, that has brightened you up, good! And was it my cousin who returned? Oh I have a mind to make you wait before I tell you more of that, dear Gervase!

However for now let me recap and remind you of how things lay with us in that spring of 1194. Of the six who had come from the East, James had now gone, but I promised you I would tell you of Walter of Fiskerton, and I shall conclude with him. I had not witnessed this myself, but Allan and Roger had. They told us that as they lay hidden outside the army camped around Southwell, they saw to their horror Walter walking into the camp. Even worse, he was demanding loudly that he be taken to someone of importance because he could lead them to Robin Hood's camp.

Sherwood
April, the Year of our Lord 1194

"God in Heaven, we thought our hearts would jump into our mouths!" Allan told the assembled gang. "I couldn't believe it! There he was, shouting so that all could hear that he'd come to betray Robin Hood to the king."

"Ungrateful bastard!" Martin instantly declared, and got approving glances for his understanding of what must have happened. However no-one was going to interrupt Allan to explain fully just yet.

"Aye, well whatever his thinking, he made enough noise that someone took notice," Allan sighed. "The next thing we know, he's being marched forward through the camp towards the main tents! I left Roger keeping an eye on John and did my best to scurry forwards. I put on a heavy limp and held my one shoulder high, to look enough of a cripple as to not be worth grabbing, and risked getting into the camp."

"By St Thomas, you took a risk, though!" said Guy, appalled.

Allan shrugged. "I know, but someone had to find out what was happening. I mean, if the camp got made known, that was going to affect us all, wasn't it? Where would we go in winter then? So I decided it had to be done. Well I managed to squirm my way through the crowds, and thank God most men weren't that bothered by him, so there wasn't that much of an audience gathering. I suspect what local men there were had a sneaking admiration for Robin Hood, and didn't want to let on; and to the men from further away he's not such an important name.

"Anyway, I got to right by the archbishop of York's tent, and there was Walter, gibbering away that he could tell them exactly where to find Robin Hood. And to my horror, then the bloody king comes striding through the crowd! God's hooks, I nearly pissed myself at that until I realised that the king had been coming to speak to his half-brother anyway! So King Richard comes up and hears Walter gibbering away, and it was only then that I realised that he couldn't understand a word."

"God be praised for his Norman arrogance!" Tuck declared fervently. "Never did I think I would be so glad that the king of England can't speak a word to his subjects in their own tongue."

"Too true!" Allan agreed and the others nodded as well. "If he had, I shudder to think what would have happened. As it was I heard him ask Lord Geoffrey what was going on, and him answer that it was just some madman. He said 'It's just about some troublesome outlaw hereabouts,' to which the king said, 'He cannot be as troublesome as my brother!' I don't think either of them grasped what a thorn in the sheriff's side we've been this last couple of years, you know. So I managed to start breathing again, and I heard Walter saying, 'I can lead you to him! Why won't you listen?' He couldn't believe, you see, that the king hadn't understood him.

"But then the king asked his brother how Walter knew about this outlaw, and Walter stupidly said that he'd been to the camp – which got translated back and forth – at which point the king said that that must make Walter an outlaw too. What no-one expected was for the king to tell Lord Geoffrey to take Walter's head off, and for the bloody archbishop to pull out his sword and do it on the spot!"

There was a collected gasp of horror from Allan's audience.

"What? He did it right there and then, in front of the king?" John asked in shock.

Allan nodded. "Right there! He had one of those beautiful swords like Will's been making. It had some edge on it, I can tell you, because it took Walter's head off like it was slicing through butter. The knights standing behind Walter weren't any too pleased, because they got the worst of the spray, but of course they couldn't say a word when the king just nodded and then carried on talking to the archbishop like nothing had happened.

"It was then that I saw Robin." Everyone gasped again. "He didn't see me. His eyes were all on the king and Walter. I think he heard every word, because he was as white as a sheet, and he certainly saw Walter's body."

"He must have thought his time had come," Gilbert sighed.

"He was definitely keeping back a bit," Allan admitted. "I think he was being very careful to stay where Walter couldn't see him."

"No wonder he was so confident when we saw him," Tuck said thoughtfully. "This might explain much, you know. Given the way Robin's faith works, he may well have thought that the Lord was watching over him, and that this lunatic idea to speak to the king was still possible, and maybe even divinely endorsed."

Will snorted in amazement. "What? You mean he thinks God is protecting him so that he can have a nice chat with the king?"

Tuck rocked a hand in ambiguity, "Mmmm, something like that. I can see from what Allan's just told us that half of the luck was simply in the king's lack of English. Had he understood anything at all of it, the outcome might have been very different. But knowing Robin, I think he'll certainly have felt the Almighty on his side for escaping like that. And can't you see that as that happened before he got on the road and saw us appearing, that will have affected how he saw that?"

Always the perceptive one of the cousins where Robin was concerned, Allan now groaned and said, "By Our Lady, what a mess! So if Robin thinks he can go and have a quick fight in Normandy with the king, then sit by some castle fire with him and tell him what's been going on in England while he's been gone. And then Robin thinks he can just stroll back home too. I mean, that's what the king's just done, isn't it? So if Robin has always intended to come back, seeing someone take his place *would* make him outraged! In his eyes it's us who've lost faith in him – he's never even got as far as thinking, as we did, what might happen in the time he's away."

Yet Guy was shaking his head. "I'm sorry, Allan. You may very well be right. But he's old enough now that he should have thought more. If when he came back, he had set on me and it had come to an actual fight – him wanting to beat me for being so faithless over him – then that would be one thing. But he was as good as handing the sheriff my head on a platter, and alongside me all those who depend on me. Don't forget that Ingulf and Big Ulf were right there in that army. I saw them, and they were a mere matter of paces away from him. To say 'Gisborne is a traitor' was going to condemn them to a death as swift as Walter's!"

"Oh sweet Jesu!" Allan gulped, and so did several of the others.

Guy grimaced. "Yes, you see it now, don't you? Thanks to Allan's courage we now know that Robin saw Walter die without so much as a trial or questioning. Do you think that same king would have been any kinder to two men-at-arms walking in his wake? Never forget that this is the same king who offered the noblemen at the siege of Nottingham the chance to buy their pardon, but hanged all the sergeants-at-arms!

"Not that I ever wanted to see Ralph Murdac hang. He was never going to win no matter what he did – the poor man was condemned either way. But also, given that the king supposedly wants men to fight with him in Normandy, it just shows what disregard he has for lesser men that he would hang those sergeants. They were the very kind of men he needs, and they'd done nothing but follow the orders of their leaders, and yet he deemed it necessary to make an example of them to show the ordinary people.

"And it shows something else too. That money was at the bottom of everything! Those poor soldiers could never have paid their way out of trouble, but it was the promise of what the noblemen could dig out of their coffers which saved their necks. Ralph Murdac's poor wife will be in rags for the rest of her life, no doubt, but at least she and his children will live, and so will he.

"But the king would've assumed that Ingulf and Big Ulf wouldn't have two ha'pennies to scrape together and taken their heads off, possibly with his own sword – and Robin should have known that! By

Our Lady, he'd bloody seen him do it not hours before! *That's* why I cannot forgive him for his thoughtlessness."

To Guy's surprise it was John who came over and put a brotherly arm around his shoulders.

"You always see to the heart of the matter," the oldest of the cousins said sadly. "I was so blinded by Robin's vision of what could be done I thought you were just nit-picking when you criticised. I'm heartily ashamed that it's taken me nearly being swept off to fight in a war I know nothing about, to see that Robin's view of the world is cock-eyed."

Tuck tutted. "No John, don't be so hard on yourself. It's more that Robin's world revolves entirely around Jerusalem and the kind of view of the world that says that defending Christendom is everything. In one way men like him are right – if defending the places Our Lord went to is all important to the salvation of all of our souls, then men like the king, who have risked their lives to try and win Jerusalem back at all costs, are to be honoured above all others. If anyone is to blame, I suspect it's me for bringing Guy very early to my Celtic view of God."

And at this Guy couldn't help but laugh. "That's truer than you know, Tuck! It certainly helped me keep my head when I was threatened with excommunication. You know that I was so condemned for being deemed to be one of Count John's men during the siege, even though I loathe the little shit?"

Tuck blinked while others gasped again. "*Duw!* Again?"

Guy nodded, "Again! I'm getting pretty angry at the way the souls of others are being bandied about in order for rich men to get what they want in this world, I can tell you!"

The others looked horrified too. To die a swift and horrible death like Walter was bad enough, but to risk going to the grave and knowing that you would be condemned to an eternal life of torment in Hell beyond that was something else – and that was what excommunication meant for anyone who died whilst in that state.

Marianne in particular was appalled. "That's an appalling risk! Why did you stay in that ca... Oh!" As light dawned for her she went bright red. "You stayed for us, didn't you? And for Robin ...because he's your cousin." Her eyes filled with tears. "I'm so ashamed I never saw it like that. Please forgive me, Guy, you were my friend long before I fell in love with Robin. I should have had more faith in you."

Guy went and pulled her to her feet from where she sat and hugged her tight. "I cannot censure you for loving my cousin, but I'm very glad that you no longer think me the heartless enemy, either." He planted a kiss on the top of her head, then held her at arm's length as he nodded towards Tuck and said,

"But he's right! It was remembering all the things Tuck said to me, right from when I first met him over in Wales. The way he always said that God sees into men's hearts, and knows who is good and who bad. That he doesn't need other men to tell him such things. When those abbots did it to me the first time, I freely admit I was bloody terrified for a moment! But especially once I'd come and talked to Tuck again, I saw them for what they were – avaricious, scheming lordlings, who care nothing for those they so casually condemn. That's how I had the heart to stay, Marianne, and that's why I'll continue to stay."

The group relaxed again, and it was only as Guy was leaving again in the morning that Robin and Siward came back into the conversation.

"How long do you think it will be before we see Siward?" Gilbert asked Guy as they were wishing him farewell.

"I don't know," Guy answered truthfully. "I hope for his sake that he leaves before the king gets much further than Northampton, because I don't think the king will linger long here. He'll be off to Normandy as fast as he can, I suspect, and that means that the closer to the coast they get, the more those around him will be on the watch for men slipping away. If they haven't got away by the time they get to Winchester it could be the last we see of them."

So there you have the account of the end of the treacherous Walter, Brother. How he came to be at Southwell at just the right time I do not know. When we came to think about it with cooler heads, we surmised that he may well have been lurking in the woodland close to his home village of Fiskerton for some time. Possibly some member of his family had been sneaking bread and beer out to him to keep him alive, because as I have said before, Walter was ill equipped for the rough life, and I cannot imagine that he survived for that long by his own devices alone. And Fiskerton was not that far from Southwell, so he may well have seen the king's passing and simply followed him to Southwell on that fateful day. Whatever the truth of that matter, Walter paid for his folly with his life, and that was a high price I would not have wished on him, despite what he had done.

And no, Brother, taking on the men Thomas and Piers had brought to us was not the same at all as Robin's recruits. For a start off, some of them had been in Normandy fighting already. They had become accustomed to the life of a soldier long before they met us. Just because we allowed Aneirin and Rhys, and Simon and Martin to step back from the life of fighting did not mean that they were as hopelessly incapable as Walter and Algar had been. Those two had known nothing but village life until fate had blown them our way, and they had stayed because they did not know what else to do. Whereas Aneirin and Rhys had had more than enough time in Normandy to understand what they were getting involved with, and came to us knowingly. And Martin and Simon had had a much shorter time in the army, but it had been enough to show them what such a life would be like for them.

Therefore they had a much better grasp of what was at stake than Walter and Algar had ever done; and you also have to allow that the few years between those two coming to us and the current newcomers had seen desperate changes in life in England. Suddenly life had become much tougher for everyone, and these lads had seen how a man could stand accused of something he had not done and no longer have recourse to the Hundred Courts or other means of justice. That was only just beginning when Algar and Walter had fallen foul of the law; the younger men had grown up with it!

As for Colm and Ed, they too understood what they were giving up far better than Algar and Walter had ever done. For all that Ed was much younger than those two, he made his decision with much greater adult appreciation of what he was going to be doing. And the only wavering anyone had seen in Colm was when Gilbert left with Robin. Once Gilbert returned, the sheer relief of having a fellow countryman around soon settled Colm, and we found that he too was quite the natural warrior. Oh, not with the sword, Brother, that was far too fine a weapon for the likes of him to have had experience of – though we soon remedied that! But Colm was another who was a dab hand with a quarterstaff. And Ed was to join Will in being a natural with a warhammer. He had the strength of arm for such a beast of a weapon, and it felt natural in his hand, he once told me, in a way that the sword never did.

So you see, Brother, we had gained men who were willing and able to join the band of fighters in Sherwood, and regardless of whether Robin ever returned, when I left that first night I was confident that the band of men apparently led by ~Robin Hood~ would continue to defend the people of Nottingham and Sherwood as best they could.

Now, Gervase, I must rest, for although I am feeling better than I did, I still feel the need for my bed after such a long day talking to you. I will gratefully continue in the morning, if you will allow me, for there is still a good deal of my life which I wish to confess. But for now I must assure you that I have told the truth. This was the way that things happened to the best of my recollection, and if I have failed in some minor detail, I hope you and God will forgive the memory of an old man. In my heart, I assure you, I have told all and kept nothing back.

I do freely confess that at times I was too harsh on my younger cousin. That fault is mine and I do heartily repent of it. But I hope you see why I was so often exasperated by his high ideals. From where I was standing he so often failed to think of what the results of his actions would be aside from those he intended. Heroes such as he and the kings he so admired often left vast amounts of misery and chaos in their wake, I have found, and may the Lord have mercy on me if I was wrong to be affronted by that. My much loved young cousin, Baldwin, had so desperately wanted to be prized and honoured by those he thought more worthy than him for all of his life, that it blinded him to the consequences. For that I was deeply sad, because I wondered if he would ever grow up enough to see what he had brought down on others in his quest for something higher?

Did he make such a confession? Truly, Gervase, I do not know. You have not heard the last of my cousin as Robin Hood, that I will tell you, but it is a tale filled with much recrimination and blame, and I do not have the strength to begin it tonight. Tomorrow I will pick up the story once more and you may judge for yourself whether I am wholly at fault. Do you feel I am so condemned to a long penance in the afterlife after today? No? I am much relieved to hear you say so, and yes, I will say those prayers you incite me to before I lay my head on my pillow and rest for the night. Goodnight, Brother Gervase.

Thank you for taking the time to read this book. Before you move on to the notes which give you a bit of background to the story, I would like to invite to to join my mailing list. I promise I won't bombard you with endless emails, but I would like to be able to let you know when any new books come out, or of any special offers I have on the existing ones.

Simply go to my website   www.ljhutton.com You will also be offered two free eBooks.

Also, if you've enjoyed this book you personally (yes, you) can make a big difference to what happens next.

Reviews are one of the best ways to get other people to discover my books. I'm an independent author, so I don't have a publisher paying big bucks to spread the word or arrange huge promos in bookstore chains, there's just me and my computer.

But I have something that's actually better than all that corporate money – it's you, my enthusiastic readers. Honest reviews help bring them to the attention of other readers better than anything else (although if you think something needs fixing I would really like you to tell me first). So if you've enjoyed this book, it would mean a great deal to me if you would spend a couple of minutes posting a review on the site where you purchased it.

Thank you so much.

Historical Notes

The description of William Longchamp comes directly from contemporary eye witnesses, particularly Gerald of Wales. He was almost certainly a dwarf by modern medical terms, but that alone did not condemn him in his contemporaries' eyes. That came from his truly villainous nature, and the fact that Queen Eleanor herself refused to leave her grandson (one of the hostages for King Richard's ransom) in Longchamp's care whilst travelling to Emperor Henry IV, speaks volumes for how bad his reputation had become by 1193. He is one of the few historical characters where it's almost impossible to overstate his villainy! Corrupt and untrustworthy, he was also almost certainly a sadist and a paedophile, and even contemporaries were baffled as to why King Richard held him in such high regard – the most likely explanation being that Richard saw him as a useful weapon, and didn't so much turn a blind eye to his actions, as never even considered the collateral damage.

Since money plays such a key part in the events of these years, it is worth explaining to all who never saw the old imperial coinage in Britain that there were 4 farthings to a penny; 12 pennies to a shilling; and 20 shillings to a pound. Therefore there were 240 pennies in a pound, not 100 as now. So the knight's-fee of 20s asked for from each knight for Richard's ransom was a pound's worth, but would have bought that knight a whole herd of 240 sheep at the time, giving you some idea of just how much was being asked for!

Also, the quarter of wheat which Guy talks about is a hard to define measurement. It was the crop of an acre of land, and therefore a variable measurement (not the much later and regulated imperial measurement of 28lbs in weight which was called a quarter; nor the dry measure of capacity, 2 gallons = 1 peck, 4 pecks = 1 bushel [56lb] and 8 bushels = 1 quarter). Likewise, the best description of the medieval 'hide' is that it was the amount of land which could sustain a family for a year. Therefore on poor land it was a far greater acreage than on good fertile land, and could vary hugely even within one county/shire.

In the early 1190s the care of Bolsover Castle was granted by King Richard to someone called Richard of the Peak (no other identification) up until the rebellion of 1194-5, when William Briwere took over the castle. Richard's name implies that he may well have been in charge of the castle of the Peak prior to that time, but as he remains an otherwise unknown I have taken artistic license with the facts and initially put William de Wendenal at the Peak in order to place him where he would be in a prime position to become sheriff – he's certainly not the best documented of the sheriffs. I have then turned the anonymous Richard into the known 'Richard Vernon of Baslow', who is later mentioned in the Pipe Rolls for 1194 as owing 100s for the 'farm' of his manor at Baslow – clearly no small place! Anyone holding a place worth that much was evidently someone of minor importance, and of the social standing which would put them in line for a post such as temporary constable of a castle – temporary in the sense that he clearly only holds it for a year or two and then disappears from the records again. However the wonderfully named Gerbod de Escalt really did hold some of the lands in and around Bolsover on behalf of the sheriff of Nottingham.

The castle of The Peak or High Peak is another puzzle at this time. It was always a key castle, sitting as it did at the base of the Pennines, but during the years of this book, who actually held it is a mystery. Apart from the anonymous Richard just mentioned I have been unable to find anyone specific, yet it was important enough to be included alongside Windsor and Wallingford as castles which John had to surrender to his brother Richard in their truce of 1193. By taking artistic license and inserting Sir Richard of Lea as another temporary constable, I have therefore retained a 'Richard' at The Peak, and also introduced the person who in some versions of the legend is credited with being Lady Marion's father, although there is no historical basis for this. There is a Richard of Lea in the Pipe Rolls for the shires, and just by the fact that he made it into such a record would imply that he was more than just a free-man farmer. The only Lea I can find in the two shires is in Derbyshire, but where the Chaward was he was being fined for remains a mystery.

It is near impossible to find exact dates for the sheriffs of Nottingham during these years. Normally one would turn to the various Pipe Rolls for such information, but because Nottinghamshire & Derbyshire had been handed to Count (Prince) John, no returns to the Exchequer were made for these shires between 1189 and 1194, all revenues going straight to John's coffers, not the Crown's! Consequently a certain amount of deduction has to go on. Fitz John certainly only held the sheriffdom for a very short while, and it was the very real and dreadful fate of the assistant constable of Nottingham Castle, Alan of Leek, which resulted in his expulsion. Quite where fitz John was when Robert of Crockston handed over Nottingham to Count John is unrecorded, but he clearly wasn't at the castle since fitz John's name (or that of de Lacy, if using his later family association in a retrospective context) is never mentioned, and he's not mentioned as leaving alongside Robert; nor do we know where he was before he returned to Nottingham after William Marshall's short stay there.

This alone gives us a starting point for William de Wendenal's tenure as sheriff, but more confusing is the reappearance of Ralph Murdac around the time of the siege at Nottingham in early 1194. The near-contemporary accounts call Murdac sheriff when the Pipe Rolls begin again in autumn 1194, but when or where he regained the post he lost upon King Richard's accession they never make clear. My big question was therefore, where had he got the money from to repurchase the office if he hadn't had it back in 1199? And it would have to have been a substantial sum, too, if he bought the office as was generally happening at the time. By this time Murdac must have known he would never find favour with King Richard, because he couldn't provide the one thing the king wanted – large quantities of money! So did he pay, or did he return almost by default?

This then makes his reticence to leave Nottingham Castle during the siege rather more believable when we come to siege of 1194, but makes it no clearer how he came to be the one in charge. It is also strange that by all contemporary accounts, Murdac and de Wendenal truly did not believe that it was the king besieging them at Nottingham. Why would they be so suspicious? I cannot prove this, but my own theory is that having had Geoffrey Plantagenet besieging Tickhill, just up the road, only six months earlier, they had every reason to think that it was the war-loving *illegitimate* Plantagenet (the archbishop) who had come, rather than the king – particularly if at some point Geoffrey Plantagenet had been making heavy use of his family name prior to that.

Even more curious, the next Pipe Roll record to appear says that Murdac was sheriff for the half-year running from Michaelmas 1193 to Easter 1194 (i.e. the time of the siege), but with no clue as to what happened to end William de Wendenal's time as sheriff! I have therefore taken the approach that Murdac must have been on hand to take over when de Wendenal met whatever fate befell him, and so have had him return as constable after fitz John's fall from grace, since that post fell vacant following Robert of Crockston's departure.

Howden's Chronicle has both Murdac and de Wendenal as joint constables of Nottingham at the time of the siege, but it seems unlikely that even a castle as big as Nottingham's would have required two constables, and the chronicles are not always one-hundred percent accurate. Moreover, de Wendenal was definitely made constable of Tickhill in 1191, but by the time of the siege in 1194 that role had been taken by Robert Delamere who, like Murdac, had once been one of King Henry's trusted men and sheriff of Oxford until Richard's accession. With him occupying the position of constable there is therefore precedence for former sheriffs becoming constables.

Whatever really happened, de Wendenal's fall from grace had to have been fast to go from being the autonomous constable at Tickhill, to being under his former boss' gaze in Nottingham castle! Therefore they are both present at the siege as documented, but with their roles in this book making the best sense I can find of what they were doing there. As for William de Wendenal, the chance was then too good to miss to make de Wendenal the first sheriff to be a casualty of Robin Hood! He disappears from all records by 1194, but normally sheriffs were men of sufficient standing to continue to be recorded, even if they retired to a different shire as Hugh Bardolf would do later. So it's a reasonable assumption to say that he died, or fell so heavily from grace as to have been reduced to virtual poverty in order for him to disappear like that – however, a dead sheriff fitted much better with the legend!

There has been much academic speculation as to why the garrison at Nottingham did not believe it was King Richard at their gates demanding their surrender, and we may never know exactly why. However, my take on the language issue isn't so farfetched. King Henry really did speak enough English to be able to converse with his subjects, and by this time many of the lesser barons would not have been speaking French as their first language – some lesser knight who did not go to court may hardly have spoken it at all. It was definitely the language of the court, but only the top tier of nobles would have been there, whereas most ordinary knights would have needed to speak English fluently in order to conduct their everyday affairs with the multitude of Englishmen around them.

What is less well known is that Queen Eleanor never learned to speak English, and neither did King Richard! Our famous king couldn't speak a word in the language of his kingdom. However King John was totally fluent because of the amount of time he spent here – unlike Richard who spent a great deal of his youth in Eleanor's Aquitaine, John grew up in England. So to those who had only experienced the old king and the youngest prince, there might well have been an expectation that King Richard would speak English.

And the constant threat of what King Henry's illegitimate son, Geoffrey, archbishop of York, would do no doubt muddied the waters considerably! We know he was at the siege because there remains a contemporary record of a spat between him and Hubert Walter (the archbishop of Canterbury) over whose cross should be carried before them there. We also know that Hubert Walter arrived on the same day that King Richard did, but that Geoffrey was already there. So it is perfectly plausible that with little communication possible in the circumstances, that the defenders couldn't work out which Plantagenet was challenging them.

It is also not entirely clear when William the Lion, king of Scotland appeared at the siege. One scenario is that he arrived in time to go to Southwell with King Richard, and then on to the Easter Court at Northampton, which makes sense. The other is that King Richard went to Clipstone on the day after the siege ended, managed to find time to hunt, and meet the king of Scotland, and then return to Nottingham all in the same day! Even allowing for the fact that people were much more used to travelling by foot and riding, the fifteen miles each way was quite a journey all by itself; and significantly there is no mention of the Scottish king at the council held at Nottingham Castle – somewhat unlikely for a man of his status, and given that he and his brother had remained loyal to King Richard. I have therefore assumed that he arrived at some point while Richard was at Nottingham, but too late to join in that council, explaining why he had to travel on with the king just to hear if his request for the lordship of Northumberland would be granted. In typical King Richard fashion, he prevaricated until the Scottish king had attended the second coronation at Winchester, then told him he could pay 15,000 marks for the shire but would not be allowed to have the castles. It was hardly the reward for loyalty King William must have been hoping for!

Yet what happened post-siege at Nottingham is every bit as difficult to untangle. By late 1194 there is no doubt that William Briwere, King Richard's loyal servant, was firmly settled as sheriff of the two shires. But what happened in between? De Ferrers appears in the list of Nottingham sheriffs, so when did he hold office? Did King Richard hand the sheriffdom to William earl Ferrers because he was considered to be responsible for his liegeman, de Wendenal (and maybe if de Wendenal had become incompetent or died, he thought that Ferrers should have taken over instead of Murdac)? It's almost impossible to tell. Some sources say that Ferrers was only sheriff for seven weeks, but who took over after that? Briwere, along with another man who would later become sheriff of Nottingham, Hugh Bardolf, were definitely out on eyre in the summer of 1194, and there is certainly mention of the fact that the eyre finally got to visit those shires which were Count John's for the first time in years. Given that a sheriff was not allowed to hold an eyre in his own county, Briwere at that stage was unlikely to be the sheriff actually in residence, but maybe in the upheaval of King Richard wanting loyal men in office, this convention was overlooked for once?

With regard to the Welsh prisoner episode, Einion Clud was one of the minor Welsh princes of the time whom we at least have some information on as the lord of Elfael – the area on the north side of the River Wye from modern day Hay. He died in 1177 but his son, Einion ap Einion Clud, otherwise known as Einion o'r Porth, left on crusade in 1188 or '9, quite possibly believing his chances of survival were better in the Holy Land! Sources vary as to when Einion o'r Porth died, but it seems likely it was in 1191, and possibly at the hands of his brother. His son, Anarawd, was one of the Welsh leaders who would take part in the battle of Painscastle (in southern Elfael), serving Gwenwynwyn, Prince of Powys. The battle was disastrous for the Welsh, and Anarawd ab Einion was one of those who are recorded in the annals as having been killed there, along with other leading Welsh lords. Anarawd's mother was the daughter of another leading Welsh prince, Rhys ap Gruffudd, whose lands lay to the east of Elfael in Deheubarth, so the children were people of some consequence even if they aren't mentioned in surviving records. An ancient tombstone in St Mary's, New Radnor, is either Einion Clud's or Einion o'r Porth's. This then was a good background to the story which brings Mariota into the gang.

Nottingham had its first town gaol built under order from Henry II. However quite where that was in the town is harder to say. All that is currently known is that the shire hall building was where a court of justice lay in the late 14th century, and a proper prison lay in the 15th. However the High Pavement area of Nottingham lies within what was the ancient Anglo-Saxon burgh of Nottingham, and therefore abutting the subsequent Norman development and in existence at the same time. Located high on the natural cliff above the River Leen, High Pavement must therefore have been thought to be one of the more secure areas of the town in those days. So it's likely that the prison and court of the high middle ages lay on the same site as an earlier town gaol. In recent years (2007) there has been the discovery of steps leading down from the later gaol to caves which appear to have been used as cells in medieval times, although whether that use dates back to Robin Hood's day is debatable. However such a gift is not to be overlooked, and so I have used this idea and am reconciled to the possibility that subsequent archaeology may prove me hopelessly wrong!

Sir Ralph fitz Stephen was the very real Keeper of the old Forest of Nottingham, and it is true that he received the office having married Maud de Caux, whose family had it as a hereditary office. He had been Keeper since 1177 – a significant date since that was the point at which Henry II had begun to make Nottingham into a suitable place for his much loved youngest son, John, to live. As fitz Stephen had been a loyal servant to King Henry, it's hardly surprising that he should have been married to the much younger Maud, and charged with taking over the role of her late father to care for the royal forest which would one day provide the youngest prince with much needed revenue.

Yet something clearly went amiss, because by the time Ralph died in 1202, King John was able to take the Keepership away from Maud and her family and use it to reward his own men. Therefore I have taken the liberty of giving Sir Ralph his injury to explain why the role of Keeper may have already slid into the hands of the sheriff in its practical terms, and why it was so easy to disenfranchise the de Cauxs a few years later.

With regard to the verderers, I have been unable to find records of specific names. However the names associated with certain places are as close to accurate as possible. So Roger de Lovetot, for instance, is attached to a very real family who were powerful in the Worksop area. There were several de Lovetot brothers living at this time, the oldest being Richard, who inherited the family manor at Worksop, but also substantial lands in Huntingdonshire. The next brother, Nigel, succeeded when Richard died without an heir, and Nigel's son would one day become sheriff. But what happened to the three younger brothers – Roger, Robert and William – is not clear, yet these were the very sort of lower ranking noble men from whom the verderers would have come. Therefore since we know that there were two verderers who dealt with matters in the northern part of the forest, it is plausible that one of the de Lovetots would have assumed that role.

What is slightly harder to unravel is the fact that in every other royal forest there were only four verderers, so why did Sherwood have six? It seems likely that the origins of the extra two would have come about when Henry II expanded the royal forest to encompass virtually the entire shire, thus creating a desperate need for more men to help with the forest courts. It is significant that the four known courts are all closer to Nottingham than the northern expanse which got given the keepership name of Rumwood; and so although the late medieval records say that this keepership had two verderers, they do not appear to have their own courts. It is possible that there were courts, but that they did not survive the shrinking of Sherwood back to its original limits at the time of Magna Carta. Therefore I have made these verderers the newcomers to the ranks of the forest officers in Guy's time, when so few records remain for the two shires of any kind.

St George didn't become the patron saint of England until 1348, well after Guy's time, but the 23rd of April wasn't officially made his feast day in England until 1222, either. This makes the choice of the twenty-third for the official reopening of the forest more than a little unusual in medieval terms, because it wasn't the feast of any particularly noteworthy saint in an era when most official days related to something within the Church. It was the feast of St Felix, but he would hardly have been as well known as many other saints. I have found no explanation for this, but have assumed that St George would have been known of from Continental sources. The previous patron saint of England was the Anglo-Saxon martyred king, Edmund, but his feast day is in November.

If anyone local to the area wonders why I did not mention Codnor Castle during the poaching incident, it is because it was not built until later in the 13th century.

Guy and Robin will return in **Broken Arrow**.